Selected Academic Papers of
Yin Qiping

殷企平
学术研究文集

殷企平 著

中国知名外语学者学术研究丛书
总策划：庄智象
Selected Academic Works of
Renowned Foreign Language Scholars of China

上海外语教育出版社
SHANGHAI FOREIGN LANGUAGE EDUCATION PRESS

图书在版编目(CIP)数据

殷企平学术研究文集 / 殷企平著. -- 上海：上海外语教育出版社，2025. -- (中国知名外语学者学术研究丛书 / 庄智象总主编). -- ISBN 978-7-5446-8476-7

I. I1-53

中国国家版本馆CIP数据核字第2025TF5338号

出版发行：**上海外语教育出版社**
（上海外国语大学内） 邮编：200083
电　　话：021-65425300 (总机)
电子邮箱：bookinfo@sflep.com.cn
网　　址：http://www.sflep.com
责任编辑：董　新

印　　刷：上海新华印刷有限公司
开　　本：710×1000　1/16　印张 34.75　字数 548 千字
版　　次：2025 年 6 月第 1 版　2025 年 9 月第 2 次印刷

书　　号：ISBN 978-7-5446-8476-7
定　　价：142.00 元

本版图书如有印装质量问题，可向本社调换
质量服务热线：4008-213-263

编委会名单

总 策 划： 庄智象

编委会成员（按姓氏拼音排序）：

戴炜栋　桂诗春　何兆熊　何自然　胡文仲
胡壮麟　黄国文　黄源深　卢思源　潘文国
石　坚　束定芳　汪榕培　王　蔷　王守仁
文秋芳　徐真华　许　钧　杨惠中　杨仁敬
张绍杰　庄智象

目 录

001 总序
001 序言
001 前言

第一编　文化与共同体

003　西方文论关键词：文化
019　文化批评的来龙去脉
034　趣味即文化：阿诺德对文学批评的贡献
050　走向公共精神：伊格尔顿的趣味观
063　西方文论关键词：共同体
078　英国文学中的幸福伦理与共同体形塑
092　英国文学中的音乐与共同体形塑
109　英国文学中的会话与共同体形塑
123　Space, Cultural Materialism and Structure of Feeling: Reflections on the Chinese Reception of Raymond Williams

第二编　文学理论

147　西方文论关键词：普通读者
163　西方文论关键词：愉悦

185	文论讲座：概念与术语　含混
200	西方文论关键词：重复
214	说"顿悟"
223	谈"互文性"
236	实验的结果是写实
	——布洛克-罗斯的小说创作和理论
246	节奏即境界：从福斯特的小说观说起
260	New Possibilities Brought About by Hypertext

第三编　作品评论

273	文化的物质性
	——哈代小说中的哥特式建筑
287	夜尽了，昼将至：《多佛海滩》的文化命题
303	走向生物共同体：《阿弗小传》的意义
316	劳伦斯笔下的彩虹
326	《黑暗的心脏》解读中的四个误区
339	Communal Pleasure in Jean Rhys's Fiction
366	The Meaning of Community under the Pen of Wordsworth
389	Where Is the West-Running Brook Flowing? Robert Frost in Taoist Perspective

第四编　教育思想

409	外国文学的"新"与"旧"：新文科浪潮下的思考
422	阐释三境界：外国文学教学的艺术之路
435	两种文化和英国高等教育（上）
444	两种文化与英国高等教育（下）
453	纽曼大学观探微

462 Teaching English Literature in China: Importance, Problems and Countermeasures

第五编　对话访谈

477　文化观念流变中的英国文学典籍研究：殷企平教授访谈录
487　"普通读者"与外国文学研究：殷企平教授访谈录
500　"共同体"与外国文学研究
　　　——殷企平教授访谈录
514　悖论文化：文学中的文化反思
　　　——殷企平教授访谈录
527　"英语专业与人文教育"二人谈

总　序

我国波澜壮阔的改革开放伟大实践即将跨入第四十个年头。四十年的历程、四十年的实践、四十年的发展、四十年的成就，令世界瞩目。这四十年，中国发生了翻天覆地的变化，经济、政治、科技、教育、文化、外交、军事和社会发展等各项事业都取得了令人骄傲的进步，成绩辉煌。中国特色社会主义革命和建设的探索、开拓和创新推动中华民族的伟大复兴步入了快车道。正如习近平总书记所指出的那样："我们比历史上任何时期都更接近中华民族伟大复兴的目标，比历史上任何时期都更有信心、有能力实现这个目标。"

伴随着时代步伐，我国外语教育事业迅猛发展，学科建设、人才培养、学术研究、社会服务、文化传承与传播以及国际交流与合作均取得了长足的进步，成绩斐然。外语教育主动对接国家发展战略、主动服务国家发展需要，全面有力地支持了改革开放的实践与发展，在各个领域都发挥了重要的作用，为经济和社会发展，做出了积极的努力和贡献，功不可没。

上海外语教育出版社全心致力于中国外语教育事业的发展，将推动外语学科建设、人才培养、学术繁荣、社会服务、文化传播、国际交流与合作以及中国文化的国际传播作为义不容辞的责任。经过近四十年的发展，外教社已成为我国最重要的外语出版基地之一，为外语教育事业的发展和进步做出了不懈的努力和积极的贡献。外教社策划出版的"改革开放30年中国外语教育发展丛书"和"新中国成立60周年外语教育发展研究丛书"，在全国外语界和出版界产生了热烈的反响，获得广泛好评，被有关媒体列为年度最有影响力的出版物之一。在即将迎来改革开放四十年这一具有特殊意义的时间节点，外教社组织策划了"中国知名外语学者学术研究丛书"，计划出版100种，诚邀国内外语界知名专家学者，请他们梳理和精选改革开放以来，在各自学术领域最具代表性的成就和成果，结集出版，记录他们在各个外语学科领域或方面的所思、所学、所想和所为。丛书内容丰富，所涉领域广泛，几乎涵盖了外国语言文学研究、外语教育、教学研究、翻译学研究、跨文化交际研究等各个重要领域，包括：语音学研究、词汇学研究、语法学研究、语用学研究、认知语言学研究、心理语言学研究、文学理论研究、文学史研究、作家研究、文学作品研究、英汉对比研究、翻译理论和与实践研究、翻译史研究、翻译家与翻译作品研究、外语教学理论与实践研究、学科建设与课程建设研究、教材与教学研究、测试理论与实践研究、跨文化交际理论与实践研究、外语复合型人才培养理论与实践研究、外语学科融合与人才培养研究等，既有理论研究和提炼，又有丰富的实践体验，充分展示了改革开放四十年来外语学科方方面面的实践与发展、成就与成果，是读者了解和研究这一代学人不可或缺的文献资料。从他们的作品中，读者可以清晰地了解外语教育四十年改革发展的历程，外语学科建设和学术研究演变的轨迹和不断发展和繁荣的过程，体察一代学人的学术追求和治学精神，尤其是他们在探索和创新中体现出的既积极跟踪国际学术研究发展，及时介绍、引进各种先进理论和方法，为我所用，又紧密结合中国外语教育的需求和实际，积极有效借鉴他人成果，针对我国外语教育、教学研究、人才培养等各方面的现实，通过学习、引进、消化、创造、创新解决现存问题，探索和建立具有中国特色的外语教育理论和实践体系，有力有效地促进和提升中国外语教育、学科、学术研究的发展的示范和引领价值。

丛书的作者大多是改革开放以来，在外语教育领域、各个学科或学术领域成就卓著的知名专家和学者。其中不少前辈亲身经历了改革开放、实践发展的风雨历程，见证了她的变化与前行，经历和体验了发展过程，主持或参与了不少外语教育改革方案的具体设计和实施，为外语教育事业的发展做出了突出的贡献。他们在几十年的学术生涯中，勤耕不辍、孜孜不倦，在各自研究的领域都取得了令人敬佩、敬仰和骄傲的成绩。他们是某一研究领域的拓荒者、奠基人，或是代表人物、主要建设者，推动、影响和引领某一学科或领域的发展，做出了特殊的贡献。如今他们大都年事已高，从改革开放启始时的青年才俊，风华正茂的外语学术栋梁，步入了古稀、耄耋之年。整理、遴选和出版他们的优秀学术成果，正是为了弘扬我国知名外语学者敢为天下先，善于探索、勇于创新的精神，继承他们那种"衣带渐宽终不悔，为伊消得人憔悴"的敬业精神，学习他们那种筚路蓝缕、坚忍不拔的创业精神。

丛书的作者们与外教社有着十分融洽的长期合作，既是外教社的杰出合作者和最珍贵的资源，又是外教社员工的良师益友。他们有的从建社一开始就是外教社不签约的"签约作者"，始终如一地关心、支持外教社的发展；有的尽管合作时间稍短，但一直对外教社的各项工作鼎力相助。他们不但将其得意之作首选外教社出版，而且始终关注国内外外语学科的发展和学术研究的繁荣，及时向外教社的编辑们提供信息，介绍成果，提想法，提建议，献计献策，有力地推动了外教社出版工作的开展，极大地支持了外教社办社水平的提升。更值得一提的是，这一代学人深厚的家国情怀，崇高的敬业精神，强烈的事业心，敢于担当的责任心，勇于开拓的进取心，实事求是的务实精神，不图虚名，谦虚谨慎，全心投身于教书育人事业的献身精神，始终激励和鼓舞着外教社人砥砺前行。他们中不少是教材编审委员会、教学指导委员会、教学研究会、考试委员会、外国语言文学等各类学术机构和团体的领导或重要成员。长期以来，他们活跃在外国语言文学、翻译、跨文化交际研究、课程设计、教材编写与评审、教师培养与发展、教学研究与评估等各个研究领域，不遗余力，不断进取，为我国外语教育事业的发展，为外语出版事业的繁荣做出了积极的努力和重大的贡献，外教社的同仁们一直心存敬畏和感激。

回顾昨天，了解历史，思考今天，直面机遇与挑战，让我们学习、继承和弘扬前辈学人学高、身正的大师风范，展望明天，拥抱未来，奋发图强，更好地肩负起历史的责任和使命，为开创外语教育事业新局面，继续前行。

上海外语教育出版社前社长、前总编辑
庄智象
2017 年 5 月

序　言

我和企平最初是在外国文学界的学术会议上见面的,至今已有三十多年了。当时企平在杭州大学执教,我们都是杭州人,专业领域相同,有一些共同的朋友,大有相见恨晚之感。企平是恢复高考后首届大学生,即 77 级。那次高考我未能参加,结果我成为 78 级的学生。就此而言,企平是我的学长。我对杭大有些特殊的感情,我小哥临安是杭大外文系的 67 届毕业生,杭大是从浙大分出去的,我家在杭大的道古桥宿舍区有不少熟人朋友,其中包括企平的硕士导师蒋炳贤先生。蒋先生的夫人是贵州遵义人,早在浙大西迁贵州时就和我母亲结为朋友。20世纪 50 年代后期,杭大道古桥宿舍区建成后,一些原住大学路和附近的浙大员工搬到那里,企平留校后一度也住道古桥,那些灰砖楼房现在已成为保护文物。

这本自选集所收论文的写作时间大致也是在这三十年间,其中不少是我拜读过的。现在它们分为五类汇集在一起,读起来的感觉竟全然不同。我不知道这本书印成后将有多少页,但是可以预期,它将十分厚重。这种分量是与企平这三十年来对外国文学学科的贡献相称的。企平待人友善谦让,进办公室和书房工作起来,却像个拼命三郎。这本自选集仅是他学术成就的一部分,但足以体现作者身上杭师大校训中"勤慎诚恕"四字的基本精神。所谓的"做学问"有不同的做法,很多人(包括我自己)抵挡不住这样那样的诱惑,有时还想走走捷径;企平则不然,他是超然独立的,心无旁骛地埋头于教学、阅读和写作,总是不惜时间和精力,把原著读得很透,甚至读了又读。这种踏踏实实的用功,自然而然地表现在大量的文本细读之中。他不计利害，不断更新自己的知识结构，在勤奋阅读文学作品的前提下源源不断地汲取各种理论的营养。他为《外国文学》杂志撰写的文论关键词系列就是他拓展视野的具体体现。

企平早在 20 世纪 90 年代中期就因《小说艺术管窥》一书得到有识之士的褒扬。当时他还在主持《英国小说批评史》（上海外语教育出版社，2001 年）的撰写，这是企平与这家著名出版社的首次合作。但是《推敲"进步"话语：新型小说在 19 世纪的英国》（商务印书馆，2009 年）有一种更深切的社会情怀，列入浙大学术精品文丛是理所当然的。从书名可知，企平有意接续黄梅的《推敲自我：小说在 18 世纪的英国》（三联书店，2003 年，修订版 2015 年）。他在序言里引用了黄梅的一段话："生活在这样的历史时刻，像是搭乘在不大稳当的高速列车上。列车摇摆颠簸，窗外景色倏忽变换，车内人不免头晕目眩，跌跌绊绊，动作变形。"接着他强调，到了 19 世纪，随着工业革命的进一步发展，这种感觉更明显了。企平调到杭州师范大学后，继续往这一方向努力，于 2013 年出版《"文化辩护书"：19 世纪英国文化批评》（上海外语教育出版社，2013 年）。他又通过阿诺德、卡莱尔、罗斯金、金斯利和莫里斯的著作揭示了"转型焦虑"。他概括了这五位维多利亚时期哲人的共同特点。他们在工业革命浪潮中不断追问：究竟什么是进步、幸福和高品质的生活？不论是在英国还是在中国，社会发展的理念和实践都因这些问题的提出而发生了根本性的调整与变化。

企平在新的岗位上很快就以他的热诚和精湛的学识在身边聚集了一批志同道合的中青年学者。在这一群体多年的共同努力奋斗下，企平主持的六卷本《文化观念流变中的英国文学典籍研究》（上海外语教育出版社，2020 年）得以顺利完成。这是一个国家社科基金重大招标项目，出版后得到学界的高度评价。为了配合杭师大外院同仁，企平现在又投入两个重大项目的写作。

英国文学研究者一般都喜欢阿诺德的诗句："徘徊于两个世界之间，／一个已经死去，／另一个还无力诞生。"阿诺德去世几十年后，人们是否感到这些诗句更贴切地反映了自己的时代？也许可以斗胆说，自从文艺复兴以来，"转型"并不属于某个时期，它可能就是一种常态。维多利亚时期的英国不断变革，维多利亚女王去世的时候，工人阶级的状况恐怕就迥然有别于 19 世纪 40 年代。一旦批评的声音与立法机构形成良性的互动，弱势群体的利益有望得到某种程度的保护，资本主义制度也会做出适度的自我调整。即使是个人主义，我们也不妨从艾伦·麦克法兰的《英国个人主义的起源》等著作看到它在社会发展过程中较为积极的一面。

　　企平喜爱"普通读者"的观念，不妨再转入这个话题。我的两本弗吉尼亚·伍尔夫的《普通读者》是企鹅版的。《普通读者》第一册和第二册先后于1925年、1932年问世，企鹅平装本推出的时间为1938年、1944年，书后各有广告，推销的商品为多维片、格雷香烟和诺维克皮鞋等等。企鹅出版社在起步阶段不得不部分依赖广告收入，或与特殊的环境相关。二战结束以后，企鹅出版社地位提高，广告就从封面上消失了，企鹅出版社的进步是明显的。在20世纪三四十年代的学生中间，买得起《普通读者》精装初版的人肯定不多，然而那时"普通读者"的规模不知要比约翰逊博士时代大多少，企鹅的成功取决于时代背景。教育的普及曾经使得维多利亚时期和20世纪上半叶维护"文化"的精英们深深担忧，现在看来，畅销书并不一定意味着低品质。1938年企鹅版《普通读者》第一册的最后是冠以"企鹅的进步"（Penguins Progress）之名的书讯，长长的书单中不乏熟悉的书名。这里的Progress一词是否能翻译成"进步"，我不很确定，但是普及型的出版公司不断将好书推向广大的市场，并使之逐步成为一种学界认可的品牌，也是一种进步。企鹅平装本延续了"人人丛书""牛津经典"等口袋精装本的传统，将书价再次压低，对低收入读者来说实在是大好消息。

　　假如卡莱尔看到那两册纸质发灰的《普通读者》，是不是会谴责作贱传统图书印制、装订艺术的企鹅出版社？那么，拷问"进步"，似也可以从另一角度来评价。在此我举一个例子。伍尔夫的父亲莱斯利·斯蒂芬年轻时经常拜访卡莱尔，但随着他入世渐深，他对卡莱尔的崇拜就打了一点折扣。1883年3月11日，他在致美国友人、哈佛大学历史上影响最大的教授之一查尔斯·艾略特·诺顿的信上说，他依然钦佩卡莱尔文辞的爆发力，这位苏格兰哲人几乎想把世上的罪恶一把火烧得干干净净，他身上的燃料足以驱动一打人的引擎。此刻斯蒂芬又有所保留："我要是想让自己在智力上醉醺醺的，我只要喝一杯卡莱尔就行了，喝多了就有点消受不了。但从没有人像他那样令我着迷。"[①] 维多利亚时

---

　　① 详见弗雷德里克·威廉·梅特兰，《莱斯利·斯蒂芬生平和书信》，伦敦，1906年，第377页至378页。

期也有不少思想家、作家在批判现实的同时投入社会改革，这一群体同样是可敬的。企平所钦佩的金斯利就是一个很好的例子。英国毕竟是工业化和现代化的开路先锋，无数工程技术的发明和新思想的出现最终都能造福人类。

我曾经在企平新居的阳台上远眺杭州西部在城市化进程中保护起来的树林，读了这本自选集，仿佛再次在他的邀请下登高望远。我深深感到，文字的风景，竟远胜自然。应该感谢企平让我优先观赏这个他自己多年来辛勤耕耘的园子。

陆建德

2024 年 11 月 22 日

前　言

人生乐趣，莫过于共享愉悦，今天向同道奉献学术研究的成果，自当属于最大乐趣之一。

庆幸以此书总结一己的学术生涯，从中记叙成长轨迹，回顾心路历程，分享心得体会，以及知识探索和思想碰撞的快意，寻觅神交的乐趣，心中充满感激。关于学术生涯，铭记有四：

首先，个人的学术兴趣须与国家乃至人类命运紧密相扣。学术研究是求知和洞察真理的过程，更是一种社会责任；离开社会责任感，任何学者都难以找寻持之以恒的动力。

其次，在研究外国文学或国外教育时，应该一只眼睛盯着国外，另一只眼睛盯着国内。世事并非孤立，只有比照和对接，才能找到真正有意义的解答。

再次，共享知识、观念与见解在学术交流中至关重要；独乐乐不如众乐乐，一个人无论取得何种学术成就，若不能分享给他人，那么这份喜悦必会大打折扣。

最后，论文写作既要坚持深度和广度，也须讲求审美维度，至少要具有可读性。要使学术话语不那么生涩难读，虽大为难事，但务必追求。

本书内容分为五个板块：1）文化与共同体；2）文学理论；3）作品评论；4）教育思想；5）对话访谈。其间互相呼应：后四个板块的选文或多或少地呼应了第一板块中"文化"与"共同体"主题，从理论与实践两个层面对英国文学与西方文论研究进行探索，也对新时代外国文学教学和大学理念提出见解。选文中既有偏重学理研究的深入讨论，也有偏重文本分析的细致操作，力求保持较为合理的平衡。在谋篇布局时，不仅服从上述主题，而且注意其中的大多数未汇集成书。

本书选文的时间跨度达三十余年，从中可以瞥见一学人的成长轨迹。早年的选文虽也围绕思想主题，但是文字与思想/情感的咬合力度相当稚嫩，而晚些时候的选文在命词遣意上较为着力。这表明后期在思想情感与文字的吻合方面的自觉性加强了。促成我增强这方面意识的人主要有卡莱尔和福楼拜。卡莱尔强调文字是思想的皮肉，比喻是思想的筋络；而福楼拜说得更为精彩："思想与形式分开，全无意义。譬如物体，去其颜色形模，所余不过一场空。思想之为思想，端赖文笔耳……文章不特为思想之生命，抑为思想之血液。"① 我国也多有类似的主张。例如，刘勰推崇文质统一，对情、文、辞、理之间的辩证关系作出了这样的阐述："情者，文之经；辞者，理之纬。经正而后纬成，理定而后辞畅。"现代学者朱光潜也推崇韩愈所主张的"惟陈言之务去"，声称视陈腔滥调为仇敌，务必在谋篇布局和命词遣意上开辟自己的蹊径。

反顾所为，深感与目标相去甚远，不过，展现成长轨迹，与读者分享经验教训，何尝不是一种乐趣？虽不能至，心向往之，这一心迹已镌刻在论文集中。选文犹如自己的孩子，虽媸妍不等，但真要作出评价，并非易事，先要看采用什么角度，倚重何种尺度。前文提到，此处所选皆服务于"文化"与"共同体"主题，因而都有收录的理由。若用文质统一的尺度来衡量，本人更青睐于《夜尽了，昼将至：〈多佛海滩〉的文化命题》《阐释三境界：外国文学教学的艺术之路》《节奏即境界：从福斯特的小说观说起》《西方文论关键词：愉悦》《文论讲座：概念与术语含混》《说"顿悟"》《英国文学中的幸福伦理与共同体形塑》《英国文学中的音乐与共同体形塑》和《英国文学中的会话与共同体形塑》这几篇。不知为什么，在写这几篇的时候，耳边总会想起清代顾炎武的忠告：文章应如"风行水止，自然成文"。为印证当初追求水到渠成境界所作的努力，我在《夜尽了，昼将至：〈多佛海滩〉的文化命题》后面附了一篇写作心得。写作

---

① 转引自钱锺书，《中国固有的文学批评的一个特点》，载《钱锺书散文》，杭州：浙江文艺出版社，1997年，第396—397页。

心得亦可看作读书心得：有文出自然的冲动，皆因前辈书籍的影响。每每读到文约旨博的文章，总会心生羡慕，甚至自觉为文面目可憎——那么旧我就如黄山谷所说，读书太少，而"不读书便语言无味，面目可憎"。

学海无涯苦作舟，而学术予人的宝贵馈赠恰载于"苦舟"之内。求学的诀窍端在苦中作乐。学人吃苦，不断丰盈内心，收获欢乐。信佛的人常说：众生皆苦，唯有自渡。我想说：学人皆苦，唯有共渡；一旦共渡，便生愉悦。

本书在酝酿阶段，承管南异、何畅、孙艳萍和金佳等诸位好友拨冗初选，斟之酌之；还蒙建德兄慷慨赐序，至感荣宠。付梓阶段，承蒙上海外语教育出版社孙玉书记、张春明和董新先生、孙静和梁晓莉女士鼎力相助，感激不尽。初稿收集和打印过程中，诸桥瑞和周城伊同学给予了宝贵支持。谨此一并鸣谢。

殷企平

2025 年 1 月

第一编

文化与共同体

西方文论关键词：文化

一、略说

"文化"（Culture）这一概念既复杂又简单。说它复杂，是由于几乎不存在比它含义更丰富的词语了。说它简单，是因为它在近三百年以来的人类社会历史中，最重要的内涵演变根植于"现代性焦虑"，即农业文明向工业文明转型而引起的焦虑。一旦我们从这一焦虑入手，把握文化的反机械主义特性，就能顺藤摸瓜，理清脉络。

二、综述

当今世界，"文化"已成为无人不知、无人不用的术语。然而，一说起它的定义，仍然令人生畏。恰如弗伊利和曼斯菲尔德所说，"很少有比'文化'更成问题的词语了"（Fuery & Mansfield 1997：xviii）。迄今为止，不成问题的文化定义还未出世。爱德华·泰勒给过一个十分出名的定义，但是它也难逃被质疑的阴影。这个定义是："（文化）是一个复杂的综合体，它包括知识、信仰、艺术、道德、法律、风俗，以及人作为社会成员所养成的其他任何能力和习惯。"（Tylor 1958：1）这样的定义显然大而无当。格林布拉特就曾批评道，泰勒的定义"几乎含糊得不能再含糊了"（Greenblatt 1995：225）。还有比这更含糊的，如在《文化：概念和定义批判分析》①一书中，上百个文化定义被逐一解析归类，"结果得出九种基本文化概念，它们分别是哲学的、艺术的、教育的、心理学的、历史的、人类学的、社会学的、生态学的和生物学的"（陆扬等 2006：3）。这样的分门别类看似全面，可是一个圈子兜下来，读者仍然找不到中心。文化的"桀骜不驯"自有其原因，威廉斯说得好：文化之所以是整个英语语言中两三个最复杂的单词之一，"部分原因在于它经历了好几种欧洲语言的历史演变，盘根错节，而主要原因是它目前已被好几个截然不同的学科用作重要的概念，而且被用在好几个互不兼容的思想体系中"（Williams 1983：87）。由此看来，文化的定义因历史时期不同而不同，因学科不同而不同。

威廉斯在《关键词》一书中从词源学的角度对文化一词的拼写及其含义的嬗变做过梳理。英语 culture 一词最早可以追溯到拉丁语 colere，后者几经变体，如 coulter 和 cultura，慢慢发展为中古英语 culter、colter 和 coulter 等词，最终于 17 世纪初叶定格为 culture，其含义也由最早的"动植物的培育"渐渐发展为"心灵的培育"等。如今常见的用法有三：其一，用来形容思想、精神和审美演变的总体过程；其二，表示一个群体、一个时期、一个民族乃至全人类的某种特定生活方式；其三，指涉思想艺术领域的实践和成果（Williams 1983：87-90）。这样的梳理虽然提供了几条比较清晰的线索，但是未能说明这样一个关键问题：对西方文学和文艺理论来说，文化概念在现代的最重要内涵是什么？

要说明上述问题，我们还得从威廉斯说起。在《文化与社会》一书中，威廉斯首次指出，19 世纪思想史的一个重要产物是关于文化概念演变的假说，即"一个时期的艺术必然跟该时期普遍流行的'生活方式'紧密相连，其结果是审美判断、道德判断和社会判断都互相紧密地联系在一起"（Williams 1958：130）。威廉斯的贡献在于：他率先勾勒了上述假说的形成轨迹，并对其背后的原因进行了鞭辟入里的分析。用他自己的话说：

> 文化一词的演变记录了人们对历史性变化的反应，即对我们的社会、

---

① 该书被不少国内外学者奉为经典，原书名为 *Culture: A Critical Review of Concepts and Definitions*（1963），作者为克洛依伯（A. Kroeber）和克拉克洪（C. Kluckhohn）。

经济和政治生活中的重大历史性变化作出的重要而持续的反应。该词的演变本身好比一种特殊的地图,从中我们可以探索那些变化的性质。①

(Williams 1958:xvi—xvii)

威廉斯此处所说的重大历史性变化是什么呢?从《文化与社会》全书的内容来看,最大的变化莫过于社会的转型,即农业文明向工业文明的转型。唯其转型,所以有社会、经济和政治乃至总体生活方式的空前变化。

确实,在过去的三百多年中,人类社会的头号变化,非工业文明的崛起莫属。由它引起的社会转型,以及随之而来的一系列现代性②问题,自然激发了文人学者们的回应,其内容和性质恰恰在文化概念的演变轨迹中得到了生动的体现。从这一意义上说,文化概念的最重要内涵是对社会转型的回应;虽然它还有许多其他内涵,但是上述内涵跟人类社会最重大的变化密切相关,因而我们的文化之旅从社会转型开始,应该是顺理成章的。

(一) 文化是焦虑

上文提到,威廉斯对文化概念演变的追踪紧扣社会转型这一线索,但是他在文字表述上没有直接使用"转型焦虑"这样的字眼。倒是哈特曼(Geoffrey H. Hartman)的有关论述更为简明扼要:"到了穆勒、阿诺德和罗斯金的时代,出自对于文明的肤浅及其悖逆自然的效应的焦虑,开始赋予'文化'一词新的价值含义。"(Hartman 1997:207)此处的关键词是"文明"和"焦虑",也就是对于工业文明的焦虑。另一组关键词是相关的人名,其中又以阿诺德最为关键。当今西方世界,凡是探讨文化定义的论著,几乎言必谈阿诺德,以及他的名著《文化与无政府状态》。该书前言中有一段引用率很高的概述,涉及文化的性质和功能:

全文的意图是大力推荐文化,以帮助我们走出目前的困境。在与我们

---

① 本书中汉语译文若无笔者或参考文献特别注明,均为笔者自译。
② 关于"现代性"话题,可参见赵一凡等主编《西方文论关键词》(外语教学与研究出版社,2006)和童明《现代性赋格》(广西师范大学出版社,2008)。

密切相关的所有问题上，世界上有过什么最优秀的思想和言论，文化都要了解，并通过学习最优秀知识的手段去追求全面的完美。我们现在不屈不挠地却也是机械教条地遵循着陈旧的固有观念和习惯；我们虚幻地认为，不屈不挠地走下去就是德行，可以弥补过于机械刻板而造成的负面影响。但文化了解了世界上最优秀的思想和言论，就会调动起鲜活的思想之流，来冲击我们坚定而刻板地尊奉的固有观念和习惯。这就是下面的文章所要达到的唯一目的。我们所推荐的文化，首先是一种内向的行动。

（阿诺德2002：208）

在这段文字中，引用率最高的又要数提及"世界上最优秀的思想和言论"的这一句，而且常常被单独用作阿诺德关于文化的定义。事实上，这一句名言一旦成为"孤家寡人"，就毫无意义。换言之，对它的理解必须结合上下文，尤其是对机械主义的批判——光是上面这短短的引文中，"机械"一词就出现了两次："我们……机械教条地遵循着陈旧的固有观念和习惯"和"机械刻板而造成的负面影响"。对机械主义的批判实际上遍布《文化与无政府状态》全书。例如，该书第一章"美好与光明"中这样强调："整个现代文明在很大程度上是机器文明，是外部文明……"，而且"在我国，机械性已到了无与伦比的地步……关于完美是心智和精神的内在状况的理念与我们尊崇的机械和物质文明相抵牾，而没有哪个国家比我们更推崇机械和物质文明。"在紧接着的一页，阿诺德再次强调："对机械工具的信仰乃是纠缠我们的一大危险。"（阿诺德2002：11—12）"机械"和"机器"等词语的出现频率如此之高，自然有其深意。阿诺德是要告诉我们：他之所以推崇文化，是因为他看到社会转型带来了问题，即新兴的工业文明仰仗的是机械力量和物质力量，缺失了精神的力量。正因为如此，他要用文化来"调动起鲜活的思想之流，来冲击我们坚定而刻板地尊奉的固有观念和习惯"——这里要冲击的，正是前文所说的"对机械工具的信仰"。也就是说，文化诞生于焦虑：社会转型引起的焦虑，或者说机械文明引起的焦虑。机械文明带有盲目性，其后果之一是社会、经济和科技的发展速度过快，导致新旧世界之间的断裂，即旧体制和旧学说遭到了废弃，而新体制和新学说还来不及诞生。这一情形在阿诺德的著名诗句中得到了生动的再现：

> 徘徊于两个世界之间，
> 一个已经死去，
> 另一个还无力诞生。
> 我的头脑无处依靠……

（Arnold, 1965: 288）

透过这些诗行，我们看到的是深深的文化焦虑：新旧世界的断裂意味着社会的畸形发展，也就是前文中哈特曼所说的"悖逆自然的效应"；而造成社会畸形发展的原因，又跟上文讨论的"对机械工具的信仰"密切相关。

在世界文化史上，阿诺德是一位继往开来的人物，他并非用文化冲击机械主义的第一人，称得上第一人的是卡莱尔（Thomas Carlyle）。虽然如前文所示，哈特曼没有提到卡莱尔，但是后者表达的对于机械文明的焦虑，更早地赋予了文化一词新的价值含义。事实上，卡莱尔最早明确地把工业化时代称作"机械时代"，这一命名首次见于他的名篇《时代的特征》："假如我们需要用单个形容词来概括我们这一时代的话，我们没法把它称为'英雄的时代'或'虔诚的时代'，也没法把它称为'哲思的时代'或'道德的时代'，而只能首先称它为'机械的时代'"（Carlyle 1967: 169）。至于"机械"的含义，卡莱尔作了迄今为止最精辟的解释：

> 目前受机器主宰的不光有人类外部世界和物质世界，而且有人类内部世界和精神世界……不光我们的行动方式，而且连我们的思维方式和情感方式都受同一种习惯的调控。不光人的手变得机械了，而且连人的脑袋和心灵都变得机械了。

（Carlyle 1967: 170—173）

在他的另一部名著《拼凑的裁缝》中，卡莱尔干脆把工业化浪潮冲击下的世界比喻成"一个巨大的、毫无生气的、深不可测的蒸汽机"（Carlyle 1987:

127）。这些批评和文化之间的关系，其实已经被威廉斯点破：

> 在卡莱尔那里，把文化看作一个民族的总体生活方式的观念明显地得到了新的增强。这种文化观是他抨击工业主义的基础：一个社会若要名副其实，维系它各个组成部分的就应该远远不止是经济纽带，应该远远超越那种以现金支付为唯一联结的经济关系。
>
> （Williams 1958：83）

这段话中有两点需要特别注意：1."现金联结"（cash-nexus）；2."把文化看作一个民族的总体生活方式的观念"。熟悉卡莱尔的人都知道，"现金联结"也是他的名言之一，被用来描述19世纪工业社会里的人际关系。这种依靠现金来联结的社会，所奉行的正是单向度发展的机械主义原则，而一个民族的理想生活方式应该是多向度的，是讲究整体性与和谐性的。换言之，对于这种机械式文明的焦虑，从卡莱尔起就已经渗入了文化概念内涵的演变过程中。

当然，卡莱尔并非凭空就具备了回应工业主义/机械主义的能力。就思想源流而言，卡莱尔直接受到了英国浪漫主义诗人尤其是柯勒律治的影响。关于浪漫主义诗人对工业化的回应，以及柯勒律治对卡莱尔的影响，威廉斯在《文化与社会》中都作了详尽的阐述。他特别指出，虽然柯勒律治没有直接使用culture一词，但是他笔下的cultivation就是文化的意思，而且"就是从柯勒律治时代开始，文化概念决定性地进入了英国的社会思想"（Williams 1958：59—62）。需要补充的是，卡莱尔还深受哈曼、赫尔德和雅各比等德国浪漫派思想家的影响，后者曾经掀起一场"反启蒙运动"，其宗旨跟机械主义思想正好相悖。[①]还须指出的是，在卡莱尔之前，歌德、席勒和诺瓦利斯等德国文学家已经在不同程度上直接表述过对于以"机械的崛起"为标志的"现代文明"的焦虑。譬如，席勒在《审美教育书简》中曾经指出，现代文明的特点是"无限众多但都没有生命的部分拼凑在一起，从而构成了一个机械生活的整体……人永远被束缚在整体的一个孤零零的小碎片上……永远不能发展他本质的和谐"（席勒

---

① 详见拙文《〈拼凑的裁缝〉为何迂回曲折?》，载《外国文学评论》2009年第2期。

1985：29—30）。不过，卡莱尔是明确地把工业化时代称为"机械时代"并对其全面解剖的第一人。从这一意义上说，他居功至伟。

更确切地说，作为批判机械主义基础的文化观在卡莱尔那里已经成熟。如前文所述，这一文化观经阿诺德之手得到了充实。这种充实在阿诺德之后并没有停顿，而是一直延续至今，途中参与充实工作的文人学者可谓群星灿烂，其中必须一提的有英国的罗斯金、莫里斯、利维斯、艾略特、考德威尔、威廉斯、霍加特、汤普森、安德森，以及意大利的葛兰西、法国的布迪厄、美国的格林布拉特、德国的本雅明、马尔库塞和阿多诺，等等。经他们之手，"文化"不断改头换面，并派生出诸如"文化霸权""文化唯物主义""文化马克思主义""文化工业批判""文化诗学""文化无意识"和"文化资本"等新术语，还引起了层出不穷的纷争。① 以笔者愚见，"文化"万变不离其宗。就其"转型焦虑"这一主要内涵而言，文化概念形成的基础性工作在19世纪已经完成。对这项基础性工作付出巨大努力的，不光有前文介绍的卡莱尔和阿诺德，还有罗斯金和莫里斯。

虽然罗、莫二人没有像阿诺德那样，直接以"文化"为标题发表过专论，但是他们的文化观几乎渗透了各自的每一部作品。跟阿诺德一样，他们几乎在自己的所有作品中都提出了与社会转型有关的问题，而且在具体表述上也与阿诺德有耐人寻味的相似之处。例如，罗斯金在《给这后来者》一书中有一个论断："治理与合作在所有事情中都是生命法则，而无政府状态与竞争则是死亡法则"（Ruskin 1997：202）。这里说的其实就是文化问题，其实质曾经被威廉斯一语道破："（罗斯金的这个论断）再次把文化与无政府状态进行了对照，只不过这一次的措辞直接对19世纪工业经济的基本原则形成了挑战"（Williams 1958：143）。威廉斯这里指的是罗斯金和阿诺德之间的巧合，后者的代表作题目本身就是《文化与无政府状态》。类似的巧合还出现在莫里斯和阿诺德之间。跟阿诺德的诗句"徘徊于两个世界之间……"一样，莫里斯也在文字上直指社会转型："我们觉得自己身处新旧世界之间……期待着变化的来临。"（Morris Vol. XXIII 1992：122）这些巧合表明，跟阿诺德与卡莱尔一样，罗斯金与莫里斯的文化情

---

① 参见赵一凡等主编《西方文论关键词》及赵一凡《西方文论讲稿续编》。

结中也带有浓浓的转型焦虑。

必须指出的是,上述焦虑不但导向了对现代文明的批评实践,而且最终化成了有关理想社会的愿景。这也构成了本文下一小节的主要内容。

(二) 批评与愿景

上一小节主要回答了一个问题,即文化是什么?任何有关文化概念内涵的探讨还须回答另一个问题:文化能做什么?实际上,这两个问题是无法截然分开的。当我们强调文化是对于社会转型的焦虑时,同时也暗示了文化的功能,即化解这种焦虑的功能。

文化怎样化解焦虑呢?其主要手段有二:一是从事批评,二是提供愿景。莱斯利·约翰逊的一段话可以作为凭证:

> 在19世纪,文化的概念大体属于文学知识分子的研究领域。当时对英国社会的不满、抗议和批判主要来自他们,并形成了一种社会思想传统,而文化是他们用来表示这一重要传统的术语。社会潮流的走向,让这些作家痛心疾首,而文化概念则表达了他们的痛苦,同时彰显了他们的社会关切,以及他们提供的建设性愿景。
>
> (Johnson 1979:1)

在约翰逊所说的文学知识分子中,最杰出的代表当属卡莱尔、阿诺德、罗斯金和莫里斯。他们都在社会批评和描绘愿景两方面作出了巨大贡献。鉴于上一小节已经涉及卡莱尔和阿诺德所从事的社会批评,此处只就罗斯金和莫里斯的有关工作略做补充。

先说罗斯金。跟卡莱尔和阿诺德一样,罗斯金也把批评的矛头对准了由工业革命所牵引的、以机械式进步为内涵的文化现象——更确切地说,是"反文化"现象。这种现象的最大特征是国家以及个人身上的某一种禀性或能力特别发达,而其他禀性和能力却急剧萎缩。在《芝麻与百合花》一书中,他哀叹英国大众已经失去了许多应有的能力,尤其是阅读和思维的能力,而祸根又恰恰是对钱财的贪欲:"眼下英国公众完完全全地不可能读懂任何思想深邃的作品——他们的贪婪是如此疯狂,以致他们变得不会思考……凡事都得有'回报'的观念已经深深地影响了我们的每一项目标……"(Ruskin 1921:93)这种"反文化"现象意味着国家和个人都失去了完整性以及和谐状态,而文化则意味着对整体与和谐的追求。我们在上一小节中提到,席勒曾经哀叹现代文明把人变成了机械生活中的碎片,这也正是罗斯金焦虑的原因。比席勒更进一步的是,罗斯金把整体性的丧失明确地归咎于现代化进程中大规模生产的分工方式:

> 分工劳动可真是伟大文明的一大发明。近来我们把它又研究并完善了一番,只不过我们给它取了一个虚假的名字。说实话,我们并不是在分工,而是在分人——人被分成了一个个片段——分解成了生命的碎片和细屑。结果,一个人的智力所剩无几,甚至不足以制造一枚别针或一颗钉子。仅仅制造针尖或钉子头就耗尽了一个人的智力。
>
> (Matteson 2002:299)

罗斯金关注的还不仅仅是因分工引起的异化。如戴维·希克瑞所说,罗斯金的批评理论分别"由以下几组分离而生成:思想与感受分离;时间与空间分离;肉体与灵魂分离;行动与意图分离;计划与实施分离"(希克瑞 2001:47)。换言之,罗斯金是站在整个文化层面上关注人类社会的整体性或和谐性遭受侵蚀这一问题的。以形形色色的"分离"为特征的异化在现代化进程中愈演愈烈,这是让罗斯金深感焦虑的根本原因,也是他批判的对象。

再说莫里斯。跟卡莱尔、阿诺德和罗斯金相比,莫里斯对现代文明的批判有过之而无不及。用他自己的话说:"我一生的主要激情过去和现在都表现为对现代文明的仇恨。"(Morris 1993:380)这种仇恨和批判精神在他的诗歌、小说和政论文中随处可见。限于篇幅,我们仅以他的早期诗歌为例。在《地上乐园》和《吉尼维亚的自辩及其他》等诗歌中,我们只看到蒸汽机、活塞(这两种意象明显指涉工业革命)、城堡、塔楼和布匹劳动产品,却看不到生产这些产品的劳动者。后者的缺席意味着创造物和创造者被无情地分割,这也正是马克思所批判的劳动异化现象,即主体与客体的分离和错位。莫里斯表现劳动异化的手法极为生动，其中给人印象最深刻的是频频出现的"手"的意象。阿姆斯特朗曾经对此做过十分精彩的评论：

> ……手也是工具符号和代理符号，因为诗中的手总是操纵着物品，经常摆弄杯子和衣服之类的消费品，或者握有盾牌和利剑，而且总是跟身体分离，让人有一种不安的感觉。这里的"手"当然是指称 19 世纪的工人。城堡、塔楼和花园的建造都要依靠工人，但是在莫里斯笔下，作为建造者符号的工人全都被不祥地清空了……清空得如此彻底，以致构成了一种揭示工人遭受压制这一状况的怪诞技巧。现代怪诞艺术无法再现工人，因为工人除了缺席以外，再也没有再现自己的手段了。
>
> （Armstrong 1993：241）

虽然阿姆斯特朗未能指明工人的缺席是一种异化劳动，但是我们不难察觉这种缺席意味着劳动主体和劳动客体之间的分离。这种异化还由手跟身体分离的情景得到了强化：劳动者不仅远离自己的劳动果实，而且连自己的手都处于游离状态，这分明是一种双重隔离和双重异化。需要特别关注的是，莫里斯与异化的抗衡是在批判机械文明的大语境中进行的：他曾经在许多场合反对机器统治人的生活方式和思维方式，强调机器"可以做任何事情，但是做不出艺术品"，而且机器"奴役人的身心"，以智慧式劳动为敌（Morris Vol. XXII 1992：149）。这些论述与卡莱尔、阿诺德和罗斯金等人的相关论述不无互动，形成了强有力的文化批评语境。

不过，批评至多只化解了焦虑的一半，另一半焦虑要靠描绘愿景来化解。上述几位批评家都描绘了理想社会的蓝图。虽然这些蓝图不尽相同，但是它们共同拥有一个基本特征：它们呈现的是一个和谐发展的有机社会。还需强调的是，从卡莱尔到阿诺德，再从罗斯金到莫里斯，这些理想蓝图的艺术元素呈现出依次递增的倾向。

相对而言，卡莱尔提出的社会蓝图是遭受诟病最多的。有关他"拥护独裁、反对民主"的指责，我们已经耳熟能详。然而，尽管他的社会主张有时带有精英主义的色彩，但是他并非一味地反对民主。即便他那最遭攻讦的"英雄崇拜"

论，也含有合理的内核——他笔下的"英雄"绝不是一个简单的身份概念，而可以是一个平民，甚至是一个黑奴；他不但在文艺作品中刻画和歌颂过普通人，而且在书评中主张"人永远是人的兄弟"。① "人人是兄弟"的原则跟卡莱尔批判的"机械时代"和"现金联结"从一破一立两个方面互相呼应，是他理想中和谐社会的鲜明特征，也是实现和谐社会的途径。除了人人是兄弟以外，理想的社会还需要人人热爱劳动，所以卡莱尔提出了与"旧福音"针锋相对的"工作福音"："在这个世界上，最新的'福音'是：了解你所要做的工作，并认真去做你所要做的工作"（卡莱尔 1999：61）。不过，他的"工作福音"带有苦行僧的味道，缺乏罗斯金、莫里斯所提倡的"艺术成分"，即艺术化劳动和创造性愉悦。② 还需指出的是，"工作福音"若强调过头，就会不利于工人阶级争取良好劳动环境的斗争，或者会被用来作为要求被剥削阶级安分守己的借口。卡莱尔文化观的瑕疵由此可见一斑。然而，瑕不掩瑜，他的远景规划闪烁着真知灼见。

在表达愿景方面，阿诺德比卡莱尔走得更远。不仅仅是在《文化与无政府状态》中，而且在《当今批评的功能》《平等》和《民主》等许多作品中，阿诺德殚精竭虑地规划文化策略，阐述文化理论，以图这些"文化理论能够跨越旧世界和新世界之间的鸿沟，并把两者连接起来，也就是保存过去的精神遗产，并用以统一振兴现代世界"（Carroll 1982：xvii）。经由"文化"与过去连接并得以振兴的世界，就是阿诺德的理想世界。在这一理想境界中，人们不必因社会转型而焦虑，因为过去的优秀精神遗产都得到了保存，而且如前一小节引文中所说，人人都能"通过学习最优秀知识的手段去追求全面的完美"。关于此处"完美"的意思，约翰逊有过恰如其分的解说："完美有三个层面：一是和谐，二是普遍，三是付诸行动。"（Johnson 1979：28）也就是说，阿诺德向往的是一个和谐社会，不仅个人与社会、个人与个人之间的关系和谐发展，而且个人的全部禀赋或潜力都能和谐发展。尤其值得注意的是上述第三个层面，即"付诸

---

① 详见拙文《卡莱尔"英雄"观的积极意义》，载《杭州师范大学学报》（社会科学版）2009 年第 6 期。
② 需要说明的是，卡莱尔在其他地方肯定过生活中的艺术元素，他的不少论述或多或少地肯定了艺术想象力对建设和谐社会的作用。例如，他在《论英雄、英雄崇拜和历史上的英雄事迹》一书中把英雄分成了六类，其中的一类就是具有艺术想象力的诗人。

行动"。阿诺德常常被贴上"抱残守缺"的标签,或干脆被贬为改革的敌人,然而他并非反对改革,而是主张"在**成为**文化人之后,才能采取行动"(Johnson 1979:28)。阿诺德还常常被扣上"精英主义"的帽子,但是他的最终目的是让人人都享受美好与光明的生活,这一点在《文化与无政府状态》中已经说得非常明白:"文化寻求消除阶级,使世界上最优秀的思想和知识传遍四海,使普天下的人都生活在美好与光明的气氛之中,使他们像文化一样,能够自由地运用思想,得到思想的滋润,却又不受之束缚。"(阿诺德 2002:31)需要强调的是,较之卡莱尔的社会图景,阿诺德的理想蓝图中多了些艺术元素,他在许多场合都流露出这样一种观念:依靠文艺想象力产生的社会图景,比依靠其他想象力构建的远景更具有优越性。限于篇幅,我们只举一例:在长诗《吉卜赛学者》中,主人公有一个远大的抱负,而且是唯一的抱负,即"在学成之后,向世人传授艺术的奥秘"(Arnold 1965:335)。通过艺术传播文化,进而建设和谐社会,这既是阿诺德的宗旨,也成了他的实践,他的创作本身就是有力的见证。

  在提供理想社会的蓝图方面,罗斯金丝毫不亚于阿诺德。威廉斯曾经高度评价罗斯金对 19 世纪英国人总体生活方式的关注,并认为他"对文化概念的丰富内涵的发展做出了主要贡献"(Williams 1958:134)。约翰逊也曾强调:"罗斯金的工作为文化意义的迁移提供了证据;作为个人精神状态的'文化'转变成了作为'总体生活方式'的'文化'"(Johnson 1979:59)。对"总体生活方式"的关注,当然首先表现为前文所说的"现代性焦虑",但是焦虑的背后是他对人类社会的整体性与和谐性的向往。前文提到,罗斯金对各种以"分离"为特征的异化深恶痛绝,此处再举一例:他强烈反对体力劳动和脑力劳动分家,并一针见血地指出了这种分离的后果,即"大众社会成员的一分为二,一类变成了病态的思想者,另一类变成了悲惨的劳动者"(Ruskin 2005:24)。为改变这一状况,罗斯金提出要建设一个理想的社会;在这样的社会中,"劳动者应该经常思考,思想者应该经常劳动"(Ruskin 2005:24)。不难看出,在这一理想图景的背后,晃动着卡莱尔"工作福音"的影子。不过,罗斯金明显要比卡莱尔棋高一着:他不但像后者一样注重劳动,而且明确地提出要消灭体力劳动和脑力劳动的差别,这显然朝社会民主的方向又迈进了一大步。另一个超过前人的特点是,他有关劳动的愿景里有着更浓厚的艺术元素。他描述的理想社会不但要求人人劳动，而且讲究劳动的艺术性——劳动者应该有自由想象和创造的空间，并从中得到愉悦。他在《威尼斯之石》一书中提出了一个重要观点，即中世纪的哥特式建筑比近、现代建筑更为可取，其原因是前者虽然粗糙，但是代表了人类早期的纯朴和自然状态，体现了普通劳动者的活力和想象力（此时的社会组织、劳动制度和价值取向还允许普通工匠在劳动的同时有一定的空间进行自由的想象和思考），而后者虽然精致，但是因机械的分工方式而压抑了普通工匠的想象力和创造性——现代资本主义的生产方式和劳动组织形式只允许工匠机械地服从设计师的规划，致使工匠失去了自由发挥想象力和创造性的余地，同时也就失去了劳动的愉悦。需要指出的是，罗斯金并非主张回到中世纪去，而是主张在未来社会里，劳动本身更多地带有艺术性，劳动者能获得更多的创造性愉悦。

继罗斯金之后，莫里斯再次向世人提供了愿景。更确切地说，文化焦虑经莫里斯的点化，演变成了更合理、更绚烂、更完美的社会图景，在他的诗篇、文章和小说中都能找到这样的图景。比较起来，他的乌托邦小说《来自乌有乡的消息》所呈现的愿景最为全面，也最为生动。在乌有乡里，人不再是机械主义桎梏下的碎片，而是与社会乃至自然和谐相处的、全面发展的、有艺术品位的劳动者。乌有乡的居民们往往一个人从事多种职业，同时还能兼顾脑力劳动和体力劳动之间的平衡。例如，故事人物罗伯特既是织工，又是排字工，还是数学家兼史学家，甚至兼任摆渡的船夫。书中最引人入胜的是劳动场面；在这些场面里，人、服饰和大自然总是完美地融为一体。① 概括地说，乌有乡的居民们把生活变成了艺术，或者说总能艺术地生活着，劳动时如此，休闲时也是如此。事实上，莫里斯有一个至今未得到足够重视的观点，即劳动和休闲之间其实没有严格的界限；在一个健康的社会中，休闲是劳动的延伸，反之亦然；而艺术则贯穿二者的始终。他在名篇《我们的生活方式与可取的生活方式》中写道："许多最出色的工作是在人们休闲时完成的，此时人们衣食无忧，乐于表现他们的特殊才能……"（Morris 1962：173）在另一篇文章中，他说得更为明白："让所有的普通人都爱艺术，都坚持把艺术变成他们生活的一部分"（Morris Vol. XXII 1992：134）。可以说，莫里斯的艺术观、道德观、政治观和自然观在

---

① 详见拙文《乌有乡的客人——解读〈来自乌有乡的消息〉》，载《外国文学》2009 年第 3 期。

他描绘的社会图景中实现了高度的结合。露思·季娜说得好：莫里斯"把艺术的道德目的与对美的追求联系在了一起，又把它的社会目的与实现他所说的智慧型劳动联系在一起"（Kinna 2000：44）。这样一种联系其实已经给"文化"概念注入了新的含义，即社会主义的含义。换言之，莫里斯的文化之旅最后通向了社会主义。让我们再引用季娜的一句评论："莫里斯对社会主义思想的最大贡献——用威廉斯的话来说——在于他对文化的欣赏，以及他对文化变革的欣赏"（Kinna 2000：17）。我们不妨反过来说：莫里斯的文化焦虑把他引向了社会主义，使他在社会主义理想中找到了归宿。

在莫里斯之后，对资本主义工业文明的批判、对机械主义的批判，以及对美好社会的憧憬，一直延续着，至今未断。后人的批判和憧憬虽然方法各异，侧重面各有不同，意识形态各自为政，但是本质上都出于同一种文化焦虑。从这一角度看，到了莫里斯时代，以转型焦虑为主要内涵的文化概念已经确立。

三、结语

文化概念在现代社会的演变史，就是对社会转型的回应史。

在以往三百年中，人类面临的最大问题，就是社会转型问题。因此，针对转型问题而形成的文化概念内涵，理应作为我们最关注的内容，在这一方面，卡莱尔、阿诺德、罗斯金和莫里斯功莫大焉。说他们功劳最大，不是因为他们已经登峰造极，而是因为他们做了基础性工作。没有他们夯实的基础，就没有20世纪红红火火的文化批评与文化研究。自莫里斯以降，文化战场烽烟四起，从"文化"而衍生的新概念五花八门。然而，凡是卷入重要"文化之争"的学者，都怀有类似的文化焦虑，都向往和谐发展的社会，尽管他们在其他方面会立场各异，甚至彼此间激烈冲突。例如，安德森和汤普森曾在20世纪60年代唇枪舌剑，前者认为"英国文化的特点是中心缺席"，其原因是缺乏"总体社会理论"指导下的工人阶级运动；而后者坚持认为，反抗资本主义工业文明的传统在英国一直很活跃（Johnson 1979：12—14）。然而他们讨论的都是社会转型期的问题，都关注人类生活的总体方式。又如，哈贝马斯在跟福柯的论战中，强调"当今社会整合力量，只能来自文化"（赵一凡 2009：739）。文化有整合社会的力量，这一观点显然与19世纪形成的文化概念十分吻合。

文化概念的内涵极为丰富，本文展现的只是冰山一角。然而，我们若能紧紧抓住"转型"和"焦虑"这两个关键词，就应该可以窥豹一斑，知其要略。

参考文献

［1］Armstrong I. *Victorian Poetry: Poetry, Poetics and Politics* ［M］. London and New York: Routledge, 1993.

［2］Arnold M. *The Poems of Matthew Arnold*. Ed. Kenneth Allott ［M］. London: Longmans, 1965.

［3］Carlyle T. *Sartor Resartus* ［M］. Oxford and New York: Oxford UP, 1987.

［4］Carlyle T. "Signs of the Times." *Socialism and Unsocialism*. Vol. 1. Ed. W. D. P. Bliss ［M］. New York: The Humboldt Publishing Co., 1967.

［5］Carroll J. *The Cultural Theory of Matthew Arnold* ［M］. Berkeley: U of California P, 1982.

［6］Fuery P & Mansfield N. *Cultural Studies and the New Humanities: Concepts and Controversies* ［M］. Melbourne: Oxford UP, 1997.

［7］Greenblatt S. "Culture." ［A］//In Lentricchia F & McLaughlin T (eds.) *Critical Terms for Literature Study* ［M］. Chicago: U of Chicago P, 1995.

［8］Hartman G H. *The Fateful Question of Culture* ［M］. New York: Columbia UP, 1997.

［9］Johnson L. *The Cultural Critics: From Matthew Arnold to Raymond Williams* ［M］. London: Routledge & Kegan Paul, 1979.

［10］Kinna R. *William Morris: The Art of Socialism* ［M］. Cardiff: U of Wales P, 2000.

［11］Matteson J. Constructing ethics and the ethics of construction: John Ruskin and the humanity of the builder ［J］. *Cross Currents*. Vol. 52. No. 3 (2002): 294-305.

［12］Morris W. "How I Became a Socialist." ［A］//Wilmer C (ed). *News from Nowhere and Other Writings* [M]. London: Penguin, 1993.

[13] Morris W. "How We Live and How We Might Live." [A] //Briggs A. (ed). *News from Nowhere and Selected Writings and Designs* [M]. London: Penguin, 1962.

[14] Morris W. *The Collected Works of William Morris.* Vol. XXIII [M]. London: Routledge/Thoemmes Press, 1992.

[15] Morris W. *The Collected Works of William Morris.* Vol. XXII [M]. London: Routledge/Thoemmes Press, 1992.

[16] Ruskin J. *On Art and Life* [M]. London: Penguin Books, 2005.

[17] Ruskin J. *Sesame and Lilies* [M]. New York: Metropolitan Publishing Co., 1921.

[18] Ruskin J. *Unto this Last and Other Writings* [M]. London: Penguin Books, 1997.

[19] Tylor E B. *The Origins of Culture* [M]. New York: Harper and Row, 1958.

[20] Williams R. *Culture and Society* [M]. London: The Hogarth Press, 1958.

[21] Williams R. *Keywords: A Vocabulary of Culture and Society* [M]. Flamingo: Fontana Press, 1983.

[22] 阿诺德.文化与无政府状态：政治与社会批评[M].韩敏中译.北京：三联书店，2002.

[23] 戴维·希克瑞.拜读罗斯金[J].李临艾，郑英锋，译.世界美术，2001，(2).

[24] 卡莱尔.文明的忧思[M].宁小银，译.北京：中国档案出版社，1999.

[25] 陆扬等.文化研究导论[M].上海：复旦大学出版社，2006.

[26] 席勒.审美教育书简[M].冯至，范大灿，译.北京：北京大学出版社，1985.

[27] 赵一凡.西方文论讲稿续编[M].北京：三联书店，2009.

（本文原载于《外国文学》2010年第3期）

文化批评的来龙去脉[*]

一、引言

在过去的四五十年中,文化批评(cultural criticism)逐渐化身为"显学"。几乎在所有的人文、社科领域里,都能见到它的身影,但是关于它的性质和特征,学界至今众说纷纭,莫衷一是。在相关专论中,最值得关注的是美国学者亚瑟·阿萨·伯杰(Arthur Asa Berger)的《文化批评关键概念入门》(*Cultural Criticism: A Primer of Key Concepts*, 1995),以及我国学者王晓路的《西方文论关键词:文化批评》(2014)。称之"最值得关注",是因为伯杰和王晓路都以流畅易懂的语言,回答了以下最基本的问题:文化批评是什么?它做什么?它怎样做?

先来看一下伯杰(1995:2)给出的定义:"文化批评是一种活动,而不是一种学科……文化批评家们运用作者在这本书中所论及的概念和理论,通过各种排列组合,把这些理论应用于高雅艺术、通俗文化、日常生活以及一大堆相关议题。我认为文化批评是一项多学科、跨学科、泛学科或元学科的事业,文化批评家们来自各种各样的学科,所用的思想也来自不同学科。"这一定义同时回答了三个问题,即文化批评是什么(一种活动/事业)、做什么(针对高雅艺

---

[*] 基金项目:本文系浙江省哲学社会科学重点研究基地资助项目"文艺批评研究院"(wypps2020002)的阶段性成果。

术、通俗文化和日常生活中的众多问题进行批评）和怎么做（把经过各种排列组合的理论应用于批评活动）。

与伯杰的阐述相比，王晓路（2014：96）给出的定义更简洁："文化批评是以文化学角度观察、分析和阐释文学文本的批评方式，以此拓展固有的文学批评模式。"定义本身虽然简洁，却有复杂的阐发紧随其后，这在其后续的几段论述中可见一斑：

> 文化批评将文本作为当代商品化的文化产品之一，在分析其构成性要素的同时，着重考察其外部要素，包括文本环境、生产与再生产体制以及传播和接受，其重点是针对文本背后的观念系统。
>
> （王晓路 2014：96）

> 文化要素的介入方式也与人们认知图式的不断扩大有关。人们在结构主义之后所关心的并不完全是知识本身，而是知识之所以成为知识的建构方式，即真理的生产与传播方式。这一点在文学研究中的反映就是对文学观念本身的追问。所以，打破二元对立的实质是对知识谱系背后权力的追问，亦是学界对于社会文化现状的学理考量。
>
> （王晓路 2014：99）

> 文化批评以学理方式关注由技术、法律、道德和艺术四类要素之间发展不平衡所构成的社会文化关系，有针对性地分析四组要素之间所形成的政治文化功能，其主要的兴奋点是历史中和当下的社会文化状况。
>
> （王晓路 2014：102）

所有这些论述都侧重于文化批评的对象——既交代了做什么，也涉及怎样做。事实上，伯杰在《文化批评关键概念入门》中也提到了这些对象，包括文本背后的观念支撑方式、意识形态、知识谱系背后的权力，以及古今社会的文化状况，等等。应该说，伯杰和王晓路所做的界定都没有错，但是它们仍然给我们留下了以下困惑：既然文化批评有那么多事情要做，那么它最主要的对象又是什么呢？是否有那么一条主线，贯穿了它所做的所有工作呢？

笔者认为，若能辨认出主线，就能走出困惑。要说清这条主线，还得从

"文化"观念说起。

二、从"文化"观念说起

在当今学界,许多阐述文化批评的人都省掉了一道工序,即对"文化批评"中的"文化"未做界定。更确切地说,如今大多数人在使用"文化"一词时,都想当然地认定别人都知道它的所指,可实际情形往往是:此文化非彼文化;论者心中想的是一种文化,而读者理解的则是另一种文化。之所以如此,是因为"很少有比'文化'更成问题的词语了"(Fuery 1997: xviii)。早在半个世纪以前,克洛依伯和克拉克洪(Kroeber & Kluckhohn)就在其名著《文化:概念和定义批判分析》(*Culture: A Critical Review of Concepts and Definitions*, 1963)中整理出上百个文化定义,并归类为"九种基本文化概念,它们分别是哲学的、艺术的、教育的、心理学的、历史的、人类学的、社会学的、生态学的和生物学的"(陆扬 等2006: 3)。我们不禁要问:在如此之多的"文化"中,哪一个可以作为文化批评的基础呢?因此,可以断言,在对文化加以清晰界定之前,任何尝试文化批评的努力难免都是以其昏昏,使人昭昭。

在众多关于文化定义的论述中,最具影响力的理论来自雷蒙德·威廉斯(Raymond Williams)(1983: 87—90)。他在《关键词》(*Keywords: A Vocabulary of Culture and Society*, 1983)一书中把"文化"最常见的用法归为三类:① 用来形容思想、精神和审美演变的总体过程;② 表示一个群体、一个时期、一个民族乃至全人类的某种特定生活方式;③ 指涉思想艺术领域的实践和成果。威廉斯的归纳虽然比前人的梳理清晰了许多,但是他仍然未能说明一个关键问题:对西方文学和文艺理论来说,文化概念在现代的最重要内涵是什么?

针对上述缺憾,笔者曾在《"文化辩护书":19世纪英国文化批评》(以下简称《辩护书》)一书中提出并论证了如下观点:现代意义上的"文化"概念在19世纪的英国经历了最重要的内涵演变,而这一演变根植于"现代性焦虑",即农业文明向工业文明转型而引起的焦虑;就这一内涵的演变而言,"卡莱尔、阿诺德、罗斯金、金斯利和莫里斯等人做了根基性的工作"(殷企平 2013: 3—4)。更具体地说,这五位"维多利亚贤哲"(Victorian saints)持续表达了对于

"现代文明"的焦虑，或者说对工业文明引起的社会转型做出了回应，其内容和性质则在文化观念的流动轨迹中得到了生动的体现。继《辩护书》之后，笔者又在《经由维多利亚文学的文化观念流变》（2017）一文中提出，上述文化观念内涵的形成不仅仅得益于托马斯·卡莱尔（Thomas Carlyle）、马修·阿诺德（Matthew Arnold）、约翰·罗斯金（John Ruskin）和威廉·莫里斯（William Morris），而且得益于几乎所有优秀的维多利亚作家；他们所作的贡献有一个共同点，即"或不约而同，或前呼后应地承担起了给'文化'和'文明'分家的工作"（殷企平 2017：85）。笔者提出这一观点，是受到了特里·伊格尔顿（Terry Eagleton）的启发。后者先后在《文化观念》（*The Idea of Culture*，2000）和《文化》（*Culture*，2016）这两部力作中描述了"文化"从其母体"文明"脱胎换骨的过程。他在《文化观念》中指出，"文化"和"文明"原先好比一家人，两者实为"同义词，都隶属于启蒙精神"，但是后来"文化观念从'文明'的同义词转变成了它的反义词"（Eagleton 2000：9）。究其原因，无非是"文明"的异化——"文明"一词原本语义为"集事实与价值于一身"，可是后来却发生了分裂（Eagleton 2000：10）。换言之，"文明"的语义原有两个基本层面：一是描述层面（关乎事实）；二是规范层面（关乎价值）。但是随着工业革命的兴起，这两个语义层面产生了分裂：描述/物质层面犹在，而规范/精神层面却丧失殆尽。为强调这一点，伊格尔顿（2016：10）在时隔16年后出版的《文化》一书中更言简意赅地指出："文明如今只关乎事实，而文化却追问价值。"也就是说，"文明"原有的价值使命，如今只能由"文化"来承担了。造成这种局面的，就是上文所说的工业革命，而后者是以"机械崛起"为特征的——我们不妨借用中国台湾学者陈德如（2006：2）的一段话来加以描述：

> 工业革命如此不满于现状而无止于积极求进……我们从此只能越来越快，快到来不及细数便忘记，快到无以再得仔细辨认方向的余裕……文明进展提升到前所未有的速度，人类不再以己身的体能与感知系统来掌握物质的速度与重力，机械之崛起从此改变了生活的内容。

机械崛起，意味着精神沦丧。不过，伊格尔顿（2016：10）还看到了事情的另一面:"与工业革命同时兴起的,是对文明本身的激烈反抗,因为后者在总体上已经精神沦丧了。"正是在这一意义上,我们可以说"是工业革命助产了文化观念"(Eagleton 2016:10)。也正是在伊格尔顿这一观点的启发下,笔者在《经由维多利亚文学的文化观念流变》一文中列举大量例子,证明了以下观点:

> 维多利亚文学家们往往以生动的故事、诗性的语言和熠熠生辉的人物形象来传达自己的文化思想,亦即构建文化观念的内涵。他们的言说往往有一个共同点,即鲜明地采取了与"文明"决裂的战斗性姿态。采取这一姿态的人数之多,影响之广,言辞之激烈,是维多利亚时期之前所未见的。这种姿态由莫里斯的一句名言得到了诠释,即:"我一生的主要激情,过去和现在都表现为对现代文明的仇恨。"可以说,"文化"与"文明"的决裂至此已经完成,而它就是文化观念成熟的标志。

(殷企平 2017:86)

伴随着上述"文化"巡礼,本文的首要立论也已显山露水:文化批评的基础恰恰是与"文明"决裂的文化。从批判"文明"弊端入手,我们就能抓住文化批评的主线。那么,这条主线是怎样贯穿文化批评的呢?本文下一小节将加以探讨。

三、文化即批判

如上所述,"文化批评"这一术语的重心是"文化"。更确切地说,文化批评的性质从一开始就被文化的本质规定了:文化即批判,即对"文明"弊端的批判。"文明"弊端五花八门,体现于生活的方方面面,但是有一个共同特点,即"分裂"。早在 18 世纪末,弗里德里希·冯·席勒(Friedrich von Schiller)(1985:29—30)就曾指出,现代文明的特点是"无限众多但都没有生命的部分拼凑在一起,从而构成了一个机械生活的整体……人永远被束缚在整体的一个孤零零的小碎片上……永远不能发展他本质的和谐"。针对这一特点,文化批评也形成了自己的特点,即用"整体"来抗衡"分裂"。换言之,文化意味着和谐性、整体性（无论就个人的发展而言，还是就社会的发展而言），意味着对片面性、机械性和功利性的批判。真正的文化批评，其具体对象可能会不同，批评方式可能会更迭，涉及的理论和领域可能会变换，但是万变不离其宗，它必然以反对"分裂"为宗旨，反对那种使人类社会的整体性或和谐性遭受侵蚀的异化现象。

下面以文化批评史上几位杰出代表为例来说明他们都是以维护"整体"、抗拒"分裂"为宗旨的。

前文提到的阿诺德是文化批评史上绕不过去的人物。他在《文学与科学》(*Literature and Science*, 1882, 1897) 一文中发表了如下论断："科学一劳永逸地摧毁了关于世界的'神秘观'，让诸多正宗的宗教变得不堪一击，因而危害了人类与周围世界的整体性。在这种情形下，人类比以往任何时候都更需要诗歌，这是因为诗歌持开放态度，它把人类所有经验都融为一体，就连古老的宗教冲动也被包含在内"（Arnold 1897: 125）。阿诺德生活在一个科学事业蒸蒸日上的年代，正当大家都在为科学进步拍手叫好（也就是在为"文明"叫好）之际，他却看到了事物的另一面：一味强调科学进步，会让人与周围世界的整体性受到危害。他写文学/诗歌与科学的关系，其实就是倡导人类社会整体性发展，反对呈"分裂"状态的单向度发展。

罗斯金曾这样评论工业革命进程中大规模生产的分工方式："分工劳动可真是伟大文明的一大发明。近来我们把它又研究并完善了一番，只不过我们给它取了一个虚假的名字。说实话，我们并不是在分工，而是在分人——人被分成了一个个片段——分解成了生命的碎片和细屑。结果，一个人的智力所剩无几，甚至不足以制造一枚别针或一颗钉子。仅仅制造针尖或钉子头就耗尽了一个人的智力"（Matteson 2002: 299）。罗斯金此处所谈，表面上跟阿诺德的上述话题风马牛不相及——罗斯金谈的是分工劳动，而阿诺德却是在谈文学和科学的关系；然而，他俩关注的问题在实质上是一样的，都是反对"分裂"，倡导"整体"。事实上，他们所关注的"分裂"现象是多种多样的。仅以罗斯金为例：他把批评矛头指向了形形色色的"分离"，包括"思想与感受分离，时间与空间分离，肉体与灵魂分离，行动与意图分离，计划与实施分离"（希克瑞 2001: 47）。这就应了我们在前文强调的观点：文化批评的具体对象可以千变万化，但是主线只有一条，即反对"分裂"。

同样的主线延续到了 20 世纪，这在托马斯·斯特恩斯·艾略特（Thomas Stearns Eliot）那里就颇具代表性。艾略特无论是在从事文学创作/批评时，还是在从事文化批评时，都十分强调"整体"和"部分"的辩证关系。说起艾略特的诗艺，许多人首先会把他作为现代主义的鼻祖，而很少有人会察觉他的灵感首先来自 17 世纪以及此前的诗坛，就像他在《玄学派诗人》（*The Metaphysical Poets*, 1950）一文中谈到的那样——他强调这一点，其实是从文化整体观出发的。在他看来，17 世纪早期的英国，哪怕是一位次要诗人，也能作为文化的表率，这是因为他在那个时期发现了"人类经验的整体性"（an integration of experience）；他发现那时人的思想和情感、高贵和平凡、精神和肉体都不被看作互不相关的，因而不需要用不同的话语来加以表述。让他感到悲哀的是，在随后的几个世纪里，人类渐渐被不同话语——如科学话语、宗教话语、社会学话语等等——分割了，或者说正在经历一种愈演愈烈的"感受力解体"（dissociation of sensibility）过程（Eliot 2001：1103）。正因为如此，艾略特积极倡导"整体感受力"（the associated sensibility），主张人类在认知/体验世界时应该兼收并蓄，或以兼容并包的态度去拥抱世界（Collini 2008：263）。

艾略特常常被看作新批评（New Criticism）的先驱，这不无道理，不过他对新批评的首要影响与其说在于诗艺，不如说在于文化批评层面。英国学者斯蒂芬·科里尼（Stephan Collini）（2008：263）曾经把艾略特的"整体感受力"和英国新批评代表人物艾弗·阿姆斯特朗·瑞恰兹（Ivor Armstrong Richards）的"联觉"（synaesthesia）、美国南方重农派观念中的"南方"（the South）以及利维斯的"有机共同体"（the organic community）相提并论，指出"它们都作为完整的形式而受到珍视，它们所对抗的是片面化、碎片化、专业化和工具化"。这一评价颇有见地，它指出上述批评家的主张和活动（实为文化批评活动）看似不同，可是都遵循了一条主线，即反对分裂，捍卫整体。须特别一提的是瑞恰兹的"联觉"——人们通常把它看作一种修辞手段，或者说一种技巧，但是科里尼指出了它的实质：联觉本身就暗示"联通"和"联合"，因而彰显了一种整体文化观。

艾略特的文化思想尤其在弗兰克·雷蒙德·利维斯（Frank Raymond Leavis）

那里得到了继承和发展。在《共同的诉求》(The Common Pursuit, 1952) 一书的前言中，利维斯借用了艾略特关于文学批评的定义，即"对真知灼见的共同诉求"(the common pursuit of true judgement)，以此强调文学批评是一种"合作性劳动"(cooperative labour)，亦即一种体现整体性的劳动（Leavis 2008: v）。在他的著述里，"合作性""集体性"和"创造性"是高频词，而且常常一起出现，这跟他的文化观和语言观有很大关系。就像英国沃里克大学教授迈克尔·贝尔（Michael Bell）（2000: 398—401）指出的那样："利维斯那兼容并包的文学观、文学史观和文学批评观都以他的语言观为支撑点。……利维斯明确关心集体的创造过程，这一过程源自无数个人的努力——这些努力未经协调，但都汇入了语言，从而成为未来言说者的资源。利维斯特别强调，个人存在于语言……"这里，利维斯的整体文化观清晰地呈现在了我们面前——个人通过语言与世界实现了连接。利维斯谈语言，谈文学，然而他分明又在批判"文明"的弊端。他的如下论述对此表现得痛快淋漓：

> 文学的重要性不仅仅是因为它本身很重要，而且还因为它蕴藏着创造性的能量；后者在现代"商业化"的社会中到处都处于守势。在文学中，或许只有在文学中，一种鲜活的、创造性地运用语言的感觉仍然显而易见，这与"大众社会"里语言和传统文化的贬值和庸俗化形成了鲜明的对比。一个社会的语言质量是其成员个人和社会生活质量最有说服力的标志：一个不再珍重文学的社会是一个致命的、封闭激情的社会，而激情创造并维持了人类文明的精华。（Eagleton 1994: 50）

此处，利维斯把语言、文学和人类社会创造力之间的整体关系阐述得十分透彻。这一思想还贯穿于他的具体文学批评实践。例如，他在评论查尔斯·狄更斯（Charles Dickens）的《艰难时世》(Hard Times, 1854) 时，针对小说中葛擂硬先生（Mr. Gradqrind）只用"第二十号"来称呼西丝·朱浦（Cecilia Jupe），导致后者在慌乱中反应迟钝这一情景，做了如下鞭辟入里的分析：西丝"对教育的迟钝反应，乃是她身上那至高无上而无法根除的人性的必然流露：正是她的美德使她不能理解，也不能默认把她当作'二十号女生'的那种时代精神,使她无法把一个人想象成一个算术上的单元"(利维斯 2002:382—383)。①透过这层分析,我们可以再次看到尖锐的文化批评:19 世纪的英国一味追求"进步",其代价之一就是把生活简化;西丝这个有血有肉的小女孩被简化成了一个干巴巴的数字。这样的简化,就是我们前面所说的"分裂",就是"文明"的弊端。

同样的文化批评主线在利维斯之后仍然不断地延伸,一直持续到了今天。本文下一小节将继续这一话题,并展望文化批评的走向。

四、文化批评的走向

要预测文化批评的走向,首先还得回顾它原来的走势。我们在前面的分析中,其实埋下了一个伏笔:最有影响力的文化批评工作,其实是由优秀的文学家们来完成的。然而,在过去的五六十年里,情形似乎发生了很大的变化。学界越来越多的人认为,文化批评已经与文学渐行渐远,这在下引叙述中可见一斑:"20 世纪 60 年代初期,'文化批评'从侧重大传统与经典研读的层面,转移到日常生活的研究上……70 年代以降,新兴的'文化批评',挟着女性主义、少数话语、后结构或后现代主义的方法及社会关怀,对好莱坞的电影、新闻广播、电视连续剧、各种娱乐节目的各种观众、机构历史、生产技术、消费行为及其效果等,均加以仔细研究……"(王晓路 2014:100—101)。就连美国最出色的文化批评家之一苏珊·桑塔格(Susan Sontag)也曾在 1965 年发文,声称已经出现了一种"新感受力",而"新感受力的首要特征,在于它不以文学作品作为典范,尤其不以小说为典范"(Sontag 2009:298)。她还断定,当代"大多数具有创造性的艺术家(小说家极少能被列入其中)……发现马修·阿诺德的文化观念已经不合时宜;无论就历史意义而言,还是就人类经验而言,都是如此,因此他们已经与这种观念决裂了"(Sontag 2009:299)。这难道是事实吗?

应该承认,如今许多以"文化批评"名义开展的活动都发生在非文学领域,但在诸多领域中,是否有一个中心呢?笔者以为,中心是存在的,而且仍然是

---

① 参照袁伟译文,部分文字作了更动。

文学。

比桑塔格稍早一点的美国杰出文化批评家莱昂内尔·特里林（Lionel Trilling）（1968：12）有一段话，可以给我们带来启发："我自己的兴趣引导我发现，文学情景就是文化情景，文化情景就是围绕道德问题而展开的伟大而艰辛的战斗，道德问题跟毫无理由地选中的私人形象不无关系，而私人形象则跟文学风格不无关系。"特里林如此看重文学，源自他的文化批评思想。在其名著《自由想象》（The Liberal Imagination，1950/2008）里，他把批评的矛头对准了自由主义及其背后的启蒙思想遗产，即理性主义和功利主义（也就是我们前面所说的西方文明的思想特征）。他指出，美国的知识阶层（the educated class）一方面"信仰进步、科学、社会立法和国际合作"，另一方面却"不见有任何一位一流作家用伟大的文学方式来处理这些思想，以及与之相一致的情感"（Trilling 2008：98）。他进而指出："在我们自由知识阶层和我们时代最优秀的文学人才之间，没有任何联系。也就是说，在我们知识阶层的政治思想和深度想象领地之间，没有任何联系"（Trilling 2008：98—99）。此处的"深度想象领地"（the deep places of the imagination）指的就是文学。特里林从文化角度给美国文明诊脉，发现它的最大弊端就是政治和文学的分离，而这在他眼里是"致命的分裂"（the fatal separation）（Trilling 2008：99）。特里林（2008：103）不仅诊断出了"文明"的毛病，而且开出了如下药方：

（文学批评的功能就是）让自由主义迷途知返，使其恢复原有的基本想象成分，即关于世界千姿百态、充满各种可能性这一现实的想象。这种想象意味着一个人在面临复杂和困难局面时，能审时度势……要做到这一点，就要依靠文学……文学这一人类活动，能给予事物的复杂性最充分、最精确的考量，既敏锐感知世间万千气象，又明察人生百味千状，因而最能应对扑朔迷离的情形。

特里林诊治"分裂"的药方就是想象力，因为无论是人类整体经验，还是全局意识的养成，都离不开想象力。更确切地说，特里林（2008：222）提倡的是一种"道德想象"（the moral imagination）：

> 就我们时代而言，道德想象最有效的手段是小说，过去两百多年皆是如此。……小说的伟大之处和实用之处在于，它坚持不懈地把读者自己卷入有道德的生活，邀请他审视自己的行为动机，暗示他反思自己对现实的认识，从而意识到现实与先前常规教育中所说的并不一样。小说教会我们认识人类的包罗万象，以及这种丰富性的价值，而其他文类还未做到这一点。

值得一提的是，特里林认为道德想象最有效的手段是文学，尤其是小说，这跟前文所述桑塔格的观点恰好相反。那么，面对这两种针锋相对的观点，我们应该接受哪一种呢？

依笔者之见，当今文化批评的主战场仍然是在文学领域。限于篇幅，我们仅以当代英国为例。

反对"分裂"，呼唤想象力，这是当代英国文学家所作文化批评的一个主要特征。例如，安东尼娅·苏珊·拜厄特（Antonia Susan Byatt）在其小说《天使与昆虫》（*Angels and Insects*, 1992）中塑造了一个"自我分裂"的人物形象：主人公威廉享受着高度的物质文明，可是他并不幸福，而是"觉得自己被分裂开来与自我作对"（拜厄特 2012：61）。同样的分裂现象见于格雷厄姆·斯威夫特（Graham Swift）的小说《此后皆如此》（*Ever After*）："世界正在散架；它的社会结构破碎了，它的经济体系濒于崩溃"（Swift 1993：4）。无独有偶，石黑一雄（Kazuo Ishiguro）的《别让我走》（*Never Let Me Go*, 2005）也呈现了一个散了架的世界，一个"更科学、更高效……却很苛刻而残酷的世界"（Ishiguro 2005：272）——科学发达了，效率提高了，可是人的幸福感却降低了，甚至丧失了，这不啻为一种残酷的"分裂症"，更是典型的"文明病"。类似的例子不胜枚举，仅再以马丁·艾米斯（Martin Amis）的《时间之箭：罪行的本质》（*Time's Arrow: Or the Nature of the Offense*）为例。该小说人物奥迪罗（Odilo）在经受第二次世界大战创伤之后（从本质上讲，战争及其灾难应归咎于主导西方文明进程的资本主义逻辑），发现自己的"人生被撕裂了，被撕碎了"（Amis 1992：116）。

面对上述"分裂症"，当代英国文学家们的文化策略是高擎想象力火炬。这方面最典型的要数彼得·阿克罗伊德（Peter Ackroyd）。他的《英国音乐》（*English Music*，1992）围绕"音乐"这条主线展开，而这"音乐"指的"就是关于民族共同体的想象"（殷企平 2016：65）。除了文学创作，阿克罗伊德还发表过一部颇有影响的专著，"想象"一词在其题目中赫然入目：《阿尔比恩：英格兰想象的起源》（*Albion: The Origins of the English Imagination*，2002）。不仅如此，他还像桑塔格关注"新感受力"那样，关注起"新文化"来，并发表《新文化札记》（*Notes for a New Culture*，1976）一书。此书堪称文化批评杰作，它关注的虽是整个文化，却颇着力于从文学作品中寻找"存在于英国文化内部的生成性力量"，如塞缪尔·泰勒·柯勒律治（Samuel Taylor Coleridge）诗作的生成性力量——阿克罗伊德对柯氏（Ackroyd 1993：31）的如下观点特别欣赏："'想象力'是人与世界的中介。"培育想象力的努力，同样出现于伊恩·麦克尤恩（Ian McEwan）（2001：3）的笔下。他在一次访谈中坦言自己写小说是为了"展示设身处地想象他人的可能性……人之所以会残酷，就是因为缺乏想象力"。另一位著名小说家斯威夫特（1997：155）也曾直言：小说创作"全是关于想象，即设身处地想象他人……我们至少要努力想象其他人的生活是怎样的；假如不这么做，我们就会失败，不光做人失败，而且导致社会的失败"。还须一提的是拜厄特，她不仅致力于呈现设身处地想象他人的可能性，还致力于点燃世人关于过去与现在之间连接纽带的想象力，这一点已经为美国学者布赖恩·芬尼（Brian Finney）（2006：85）所道破："拜厄特跟阿克罗伊德分享了一个信念，即'过去与现在能有效地互相渗透'。"显然，以想象力为武器，抗拒以"分裂"为特征的文明，已经成为一种文化批评的主要策略，而在这方面做出表率的仍然是文学家，至少在英国是如此。

让我们再回到桑塔格。前文提到，她认为当代文化批评已经"不以文学作品作为典范"。桑塔格是在1965年发表这一观点的，不过时隔30年，她在《反对阐释》1996年版的后记（2009：312）中做了反思："当年我在谴责某种浅薄的道德说教时（如在关于科幻电影和卢卡奇的论文中），是以一种严肃态度的名义——比那种道德说教更带有警觉性的态度，并且不那么沾沾自喜。可是我当时未能理解的是（那时候的我肯定理解不了），严肃本身在整个文化中已经开始失去其可信度。我当时很享受某些较为出格的艺术，殊不知这些东西会强化轻浮的出格行为，会强化消费主义行为。"从中我们似乎能读出这样一层深意：当年桑塔格所提倡的"新感受力"——对于（排斥文学的）出格艺术的感受力——有悖于文化批评的初衷。从桑塔格的反思中，我们可以瞥见文化批评的走向：它仍将沿着阿诺德等人划定的路线前行。

五、结语

总之，欲知晓文化批评的来龙去脉，须从"文化"与"文明"的分野入手。文化批评，即针对"文明"弊端的批评活动。它反对"分离"，抗拒异化，关注人类社会的整体性与和谐性。对整体性与和谐性的诉求离不开想象力，而文学是最具想象力的学科。因此，文化批评的手段尽管是跨学科、多学科和超学科的，却需要以文学为中心，否则有可能流于肤浅。

参考文献

[1] Ackroyd P. *Notes for a New Culture* [M]. London：Alkin Books, 1993.

[2] Amis M. *Time's Arrow: Or the Nature of the Offense* [M]. New York：Vintage Books, 1992.

[3] Arnold M. Literature and Science [A] //Lewis E. Gates（ed.）. *Selections from the Prose Writings of Matthew Arnold* [M]. New York：Henry Holt, 1898.

[4] Litz, A W. *The Cambridge History of Literary Criticism（Vol. 7），Modernism and New Criticism* [M]. Cambridge：Cambridge University Press, 2000.

[5] Berger A A. *Cultural Criticism: A Primer of Key Concepts* [M]. London：Sage Publications, 1995.

[6] Collini S. *Common Reading: Critics, Historians, Publics* [M]. Oxford：Oxford University Press, 2008.

[7] Eagleton T. *Culture* [M]. New Haven and London：Yale University Press, 2016.

[8] Eagleton T. *The Idea of Culture* [M]. Oxford：Blackwell, 2000.

[9] Eagleton T. The Rise of English [A] //David H. Richter（ed.）. *Falling

into Theory [M]. Boston: St. Martin's Press, 1994.

[10] Eliot T S. The Metaphysical Poets [A] //Vincent B. Leitch (ed.). Norton Anthology of Theory and Criticism [M]. New York: W. W. Norton, 2001.

[11] Finney B. *English Fiction Since 1984: Narrating a Nation* [M]. New York: Palgrave Macmillan, 2006.

[12] Fuery P, Mansfield N. *Cultural Studies and the New Humanities: Concepts and Controversies* [M]. Oxford: Oxford University Press, 1997.

[13] Ishiguro K. *Never Let Me Go* [M]. New York: Knopf, 2005.

[14] Leavis F R. *The Common Pursuit* [M]. London: Faber and Faber Ltd., 2008.

[15] Matteson J. Constructing ethics and the ethics of construction: John Ruskin and the humanity of the builder [J]. *Cross Currents*, 2002 (3): 294 – 305.

[16] McEwan I. Review: Interview: At Home with His Worries [N]. Observer, 2001 – 09 – 16 (3).

[17] Sontag S. *Against Interpretation and Other Essays* [M]. London: Penguin Books Ltd., 1996/2009.

[18] Swift G. *Ever After* [M]. New York: Vintage, 1993.

[19] Swift G. Graham Swift in interview on last orders [J]. Anglistik, 1997 (8): 155 – 160.

[20] Trilling L. *Beyond Culture: Essays on Literature and Learning* [M]. New York: Viking Adult, 1968.

[21] Trilling L. *The Liberal Imagination* [M]. New York: New York Review Books, 1950 /2008.

[22] Williams R. *Keywords: A Vocabulary of Culture and Society* [M]. Flamingo: Fontana Press, 1983.

[23] 安东尼娅·苏珊·拜厄特. 天使与昆虫 [M]. 杨向荣, 译. 海口: 南海出版公司, 2012.

[24] 陈德如. 建筑的七盏明灯: 浅谈罗斯金的建筑思维 [M]. 台北: 商务印

书馆，2006.

[25] 戴维·希克瑞.拜读罗斯金[J].李临艾等，译.世界美术，2001（2）：45-48.

[26] 弗兰克·雷蒙德·利维斯.伟大的传统[M].袁伟，译.北京：生活·读书·新知三联书店，2002.

[27] 弗里德里希·席勒.审美教育书简[M].冯至等，译.北京：北京大学出版社，1985.

[28] 陆扬，王毅.文化研究导论[M].上海：复旦大学出版社，2006.

[29] 王晓路.西方文论关键词：文化批评[J].外国文学，2014（3）：98-106.

[30] 殷企平.经由维多利亚文学的文化观念流变[J].浙江外国语学院学报，2017（5）：83-91.

[31] 殷企平."文化辩护书"：19世纪英国文化批评[M].上海：上海外语教育出版社，2013.

[32] 殷企平.英国文学中的音乐与共同体形塑[J].外国文学研究，2016（5）：58-68.

（本文原载于《英语研究》2020年第2期）

趣味即文化：
阿诺德对文学批评的贡献[*]

关于阿诺德（Matthew Arnold，1822—1888）对文学批评的贡献，学界至今仍仁者见仁，智者见智。在贬损他的声音中，有两种观点最具影响：1. 阿诺德是精英主义者，他的文学批评思想只为统治阶级服务；2. 阿诺德虽对文学批评有贡献，却称不上批评家。前一种观点的代表人物是伊格尔顿（Terry Eaglton，1943—　　），后一种观点的代表则是艾略特（T. S. Eliot，1888—1965）。后者虽然早已过世，但是他的相关论点仍被不少在世学者沿袭。

倘若上面两种观点成立，那么我们就很难解释如下现象：几乎在所有世界文学批评史专论中，阿诺德都是一位绕不过去的人物。以美国芝加哥大学教授里克特（David H. Richter）主编的鸿篇巨制《批评传统：经典文本与当代趋势》（*The Critical Tradition: Classical Texts and Contemporary Trends*，2005）为例，阿诺德所占篇幅在30页之上。除里克特之外，还有不少著名学者通过专门著述积极评价阿诺德在文学批评史上的功绩，如利维斯（F. R. Leavis，1895—1978）的《作为批评家的阿诺德》（*Arnold as Critic*，1938）、特里林（Lionel Trilling，1905—1975）的《马修·阿诺德》（*Matthew Arnold*，1939）和斯通（Donald Stone，

---

[*] 基金项目：国家社科基金一般项目"英国文学中的'趣味'理论变迁研究"（16BWW011）；浙江省哲学社会科学重点研究基地"文艺批评研究院"资助（wypps2020002）。

1942—2021)的《与未来沟通:对话中的马修·阿诺德》(*Communications with the Future: Matthew Arnold in Dialogue*,1997)等。这种现象不仅意味着艾略特和伊格尔顿等人的观点有误,也要求我们深入地、多角度地从事阿诺德研究,进而更具体地说明艾略特、伊格尔顿等人对阿诺德的诟病为何有失偏颇。依笔者之见,若要对阿诺德文学批评思想做出较公允的评价,就得从他的趣味观入手。本文以下的三个小节都将围绕"趣味"这一关键词而展开。

一、趣味:阿诺德文化蓝图的中枢

阿诺德的文学批评是他文化蓝图的核心部分,而趣味则可谓核心的核心。

作为关键词的"趣味"(taste),常常出现在阿诺德的文学评论中。例如,他在评论格雷(Thomas Grey,1716—1771)、华兹华斯(William Wordsworth,1770—1850)和雪莱(Percy Bysshe Shelley,1792—1822)等人的作品时都讨论了趣味问题。[①] 至于他的批评理论,那就更离不开趣味话题了。利维斯在《作为批评家的阿诺德》中曾讨论他的《诗歌研究》("The Study of Poetry",1880),认为它"之所以令人难忘,是因为它树立了维多利亚时期的趣味标杆"(Leavis 1968:260)。这一评价是十分中肯的。为进一步探究趣味跟阿诺德的文学批评/文化思想之间的关系,我们以下将从他给文学批评下的定义说起。

阿诺德在其《批评在当前的功能》(The Function of Criticism at the Present Time,1864)一文中,曾经这样界定文学批评:"可以说,我把批评界定为一种非常微妙而间接的行动,它拥抱印度式的超然美德,置身于实用生活领域之外〔……〕讲求实用的人不擅长对事物作细微的区分,而恰恰是在这些区分中,真理和最高层次的文化才能够体现其不凡价值。"[②] 这一定义虽未直接使用"趣味"(taste)一词,但说的就是趣味问题——强调"非常微妙而间接的行动",以及"对事物作细微的区分",并在真理和文化层次上体现"不凡价值",这其实就是强调文学批评中的趣味。正如朱光潜先生所说,"鉴别力就是趣味",而

---

① 参见 Arnold, *Essays in Criticism: Second Series*, pp. 75, 77, 125, 129, 239。
② 参见 Arnold, *Lectures and Essays in Criticism*, pp. 274-275。后文凡出自该著作的引文,随文仅标注具体页码,不再另行做注。

文学创作"在命意布局遣词造句上都须辨析锱铢，审慎抉择"（朱光潜 2006：97）。此处的"辨析锱铢"就是阿诺德所说的"细微的区分"。又如日本美学家竹内敏雄所说，"趣味"是指"享受美的对象、判断它的价值的能力"（转引自李春青 2014：3），而阿诺德心目中的文学批评正是对批评/审美对象做出价值判断。

在《批评在当前的功能》中，阿诺德还给文学批评的"任务"（business）下了一个定义，即"了解世界上最优秀的知识和思想，进而宣传它们，以创造真实而鲜活的思想洪流"（阿诺德 2008：270）。这个关于文学批评"做什么"的定义跟上面那个"是什么"的定义是紧密相连的。从某种意义上说，此处"是什么"跟"做什么"是同一个定义的两个方面。正因为如此，美国学者斯通在总结阿诺德的批评观时做了这样的表述："用阿诺德自己的话说，批评是一种行动的形式，即向公众展示'世界上最优秀的知识和思想，进而宣传它们，以创造真实而鲜活的思想洪流'〔……〕它（笔者按：指文学批评及其机构）的使命是提升英国人的趣味"（Stone 1997：15）。此处特别值得一提的是，"世界上最优秀的知识和思想"一语不仅多次出现在阿诺德的文学批评作品中，还常常被他单独用作关于文化的定义。例如，他的名著《文化与失序》①（*Culture and Anarchy: An Essay in Political and Social Criticism*, 1867—1869）前言中就有一段涉及文化性质和功能的概述：

> 全文的意图是大力推荐文化，以帮助我们走出目前的困境。在与我们密切相关的所有问题上，世界上有过什么最优秀的思想和言论，文化都要了解，并通过学习最优秀知识的手段去追求全面的完美。我们现在不屈不挠地却也是机械教条地遵循着陈旧的固有观念和习惯；我们虚幻地认为，不屈不挠地走下去就是德行，可以弥补过于机械刻板而造成的负面影响。但文化了解了世界上最优秀的思想和言论，就会调动起鲜活的思想之流，来冲击我们坚定而刻板地尊奉的固有观念和习惯。〔……〕我们所推荐的文化，首先是一种内向的行动。（阿诺德《文化与无政府状态》185—186）

---

① 该著题目一般被译为《文化与无政府状态》，但是笔者认为"失序"更贴近书中 anarchy 的原义。

这一关于文化的定义中不仅反复强调了"最优秀的思想和言论"及"最优秀知识",而且强调要"调动起鲜活的思想之流",这几乎跟前述文学批评的定义一模一样。也就是说,在阿诺德心目中,文学批评就是文化的一部分,而且是其核心部分。更须指出的是,无论是阿诺德的文化,还是他的文学批评,都是以趣味为轴心的。对这一点的理解必须结合阿诺德对机械主义的批判——上引文字中两次出现了"机械"一词:"机械教条地遵循着陈旧的固有观念和习惯",以及"机械刻板而造成的负面影响",而机械主义者显然是趣味低下的,甚至是毫无趣味的。熟悉阿诺德的人都知道,他一生都把批判矛头对准了信奉机械主义的英国中产阶级,并称后者为"非利士人"(Philistines),这一带有贬义的外号在《文化与失序》一书中俯拾皆是。英国学者琼斯曾经根据《文化与失序》中的阐述,指出非利士主义的主要特征之一就是"趣味平庸低俗"(Jones 1998:2—3)。换言之,文化的批评对象就是非利士主义,而后者的特征就是低级趣味。这在阿诺德的另一部名作《海因里希·海涅》中写得更为明白:文中把"非利士人"描述为"单调乏味、墨守成规、与光明为敌的人;这种人愚昧成性,压制持不同意见者,但是势力很大"(Arnold, *Heinrich Heine* 1962:112)。令人回味的是,阿诺德把"单调乏味"用来作为英国中产阶级——光明/文化的敌人——的首要修饰语,可见趣味在他的文化考量中有多重要。

简而言之,要了解阿诺德的文学批评观,就须了解他的文化观。然而,他所说的"文化"曾频遭攻评。例如,伊格尔顿就视阿诺德为艾迪生(Joseph Addison, 1672—1719)一类的"精英主义"文人兼批评家,并认为后者的"文化就是帮助巩固英国统治集团的东西,而批评家则是这一历史性任务的承担者"(Eagleton, *The Function of Criticism* 12)。基于这一立场,伊格尔顿断定阿诺德的文学批评使命是"把中产阶级意识形态这一药剂裹上文学糖衣"(Eagleton, *Literary Theory* 1983:26),或者说是帮助没落贵族阶级向它的中产阶级新主人提供精神库存:"中产阶级自己无法炮制出一套丰富而精致的意识形态,以此巩固自己的政治和经济权力,因此在阿诺德看来,社会的当务之急是用'希腊精神'来教化粗俗的中产阶级〔……〕"(Eagleton, *Literary Theory* 1983:24)言下之意,刚从贵族阶级那里夺得政治、经济领导权的英国中产阶级/资产阶级急需进一步夺取文化领导权。伊格尔顿的下述定论至今还颇有影响："安东尼奥·葛兰西为现代无产阶级所作的诉求——主张无产阶级不但要争取物质权利，而且要争取'道德与精神领导权'——正是阿诺德为维多利亚资产阶级所作的诉求"（Eagleton *The Eagleton Reader* 1998：172）。情形果真如此吗？

假如伊格尔顿所述属实，那么阿诺德怎会用极其激烈的言辞来抨击"非利士人"呢？他眼中那些"单调乏味""愚昧成性""与光明为敌的人"即便能接受"希腊精神"的教化，恐怕也不配拥有文化领导权吧？换言之，只从意识形态的视角死抠问题，无异于戕害阿诺德文化思想的精髓。任何作家都会在不同程度上受到所处时代、社会和阶级的局限，但是出类拔萃者总会试图超越这些局限性，阿诺德就是这样一位超越者。他的大量著述都表明，他最关心的问题不是由哪个阶级来掌握文化领导权，而是如何实现新旧社会之间的完美过渡；不仅如此，他还在许多场合表达了对各个阶级中"异己分子"——亦即各社会阶层中"最优秀的自我"——的欣赏。① 历史上有不少人批评他的"精英主义"意识，但是如果我们参考一下《牛津英语词典》（*Oxford English Dictionary* 2009），就会发现"精英主义"（élitism）这一词条的释义是"提倡或依靠（社会或任何团体或阶级的）精英的领导"。换言之，这样的精英并非必然来自某个固定的社会阶层。如果我们做进一步考察，就会发现阿诺德曾在《伦敦东部》（"East London"，1867）和《伦敦西部》（"West London"，1867）等诗作中表明，身处社会底层的小人物也可以是精英。《伦敦西部》中就这样写道：一位身处社会最底层的流浪女子"拒绝来自大人物的冰冷的施舍，／因为大人物对无名小人物并不体谅。／她指引我们向往胜过这个时代的美好时光"（Arnold, *West London* 1949：566—567）。当然，小人物也好，大人物也好，都必须具备阿诺德所提倡的"世界上最优秀的知识和思想"，而这里"最优秀"一词指的就是对完美的追求。

正是在对完美的追求中，阿诺德看到了文学批评的作用，看到了趣味的作用。这其中微妙的关系，在英国学者加里·戴的一段评述中可见一斑：

---

① 参考拙著《"文化辩护书"：19世纪英国文化批评》（上海外语教育出版社，2013年，第81—91页），其中论证了这样一个观点："阿诺德所考虑的核心问题不是如何帮助贵族阶级与资产阶级争夺文化领导权，而是如何实现物质文明和精神文明的同步发展，以及如何实现新旧社会之间的完美过渡。"

> 在18世纪，文学批评的正当性由当时存在的公共领域得以确立，后者得益于理性的统御。研究有关趣味的事物，讨论日常问题，讲解文学作品，这一切都加强了理性的普遍性，并把那些参与这种文明交流的人确认为开明的主体。到了19世纪，这种公共领域消失了，文学批评家也随之陷入了孤立。文学批评也就多了一项新任务，即预防社会的失序。(Day 1993: 1)

这段话有两处最值得留意：一是把"研究有关趣味的事物"看作文学批评的首要任务，二是强调19世纪后文学批评的新增任务是"预防社会的失序"。我们知道，"失序"（anarchy）正是阿诺德的《文化与失序》——他的文化蓝图最倚重的力作——题目中的关键词之一，也是全书的关键词之一。至此，我们已经看清了这样一层关系：阿诺德描绘文化蓝图，是为了预防社会的失序；他从事文学批评，也是为了预防社会的失序；描绘文化蓝图也好，从事文学批评也好，都需要趣味来发挥中枢作用。

一言以蔽之，欲熟谙阿诺德文学批评的精髓，须着眼于作为他文化蓝图中枢的趣味。

二、文学批评的权威与标准

什么是文学批评的权威和标准？这是阿诺德研究中的另一个热点问题，而且又跟趣味有关。

前文提到，阿诺德的《诗歌研究》曾被誉为"趣味标杆"。这篇长文中多次出现了"试金石"（touchstone）一词，如在下面这段论述里那样："让我们永远记住大师们的诗行和词语，并把它们用作检验其他诗歌的试金石，再也没有比这更有助于发现哪些诗作堪称一流了，因而再也没有比这更有益于我们了"（Arnold, *Essays in Criticism* 1913: 17）。然而，阿诺德的"试金石"说在过去的一个世纪里频遭攻击，以致加里·戴干脆斥之为"臭名昭著"（Day 1993: 34）。加里·戴等人主要是沿袭了艾略特的观点，后者曾这样给阿诺德定性："与其说他是一位批评家，不如说他是文学批评的宣传家"（Eliot, *The Sacred Wood* 1）。言下之意，阿诺德在文学批评实践方面还不够水准，或者说拿不出评价文学作品的具体标准。无独有偶,加里·戴也这么说:"阿诺德显然是一位文学的'高级理论家',而不是实践型的批评家。他与约翰逊和柯勒律治不一样,并没有批评方法"(Day 1993:35)。当然,加里·戴承认阿诺德提出过"优美格调"(the accent of beauty)和"高度严肃"(high seriousness)等标准,但是在加里·戴看来,这些只是"最武断的标准",其基础是由"雅趣之士"(men of taste)"建构起来的共识",而"由此得出的特定判断没有文本支撑,没有任何关于文学文本形式特征的展示"(Day 1993:34—35)。加里·戴还一再强调"他(笔者按:指阿诺德)未能通过展示文本分析来做出判断",因而"只能依靠'标准''感受力'和'趣味'等强制性的、冠冕堂皇的辞令"(Day 1993:35)。可是加里·戴们这样的评价公允吗?

依笔者之见,对阿诺德的上述诟病至少有两点值得商榷。

其一,阿诺德生活在 19 世纪,不能用后世的眼光来衡量他。由上文所示,阿诺德的"罪名"是未能展示文学文本的"形式特征"(the formal properties),这显然是以形式主义或英美新批评为评价标准的。事实上,就在上引文字所在的同一段落中,加里·戴称赞了新批评代表人物瑞恰慈(I. A. Richards, 1893—1979),肯定其"含有分析方法的准科学语言",并表扬利维斯传承了这一传统,"坚持对文本做艰苦而细致的解析,正是这种批评实践成了文学季刊《细察》中批评方法的主要基石"(Day 1993:35)。诚然,瑞恰慈和利维斯在文本细读方面极大地丰富了文学批评方法(此前艾略特已经做了类似的开拓工作),但是这些具体的操作方法和手段在阿诺德时期显然是不具备的,因而我们不能苛求他。

其二,阿诺德的"趣味"说也具有操作性,并且足以作为文学批评实践的一种标准,甚至是具有权威性的参照标准,而不是所谓"冠冕堂皇的辞令"。就这一点而言,我们可以用"艾略特之矛"攻"艾略特之盾"。在《诗歌的用处与批评的用处》(*The Use of Poetry and the Use of Criticism*, 1933)一书中,艾略特对阿诺德有过如下褒奖:"然而,你只要读了他的论文《诗歌研究》,就会折服于他所引用的那些诗文,引用得那样精当妥帖;一个人趣味高雅,最好的证明就是能像阿诺德那样得体地引经据典。那篇论文是英国文学批评的经典:言简意赅,虽惜墨如金,却颇具权威性"("The Use of Poetry"188)。事实上,阿诺德从事文学批评最常用、最典型的方法就是引经据典,用所引诗文来对照手头的研究对象，让后者的优劣高低，在比对中得以彰显。他常用的"试金石"包括以荷马（Homer, c. 800—c. 701 BC）、品达（Pindar, 518—438 BC）、但丁（Dante Alighieri, 1265—1321）、莎士比亚（William Shakespeare, 1564—1616）和弥尔顿（John Milton, 1608—1674）等人的作品为标杆。试问，用经典作为衡量标准，不厌其烦地比对，这何尝不是一种批评方法呢？有比较才有鉴别，才有趣味，只是它有一个前提，即批评家须熟读"经书"，其难度可想而知。也就是说，阿诺德不是没有批评方法，而是具有常人所难以掌握的方法。根据安德森（Warren D. Anderson, 1920—2001）的考证，"阿诺德不仅是首位真正熟谙欧洲研究领域的英国文学家，而且率先掌握了古典文学知识，并把它作为一种连续体来运用"（Anderson 1988: 171）。此处所说的"古典文学知识"显然也包括了关于文本形式的知识，阿诺德在大量引用——引用即展示——经典文本时不可能不展示文本的形式特征。

可能有人会说，上述"展示"只停留在不言自喻的层面，而没有指出具体的形式特征。可是情形并非如此。阿诺德曾经为自己 1853 年所出的诗集写序，其中列举了最优秀的古希腊文学技巧，对此，安德森作出总结："布局清晰、结构严谨、风格简洁"，这些都显示了一种"自我克制，可谓严格，一丝不苟"（Anderson 1988: 50）。这里，"自我克制"（self-restraint）显然是一种趣味，体现于严谨的结构。如安德森所说，阿诺德很关注文学作品的形式结构，"关注结构的整体需求，追求一种总体感，而非'醒目段落'的随意聚合"（Anderson 1988: 50）。当然，那些惯于挑剔的人仍然会觉得不够具体。例如，艾略特（就在紧接着赞扬阿诺德"得体地引经据典"那段文字之后）就批评阿诺德"对韵文的音乐品质不那么敏感"："在我的记忆中，他从来就不在从事文学批评时强调诗体的这一长处，音乐性可是诗体的基本优点啊！他不擅长我所说的'听觉想象'，即对音节和节奏的感觉〔……〕"（Eliot, 1933: 188）这一判断显然有失公允，对此我们只消参照一下阿诺德的《莫里斯·德·格兰》（"Maurice de Guérin", 1865）一文便知。该文一开篇就讨论了法国作家莫里斯·德·格兰（Georges Maurice de Guérin du Cayla, 1810—1839）的一个句子的韵律，接着通过跟莎士比亚、华兹华斯、济慈（John Keats, 1795—1821）、夏多布里昂（François-René de Chateaubriand, 1768—1848）和赛南库尔（Étienne Pivert de

Senancour，1770—1846）等人的诗行进行的对比，一方面指出格兰的散文作品也能（因其音乐性）"无比优越地展示诗歌魔力"（Arnold, "Maurice de Guérin" 14），另一方面指出他的诗歌不如他的散文，其原因是采用了亚历山大格律（Alexandrine）。阿诺德花了相当大的篇幅来讨论格律问题，仅摘录数句如下：

> 在我看来，法语中这种已有的格律——亚历山大格〔……〕作为一种高雅诗歌格律，它与六步格或希腊抑扬格（举例来说）或英国无韵诗相比都极为逊色……拉辛比不上索福克勒斯或莎士比亚，他在与舒波哀相比时也同样如此。这一点同样适用于我国18世纪的诗人们，这个世纪为其最高水准的诗歌提供的主要诗格就是一种不恰当的格律（与法国的亚历山大格一样，所采用的方式也几乎相同）——十音节对句格〔……〕
>
> 与卢克莱修的自然诗相比，蒲柏的《人论》（*Essay on Man*）要逊色一些，因为卢克莱修用了一种恰当的格律，而蒲柏没有。（阿诺德 2017：80—81）

阿诺德所做的这些评述足以说明艾略特评价的谬误。这些评述说明阿诺德的趣味还体现于对诗词格律的甄别，这自然包括了他对音节和节奏的感觉。

上引（关于格律的）文字还说明了阿诺德的另一个重要观点，即评价作品并非全凭个人的趣味，而更多地取决于作家所处时代，以及不同时代、不同国度之间的互鉴。正如斯通所说，阿诺德在趣味/鉴别作品方面"维护的是集体标准和理想"（collective standards and ideals）（Stone 1997：9）。此处，"集体"指的是全世界，而这跟阿诺德的文化观十分契合——前文提到，他曾把文化界定为"世界上最优秀的思想和言论"，其中自然包括了体现最佳文学趣味的思想和言论。斯通在论及上述文化定义时曾经指出："此处，阿诺德对'世界'的强调不亚于对'最优秀'的强调"（Stone 1997：3）。我们不妨加上一句：阿诺德对"集体"的强调不亚于对"标准"/"权威"的强调。也就是说，在阿诺德眼里，最具权威性的标准来自世界各国文学的荟萃。在上面那段鉴别诗歌格律的论述中，他不仅把眼光投向了英国和法国，而且投向了德国、古希腊和古罗马。事实上，几乎在所有批评实践中，他都博采众长，这意味着他的趣味和标准并非一成不变的，而是像斯通所说，"永远有待于完善，有待于更新"（Stone

1997：3）。从这一角度看，那种把"武断"这顶帽子扣在阿诺德头上的做法也是错误的。

说到"集体标准和理想"，阿诺德还有一个相关主张值得一提，即建立一个像法兰西学院（the French Academy）那样的"趣味中心"："要建立一个公认的权威机构，以便为我们树立思想和趣味方面的高标准"（Arnold, The Literary Influence of Academies, 1962：235）。阿诺德是在《学院的文学影响》（Arnold, The Literary Influence of Academies, 1865）一文中提出这一主张的，并一再称赞"法兰西学院这个体现最佳文学观点的最高机构，一个思想格调和趣味方面的公认权威"（Arnold, The Literary Influence of Academies, 1962：257）。在该文中，"趣味"一词出现了十来次，而且都服务于"集体标准和理想"。阿诺德这样主张，不仅是为了防止个人趣味的盲目性和武断性，更是为了防止整个国家妄自尊大。事实上，这篇文章的直接起因是麦考莱（T. B. Macaulay, 1800—1859）的一句"豪言壮语"："现存英语文学的价值，要远胜于三百年前形成于全世界所有语言中的文学"（同上：232）。阿诺德从中看到了"一种小家子气"（a note of provinciality），视其为"正当趣味"（correct taste）的敌人，因此提出要建立一个"趣味中心"，"要有一个正确信息、正确判断和正当趣味的中心，它对一种文学的影响越少，我们在这种文学里发现的小家子气就越多"（同上：245）。可以说，阿诺德"趣味中心"论是一种悖论；它不是要建立一种君临其他国家文学的权威，而是要防止自己的同胞狂妄自大。

让我们援引《学院的文学影响》的结束语作为本小节的结束语："像我在本文开头用麦考莱勋爵语录所示的那样，对我们自己或我们文学的一切简单称颂都是低俗的，低俗之余，还让我们停滞"（同上：257）。阿诺德此处所说的"低俗"（vulgar），正是他所说趣味的对立面，从中我们不难感受到一种对权威/标准的重视。

三、趣味的完美点

前文提到，阿诺德是一位优秀的文学批评家，他擅长得体地引经据典，这足以体现他的趣味。可能有人还会问：此处的"得体"有具体的衡量标准吗？

要回答这一问题，我们似乎可以从阿甘本（Giorgio Agamben，1942— ）说起。

阿甘本曾就趣味性问题提出一个有趣的术语，即"完美点"（the point de perfection）。阿甘本是在论述"雅趣之士"（the man of taste）时提出这一概念的："大约在 17 世纪中期，欧洲社会出现了雅趣之士的身影，即具备一种特殊禀赋的人物。按照当时的说法，这种人物几乎带有第六感觉，足以使他把握艺术的完美点——抓住了这一完美点，就抓住了任何艺术品的特点"（Agamben 1999：13）。阿甘本还说，一个人若能感受并热爱上述完美点，他/她就有了"完美的趣味"（a perfect taste）；"凡是艺术，皆有完美点，就像大自然中的事物总有某一点能反映她的美好和完整。不管是谁，只要能感觉并热爱这一完美点，就拥有了完美的趣味。反之，如果感受不到这个完美点，或是所爱达不到那个完美点，或是越过了那个点，那就是缺乏趣味"（Agamben 1999：13）。依笔者之见，我们可以借用阿甘本的学说，来形容阿诺德的批评实践。理由是，阿诺德虽然没有用这一概念表述他的标准，但实际上正是依循是否具备"完美点"来评价文学作品，从而展示"完美点"所体现的趣味。

一个最典型的例子可以在《但丁与比阿特丽斯》（"Dante and Beatrice"，1862）一文中找到。在这篇论文中，阿诺德就但丁笔下人物比阿特丽斯的象征意义提出了独到的见解。此前许多评论家——尤其是翻译家马丁（Theodore Martin，1816—1909）——都过于强调现实生活中的比阿特丽斯与但丁之间的关系：相传但丁在 9 岁时，就对比阿特丽斯一见倾心；九年后两人在佛罗伦萨的一座老桥上再次相见，但丁于是魂不守舍；虽然他俩从未直接有过交谈，而且比阿特丽斯在嫁与他人后不久身亡，可是但丁对她的倾慕却伴随一生。在但丁的《新生》和《神曲》这两部作品中，都出现了比阿特丽斯这一人物，而评论家们往往把她仅仅看作但丁实际生活中的感情寄托，并据此揣测但丁生前的种种琐事，尤其是他跟妻子之间的关系。换言之，不少评论家们热衷于寻找但丁作品与他私人生活之间的一一对应关系。针对这一情形，阿诺德发表了如下观点：

> 是的，一个真实的比阿特丽斯无疑存在过。但丁见过真人，见过她从眼前走过，而且因她而激情澎湃。他从实际生活的外部世界里汲取了这一基本事实：这一基础对于他是必不可少的，因为他是一位艺术家。

然而，作为艺术家，他有以下事实做基础就足够了：见过比阿特丽斯两三次，跟她交谈过两三次，感受到了她的美、她的魅力，因她的婚姻和死亡而动情——这些就够了。艺术要以事实做基础，但是也要尽可能自由地处理现实基础。当艺术处理的对象太接近、太真实时，想要最洒脱地加以处理的愿望就会受挫。可以说，假如但丁把自己跟比阿特丽斯的关系描述得更确定、更亲密、更长久，更按当时的实际情形来描述对她的爱慕，那么多少会妨碍这些关系的自由运用，也就有损艺术效果。（Arnold, Dante and Beatrice 1962: 5）

阿诺德此处论述的是艺术和素材之间的辩证关系：艺术必须从实际生活中汲取素材，少了不行；然而，若是拘泥于炮制生活实际的翻版，那就有损艺术效果。阿诺德这样论述，不就意味着需要定格于一个"完美点"吗？如果现实基础少了，那就是阿甘本所说的"达不到那个完美点"；而强调现实基础过了头，则是"越过了那个点"。二者都是"缺乏趣味"。

阿诺德心中有一条"完美线"。更确切地说，他在判断一部作品是否具有良好趣味时，会看它有没有"越线"（cross the line）。例如，金克莱（Alexander William Kinglake, 1809—1891）曾经因《克里米亚入侵》（Invasion of the Crimea, 1863—1887）的前两卷（共有八卷）而一炮走红，人们纷纷赞扬该书的文体风格，可是阿诺德却批评他的文风还有失"雅兴"（Attic taste），原因是"他有时候会因爱国情绪而愤怒，头脑有点儿发热，于是便越过了那条线，失去了完美的分寸感"（Arnold, The Literary Influence of Academies 1962: 256）。这里，"越过了那条线"可谓与阿甘本的"越过了那个点"异曲同工。

在上引文字中，"完美的分寸感"值得特别留意。阿诺德在许多场合都强调文风的分寸感、适度感、节制感和平衡感。他在上文所提对金克莱的批评中，还用梯也尔（Marie Joseph Louis Adolphe Thiers, 1797—1877）做对照，称后者受过良好教育，因而"文风优越"，体现了一种"健康的节制感（wholesome restraining）"（Arnold, The Literary Influence of Academies 1962: 255）。阿诺德还曾拿当时伦敦的文学批评家跟巴黎的批评家相比较，发现后者远胜于前者，皆因后者更有"持重感"（sobriety）和"分寸感（measure）"（Arnold, The

Literary Influence of Academies 1962：254）。他还对法国作家朱伯特（Joseph Joubert，1754—1824）赞赏有加，认为斯塔尔夫人（Anne Louise Germaine de Staël-Holstein，1766—1817）"够不上他的趣味"，原因是斯塔尔夫人"激情有余，真理不足；热度有余，光亮不足"（Arnold, Joubert 1962：186）。另一个例子可以在他对罗斯金（John Ruskin，1819—1900）的点评中找到。尽管阿诺德承认罗斯金常常语出惊人，甚至有"精湛的文风"（Arnold, The Literary Influence of Academies 1962：251），但是后者对莎士比亚笔下众多人物名字背后的语源学考证却引起了阿诺德的不满：罗斯金曾不厌其烦地追根寻源，试图证明相关人物名字的意义，如哈姆雷特（Hamlet）的名字暗含"带有家庭特点的"（homely）意思，而"整个悲剧事件恰好以对家庭义务的背叛为轴心"（Arnold, The Literary Influence of Academies 1962：252）。阿诺德对这样的文本解读提出了如下批评："〔……〕这样的解读真是夸张得离谱！我不是说莎士比亚笔下人物名字的意思（姑且不论罗斯金先生的语源学考证是否正确）对作品的理解毫无影响，因而可以完全忽略。然而，把人名解读提升到那样显著的程度，这犹如异想天开，置适度性和均衡性于全然不顾，完全失去了思想的平衡。这样的批评解读过分牵强，尽显小家子气"（Arnold, The Literary Influence of Academies 1962：252）。我们由此再次瞥见了阿诺德关于"完美点/线"的尺度：文学人物名字的意思固然不可忽视，但是强调过头了，那就过犹不及。换言之，他对文学人物名字的解读，就像对其他（文学作品）细节的解读一样，心里有一条完美线——忽视人物名字的寓意，那就是不及完美线；而过分重视，那就是越线。两者都不完美。阿诺德的趣味由此可见一斑。

最后还须指出的是，阿诺德在文学批评实践中讲求"完美点/线"，这跟他文化蓝图中描绘的总目标是一致的。本文第一小节中提到，阿诺德心目中的"文化"意味着对"完美"的研究和追求，而这"完美"离不开以适度感、分寸感为核心意蕴的趣味。让我们再引用《文化与失序》中的一段论述，作为印证：

就在我们的自由、体格锻炼和工业才能开始得到世界的瞩目时，世界却没有因为看到我们的这些长处而表现出热爱、钦羡……原因难道不正是我们那种机械的行为方式吗？我们将自由、强健的体魄和工业技术本身当作了目的来追求，而没有将这些事情同人类臻于完美的总目标联系起来……英式的自由，英式的工业，英式的强健，我们一概都在盲目地推进，我们把握这些事物时根本没有适度感、分寸感，因为我们的头脑里缺乏人类和谐发展、达到完善的理想，我们并不是在这理想的促使下开始行动，不是用理想来指导我们所做的工作。（马修·阿诺德《文化与无政府主义》2008：130）

在这段话里，"人类臻于完美的总目标""适度感"和"分寸感"这几个关键词跟本小节的论证不是很契合吗？当阿诺德从事文学批评，尤其是探究审美趣味时，他关心的是文化问题，其中的奥妙曾被高晓玲点明：跟同时代的穆勒等人相比，"阿诺德则更忧虑审美趣味的庸俗化和道德失序问题，倡导以'最优秀的思想与言论'引领时代精神，塑造'最好的自我'，借助诗歌和文化实现大众的精神救赎"（高晓玲 2018：54）。此处，趣味和文化的关系已经被勾勒得非常清楚。

我们不妨用阿诺德论文学批评功能的一段话作为本文的结束语："文学批评最重要的功能是检验文学图书，考察它们是否对某个民族或全世界的总体文化产生了应有的影响。文学批评是上述文化的特聘护卫，而且我们可以这样构想：所有文学作品都以这样或那样的方式对相关文化产生了作用"（Arnold, The Bishop and the Philosopher 1962：41）。还得加上一句：没有趣味，就没有批评，也就没有文化。

参考文献

[1] Agamben G. *The Man Without Content*. Translated by Georgia Albert［M］. Stanford, CA：Stanford UP, 1999.

[2] Anderson W D. *Matthew Arnold and the Classical Tradition*［M］. Ann Arbor, MI U of Michigan P, 1988.

[3] Arnold M. *Essays in Criticism: Second Series*［M］. London：Macmillan and Co., 1913.

[4] ——. "West London." *Victorian and Later English Poets*, edited by James Stephens *et al.* [M]. New York: American Book Company, 1949: 566-567.

[5] ——. "Dante and Beatrice." *Lectures and Essays in Criticism*, edited by R. H. Super [M]. Ann Arbor: Michigan UP, 1962: 3-11.

[6] ——. "Joubert." *Lectures and Essays in Criticism* [M]. Ann Arbor: University of Michigan Press, 1962.

[7] ——. "Maurice de Guérin." *Lectures and Essays in Criticism*, (ed.). R. H. Super [M]. Ann Arbor, University of Michigan Press, 1962.

[8] ——. "The Bishop and the Philosopher." [A] //*Lectures and Essays in Criticism*, edited by R. H. Super and T. M. Hoctored [M]. Ann Arbor: U of Michigan Press, 1962, pp. 40-55.

[9] ——. "The Function of Criticism at the Present Time." *Lectures and Essays in Criticism*, (ed.). R. H. Super [M]. Ann Arbor, University of Michigan Press, 1962.

[10] ——. "The Literary Influence of Academies." *Lectures and Essays in Criticism*, (ed.). R. H. Super [M]. Ann Arbor, University of Michigan Press, 1962.

[11] 马修·阿诺德. 文化与无政府状态: 政治与社会批评 [M]. 韩敏中, 译. 北京: 三联书店, 2008. [Arnold, Matthew. *Culture and Anarchy: An Essay in Political and Social Criticism*. Translated by Han Minzhong, SDX Joint Publishing Company, 2008.]

[12] ——: 莫里斯·德·格兰. 批评集: 1865 [M]. 杨果译. 北京: 中央编译出版社, 2017: 76-111. ——. ["Maurice de Guérin." *Essays in Criticism: 1865*. Translated by Yangguo, Central Compilation & Translation Press, 2017, pp. 76-111.]

[13] Day G. *The British Critical Tradition: A Re-evaluation* [M]. New York: St. Martin's Press, 1993.

[14] Eagleton T. *Literary Theory: An Introduction* [M]. Minneapolis: Minnesota UP, 1983.

[15] ——. *The Eagleton Reader*. Stephen Regan (ed) [M]. Oxford: Blackwell, 1998.

[16] ——. *The Function of Criticism*. [M]. London and New York: Verso Press, 2005.

[17] Eliot T S. *The Sacred Wood* [M]. London: Methuen, 1920.

[18] Eliot T S. *The Use of Poetry and the Use of Criticism* [M]. London: Faber and Faber Limited, 1933.

[19] 高晓玲. 诗性真理: 转型焦虑在19世纪英国文学中的表征 [J]. 外国文学研究, 2018 (4): 47—57. (Gao Xiaoling. Poetic truth as the expression of anxiety in the 19th-century English literature. [J]. *Foreign Literature Studies*, 2018, (4): 47-57.)

[20] Jones T E. Matthew Arnold's "Philistinism" and Charles Kingsley [N]. *The Victorian Newsletter*, Spring, 1998, pp. 2-3.

[21] Leavis, F R. "Arnold as Critic." *A Selection from Scrutiny*, vol. 1, F. R. Leavis (ed.). [M]. Cambridge: Cambridge UP, 1968, pp. 258-268.

[22] (李春青. 趣味的历史: 从两周贵族到汉魏文人 [M]. 北京: 三联书店, 2014.) Li Chunqing. *The History of Taste: From the Aristocracy of the Zhou Dynasties to the Literati of Han and Wei Dynasties* [M]. Beijing: SDX Joint Publishing Company, 2014.

[23] *Oxford English Dictionary*. 2nd Edition on CD-ROM (v. 4.0) [M]. Oxford: Oxford UP, 2009.

[24] Stone D. *Communications with the Future* [M]. Ann Arbor: U of Michigan P, 1997.

[25] 殷企平. "文化辩护书": 19世纪英国文化批评 [M]. 上海: 上海外语教育出版社, 2013年. [Yin Qiping. *An Apologia of Culture: Cultural Criticism in the 19th-Century Britain*. Shanghai Foreign Education Press, 2013.]

[26] 朱光潜. 谈美 [M]. 桂林: 广西师范大学出版社, 2006. [Zhu Guangqian. *On Beauty*. Guangxi Normal UP, 2006.]

(本文原载于《外国文学研究》2011年第5期)

走向公共精神：伊格尔顿的趣味观*

伊格尔顿（Terry Eagleton）的趣味观值得研究。迄今为止，学界对伊格尔顿各种学术观点的评论大都停留在理论层面，鲜有从趣味观切入的专论。我国学者近年来曾发表以趣味为主题的文章，如刘晖（2017：48—67）和翁洁莹（2015：67—74）都简短引述了伊格尔顿的《美学意识形态》（*The Ideology of the Aesthetic*）一书，但是相关文字中都未出现"趣味"（taste）一词。事实上，"趣味"不仅几十次地出现在了《美学意识形态》一书中，而且不断出现在伊格尔顿的大多数著作中。不过，他从未系统地就趣味而论趣味，而是常常通过妙趣横生的文字来从事理论分析和文学批评，从而展现自己的趣味观。虽然在西方文学史和美学史上，"趣味"主要跟"美"（beauty）的辨认和判断有关，但是就其基本含义"鉴别力"（朱光潜 2006：97）而言，它也可以在各类学术著作中大显身手，更何况在伊格尔顿看来，"撰写评论或理论本身就应该是一门艺术"（*Saint Oscar* 1）。我国有学者曾经指出，伊格尔顿"属于那种少见的具有强烈风格意识的理论家"，他的文章品质可以称为"伊格尔顿体"（Eagletonism）（马海良 2016：91）。这里所说的风格，在很大程度上体现了一种趣味。应该说，这种趣味/风格不仅体现于伊格尔顿的理论表述之中，而且体现于他的文学批评之中。有鉴于此，本文将从他的理论著述和批评实践两方面入手，探究"伊格尔顿体"含有的趣味。

---

* 基金项目：浙江省哲学社会科学重点研究基地"文艺批评研究院"资助项目（wypp2020001）。

一、甄别的辩证法

在伊格尔顿笔下，"趣味"的涉及面很广，上至信仰、价值（value）、意识形态和审美标准，下至日常生活的方方面面，尤其是风俗习惯，不过其核心内涵则是价值判断/鉴别。在《文学批评与意识形态》（*Criticism and Ideology*）一书中，伊格尔顿曾把"价值问题"（the value-question）与"趣味"相提并论，认为价值问题"可以被解释为'趣味'"（Eagleton 1978：163）。事实上，若要领略"伊格尔顿体"的趣味，就须从它对于各种价值问题的甄别艺术入手。无论是进行高深的理论辨析，还是对具体的作品解读，伊格尔顿都显示了不可多得的鉴赏力，而其中的诀窍可以归结为三个字：辩证法（dialectics）。在哲学领域，辩证法的含义相当丰富，本文主要取其"对立统一"之义（宋原放等 1982：1100），即从事物的普遍联系和发展来看待问题，在甄别不同事物和观点时不机械、不片面、不走极端，从而在看似矛盾的事物之间找到内在联系。下面就让我们来看一下伊格尔顿甄别艺术的几个具体实例。

先说伊格尔顿是如何处理艺术和意识形态之间关系的。伊格尔顿的名字常常跟"意识形态"联系在一起，且不说他那流传甚广的不少相关观点，就连他的一些著作也直接用"意识形态"冠名，如《文学批评与意识形态》（*Criticism and Ideology*）《美学意识形态》（*The Ideology of the Aesthetic*）和《意识形态导论》（*Ideology: An Introduction*）。然而，学界常有人误解他对"意识形态"这一术语的界定，误以为他把"意识形态"与"虚假意识"（false consciousness）等量齐观。受这一曲解的影响，一些学者在解读外国文学作品时，一味地挖掘其背后的意识形态，结果总能得出某部作品"为统治阶级服务"这样的结论，几乎给人以千篇一律的印象。事实上，伊格尔顿对艺术/文学作品和意识形态之间关系的理解远不是那样简单。诚然，他认为"一切艺术都起源于在意识形态层面对世界的构想"（Eagleton, Marxism and Literary Criticism, 1976：17）。基于这一立场，他曾批评艾迪生（Joseph Addison）等"精英主义"文人兼批评家，原因是后者的"文化就是帮助巩固英国统治集团的东西，而批评家则是这一历史性任务的承担者"（Eagleton 2005：12）；同样，他还批评阿诺德（Matthew

Arnold），说他的文学批评使命是"把中产阶级意识形态这一药剂裹上文学糖衣"（Eagleton 1983：26）。然而，这些并非伊格尔顿从意识形态角度从事文学艺术批评活动的全貌，他对其间关系的理解要全面得多。要说明这一点，还得从他对马克思主义文艺思想的继承说起。

伊格尔顿继承了恩格斯在《路德维希·费尔巴哈和德国古典哲学的终结》中的观点，即"意识形态不是一套教条，它意指人们在阶级社会里践行的角色，意指那些把他们束缚于社会功能的价值观、思想和形象，这些东西阻碍他们真正地了解整个社会"（Eagleton, Marxism and Literary Criticism, 1976：17）。不过，伊格尔顿同时还意识到，"恩格斯的言论表明，艺术跟意识形态的关系比法律和政治理论跟它的关系更为复杂，而法律和政治理论比较透明地体现了统治阶级的利益"（Eagleton, Marxism and Literary Criticism, 1976：17）。那么，艺术和意识形态之间到底是一种什么关系呢？伊格尔顿认为，要辨清它们的关系，就要首先防止两种极端的倾向。第一种倾向认定"文学仅仅是以某种艺术形式出现的意识形态——文学作品只不过是所在时代不同意识形态的表现而已。它们是'虚假意识'的囚徒，因而无法实现超越而抵达真理"。在伊格尔顿看来，这一倾向代表了"典型的'庸俗马克思主义'文艺批评立场"，是不可取的，因为它"无法解释为什么那么多文学作品事实上对所在时代的那些意识形态设想进行了挑战"。另一种倾向则坚信"货真价实的艺术总能超越所在时代意识形态的局限，从而让我们洞察现实，不再让现实被意识形态遮蔽"（Eagleton 1978：17—18）。这一观点也被伊格尔顿视为过于机械。他认为"文学作品是意识形态结构的一部分"，因此批评家们应该"依据意识形态结构来解释文学作品，不过文学作品又通过自己的艺术改造了意识形态结构"；更具体地说，文学作品中有一种成分，"它既把作品束缚于意识形态，又使作品跟意识形态保持距离"，而批评家的使命就是"搜寻出这种成分"（Eagleton 1978：19）。就这样，伊格尔顿揭示了文学艺术和意识形态之间的辩证关系，从而也使这种辨析工作平添了不少趣味。

为揭示不同事物之间的辩证关系，伊格尔顿十分注重相关概念的甄别。例如，他对"意识形态"这一术语的多义性保持着高度警觉，而不是像很多学者那样，在了解它的部分含义后就"果断"地使用它。他清醒地认识到，"关于意识形态,还没有人拿出一个为大家所接受的全面定义,这是因为当初这一术语应运而生时,就是被用来为各种各样的目的服务的,其中许多用法很有用,但是它们并非全都互相兼容"(Eagleton 1994:20)。同样,对于"艺术"这一概念的多义性,他也能恰当地予以鉴别。虽然他认为艺术作品都脱离不了意识形态,但是他同时还看到了艺术呈现美好生活的一面,这在他的《文学事件》(*The Event of Literature*)里可见一斑:

> 难道每一部文学作品都是强势意识形态的女仆,是用来方便地解决冲突的吗?这样看待文学,实在是太消极了。无论艺术作品有多大能耐与压迫形式共谋,依然只是人类实践的一种实例,因此可以向我们示范如何更好地生活。在这个意义上,政治批评所包含的内容应该不限于怀疑阐释学。它也应该铭记威廉·布莱克对美好生活的憧憬:"艺术,以及有共同之处的一切。"(Eagleton 1978:224)

强调艺术能向世人示范美好生活,就是肯定它的价值。须特别留意的是,伊格尔顿在鉴别事物的价值时,从不简单地行事,而总是有一个较全面的观照。例如,他在肯定艺术价值的同时,还看到其间的复杂性,如上引文字中所说的"与压迫形式共谋",也就是容易被统治阶级的意识形态利用。同理,他在主张"依据意识形态结构来解释文学作品"时,又强调文学艺术有改造意识形态之功,这就肯定了意识形态视角在文学批评中的价值,同时还指出了艺术对它的反作用,从而自然而然地展现了文学批评的趣味。

再来看一下伊格尔顿是如何鉴别"现实主义""自然主义"和"形式主义"的,以及他是如何分出它们各自价值高低的。他跟卢卡奇一样,把现实主义文学看成一种"辩证的艺术形式"(the dialectical art-form)(Eagleton, Marxism and Literary Criticism, 1976:31),理由是"这一艺术抗拒异化的、分崩离析的资本主义社会,树立完整的人类形象,具有丰富性和多面性"(Eagleton 1978:28)。他还赞赏卢卡奇把现实主义作家看作"最伟大的艺术家",指出对"马克思主义者卢卡奇来说,最伟大的艺术家是那些能重新捕捉并重新创造和谐的、全面的人类生活的人。资本主义的'异化'日益撕裂了一般与特殊、知性与感性、社会与个人之间的关系。就是在这样一个社会里，伟大的作家辩证地看待那些关系，把那些撕裂了的东西重新整合起来，使之形成一个完整的复合体"（Eagleton 1978：27—28）。

除此之外，伊格尔顿还强调现实主义的历史条件，或者说"为其形式成就奠定基础的历史'内容'"。他接着说，"现实主义一旦被剥夺了它赖以产生的历史条件，它就分化并衰退了，要么退化成'自然主义'，要么退化成'形式主义'"（Eagleton 1978：30）。许多拿"现实主义""自然主义"和"形式主义"作比较的论著，洋洋洒洒地写上数千字后仍然没把问题说清楚，可是伊格尔顿寥寥数语，就勾勒出了它们的分野，还分出了它们的高低。许多本来艰涩的理论，到了他的手里就会变得简洁，甚至生趣盎然。例如，他把自然主义描述成"一种异化的现实观，把作者从历史进程的积极参与者变成了诊所里的观察者"。又如，在形式主义作家的笔下，"人被褫夺了历史环境，除了自我，再无现实；人物性格被溶解为心理状态，客观现实沦为一片混沌，无人能懂。就像在自然主义作家那里一样，人的内部世界和外部世界的辩证统一性被摧毁了，结果个人和社会的意义都被掏空了。"在这些清新的文字背后，是不无趣味的辩证思想。在下面这段文字中，伊格尔顿再次使用了"辩证的"（dialectical）一词："如果说自然主义是一种抽象的主观性，那么形式主义就是一种抽象的客观性；二者都偏离了真正辩证的艺术形式（现实主义）。正是现实主义艺术形式在具体和一般、本质和存在、类型和个体之间起着调和作用"（Eagleton 1978：31）。

在解读具体文学作品时，伊格尔顿也同样会巧用辩证法。例如，他在评论勃朗蒂三姐妹的作品时，一方面强调要注重历史事件，如当时如火如荼的工业革命、蓬勃兴起的棉花厂、圈地运动、饥荒现象和阶级斗争等，另一方面还特别强调当时"正在形成一种全新的情感文化，此时英格兰正破天荒地变成以城市为主的社会，因此那种情感文化很适合它。这意味着学习新的学科，养成新的情感习性，适应新的时间节奏和空间布局，以新的形式克制自己，尊重他人，自我形塑"（Eagleton, Myths of Power: A Marxist Study of the Brontës, 2005: xiii）。伊格尔顿这样强调的目的，是要防止单方面地从政治、经济的角度来评判勃朗蒂姐妹的作品，主张情感文化同样是"历史条件"，提倡在两者互动的语境下从事作品解读，从中我们可以感受到一种辩证思维，品尝到一种趣味。这在下面的论述中更为明显:"一种全新的人类主观状态正在形成,这就像夏洛特小说中那些自我分裂的主人公那样,既志存高远,又灰心丧气;既流离失所,又足智多谋;既形单影只,又自强不息"(Eagleton, Myths of Power: A Marxist Study of the Brontës, 2005: xiii)。如此鞭辟入里的人物分析,是任何没有趣味的人都无法企及的。

让我们再以伊格尔顿对狄更斯作品的分析为例。关于狄更斯,一个常见的批评是他笔下人物往往缺乏深度,缺乏性格层次上的变化,也就是像福斯特(E. M. Forster)所说的"扁平人物"(Forster 1955: 67—68)。诚然,狄更斯小说中人物众多,常常是"你方唱罢我登场",给人以目不暇接的感觉,自然就谈不上性格上的深度挖掘。然而,这难道是一种缺陷吗?伊格尔顿从历史唯物主义和辩证法的角度,指出上述现象应该放在工业革命带来的城市化背景下加以审视:

> 城市加速了生活节奏……城市居住者需要警惕、应变,善于应付生活的多变性和不连贯性。他/她长出了新的身体,演化出了新的感觉器官。逐渐演进的历史让位于一系列互不搭界的瞬间。城市加快了我们感官的反应,但是也使它们捕捉到的东西变得稀薄,因此世界显得既很生动,又二维化(two-dimensional);既很真切,又很虚假。我们的身体不得不学着在密集的他人身体堆里迂回穿行,这是一些既亲近又陌生的身体,让我们自己的身体缺乏安全感,不得不加强自我保护。从某种意义上说,乡村的空间是绵延的,而城市空间则变幻不定,不是遭受切割,就是遭受阻隔。(Eagleton, The English Novel: An Introduction, 2005: 144)

伊格尔顿的这段分析有一个弦外之音:狄更斯笔下人物之所以扁平,是因为工业化/城市化浪潮下的世界变得扁平了——上引文字中的"二维化"即"扁平"的意思。可见,狄更斯塑造的众生相看似没有深度,却精准地捕捉住了历史真实和社会现实。换言之,伊格尔顿对狄更斯刻画的人物做出了悖论式的、不无趣味的价值判断。上引文字中关于身体的那几句评论尤为精彩,简直就是一种艺术创造:在城市化的漩涡中,人"长出了新的身体,演化出了新的感觉器官",不得不在"既亲近又陌生的""他人身体堆里迂回穿行"。这是用创造性的文字肯定狄更斯笔下人物形象的价值，读来趣味横生。

不过，伊格尔顿不是为趣味而趣味。他的趣味观服务于一个目的，即提倡公共精神（public spirit）。这将是我们在下一小节所要探讨的内容。

二、走向公共精神

上一小节的许多内容，其实都隐含了伊格尔顿对公共精神的诉求。例如，他跟卢卡奇一样，把现实主义作家看作最伟大的艺术家，理由是他们"能重新捕捉并重新创造和谐的、全面的人类生活"，这其实就是依照公共精神来评判作家。又如，他关注狄更斯笔下"扁平人物"，就是要揭示工业革命浪潮下普通大众的生活状况，这里面也体现了公共精神。问题也就来了：在伊格尔顿那里，趣味和公共精神究竟是一种什么关系呢？

伊格尔顿常常把"趣味"一词与"公共领域"（the public sphere）、"精神共同体"（spiritual community）、"情感共同体"（community of sensibility）和"普遍共同的感觉"（universal common sense）这样一些词汇相提并论。这一做法本身就在告诉世人：他是要在趣味和公共精神之间架一座桥梁。在《美学意识形态》中，伊格尔顿干脆把审美趣味与精神共同体等量齐观："审美趣味的全部意义在于，它作为精神共同体的模式，是不可能强加于人的"（Eagleton 1978：63）。在同一本书的第二章，他对18世纪英国形成的公共领域进行了分析，并强调"比起道德方面的努力或意识形态方面的说教，趣味、情感和舆论更雄辩地证明，让人产生共鸣的是某种普遍共同的感觉"（Eagleton 1978：32）。在同一段落中，他两次直接使用"公共领域"这一词汇，还使用了"情感共同体"这一语汇，这些都说明在他心目中，趣味和共同体/公共精神之间的联系是多么重要。

事实上，无论是投身理论建树，还是从事文学批评，伊格尔顿对趣味的关注最终总要落实到公共精神。例如，他在研究18世纪英国文学批评的状况时也曾谈到趣味，不过这里的趣味不是个人的趣味，而是"社会趣味"（social taste）：文学批评的历史使命是"把新兴阶级和不同派别在文化层面上团结起来，达成社会趣味方面的共识，建构共同的传统，推广统一的习俗"（Eagleton 1978：19）。此处，"社会趣味方面的共识"和"共同的传统"以及"文化层面上"的团结紧密相关，其中包含的公共精神和共同体考量不言自喻。此外，伊格尔顿还强调文学批评"对秩序、均衡和得体的诉求，对社会凝聚力的呼求"，这显然也与公共精神不无关系。正是本着这一精神，他特别关注文学理论中具有共性的东西。例如，他在《文学事件》的前言里坦言，该书实际上"首次引人关注几乎所有文学理论的共同点"（Eagleton 2012：xii）。之所以要研究所有文学理论的共同点，不光是因为个人的学术兴趣，更是因为要服务于所有文学理论的受众，这自然又体现了一种公共精神。

除了以上所说，伊格尔顿的公共精神还体现于他为普通读者著书立说的实践。他的两部专著《如何读诗》（*How to Read a Poem*）和《如何读文学》（*How to Read Literature*）就是明证。在《如何读诗》的前言中，他直言自己写作的对象是"学生和普通读者"（Eagleton 2007：vii）。为了帮助普通读者，他在语言文字的解读方面颇为着力，颇为精细，细到语调、音调、节奏、质地、句法、标点以及行文的速度和情感、声音的强度。所有这些都牵涉趣味话题，如伊格尔顿对维多利亚时期女诗人勃朗宁（Elizabeth Barrett Browning）一首爱情诗的分析。兹取该书中译本节选如下：

> 我如何爱你？让我细数究竟。
> 我爱你到我的灵魂所能达到的
> 深邃、广阔和高度，同时感到超出了
> 人的目标和理想的恩惠。
> 我爱你到每日最朴素的需要的
> 程度，在阳光和烛光里。
> 我自由地爱你，像人们为正义而战。
> 我纯粹地爱你，像人们拒绝赞美……（伊格尔顿《如何读诗》2016：175）

伊格尔顿这样评价这首诗的情感强度："这对现代趣味来说太热切、太高尚了"，"不过，可以假定的是，维多利亚时代的人可不会觉得这首诗的情感强度过分了"（Eagleton 2007：118）。伊格尔顿这里讨论的，显然是公众的趣味。

事实上，伊格尔顿对文学作品的分析大都有一个着眼点，即该作品的公共性（communality）。前文提到，他在语言文字的解读方面颇为着力，这是因为语言本身具有公共性。一般人提到伊格尔顿，首先会想到他是一个政治倾向十分强烈的文论家，可是他在《如何读文学》的前言中这样强调："如果一个人对语言没有一定程度的敏感性，那么他/她就提不出关于文学文本的政治或理论问题。"（Eagleton 2014：ix）可见，他关心语言文字，其实就是关心政治或理论等公共问题。即便是一些多半具有私人属性的文字，在他那里也具有公共性。例如，一些描述苦难的文字通常被视为具有私密性，但是伊格尔顿不会错过其中的公共意义，这在他对奥登（W. H. Auden）的诗作《美术馆》（"Musée des Beaux Arts"）的分析中可见一斑：

> 在诗的第二节中，奥登明确地把对人类灾难的冷漠比作阳光，好像前者与后者一样，都是自然而然的。然而，这首诗发表于1940年，那时欧洲已经经历过西班牙内战（奥登短暂地参与过），正处于反法西斯的全球战争的苦痛中。这种苦难确实并不总是私人的、秘密的事。相反，它可能是一种集体经验。如果死亡和悲痛在人们中间显示出了无法消除的裂隙，那么它们也是能被公开分享的现实。灾难和日常生活，在不列颠城市的轰炸中一起到来。苦难并不像个人爱好一样是人们私下去面对的事；一定程度上，在受难者与旁观者、士兵与市民之间，有着共同的语言。（伊格尔顿《如何读诗》2016：8）

上面这段分析传递的公共精神以及对人世间苦难的悲悯之情，经由"共同的语言""公开分享的现实"和"集体经验"等词语的烘托，给人以一种强烈的冲击。

对伊格尔顿来说，文学作品的公共性跟道德意义紧密相连，而道德意义又跟虚构性或"虚构化"（fictionalize）紧密相连。前文提到，伊格尔顿的论述充满着辩证意味，这也体现于他对于真实生活中的道德与虚构化的道德之间关系的阐释。在他看来，虚构化的道德比真实生活中的道德更胜一筹，原因是前者比后者更能惠及公共生活。他曾经举了一个真实生活中有关道德趣味的例子，即从实际生活中撷取的一句道德陈述："某些王室成员趣味平庸，智商太低，真是愚不可及"（伊格尔顿《如何读诗》2016：31）。由此我们可以追问：这类本来具有道德真实意义的表述一旦进入了诗歌或小说，也就是被虚构化了，是否就不真实了呢？伊格尔顿的回答恰恰相反：

> 所谓"虚构化"，就是把一部作品从直接的经验语境中抽离出来，并发挥它更广泛的用途（wider uses）。把某样东西称作一首诗，就是让它广泛流通（general circulation），这是用一张洗衣单而无法做到的。写诗这种行为，不管素材多么私密，都是"道德的"行为，原因是它隐含了某种反应的公共性。这并不是说，读者的反应会是千篇一律的。单凭纸面上的实际安排，诗歌就提供了可被分享的（sharable）潜在意义。（伊格尔顿 2016：31—32）

在上引文字中，伊格尔顿一口气连用了"更广泛的用途""广泛流通""公共性"和"可被分享的"等词汇，其间的道德趣味耐人寻味。也就是说，不从公共精神的角度切入，任何对伊格尔顿趣味观的认识都会大打折扣。这在他跟布尔迪厄（Pierre Bourdieu）的交集中也可见一斑。

伊格尔顿与布尔迪厄曾在 20 世纪末有过一场面对面的讨论，这次对话的文字记录后来以《信念与普通生活》（Doxa and Common Life）为题发表。信念、普通生活以及那场对话中被频频提及的意识形态都跟趣味有关。我们知道，布尔迪厄曾以挑战康德关于审美趣味的理论而出名。康德强调无功利、先验性的纯形式审美，把趣味判断局限于上层建筑；而布尔迪厄则更重视趣味判断的物质基础和社会历史条件，主张把"趣味"放在人类学意义上的"文化"层面来理解："'文化'的普通用法局限于它的规范意义，除非它回归到人类学意义上的'文化'，除非人们对于最精美物品的高雅趣味与人们对于食物口味的基本趣味重新得以联系，否则人们便不能充分理解文化实践的意义"（Boudieu and Eagleton 1992：1）。伊格尔顿跟布尔迪厄一样，也很看重"趣味"的物质性、社会性，尤其重视它的文化实践意义。需在此强调的是，他俩理解的"文化"含义基本相仿，即威廉斯（Raymond Williams）所说的体现"普通生活"（the common life）的"共同文化"（the common culture），这在伊格尔顿充满欣赏口吻的赞词中得到了印证："您的工作体现了一种强有力的奉献精神，虽不总是很明显,却一直作为一种感染力而存在,它使您致力于可以称作'普通生活'的东西,不过这样称它或许还不到位。这是您的工作和雷蒙德·威廉斯在这个国家所从事工作相似的许多方面之一"(Boudieu and Eagleton 1992:117)。不过,在赞扬了布尔迪厄之后,伊格尔顿口风一转,批评后者的"信念"(doxa)过于消极和悲观——在布尔迪厄所描绘的"普通生活"中,"行动者"(the actor)往往受制于社会场域(field)、惯习(habitus)和资本(capital)等因素,缺乏反抗社会不公的意愿,更谈不上解放自己乃至全人类的动力,从而沦为被动的、无能为力的、不无讽刺意义的"主体",因此伊格尔顿当面向他强调"马克思主义思想会坚守一个观念,即凡是有邪恶出现,行动者就要进行反抗。您的信念让您失去了这种斗争精神;您压根儿没有意识到问题所在——在您的信念里没有求解放的欲望(drive to emancipation)"(Boudieu and Eagleton 1992:121)。这里所说的"求解放的欲望",显然是马克思关于解放全人类的诉求。对作为马克思主义者的伊格尔顿来说,这一诉求是"普通生活"和"共同文化"的最高体现,也是趣味的最高体现。

在《文化观念》(*The Idea of Culture*)一书中,伊格尔顿再次谈到趣味和共同文化之间的关系。该书最后一章"走向一种共同文化"(Towards a Common Culture)中,他把威廉斯关于共同文化的理论跟"杂糅论者"(hybridists)和"多元论者"(pluralists)的"当代文化主义"(contemporary culturalism)做了比较,其中直接使用了"趣味"一词:

> 威廉斯的共同文化理论……不会受到激进主义杂糅论者和自由主义多元论者无保留的欢迎,这是因为它必然需要一种信仰和行动的公共性,而这几乎是不合他们趣味的(hardly to their taste)。威廉斯的立场是一个悖论:这种复杂的文化发展的条件,只有通过在政治上确保某种手段才能设定——他把后者相当含糊地称作"共同体手段",而实际上他指的就是社会主义的公共机构。这样做就肯定需要公共的信仰、承诺和实践。只有通过充分的民主参与,包括调节物质生产的民主制度,才能充分开放民主参与的通道,从而充分表达这种文化的多元性。简而言之,要确立真正的文化多元主义,就需要齐心协力的社会主义行动。当代文化主义未能明白的,

恰恰是这一要点。(Eagleton 2000：121—122)

至此，我们已能清楚地看到，合乎伊格尔顿趣味的就是"信仰和行动的公共性"，或者说"社会主义行动"所体现的"齐心协力"，也就是本小节一再强调的公共精神。对于形形色色的自由主义者来说，无论他们如何高唱"民主"和"多元"，无论他们显得多么激进，公共精神"几乎是不合他们趣味的"。也就是说，趣味是有高低之分的。对伊格尔顿来说，趣味的最高境界就是公共精神。

综上所述，伊格尔顿的趣味观既体现于他的理论辨析，也体现于他的批评实践。在他那里，趣味是一种魅力四射的风格，是一种充满辩证法的鉴别力，更是一种激励人心的公共精神。为进一步理解这种公共精神，我们不妨引用一下他为《马克思主义与文学批评》（*Marxism and Literary Criticism*）所写的结束语："马克思主义文学批评不仅仅是阐释《失乐园》或《米德尔马契》的另类技巧，它是我们反抗压迫、获得解放这一努力的一部分。这就是为什么它值得我们花整部书的篇幅来给予讨论"（Eagleton 1976：76）。把趣味提升到人类解放的高度，这难道不就是"伊格尔顿体"的精髓吗？

参考文献

[1] Boudieu, P and Eagleton T. In Conversation：Doxa and Common Life [J]. *New Left Review* 191.1 (1992)：111-121.

[2] Boudieu P. *Distinction: A Social Critique of the Judgment of Taste*. Trans. Richard Nice [M]. Cambridge：Harvard UP, 1984.

[3] Eagleton, Terry. *Criticism and Ideology: A Study in Marxist Literary Theory* [M]. London：Verso, 1978.

[4] —, ed. *Ideology* [M]. London：Longman, 1994.

[5] —. *How to Read a Poem* [M]. Oxford：Blackwell, 2007.

[6] —. *How to Read Literature* [M]. New Haven：Yale UP, 2014.

[7] —. *Literary Theory: An Introduction* [M]. Minnesota UP, 1983.

[8] —. *Marxism and Literary Criticism* [M]. Berkeley：U of California P, 1976.

[9] —. *Myths of Power: A Marxist Study of the Brontës* [M]. Palgrave：

Macmillan, 2005.

[10] —. *Saint Oscar and Other Plays* [M]. Oxford: Blackwell, 1997.

[11] —. *The English Novel: An Introduction* [M]. Oxford: Blackwell, 2005.

[12] —. *The Event of Literature* [M]. New Haven: Yale UP, 2012.

[13] —. *The Function of Criticism* [M]. London: Verso, 2005.

[14] —. *The Idea of Culture* [M]. Oxford: Blackwell, 2000.

[15] —. *The Ideology of the Aesthetic* [M]. Oxford: Blackwell, 1990.

[16] Forster, E. M. *Aspects of the Novel* [M]. Orlando: Harcourt, 1955.

[17] 刘晖. 从趣味分析到阶级构建：布尔迪厄的"区分"理论 [J]. 外国文学评论, 2017, (4): 48-67. [Liu, Hui: "From the Analysis of Taste to the Construction of Classes: 'Distinction' and Bourdieu's Sociology of Art." *Foreign Literature Review* 4 (2017): 48-67.]

[18] 马海良. 伊格尔顿与经验主义问题 [J]. 外国文学评论, 2016, (4): 78-95. [Ma, Hailiang. "Terry Eagleton and the Problem of Empiricism." *Foreign Literature Review* 4 (2016): 78-95.]

[19] 宋原放等. 简明社会科学词典 [M]. 上海：上海辞书出版社, 1982. [Song, Yuanfang, et al., eds. *Concise Dictionary of Social Sciences*. Shanghai: Shanghai Lexicographical, 1982.]

[20] 翁冰莹. 审美趣味的演绎与变迁——兼论布尔迪厄对康德美学的反思与超越 [J]. 厦门大学学报, 2015, (3): 67-74. [Weng, Bingying: "Deduction and Vicissitudes of the Aesthetic Taste: On Bourdieu's Inheritance and Transcendence of Kant's Aesthetics." *Journal of Xiamen University* 3 (2015): 67-74.]

[21] 伊格尔顿. 如何读诗, 陈太胜译 [M]. 北京：北京大学出版社, 2016. [Eagleton, Terry. *How to Read a Poem*. Trans. Chen Taisheng. Beijing: Peking UP, 2016.]

[22] 朱光潜. 谈美 [M]. 桂林：广西师范大学出版社, 2006. [Zhu, Guangqian. *On Beauty*. Guilin: Guangxi Normal UP, 2006.]

（本文原载于《外国文学》2022年第6期）

西方文论关键词：共同体*

一、略说

"共同体"（Community）一词源于拉丁文 communis，原义为"共同的"（common）。自柏拉图发表《理想国》以来，在西方思想界一直存在着思考共同体的传统，但是共同体观念的空前生发则始于 18 世纪前后。这是由于在工业革命和资本主义全球化之际，人们突然发现周围的世界/社区变得陌生了：传统价值分崩离析，人际关系不再稳定，社会向心力逐渐消失，贫富差别日益扩大。换言之，就是人类社会对共同体的需求已迫在眉睫。作为对这一需求的回应，欧洲各国相继涌现出一批探索并宣扬共同体观念的仁人志士。他们或在哲学、社会学等领域里著书立说，或用文学形式推出关于共同体的想象，在两者形成的互动中，共同体观念随之嬗变演进。其中从黑格尔到马克思，从滕尼斯（Ferdinand Tönnies）到威廉斯（Raymond Williams），把有机/内在属性看作共同体主要内涵的观点一直占据共同体思想史的主流地位。在威廉斯之后，由于布朗肖（Maurice Blanchot）、南希（Jean-Luc Nancy）和米勒（J. H. Miller）等人的影响，文学批评理论界对共同体有机/内在属性的质疑甚嚣尘上，共同体观念的多义性因此日益彰显。为了厘清概念，对这些质疑进行梳理已然成为学界当务之急。

---

* 基金项目：国家社科基金重大项目"文化观念流变中的英国文学典籍研究"（12&ZD172）。

二、综述

根据威廉斯在《关键词：文化与社会的词汇》中的考证，英语 Community 一词在不同时期分别衍生出以下四个基本含义：一、平民百姓（14—17 世纪）；二、国家或组织有序的社会（14 世纪起）；三、某个区域的人民（18 世纪起）；四、共同拥有某些东西的性质（16 世纪起）。跟本文关系最密切的考证见于威廉斯如下的表述："从 18 世纪起，**共同体**比**社会**有了更多的亲近感……这种亲近感或贴切感是针对巨大而庞杂的工业社会语境而蓬勃生发的。人们在寻求另类的共同生活方式时，通常选择**共同体**一词来表示这方面的实验"（Williams 1988：75）。威廉斯还认为，作为术语的共同体有一个更重要的特征："不像其他所有指涉社会组织（国家、民族和社会等）的术语，它（共同体）似乎总是被用来激发美好的联想……"（Williams 1988：76）这一立论与德国社会学家、哲学家滕尼斯的共同体学说形成了呼应，后者曾经在与"社会"相对的意义上，给共同体下了一个经典性定义："共同体意味着人类真正的、持久的共同生活，而社会不过是一种暂时的、表面的东西。因此，共同体本身必须被理解为一种生机勃勃的有机体，而社会则是一种机械的聚合和人工制品"（Tönnies 2001：19）。滕尼斯是共同体思想的集大成者，他对于共同体的研究适逢文化观念内涵（共同体观念是文化观念的主要内涵之一）演变的最重要时期。或者说，在他那个时期，现代意义上的"文化"概念经历了最重要的内涵演变，① 而这一演变根植于"现代性焦虑"，即农业文明向工业文明转型而引起的焦虑。

在形成上述共同体观念的过程中，滕尼斯受到了洛克、卢梭、黑格尔和马克思等许多思想家的启发，其中黑格尔和马克思对他的影响最大。西班牙科尔多瓦大学教授赫弗南（Julián Jimnénez Heffernan）曾经指出，滕尼斯用以描述自己思想的关键术语都是从黑格尔那里借来的，如"社会"（Gesellschaft）和"共同体"（Gemeinschaft），以及"有机的"和"机械的"，等等（Heffernan 2013：8—16）。如上文所示，滕尼斯在界定共同体时，强调它是一种有机体，其对立

---

① 在过去的四百多年中，文化概念的最重要内涵是"转型焦虑"和"愿景描述"。关于这一观点的论证，请参考拙著《"文化辩护书"：19 世纪英国文化批评》（上海外语教育出版社，2013）。

面则是作为机械聚合体的社会,而黑格尔在其著作中"常常把有机纽带和聚合看作对立面,前者把一切融入活生生的整体,而后者仅仅用机械的方式把一切拼凑在一起"(Heffernan 2013:8)。相对于黑格尔,马克思对滕尼斯的影响更深刻、更具体。如赫弗南所说,马克思"渴望有一个由众多相互团结的、不弃不离的个人所组成的同质共同体"(Heffernan 2013:11)。确实,马克思对理想的共同体即共产主义社会的憧憬尤其强调个人与共同体之间的辩证关系:他既重视个人对共同体的责任,又主张共同体是个人全面发展的保障。在《德意志意识形态》一书中,他提出了"全人共同体"(the community of complete individuals)这一概念(Marx 1996:173—174),并强调"只有在共同体中,每个人才有全面发展自己能力的手段;因此,只有在共同体中,人的自由才有可能……在真正的共同体中,个人在联合的状态下通过联合获得自由"(Marx 1996:171)。类似的观点在《共产党宣言》里也曾出现:"代替那存在着阶级和阶级对立的资产阶级旧社会的,将是这样一个联合体,在那里,每个人的自由发展是一切人的自由发展的条件"(马克思,恩格斯 1972:273)。这里说的"联合体"就是共同体,"每个人的自由发展是一切人的自由发展的条件"就是滕尼斯所说的有机联系,而"阶级和阶级对立"则是机械聚合的重要表现形式之一。

在滕尼斯之后,一直有人继承他的共同体思想,并努力将其发扬光大。除上文所说的威廉斯以外,在这方面有较大影响的是安德森(Benedict Anderson),后者在其《想象的共同体》一书中把共同体的有机/内在属性寄托于想象,这是"因为即便在最小的民族里,每个成员都永远无法认识大多数同胞,无法与他们相遇,甚至无法听说他们的故事,不过在每个人的脑海里,存活着自己所在共同体的影像"(Anderson 1991:6)。所有这些思想跟文学家们对于共同体的想象形成了互动。① 不过,由于后现代主义尤其是解构主义思潮的兴起,文学创作和文学批评领域风向骤变,对共同体有机/内在属性的质疑和解构成了一种时髦。这股风在我国学界也吹得十分强劲,有学者最近撰文论证美国作家品钦的《秘

---

① 分别参见拙文《"朋友"意象与共同体形塑——〈我们共同的朋友〉的文化蕴涵》,载《外国文学研究》2013 年第 4 期;《想象共同体:〈卡斯特桥镇长〉的中心意义》,载《外国文学》2014 年第 3 期;《"多重英格兰"和共同体:〈荒凉山庄〉的启示》,载《外国文学评论》2014 年第 3 期;《华兹华斯笔下的深度共同体》,载《杭州师范大学学报》2015 年第 4 期;《丁尼生的诗歌和共同体形塑》,载《外国文学》2015 年第 5 期。

密融合》如何"表现了虚构共同体的自毁性",其前提是默认"文学呈现的是一种共同体的不可能性"(但汉松 2015:10)。这股思潮的最大推手是法国哲学家南希,下文就从"南希之辩"说起。

三、南希之辩

1983 年,南希发表长文《不运作的共同体》("La communauté désoeuvrée"),其宗旨是解构共同体这一概念,其核心观点是共同体只有在不运作——该文题目中的 désoeuvrée 意指"不运作""不操作""不运转"或"被闲置",英语通译为 inoperative——的时候才是真正的共同体。"南希的哲学揭示了一个悖论:真正的共同体是不可能存在的,但人类却生活在对它的虚构中"(但汉松 2015:9)。除了这个总悖论之外,南希这篇长文中还有许多小悖论,或者说惊人之语,如"共同体还没有发生过"(Nancy 1991:11),"共同体仍然没有被思考过"(Nancy 1991:26),"共同体不可能产生于工作领域"(Nancy 1991:31),"共同体在他人的死亡中得以显现"(Nancy 1991:15),"(共同体的)内在属性、集体融合含有的逻辑就是自杀逻辑;除此之外,共同体不受任何逻辑的支配"(Nancy 1991:12),等等。此文一出,响应者众,批评声也不少,学界称之为"南希之辩"(the Nancy debate)。

南希此论的直接思想来源是巴塔耶(George Bataille),后者"在形而上的层面上重燃关乎共同体的辩论",并引导南希围绕七个范畴来探讨共同体的属性,这些范畴分别为"死亡"(death)、"他异性"(alterity)、"超越"(transcendence)、"独体/单体"(singularity)、"外在性"(exteriority)、"交流/传递"(communication)和"有限性"(finitude)(Heffernan 2013:19—20)。所有这些范畴都是为解构所谓共同体的"内在性"(immanence)——在南希看来,滕尼斯以及许多文学家(如乔治·爱略特)所提倡的共同体都基于它的内在性,即内在的有机属性——而设立的。南希认为,共同体的内在性是不存在的,因此以内在性为基础的共同体是不真实的。

换言之,南希把滕尼斯、威廉斯和安德森看重的有机/内在属性视为共同体思想的障碍,进而提出要沿着"非内在性"(non-immanent)的思路重新思考共同体:"从某种意义上说,共同体就是抵制本身,即对内在性的抵制。因此,共同体就是超越,不过这'超越'不再具有任何'神圣的'意义,而只是精确地表示对内在性的抵制"(Nancy 1991:35)。除了 immanence,南希的笔下还有一个关键(动)词 expose,与其对应的名词同时为 exposition 和 exposure,分别表示"揭示/展露"和"暴露/易受伤(性)/脆弱性"的意思。这一关键词的使用也旨在解构上述"共同体的内在性",或者说共同体内在的纽带和交融。对此,有学者做过精辟的解释:

> 在南希的理论中,共同体的成员不是个体(individuality),而是单体(singularity);单体之间的最重要关系是"你和我",但其中的连接词"和"并不表示"并列关系"(juxtaposition),而是"揭示关系"(exposition)——你向我揭示你(expose),也就是对自我进行阐述(exposition)。这样,所谓交流也无法形成内在的纽带和交融,而只是向外进行表述。这种共同体实质上是分崩离析的堆砌。(程朝翔 2015:8)

如果说上述诠释偏重于 expose 中 exposition 的含义,那么赫弗南的以下解释则侧重其 exposure 的含义:

> 按照巴塔耶的观点,他异性成了……共同体生发的原因本身。当不同的自我共同暴露于相互间的他异性时,真正的共同体就产生了。这种暴露在死亡周围达到了高潮。这是因为只有他者的死亡,而非我们自己的死亡(因为它不可能被体验回味),才能最好地传递我们因自身属性无效而产生的狂喜。因此,狂喜、交流和牺牲(作为共享的死亡体验)是超越内在性并培育共同体的三种对等方式。(Heffernan 2013:19—20)

此处对"狂喜"(ecstasy)和"牺牲/死亡"的强调,令人想起尼采在其《悲剧的诞生》中所描述的"个体原则"被酒神精神粉碎/遭"翻船"的那一刻:"尼采说,'个人原则'被粉碎,先是惊骇,接下来是喜悦"(童明 2008:166)。然而,在这狂喜之后,共同体如何建构呢?南希于此则语焉不详。确切地说,南希认为狂喜/死亡后余下的只是不再运作的共同体。

以上两个段落的引文已经涉及南希想要揭示的他心目中"真正共同体"的七个范畴中的五个,即死亡、他异性、超越、独体/单体和交流/传递。至于另外两个,即外在性和有限性,我们不妨参照一下《不运作的共同体》的前言,因为在那里可以找到较为简明的解释。先来看一下外在性:"'被揭示/暴露'意味着'被放置于'外在性之中。说一个事物有外在性,是因为在它的内部也有一个外部,而且这外部就处于那内部的私密之处。……现实是'我的'脸总是暴露给他人,总是朝向某个他者,总是被他或她面对,而从不面对我自己"(xxxvii—xxxviii)。再来看有限性:"有限性,或者说无限同一性的无限缺失,是构成共同体的要素……发生在'交流'中的是**揭示**:有限的存在暴露于另一种有限的存在,两者互相面对,同时揭示自己"(xxxii—xl)。也就是说,这种"揭示"和"交流"仅仅作为"自身之外"而发生,并不触及人的"内部",即内心深处;即便进入了"内部",也只是进入了那"处于内部私密之处"的"外部",因而相关的交流都是有限的。

南希的理论在学界引起了极大反响。作为响应者,布朗肖在《不运作的共同体》问世的当年就发表《不可言说的共同体》(*La communauté inavouble*)一书,继续在"他异性"和"死亡"这两个母题上大做文章,以证明世上只存在"负面共同体"(the negative community)。该书第一章的小标题就是"负面共同体",此处的"负面"有否定的意思。布朗肖在书中强调"孤立的存在"(the isolated being),亦即前文所说的"独体",须由"狂喜",即死亡,而被否定。言下之意是人只有通过死亡才能摧毁他异性、单一性和有限性,才谈得上跟他人的真正融合,才谈得上共同体,不过这时的共同体已经是 the unworked community,即前文提到的南希所说的 the inoperative community(Blanchot 1988:18)。该书还试图证明世上只有"没有共同体的人所拥有的共同体"(the community of those who have no community),并将巴塔耶的这句话作为书的开篇。用布朗肖的原话说,"没有共同体的人所拥有的共同体"是"共同体经验的终极形式"(Blanchot 1988:25)。尽管布朗肖这部书的影响很大,许多学者在解读文学作品时都套用了他的一些词汇,但是如赫弗南所说,该书"与其说以分析见长,不如说只是提供了一些证据……它对那场辩论①的唯一显著贡献是强调在集

---

① 指南希之辩。

体交流的根基处存在着秘密，一种深藏而无法言说的秘密，因此是不可能被揭示的"（Heffernan 2013：28）。我们知道，共同体的一个根本前提就是人与人之间的深度沟通/交流。威廉斯曾经在《漫长的革命》一书中指出，只有在"深度共同体"（the deep community）中，"沟通才成为可能"（Williams 1961：65）。不妨反过来说：没有深度沟通，就没有深度共同体。布朗肖和南希等人咬定人类"秘密"的"不可言说"性，把沟通/交流锁定在外在层面，其实就是否定了深度沟通，也就否定了深度共同体。

若作深究，南希的思想还应追溯到海德格尔，后者在《存在与时间》中把"此在"（Dasein）——即人类特有的存在体验——区分成"真实的此在"和"不真实的此在"：前者是一种独体，始终保留自己的独特性和有限性；后者则丢失了自我，迷失/湮没于"他们"（das Man），即日常性的存在，其显著表征是人们关于日常共享经验的话语，海德格尔称之为闲话（Gerede）。对此米勒曾经有过简洁的解释："对于海德格尔来说，处于共同体就是迷失于'他们'，而挣脱共同体就是为了变成真实的此在，而我们本来就具备成为此在的潜在性"（Miller 2015：13）。在《不运作的共同体》中，南希多次借用海德格尔的观点来强调共同体的"独体性"（singularity），以及它和"死亡""他者"的相互依存关系，认为"独体是激情式的存在"，并主张"在跨越共同体的门槛时就要通过死亡来辨认他者……只有在他者的死亡里，共同体才让我触及它的本真"（Nancy 1991：33）。鉴于南希和海德格尔的有关表述都十分晦涩，我们不妨参照米勒的再阐述来加以理解：

> 海德格尔在《存在与时间》《形而上学的基本概念》中断言 Mitsein，即"共在"，是 Dasein——他给人类"存在"取的名字——的原始特征。然而，他把人类日常共享经验的话语谴责为 Gerede，即"闲话"，这使他招来了恶名。他认为，Dasein 在某些瞬间会意识到自己的独特性和有限性，会意识到自己的 Sein zum Tode（"向着死亡而存在"），而这些正是他最珍视的瞬间。这样的 Dasein 于是会"想要有良心"，进而决定负起自己的责任。在威廉斯看来，像哈代的《无名的裘德》中的裘德·福利或《还乡》中的克林·姚伯这样的人物所经历的异化是件坏事，而在海德格尔看来正是真

实的基本状况。真实意味着在孤独中把握住自己的 Dasein，而不是屈从于 das Man，即"他们"。海德格尔的评价刚好与威廉斯的截然相反。（Miller 2015：7）

此处唯一让人心头一热的是"良心"和"责任"，这似乎跟马克思、滕尼斯和威廉斯等人所提倡的有机共同体——没有阶级等差别的共同体——相当契合。然而，就像米勒所指出的那样，海格德尔、南希等人所谓"良心的召唤是无法向任何另一个人证明的"（Miller 2015：15），因而这种"良心"和"责任"的最终指向只能是独体，而非共同体。

南希等人的"共同体"实为独体，他们的理论影响了当今一大批学者和文人。例如，米勒虽然声称自己"分享威廉斯对乌托邦的憧憬"（Miller 2015：4），但是他表示无法相信后者所说共同体的真实性："我全心希望我能够相信威廉斯笔下那种没有阶级的共同体，但是真正的共同体恐怕更像德里达描述的那样，是一种自我毁灭性的自动免疫体①"（Miller 2015：17）。米勒还在2015年发表专著《小说中的共同体》（*Communities in Fiction*），其中对特罗洛普（Anthony Trollope）、哈代、康拉德、伍尔夫、品钦和塞万提斯等人作品的解读在很大程度上借力于南希。例如，其中对特罗洛普的《巴塞特的最后记事》（*The Last Chronicle of Barset*）的解读无非是印证了南希的"独体理论"："我的结论是：《巴塞特的最后记事》出人意料地提供了——尽管是以一种间接的、模棱两可的方式——南希所说的第二种共同体②的范例，即由独体构成的共同体；就这些独体最深的层次而言，他们毫无共同之处"（Miller 2015：91）。

总之，沿着米勒和南希等人的思路，我们永远走不出独体这一怪圈，或者说只能在共同体和独体之间画上等号。难道我们只能在这样的怪圈里就范吗？本文下一小节将试作回答。

---

① 德里达假定在每个共同体中都有一种自杀倾向，并称之为"自动免疫"（autoimmunity）："不在自身中培育自动免疫的社群/共同体是不可能存在的。这种自动免疫自我牺牲，自我破坏，是一种毁灭自我保护原则的原则"（Derrida 87）。

② 根据南希的分类，在"第一种共同体"中，人们拥有共同的信念、理想和价值观，不过南希否定了这种共同体的真实性。

四、走出"独体"怪圈

应该承认,独体理论并非一无是处,它至少有两个积极作用。其一,它指出了现代性语境下的"此在",或者说"真正的共同体"容易湮没于"他们",湮没于所谓的"日常习俗""共享经验"和"日常话语",而这些都已经被工具理性、大众文化和全球性扩张的资本所操纵。它企图通过良心把"此在"从湮没于"他们"的状态中解救出来,这本身无可厚非。其二,它起到了解构形形色色的伪共同体的作用。例如,米勒在《小说中的共同体》中就曾有力地批评美国,指出它不是一个真正的共同体,"当然,如果你把当今的美国看作一个巨大的共同体,那么与其说它是威廉斯所说的那种由亲密无间的善良人们组成的共同体,不如说它是德里达所说的自我毁坏的自身免疫性共同体"(Miller 2015:17)。显然,具有自我毁灭倾向的共同体不是理想的共同体。然而,独体理论有三大要害:混淆/偷换概念;以偏概全;解构有余,建构不足。下文将逐一分析。

首先,从巴塔耶到南希,从海德格尔到米勒,都是在混淆或偷换概念。用来遮掩这一手段的,是他们在逻辑推理方面高超的隐秘性。乍看上去,推演十分严谨,丝丝入扣,可是其前提往往值得商榷。就共同体这一概念而言,他们以"形而上层面"的思考为前提,开始了从概念到概念的推理,其中不乏解构主义者惯用的"能指置换"游戏,其逻辑不可谓不严密。如上文所示,推理的结果是"奇迹"般地把共同体换成了独体。然而,共同体本来就不是也不应该是纯粹的形而上概念。马克思当年对先前哲学家们的批判也适用于那些只在形而上层面推演/解释共同体的学者和文人:"哲学家们只是用不同的方式**解释**世界,问题在于**改变**世界"(马克思,关于费尔巴哈的提纲,1972:19)。无论是马克思主义哲学家,还是无数优秀的文学家,他们在倡导/想象共同体时并不仅仅把它看作一个形而上的概念,而是更多地把它看作一种文化实践。这种实践作为一种社会活动乃至运动,在19世纪已经蔚为壮观。参与这种实践的除马克思和恩格斯之外,还有英国的华兹华斯、卡莱尔、狄更斯、乔治·爱略特、哈代、丁尼生、罗斯金和莫里斯等,以及法国的涂尔干、德国的韦伯和滕尼斯等。以滕尼斯为例,他认为一切有利于共同体的人类活动"都是一个有机的过程",

而且"都跟艺术有着亲缘关系"(Tönnies 2001：80)。此处对"活动"和"有机过程"的强调表明共同体并未定型，而是动态的、不断生长的、具有开放性的，因而不可能是南希等人所说的那种封闭型独体。美国学者格雷弗（Suzanne Graver）曾经细致地研究过 19 世纪的共同体思想，尤其是滕尼斯的思想，对乔治·爱略特的影响。她强调后者的写作"不是提供解决（文化失序等问题）的方案，而是培育有关手段的意识——通过这些手段我们可以实现无穷无尽的解决方案"(Graver 1984：9)。也就是说，乔治·爱略特想象共同体的出发点跟马克思的一样，是为了改造整个世界。她致力于构建"情感共同体"(community of feelings)①，并"坚信艺术有力量扩展读者的胸怀，使之更有同情心和反应能力；她的美学旨在全面改变人的感受力，进而最终改变社会"(Graver 1984：11)。可见共同体概念最重要的属性是文化实践，意在改造世界。它怎能允许被形而上的推演轻易地加以置换呢？

其次，独体理论往往以偏概全。最明显的要数南希和布朗肖的"秘密说"，即所谓"揭示"和"交流"只能在"自身之外"发生，并不触及人的"内部"，或者说"集体交流的根基处存在着秘密"，而且这种秘密"是不可能被揭示的"（参见上一小节第 4—5 段）。诚然，每个人的心底都可能有一些秘密，但是这些秘密往往只占每人心思的很小一部分；在绝大多数情况下，这些小秘密不会影响人们在"共同体的第三支柱"② 方面——信念、理想、志趣、情感和观念等——达成一致。换言之，共同的事业需要人们志同道合，甚至肝胆相照，但是这并不要求也没有必要要求人们和盘托出内心的秘密；对于公共事业来说，许多私人的秘密无关大局。诡辩者们以人们有一些小秘密（哪怕只占全部心思的一个角落）为由，就说人与人之间无法沟通、交流，并据此推导出共同体为独体的结论，这明摆着是以偏概全，混淆视听。令人遗憾的是，就连米勒这样的饱学之士也深陷独体论泥淖。且看他对《巴塞特的最后记事》的如下解读："特罗洛普对亨利·格兰特利和格蕾丝·克劳利之间的恋情巧妙地作了戏剧化处理，微妙地揭示了他俩互相暴露于对方的独体性和他异性，同时也把各自

---

① 据格雷弗的研究，这一概念出自华兹华斯。
② 滕尼斯界定了共同体的"三大支柱"(three pillars)，即"血缘"(blood)、"地缘"(place)和"心缘"(mind)，其中作为第三支柱的"心缘"包括共同的信念、理想、志趣、情感和观念等。

的秘密和他异性暴露给了自己"（Miller 2015：76）。这样的解读也是以偏概全的产物。从小说的情节来看，亨利和格蕾丝之间的恋情虽然经历了种种曲折，但是他俩终成眷属，这是不争的主旋律，米勒所说的"独体性"和"他异性"并未妨碍他俩真诚相爱。小说中有一段叙述可以用作对米勒的回应："要是说爱情产生争吵，那可是错误的，但是爱情确实产生亲密的关系，而争吵经常是这种关系的后果之一……一位兄弟可能会指责另一位兄弟，但是相互间从未发生龃龉的兄弟恐怕不存在吧？"（Trollope 2012：531）同理，在大多数情况下，恋人之间，或兄弟之间，即便有这样或那样的私密，也不会在总体上影响恋情或兄弟情，这其实是常识。独体理论的推崇者置常识于不顾，自然会制造出种种奇谈怪论。以偏概全的错误还常常跟偷换概念的错误相重合。例如，南希和米勒都推崇的德里达很不喜欢"共同体"一词，其理由是它带有"融合"（fusion）的含义，而"融合"意味着"责任的消除"（Salas 2013：160）。这一观点跟海德格尔的"此在"说和"他们"说如出一辙。如前文所述，在海德格尔看来，处于共同体就是迷失于"他们"，湮没于受工具理性、大众文化和全球化资本支配的"日常习俗""共享经验"和"日常话语"，也就是迷失于德里达所说的"融合"。事实上，人类的普通经验已经告诉我们，处于共同体的"他们"中虽然鱼龙混杂，但是绝非每个人都不负责任，否则这个世界早就灭亡了。因此，海德格尔所说的"他们"本应既包括负责任的共同体成员，也包括不负责任的"混混"们，前者应该看作融合，而后者则是混合。在德里达和海德格尔的词典里，把"混合"无限扩大，变成/取代了"融合"，这既是以偏概全，又是偷梁换柱。

再次，独体理论解构有余，建构不足。这一点在那些运用独体理论解读文学作品的批评活动中表现得非常明显。限于篇幅，我们仅以维勒-阿盖兹（Pilar Villar-Argáiz）对乔伊斯（James Joyce）短篇小说《死者》（"The Dead"）的解读为例。维勒-阿盖兹声称自己的

  主要目的是审视乔伊斯如何呈现南希和布朗肖这两位法国思想家所讨论的两种共同体模式：一种是"有着被所有成员都接受并遵循的固定法律、机构和习俗的可运作的共同体"（米勒语）；另一种是让前一种停顿使之不可运作的共同体，南希称之为"不运作的共同体"，而布朗肖则称之为"不

可言说的共同体"或"没有共同体的人所拥有的共同体"。（Villar-Argáiz 2013：48）

维勒-阿盖兹进而断言"乔伊斯在许多方面瓦解了有机共同体中固定的习俗"（Villar-Argáiz 2013：59），或者说"聚焦于那些据称有凝聚力的共同体内部的许多缝隙，这些缝隙的口子越开越大"（Villar-Argáiz 2013：49）。在维勒-阿盖兹引为论据的诸多例子中，最典型的要数加布里埃尔和格蕾塔的婚姻（婚姻也是一种共同体）。在格蕾塔逝世之前，他俩其实没有深度交流，而加布里埃尔一直以为"她是他的"（Joyce 2000：216），自己能够"征服她"（Joyce 2000：218）。直到故事结尾，加布里埃尔才意识到妻子另有所爱。维勒-阿盖兹由此得出的结论是："只有当他［加布里埃尔］认识到格蕾塔是一个他者，一个独立于他、与他分离的自我时，'真爱'才可能出现在他俩之间。这种暴露于他异性和有限性的状况会培育透明交际的可能性"（Villar-Argáiz 2013：59）。维勒-阿盖兹还指出加布里埃尔经历了一次"精神上的觉醒"，而这觉醒"发生在死亡瞬间"（Villar-Argáiz 2013：61）。确实，通过迈克尔之死以及对他悲惨人生的了解，加布里埃尔意识到迈克尔比自己更爱格蕾塔，并意识到自己私心过重（他对格蕾塔的爱其实是一种占有欲），因而经历了一次成长。维勒-阿盖兹看到了这一点，所以他说上述经历帮助加布里埃尔"摆脱了自我万能的感觉"（Villar-Argáiz 2013：61）。然而令人遗憾的是，维勒-阿盖兹未能在解构那个虚假共同体——加布里埃尔和格蕾塔的婚姻共同体有许多虚假成分——的基础上，进一步阐发《死者》所隐含的积极的建构意义，即加布里埃尔经由"死亡"走出了自我，今后有可能融入一个具有真爱的共同体，甚至会积极投身于这类共同体的建设；相反，维勒-阿盖兹笔锋一转，强调这一故事"描写了一个由死亡的迫近所界定的不运作的共同体"（Villar-Argáiz 2013：61）。事实上，维勒-阿盖兹在引言部分就强调了贯穿全文的一个观点，即加布里埃尔只是在死亡瞬间"才瞥见了一种更真实的交流，即不同独体之间的交流"（Villar-Argáiz 2013：49）。跟乔伊斯同时代的艾略特（T. S. Eliot）曾经谈到"对死者的虔敬"对于文化、家庭和共同体（家庭概念跟共同体概念有关）建设的重要性："当我说到家庭时，心中想到的是一种历时较久的纽带：一种对死者的虔敬，即便他们默默无闻；一种对未出生者的关切，即便他们出生在遥远的将来。这种对过去与未来的崇敬必须在家庭里就得到培育，否则将永远不可能存在于共同体中，最多只不过是一纸空文"（Elliot 1948：44）。言下之意，死者虽逝，活力尚存——只要虔敬还在，共同体的纽带就在；这种虔敬会化作历史悠久的、具有建构意义的无形力量。在南希等人的理论里，正因为这种虔敬严重缺席，所以才有"不运作的共同体"之说。

一言以蔽之，只要我们澄清概念，不以偏概全，并在解构的同时积极建构，就能走出"独体"怪圈。独体消亡之时，才是共同体振兴之日。

五、结语

作为一个术语，"共同体"的含义还会不断增殖，关于这些含义的大辩论还会持续。就文学领域而论，讨论共同体的理由首先来自普遍存在的"共同体冲动"。大凡优秀的文学家和批评家，都有一种"共同体冲动"，即憧憬未来的美好社会，一种超越亲缘和地域的、有机生成的、具有活力和凝聚力的共同体形式。自18世纪以降，在许多国家的文学中，这种冲动烙上了一种特殊的时代印记，即群起为遭遇工业化/现代化浪潮冲击而濒于瓦解的传统共同体寻求出路，并描绘出理想的共同体愿景；而在其背后，不乏社会转型所引起的焦虑，为化解焦虑而谋求对策。由于解构主义思潮的兴起，声讨共同体的有机/内在属性突然成了一种时髦。共同体，还是独体？这居然成了问题。不解决这个问题，文学中的共同体想象就很难想象。也就是说，对共同体观念的内涵和外延进行梳理实在是燃眉之急，而解决问题的关键，在于走出"独体"怪圈。要走出这一怪圈，则关键在于抓住本文所分析的"三大要害"。

参考文献

[1] Anderson B. *Imagined Communities: Reflections on the Origin and Spread of Nationalism* [M]. London：Verso，1991.

[2] Blanchot M. *The Unavowable Community*. Trans. Pierre Joris [M]. New York：Station Hill，1988.

[3] Childers J.，Hentzi G. *Columbia Dictionary of Modern Literary and Cultural*

Criticism. [M]. New York: Columbia UP, 1995.

［4］ Derrida J. "Faith and Knowledge: The Two Sources of 'Religion' at the Limits of Reason Alone." ［A］// *Acts of Religion.* Trans. Samuel Weber. Ed. Gil Anidjar [M]. New York: Routledge, 2002. 40 – 101.

［5］ Eliot T S. *Notes towards the Definition of Culture* [M]. Croydon: Faber, 1948.

［6］ Graver S. *George Eliot and Community: A Study in Social Theory and Fictional Form* [M]. Berkeley: California UP, 1984.

［7］ Heffernan J J. "Introduction: Togetherness and its Discontents." ［A］// *Community in Twentieth-Century Fiction.* Ed. P. M. Salván, et al. [M]. London: Palgrave, 2013. 1 – 47.

［8］ Joyce J. "The Dead." *Dubliners* [M]. London: Penguin, 2000. 172 – 225.

［9］ Marx K. *The German Ideology* [M]. Cambridge: CUP, 1996.

［10］ Miller J H. *Communities in Fiction* [M]. New York: Fordham UP, 2015.

［11］ Nancy J. *The Inoperative Community.* Trans. Peter Connor, et al. [M]. Minneapolis: Minnesota UP, 1991.

［12］ Salas G R. "When Strangers Are Never at Home: A Communitarian Study of Janet Frame's *The Carpathains.*" ［A］// *Community in Twentieth-Century Fiction.* Ed. P. M. Salván, et al. [M]. London: Palgrave, 2013. 159 – 176.

［13］ Tönnies F. *Community and Civil Society.* Trans. Jose Harrisand and Margaret Hollis [M]. Cambridge: CUP, 2001.

［14］ Trollope A. *The Last Chronicle of Barset* [M]. London: Penguin, 2012.

［15］ Villar-Argáiz P. Organic and Unworked Communities in James Joyce's 'The Dead.' ［A］// *Community in Twentieth-Century Fiction.* Ed. P. M. Salván, et al. [M]. London: Palgrave, 2013. 48 – 66.

［16］ Williams R. *Keywords: A Vocabulary of Culture and Society* [M]. London: Fontana, 1988.

［17］ Williams R. *The Long Revolution* [M]. Harmondsworth: Penguin, 1961.

[18] 程朝翔. 无语与言说、个体与社区：西方大屠杀研究的辩证——兼论大屠杀研究对亚洲共同体建设的意义 [J]. 社会科学与研究, 2015, (6): 2-14. [Cheng, Zhaoxiang. "Silence and Speech: the Individual and Community: The Dialectics of the Research on the Holocaust in the West—With a Subsidiary Probe into the Significance of Community Building in Asia." *Social Sciences and Studies* 6 (2015): 2-14.]

[19] 但汉松. "卡尔"的鬼魂问题——论品钦《秘密融合》中的共同体和他者 [J]. 当代外国文学, 2015, (4): 5-11. [Dan, Hansong. "Carl's Problematic Ghostliness: On Community and the Others in Pynchon's 'Secret Integration.'" *Contemporary Foreign Literature* 4 (2015): 5-11.]

[20] 马克思, 恩格斯. 共产党宣言. 载《马克思恩格斯选集》第一卷 [M]. 杭州：人民出版社, 1972: 250-286. [Marx, Karl, and Friedrich Engels. *The Communist Manifesto. Selected Works of Marx and Engels.* Vol. 1. Hangzhou: People's, 1972. 250-86.]

[21] 马克思. 关于费尔巴哈的提纲. 载《马克思恩格斯选集》第一卷 [M]. 杭州：人民出版社, 1972: 16-19. [Marx, Karl. *An Outline on Feuerbach. Selected Works of Marx and Engels.* Vol. 1. Hangzhou: People's, 1972. 16-19.]

[22] 童明. 现代性赋格：19世纪欧洲文学名著启示录 [M]. 桂林：广西师范大学出版社, 2008. [Tong, Ming. *Modernity in Fugue: Inspirations from Masterpieces of the 19th Century European Literature.* Guilin: Guangxi Normal UP, 2008.]

（本文原载于《外国文学》2016年第2期）

英国文学中的幸福伦理与共同体形塑[*]

近年来，关于英国文学中共同体形塑的研究日渐增多，但是此项研究并未摆脱一个困境，即如何应对解构主义思潮对共同体真实性、内在性、和谐性的质疑——解构主义思潮影响所及，居然使共同体究竟是否存在成了问题。针对这一问题，笔者曾发表《西方文论关键词：共同体》一文，以梳理共同体观念的内涵和外延，并反驳了南希（Jean-Luc Nancy, 1940— ）、巴塔耶（George Bataille, 1897—1962）、布朗肖（Maurice Blanchot, 1907—2003）和米勒（Joseph Hillis Miller, 1928— ）等人把"共同体"等同于"独体"的观点。不过，这篇文章还有一个不足之处，即未能从幸福伦理（ethics of eudaimonia）的角度探讨共同体话题，而要走出上述困境，我们还可从历来英国文学家们对幸福伦理的探究入手。[①] 伦理和幸福宛若一对孪生姐妹，这在聂珍钊教授所梳理的伦理思想史中可见一斑：霍布斯等哲学家在"完成……从中世纪伦理思想到近代伦理思想的真正转变"时所做的一项主要工作就是"规定幸福的内容"（聂珍钊 117—119）。哲学家们是如此，文学家们更是如此。从奥斯汀（Jane Austen, 1775—

---

[*] 本文系国家社会科学研究基金重大项目"文化观念流变中的英国文学典籍研究"【项目批号：12&ZD172】的阶段性成果。

[①] 详见拙文《西方文论关键词：共同体》，载《外国文学》2016 年第 2 期，第 70—79 页。

1817)到乔治·艾略特（George Eliot, 1819—1880），从狄更斯（Charles Dickens, 1812—1870）到乔治·吉辛（George Gissing, 1857—1903），再从普里斯特利（J. B. Priestley, 1894—1984）到拜厄特（A. S. Byatt, 1936—　），英国文学家们都把幸福和伦理结合起来考量，并把幸福伦理看作通向共同体的一把钥匙；通过如椽之笔，一股股川流不息的诗性叙事，全都流向"秩序"与"自由"之间平衡的渊薮，而这平衡的关键在于进行幸福伦理的建构，在于以情感文化为基石而树立的社会责任感。

要说清"秩序"与"自由"之间的关系，还得从"霍姆斯之辩"说起。

一、霍姆斯之辩

跟南希等人一样，美国学者霍姆斯（Stephen Holmes）否认以黑格尔、马克思、滕尼斯、威廉斯和麦金泰尔（Alasdair MacIntyre, 1929—　）为代表的主张个人与共同体之间辩证关系的思想，即既主张个人对共同体负有责任，又主张共同体是个人全面发展的保障，就如马克思在《德意志意识形态》中所说的那样，"只有在共同体中，每个人才有全面发展自己能力的手段；因此，只有在共同体中，人的自由才有可能……在真正的共同体中，个人在联合的状态下通过联合获得自由"（Marx 1996: 171）。此处，尤其值得关注的是"自由"一词——个人在共同体中分明是自由的；共同体似和谐之水，而个人则如鱼处其中。用麦金泰尔的话说，共同体模式的社会秩序不仅向社会成员提供了基本的生活福祉，而且使"厚实的自我"（thick self）牢牢地扎根于自己所在的环境，因此"既过得很好，又干得很好"（MacIntyre 1966: 139）。然而，霍姆斯不认同这样的共同体理想。他在《反自由思想的永久性结构》（*The Permanent Structure of Antiliberal Thought*, 1989）一文中，把上述共同体图景描绘为"不真实的"，或者说是"有悖于情理的"（implausible），并把上述"个人扎根于自己所在环境"的共同体模式定性为"镶嵌性模式"（embeddedness），而这种"镶嵌"又无异于"限制"（restriction）或"遏制"（restraint）（Holmes 1989: 159—182）。用意大利学者瓦莱丽·温赖特（Valerie Wainwright）的话说，霍姆斯这样的"自由主义者把'镶嵌'阐释为限制和遏制；他们认为，一旦人们追求归属于某个团体,个人自由和个性发展等开明目标就会被丢弃"(Wainwright 2007:110)。也就是说,在霍姆斯的词典里,共同体/秩序诉求必然意味着个人自由的丢失。

霍姆斯的"镶嵌论"可以追溯到海德格尔(Martin Heidegger,1889—1976)的"湮没论"。后者在《存在与时间》(Sein und Zeit,1927)中提出,"自我"/"此在"(Dasein)有湮没于"他们"(das Man)的危险;他把"此在"——即人类特有的存在体验——区分成"真实的此在"和"不真实的此在",前者是一种独体(始终保留自己的独特性和有限性),而后者则丢失了自我,迷失/湮没于"他们"(das Man),即日常性的存在(Childers & Hentzi 70)。关于这一点,米勒曾经有过简洁的解释:"对海德格尔来说,处于共同体就是迷失于'他们',而挣脱共同体就是为了变成真实的此在,而我们本来就具备成为此在的潜在性"(Miller 2015:13)。情形果真如此吗?共同体/秩序诉求必然意味着个人自由的丢失吗?

诚然,没有个人的自由,就无所谓共同体,反之亦然。个人自由和共同体互为依存,相辅相成,彼此是一种辩证的关系,这本来是一种常识,可是到了那些自命高深的哲学家/批评家手里,却成了水火不相容的东西。这种非此即彼的思维方式,究其根源,与启蒙现代性不无关系——启蒙思想家们过度依赖工具理性,过度"热衷于个人对福祉的主观感受"(Norton 2012:10),因而使个人自由/幸福与共同体/秩序诉求截然对立,导致现代幸福观念中认知维度和伦理维度的分裂。用麦金泰尔的话说,"责任和幸福的纽带逐渐被撕裂了……原先幸福定义中的满足感,要根据主导社会生活形态的标准来衡量,而如今幸福不再根据那种满足感来界定了,而是仅仅从个人的心理感受层面来界定"(MacIntyre 1966:167)。换言之,责任本来应该是幸福伦理的核心要素,可是如今它已游离了许多现代西方人的幸福观念;在启蒙现代性语境下,自由主义者往往无视个人对社会的责任。那么,履行个人对社会的责任,追求具有良好秩序的共同体,是否就必然意味着个人自由和幸福的丧失呢?事实上,从19世纪至今,英国文学家们对此一直进行着不懈的探讨。他们在想象共同体时,已经对如何保持"秩序"与"自由"之间的平衡这一问题有深入的思考。无论是19世纪的奥斯汀、狄更斯、乔治·艾略特和乔治·吉辛,还是当代的麦克尤恩(Ian McEwan,1948—)、斯威夫特(Graham Swift,1949—)、阿克罗伊德

(Peter Ackroyd，1949— ）和拜厄特，英国文学家们描绘了一幅幅呈现上述平衡的共同体图景，而维系这种平衡的关键在于他们所主张的幸福伦理。

为探究上述小说英国文学家们所构建的幸福伦理，我们不妨从"另一个穆勒"说起。

二、"另一个穆勒"

就"幸福"和"自由"这两个文化命题而言，英国文学史上有一个绕不过去的人物，即穆勒（John Stuart Mill，1806—1873）。这位横跨文学和哲学两大领域的思想家通常被视为西方自由主义的鼻祖，他的《论自由》（*On Liberty*，1859）总会被列入西方大学课程的必读书目，就像芝加哥大学的卡汉（Alan S. Kahan）博士所说的那样："假如您只能通过阅读一本书来了解现代西方文化，那么《论自由》会是一个很好的选择"（Kahan 2008：2）。然而，正如美国学者希梅尔法勃（Gertrude Himmelfarb）所说，穆勒的思想还有另一面，或者说存在着"另一个穆勒"，"而对这个穆勒来说，思想自由和言论自由本身并非目的，甚至不是通向真理这一更高目标的手段；个性自由本身既不构成善，也不足以成为手段来使人类臻于完善；社会并非个人的天敌"（Himmelfarb 2006：102）。此处的"社会"跟我们在上文中所说的"秩序"同义，因此也就是肯定了"自由"与"秩序"共存的可能性，或者说暗示了两者相辅相成的辩证关系。在这一思想的基础上，穆勒还表达了下面这一观点：

> 人们来到世上，并非为了实现某个单一目的；任何单一目的，即便完满地实现了，也不能使人幸福。（Himmelfarb 2006：102）

这段话的关键词是"幸福"。结合前面的那段引文，我们可以这样来理解穆勒的意思：若把自由本身当作目的，人类就无幸福可言。

穆勒的上述观点在他的《自传》（*Autobiography* 1873）——该书是英国文学史上公认的佳作——里得到了更加生动的表述。《自传》中最富有戏剧性的事件是穆勒20岁那年经历的一场精神危机：他深受父亲詹姆斯·穆勒和偶像人物边沁的影响，全身心地投入了以"人类自由"为目标的社会改革，然而他突然迟疑了，甚至患上了忧郁症，其起因源于他对幸福命题的思考。他在书中这样回忆道：

> 我对自己直接发问："假设你生活中的所有目标都实现了，你所期待的所有机构改革和思想变更都能在这一刻得以完成，你会因此而欢欣鼓舞并感到幸福吗？"一个不可压抑的自我意识清楚地答道："不！"我的心随之下沉了，支撑我生命的全部基础轰然倒塌。我全部的幸福原本都寄托于对上述目标的不懈追求。既然目标已经失去了魅力，那么对手段的兴趣又何以为继呢？我生活的意义似乎荡然无存了。（Mill 2015：112）

此处，穆勒以"幸福"为标准，对边沁和老穆勒所发动的"机构改革和思想变更"——这些变革总是打着"自由"的大旗——进行了深刻反思。谓其深刻，是因为穆勒把矛头对准了边沁的"幸福原则"，即所谓"最大多数人的最大幸福"——边沁把它简单地归结为"自由放任"（laissez faire）的工商业政策、"公平竞争"和市场供求关系等（Bentham 2003：17—20）。事实上，上述改革并未给最大多数人带来最大幸福，而是如阿诺德当年所批评的那样，造成了如下自由而无序的状况：

> 就在我们的自由、体格锻炼和工业才能开始得到世界的瞩目时，世界却没有因为看到我们的这些长处而表现出热爱、钦羡……原因难道不正是我们那种机械的行为方式吗？我们将自由、强健的体魄和工业技术本身当作了目的来追求，而没有将这些事情同人类臻于完美的总目标联系起来……英式的自由，英式的工业，英式的强健，我们一概都在盲目地推进，我们把握这些事物时根本没有适度感、分寸感，因为我们的头脑里缺乏人类和谐发展、达到完善的理想，我们并不是在这理想的促动下开始行动，不是用理想来指导我们所做的工作。（阿诺德 2014：145）

穆勒正是因为看到这种"自由"无法给世人带来幸福，所以才重新思考

"幸福"的要义。经过反思,他总结出了幸福生活的要素,其中包括"阳光、空气和书籍",以及"与人交谈"和"公共事务"所带来的欢乐(Mill 2015:117);他还特别强调"美感激荡下的情感状态,以及带有感情色彩的思想",并把后者称为"情感文化",进而从中发现了"幸福的永久源泉"(Mill 2015:121)。

须特别指出的是,穆勒认定的幸福观有着坚实的伦理维度,这体现于他对"与人交谈"和"公共事务"的强调。如本文第一小节中所述,幸福伦理的核心要素是责任,而穆勒强调"与人交谈"和"公共事务",这显然表达了两层意思:1)对他人和公共事务的高度责任感(任何社会/共同体秩序都需要这种责任感);2)这种责任不但没有让人感到不自由,而且还给人带来欢乐。换言之,穆勒在摆脱了(前文所说的)精神危机之后,找到了通向自由与秩序之间平衡的一把钥匙,即以上述责任感为前提的幸福伦理。

还须进一步指出的是,上述责任感并非纯粹地为责任而责任。前文提到,穆勒在陷入精神危机之前就是富有责任心的人,他对于社会/政治改革的抱负就说明了这一点,但是那时他却缺乏幸福感,因此导致他的抱负难以为继;后来之所以能重获幸福感,是因为他学会了把责任建筑在"情感文化"的基础之上,也就是使自己的责任感处于"美感激荡下的情感状态",并"带有感情色彩的思想"。此处所说的"情感文化"原文为 the culture of feelings,其含义跟伯克(Edmund Burke,1729—1797)所说的 sensibility 十分吻合(Burke 2004:281),两者其实就是同义词。美国弗吉尼亚大学教授麦克甘恩(Jerome John McGann,1937—)曾在追溯以 sensibility 为关键词的诗学传统时提出,"情感诗学"(the poetics of sensibility)标志着"文学风格的一场革命",[①] 但是他只在一处提到了伯克,并把后者的思想概括为"多愁善感的伯克式意识形态"(sentimental Burkean ideology),甚至把它跟"浅薄的阅读"联系在一起(McGann 1996:186)。事实上,伯克所提倡的 sensibility 跟浅薄的多愁善感大相径庭,他在《法国革命回想录》(*Reflections on the Revolution in France*,1790)中有一段相关论述:"真正的立法者应该心中充满情感。他应该热爱同胞,尊重同胞,并对自我

---

① 麦克甘恩所著《情感诗学》一书的副标题就是"文学风格的一场革命"(A Revolution in Literary Style)。

保持警觉"（Burke 2004：281）。此处，"心中充满情感"一语的原文为 to have a heart full of sensibility——笔者出于不得已，把 sensibility 译成了"情感"，其实它有着很丰富的含义，既指感受/甄别他人情感的能力和敏感性（尤指不伤害别人的感情），又指上引文字中"热爱同胞""尊重同胞"以及"对自我保持警觉"等品质。一言以蔽之，sensibility 意味着既有感情，又懂感情。在这一意义上，它跟穆勒所说的"情感文化"别无二致。正是这种情感文化，构成了幸福伦理所需责任感的前提。

参与上述情感文化建设的不光有穆勒、伯克，还有许多其他英国文学家。这将是本文下一小节的话题。

三、情感文化：幸福伦理的关捩

幸福伦理的关捩在于情感文化。在英国历史上，无论是 19 世纪的奥斯汀、狄更斯、乔治·艾略特和乔治·吉辛，还是 20 世纪的普里斯特利，或是仍然活跃在 21 世纪的拜厄特、麦克尤恩、斯威夫特和阿克罗伊德，都用生动的文学语言参与了情感文化的建设，而这又是一种共同体形塑。

先说奥斯汀。她的名著《理智与情感》（Sense and Sensibility，1811）标题中就有 sensibility 一词，目前国内一般都把它译为"情感"，但是如前文所述，它的实际含义是情感文化。也就是说，当年奥斯汀就已经十分重视情感文化的建设。仅就《理智与情感》而言，女主人公玛丽安的情感就经历了一个成长过程，而这正折射了奥斯汀在情感文化建设方面的思考。在学界，我们常常听到有人简单地把玛丽安说成小说题目中 sensibility 的化身，进而认为她之所以遭受情感挫折，是因为情感过多。例如，孙致礼先生就说"玛丽安是吃了'感情有余、理智不足'的亏"（孙致礼 2017：2）。依笔者之见，故事的寓意远非那样简单。玛丽安之受挫于初，并非因为她情感太丰富，而是因为她不太懂感情，不善于感受或甄别他人的情感。更具体地说，她起先根本就不具备察觉/甄别布兰登上校和威洛比各自真实情感的悟性——布兰登真心爱她，她却感受不到这份感情的力量；而威洛比只是逢场作戏，她却真心相许。有一次，玛丽安在巴顿庄园为众人演唱，其他人都假装"听得欣喜若狂"，而"上校只是怀有敬意地听着"，此时玛丽安虽然看穿了其他人的虚情假意，但是并未察觉布兰登上校的"敬意"背后有着真情；她"非常通情达理地认为，一个三十五岁的男人可能早已失去了敏锐的情感和高度的鉴赏力。她完全可以理解上校的老成持重"（奥斯汀 2017：31）。玛丽安未能感受布兰登蕴蓄着深情的"敬意"，皆因她本人的情感未经淬砺，以致流于浅薄。正因为如此，她跟威洛比反而几乎一见如故：

> 她问起他的读书情况，搬出了她最喜爱的几位作家，而且谈得眉飞色舞……他们有着惊人相似的兴趣。两人崇拜相同的书籍、相同的段落，一旦出现差别和异议，只要经她一争辩，眼睛一闪亮，就都烟消云散。凡是她所决定的，他都默认；凡是她所热衷的，他都喜爱。早在访问结束之前，他们就像故友重逢般亲切交谈着。①（奥斯汀 2017：40—41）

熟悉奥斯汀文风②的读者都能看出上引文字的反讽意味：威洛比明明是在投其所好，玛丽安却一厢情愿地以为情投意合。在这一阶段，玛丽安和威洛比都完全地按自由意志行事：玛丽安一味地想入非非，以为自己找到了知音，而不顾姐姐埃丽诺的警告，更不考虑自己可能给布兰登带来的痛苦，而威洛比则根本就是逢场作戏，寻欢取乐；他俩的行为在不同程度上都意味着对家庭/社会秩序的破坏。不过，玛丽安最终学会了反思，并选择了布兰登，这表明她的情感发生了升华，终于具备了鉴赏力；随着这一故事结局的出现，一种家庭和睦、社会祥和的秩序感也从而凸显。换言之，玛丽安的故事含有如下寓意：不经过情感的淬砺，没有人能具备上述鉴赏力，即情理交融的文化素质，而这种文化素质正是一个共同体所深为倚赖的。

在狄更斯的《艰难时世》（*Hard Times*，1854）中，也有一个威洛比式的人物，即哈特豪斯。后者跟前者一样，是个只顾个人自由、不顾他人感受的人，或者说是个置权利、欲望于责任之上的人。对这样的人来说，自由的确与秩序格格不入，因而也就毫无幸福伦理可言。那么，问题也就来了：人总是有欲望/

---

① 笔者根据原文，对译文的个别文字作了更动。
② 奥斯汀惯用"戏剧反讽"（dramatic irony），即现实是一回事，而故事人物对现实的理解又是一回事，两者往往大相径庭，甚至截然相反。

意愿的，而意愿/自由难免跟责任/秩序发生矛盾，这难道就意味着两者必然形同水火、不能相容吗？狄更斯自有其思考，或者说找到了答案——他刻画了两位与哈特豪斯形成鲜明对照的人物，即具有高度社会责任心的西丝和蕾切尔。用意大利学者温赖特（Valerie Wainwright）博士的话说，"哈特豪斯的恶意皆由冲动所致，纯属心血来潮，因而于秩序有百害而无一利，而由西丝和蕾切尔作为化身的善意则既有自由，又有约束"（Wainwright 2007：119）。温赖特此处把人性的意愿分成了两类，一类是"恶意"（wanton will），另一类是"善意"（good will）。言下之意，只要有善意，自由与秩序即便发生矛盾，也是可以化解的，或者说人的自由是能够与秩序保持平衡。温赖特的这一见解受益于美国普林斯顿大学哲学教授法兰克福（Harry Frankfurt）的启发。后者把有理性的人分成了两类，一类是"有理性的恣意妄为者"（the rational wanton），另一类是普通"理性施动者"（rational agents），他认为："有理性的恣意妄为者不同于其他理性施动者，前者只顾自己的意愿，而不关心其是否可取。他根本就无视这样一个问题：他的意愿会变成什么？"（Frankfurt 1988：16—17）在《艰难时世》中，哈特豪斯从不问问自己的意愿是否可取，但是西丝和蕾切尔则相反——她们虽然也有强烈的个人意愿，但是在与他人利益或社会秩序发生矛盾时，她们总能妥善地予以化解。限于篇幅，我们仅以西丝为例：西丝被父亲送到葛擂硬的学校去念书，但是她发现那座学校简直就像监狱，因而产生了"想要逃离的强烈冲动"（Dickens 1969：95）；然而，这种追求自由的愿望却受制于一种更强烈的愿望，即想要让父亲安心——父亲含辛茹苦地把她养大，一心指望她能上学成才，而中途辍学必然会使父亲伤心。换言之，西丝对父亲的爱（包括她对父亲的责任感）是一种更强烈的意愿，促使她战胜了一己私欲。必须指出，不无悖论的是，西丝限制自己自由的意愿其实是自由的，或者说是一种更大的自由。用小说叙述者的原话说，"这种限制是自我强加的"（Dickens 1969：95），因而是一种自由选择，反倒使她获得了幸福，而且是伦理意义上的幸福。

简而言之，西丝的故事生动地演绎了一种幸福伦理观，即一个人能够通过限制自身的自由、付出爱心来履行责任，从中获得幸福感，进而在更高的境界上实现自由与秩序的平衡。这种幸福伦理观也体现于乔治·艾略特的作品，尤其体现于她所著《米德尔马契》（*Middlemarch*，1871—1872）中多萝西娅和利德盖特在履行责任方面所表现出来的不同特点。从表面上看，萝西娅和利德盖特都不会逃避责任，但是他俩在履行责任时的心态却有不同。就利德盖特而言，一个典型的事例发生在他救助银行家布尔斯特罗德之时：在一次市政会议上，布尔斯特罗德贪赃枉法的丑行败露，身心崩溃的他站立不稳，此时作为医生的利德盖特立即起身去搀扶他，"但是他的这一举动此刻竟夹杂着难言的苦涩……可怜的利德盖特只是出于道德心，无奈地护送布尔斯特罗德先生回到了银行……"（Eliot 1981：783—784）此处值得留意的是"无奈地"一词，它表明利德盖特虽然在表面上履行了职责，却没有幸福感。这就又把我们带回到了前文所提的问题：履行个人对社会/他人的责任，是否就必然意味着个人自由和幸福的丧失呢？利德盖特和布尔斯特罗德的故事似乎给出了肯定的回答。然而，《米德尔马契》中还有一起与此相对照的事例，即多萝西娅帮助罗莎蒙德（利德盖特之妻）的事例。当罗莎蒙德与利德盖特的婚姻出现了裂缝之际，多萝西娅决定帮助他们和解，但是就在这过程中却发现罗莎蒙德跟威尔（多萝西娅的恋人）有一些暧昧的举动，这使她陷入了痛苦，不过她最终仍然鼓起勇气，满怀热情地去找罗莎蒙德谈心，澄清了后者与利德盖特之间的误会，而自己也从中获取了幸福感。书中关于她鼓足勇气之前的描写一连用了两个"迫使自己"（forcing herself）这一词组来形容："她现在又把昨天上午的事情从头至尾地回顾了一遍，**迫使自己**审视当时的每一个细节，思考这些细节可能意味着什么。难道那一幕只涉及她一个人？只是她一个人的际遇吗？她**迫使自己**把整个事件跟另一个女人的生活结合起来考虑……"①（Eliot 1981：845）这两个"迫使自己"表明，多萝西娅是主动而积极的（英语原文用的是主动语态），而上文中的利德盖特则是消极被动的（英语原文 was forced to 用的是被动语态）。从这一对比中，艾略特的幸福伦理观再清晰不过：一个人在履行责任时是否有幸福感，关键在于他/她是否出于积极主动。

以上分析表明，幸福伦理的前提是情感文化，即以懂感情、有善意、尊重人、有爱心为内涵的 sensibility。这既是一种深切的感受力，又是一种无私的想象力，或者说是一种设身处地为他人着想的情愫，而这正是任何共同体的立足

---

① 此处的黑体为笔者所加。译文参考了项星耀的译本（人民文学出版社 1987 年版）。

之本。从这一意义上说，弘扬情感文化，就是从事共同体想象。在艾略特和狄更斯之后，书写情感文化——亦即共同体形塑——的传统从未消失，一直延续至今。例如，在乔治·吉辛的《文苑外史》（*New Grub Street*, 1891）中，情趣高雅的毕芬因生活所迫而选择自杀，但是他即便在万念俱灰之际，也仍然想到了别人——为了不连累房东，他选择了人烟稀少的森林作为自杀场所（Gissing 2016：436—437）。又如，在普里斯特利的《好伙伴》（*The Good Companions*, 1929）中，特兰忒小姐依靠爱心、友情和事业心来管理歌舞剧团；她赔上了所有的积蓄，换来了剧团成员们同甘苦、共患难的生机，因此获得了莫大的幸福感。再如，阿克罗伊德在《英国音乐》（*English Music*, 1992）中描写了哈库姆先生、玛格丽特和伯登等小人物，他们常常互相帮助，并且只要"发现大家都在一起"，就能"突然找到通向幸福的秘诀"（Ackroyd 1993：56）。无论是哈库姆等人的"幸福秘诀"，还是特兰忒小姐寻找幸福感的方式，或是毕芬选择自杀场所的举止，都显示着伦理维度，而其中又都融入了前文所说的想象力，即设身处地为他人着想的悟性。可以说，如今英国文学家们比以往更强调想象力的重要性。布克奖得主斯威夫特就认为小说创作"全是关于想象，即设身处地想象他人……我们至少要努力想象其他人的生活是怎样的；假如不这么做，我们就会失败，不光做人失败，而且导致社会的失败"（Swift 1997：155）。另一位布克奖得主麦克尤恩也说，他写小说的目的就是"展示设身处地想象他人的可能性……人之所以会残酷，就是因为缺乏想象力"（Atonement 3）。这种想象力显然是 sensibility（情感文化）的前提。

还须强调的是，情感文化层面的想象力往往表现为得体的言行举止。当代英国小说家拜厄特就曾把"得体"（decorum）提到构筑"人类共同体"（the human community）的高度，这在她关于自己父亲临终前情形的一段描述中说得很明白（她父亲死于一家荷兰临终医院，那里的医生和护士都言行得体，举止文雅）："我想我看到的是一个很复杂的人类共同体意象。这个共同体的维系体现于得体的言行、良好的举止；当人们相互传递精心烹调的食物时，或是周到而体贴地相互交谈时，或是恪守某些规矩时，共同体就得以维系了。……我指的是修养，是良好的举止，这些极其重要"（Byatt 2003：5—6）。拜厄特关于"得体"的见解，不仅融入她自己的作品中，而且代表着英国文学/文化中一个较为悠久的思想传统。鉴于笔者已在《英国文学中的会话与共同体形塑》①一文中曾经对此有所论述,此处不再赘述。本文所要强调的是,我们在讨论作为幸福伦理前提的情感文化时,"得体"不失为一条贯穿其中的重要线索。

四、结语

要探究英国文学中的共同体书写,可以从幸福伦理这一角度入手。两百多年以来,英国文学史上不乏有关幸福伦理的诗性叙事,后者有一个共同的旨归,即共同体形塑。进一步说,能否理解英国文学中幸福伦理与共同体之间的关系,关键在于能否捕捉以情感文化为基石的责任感。哲学家们或许有更宏大的"幸福话语"和"共同体话语",但是文学中的相关叙事和画面不容忽视,甚至会更生动,更富有诗意,更具有感染力。

参考文献

[1] Ackroyd P. *English Music* [M]. London: Penguin Books, 1993.

[2] Arnold M. *Culture and Anarchy: An Essay in Political and Social Criticism* [M]. Beijing: People's Press, 2014.

[3] Austen J. *Sense and Sensibility* [M]. Beijing: People's Press, 2014.

[4] Bentham J. "An Introduction to the Principles of Morals and Legislation." [A] // *Utilitarianism and On Liberty Including Mill's "Essays on Bentham" and Selections from the Writings of Jeremy Bentham and John Austin*. Ed. Mary Warnock [M]. Oxford: Blackwell Publishing, 2003: 17-20.

[5] Burke E. *Reflections on the Revolution in France* [M]. London: Penguin Books, 2004.

[6] Byatt A S. Editor's notes Interviewed by Jean-Louis Chevalier [J]. *Journal of the Short Story in English*, 2003, (41) Autumn: 1-10.

[7] Childers, J. & Hentzi G. *Columbia Dictionary of Modern Literary and Cultural*

---

① 参见《英美文学论丛》第 24 辑(2016 年春)第 40—55 页。

Criticism [M]. New York: Columbia UP, 1995.

[8] Dickens C. *Hard Times* [M]. Harmondsworth: Penguin, 1969.

[9] Eliot G. *Middlemarch* [M]. Harmondsworth: Penguin, 1981.

[10] Frankfurt H. *The Importance of What We Care About* [M]. New York: Cambridge UP, 1988.

[11] Gissing G. *New Grub Street* [M]. Oxford: Oxford UP, 2016.

[12] Himmelfarb G. *The Moral Imagination* [M]. Chicago: Ivan R. Dee, 2006.

[13] Holmes S. TWELVE. The permanent structure of antiliberal thought [J]. Semantic Scholar DOI: 10.4159/HARVARD.9780674864443.c16. 1989.

[14] Kahan A S. "Introduction." *On Liberty by John Stuart Mill with Related Documents*. Ed. Alan S. Kahan [M]. Boston: Bedford/St. Martin's, 2008.

[15] MacIntyre A. *After Virtue: A Study in Moral Theory* [M]. London: Duckworth, 1981.

[16] MacIntyre A. *A Short History of Ethics: A History of Moral Philosophy from the Homeric Age to the Twentieth Century* (2nd edition) [M]. Notre Dame: Notre Dame UP, 1966.

[17] Marx K. *The German Ideology, in Early Political Writings*. Ed. Josepn O'Malley [M]. Cambridge: Cambridge UP, 1996.

[18] McEwan I. Review: Interview: At Home with His Worries — Interview with Kate Kellaway [J]. *Observer*, 2001, 16 (9): 3.

[19] McGann J. *The Poetics of Sensibility: A Revolution in Literary Style* [M]. Oxford: Clarendon Press, 1996.

[20] Miller J H. *Communities in Fiction* [M]. New York: Fordham UP, 2015.

[21] Mill J S. *Autobiography* [M]. London: Penguin Books, 1989.

[22] Morgan O K. *The Oxford History of Britain* [M]. Oxford: Oxford UP, 2001.

[23] Nie Zhenzhao. *Introduction to Ethical Literary Criticism* [M]. Beijing: Beijing UP, 2014.

[24] Norton B M. *Fiction and the Philosophy of Happiness: Ethical Inquiries in the Age of Enlightenment* [M]. Lewisburg: Bucknell UP, 2012.

[25] Sun Zhili. "Introduction," in Jane Austen, *Sense and Sensibility*. Trans. Sun Zhili. [M] Beijing: The Publishing House of People's Literature, 2017.

[26] Swift G. Graham Swift in Interview on Last Orders — Interview with Bettina Grossmann, Roman Haak, Melanie Romberg and Saskia Spindler [J]. *Anglistik*, 1997, 8 (2): 155–160.

[27] Wainwright V. *Ethics and the English Novel from Austen to Forster* [M]. Aldershot: Ashgate Publishing Limited, 2007.

[28] Williams R. *Key Words* [M]. London: Fontana Press, 1976.

[29] 阿诺德. 文化与无政府状态: 政治与社会批评 [M]. 韩敏中, 译. 北京: 三联书店, 2002.

[30] 奥斯汀. 理智与情感 [M]. 孙致礼, 译. 北京: 人民出版社, 2017.

[31] 聂珍钊. 文学伦理学批评导论 [M]. 北京: 北京大学出版社, 2014.

[32] 孙致礼. 译序 [A] // 载奥斯汀. 理智与情感 [M]. 北京: 人民文学出版社, 2017.

(本文原载于 Interdisciplinary Studies of Literature, Vol. 3, No. 2, 2019)

英国文学中的音乐与共同体形塑*

十年前，英国威尔克斯大学教师菲莉丝·韦利弗（Phyllis Weliver）发表《英国小说中的音乐群体，1840—1910：阶级、文化与民族》一书，审视英国小说中有关音乐事件/场景的描写，并使之与想象共同体的方法相联系。此前已有学者关注英国文学与音乐的相关性，也有学者关注英国文学中的共同体形塑问题，但是把两者结合起来研究的当首推菲莉丝。她不仅率先用小说的镜头来聚焦音乐和共同体想象之间的关系，而且在研究方法上独辟蹊径，尝试从（音乐会等）观众的角度来探讨音乐在形塑共同体方面的作用。鉴于菲莉丝的研究仅限于1840年至1910年的时段，并且仅限于小说体裁，本文拟从更宽广的角度来论证如下观点：通过音乐来想象共同体，是英国文学中古往今来的普遍现象。

一、音乐与公共领域

菲莉丝著作中的一个关键词是音乐厅（the concert hall），因为它"作为公共领域的一部分而颇具价值"（Weliver 2006：45）。这一观点的灵感来自哈贝马斯。后者把公共领域界定为现代性状况下的新型话语空间，这已经是学术界的一个常识。美国耶鲁大学的本哈比卜在哈贝马斯的基础上对公共领域或"公共

---

* 本文系国家社会科学研究基金重大项目"文化观念流变中的英国文学典籍研究"【项目批号：12&ZD172】的阶段性成果。

空间"(the public space)作了进一步的界定:"(公共空间)不是任何地形或机构意义上的空间;即便在市政厅或城市广场,如果人们没有'同心协力',那么它们也称不上公共空间。反之……一片田野或森林也能成为公共空间,只要它们是人们'同心协力'的对象或场所。例如,人们可能在上述地方集会,抗议在那里建公路或军事基地,这时就形成了公共空间"(Benhabib 1992:93)。此处的"同心协力",其原文是"act in concert",而"concert"还有音乐会的意思。菲莉丝由此看到了学界的一个盲点,即只关注19世纪文学中有关政治/城市集会的描写如何影响哈贝马斯关于公共领域的思考,而忽视了作品中的音乐话语/意象如何助推了哈氏相关概念和思想的形成。鉴于此,菲莉丝仔细研读了上自勃朗特下至福斯特等人的作品,并指出它们都"介入了一场辩论",其中心议题恰好是以下两个:"公共领域是什么?应该怎样对它做出反应?"(Weliver 2006:55)在菲莉丝所做的工作中,最有意思的是她围绕公共领域——共同体的核心领域——的建构方法所展开的论述,而这又要从她所引入的"全景敞视型监狱"(the Panopticon)这一概念说起。

菲莉丝认为,19世纪50年代以降的许多英国小说都可以看作对边沁及其功利主义思想的回应。众所周知,边沁对于社会——其内涵包括我们如今所说的公共领域——的管理提出过一套重理性、重监视、重惩戒的办法。福柯在探讨现代性特征时就一直追溯到边沁,并在《规训与惩罚》一书中这样评论边沁所谓的"全景敞视型监狱"及其背后的管理思想:"对于边沁来说,这种具备一座有权力的和洞察一切的高塔的著名的透明环形铁笼,或许是一个完美的规训机构的设计方案。……全景敞视结构提供了这种普遍化的模式。它编制了一个被规训机制彻底渗透的社会在一种易于转换的基础机制层次上的基本运作程序"(福柯 2003:234—235)。福柯虽然洞察了"全景敞视型监狱"对现代社会的影响,却忽视了与边沁同时代的文人们对其提出的质疑。换言之,早在福柯之前,英国文人们就批判了"全景敞视型监狱"所隐含的管理范式。菲莉丝指出了这一点,因此她所做的工作可以看作对学术史的一种修正。有意思的是,她所援引的第一个例子并非小说家,而是随笔作家黑兹利特。后者在《时代精神》里直接批评边沁的"全景敞视型监狱"这一概念,并接着发问:"当一个人皈依伟大的功利原则之后,他在边沁的眼皮底下时会被迫工作,但是一旦离开了边沁的视线，他还会照样工作吗？"（Hazlitt 1825：20） 如菲莉丝所说，"黑兹利特反对全景敞视型监狱，其最终目的是想说明社会的凝聚力并非来自'惩罚与规训'，而是来自'同情心'"（Weliver 2006：33）。黑兹利特与边沁之争实际上围绕着一个焦点问题，即公共领域的建构——或公共凝聚力的形成——最应依靠的是监视、规训和惩罚等刚性力量呢，还是信念、情操、爱心和想象力等柔性力量？

除了黑兹利特，菲莉丝还提到了穆勒。后者早期追随边沁，可是后期与之渐行渐远，其主要原因是边沁的幸福观里缺少了下文所说的"情感文化"。穆勒以华兹华斯的诗歌为例，"华兹华斯的诗歌……似乎正是我所追求的情感文化，从中似乎能汲取源源不断的内心欢乐，一种人和万物一体同仁的愉悦。这种愉悦可以由全人类共享；它跟争斗或瑕疵毫不相干，却可以因人类的物质和社会状况的每一点改善而变得更为丰富。即便在生活中所有较大的邪恶都被祛除之后，我似乎仍然可以从这些诗歌中找到幸福的永久源泉"（Mill 1989：121）。我们知道，边沁也追求人类共同体的福祉，但是他的幸福观只关注客观世界的改造，而穆勒的幸福观则兼顾了人类主观世界的改造，因而后者要丰富得多，深刻得多。正因为如此，才有了"情感文化"一说，也就是上文所说的柔性力量——穆勒把"情感"（feelings）跟"文化"（culture）搭配，也就是把情感提到了文化的高度，可谓用心良苦。穆勒是在《自传》（*Autobiography*，1873）里表述"情感文化"的。菲莉丝注意到了这部书，但是她未留意"情感文化"，更未留意穆勒对音乐的强调，如下面的这段话："……音乐的最佳效果在于激发热情（就这一点而言，它也许胜过其他任何艺术），在于唤醒人类品格中潜在的那些高尚情感，并提升其强度。这种兴奋状态赋予升华了的情感一种光和热，后者最强烈的状态虽然短暂，却能持续维持这种升华的情感，因而弥足珍贵"（Mill 1989：119）。从这字里行间，我们不难感受到穆勒主张用音乐营造公共文化、建构公共领域（虽然他未用"公共领域"这一术语）的热情。还须一提的是，《自传》就像黑兹利特的随笔一样，虽然属于文学范畴，但是已经超出了菲莉丝的研究范畴。换言之，对边沁做出回应的不仅有菲莉丝笔下的那些小说，而且有同时期的其他文学样式。

在菲莉丝所重点分析的小说中，要数勃朗特的《维莱特》和萧伯纳的《爱在艺术家中间》最能反映音乐和公共领域之间的关系。这两部作品中都有许多描述音乐厅及其所含活动的场景。菲莉丝对它们的分析，旨在说明"音乐厅是公共领域的宝贵部分"（Weliver 2006：45）。确实，勃朗特和萧伯纳都通过音乐场景表达了各自有关公共领域建构/管理的思想，而且都刻画了两类音乐群体/观众：一类只关注音乐场所的规矩、音乐演奏的技巧、音乐家及其作品的市场价值、音乐会期间的服饰/座次等显示的身份和地位，甚至只对如何监视别人的行为感兴趣；另一类也服从音乐会的礼仪和规矩，或者欣赏音乐演奏的技巧，但是更多地随着音乐去想象，去感受情感的升华。前者正好与边沁重理性、重监视的管理思想契合，而后者则与黑兹利特、穆勒等人重情操、美感、爱心和想象力的公共文化思想相匹配。例如，《维莱特》的女主人公露西在第一次参加音乐会时比较注重理性规范，然后在随后的几次中"更多地向情感生活的信条偏移"，而陪伴露西出席音乐会的"约翰医生和其他几位公共集会的成员则试图通过公共监视来调节行为"（Weliver 2006：42—46）。又如，《爱在艺术家中间》有两类音乐家和音乐迷：一类以作曲家杰克为代表，他们把音乐跟人类大同世界的梦想相联系；另一类以"音乐精英"菲普森为代表，后者"总是仔细地阅读配有分析的节目单"（Shaw 1900：270），或者说总是拘泥于音乐的规则。杰克对这后一类人嗤之以鼻，并曾这样讽刺他们所喜欢的一个名叫"安提恩特·俄耳甫斯"的乐队："他们文雅过度了。他们害怕展露自己的个性，好像他们自己就是那些常见的绅士"（Shaw 1900：181）。对此菲莉丝有过如下分析："他们的演奏风格表明，附庸风雅的行为是有问题的，但又是'常见'的——循规蹈矩地寻求同质效应，这种常见的现象不无讽刺意味。用文雅和平静的掌控当作衡量音乐的标准，这样的理解未免过于平庸，不免成为英国音乐前进道路上骇人的绊脚石；在这种对音乐的理解背后，显露的是一种由规训和理性构筑的公共领域，而不是有机生成的、充满激情的公共领域"（Weliver 2006：138）。这一分析可谓切中肯綮。

不过，比上述两部小说更值得重视的是狄更斯的《艰难时世》。不知为什么，菲莉丝没有把它作为重点分析的对象。这部小说有许多音乐意象。例如，西丝父亲所在的马戏团每次表演时总是要以音乐开场；它第一次在书中露面时就伴随着音乐：当时葛擂硬先生正走近马戏团，"音乐声侵入他的耳朵，原来是乐队的打击乐声……"（Dickens 1994：14）这里的"侵入"一词十分传神，它表明音乐跟葛擂硬格格不入。菲莉丝注意到了这一点，并且指出"'乐队的打击乐声'宣告了马戏团的存在，一种与功利主义相对立的生活方式的存在"（Weliver 2006：35），但是她未能进一步结合故事中隐含的监狱意象来探讨音乐意象。事实上，利维斯早在《伟大的传统》中就以"监狱"来比喻葛擂硬所代表的"管教体制"："马戏团获取意义的方式出色地阐明了狄更斯手法的诗意——戏剧化的特征。葛擂硬先生从功利主义的教室走回他功利主义的寓所——石屋。狄更斯笔下的石屋让我们深刻而具体地认识到了那个模范管教体制是一副何等样的面目：对于小葛擂硬们（包括马尔萨斯和亚当·史密斯）来说，它简直就是一座难以逃脱的监狱"（利维斯 2002：385）。此处的"监狱"就是边沁推崇的、黑兹利特/福柯所批判的"全景敞视型监狱"。它意味着一种强制性的管理方式，也意味着一种压抑美好情感的生活方式和思维方式。在这种思想氛围下营造出来的公共领域必然像一座监狱，而《艰难时世》中的音乐和马戏团可以看作与之相对峙的合成意象，其背后的价值取向在下面这段描述中得到了生动的体现："……即便把全团人的学问合在一起，也换不来任何一门学科的合格证书。然而，这些人温良敦厚，天真无邪，不屑于任何诡诈行为；他们互相怜悯，助人为乐，有求必应。他们在日常生活中表现出来的美德，足以与世界上任何一个阶层媲美；再多的尊敬，再大的褒奖，对于他们都不过分"（Dickens 1994：46）。这里，马戏团成员的行为方式跟前文所说的"同心协力"正好契合，因而构成了一个理想的公共领域；他们和睦相处，形成了一个理想的共同体。狄更斯的这些描写，显然可以为哈贝马斯有关公共领域的概念和思想提供养料。

　　本文所要强调的是，上述文学现象远远超出了菲莉丝的研究范围。例如，普里斯特利的代表作《好伙伴》就是一部以音乐主线贯穿全书的小说。不仅如此，它还堪称共同体想象的典范。英国曼彻斯特大学教授盖尔就曾赞扬该书，其理由是"深深镶嵌在小说中的共同体意识"（Gale 2008：126）。瑞士巴塞尔大学的哈伯曼教授也关注了《好伙伴》的共同体情结，并且把它跟音乐会挂上了钩："音乐厅表演会是普里斯特利笔下英格兰共同体生活的关键性象征"（Habermann 2010：50）。确实，《好伙伴》中的音乐厅表演会属于典型的音乐事件，也不失为想象共同体的诸多方式之一，但是若要使它真正成为共同体生活的象征，还须满足一个前提，即参与者和组织者都拥有共同的生活目标和价值取向。更具体地说，必须具备前文所述公共领域的一大要素，即"同心协力"。小说中的歌舞剧团（同时也是音乐团体）——取名为"好伙伴"——正好具备了这一要素。书中人物乔利芬特在讨论剧团名称时，最强调的就是"好伙伴的情谊"和"齐心合力"（Priestley 2000：277）。在"好伙伴歌舞剧团"成立之前，乔利芬特、特兰忒小姐、奥克劳侬特和苏茜等主要人物就像一个个孤岛，但是在剧团成立之后，他们逐渐形成了一个名副其实的共同体，不仅在内部形成了很强的凝聚力，而且通过音乐/舞蹈表演在社会上形成了公共影响力。这在他们一次义演所呈现的不凡吸引力中可见一斑："……本该待在医院里的人来了，本该待在监狱里的人也来了，本该去维多利亚街卫斯理教堂听音乐会的人也来了……各行各业的人都来了……"（Priestley 2000：550）这吸引力自然跟音乐/歌舞的感染力有关。下面就是关于那次义演的一段描述：

> 幕布要拉开了吗？不，他们先要放一段音乐；他们总是如此。音乐来了：拉姆啼—嘀—啼嘀—嘀，拉姆啼—嘀—啼嘀。观众中有人熟悉这曲调。它是一首名叫《轻快地旋转》的歌曲……从神奇的灯光照射下的幕布后面，传来轻柔妙曼的歌曲。此时，那旋律淘气得就像酵母，对台下黑乎乎的那片观众产生着潜移默化的作用。那旋律真美妙！是爱心和平常心的狂想曲！它传递着来自另一个世界的消息，那世界比我们的更光明——在我们这个世界里，大家只忙着分工资。在翩翩起舞的乐曲声中，加特福德剧院消失得一干二净；周围的街道、厂房和商店、成排的房屋、有轨电车和卡车、丑陋的小教堂和鬼鬼祟祟的酒吧全都消失了；它们起先颤抖了一阵，然后开始摇摆，接着是剧烈的晃动，最后消逝得无影无踪，全都旋转到某个硕大而难以想象的角落里去了。乐曲声更响了一些，好似凯旋。一切都消失了，只留下朗朗大地和星光闪耀的天空，还有那轻快的旋律和节奏……（Priestley 2000：550—551）

这段描述分明是对"比我们的更光明"的世界的想象，是对"朗朗大地"的想象，也就是对美好共同体的想象，而这想象的翅膀显然是音乐赋予的。整段叙述采取观众感受的视角,为的是传递出他们怎样因音乐的感染而产生强烈的情感共鸣,进而凸显了音乐在促进公众的对共同体认同感方面的作用。与此形成互动的是小说的情节:特兰忒小姐出任经理时,剧团已债台高筑,她赔上了所有的积蓄,帮助还清债务并发放工资,同时还要负担剧团的运行费用;在她的带领下,剧团成员们同甘苦,共患难;每当某个演员因疾病等意外情况而上不了舞台时,总有其他成员挺身而出,无偿地加班加点工作。换言之,特兰忒小姐管理剧团靠的是爱心、友情和事业心,而不是前文中"监狱"意象所隐含的强制手段。

类似的例子在当代也能找到。杰出的女作家拜厄特就喜欢通过音乐来想象共同体。仅以她的小说《孩子们的书》为例:书中频频出现音乐意象,甚至连战地的描写都有歌声相伴,如朱利安在野战医院"想到人们唱的那些歌,既残忍又欢乐"(拜厄特 2014:707)。最引人注目的是书中人物演出莎士比亚戏剧《仲夏夜之梦》的场景——从排练到演出,整段叙述长达10页,中间有许多插叙,大都跟共同体的想象/建设有关。又如,"爱德华·皮塞成立了新生活同人会,年轻的威尔伍德夫妇参加过这个组织的好几次集会。他们在那儿以及民主联盟里讨论失业劳工的组织、寄宿学童的伙食、厂矿和铁路的国有化乃至公共机构建立民居等问题"(拜厄特 2019:42)。此处"公社""公共机构""国有化""大学工人辅导班"和"新生活同人会"等显然是共同体意象,有关人物所从事的活动显然构成了公共领域;把它们穿插在《仲夏夜之梦》——该剧有许多音乐场景——的排练、准备和表演过程中,这显然是在暗示共同体/公共领域的建构需要音乐所唤起的那种美好情感和奉献精神。

上述例子还给了我们一个新的启示:凭借音乐想象共同体的思想雏形是否早就存在?至少在莎翁时代就已存在?《仲夏夜之梦》从表面上看,是一个浪漫神奇的爱情故事,其实却关乎国家/社会的治理这一重大问题。雅典少女赫米娅爱上了拉山德,不肯嫁给狄米特律斯,而这违抗了父命;雅典公爵忒修斯按照法律做出裁决,命令赫米娅在四天内服从父命,否则将受死或做修女。这是一种十分严酷的规训,即便赫米娅屈服了,其结果也不可能给任何人带来幸福。好在忒修斯后来回心转意(他被赫米娅和拉山德、海丽娜和狄米特律斯这两对有情人的忠贞所打动),不仅劝说伊吉斯(赫米娅之父)放弃"依法惩办"(莎士比亚 1984：347）的念头，而且提议三对新人（包括他自己和希波吕忒）共同举行婚礼。就在忒修斯改变主意之前，出现过接二连三的音乐画面：先是仙王奥布朗反复下令奏乐，然后是迫克声称"听见云雀歌吟"，接着是忒修斯要求希波吕忒"听一听猎犬的音乐"，并同他一起"领略猎犬们的吠叫和山谷中回声应和的妙乐"，而希波吕忒则回应说自己"从来不曾听见过那样谐美的喧声，那样悦耳的雷鸣"；其间忒修斯还表白自己"已把五月节的仪式遵循"（莎士比亚 1984：345—346）。此处特别值得一提的是，按英国旧俗于"五月节"（May Day）这一天早起，以露盥身，采花唱歌，因而它是一个融音乐与共同体意识于一体的象征。正是在"五月节"这一象征以及上述音乐意象所营造的氛围中，忒修斯选择了支持真诚的爱情，并对伊吉斯说了一句意味深长的话："你的意志只好屈服一下了"（莎士比亚 1984：348）。这里的"意志"其实与后来福柯所说的"规训与惩罚"不无相通之处，而剧中"谐美的"音乐则跟哈贝马斯所说的公共领域十分契合。

当然，无论是莎士比亚，还是后来的狄更斯，甚至是 20 世纪的普里斯特利，都不可能使用"公共领域"这样的术语。然而，他们描绘的有关图景及其展示的信念、情操、爱心和想象力，为后人想象音乐与共同体/公共领域之间的关系提供了启示。

二、音乐与民族认同感

作为表意形式的音乐，除了能参与公共领域的建构之外，还具有促进民族认同感的重要作用，这也是菲莉丝的主要观点之一。当然，在她之前，已有不少学者探讨过音乐在促进民族大团结方面的功能。菲莉丝的独特之处有二：1）通过小说的镜头来聚焦音乐和共同体/民族形塑之间的关系；2）强调一个民族想象共同体的方法有赖于其成员对音乐的反应能力。换言之，菲莉丝为小说文本的解读开辟了一个新视角，即着眼于相关人物如何对音乐做出反应，以此展示他们如何想象共同体，如何认同自己的民族。菲莉丝的贡献还在于揭示了如下情形：对于民族的想象，会因某个成员所在阶级的不同而不同，而这一点可以由其对音乐的不同反应而得到折射。

在菲莉丝分析的小说中，最能说明上述观点的是梅瑞狄斯的《桑德拉·贝诺利》。故事发生在19世纪40年代中期的英国，而女主人公埃米莉亚则来自意大利，其时后者正处于反抗奥匈帝国的民族解放运动之中。埃米莉亚歌喉出众，弹一手好琴（竖琴），而且还能自己作曲。书中最先表示欣赏她的是波尔家四姐弟（阿拉贝拉、科妮莉亚、阿黛拉和威尔弗里德，其父靠经商发家），以及百万富翁佩里科尔斯。他们对埃米莉亚示好，并非出于对音乐的确切理解，而是想做后者的赞助人，并借此捞取社会声誉。更复杂的是，威尔弗里德和佩里科尔斯还打着更多的小算盘——前者开始追求埃米莉亚，而后者完全是想占她的便宜。小说第二章围绕埃米莉亚在林中月下唱歌、弹奏的场景而展开（本是独自练习，却引来了波尔家姐弟和佩里科尔斯等人的围观），在唱其中的一首歌曲时埃米莉亚"热血沸腾，激情四射，甜美歌声的深处缭绕着悲伤，这分明是现代意大利的标志"（Meredith 1914：11）。埃米莉亚身在英国，心系意大利的民族解放运动，所以有"现代意大利的标志"一说，然而这音乐声中的政治元素根本未被察觉——威尔弗里德和三姐妹听完埃米莉亚表演以后的中心话题只是"她歌声中有没有伤感之情"（Meredith 1914：13）。与此形成鲜明对照的是书中劳动阶层对埃米莉亚演唱的反应。在第十一章中，有一个埃米莉亚（在用作酒吧的临时窝棚里）为穷苦大众演唱的场景，当时"所有的人都很虔敬……大家的表情看上去就像在听一首喜爱的国歌那样"（Meredith 1914：94—95）。埃米莉亚起先唱的是意大利歌曲，然后她意识到在座的都是英国人，所以主动要求听众挑一首大家喜欢的歌曲，接着就出现了如下场面："埃米莉亚开始演唱那首为人熟知的歌曲，序曲刚奏响，窝棚内就沸腾起来；观众们开始手舞足蹈，并用手指打起了拍子。他们的身体全都听命于她的旋律，随时准备扭动、伸展或弯曲。她完全捕捉住了他们的心"（Meredith 1914：96）。显然，此处的听众在乐曲声感召下形成了一股凝聚力。菲莉丝曾经把这一场景跟先前埃米莉亚在林中月下唱歌的情景加以比较，并指出"这两个不同的场景首先揭示了新兴资产阶级的无知，然后……表现出工人阶级自然具有的洞察力"（Weliver 2006：88）。事实上，菲莉丝花了很大的篇幅对此做了分析，其中较有说服力的是她对历史原因的考察——从1848年到1870年期间，英国工人阶级对意大利的独立运动给予了积极的支持（所以故事中劳动者从埃米莉亚那里听到的不仅是热烈的旋律，而且是政治热情），而英国的资产阶级和贵族阶级当时则与奥匈帝国的统治者沆瀣一气（波尔家有亲戚在奥地利的骑兵队伍里服役；威尔弗里德自己在印度当过英帝国骑兵队的掌旗官，其帝国情结与意大利民族解放运动格格不入，因此他对埃米莉亚歌声中的民族主义元素充耳不闻）(Weliver 2006: 85—129)。鉴于菲莉丝在这方面已经作了很详尽的探讨，本文不再赘述。

假如菲莉丝在上述分析中采用了已故剑桥大学教授热尔韦的观点，那么她本来可以更全面地把握《桑德拉·贝诺利》所展现的共同体形塑问题，可惜她未能在这方面深入地加以探讨。热尔韦曾经提出"多重英格兰"一说，并赞扬诗人爱德华·托马斯把目光投向了"漏洞与边角里的英格兰"，即"在官方地图上找不到的一个英格兰"(Gervais 1993: 2—28)。言下之意，在统治阶级把持的官方话语中，英国的下层阶级并不属于英格兰，或者说只存在于官方话语/统治阶级心目中的漏洞和边角里。虽然《桑德拉·贝诺利》属于热尔韦的研究范围，但是它跟托马斯的诗歌一样，也呈现了被遗忘在"漏洞与边角里的英格兰"——那些随着埃米莉亚的歌声手舞足蹈的穷苦百姓就生活在漏洞与边角里。书中有许多这方面的描写。例如，在埃米莉亚去酒吧窝棚演唱之前，波尔家三姐妹曾极力劝阻，双方因此展开了激烈的争辩。从这些指责中，我们可以看到波尔家姐妹是如何看待共同体的。她们心目中的"社会"根本就不能容忍所谓的"粗人"和"乡巴佬"，而埃米莉亚的歌声则强烈地反衬出这种"伪共同体想象"的荒谬之处。

放眼通观英国文学史，我们会发现通过音乐意象来唤醒民族认同感，这远远不止是菲莉丝笔下那些小说家的使命，而是古往今来英国文学中的一个亮点。这方面最典型的例子当推阿克罗伊德的小说《英国音乐》。它不仅以"音乐"命名，而且以音乐意象贯穿全书。小说主人公蒂莫西从小受父亲的熏陶，终身热爱音乐。在蒂莫西——其实是阿克罗伊德——的眼中，"音乐"和"文学""历史"和"绘画"是同义词。

英国利物浦约翰摩尔大学的史密斯曾经承认，阿克罗伊德作品的"中心主题是过去——尤其是英国的过去——与现在之间的牢固关系"(Smyth 2008: 172—173)，不过他在涉及《英国音乐》具体文本时却话中有话："'英国音乐'这题目……看上去指的是一种贯穿英国历史的精神；更具体地说，一种似乎有史以来一直持续的、特殊的文化想象"（Smyth 2008：173—174）。史密斯此处接连用了"看上去"和"似乎"两个词语，其用意无非是否定"贯穿英国历史的精神"的存在——在他看来，宣扬这种精神的话语隶属于本质主义，或者说是一种"本质话语"（discourse of essence），而"英国音乐"所隐含的"英格兰特性"（Englishness）其实是一种人为的建构，是一种可以被不断抹去而重新建构的东西，因而也就谈不上有任何本质。为这一观点他作了如下阐述：

> 蒂莫西·哈库姆在故事里所经历的一切都导向了他最后的顿悟，这在小说的末句里得到了概括："我听到了音乐。"这一陈述看似简单，却涵盖了一系列复杂的历史、政治进程。它跟弥漫于全书的本质话语是格格不入的……换言之，作者召唤音乐固然有其目的，然而音乐此处并不为他的目的服务："英国音乐"的"英国特性"永远是一种正在被抹去的能指。（Smyth 2008：176）

言下之意，阿克罗伊德所提倡的"英国音乐"只是一种无根的能指，它没有任何坚实的所指与之匹配。若要评判史密斯是否说得在理，我们必须细察小说结尾的那一句，即"我听到了音乐。"史密斯单独把这一句拎出来，不顾它的上文，强行使用时髦的解构理论，便得出了上面那段引语中的结论。事实上，在"听到了音乐"之前，蒂莫西刚经历了史密斯所忽视的一桩轶事：年事已高的蒂莫西帮助朋友爱德华的小孙女塞西莉亚埋葬了一只死去的小鸟，然后就有了全书的结尾段落（第二人称"您"指读者）：

> 于是我们蹲了下来，我为这只死鸟的灵魂作了祷告。我不知道我为何要在结尾时给您讲那么简单的一个故事，不过那也许是我如今所做的最好的事情——简单的事情，就像葬鸟。我们祷告以后，另一只鸟从我们前面的一棵树上飞了下来，栖息在我家花园的门上。没过多久，它也吟唱起来，歌声在整条小径上回荡。所以您明白了吧，就像我先前解释的那样，我已经不再需要从旧书中去寻找音乐。我听到了音乐。（Ackroyd 1993：400）

这是一个极具象征意味的结尾。葬鸟的小姑娘跟蒂莫西的母亲（她在蒂莫西出生那天因难产死去，生前擅长弹奏曼陀林）同名，而她俩又跟音乐主保圣人圣塞西莉亚（Saint Cecilia, ? —230?）同名。从古代的圣塞西莉亚到蒂莫西的母亲，再从后者到小姑娘塞西莉亚，古人虽已死亡，但是象征音乐精神的名字却代代相传，就如会唱歌的小鸟一样，先前的死了，却总有后来者接替。小说的所有章节都跟这一段形成了呼应，其中最直接的要数第九章——音乐教师阿米蒂奇询问了蒂莫西（他在外祖父的家乡上学）母亲的名字，并告诉他这一名字跟圣塞西莉亚的关系，还在课堂上发表了一通议论："我们可以把英国音乐的开端追溯到16世纪，从此它一直实实在在地持续着……这音乐还活着。你们听过埃尔加和沃恩·威廉斯①的音乐吗？……这音乐是不朽的。古老的音乐仍然是我们的一部分。它永远是我们的一部分。几百年来，同样的旋律总是在重复着，传给了一代又一代"（Ackroyd 19993: 196）。书中与此明显相似的表述还有许多。例如，第六章中斯莫尔伍德（一个长得很像福尔摩斯的侦探）对蒂莫西这样说："英国音乐很少变化。乐器会更换，形式会变更，但是精神似乎永远不变。精神永存。我想，我们所说的和谐就是这个意思"（Ackroyd 1993: 128）。又如，在第十二章里，贺加斯（他把绘画与音乐相提并论）在蒂莫西的梦境中强调"音乐有其线条美"，强调自己的工作是"描绘我们英格兰民族的风俗习惯，使之保留到未来"，并这样抒发自己的理想："我们的英国音乐必须持续，直到我们到达最后一个音符"（Ackroyd 1993: 268）。这里，通过音乐/绘画来促进民族认同的热情跃然纸上。

也就是说，阿克罗伊德所说的"英国音乐"并非没有坚实的所指与之匹配——这所指就是关于民族共同体的想象。这想象虽然不可触摸，而且形式多变，可是其精神却异常坚固。阿克罗伊德的这一思想跟安德森的共同体理论十分契合。后者在其《想象的共同体》一书中强调了想象在共同体形塑方面的作用；他认为虽然一个民族的绝大多数成员无法彼此相识，甚至彼此之间的关系并不平等，但是他们可以通过想象来分享"一种深度的、平行的同志情谊"（Anderson 1991: 7）。跟安德森一样，阿克罗伊德也有着对"深度共同体"（the

---

① 埃尔加（Edward Elgar, 1857—1934）和威廉斯（Ralph Vaughan Williams, 1872—1958）都是英国作曲家。

deep community)① 的诉求，而且将其与民族想象紧紧地联系在一起。阿克罗伊德曾经发表《阿尔比恩：英格兰想象的起源》一书，其中第 53 章的标题为"英国音乐"，其实就是以音乐来形容民族想象。"阿尔比恩"（Albion）是古代不列颠或英格兰的指称，阿克罗伊德用它来冠名全书，自然是指"英格兰想象"源远流长。该书开篇之处就把这想象比作"河流"，紧接着又把它比作"风竖琴"（Ackroyd 2002：xix），然后又在第 53 章与之呼应——在列举多位音乐家（包括前文所提的伯德和沃恩·威廉斯）之后，出现了下面这段文字：

> （沃恩·威廉斯的音乐）既拥抱现在，又拥抱往昔；在这乐曲声中，对英国古代文化的兴趣变成了一种魔力，催生出一种亘古永恒的品质。艾略特从英国山水中感悟到的就是这样一种品质，他在诗歌《四重奏》中令人难忘地展现了这一品质："就在此刻，就在英格兰"。那感觉就像比德②在《英格兰人教会史》中描绘的那只小鸟，穿越了盎格鲁-撒克逊宴会厅，吸到了户外的空气，变成了在沃恩·威廉斯的乐队背景中腾飞的百灵鸟。它就是雪莱诗中的云雀，"啼声婉转如清澈的溪流"。这同一只鸟还出现在乔治·梅瑞狄斯的诗行中，沃恩·威廉斯借用过这些诗行："飞腾而起，继而盘旋，/她的歌声宛如银链，/环环相扣，一环又一环。"这牢不可破的银链就是英国音乐之链。（Ackroyd 2002：440）

类似的描述也见于《英国音乐》。该书第 16 章第一句就把"阿尔比恩"跟"英国音乐"联系在了一起："苏醒吧，阿尔比恩，倾听英国音乐那永无休止的曲调……"（Ackroyd 1993：349）这一章取名为"阿尔比恩之歌"，并模仿布莱克的笔法（第 15 章以蒂莫西倾听父亲朗诵布莱克诗歌的情景结尾，诗中有"苏醒吧，阿尔比恩，苏醒！"这一句），全用歌谣体写成。在这一章中，"阿尔比恩"一词的出现频率高达二十二次，且多与英国史上的伟大文学家相连，如涉及乔叟的这些诗行："……神圣的气息进入阿尔比恩，/时光轮回，英格兰苏醒复

---

① 威廉斯（Raymond Williams）语，详见他的 *The Long Revolution*（Harmondsworth：Penguin Books，1961）65。
② 比德（Saint Bede，627—735），盎格鲁—撒克逊神学家、历史学家。

生,/这复苏的生命在乔叟的诗中永存"(Ackroyd 1993:350)。又如涉及莎士比亚的这几句:"莎士比亚俯察人世,融入了人世。/他融入了自己的文字:他脱胎换骨,/一如节奏和音节再造了他的激情……锻造了铿锵文字,供阿尔比恩居住……所有的忧伤痛苦,所有的友情亲缘,/在这里刻入了英国音乐的作品。/莎士比亚从露珠般的卧榻起身,阿尔比恩则留在身后,/永远被他的诗文环绕"(Ackroyd 1993:352)。此处需要留心的是"在这里刻入了英国音乐的作品"一句:"在这里"显然指的是莎士比亚的诗句,而后者又被等同于"英国音乐",从中我们可以瞥见文学、音乐和民族/共同体想象之间的关系。

还须一提的是,"阿尔比恩之歌"中几乎每位诗人都负有承前启后的"音乐"使命。例如,布莱克不但"听到了把代代相连的音乐",而且"为后来者铺平了道路:/不,不是为克雷布①……而是为柯勒律治和华兹华斯"(Ackroyd 1993:356)。不久,我们看见"拜伦随后崛起",然后"雪莱继承了那音乐",紧接着我们又看到济慈在吟唱:"美即真,真即美,/想象不是心态,而是人类存在的形态。/大自然没有轮廓,唯有想象本身,/因为语言即永恒,它源自阿尔比恩的嘴唇"(Ackroyd 1993:357—358)。当然,除了"美即真,真即美"那一句是出自济慈之外,此处的诗行是阿克罗伊德杜撰的。不过,他借此点明了想象——尤其是代代相传的想象——在民族/共同体形塑中的重要作用,而"音乐"则是想象的代名词。

除了过去、现在乃至未来的彼此沟通之外,民族认同感的形成还有赖于许多其他复杂的因素。例如,不同的阶级和种族在想象共同体方面或多或少会有不同。正是在这方面,阿克罗伊德不免会受到攻讦。美国罗德岛大学英语系主任特里姆就曾批评《英国音乐》反映的民族文化遗产观"在政治上排斥少数族裔",或者说"掩盖了移民的存在"(Trimm 2011:251—257)。确实,阿克罗伊德未能在他的"音乐"中思考由少数族裔——尤其是当代大量移民的涌入而带来的问题。然而,我们不应该仅凭这一缺憾就否定《英国音乐》在民族想象方面的积极意义。阿克罗伊德至少表达了通过文化遗产来促进民族认同感的强烈愿望,而且表达得十分生动。此外,他还跟爱德华·托马斯和梅瑞狄斯一样,

---

① 克雷布(George Crabbe, 1754—1832)。

把目光投向了"漏洞与边角里的英格兰"——《英国音乐》中真正爱好音乐的全都是些小人物。哈库姆先生（蒂莫西的父亲）一生贫困，那些常常聚在他周围的人也全是些穷苦的老百姓，如靠做清洁工为生的小矮人玛格丽特和餐馆侍者伯登。他们并没有出众的音乐天赋和造诣。玛格丽特"唱歌时声音很高，但是嗓子有些破"（Ackroyd 1993：56），就连哈库姆先生也"在音乐表演方面并不专业"（Ackroyd 1993：3）。然而，他们都很善良，常常互相帮助，并且只要他们"发现大家都在一起"，就能"突然找到通向幸福的秘诀"（Ackroyd 1993：56）。书中有很多类似的描写，从中不难瞥见共同体情怀。

还须强调的是，阿克罗伊德的音乐情结远非当代英国文坛上的孤立现象，而且他的缺陷因其他一些作家——如拉什迪和石黑一雄等移民作家——的贡献而得到了弥补。这些作家常常把目光投向移民或侨民，后者的生活大都漂泊不定，但是他们也有共同体诉求；他们的共同家园之路，跟阿克罗伊德笔下的情形相比，往往要艰难得多，不过他们也总能从"音乐"中找到一丝希望。限于篇幅，本文仅以拉什迪的《她脚下的土地》为例。这部小说的男女主人公奥默斯和维娜都是摇滚乐手，他们居无定所，浪迹孟买、伦敦和纽约等地，可是他们从未放弃对共同文化遗产的追求，这在奥默斯的一次表白中可见一斑："……不管我们在哪里，不管我们的母语是什么，不管我们最先学会的是哪一种舞蹈，那种流动在我们血液里的占有并激励我们的音乐说着全人类的秘密语言，它就是我们的共同遗产"（Rushdie 1999：89）。这里，我们可以看见对阿克罗伊德的民族共同体思想的一种补充：在一个健康的社会里，民族认同感应该包括对"全人类""共同遗产"的诉求。

综上所述，通过音乐来想象共同体，这是英国文学史上的一大特色。我们可以在菲莉丝所做工作的基础上，把视角从1840年至1910年的英国小说扩大到整个英国文学史。在本文涉及的文学作品中，无论是音乐事件，还是音乐场景，抑或是音乐意象，都强烈地呼唤着民族认同感，都为公共领域的构建、公共文化的建设提供了启示。在这些音乐事件/场景/意象的背后，是各种社会/政治话语的交集和互动，是世代文学家为重塑共同体的不断努力——它们汇成了此起彼伏的强音。

参考文献

[1] Ackroyd P. *Albion: The Origins of the English Imagination* [M]. London: Chatto & Windus, 2002.

[2] Ackroyd P. *English Music* [M]. London: Penguin Books, 1993.

[3] Anderson B. *Imagined Communities: Reflections on the Origin and Spread of Nationalism* [M]. London: Verso, 1991.

[4] Benhabib S. *Situating the Self: Gender, Community and Postmodernism in Contemporary Ethics* [M]. New York: Routledge, 1992.

[5] Dickens C. *Hard Times* [M]. Beijing: Foreign Language Teaching and Research Press, 1994.

[6] Gale M B. *J. B. Priestley: Modern and Contemporary Dramatists* [M]. London & New York: Routledge, 2008.

[7] Gervais D. *Literary Englands: Versions of "Englishness" in Modern Writing* [M]. Cambridge: Cambridge UP, 1993.

[8] Habermann I. *Myth, Memory and the Middlebrow: Priestley, du Maurier and the Symbolic Form of Englishness* [M]. Hampshire: Palgrave Macmillan, 2010.

[9] Hazlitt W. *The Spirit of the Age: Or Contemporary Portraits* [M]. London: Colburn, 1825.

[10] Meredith G. *Sandra Belloni* [M]. London: Constable, 1914.

[11] Mill J S. *Autobiography* [M]. London: Penguin Books, 1989.

[12] Priestley J B. *The Good Companions* [M]. London: Arrow Books, 2000.

[13] Rushdie S. *The Ground Beneath Her Feet* [M]. New York: Henry Holt and Company, 1999.

[14] Shaw G B. *Love Among the Artists* [M]. New York: Herbert S. Stone and Company, 1900.

[15] Smyth G. *Music in Contemporary British Fiction: Listening to the Novel* [M]. New York: Palgrave Macmillan, 2008.

[16] Trimm R S. Rhythm nation: Pastiche and spectral heritage in *English music*. [J]. *Critique: Studies in Contemporary Fiction*, 2011, 52 (3) June: 249-471.

［17］Weliver P. *The Musical Crowd in English Fiction*, *1840 – 1910*: *Class*, *Culture and Nation* ［M］. Houndmills: Palgrave Macmillan, 2006.

［18］拜厄特. 孩子们的书 ［M］. 杨向荣, 译. 海口: 南海出版公司, 2014.

［Byatt, A. S. *The Children's Book*. Trans. Yang Xiangrong. Haikou: Nanhai Publishing House, 2014.］

［19］福柯. 规训与惩罚 ［M］. 刘北成 杨远婴, 译. 北京: 三联书店, 2003.

［Foucault, Michel. *Surveillance and Punishment*. Trans. Liu Beicheng and Yang Yuanying. Beijing: The Joint Publishing Company, 2003.］

［20］利维斯. 伟大的传统 ［M］. 袁伟, 译. 北京: 三联书店, 2002.

［Leavis, Frank Raymond. *The Great Tradition*. Trans. Yuan Wei. Beijing: The Joint Publishing Company, 2002.］

［21］莎士比亚. 仲夏夜之梦 ［M］. 朱生豪, 译, 《莎士比亚全集》第 2 卷. 北京: 人民文学出版社, 1984.

［Shakespeare, William. *A Midsummer Night's Dream*. Trans. Zhu Shenghao. *Collected Works of Shakespeare*. Vol. 2. Beijing: People's Literature Publishing House, 1984.］

(本文原载于《外国文学研究》2016 年第 5 期)

英国文学中的会话与共同体形塑[*]

  30多年来，批评界对英国文学中共同体形塑这一话题的关注逐渐增多，但是从会话这一角度加以探讨的很少。四年前，英国华威大学（现约克大学）的乔恩·米（Jon Mee）教授出版《会话世界：文学、争辩与共同体，1762—1830》(*Conversable Worlds: Literature, Contention and Community 1762 to 1830*, 2011) 一书，揭示了"会话"与"共同体"之间的天然联系，并把会话看作英国文人用以创建共同体的模式和文化实践。该书堪称这方面的开山之作，不过它的视野仅局限于18世纪下半叶和19世纪上半叶的英国文学。可是事实上，近三百年的英国文学史都可以看作一部会话和共同体的交融史。无论是在1830年之前，还是在其后，英国文学家们对于共同体的构想从来都是充分运用会话元素的。有鉴于此，本文拟从更宽广的角度考察英国文学家们是如何通过会话的诸多形式来想象/塑造共同体的。

一、会话与共同体的血缘关系

  作为一般概念，"会话"与"共同体"自来有着血缘关系。根据《牛津英语词典》，"会话"（conversation）最早包括"相处""交往""交流""社交"

---

  * 基金项目：本文系国家社科基金重大项目"文化观念流变中的英国文学典籍研究"（项目编号：12&ZD172）的阶段性成果。

"亲密""跟他人结交或打交道"以及"在某个地方或某些人中间生活或生存"等含义,这跟我们如今所说的"共同体"——"真正的、持久的共同生活"(Tönnies 2001：19)——在语义上密切关联。本文所要强调的是会话和共同体的亲缘关系还须从文化层面上来理解。

在英国文学史上,最早把"会话"跟"文化"相提并论的恐怕是 18 世纪的诗人柯珀(William Cowper,1731—1800)。柯珀在其题为《会话》("Conversation",1782)的一首诗中直接用了"文化"(culture)一词:"虽然大自然权衡我们的才能,施予/每个人些许判断力,/而且臻于佳境的会话源于天赋而非艺术,/但是会话在很大程度上取决于文化,/就如播种取决于耕种者的耕耘那样"(Cowper 1980：354)。大概是受了柯珀的启发,乔恩·米在其著述中把会话直接跟文化挂上了钩,并多次使用了"文化会话"(conversation of culture)、"作为会话的文化"(culture as conversation)和"以会话为形式的文化"(culture as a form of conversation)这类说法(Mee 2011：30—32)。也就是说,作为文化观念内涵的会话在乔恩·米笔下得到了较充分的论证。然而,令人遗憾的是,乔恩·米没有提出"作为共同体的文化"(culture as community)这样的说法。依笔者之见,共同体也属于文化观念的范畴。假如乔恩·米当初把共同体和会话同时作为文化观念的内涵加以论证,那么两者之间的血脉就会更加清晰。笔者在《"文化辩护书":19 世纪英国文化批评》(2013)一书中曾经提出,在过去的三百多年中,文化观念最重要的内涵"是对社会转型的回应,是对于社会转型的焦虑,以及化解这种焦虑的对策"(殷企平 2013：239)。此处所说的"转型焦虑",是指农业文明向工业文明转型而引起的焦虑,它散见于诸多英国文学家们的笔下。换言之,许多优秀的英国文学作品对上述社会转型做出了回应,其用以化解焦虑的思想和策略往往表现为对美好共同体的想象和憧憬,以及在此基础上通过文学话语从事文化实践或相关探索。正是在这一意义上,会话对于共同体形塑的作用得以凸显,文学家们给予会话的诉求也就顺理成章了。

我们在上文中引用了柯珀的诗行,紧随其后的几句也颇值得一读:"死记硬背的文字,连鹦鹉都能演习,/然而谈话并非总是会话,/就如乡野里不停的嘎吱声/与神圣的和谐境界相去甚远……"(Cowper 354)。这些诗行其实可以看作一种文化新现象的标志,即当时的英国文人们已经开始区分会话与谈话

(talking) 的不同含义。进行这种区分的努力更早见于沙夫茨伯里（Anthony Ashley Cooper, 3rd Earl of Shaftesbury, 1670—1713）、艾迪生（Joseph Addison, 1672—1719）和斯梯尔（Richard Steele, 1672—1729）的言论，他们多次提醒世人要警惕"闲言碎语的危害性"，并且主张以有品位的会话来与之抗衡，强调"会话不仅仅是社交界的原则，而且是创建主体性过程的一部分"（Mee 2011：45）。艾迪生和斯梯尔还在他们先后创办的刊物《闲话报》（*The Tatler*）和《旁观者》（*The Spectator*）上界定会话的性质，将其等同于思想情感的"流畅的循环"，并将其功能界定为树立"人类的榜样，使之传播并广受模仿"，"深化人们对文雅的体验"，乃至"加强公民社会的基础"（Money 1993：361）。此处，会话明显地被提到了文化生活的高度，或者说共同体/公民社会生活的高度。不过，要达到这样的高度并非易事，因为斯梯尔等人面临着一个难题，即"如何在一个攫取、挥霍的世界里树立公共价值观"（Mee 2011：44）。在斯梯尔关于会话及其功能的诸多论述中，有一句话令人回味："我们应该提升公共娱乐的品位，改善享受生活的方式，使之与我们在国力和荣耀方面的进步相匹配"（Steele 1987：104）。言下之意，英国人的文化/精神生活跟他们的物质生活不相匹配，这种畸形的发展是产生我们在前文所说的"转型焦虑"的根本原因。对斯梯尔等人来说，18世纪英国的物质文明与精神文明严重脱节的症状表现为会话品味的缺失、沟通能力的丧失以及语言质量的堕落。对于这种现象的焦虑，乔恩·米有过以下总结：（当时的英国见证了一种）"与日俱增的焦虑，即担忧日常语言过于腐败，无法作为情感传递的真正媒介"（Mee 2011：78）。对此，我们还须补充一句：语言的堕落还必然影响思想的交流、真理的诉求和知识的传播，而这些交流、诉求和传播都是共同体的建构所不可或缺的。正因为如此，斯梯尔等人除了对会话的词义进行甄别等工作以外，还用文学形式展示出什么样的言谈才称得上会话。《旁观者》从第二期开始，刊出了许多属于小品文样式的人物特写，这些人物（其中罗杰·德·科弗利爵士成了不朽的文学人物）来自社会各界，并常常聚在一起讨论关乎公共生活的一些事情。就在这些普普通通的会话场面中，细心的读者不难体会到感人的共同体情怀，因此《旁观者》的人物特写常被誉为"现代小说的先声"（Long 1909：279）。

我们在上文中使用了"因此"一词，无非是要传递这样一层意思：英国现代小说从一开始就带有共同体冲动。享有"现代小说之父"美誉的菲尔丁（Henry Fielding, 1707—1754）除了在小说中展示出丰富多彩的会话形式之外，还专门在一篇以《论会话》（"An Essay on Conversation", 1743）为题目的小品文中把会话界定为"思想的互惠交流，由此真理得以审视，事物得以改变，我们所有的知识得以相互传递"（Fielding 120）。自菲尔丁以降，以会话见长的英国小说家层出不穷。以"会话女元老"（the doyenne of conversation）著称的奥斯汀（Jane Austen, 1775—1817）自不消说，从 19 世纪的乔治·艾略特（George Eliot, 1819—1880）到世纪之交的詹姆斯（Henry James, 1843—1916），直至当代的拜厄特（A. S. Byatt, 1936—2023）和德拉布尔（Margaret Drabble, 1939—　），他们都在各自的小说里展现了会话的风采，并借此抒发了共同体情怀。也就是说，英国小说家们以会话来形塑共同体的努力从来就没有停止过。曾在 20 世纪叱咤英国文坛的利维斯（F. R. Leavis, 1895—1962）一贯提倡"有机共同体"，这已经是文学界的常识。他所抱持的共同体情怀常常表现为对文学作品中会话的关注。例如，他在分析詹姆斯的《波士顿人》（The Bostonians, 1886）中维芮娜和奥莉芙之间的会话以后，给出了这样的赞扬："在女性主义与良知的关系上，詹姆斯把握得很好……在奥莉芙·钱斯勒身上，他把良知、女权主义、文化以及教养联系在了一起"（利维斯 2002：226）。此处的"良知""女权主义""文化"和"教养"显然都是跟共同体密切相关的话题。利维斯的女弟子德拉布尔继承了利维斯的共同体思想，她的 17 部长篇小说都凸显了共同体情怀，而且都体现在她对会话的处理上。例如，《光辉灿烂的道路》（The Radiant Way, 1987）的情节主线是莉兹、艾丽克斯和艾斯特三人之间的关系，小说叙述者称之为"几十年机缘巧合的友谊"（Drabble 1987：81—82），但是依笔者之见，在这"巧合"中有其必然性，即共享的理念、情感和价值观。书中有很多她们三人之间的会话以及她们跟各自亲友之间的会话，其话题包括"钢铁工人的罢工……紧随其后的矿工们的罢工……失业率的稳步增长"（Drabble 1987：163），这些都关乎公众的利益，也就涉及共同体的建构。一段最典型的会话发生在莉兹和斯蒂芬之间，后者在解答莉兹有关"实用政治纲领"的疑问时，直接用了"共同体"一词："如果得以实施，它更能够造福于整个共同体，以及组成共同体的个体成员；更有助于健康、财富和幸福"（Drabble 1987：250）。也就是说，从菲尔丁到德拉布尔，以会话促进共同体建设的努力从未停止过。

当然，会话与共同体的亲缘关系不仅体现于小说，而且体现于诗歌和戏剧等文类。英国的诗人和剧作家们在这方面的建树，理应受到同等的重视，但是由于篇幅有限，本文只能割爱。不过，有一种文类值得格外重视，即"会话体随笔"（the conversation piece）。有趣的是，乔恩·米在其书中也谈到了"会话体随笔"，然而只是把它作为"在18世纪20年代和30年代崛起的一种重要的视觉艺术样式"（Mee 5）。把它作为文学样式来探讨并颇有建树的是著名诗人兼批评家戴维（Donald Davie，1922—1995）。他不无道理地指出，虽然会话体随笔在英国"奥古斯都时期的作家"（the Augustans）中颇为盛行，而且算不上新生事物（因为它明显地带有柏拉图对话体的痕迹），但是它在17至18世纪成了英国作家们培育"诚恳"（candour）和"礼貌"这两种美德的常见手段，因而它具有"一种新增的力量"（Davie 1964：93）。这股新力量的主要推手是伯克利（George Berkeley，1685—1753），他用会话体随笔把文学和哲学完美地融为一体，或者说"把'优质会话'引入了哲学作品"（Davie 1964：92）。他不但用优质会话来传递哲学思想，而且用实例来展示什么是优质会话。就后者而言，最杰出的要数《希勒斯和斐洛诺斯三对话》（*Three Dialogues between Hylas and Philonous*，1713）。下面这段对话可以作为凭证：

斐洛诺斯：然而全世界都被骗了，都愚蠢地相信自己的感官，这难道不奇怪吗？我真不明白人们何以心安理得地吃喝、睡觉、处置生活中的所有事务，好像他们说什么就懂什么似的。

希勒斯：的确如此。不过，你知道普通的实践不需要精妙的思辨性知识。因此，庸俗者尽管一错再错，却总能设法在生活中弄出些声响。

斐洛诺斯：但是哲学家比较明智。

希勒斯：你是说他们知道自己什么都不懂。

斐洛诺斯：那才是人类知识的最高境界。（转引自 Davie 1964：96）

这是一段浸润着睿智的语言，其核心思想是提倡谦卑的美德，而这正是任何共同体都不可或缺的。这段会话的口气也值得回味：会话者的口气带着坦率（如对世人的愚蠢自负的讽刺），而这也是共同体所倚赖的美德。此外，会话内容还涉及知识、思辨和心智的培育，这些都跟共同体的建构关系密切。如上文举例所示，伯克利笔下的会话内容远远超越了个人的私利；虽然他的观点未必都正确，但是他通过会话形式提出的问题是每个有志于共同体建设的人所不能回避的。正如戴维所说，伯克利的"对话除了其他优点以外，堪称良好教养和无私行为的典范"（Davie 1964：95）。

伯克利对后人产生过很大影响，尤其是对休姆（David Hume，1711—1776）和伯克（Edmund Burke，1729—1797）。虽然休姆和伯克似乎没有留下著名的会话体作品，但是他们对会话思想及其形式的贡献非常大，对此乔恩·米在《会话世界：文学、争辩与共同体》中已有详细论述（令人费解的是他对伯克利只字未提），此处就不再赘言。本文要强调的是，伯克利也好，休姆和伯克也好，他们对会话的关注都持有共同体情怀。威廉斯（Raymond Williams，1921—1988）曾经直言休姆和伯克在事业上都是"失败"的，但是他的下列评价却十分中肯："像伯克的事业一样，休姆的事业强调共同体，因而化作了思想的溪流，超越了局部性的失败"（Williams 1964：144）。威廉斯的评价其实也适合伯克利。

正是像上述所有作家那样的无数涓涓细流汇成了英国史上会话/共同体的思想洪流，不弃涓涓，终成江河。

二、分寸的拿捏

会话的共同体精神还体现在对会话分寸的拿捏方面。会话者能否成功地交流思想和情感，往往取决于他们的态度、语气和措辞是否得体。英国文学家们对分寸的关注程度是世界上最讲究的，在会话方面尤其如此，而这跟他们对于共同体的想象有关。

一个民族对于共同体的想象必然涉及对于民族特性的想象。两百多年来，英国历史上关于"英格兰特性"（Englishness）的争论从来就没有停止过，而且在近几十年来愈演愈烈。依笔者之见，在所有相关的解说中，要数美国小说家库珀（James Fenimore Cooper，1789—1851）的观点最值得参考："英格兰是一个讲究举止得体的国度。如果我必须用一个单词来形容，那么我就会选择'得体'

一词，这是因为它最接近英格兰的民族特性"（转引自 Langford 2000：157）。库珀的判断不一定精确，不过英国文学中有关"得体"的探究和描写至少堪与任何国家媲美。就会话而言，对"得体"的诉求常常表现为对于"说真话"和"礼貌"之间分寸的拿捏，这看似小事，却关乎共同体的健康发展。共同体的建构有赖于思想的交流、真理的审视和知识的传播，这些都要求会话者既说真话，又讲礼貌，可是实际生活中会话的目的、语境和参与者的背景千变万化，因而说真话与讲礼貌之间的分寸并不容易把握，会话者顾此失彼的现象成为生活常态。更确切地说，真诚/坦率与礼貌/文雅在现实生活中是一对矛盾。

针对上述矛盾，英国历史上曾经有过一场"两种模式之争"，即"礼貌会话模式"（the polite model of conversation）和"交锋会话模式"（the combative model of conversation）之争。推崇"礼貌模式"的文人学者主要有艾迪生、斯梯尔、休姆、理查逊（Samuel Richardson，1689—1761）和斯密（Adam Smith，1723—1790）等，他们或主张"压制分歧，把各种特殊意见带入平衡状态"（Mee 2011：42），或提倡在会话中凸显"人类中优雅的那一部分"（Mee 2011：62），或强调"会话和社交的极大愉悦""见解的契合"和"心智的某种和谐"（Smith 1984：23）。这方面最典型的可能要数理查逊，他在小说《查理士·格兰狄生爵士的历史》（*The History of Sir Charles Grandison*，1754）中写道：会话能使人变得"有教养，变得平易近人、和蔼可亲"（Richardson 1972：250）。所有这些主张都有一个共同点，即注重会话的礼貌、文雅、和谐等要素，因而可以概括为"礼貌会话模式"，或称"休姆范式"（the Humean paradigm）。

跟休姆等人不同，沃茨（Isaac Watts，1674—1748）、约翰逊（Samuel Johnson，1709—1784）和葛德汶（William Godwin，1756—1836）等提出了"交锋会话模式"。在他们看来，会话的首要功能是追求真理、传播知识，而这少不了思想的交锋和争斗。他们不仅"把会话看作知识的生产形式"和"真理的中转渠道"，而且直接向上述"休姆范式"挑战，直言"须警惕过于讲究礼貌或趣味的倾向"（Mee 2011：38）。较早提出这一主张的是沃茨，不过持相同主张的约翰逊在这方面的影响最大。后者有一个美称，即"用会话巩固英国文化的不朽典范"（Mee 2011：31），而为他赢得这一美称的是他提出的一系列的口号（他在文学俱乐部等地的会话实践除外），如："需要创造性的碰撞"（Mee 69），

"为胜利而交谈"（talking for victory），以及"把会话当作思想斗争的形式"，等等（Mee 2011：82）。继约翰逊之后，葛德汶也大力提倡"交锋会话模式"，并提出了以下理由："如果存在着真理这东西的话，那么它必然在心智与心智的碰撞中得以产生，除此，别无他法"（Godwin 1993：15）。在所有这些主张中，真理/知识和交锋/碰撞之间几乎画上了等号。

细心人不难察觉，上述"两种模式之争"实际上隐含着一种非此即彼的偏执型弊病。"文雅派"也好，"交锋派"也好，他们在推行自己的观点时，都忽视了这样一个事实：如果一味追求"说真话"而不顾礼貌，那么很有可能伤人，因而也就达不到思想交流的目的；相反，过于"讲礼貌"而言不由衷，那更谈不上真正的交流。理想的会话应该既说真话，又讲礼貌。同理，共同体的建设既需要真诚坦率，又需要文雅礼貌。然而，如前文所示，在实际生活中，会话者顾此失彼的情况常有发生。换言之，对于真诚与礼貌之间分寸的拿捏远非易事。该如何破解这一难题呢？为寻求答案，不少英国文学家做出过不懈的努力，其代表人物当首推奥斯汀。乔恩·米在论及奥斯汀对会话的贡献时曾经注意到小说《爱玛》（*Emma*，1816）中的一段对话（爱玛称赞丘吉尔的会话才能，但是奈特利不予认同）：

> "我的看法是，他能根据每个人的趣味调整会话内容。他既有让大家都愉快的愿望，又有让大家都愉快的能力。跟你，他会谈农业。跟我，他会谈绘画和音乐。不管是谁，他都能投其所好。不管是什么话题，他都有个大致的了解，因而总能搭得上话，或引领某个话题，而且谈吐得体，每个话题都处理得极佳。这就是我对他的看法。"
>
> 奈特利热切地答道："在我看来，假如他真的如你所说，那他就是世上最难以容忍的家伙！……"
>
> （Austen 1981：138）

乔恩·米援引上述对话，为的是强调"奈特利的回应……旨在表明随机应变的礼貌会牺牲太多的诚恳"（Mee 2011：205）。在笔者看来，上述对话中最值得关注的是"得体"一词。奥斯汀此处不仅像乔恩·米所说的那样，指出了过分的礼貌会以牺牲诚挚为代价,更重要的是引出了"得体"的话题,即如何在真诚与礼貌之间拿捏分寸的话题。不过,上引对话中的"得体"是反其意而用之——丘吉尔那以牺牲真诚为代价的文雅恰恰是不得体的。

那么,怎样的会话才是得体的呢?事实上,奥斯汀向世人展示过分寸拿捏得当的会话,只不过恰恰被乔恩·米忽视罢了。依笔者之见,最佳的例子见于《傲慢与偏见》(*Pride and Prejudice*, 1813)。在小说第38章中,有一段柯林斯先生向伊丽莎白吹嘘自己婚姻美满的插曲:"我亲爱的夏洛特跟我同心同德。不管遇到什么事儿,我们都情投意合,这真是少见的缘分。我们就像是天生的一对"(Austen 2003:185)。读过这部小说的人都知道,夏洛特是迫于生计才嫁给柯林斯的,根本谈不上同心同德,只不过柯林斯比较愚钝,毫无察觉罢了。作为夏洛特闺蜜的伊丽莎白对此心知肚明,可是她若一味地求真,直言柯林斯夫妇同床异梦,那不免有失礼貌(更何况此时的她正在柯林斯家做客——后者尽管俗不可耐,却尽了地主之谊);相反,她若只顾礼貌,一味地应和,那又会流于虚假。这真是两难啊!且看伊丽莎白如何作答:"伊丽莎白不失礼貌地答道:那样的婚姻确实幸福美满;她还带着同等的真诚补充说,她坚信他很享受家庭生活,并且为他感到高兴"(Austen 2003:185)。此处的分寸拿捏得十分精妙:伊丽莎白礼貌地祝福了柯林斯,同时又不失真诚——她所承认的美满婚姻只是"那样的婚姻",而非柯林斯和夏洛特实际拥有的婚姻;她"坚信他很享受家庭生活",所强调的是"他",并不包括夏洛特,因而伊丽莎白始终保持了真诚。奥斯汀通过伊丽莎白之口,向世人提供了一个鱼和熊掌兼得的会话范例。

会话时最难拿捏的分寸,莫过于批评方式的选择。《傲慢与偏见》在这方面提供的范例也堪称上乘。在第31章中,有一段达西和伊丽莎白之间的对话:

> 达西说:"有些人很善于跟陌生人攀谈,我可没有那样的才能。跟先前从未见过的人会话时,我无法捕捉他们的语气,无法跟着他们的兴趣转。我经常看到有人能那样做,可我做不到。"
>
> 伊丽莎白答道:"我看到许多女子弹钢琴时指法娴熟,而我的手指却不那么听使唤。它们达不到相同的力度和速度,因而不具有相同的表现力。然而,我一直认为那是我主观上不够努力的缘故——是我没有花足够力气

练习的缘故。我并不认为自己的手指天生就不如那些指法高明的女子。"

(Austen 2003: 151)

此处，伊丽莎白其实是在批评达西的矜持与傲慢——他不愿意跟生人交谈，还找客观理由来为自己辩护。虽然是批评达西，但是她选择了从批评自己的方式切入。达西足够聪明，应该能听出她的言下之意：就像伊丽莎白应该多练习钢琴指法一样，达西应该多练习跟人交谈，尤其是跟生人交谈，而不应该用客观理由来为自己开脱。这样的方式显然非常得体，容易被人接受。

在上面的例子中，文雅跟坦诚结合得完美无瑕。然而，批评/会话形式在实际上是多种多样的，有时候并非一定要那样文雅，甚至有必要以激烈的形式呈现，此时的分寸应该如何拿捏呢？乔治·艾略特的《丹尼尔·德隆达》(*Daniel Deronda*, 1876) 在这方面为我们提供了启示。女主人公关德琳曾去音乐家克莱斯摩尔那里拜师，后者在听完她的演唱之后，给出了如下批评："你未被教好。这并不是说你没有天赋。你的调子很准，而且音色很美，但是你的发声不好，所选择的曲调趣味低下。这类形式的旋律表现了一种幼稚的文化——是一种虚张声势的玩意儿，表现了那种没有开阔视野的人的情感和思想。这种曲子的每一个乐句都带有愚蠢的自满情绪：没有深切而神秘的激情的爆发，没有冲突，没有对大千世界的感受。听这种乐曲的人会变得渺小。唱点儿豪放的曲子吧……"(Eliot 1984: 42—43) 此处的"未被教好""趣味低下"和"愚蠢的自满情绪"等措辞相当激烈，语气也同样激烈，可是它们的冲击力经由"调子很准"和"音色很美"等词语的缓冲，让关德琳在感到羞耻的同时，还能感受到克莱斯摩尔的公允。此外，"唱点儿豪放的曲子"这样的建议透着关爱和不凡学识，不能不让人佩服，因而加强了整个批评意见的可接受度。换言之，即便是激烈的批评，也需要拿捏分寸，甚至比一般会话更需要拿捏得体。从《丹尼尔·德隆达》的情节来看，这类激烈而又得体的批评是行之有效的——正是在受克莱斯摩尔的影响之后，关德琳第一次学会了"在普通水平上看待自己"（殷企平 2015：76）。可以说，艾略特继承了奥斯汀的会话思想传统，并将其发扬光大。

上述传统一直延续到了当代。如今仍然活跃在英国文坛的杰出小说家拜厄特在 21 世纪的一次访谈中，就曾把"人类共同体"（the human community）、

"得体"（decorum）和"会话"（conversation）相提并论——触发话题的是她的短篇小说《糖》（Sugar，1987）以及她父亲临终前的情景（她父亲死于一家荷兰临终医院，那里的医生和护士"做得很得体，既悉心照料他，又不让他因倚赖他人而没有自尊"）；跟这一情景交融的是拜厄特跟父亲的"最后一次会话"，其间后者"试图建构一个故事，一个神话，一种令人满意的、有关他自己人生的叙述"（Byatt 2003：5）："我想我看到的是一个很复杂的人类共同体意象。这个共同体的维系体现于得体的言行、良好的举止；当人们相互传递精心烹调的食物时，或是周到而体贴地相互交谈时，或是恪守某些规矩时，共同体就得以维系了。……我确实很钦佩我的父亲……他不停地讲着人类的历史，其中既有他亲身经历过的，也有他从书本中体验到的，一直从第一、第二次世界大战讲到狄更斯、乔治·艾略特和夏洛特·勃朗特。参与那场有趣会话的还有那些荷兰医生，他们非常文雅。他们不会在接诊时糊弄一番了事，而会停下来，站着跟他谈读书心得。这些举止并没有减少我们因他去世而产生的悲痛，但是让我们获得了人的尊严，这才是那些得体举止的意义所在。……我指的是修养，是良好的举止，这些非常非常重要"（Byatt 2003：5—6）。修养/得体的举止跟会话和共同体之间的关系，在这里被阐述得再清楚不过了。如果我们结合拜厄特的创作实践，就会发现她对"得体"的理解还有赖于会话者共通的才思与见解，这在小说《占有》（Possession，1990）中艾什跟拉蒙特之间的书信里可见一斑——这些书信的第一封（出自艾什之手）就是由一次会话引发的："亲爱的女士：自从我们那一次令人惊喜的谈话以后，我的脑中就再也容不下其他思绪。对于身为诗人的我……竟能体验到如此心领神会的共鸣，如此共通的才思与见解……"（拜厄特 2012：6）触发艾什跟拉蒙特之间恋情的是得体的会话，而这得体则是以共通的修养——共通的才思与见解——为前提的。《占有》中还有一个细节值得注意：贝雅特丽斯曾经写过一篇专论，其中"她唯一引以为豪的字词就是'交谈'"，而这交谈所追求的情景"同时融合了高尚的谈吐以及不加掩饰的热情"（拜厄特 2012：146）。高尚的谈吐和不加掩饰的热情也好，共通的才思与见解也好，它们都是会话分寸得以恰当拿捏的基本保证。透过这种分寸的拿捏，我们还应看到拜厄特的共同体情怀，或者用她自己的话说，看到"一个很复杂的人类共同体意象"（Byatt 2012：5）。

同样善于把握会话分寸的当代英国作家还有许多。篇幅有限,仅再以德拉布尔为例。上一小节曾用了《光辉灿烂的道路》中的例子,说明德拉布尔以会话为促进共同体建设所做的努力。这种努力还见于她的另一部小说《七姐妹》(*The Seven Sisters*, 2002)。女主人公坎迪达遭丈夫背叛,又因社会风气的败坏,逐渐陷入自我封闭的境地;随后她在各种外因和内因的促使下奋力走出了自我,开始跟其他六位不同身份的妇女交往,还结伴赴意大利旅游。途中她们情同姐妹,完成了一次共同体之旅。七姐妹的许多会话都投射出拿捏分寸的重要性,其中最耐人寻味的一次发生在坎迪达和杰罗尔德太太之间:坎迪达第一次造访杰罗尔德太太(一年前坎迪达曾修过她的夜大课程),离开时适逢下雨;杰罗尔德太太要把自家的雨伞借给坎迪达,但是后者不肯接受,于是杰罗尔德太太说:"如果我把伞借给了你,你就会再来我家了。你就不可能一消失就是一年了。我想再跟你见面"(Drabble 2002:106—107)。此处,杰罗尔德太太其实是在批评坎迪达自我封闭,可是她捕捉了借雨伞的话题而乘势发挥,拿捏得既圆熟自如又感人至深。因此,坎迪达不仅接受了雨伞,而且频频与杰罗尔德太太来往,进而渐渐地把社交圈扩大为七姐妹旅行团。这足以说明,一次得体的会话,埋下了形成美好共同体的种子。

正是有了无数像上述作家那样的精细推敲,英国文学中以会话促进共同体的传统才绵延不断、绚丽多彩。正所谓精诚所至,金石为开。

参考文献

[1] Austen J. *Emma* [M]. Toronto: Bantam Classic, 1981.

[2] Austen J. *Pride and Prejudice* [M]. New York: Bantam Classic, 2003.

[3] Byatt A S. Editor's notes interviewed by Jean-Louis Chevalier [J]. *Journal of the Short Story in English*, 2003, 41 (8): 1 - 10.

[4] Cowper W. *The Poems of William Cowper*, Vol. I. John D. Baird and Charles Ryskamp. (eds.) [M]. Oxford: Oxford UP, 1980.

[5] Davie D. "Berkeley and the Dialogue." *The English Mind*. Hugh Sykes Davies and George Watson (eds.) [M]. Cambridge: Cambridge UP, 1964: 90 - 106.

[6] Drabble M. *The Radiant Way* [M]. New York: Ivy Books, 1987.

[7] Drabble M. *The Seven Sisters* [M]. Orlando: Penguin Books, 2002.

[8] Eliot G. *Daniel Deronda* [M]. Oxford: Clarendon, 1984.

[9] Fielding H. "An Essay on Conversation." *Miscellanies*, Vol. I. Henry Knight Miller (ed.) [M]. Oxford: Clarendon Press, 1972: 119-162.

[10] Godwin W. *Political and Philosophical Writings of William Godwin*, Vol. III. Mark Philip (ed.) [M]. London: William Pickering, 1993.

[11] Langford P. *Englishness Identified: Manners and Character 1650-1850* [M]. Oxford: Oxford UP, 2000.

[12] Long W J. *English Literature: Its History and Its Significance for the Life of the English-Speaking World* [M]. Boston: Ginn and Company, 1909.

[13] Mee J. *Conversable Worlds: Literature, Contention, and Community 1762 to 1830* [M]. Oxford: Oxford UP, 2011.

[14] Money J. The Masonic Movement: Or Ritual, Replica, and Credit: John Wilkes, the Macaroni Parson, and the Making of the Middle-Class Mind [J]. *Journal of British Studies*, 1993, (4): 358-395.

[15] Richardson S. *The History of Sir Charles Grandison*, Vol. III. Jocelyn Harris (ed.) [M]. Oxford: Oxford UP, 1972.

[16] Smith A. *The Theory of Moral Sentiments*. D. D. Raphael and A. L. Macfie (eds.) [M]. Indianapolis: The Liberty Fund, 1984.

[17] Steele R. *The Tatler*, Vol. I. Donald F. Bond (ed.) [M]. Oxford: Clarendon, 1987.

[18] Tönnies F. *Community and Civil Society*. Trans. Jose Harris and Margaret Hollis [M]. Cambridge: Cambridge UP, 2001.

[19] Williams R. "David Hume: Reasoning and Experience." *The English Mind*. Hugh Sykes Davies and George Watson (eds.) [M]. Cambridge: Cambridge UP, 1964: 123-145.

[20] 拜厄特. 占有 [M]. 于冬梅, 宋瑛堂, 译. 海口: 南海出版公司, 2012.

[21] 利维斯. 伟大的传统 [M]. 袁伟, 译. 北京: 三联书店, 2002.

[22] 殷企平.从自我到非我:《丹尼尔·德隆达》中的心智培育之路[J].外国文学研究,2015,(2):71—82.

[23] 殷企平."文化辩护书":19世纪英国文化批评[M].上海:上海外语教育出版社,2013.

(本文原载于《英美文学研究论丛》2016年第1期)

Space, Cultural Materialism and Structure of Feeling: Reflections on the Chinese Reception of Raymond Williams

THE LAST DECADE HAS WITNESSED a burgeoning literature on Raymond Williams in China. In addition to over fifty articles, three book-length studies have been published since 2001, whereas prior to 2001 there were only two essays and one book of this kind. The themes that are privileged in the Chinese discourse on Williams include the principal categories in Williams's theories: the concepts of the knowable community and of cultural materialism. The latter, which has become a focus of the debates on Williams in China, is often discussed in terms of canon, institution, mediation, totality, ideology, hegemony, the base-superstructure model, and, above all, structure of feeling.

Interestingly, the concept of cultural materialism has also found echoes to a greater or less extent in almost all the works that Chinese critics have written on Williams. Even more significantly, up to now it has invariably found positive responses. In each of the four monographs produced in China dealing with Williams we find a whole chapter devoted to cultural materialism, and many of the articles concerned actually have the words "cultural materialism" in their titles, such as "A Mirror to History: An Analysis of Raymond Williams's Cultural Materialism",① "Theories of Cultural Materialism: A Field That Is Worthy of Continuing Attention — Reading Raymond Williams's *Marxism and Literature*",② "Cultural Materialism: A Theoretical Exploration on Raymond Williams's Marxism",③ to name only a few. Cultural materialism, as Williams says in *Marxism and Literature* (Oxford 1977), is a position which it took him years to reach and "which can be briefly described as ... a theory of the specificities of material cultural and literary production within historical materialism" (p. 5). In *Problems in Materialism and Culture* (London 1980), he gives a more elaborate definition: "I would now claim to have reached ... a theory of culture as a (social and material) productive process and of specific practices, of 'arts', as social uses of material means of production (from language as material 'practical consciousness' to the specific technologies of writing and forms of writing, through to mechanical and electronic communications systems)" (p. 243). It is this emphasis on the materiality of culture and its socio-historical aspects, and the implied critique of the "orthodox" Marxist theory of culture, that has ignited the most enthusiastic response from the interpretative community in China. A typical example can be found in *The Cultural Politics of New Left: Raymond Williams's Theory of Culture*, recently published by Zhao Guoxin:

> On the one hand, cultural materialism is a reaction to the Leavisite mode of criticism which overemphasizes the text to the neglect of its social and historical backgrounds. On the other hand, it is a sublation of the orthodox Marxist theory of culture. It is materialistic because it brings into prominence the important role of social production and historical contexts in the production of culture. ④

---

① Published by Zhang Pinggong in *Academic Research*, 8 (2003).
② Published by Ma Chi in *Heilongjiang shehui kexue* [*Heilongjiang Social Sciences*], 1 (2009).
③ Published by Yin Xuhui in *Qinghai shifan daxue xuebao (zhexue shehui kexue ban)* [*Journal of Qinghai Normal University (Philosophy and Social Sciences)*], 6 (2009).
④ Zhao Guoxin, *Xinzuopai de wenhua zhengzhi: leimengde weiliansi de wenhua lilun* [*The Cultural Politics of New Left: Raymond Williams's Theory of Culture*] (Beijing 2009) p. 24.

Embedded in this passage is a tone of affirmation and appreciation, and this is far from an isolated case. Wu Yeping, for instance, has given effusive praise to Williams's cultural materialism, which she sees as "representing a praxis par excellence in analysing cultural phenomena in their social and historical contexts". ① Tribute is also paid to Williams in another recently published article because his cultural materialism "has perfected 'the base-superstructure formula' in traditional Marxist theory and has overcome a mechanical theoretical tendency". ② A similar view is held by Fu Degen, who also praises Williams for "criticising the reductive economism", and for having, after he "discussed the base-superstructure proposition", "disagreed with its orthodoxy in theorising and its rigidity in application". ③

Interestingly, most of those who embrace the notion of cultural materialism see it as a development of Marxism rather than a deviation from it. Qiao Ruijin and Xue Ji, for instance, have argued that Williams's "effort to deconstruct the antithesis between base and superstructure ... seems to have deviated far away from Marxism, but rather than 'stepping beyond Marxism', his cultural materialist views are in line with Marxist philosophy and are actually its extension and development in the cultural sphere". ④ Such instances point to an exceptionally strong interest in, and warm appreciation of, Williams's theory of cultural materialism.

But why has there been such a warm response?

The answer lies in China's historical and cultural circumstances. Many Chinese scholars see in cultural materialism, which presupposes the elimination of the rigid dichotomy of the base and the superstructure, a way out of their cultural impasse. As a

---

① Wu Yeping, *Leimengde weiliansi de wenhua lilun yanjiu* [*A Study on Raymond Williams's Cultural Theory*] (Lanzhou 2006).
② Yin Xuhui, "Wenhua weiwu zhuyi de changshi" ["Cultural Materialism: A Theoretical Exploration – On Raymond Williams's Marxism"], *Qinghai shifan daxue xuebao (zhexue shehui kexue ban)* [*Journal of Qinghai Normal University (Philosophy and Social Sciences)*], 6 (2009) p. 16.
③ Fu Degen, "Zouxiang wenhua weiwu zhuyi" ["Towards Cultural Materialism"], Ph.D thesis (Beijing 1998) p. iv.
④ Qiao Ruijin and Xue Ji, "Leimengde weiliansi weiwu zhuyi wenhuaguan jiexi" ["An Anatomy of Raymond Williams's Materialist Views on Culture"], *Makesi zhuyi yu xianshi* [*Marxism and Reality*], 3 (2007) pp. 154 – 7: 155.

matter of fact, various people have drawn attention to the need to apply cultural materialism to the reality in China. Ma Chi, for example, believes that it applies to China at least in the sense that it stimulates people to think about the following question: "What should a Chinese scholar, in the fields of Marxist literary theories and cultural studies, really do?"[1]

Another appeal for the use of Williams's theory is made in an article by Zhang Pinggong: "Williams's cultural materialism is conducive to an adequate understanding and mapping of the cultural context of contemporary China, and to the analysis and critique of our own literary traditions and cultural experience."[2] Compared with Zhang Pinggong's and Ma Chi's comments, Fu Degen is more explicit and more specific:

> For years excessive importance was attached in our country to the relationship of literature to economics and politics, due to the influence of Soviet Union's research model. Since the Reform and the introduction of the opening-up policy, multifarious trends of Western thought in art and literature have arrived in China, hence the emergence of various "new methods". Perhaps as an over-rectification of those formerly prevalent research methods, these "new methods" have more or less "formalist" leanings and tend to overlook external factors underlying art and literature. Raymond Williams's cultural materialist thought has a role to play in helping us overcome both the tendency to the rigid reliance on politico-economic factors and the tendency to formalism, thus providing us with a frame of reference and enabling us to rebuild the relationships between literature and society on a higher level.[3]

---

[1] Ma Chi, "'enhua weiwu lun': yige zhide jixu guanzhu de lingyu – du leimengde weiliansi de *makesi zhuyi yu wenxue*" [" 'Theories of Cultural Materialism': A Field That Is Worthy of Continuing Attention – Reading Raymond Williams's *Marxism and Literature*"], *Heilongjiang shehui kexue* [*Heilongjiang Social Sciences*], 1 (2009) pp. 84 – 7: 87.

[2] Zhang Pinggong, "Lishi zhi jing: xi leimengde weiliansi de wenhua weiwu zhuyi" ["A Mirror to History: An Analysis of Raymond Williams's Cultural Materialism"], *Xueshu yanjiu* [*Academic Research*], 8 (2003) pp. 70 – 3: 73.

[3] Fu Degen, "Towards Cultural Materialism", p. 100.

Although Fu Degen has set a specific target, such as is lacking in Ma Chi's and Zhang Pinggong's remarks, of putting into practice Williams's thought, we are still not very clear about how that target can be reached. Despite this deficiency, the efforts made by Fu Degen, as well as by Ma Chi and Zhang Pinggong, are praiseworthy in so far as they have brought home to us a sense of the urgency of the issue.

A new trend, in the midst of all the calls to apply Williams's thought to China, manifests itself in "Political Science of Words", an article by Lu Jiande who has pinpointed the area of words where true inspiration can be drawn from Williams. Although he does not mention even once the term "cultural materialism", he nevertheless demonstrates, in a thought-provoking manner, the way in which Chinese culture can be approached as a (social and material) productive process and in which the use of keywords can be an effective method of investigation. "Our society is obsessed", he says, "with concepts and labels". It is a task of crucial importance, therefore, "to discuss and redefine as Williams did, in a critical spirit and with a historical consciousness, the keywords that have made a tremendous impact on our society, which is the prerequisite for the protection of our cultural ecology".[①] Unlike many others who have called for the necessity of drawing upon the intellectual resources of Williams's works but left the implications unexplored, Lu Jiande has made concrete efforts to probe into some of the keywords that are prevalent in Chinese cultural life but often go unquestioned, words such as "intelligentsia", "democracy", "science", and "revolution". Of all his investigations, the most noteworthy is his enquiry into the word "institution" which, when translated into Chinese, often loses one of its important meanings, i.e., the norms, principles, and customs that are often unstipulated in any written form, but have nevertheless struck deep roots in a group, community, and society. More specifically, it is often translated as 制度 which, when translated back into English, can never be "institution" again but will appear as "order" or "system", words which put the emphasis on a form that is written down or that is visible and

---

① Lu Jiande, "Ciyu de Zhengzhixue (Dai Yixu)" ["The Political Science of Words (As an Introduction to the Translation)"], in *Guanjianci* [*Keywords*] (Beijing 2005) pp. 9, 11.

quantifiable. Lu Jiande seizes upon this problem in translation and turns it into a significant cultural issue:

> More often than not, behavioural norms (or patterns) that have been long in existence and are widely accepted are not in black and white, but they can all be called "institutions". For example, bribing others with silver dollars (so as to seek interests and to extend power), as described in *All Men Are Brothers*,① was an institution at that time … Every society has its own customary rules, and things established and accepted through common practice, that give expression to the basic values underpinning people's conduct and are far more vital than written rules and laws. The implementation of written rules and regulations often depends on social customs and usages, and depends on the "institutions" that grow in specific historical circumstances. Over the past century, an obsession with the magic power of written rules and commands has taken a grip on many of the Chinese intelligentsia who mistakenly believe that various long-standing abuses and malpractices can be removed by reforms on the level of "systems", whereas the "systems" concerned are merely documents containing ineffective rules, orders, and so on. Some experts (especially "economists"), who are favourites with the media, are blind to the power of customs in shaping and transforming a human being. Their reform designs and schemes, therefore, simply overlook deep-rooted cultural factors. Hopefully, *Keywords* can help our academics, in the field of social sciences and humanities, examine the "institutions" that are invisible but ubiquitous in our society. ②

The significance of this passage lies in the insight it gives into the root cause of one of the inveterate problems in Chinese social and cultural life, and in showing us how the problem can be tackled by borrowing from Raymond Williams an investigative tool,

---

① One of the most famous Chinese classical novels, written by Shi Naian (1296 – 1370).
② Lu Jiande, "The Political Science of Words", p. 7.

namely the method of analysing keywords. It should be further pointed out that Lu Jiande has actually adopted a position within cultural materialism here, for his work implies a firm belief in the dynamic role of the superstructure, such as the social sciences and humanities, in shaping the base. Moreover, he has demonstrated a way of understanding the diverse social and material production of such works as *All Men Are Brothers* to which connected categories of ideas and values can be historically applied.

But there is still a long way to go before Williams's cultural materialism really materialises. There are hidden shoals and reefs ahead. For example, the misunderstanding or misinterpretation of Williams's views gives rise to confusions over the status of literature in his cultural theory. In other words, there has been a strong tendency among Chinese critics to indiscriminately put Williams on a par with those who pride themselves on de-canonising and de-aestheticising literary works. Wu Yeping, for instance, praises Williams for having "initiated a concept of literature as 'forms of writing' ",[1] and she gives a very revealing title to one of the sections of her book, namely "The Challenge Cultural Materialism Poses to Literary Studies". She then goes on to elaborate a dichotomy between "aesthetic judgements", which she associates with the traditional concept of literature, and "the ability to read and write", which she implicitly conceives as an innovative notion of literature:

> Subordination to class norms of aesthetic judgements can be designated as an important characteristic of the concept of traditional literature. The ability to read and write, within the theoretical framework of cultural materialism, constitute a culturally and politically emancipatory mode, unifying education and politics ... Williams regards literature as a historical and relative being with neither permanent essence nor universality ... Reading and writing are the most basic means of culture, as well as literature's basic modes of existence. In Williams's view, in fact, literature is no more than a cultural phenomenon.[2]

---

[1] *A Study on Raymond Williams's Cultural Theory*, p. 157.
[2] *A Study on Raymond Williams's Cultural Theory*, pp. 166–167.

All this gives us a false impression that Williams equates literature with non-literary, though cultural, documents.

A similar argument can be found in Zhao Guoxin's *Cultural Politics of New Left*, in which Williams's cultural materialism is compared to New Historicism: "Both cultural materialism and New Historicism ... attach great importance to non-literary documents and upgrade them to such an extent that they can make rival claims as an equal with literature."① Such examples are actually so numerous in both Zhao's book and in other people's works that we need not elaborate them further here.

But one related point has to be made: some critics do not explicitly put Williams into the category of those who mention literature and nonliterary works in the same breath, but they have created confusion by overemphasising the political aspect of his work. Zhang Pinggong's article, for instance, produces an impression that Williams relies exclusively on a political interpretation of literary works, while leaving completely out of account their aesthetic dimensions: "Williams first applied his theory of cultural materialism to research on English literature in the Renaissance period, especially the classic works by Shakespeare ... The success of Shakespearian plays, therefore, lies in their political tendency to criticise current malpractices rather than their transcendental aesthetic appeal".② Even when there is no deliberate attempt to belittle the aesthetic function, the actual absence of aesthetic dimensions is often a feature of the works that deal with Raymond Williams. An interesting example, by no means isolated, can be found in Li Zhaoqian's article "Raymond Williams's Reflections on Literary Paradigm", whose central argument is that Williams's great contribution lies in the development of "a working definition of literary paradigm" which "is a growing historical continuum".③ Williams's "cultural materialism", he goes on to argue, "is at the beginning of a new dominant literary paradigm". For all its focus on literature, however, the article does not touch at all on the aesthetic aspect of literature.

---

① *The Cultural Politics of New Left*, p. 151.
② "A Mirror to History", p. 72.
③ Li Zhaoqian, "Leimengde weiliansi de wenxue fanshi sikao" ["Raymond Williams's Reflections on Literary Paradigm"], *Shijie wenxue pinglun* [*World Literatures Review*], 2 (2009) pp. 236–40: 236.

In short, the current state of Williams's reception in China is marked by a tendency either to eliminate the distinction between literary works and non-literary documents, or to denigrate the aesthetic values which would otherwise be central to literature. Such a tendency is in fact part of an international trend to politicise, de-canonise and de-aestheticise traditional classics, especially when it comes to the evaluation of Williams's work, as reflected in an article by Stanley Aronowitz, who has come to the following conclusion:

> Williams is less interested in the intrinsic merit of the work in terms of criteria of aesthetic value such as felicitous writing style, formal innovation, or narrative elegance than in the extent to which it is *signifying practice* of a concrete historical conjuncture. His object is whether the novel or poem provides *knowledge* of what he calls the "structure of feeling" of a specific historical moment, and even more concretely of a given *class*, not whether it is a source of pleasure. ①

Furthermore, we should see that trend as one of the symptoms of a worldwide crisis of the humanities, a crisis given a succinct summary by Zhang Longxi in his most recent article: "what poses a more serious challenge, or what has been called a crisis of the humanities, is not just an unpropitious time and environment, but an internal questioning of the value and legitimacy of culture and tradition by literary scholars and cultural theorists themselves". It is this internal questioning that Zhang Longxi regards as the greatest threat to classics: "Classics, traditionally understood as the repositories of moral, social, and spiritual values, what Sainte-Beuve in an earlier time called the 'temple of taste', are under attack as embodiments of repressive ideologies of the patriarchy, the ruling elites, or the colonialist empire". ② In this general context, the

---

① Stanley Aronowitz, "Between Criticism and Ethnography: Raymond Williams and the Invention of Cultural Studies", in Christopher Prendergast (ed.), *Cultural Materialism: On Raymond Williams* (Minneapolis 1995) pp. 320–39: 321.
② Zhang Longxi, "Valeurs, défense, crise et avenir des sciences humaines", *Diogène*, 229–30 (Jan.–June 2010) pp. 11, 15.

rubbishing, de-canonisation, and politicisation of literature have become a popular game among many of our literary critics.

But is Raymond Williams also one of those fanatical game players?

To answer this question we need to look into whether literature is a legitimate discipline and whether there is still such a thing as a classic or a literary canon in the first place. Here again, we may turn for reference to Zhang Longxi, who responds enthusiastically to Frank Kermode's Tanner Lectures at the University of California at Berkeley, presented in November 2001 and published in 2004, in which Kermode holds it "to be a necessary though not obvious requirement of the canon that it should give pleasure".① Aesthetic pleasure is one of the prerequisites for any person who chooses to talk about literature as such. "The point may be a simple one", argues Zhang Longxi, "if you don't find pleasure in literature, don't pretend to be a literary critic—but it becomes important to emphasise aesthetic pleasure at this particular time when literary works are often used as so many social, historical, or political documents to comment on other subjects and for other purposes".② To argue for aesthetic pleasure is not to deny a political, ideological, or any other dimension of literature. On the contrary, a moderate dose of political and ideological sensitivity is a wholesome contribution to literary and cultural studies as a whole, but an ideological over-interpretation of any literary work or a carnival-like blurring of the boundary between literature and non-literature could only create chaos. While it is true that cultural studies is a problem-based academic pursuit and is often interdisciplinary, it does not follow that it should neutralise any of the distinctive elements of any discipline. Although cultural studies cannot but be interdisciplinary and cross-disciplinary, there has to be a discipline from which it can cross to another. The same is true of the literary critics who pursue cultural studies.

Now let us return to the question of Williams and de-canonisation. Does Williams leave aesthetics out of account when he approaches literary works?

---

① Frank Kermode, *Pleasure and Change: The Aesthetics of Canon*, ed. Robert Alter (Oxford 2004) p. 20.
② Zhang Longxi, "Valeurs, défense, crise et avenir des sciences humaines", p. 17.

The titles of some of his major works suggest a strong passion in Williams for literature: *Drama from Ibsen to Eliot*, *Drama in Performance*, *Modern Tragedy*, *Drama from Ibsen to Brecht*, *The English Novel from Dickens to Lawrence*, *Orwell*, and *Marxism and Literature*. Even in the works whose titles do not highlight literature, such as *Culture and Society*, *The Long Revolution*, *The Country and the City*, we often find page upon page, nay, chapter upon chapter, devoted to it. In *The Country and the City* (London 1985), for instance, over a hundred writers, plus a far greater number of their literary works, are discussed and analysed with exquisite literary taste, regardless of the fact that Williams's literary taste is intertwined with philosophical, social, historical, and political insight. Let us take "Surviving Countrymen", Chapter 21 of *The Country and the City*, for example. One of its foci is on how the so-called "regional novel" develops from one mode, with George Eliot/Thomas Hardy as its representative and landscape description/nature poetry as its typical forms, into another mode which focuses on feelings about the earth and about natural growth, and which contains central imagery of human relationships, especially of love and desire. Here is an excerpt in which George Eliot is compared with Meredith:

> Her uncritical transition from Germany to England, where there were no "peasants", is notable enough. But what is more important is that within the fastidious phrases a stock figure can be seen as emerging, and we have been hearing his grunts ever since. Honest grunts though; that is usually the point. He is not the simple natural figure of Wordsworth; he is something that is about to be called elemental. Rough land, rough grappling with nature, rough feelings, rough honesty...
>
> Meredith in his novels sticks mainly to the limitations; the countryman is hard, stubborn, enduring, confined. But the virtues of Earth, in the new fertile sense, were about to break through. If you read *Rhoda Fleming* you can already see the outlines of many later novels, but if you read the poems you can hear the new rhythm itself... (*The Country and the City*, pp. 250 – 251)

The whole passage reads like a pleasurable piece of literature. Look at this line: "Rough land, rough grappling with nature, rough feelings, rough honesty". An extraordinary sense of beauty is revealed here: remarkable alliteration, symmetrical pairings, majestic parallels, melodious rhythm, all working to evoke aesthetic feelings. There are many more instances, even within this short passage, which point to Williams's sensitivity and sensibility with regard to the aesthetic elements of literature. His taste for characterisation vividly manifests itself when he sees "a stock figure" "emerging", and when he nudges us into an auditory literary experience: "and we have been hearing his grunts ever since". This taste is also evident in "the simple natural figure of Wordsworth". When he comes to dwell on Meredith, he talks about "the virtues of Earth" which "were about to break through", emphasising "the new fertile sense" — only those who are aesthetically susceptible could have come up with such a collocation! And the last line of the above-quoted passage testifies once more to his taste for poetic rhythms. Such instances abound. The following is but one more of the many paragraphs in this book whose sensuous qualities are unmistakable:

> This now conscious intercourse with the Earth became, in its fusion of agricultural sexual imagery (see Lawrence's descriptions of ploughing and milking in the first chapter of *The Rainbow*) a dominant mode; dominant also in the special sense that the imagery is male, to the female Earth. The emotional basis for the rough peasant lover, the deep passions of this life of the soil, is to be found here but is only one of its figures. (p. 251)

We should hasten to add that Williams is not merely dealing with the aesthetic aspects of the novels by George Eliot, Meredith, and Lawrence. The immediate context of the two above-quoted passages is the evolution of country houses, which in turn indicates the social, historical, and political changes taking place in the course of industrialisation. Here is a contextualising passage within the same chapter:

But there is an obvious change in, for example, the country-houses of Henry James, which have become the house-parties of a metropolitan and international social round ... Its determining dimension is now not land but money; houses, parks, and furniture are explicitly objects of consumption and exchange. People bargain, exploit and use each other, with these houses as the shells of their ambition and intrigue. Money from elsewhere is an explicit and dominant theme. Social cultivation, still linked in Jane Austen with the general process of improvement, is now a complicated process that flows from a wider society. Detached capital, detached income, detached consumption, detached social intercourse inhabit and vacate, visit and leave, these incidentally surviving and converted houses. (p. 249)

It goes without saying that Williams has a strong social, economic and political concern here, but socio-economic concerns need not exclude aesthetic concerns. As a matter of fact, these different dimensions in Williams's analysis often go hand in hand and are even intertwined to a nicety. The following comment on Lawrence is a good example:

he saw quite clearly as an enemy a materialist and capitalist industrial system ... His is a knot too tight to untie now: the knot of a life under overwhelming contradictions and pressures. But as I have watched it settle into what is now a convention — in literary education especially — I have felt it as an outrage, in a continuing crisis and on a persistent border. The song of the land, the song of the rural labour, the song of delight in many forms of life with which we all share our physical world, is too important and too moving to be tamely given up, in an embittered betrayal, to the confident enemies of all significant and actual independence and renewal. (p. 271)

A social and political overtone pervades the whole passage here, but into the socio-political strands are woven aesthetic ones, what with a striking image of "knot" and an emphasis on "delight in many forms of life", further accentuated by the parallel constructions with a recurring motif of "song", which cannot but appeal to our aesthetic senses.

In his other works, too, we can find Williams bringing his aesthetic judgement to bear on his evaluation of various works of art and literature, and of various literary schools. Let us take a look at Chapter 7 of *The Long Revolution* (Harmondsworth 1965), in which Williams gives a comment on James Joyce:

> And to mention this remarkable work [*Portrait of the Artist*] is to acknowledge the actual gain in intensity, the real development of fictional method... A world is actualized on one man's senses: not narrated, or held at arm's length, but taken as it is lived. Joyce showed the magnificent advantages of this method when in *Ulysses* he actualized a world not through one person but through three; there are three ways of seeing, three worlds, of Stephen, Bloom, and Molly, yet the three worlds, as in fact, compose one world, the whole world of the novel. *Ulysses* does not maintain this balance throughout... (p. 310)

What is particularly notable here is Williams's emphasis on the balance between the general way of life and individual persons, that he considers to be the essence of the method of realism and the centre of value: "Every aspect of personal life is radically affected by the quality of the general life, yet the general life is seen at its most important in completely personal terms. We attend with our whole senses to every aspect of life, yet the centre of value is always in the individual person — not any one isolated person, but the many persons who are the reality of the general life" (p. 305). The acute sense of balance and harmony revealed here is both of socio-political and aesthetic significance.

We should further emphasise that Raymond Williams attaches great importance to literature as such. In *Problems in Materialism and Culture* (1980), for instance, he maintains that there should be "a simultaneous realization of and response to" what he calls "structures of feeling ... in some of the greatest literature", which implies a sense of hierarchy, contrary to many critics who describe him as keen on pulling down literature to the level of "ordinary culture". More importantly, he has expounded his views on "the specific literary phenomenon: the dramatization of a process, the making of a fiction, in which the constituting elements, of real social life and beliefs, were simultaneously actualized and in an important way differently experienced, the difference residing in the imaginative act, the imaginative method, the specific and genuinely unprecedented imaginative organization" (pp. 24−25). What we have here is virtually a definition of the literary genre with imagination as its distinctive element. Who can say that there are no aesthetic seeds in those imaginative acts, imaginative methods, and imaginative organisations?

Moreover, Williams has dwelt directly on the aesthetic. The second chapter of Part III in his *Marxism and Literature* (Oxford 1977) is entitled "Aesthetic and Other Situations". Here is one of the most important statements in that chapter:

> Thus we have to reject "the aesthetic" both as a separable abstract dimension and as a separable abstract function. We have to reject "Aesthetic" to the large extent that it is posited on these abstractions. At the same time, we have to recognize and indeed emphasize the specific variable intentions and the specific variable responses that have been grouped as aesthetic in distinction from other isolated intentions and responses, and in particular from information and suasion, in their simplest sense. (p. 156)

It should by now be clear that Williams not only recognises but also emphasises the importance of specific aesthetic intentions and responses, although he is strongly opposed to empty talk of "the aesthetic" as an abstract notion.

To divorce Williams from literature and the aesthetic is, therefore, to deny his fundamental contribution to cultural study which, in his case at least, relies on a thorough command of and a great passion for literature. As Lu Jiande says:

> Williams loves art and literature; without his outstanding comprehension of literature there would have been no *Culture and Society* and *Keywords*... He differs from Leavis in that he is concerned with and studies various unwritten forms of communication (such as movies and television), and in that he is opposed to any narrow and shallow understanding of the word "literature". But if cultural study goes so far as to separate itself from the literary heritage and takes pride in so doing, Williams as its founding father would disinherit some of his disciples of the cultural wealth. ①

This is an apt rejoinder indeed to those who celebrate the disappearance of the distinction between literature and non-literature when talking about Williams.

It is implied in the foregoing discussion that there has emerged in China (for example in the article by Lu Jiande) a new tendency to emphasise the importance of Williams's literary criticism as his core contribution to cultural studies, despite the general disparagement of the role of literature in Williams's academic pursuits and the conspicuous absence or dilution of the aesthetic dimension in the overall critical and interpretative discourse on Williams. While this new tendency is certainly a move in a right direction, a nagging issue still needs to be addressed: in what way do literary works excel in their function as cultural critique? The answer seems to have been suggested by Liu Jin in his article "On Raymond Williams's Spatial Criticism of Modern British Literature". Williams's "spatial criticism", Liu Jin argues, is "the most characteristic and most valuable part of his cultural-literary criticism", and he praises Williams for "mapping modern British literature in the light of three kinds of space formation, namely 'the country', 'the city' and 'the border', and their interrelationships as well as their historical evolution". ② It should be pointed out that Williams himself never used the term "spatial criticism" as such, and that Liu Jin took

---

① Lu Jiande, "The Political Science of Words", p. 10.
② Liu Jin, "Lun Leimengde weiliansi dui xiandai yingguo wenxue de kongjian piping" ["On Raymond Williams's Spatial Criticism of Modern British Literature"], *Waiguo wenxue* [*Foreign Literature*], 3 (2007) pp. 105 – 14: 114.

his cue from Philip E. Wegner's ideas concerning this. In his article "Spatial Criticism", Wegner argues that the project advocated by people like Lefebvre and Foucault, which challenges the tradition of privileging temporality and history over space and which sees space itself both as a production shaped by social processes/ human interventions and a force shaping ways of human being in the world, "is already evident in Raymond Williams's classic survey of modern British literature, *The Country and the City*". ① Of particular significance is Wegner's comment on "structures of feelings":

> Williams examines the changing "structures of feelings" concerning the relationships between the "city" and the "country", as well as the transformations and expansions that occur in the very definition of each of these inseparable conceptual poles, as these are negotiated in the tradition of modern British literature, a tradition he traces from the country-house poems of the sixteenth century up through the global literatures of the present day. ②

What is significant about this comment is that Wegner, perhaps for the first time, relates the concept of "structure of feeling" to spatial criticism. But Wegner's comment is simply too brief and, having pointed out the possible relationship, he leaves it unexplored. The thread, however, is aptly picked up by Liu Jin, who devotes a whole chapter in his book *Literature and "Cultural Revolution"* to what he calls "The Literary Space for Cultural Revolution". His purpose, he says, is to prove that "Williams's study of the theme of 'the country and the city' in modern British literature is not merely to map the transformations of a geographical space but, more importantly, to map the metamorphoses of a cultural space, i. e. to probe deeply into the vicissitudes of

---

① Philip E. Wegner, "Spatial Criticism: Critical Geography, Space, Place and Textuality", in Julian Wolfreys (ed.), *Introducing Criticism at the 21st Century* (Edinburgh 2002) pp. 179 – 201: 182 – 6.
② Ibid., p. 186.

'structures of feeling' within those changed and changing spaces of culture". ① What Liu Jin does, in other words, marks an integration of spatial criticism into the analysis of structures of feeling.

The phrase "structure of feeling", as we know, occurs in much of Williams's writing, and it is in fact a dominant concept throughout all of his work. In *Marxism and Literature* he gives it a concise definition: "For structures of feeling can be defined as social experiences *in solution*, as distinct from other social semantic formations which have been precipitated and are more evidently and more immediately available" (pp. 133 - 134). He also emphasises that "as a matter of cultural theory", structure of feeling is a way of defining forms and conventions in art and literature as inalienable elements of a social process: not by derivation from other social forms and pre-forms, but as social formation of a specific kind which may in turn be seen as the articulation (often the only fully available articulation) of structures of feeling which as living processes are much more widely experienced. (p. 133).

It is exactly this "formation" that becomes the keyword in Liu Jin's hands, although he calls it "space formation", rather than "social formation", which can nonetheless be examined as the articulation of structures of feeling. What fascinates him is how "the country", "the city", and "the border" are regarded by Williams "not as static and solidified geographical spaces, but as cross-stratifications of cultural spaces that are in a state of flux and full of tensions between heterogeneous cultural forces". ② Of particular relevance to my argument is what is here described as "cross-stratifications of cultural spaces", where literature and literary criticism, more than other cultural documents, are likely to excel.

Literature excels in exploring cross-stratifications of cultural spaces mainly for two reasons: first, its extraordinary capacity to represent their complexity, and second, its

---

① Liu Jin, *Wenxue yu "wenhua geming": leimengde weiliansi de wenxue piping yanjiu* [*Literature and "Cultural Revolution": A Study on Raymond Williams's Literary Criticism*] (Chengdu 2007) p. 244.

② Liu Jin, *Wenxue yu "wenhua geming": leimengde weiliansi de wenxue piping yanjiu* [*Literature and "Cultural Revolution": A Study on Raymond Williams's Literary Criticism*] (Chengdu 2007) p. 244.

unique function of aesthetic appeal which makes exploring those complex cultural spaces a more intense experience.

Let us take for example a paragraph from *The Country and the City*, an analysis of the nineteenth-century British countryside which Williams, with reference to Meredith's fiction and poems, sees as a space[①] undergoing physical and spiritual regeneration:

> A working country, that is to say, was becoming, yet again but in a new way, a place of physical and spiritual regeneration. It was now the teeming life of an isolated nature, or the seasonal rhythm of the fundamental life processes. Neither of these feelings was new in itself. What was new was their fusion into a structure of feeling in which the earth and its creatures — animals and peasants almost alike — were an affirmation of vitality and of the possibility of rest in conscious contrast with the mechanical order, the artificial routines, of the cities. At its strongest this was a socially adapted pantheism. At its strangest it was a displacement of sexual feeling, in the awkward course of the Victorian liberation: a transitional imagery, in which sex was ploughing, a bed of bluebells was a breast: neither activity quite stated, neither feature quite seen; the intensity part of their confused secret. Yet if you turned to doubt, there was the cold sick nerve of money and the city; property and repression and ugliness; the frustration of worldly conventions and routines. (p. 252)

Here the complexity of various lived experiences, of crisscrossed heterogeneous cultural forces, and of different old feelings fused into a new structure of feeling, is so enormous that it can only be adequately treated by literary means. Meredith has done it. Williams has affirmed it. And Liu Jin is sensitive enough to have seized upon it and given the following comment, after quoting Williams's analysis above: "The 'country' under the pen of Meredith is at once brimming with vitality and full of misery, at once filled up

---

① Williams used the word "place", but Liu Jin has rightly translated it as {空间}, which really means "space". See Liu Jin's translation, ibid., p. 260.

with 'romantic sentiment' in its critique of the 'city' and permeated with a sense of helplessness and feelings of bitterness with regards to the status quo of the 'country.' "① This is certainly a succinct comment, but there is one important dimension lacking: whereas the complexity of the space formation of the "country", subsuming intricate structures of feeling, is duly pointed out, the implications of the aesthetic are left unexplored or simply ignored. And this is not an isolated case. Throughout both his book and the article quoted earlier, Liu Jin leaves the aesthetic dimension of Williams's work by and large untouched. That is to say, for all the progress he has made, his work is still symptomatic of the nationwide, nay the international, trend to de-aestheticize Williams's intellectual work.

As previously noted, however, the exploration of complex cultural spaces will be a more intense experience if the aesthetic is brought into play. Let us return, therefore, to the above quotation concerning Meredith. Williams's aesthetic susceptibilities are undoubtedly revealed in his felicitous writing style embodied by poetic diction and images, such as "teeming life", "seasonal rhythm", "ploughing", and "a bed of bluebells". To top it all, "an affirmation of vitality and of the possibility of rest in conscious contrast with the mechanical order, the artificial routines" suggests a striking antithesis between beauty and ugliness, both elements being active in those dynamic fluid cultural spaces and in the equally dynamic vital structures of feeling which in turn suggest a superb example of aesthetic judgement. In other words, the happy marriage of the aesthetic and the socio-historical or the socio-political is a hallmark of Williams's literary and cultural criticism. Only by affirming this conjunction can we do justice to Williams, be it in China or elsewhere.

To conclude, the existing interpretations and commentaries by Chinese critics, especially with regard to cultural materialism, have brought new insights and a Chinese perspective to bear on a continued engagement with Williams, but they are more or less vitiated by the conspicuous absence of the aesthetic dimension, which is symptomatic of

---

① Williams used the word "place", but Liu Jin has rightly translated it as {空间}, which really means "space". See Liu Jin's translation, ibid., p. 260.

an international trend to de-canonise and politicise literary classics. A wholesome antidote is suggested by the call, in Lu Jiande's article, for attention to the inseparability of cultural studies and literary heritage, and by Liu Jin's endeavour to integrate spatial criticism into the analysis of structures of feeling, although it would have been more appealing had an aesthetic dimension been fused into his critical discourse on Williams.

(本文原载于 The Cambridge Quarterly, Volume 41, Issue 1, 2012)

第二编

文学理论

西方文论关键词：普通读者[*]

一、略说

"普通读者"（the Common Reader）作为西方文论的一个关键词，关乎文学与文学批评的性质、对象、目的和方法，关乎文学批评的伦理维度，关乎文学批评家的责任与使命，还关乎以下几个重大问题：文学经典从何而来？文学的经典性（canonicity）何在？经典性与经典化（canonization）的区别何在？该怎样应对去经典化（decanonization）思潮？有鉴于此，不少西方文人学者致力于建构普通读者传统，作出了艰苦卓绝的努力。这一传统可以从克莫德（Frank Kermode）追溯到伍尔夫（Virginia Woolf）和约翰逊（Samuel Johnson）：他们强调批评家与普通读者的良性互动，要求批评家既传播学术，又从普通读者那里寻求启迪；既促进学术，又引领有着广泛文化需求的普通读者；既尊重普通读者，又帮助他们提升阅读水平。这种良性互动本为天经地义，为文学批评活动的必要环节，可是在过去四五十年中，始终泛滥着轻视乃至敌视普通读者的倾向，并且汇成了国际潮流，致使学府和研究机构的高墙内外，西方文论曲高和寡。更不幸的是，一些对文学本身并无热肠的人竟窃据了评判文学作品的权位，他们不懂世人为何需要文学，而且从来就不愿文学诞生。对此，去经典化思潮难辞其咎，其背后推手卡勒（Jonathan Culler）等人所鼓

---

[*] 基金项目：国家社科基金重大项目"外国文学经典生成与传播研究"（10&ZD135）。

噪的去审美化、泛政治化言论应予反驳，否则世间就不可能重现普通读者的亲切身影。

二、综述

在西方文学批评史上，英语 the Common Reader 一词得以登堂入室，要归功于大文豪约翰逊。他在名篇《葛雷传》（"Life of Gray"，1779）中这样写道："我欲与普通读者达成一致，并为此而欢欣鼓舞。凡欲饮誉诗坛者，其资格须由读者的常识决定。饱学之士会对诗人评头论足，并在条分缕析中尽显风雅，或者会借教条来摆弄学问，但是诗坛荣耀的决定权应属于那些不带偏见的普通读者"（Johnson 1878：466）。这番话看似寥寥数语，却饱含深刻思想，其中既有对文学与文学批评的性质、对象的思考，又有对文学批评的伦理关怀，还有对文学评判标准的洞见。约翰逊是在论及格雷（Thomas Gray）的《墓畔哀歌》（*Elegy Written in a Country Churchyard*，1751）时发表以上观点的。诗中，格雷面向穷苦大众讴歌那些长眠于墓地、无人凭吊的安息者，指出他们中间"也许有缄口的弥尔顿，从没有名声"，只是因为"'贫寒'压制了他们高贵的襟怀，／冻结了他们从灵府涌出的流泉"，就像"世界上多少晶莹皎洁的珠宝／埋在幽暗而深不可测的海底"（格雷 1989：367）。约翰逊赞扬这首为普通人谱写的诗歌，并渴望就此"与普通读者达成一致"，其用意不言自喻。在他之后，又一位大文豪——这一回是女中豪杰伍尔夫——站出来，为普通读者摇旗呐喊。她先后于 1925 年和 1935 年发表了两部散文集，都冠名为《普通读者》（*The Common Reader*），其中第一集首篇的标题仍然是《普通读者》。该篇开宗明义，呼应了约翰逊的观点，并细致地描述了普通读者的特点："他从事阅读，与其说是为了传授知识或纠正他人的见解，不如说是为了自己的愉悦。最重要的是，他虽然零敲碎打，却能凭直觉形成某种总体看法——在脑海中形成某个人的肖像、某个时代的素描、某种写作艺术的理论"（Woolf 2010：3）。伍尔夫还谦虚地把自己列入普通读者的行列，并给出了撰写上述散文集的理由："如果他（指普通读者，包括伍尔夫自己）如约翰逊所说，在最终裁定诗坛荣耀方面有某种发言权，那么我们就值得写下自己的思想和见解。尽管它们本身微不足道，却能促成一种巨大的效果"（Woolf 2010：4）。伍尔夫此处发展了约翰逊的文学批评思想：约翰逊虽然努力与普通读者达成一致，但是他并未把自己等同于后者；而伍尔夫则干脆视自己为普通读者中的一员，这其实是指出了批评家和普通读者的共同之处、重合之处。诚然，批评家和普通读者在评价作品的功能方面有所不同，但是也有不少重合之处，而这一点常受到学术界忽视。伍尔夫指出了这一点，确实功不可没。

伍尔夫和约翰逊的可贵之处，在于强调批评家与普通读者的良性互动，这是文学批评健康发展的必要一环。所谓良性互动，是指批评家既传播学术，又从普通读者那里寻求启迪；既促进学术，又引领有着广泛文化需求的普通读者；既尊重普通读者，又帮助他们提升阅读水平。故此，伍尔夫的《普通读者》第二集末篇就以《我们该怎样读书》（"How Should One Read a Book"）为题，向广大读者提出了有关阅读的"唯一忠告"："关于阅读，一个人能给另一个人的唯一忠告就是跟直觉走，开动脑筋，得出自己的结论。如果我们之间能达成这一默契，那么我就会斗胆提出一些想法和建议。因为有了这种默契，所以你们不会让我的建议束缚你们的独立判断，而独立判断才是读者应拥有的首要品质"（Woolf 2010：525）。此处的关键词是"独立判断"，它既体现了伍尔夫对普通读者的引导，又体现了她对后者的尊重。这样的良性互动，本应是文学批评活动所不可或缺的，因为它关乎文学与文学批评的性质，尤其是文学批评的伦理维度（批评家的责任与使命）。然而，在过去四五十年中，曾经备受尊重的普通读者渐渐消失了，不在批评家们的考虑范围之内了。无论是在高校课堂里，还是在学术刊物上，教授和批评家们"常做的第一件事情是宣扬自己的'主体立场'"（Knight 2003：4），或者痴迷于挖掘文学作品背后的"意识形态"（不管是否真有这样的意识形态），甚至醉心于学术特技表演，而全然不顾跟普通读者的沟通。当今世界，这一现象有愈演愈烈的趋势，它其实是一种文化症候：普通读者的消失，标志着文学批评的异化。

三、文学批评的异化

新千禧年伊始，有西方学者说又见普通读者的身影。例如，伯马（Rachel

Sagner Buurma)和赫弗南(Laura Heffernan)就曾写道:"新千禧年里,一个新的身影——普通读者的身影——在向文学批评家们示意。我们大家从眼角望去,就可以看见她在教室窗外,或正从演讲厅的后排走开;我们可以在公共图书馆的书库里瞥见她……在博客评论中,在亚马逊书评里,都留下了她的痕迹"(Buurma and Heffernan 2012:113)。依笔者之见,他们所见充其量只能算作并未还魂的幽灵。这是因为在过去几十年中,轻视乃至敌视普通读者的倾向已经酿成了国际潮流,在学府和研究机构的高墙内外,西方文论曲高和寡。更可悲的是,当年瓦雷里(Paul Valéry)哀叹的扭曲世态依然存在:"有些人对诗歌从无热肠,他们不懂世人为何需要诗歌,而且从来就不愿让诗歌诞生,然而不幸的是,其中一部分人竟然鬼使神差地窃据了评判诗歌的权位……据以传播自身一窍不通的东西,用出全身解数,倾尽全部热情,其后果可想而知,只能是更加让人恐慌"(Kermode 1989:title page)。如此糟糕的情形是否已经很普遍,这还有待于探究,但是文学批评的异化现象早已司空见惯。此处所说的异化,指文学批评背离了它本应有的宗旨,即从事"文学作品的界定、分类、分析、阐释和评价"(Abrams 1999:49—50)。这一宗旨显然是要为所有文学爱好者——不管是专业读者还是普通读者——服务的,但是如今的文学批评很少是为普通读者服务的。就如英国学者雅尔丁(Lisa Anne Jardine)所说,"普通读者不复存在了"(Kaplan and Rose 1990:377)。为什么会这样呢?

问题就出在被无限拔高的"理论"。曾几何时,不少文学"理论"不再为文学服务,更谈不上为文学爱好者服务。克莫德就曾经这样感叹:"能够指望普通读者听懂理论的教授们高谈阔论的时代早已过去了;理论家们假如跟普通读者扯上了关系,就会觉得自己的尊严被触犯了,这就是我们所面临的奇怪情状。那些理论家自诩为专家,不再对普通读者负有义务……许多书籍被划入文学批评类别,其供应量日益增多,可是文学爱好者中很少有人能读懂这些书,就连专业读者也不都懂"(Kermode 1989:8)。不光克莫德作如是说,即使是美国学者奈特(Christopher J. Knight)也发出过同样的感叹,说文学批评家们"有一个坏习惯,即关心理论的程度超过了诗歌或戏剧,因此他们必然会冷落文学本身,尽管后者表面上是他们的研究对象"(Knight 2003:10)。奈特的如下批评更为尖锐:"文学研究明显地游离了文学本身,偏向了文学的理论化,以致我们要问,如今的理论家……究竟是文学的朋友呢,还是敌人?我们这样提问,似乎并没有无礼"(Knight 2003:16)。奈特此处所说的,就是我们在上文中所说的文学批评的异化现象,这种现象在布雷德伯里(Malcolm Bradbury)那里也遭到过抨击:"文学批评已经远离公共领域,躲进了大学的象牙塔,在那里变成了另一种东西。它不喜欢原先意义上的评判工作,结果变成了现在的文学理论:作为文学的一种变体,它一味迎合各种时髦的意识形态,热衷于拉山头、占地盘,充斥着专业话语"(Bradbury 1999:52)。这种敌视文学本身的"文学批评"或"文学理论"若要追根溯源,可以在柏拉图那里找到根子。犹如美国弗吉尼亚大学教授埃德蒙森(Mark Edmundson)所说,"文学批评始于要文学消失的意愿,柏拉图反对荷马的主要理由就是荷马本人的存在"(Edmundson 1995:1)。当然,柏拉图当初的激进主张并未阻遏文学的生长,所以在随后的千百年里,文学与文学批评相辅相成、共同繁荣的情形才有目共睹,但是在近来四五十年里,"柏拉图的传人们再次变得强势了"(Knight 2003:16),后果便是前文揭示的"理论繁荣"。用克莫德的话来说,过去几十年可以视作"文学理论全盛期"(the efflorescence of literary theory),可是"这文学理论全盛期似乎势必意味着对'文学'的冷漠乃至敌视"(Kermode 1989:5),或者说"理论正在淹没文学"(Kermode 1989:7)。那么,这对文学爱好者/读者尤其是普通读者又意味着什么呢?

理论淹没了文学,也就淹没了广大读者,拒后者于千里之外。奈特有一句名言:"理论不仅打败了普通读者,而且打败了文学"(Knight 2003:19)。这句话也可以倒过来说:理论打败了文学,因而打败了普通读者。更具体地说,"人们实际阅读的文学并非评论家们所讨论的文学"(Kermode,1989:52)。既然如此,普通读者听不懂理论教授,也就在所难免了。倘若理论教授们意识到其中的问题,那情形还不至于太糟糕,可是"评论家和小说与小说爱好者之间的沟壑成为既成事实,无人想去弥合","至于普通读者为何跟我们(指专业读者/批评家)格格不入,则无人想要弄明白"(Kermode 2003:55—56)。更令人担忧的是,上述鸿沟甚至横亘在许多大学的文学课堂上,横亘在学生与教授之间,前者一心想读懂文学原著,而后者则一味地沉迷于高深理论。对于这一现象背后的原因,奈特有过一针见血的分析:

> 理论并非简单地需要读者，它需要的是弟子，而寻找弟子的最佳场所就是专业院校。一个典型的例子就是保罗·德曼（Paul de Man），他把教室变成了培养弟子的皮氏培养皿①……凡是弟子，都不必把千百个文本读上千百遍，而只需要某种便携式理论，它不管应用于哪个文本，都同样灵验，这正好跟德曼的解构主义理论相契合，后者声称每个文本都是同一个文本的变体。（Knight 2003：43）

也就是说，在德曼式课堂上，教授们从未担负起培养文学读者的使命。在这种情况下，还能指望他们担负起对课堂外普通读者应尽的责任吗？上述情形并非不可逆转，但是若要实现逆转，就要从根子上解决问题。就现当代而言，理论打败文学，把普通读者拒之门外，这一现象背后的最大推手是去经典化思潮。

四、去经典化：文学批评异化的根源

文学批评发生变异，其根源在于去经典化思潮。前文提到，文学批评的宗旨之一是为普通读者服务，这意味着批评家有义务就文学经典价值与普通读者达成共识。一方面，批评家有责任用经典作品去引导普通读者；另一方面，普通读者的取舍是检验经典性的最高标准，一部作品能否成为经典，最终要看它能否超越时空，在不同时空里为广大读者所接受。然而，自20世纪中叶以来，经典竟成了问题：不仅给经典下定义成了问题，而且经典这一名称的魅力，尤其是对普通读者的魅力，也成了问题。背后，是一股十分强大的世界性潮流，即把所有的经典作品政治化、去经典化、去审美化。更具体地说，诸多打着各种"理论"旗号的学术流派都加入了一场针对文学经典的"颠覆性狂欢"。这股潮流的推动者操持着颇能蛊惑人心的理由："经典作家的声誉并非来自作品内在的优点，而是来自复杂的外部环境。在环境复合体的作用下，一些文本得以进入人们的视野，进而维持自己的优越地位"（Tompkins 1985：39）。从这一理由派生出来的观点可谓五花八门，可是万变不离其宗，其基本立场都可以归结为

---

① 皮氏培养皿（petri dish）是实验室用于培养细菌的小玻璃盆，以德国微生物学家 Julius Petri（1852—1922）命名。

"权力""利益"和"意识形态"这几个关键词。按照这些关键词的逻辑推理，经典之所以是经典，无非是外部利益集团使然，是意识形态使然，是把持话语权的学术界权威、评奖机构、出版商和新闻媒体使然。换言之，经典"都被当作了父权社会、精英统治或殖民帝国中的那些压迫人的意识形态的代表"（Zhang 2010：15）。顺着这一逻辑，揭示经典背后的意识形态就成了文学批评的主要任务，而普通读者最关心的经典本身及其内在审美维度则淡出了文学批评家的视野；其连带后果就是普通读者的淡出，或者说批评家已无暇对普通读者言说，甚至根本不屑于对普通读者言说了。

更糟糕的是，热衷于"理论"的教授、批评家们不但无视上述情形，还变本加厉，为之辩护。例如，卡勒在坦承很少有人能读懂当代文论之际，竟认为"事情本来就应该如此"（qtd. in Kermode 1989：8）。在卡勒看来，值得从事的文学批评应该有"新型的研究对象、新型的文本"，而后者都有一个特点，即晦涩！因此，他大张旗鼓地宣扬"晦涩的长处"（the virtues of obscurity），还批评有些教师怂恿学生屈服于"奉清晰为圭臬的意识形态"（the ideology of lucidity；同上），公然宣扬晦涩是正道，而清晰则成了邪道。既然晦涩成了正道，那么普通读者无疑被关在了门外。

文学批评如此变质引起不少诟病，卡勒于是在《框定符号：批评及其机构》的第一章第一段里辩护道："许多人声称文学批评已不再是一种谦卑的、审慎而明智的活动，不再为文学及其读者服务，而变得张扬和混乱，变成了不同理论相互角逐的场域，这些理论常常玄而又玄，以致人们为此付出了太多的精力，而这些精力原本是可以用于文学本身的"（Culler 1988：3）。乍一看去，卡勒似乎是要对"玄而又玄的理论"（abstruse theories）提出批评，然而情形恰恰相反，他是要为其辩护。在《框定符号》的前言中，他开宗明义地见证了"理论"的繁荣，或者说文学批评的一个"质变"，并为此欢欣鼓舞。更具体地说，文学批评的变化以20世纪80年代为界，此前"以进口理论模式为主业"（in the business of importing theoretical models），而此后则变成了"理论话语的出口行业"（an exporter of theoretical discourse）：

在20世纪60年代和70年代，文学研究似乎以进口理论模式为主业，主要从语言学、人类学、哲学、观念史和精神分析等领域引进问题和视角。然而，到了20世纪80年代，似乎旧貌已换新颜：一方面，文学研究已经变成理论话语的出口行业，这是因为法律、人类学、艺术史乃至精神分析等其他领域都注意到了文学批评家们所说的"理论"及其进展，并转而从中汲取动力；另一方面，文学批评家们自己也因跨学科研究而变得自信了、老练了，他们笔下的现象越来越多地超越了传统文学研究的边界。（Culler 1988：xii）

批评理论带有跨学科特色，这本来是值得大力提倡的，但是卡勒所提倡的并非仅仅跨学科，而是一直要"跨"到文学批评变质为止，这又从何说起呢？

这还得从卡勒的一个基本观点说起。他笃信文学批评因其"跨学科特性"（interdisciplinarity）而变成了"一种新型的、扩张了的修辞学"，或者说"一门关于文本结构和策略的学问，以及关于它们跟表意系统（systems of signification）和人类主体之间关系的学问；在这门学问中，文学起着核心作用，不过其重要性在于它跟各种人类经验息息相关，跟表意（signification）方面的问题息息相关"（Culler 1988：17）。卡勒紧接着还引用了美国学者费德勒（Leslie Fiedler）的一句话："文学批评总是在变成'另一种东西'，其原因很简单——文学永远是'另一种东西'"（qtd. in Culler 1988：17）。那么，这"另一种东西"究竟是什么东西呢？卡勒自有其解说。他先援引了罗蒂（Richard Rorty）的下面这段话："从歌德、麦考莱、卡莱尔和爱默生的时代起，一种文类开始形成；它既不是对文学作品的评价，也不是观念史；既不是道德哲学，也不是社会预言，而是所有这些东西的混合，形成了一种新文类"（new genre；Rorty 66）。然后，他接过了罗蒂的"新文类"一词，给出了自己的解说："对于这一新文类，最方便的称呼就是'理论'。如今，'理论'这一绰号已被用来指称那些挑战并重新定位思想的著作，它们表面上属于文学领域，但是由于它们在分析语言、思想、历史或文化时提供了关于表意的新解释，而且具有说服力，因此它们实际上大显身手的地方是那些文学以外的领域"（Culler 1988：15）。至此，卡勒所青睐的"另一种东西"已经水落石出：它原来是在"文学以外"。

需要指出的是，卡勒实际上使用了瞒天过海的伎俩，把罗蒂和费德勒所说的"新文类"和"另一种东西"变本加厉地改变性质。此"另一种"非彼"另一种"是也，因为罗蒂也好，费德勒也好，并没有排斥文学本身，都没有排斥对文学作品做全方位的评价。我们仔细揣摩费德勒的话就会发现，他所说的"另一种东西"永远是以文学为前提的；既然文学永远是"另一种东西"，那么这"另一种东西"就永远离不开文学，二者互为表里，可谓二律背反。也就是说，费德勒无非是说文学既是文学，又是另一种东西。同样，当罗蒂强调"新文类"时，他强调的只是"所有这些东西的混合"，其中仍然包含着文学，尤其是包含"对文学作品的评价"。然而，到了卡勒那里，文学已不复文学，批评亦不复批评；文学失去了经典性，而文学批评则变成了冠以"理论"的另类；批评家们不再对文学作品做全方位的评价，更无须就作品的经典性达成共识，而只要一根筋地抛开作品，挖掘其背后的意识形态即可。更透彻地说，卡勒看到的不是文学作品，而只是作品中的"表意逻辑"（the logic of signification）：在本文上一段的两处引文中，卡勒就一连三次使用了"表意"一词，而"表意逻辑""表意系统"和"表意机制"（mechanisms of signification）等也都高频率地出现在《框定符号》一书中。挖掘"表意逻辑"，就是挖掘所谓的"意识形态"。卡勒及其追随者发现，一旦逮住了"意识形态"，他们的"理论"就无往而不胜。用克莫德的话说，"理论"其实只有一个法宝，即"格外擅长发现暗藏的意识形态"，或者说"总能在任何经典里发现某种骇人的审美意识形态"，因此，只要预先认定经典窃据了"宝典"——即"作为储存已知真理和通行价值观的宝典"——这一位置，"理论"就"总能有所斩获"（Kermode 1989：13）。可想而知，如此一味追踪暗藏意识形态的"理论"及其批评活动，岂能把普通读者放在眼里？事实上，卡勒有过许多对普通读者表示不屑的言论，其中最直白的就是把普通读者打入"传奇"一类。他曾带着赞许的口吻援引詹森斯（G. A. M. Janssens）的话："（一些书评）直率地服务于学术受众，而不是传奇中的'普通读者'"（qtd. in Culler 1988：10）。言下之意，普通读者只是不登学术大雅之堂的虚幻传奇，可谓根本就不存在，当然可以忽略不计。

总之，普通读者之所以不受待见，是去经典化思潮作祟的缘故。因此，要重塑普通读者，就要从辨明去经典化思潮的要害做起。

五、揭露去经典化潮流的谬误：重塑普通读者的必由之路

既然不对去经典化潮流作出切实的回应就不可能重现普通读者的亲切身影，那么去经典化究竟谬误在什么地方呢？去经典化思潮的要害可以概述为"简化两步法"：第一步，把经典的形成过程简化为"经典化"；第二步，把"经典化"进一步简化为权力运作的结果。这第一步简化法，其实是偷梁换柱的诡辩，即把"经典化"和"经典性"混为一谈。须知经典化是经典形成的外在因素，而经典性则是其内在因素，两者缺一不可，这本来是常识，可是在去经典化旋风的肆虐之下，经典性竟遭横扫，而经典化则摇身一变，成了经典形成的唯一因素。如美国学者科尔巴斯（E. Dean Kolbas）所说，所有鼓吹去经典化的人有一个共同问题，即混淆经典化和经典性这两个概念——前者常被说成"与社会现状沆瀣一气的机构化过程"，而后者则指"对一部作品的认知内容的审美判断"（Kolbas 2001: 106—11）。诚然，一部经典的登堂入室，有其外在因素，但是归根结底，是其内在因素使然，是其审美维度使然。可是去经典化的始作俑者在操作经典化的第一步时，就排除了经典的内在实质。

上述第二步简化法反过头来又拿经典化本身——即经典形成的外在因素——开刀。经典化本是一个十分复杂的过程，但是经由卡勒等人之手，它被简化成了权力运作，因而被等同于上文所说"与社会现状沆瀣一气的机构化过程"。不可否认，任何一部蜚声文坛的作品，都可能得益于经典化过程中的诸多环节和机缘，甚至会掺杂意识形态和权力话语等因素。然而，在导致经典形成的外在因素中，难道只有权力、利益和意识形态吗？显然不是这样。如今的所谓"理论"，只要涉及经典化，就把目光局限于学术界权威、评奖机构、出版商和新闻媒体，殊不知这些只构成了文学受众的少数，而在把持话语权的利益集团之外，还存在着广大普通读者。少数"权威"的裁定，纵然能使一个作家声名显赫，也只能昙花一现，而真正的经典须能超越时空，直抵广大读者的心灵。就如约翰逊和伍尔夫当年所说，诗坛桂冠由谁摘得，最终取决于普通读者。

上述两步简化法都把普通读者排除在了文学批评活动之外：第一步排斥经典性，排斥文学的审美维度，这对普通读者来说无异于釜底抽薪——普通读者最

敏感、最有发言权的地方正是审美维度；第二步干脆剥夺了普通读者对于经典化的参与权。有鉴于此，我们有必要进一步为经典性辩护，并充分审视普通读者在经典化过程中的作用。

要为经典性辩护，就要先考察那些否定经典性的人拿出了什么理由。否认经典性，否认文学具有独特的内在本质，否认它的审美维度，把它等同于一般的"写作形式"或任何非文学文献，这一观点凭借着一个极具煽动性的理由，即"平等"和"民主"。用新历史主义代表人物格林布拉特（Stephen Jay Greenblatt）的话说，"社会能量的循环"（the circulation of social energy）给了所有文本"平等的认知潜能"（equal cognitive potential）（Greenblatt 1988: 129—163）。素有"文学社会学旗手"之称的米尔纳（Andrew Milner）说得更为直露：要人们相信某些作品比另一些作品更"牢固地拥有'根本的审美价值'，已经变得不可能了"，因此人们"应该完全地放弃经典这一概念"（Milner 1996: 178）。这些理由和观点反映在阅读策略上，就表现为对所谓"文本性"（textuality）的倚重，而把审美维度一笔勾销，似乎所有的书写文本都可以统一在文本性的基础上。格林布拉特用以解读莎士比亚戏剧的策略就是一例。他在解读《暴风雨》时，无视该剧的审美维度，一味地强调该剧的档案功能或"记忆"功能，即帮助后世记住"在伊丽莎白一世时代和詹姆士一世时代的英国社会，处于经济生活和意识形态中心的是……劳动者和统治者之间的区别"（Greenblatt 1988: 149）。针对这种阅读策略，科尔巴斯曾做出如下批评："把《暴风雨》这类经典文艺作品的内容简化为纯粹的文本性，无异于把人类的痛苦也仅仅当作往昔的文本现象，好像这些作品除了档案价值之外，对现今人类社会再无意义可言。这样做不仅是违背良心的，而且危害了文学艺术描述愿景的功能——文学艺术能展望摆脱了不公和残酷现象的未来社会，而这样的愿景非依靠想象力不可"（Kolbas 2001: 115）。科尔巴斯的这一批评可谓切中肯綮。不过，他对经典性/形式审美特征的强调，只停留在理论层面，未能落实于具体作品的分析。因此，我们不妨以当代美国作家厄普代克（John Updike）为例，看一下经典作品是如何以形式审美特征取胜的。

厄普代克曾两度获得普利策奖，但是关于获奖原因，却仁者见仁，智者见智。无论是赞扬他的人还是批评他的人，往往专注于某个思想主题，而置审美维度于不顾。例如，对他的抨击主要集中在他对"性"主题的关注上，而对他的褒奖则往往立足于他对社会历史的记载——他的"兔子四部曲"展示了两次世界大战以后四十多年的历史画卷，获得了"美国断代史"的美称。然而，即便厄普代克所选的都是重大思想主题，他的取胜之道仍然是审美维度，否则他至多产出了优秀的社会历史文献，而非文学经典。他至今被人们津津乐道，是因为其作品具有超越时空的审美维度。更具体地说，他的作品常以顿悟（epiphany）取胜，常能超越个体经验和局部人生，进而上升到对整个人生真谛的领悟；而这种顿悟又离不开情节、人物、比喻、象征和叙事结构的妙用，离不开时间和场景中的细节，如姿态、声响和色彩，等等。仅以他的《兔子，跑吧》（*Rabbit Run*）为例。小说主人公哈利（绰号为"兔子"）离家出走，牧师埃克里斯借邀他打高尔夫球的机会，劝他回到妻子身边，遭到了他的拒绝。埃克里斯不依不饶，连珠炮似地追问原因，并极尽挖苦之能事，逼得哈利十分尴尬，无言以对，于是干脆憋足气，使劲儿抡起了高尔夫球棒，想趁早收场脱身；不料就在击球后的一刹那，他竟然找到了答案：

> 他十分利索地把球棒挥过肩膀，然后朝球打下去。撞击的声音空洞、单调。他还从来没听到过这样的声音。由于他双臂用力较猛，头也顺势抬得很高。只见那只球悬在老远的地方，其宛若月光的银灰色背后衬着一片片美丽的雨云，蓝幽幽的。那是他外祖父的颜色，浓浓地抹在东方的天际。球沿着一条笔直的线渐渐远去。一下打去，这球恰如流星赶月，眨眼间变成一个小白点儿。球迟疑了一下，"兔子"以为它要消失了，但是他上了当。那一迟疑只是一种依托，球在此基础上又作了最后一跳。就在它落下消失之前，那球分明是带着啜泣最后咬了太空一口。"就是这个！"他大叫起来，然后喜笑颜开地转过身来，对埃克里斯重复了一句："就是这个。"
>（厄普代克 1987：186—187）

这是一段诗意的描写。打高尔夫球原本是一桩很普通的事情，但是就在那平平常常的一挥、一击、一看之间，哈利经历了一次顿悟：他生活中所缺少的正是那种流星赶月般的激情和壮美。读者也随之感悟到了小说的基本含义："兔子"之所以要跑，要离家出走，是因为他想逃离人世间的平庸。高尔夫球虽小，但是它运行的姿态、声响、色彩以及它与太空融为一体的情景却蔚为壮观。此时，哈利的心灵已经得到了升华，他的胸襟气韵分明已经贯注于天地万物之间。也就是说，此时此刻的哈利暂时超越了个体生命，而读者亦可借对这一境界的观照而忘却小我，进入人和万物一体同仁的状态，形成物我的回响交流。

上述顿悟的产生，以及诗意的构成，离不开喻象的巧用。一只普通的高尔夫球，竟然带有"宛若月光的银灰色"，而且"如流星赶月"，甚至"带着啜泣最后咬了太空一口"。此处的比喻，尤其是通感①，分明是一种诗性语言。在上引文字中，不光是那只小小的高尔夫球，而且整个打高尔夫球的场景原本都很寻常，但是经由厄普代克的生花妙笔，顿时焕发出永恒之美的光辉，或如当年乔伊斯笔下的斯提芬所说："最寻常的事物似乎辐射出了灵光"（殷企平 1995：90—104）。这种情形在那些毫无审美情趣的文献资料里是根本不可能发生的，而在厄普代克的笔下却频频发生。熟悉《兔子，跑吧》的读者，首先会被它的文字魅力所吸引，被它那跌宕起伏的情节、鲜活的人物形象和生动的喻象所吸引，被它幽默的语言风格所打动，并因此而产生审美愉悦。这就应了克莫德关于经典的前提一说："经典的必要前提是它能给人愉悦，尽管这一前提不那么明显"（Kermode 2004：20）。正是因为有了这种审美愉悦，《兔子，跑吧》的读者才能顺势寻找故事背后的重大意义："兔子"哈利的奔跑不仅隐含对美国彼时彼地社会的关切，而且隐喻对生命意义的追问，跟赶月的流星、宛若月球并融入太空的高尔夫球形成了交响，实现了时空的穿越，至今仍在对人类——不仅仅是美国人——言说着。

以上分析表明，经典性的内涵十分丰富，而在这诸多内涵中，审美愉悦是先决条件。这本来是一个简单的道理，可是在去经典化风潮的影响下，简单道理变得复杂了，因此需要重正视听。关于这一点，张隆溪曾一语中的："道理本来很简单：如果你在文学中找不到愉悦，就不要假装是文学评论家。但是在如今的特殊时期，对审美愉悦的强调显得尤其重要，因为现在文学作品经常被当作社会、历史或政治的文档使用，借以批判某些话题，或达到某些目的"（Zhang

---

① "带着啜泣最后咬了太空一口"那一句的英文原文是 with a kind of visible sob takes a last bite of space。Visible sob 显然是一种通感或联觉（synaesthesia）："啜泣"（sob）原本诉诸听觉，此处却诉诸视觉。

2010：17）。我们还须补充一句：审美愉悦的试金石恰恰是普通读者；如果一部作品能在不同时代、不同国度的普通读者心中唤起审美愉悦，那么它就满足了经典性的先决条件。让我们重温一下伍尔夫的名言："（普通读者）从事阅读，与其是为了传授知识或纠正他人的见解，不如说是为了自己的愉悦。"从这一角度看，那些得不到审美愉悦，却又藐视善于获得审美愉悦的普通读者的高深理论家们，无非是假冒的文学评论家而已。

至于普通读者在经典化过程中的作用，一个关于狄更斯的例子就颇能说明问题。在小说《老古玩店》（*The Old Curiosity Shop*）临近杀青时，狄更斯每天都要收到读者的来信，不仅来自国内，而且来自国外，尤其是美国。更值得注意的是，这些信大都出自长满老茧、晒得乌黑的劳动人民之手。他们对小说女主人公耐儿的故事反响之热烈，从狄更斯于1842年在波士顿的一次演讲中可见一斑：

> 这位早年夭折的小女孩儿在大西洋彼岸竟引起了如此浓厚的兴趣，这使我喜不自胜，禁不住要表达这一愉悦之情。在英格兰时，我曾经收到许多来自远在地球西边的美国的信件，写信者都居住在沼泽地带和密林深处的那些小木屋里。许多被斧头和铁锹磨炼得非常坚定的手，许多被夏日骄阳晒黑了的手，拿起了笔杆子，向我叙述一个个有关普通人家悲欢离合的小故事。我不无自豪地告诉你们：这些叙述总是伴随着对我的那个小小故事的兴趣，或是流露出从中得到的安慰或欢乐的情感……许多母亲——我现在已不是成个成双地数她们，而是成十成打地数她们——也同样给我写信……（狄更斯2015：18）

透过这字里行间，我们看到的是小说家和普通读者之间一种天然而健康的关系，一种真诚的、双向的心灵交流。只有在这种双向、健康、大范围的互动关系中，小说才能最大限度地发挥它强大的生命力，才能真正地登上经典宝座。与之相比，那些商业炒作以及权威机构的"盖棺论定"又能算什么呢？

六、结语

普通读者的消失，是去经典化思潮作祟的缘故。因此，要重塑普通读者，就要从彻底揭露去经典化思潮的谬误做起。去经典化的要害有二：其一，把经典性和经典化混为一谈，进而排斥经典性，排斥文学审美维度，这对普通读者来说无异于釜底抽薪；其二，剥夺普通读者对于经典化的参与权，从而否认普通读者是检验经典性的最高标准。有鉴于此，我们完全有必要维护经典性的神圣地位，重申普通读者在经典化过程中的重要性。经典性的内涵十分丰富，而在这诸多内涵中，审美愉悦是先决条件。作为审美愉悦的试金石，普通读者在文学批评活动中的地位不可小觑。在文学批评异化日益严重的今天，还普通读者应有的地位，已成当务之急。

参考文献

[1] Abrams M H. *A Glossary of Literary Terms*. 7th ed. [M]. Fort Worth: Harcourt, 1999.

[2] Bradbury M. A Stern and Righteous Reader [J]. *New Statesman*, 12 Feb. 1999: 52–53.

[3] Buurma R and Heffernan L. The Common Reader and the Archival Classroom [J]. *New Literary History* 2012, 43 (1): 113–135.

[4] Culler J. *Framing the Sign: Criticism and Its Institutions* [M]. Norman: Oklahoma UP, 1988.

[5] Edmundson M. *Literature against Philosophy, Plato to Derrida: A Defence of Poetry* [M]. Cambridge: Cambridge UP, 1995.

[6] Greenblatt S. *Shakespearean Negotiations: The Circulation of Social Energy in Renaissance in England* [M]. Berkeley: U of California P, 1988.

[7] Johnson S. "Life of Gray." *The Six Lives from Johnson's "Lives of the Poets" with Macaulay's "Life of Johnson."* Ed. Matthew Arnold [M]. London: Macmillan, 1878. 455–466.

[8] Kaplan C. and Rose E C. *The Canon and the Common Reader* [M]. Knoxville: U of Tennessee P, 1990.

[9] Kermode F. *An Appetite for Poetry* [M]. Cambridge: Harvard UP, 1989.

[10] Kermode F. *Pleasure and Change: The Aesthetics of Canon* [M]. Oxford:

Oxford UP, 2004.

[11] Knight C. *Uncommon Readers: Denis Donoghue, Frank Kermode, George Steiner, and the Tradition of the Common Reader* [M]. Toronto: U of Toronto P, 2003.

[12] Kolbas E D. *Critical Theory and the Literary Canon* [M]. Boulder: Westview, 2001.

[13] Milner A. *Literature, Culture and Society* [M]. London: UCLA P, 1996.

[14] Rorty R. *The Consequences of Pragmatism* [M]. Minneapolis: Minnesota UP, 1982.

[15] Tompkins J. *Sensational Designs: The Cultural Work of American Fiction 1790 – 1860* [M]. Oxford: Oxford UP, 1985.

[16] Woolf V. *The Common Reader* [M]. Shanghai: Shanghai World, 2010.

[17] Zhang, Longxi. Valeurs, Défense, Crise et Avenir des Sciences Humaines [J]. *Diogène* 2010, 1 – 2: 6 – 23.

[18] 狄更斯. 狄更斯演讲集 [M]. 殷企平等, 译. 上海：三联书店, 2015. [Dickens, Charles. *Collected Speeches by Charles Dickens*. Trans. Yin Qiping et al. Shanghai: SDX Joint, 2015.]

[19] 厄普代克. 兔子, 跑吧 [M]. 李力, 李欣, 译. 重庆：重庆出版社, 1987. [Updike, John. *Rabbit Run*. Trans. Li Li and Li Xin. Chongqing: Chongqing, 1987.]

[20] 格雷. 墓畔哀歌. 载《英诗金库：英语最佳歌谣及抒情诗之金库 [M]. 卞之琳, 译. 成都：四川人民出版社, 1989. [Gray, Thomas. "Elegy Written in a Country Churchyard." *A Golden Treasure-House of English Poetry: Best English Lyrical Ballads and Poems*. Trans. Bian Zhilin. Chengdu: Sichuan People's, 1989.]

[21] 殷企平. 小说艺术管窥 [M]. 天津：百花文艺出版社, 1995. [Yin, Qiping. *Glimpses into the Art of Fiction*. Tianjin: Baihua Literature and Art, 1995.]

（本文原载于《外国文学》2019 年第 6 期）

西方文论关键词：愉悦[*]

一、略说

"愉悦"（pleasure）作为西方文论的核心概念，可谓源远流长。自柏拉图以降，它的内涵、外延一直在演变，但是最剧烈的演变发生在20世纪。曾几何时，"愉悦"已不再愉悦，甚至导致愉悦话题变成了雷区，其原因大致有二：一是政治、经济等社会历史原因，如资本主义商品化浪潮下的"愉悦消费"；二是在某些"前卫"理论的作用下，"快感"取代"美感"，造成了空前困惑。

有鉴于此，我们有必要重拾愉悦话题，重估其不凡价值。要做到这一点，就要认识它的三个命题：1）何为愉悦？2）为何愉悦？3）愉悦何为？这些命题你中有我，我中有你，对其间的复杂性和相关性不可不察。

愉悦究竟为何物？就西方文论而言，最富魅力的相关学说来自康德。他把"普遍可传达的愉快感"等同于"美"，强调愉悦"不带任何利害"的特点（康德2017：29—42），此论看似在宣扬愉悦的"百无一用"，但实际上为后来华兹华斯等人倡导愉悦的重要性和深广功用铺平了道路。从华兹华斯到克默德，我们可以看到一条思想脉络，即强调愉悦关乎人类尊严，关乎生命的奥秘。从亚里士多德到马尔库塞、詹明信和伊格尔顿，我们看到了一个传统，即不断拓宽

---

[*] 基金项目：国家社科基金重大项目"西方文论核心概念考绎"（19ZDA291）；浙江省哲学社会科学重点研究基地"文艺批评研究院"资助（wypps2020002）。

并深化愉悦功用的努力。这一传统宛若波澜壮阔的大河，在奔腾途中泛起无数浪花，其中最璀璨的有两朵，即启蒙运动旨在提升趣味的课题，以及西方马克思主义者把愉悦与人类解放相结合的理想。在浪花深处，我们分明听到了一首交响曲，它的主旋律为共享愉悦，它的母题则是共同体。

二、综述

（一）"愉悦"不再愉悦

19世纪末，王尔德（Oscar Wilde, 1854—1900）曾语出惊人："愉悦是唯一值得进行理论探讨的东西"（Wilde 2006: 67）。这话可以看作一种预言："愉悦"概念在其后一百多年里，会经历内涵与外延的剧变，以致越来越不那么令人愉快了。这种变化，主要来自两方面的压力，一是社会变化导致普通人对愉悦的理解发生质变；二是理论家们不断"创新"，使得原本充满愉悦的文学批评活动变得越来越严肃，甚至枯燥无味，不仅让普通读者望而生畏，而且使许多文学课堂/课本起而放逐了愉悦女神（殷企平 2019: 52—53）。这一现象不无反讽意味：文学及其探究本应给人愉悦，可是经很多"专家"操弄竟走向了反面。20世纪末，西英格兰大学教授玛丽·罗伯茨（Marie Mulvey Roberts）指出，愉悦概念"被它自己沉重的复杂内涵给拖累了"，"就像我们如今都十分清楚的那样，愉悦经常是一个令人不安的话题，我们必须对它这样发问：它在环境意义上安全吗？它在道德意义上能被接受吗？它所含的思想健康吗？它是否政治正确？"（Roberts 1996: ix）这类问题暴露了不少人这样一种心态：如今愉悦话题俨然雷池，论者须战战兢兢避免逾越。

早在罗伯茨之前，罗兰·巴特（Roland Barthes, 1915—1980）就曾风趣地形容愉悦话题呈现的困境："只要谈及文本的愉悦，就会有两个警察伺机扑向你：一个是政治警察，另一个是精神分析警察；前者视愉悦为一种阶级观念，而后者则视其为幻觉。不管是哪一种情形，愉悦都会被判定为无用乃至有罪：不是无聊，就是虚幻"（Barthes 1975: 57）。有意思的是，虽然巴特此处揶揄了"精神分析警察"和"政治警察"，但是他本人却是从精神分析和政治学角度对愉悦概念进行改造的最大推动者，而且也正是他给关注愉悦的文学研究者带来了莫大困惑。他的名作《文本的愉悦》(Le plaisir du texte, 1973)就是最好的例子。首先是把写作和阅读的愉悦跟性高潮带来的愉悦相类比——正如许多学者已经指出的那样,他所说的 plaisir(愉悦、快乐)更多地意指一种 jouissance(性快感),这就彻底颠覆了传统意义上的审美愉悦之说。在一次接受访谈时,巴特简洁地说明了"文之悦"(笔者按:"文本的愉悦"的另一种译法)的蕴意,并且直言自己表述的愉悦"不具审美价值",而"纯粹是就精神分析的意义立论的"。① 据此,可以说,巴特"伙同"弗洛伊德抽空了愉悦概念的审美维度,这不啻是对后者的空前颠覆。

其次,巴特还在政治层面对愉悦概念进行了改造。关于这一点,詹明信(Fredric Jameson, 1934—)曾经在《愉悦:一个政治问题》("PLEASURE: A Political Issue", 1983)一文中说得很明白。詹氏指出,对巴特来说,"'愉悦'具有作为政治标语的价值"(Jameson 1983: 8)。之所以这么说,是因为"《文本的愉悦》可以看作他重又回到了早年在《零度写作》(1953)中全神贯注的问题",即如何使文学语言摆脱阶级局限性的问题(Jameson 1983: 8)。按照詹氏的分析,《零度写作》(Le degré zéro de l'écriture)重拾了萨特(Jean-Paul Sartre, 1905—1980)《何为文学》("Qu'estce que la littérature?", 1948)中的话题:巴特跟萨特一样,都认为历史充满了血腥的罪恶,而由于以往所有文学语言都必然局限于相关群体或阶层,因此所有文学实践"都象征着对阶级暴力的许可"(Jameson 1983: 8)。不过,巴特和萨特解决上述问题的方法不同:萨特寄希望于"作为史上最后一个阶级的无产阶级",进而开启"史上首次出现真正普世大众的可能性",而巴特则希望借助他的"零度写作"——即摆脱所有意识形态的写作——来"消灭文学作品中的所有阶级印记:这是一种白色或漂白了的写作,一种没有阶级倾向的乌托邦实践"(Jameson 1983: 8)。事实上,巴特在《文本的愉悦》中把"零度写作"推向了极致,他不仅自己纵情于"性高潮般的文字游戏",而且"教导我们用身体阅读,而且还经常用身体写作"(Jameson 1983: 5—9)。对于此,詹氏持十分矛盾的态度。他一方面批评上述主张和实践是一种"自我沉溺",并称其为"巴特式享乐主义"(Barthesian hedonism),另一方面又

---

① 转引自屠友祥,"中译本弁言",《文之悦》,上海:上海人民出版社,2009 年,第 4 页。

肯定了巴特作品的政治价值："巴特论说文的巨大优点是让感官愉悦的体验重获了某种政治象征价值，使得人们无法卒读那些肉体狂欢式的文字，除非把后者解读为对政治和历史窘境的回应"（Jameson 1983：9）。詹氏的意思是，巴特式写作/阅读方式虽然是对政治、历史现实（即现存文学语言全都有阶级局限性的现实）的逃避，却也是对这些现实的一种回应。确实，巴特意在"削弱在语句乃至文学机构中占统治地位的意识形态"，"这一'削弱'本身被颂扬为革命行动"（Jameson 1983：8）。然而，巴特的"革命行动"能够奏效吗？他在无限拔高肉体快感的同时，彻底放逐了美感（亦即审美愉悦），这其实是一种悲哀（下文我们还会回到这一话题）。

但是，不管怎么说，巴特毕竟是有贡献的。他至少使更多人看清了上文提及的政治历史现实。不过，关于这一现实，詹明信其实比巴特看得更清楚。他发现在后工业社会——詹氏称之为"晚期资本主义"（late capitalism）社会——中，"许多东西都变了，包括愉悦本身及其意象和功能"（Jameson 1983：4）。这一变化的明显标志是人们已经无法区分真正的愉悦（pleasure）和纯粹的消遣（diversion），其最大原因则是冲击一切的商品化浪潮，就连人类最私密的愉悦也被商品化了："不管是两性交媾，还是阅读活动，这些先前私密的愉悦体验都被打上了消费品烙印，变成了商品形式，而人的空闲时间也堕落成了商品，却美其名曰'休闲'"（Jameson 1983：3）。透过愉悦/休闲商品化的现象，詹氏还看到了"晚期资本主义的扩张"和"文化产业"的运作：

> 我们的分析有赖于对晚期资本主义惊人扩张的全面而系统的描述。这种扩张如今有多种改头换面的方式，或表现为"文化产业"，或表现为"意识产业"。在资本主义制度内部，原先还有两块保留着前资本主义自然特色的飞地，可是其中的一块——即人的无意识——如今也被侵犯了。（另一块飞地是第三世界的前资本主义农业和乡村文化）。(Jameson 1983：3)

詹氏的分析可谓鞭辟入里：资本主义扩张不仅侵蚀了人类精神领域，而且侵蚀了这精神领域中最隐秘的部分，即无意识领域。正是在这样的背景下，愉悦成了一种"商品癖"（a commodity fix），詹氏为此发出了惊呼："除了是一种商品癖以外，愉悦什么都不是，该怎样对付这种毒瘾呢？"（Jameson 1983：3）更可怕的是，人们并未意识到这类无意识的毒瘾，而是更多地在从事"有意识的'愉悦'消费，詹氏称其为"虚假意识"（false consciousness）（Jameson 1983：3）。显然，当"愉悦"沦为虚假意识时，它已不再是愉悦了。

　　我们以上讨论了"愉悦"异化的两大原因，一是政治、经济等历史原因（如资本主义的扩张、商品化浪潮的冲击），二是学界某些理论思潮的误导（如弗洛伊德、巴特等人用"快感"取代"美感"）。造成"愉悦"异化的原因其实还有很多，鉴于篇幅有限，我们只能有所取舍。即使这样，还有一个原因不能不提，那就是愉悦新形式的无序增殖，以致学者们突然有一天发现，愉悦形式竟然穷尽了，或者说再也找不到"新愉悦"（new pleasures）了，这在福柯（Michel Foucault, 1926—1984）的如下论述中可见一斑：

> 经常有人说我们已经不能想象任何新愉悦了。我们至少发明了一种不同的愉悦：因愉悦真相而带来的愉悦，了解那种真相的愉悦，发现并揭示它的愉悦，为洞见并辨认它而入迷，而且用它来让别人着迷，或私下吐露这种真相，或通过循循善诱，当众探明真相，这些都会让人乐此不疲——这是一种特别的愉悦，一种能真正谈论愉悦的愉悦。（Foucault 1990：65）（殷企平译）

福柯还把这种"新愉悦"称为"分析的愉悦"（pleasure of analysis）（66）。就以上引文的表述来看，我们不妨把它称作"元愉悦"，即关于愉悦的愉悦。愉悦本身已经难以产生，于是人们通过讨论或分析愉悦来获得一种所谓的"新愉悦"，这其实是无可奈何，确切地说是一种悲哀。

　　福柯所说的"新愉悦"也好，巴特提倡的"文之悦"也好，都反映了愉悦的缺失。凡是有实际体验的人都不难发现：如今无论是在学术会议，还是高校的文学课堂，愉悦越来越难觅踪迹了，而追求类似"新愉悦"／"文之悦"的结果往往是困惑和郁闷。这一情形在美国学者奥尔特（Robert Alter）的如下评论中也得到了折射："对游戏性的忽略是一种症状，它表明我们的知识氛围过于沉闷。例如，在哈罗德·布鲁姆的《西方正典》里面就没有游戏性的立足之处……"（Alter 2004：11）就文学领域而言，奥尔特所说的"游戏性"首先应该是审美愉悦，可是对我们来说，审美愉悦已经渐行渐远了。如今常有谈"美"色变的情形：当你以"审美愉悦"为题提交论文或发言稿时，难保不会遭到"政治""历史"大棒的挞伐，仿佛只要审美，就必然排斥政治和历史。有鉴于此，我们有必要重拾愉悦话题，探讨其复杂的内涵外延，进而重估愉悦的价值。

（二）愉悦三命题

要探究愉悦的内涵和外延，就要认识它的三个命题：1）何为愉悦？2）为何愉悦？3）愉悦何为？这三个命题其实不能截然分开，而是你中有我、我中有你。我们将在阐述时尽量顾及其复杂性和相关性。

1. 何为愉悦

在西方文化语境中，"愉悦"是多义词。以英语 pleasure 一词为例，它既有"高兴/快乐"（a feeling of happy satisfaction and enjoyment）的语义，又有"快感"（sensual gratification）的语义，甚至有"带来性满足"（give sexual enjoyment or satisfaction）的意思（Pearsall 1097—1098）。与此相仿，法语 plaisir 一词除"高兴/快乐"（État de contentment que crée chez qqn la satisfaction d'une tendance）等意思之外，也有"性的满足/快感"（satisfaction sexuelle）的语义（薛建成 2001：1465），这就是巴特要拿它来跟 jouissance 互换的原因之一（参见前文）。大概是因为该词具有歧义性这一"先天缺陷"，加上本文上一节所提的诸多原因，它竟然未被收入一些重要的参考书。例如，在艾布拉姆斯（M. H. Abrams）的《文学术语汇编》（A Glossary of Literary Terms, 1999）和威廉斯（Raymond Williams）的《关键词》（Keywords：A Vocabulary of Culture and Society, 1976）中，"愉悦"都严重缺席了。不过，它又因此而格外显眼，似乎是在召唤广泛的关注。

愉悦究竟为何物呢？就西方文论而言，最富魅力的相关学说来自（审美）愉悦观的集大成者康德（Immanuel Kant, 1724—1804）。他在《判断力批评》一书中，把愉悦跟"想象力""知性""游戏"和"美"这些关键词联系在了一起："鉴赏判断是想象力和知性这两种认识能力的自由协调活动或'游戏'，它所判定的是普遍可传达的愉快感，这就是'美'"（邓晓芒2017：2）。此处，康德分明把"普遍可传达的愉快感"等同于"美",还把它界定为审美判断的对象,并且强调愉悦需要"想象力和知性这两种认识能力的自由协调活动",亦即"游戏"。他还提出了"愉快的两个特点,即无利害的快感和概念的普遍性",并且为其找到两个"先天根据,即无目的的合目的性形式和人类的共通感"(邓晓芒 2017:2)。康德的这一思想,如果换作我国学者朱光潜先生的说法,那就会更加简洁易懂:愉悦就是"无所为而为的玩索(disinterested contemplation)"(朱光潜 2006:79),或者说是一种"不沾小我利害的超脱"(朱光潜 2006:89)。朱光潜还把这种见解一直追溯到柏拉图和亚里士多德笔下"至高的善"(朱光潜 2006:79)。确实,亚里士多德曾经认定"愉悦是一种灵魂状态",而"对每个人来说,他的所爱就是愉悦"(朱光潜 2006:16)。此处的"所爱"就是亚里士多德推崇的美德,他认为愉悦就在德行之中;"德行本身必然使人愉悦"(朱光潜 2006:17)。两千多年以后,休姆(David Hume,1711—1776)用不同的表述呼应了这一观点:"道德情操或激情产生了愉悦,而不是产生于愉悦。我为一个朋友行善,因此感到愉悦,那是因为我爱他,但我不是为了愉悦的缘故才爱他的"(Hume 1985:85—86)。显然,这些思想都已带有"超脱小我利害"的特征。

在康德之后,把愉悦与善相提并论的人还有许多。例如,济慈的恩师亨特(Leigh Hunt,1784—1859)就坚持"把愉悦等同于善"(Mizukoshi 2001:25)。再如,毛姆(W. Somerset Maugham,1874—1965)曾经断定"愉悦本身善莫大焉,一切愉悦皆如此"(Maugham 1940:6)。愉悦除了与善有不解之缘以外,还与美难解难分(这一点上文已经提及)。更进一步说,它内核中还有"真"的成分,而发现真理或真相的愉悦则离不开康德所说的"知性"(见上文)。此外,毛姆的说法也颇具代表性:"知性愉悦最能带来满足感,也最能持久;凡是能发现这一点的人,就是同时代人中的智者"(Maugham 1940:6)。顺着这样的思路,我们似乎可以说:愉悦亦真亦善亦美。文学如此,哲学和科学亦如此。朱光潜就曾这样说过:"哲学和科学穷到极境,都是要满足求知的欲望……真理在离开实用而称为情趣中心时就已经是美感的对象了……善与美是一体,真与美也没有隔阂"(朱光潜 2006:80)。

在西方文论史上,有不少人认为愉悦有高低、雅俗之分,持这一主张的思想家包括柏拉图、亚里士多德、卡莱尔、穆勒和康德。① 进入现当代社会以后，还是有不少人持类似主张，如美国学者弗罗斯特（Laura Frost）的如下见解："有两种愉悦，一种是通过习得和认知而来的雅趣，另一种则是感官易得的愉悦；旗帜鲜明地用前者取代后者，同时摒弃后者，这被奉为一种审美原则"（Frost 2013：22）。不过，由于本文第一节所说的原因，基于这种审美原则的愉悦已经离人类渐行渐远，而感官愉悦——尤其是弗洛伊德/巴特们崇尚的"快感"（jouissance）——则越来越有市场，造成了越来越多的困惑。然而，那些有类似困惑的人，可能多半是由于没有拜读过朱光潜的如下精彩论述：

> 弗洛伊德的文艺观还是要纳到享乐主义里去，他自己就常喜欢用"快感原则"这个名词。在我们看，他的毛病也在把快感和美感混淆，把艺术的需要和实际人生的需要混淆。美感经验的特点在"无所为而为"地观赏形象。在创造或欣赏的一刹那中，我们不能仍然在所表现的情感里过活，一定要站在客位把这种情感当作一幅意象去观赏。……弗洛伊德派的学者的错处不在主张文艺常是满足性欲的工具，而在把这种满足认为美感。美感经验是直觉的而不是反省的……如果自己觉得快感，我便是由直觉变而为反省，好比提灯寻影，灯到影灭，美感的态度便已失去了。（朱光潜 2006：20）

确实，只要我们能够像这样区分美感和快感，就不难辨认审美愉悦的特点，即"无所为而为"地欣赏文学艺术乃至生活中的一切美好事物，从中获得乐趣或喜悦。只有在这一前提下，我们才能进入下一小节的话题。

2. 为何愉悦

史上许多文学/批评家都十分看重愉悦。这是为什么呢？华兹华斯（William

---

① 分别参考 Plato, *Philebus*, tr. Robin H. Waterfield (New York and London: Penguin Classics, 1983); Aristotle, *The Nicomachean Ethics*, tr. David Ross (Oxford: Oxford University Press, 1998); Thomas Carlyle, *Latter-Day Pamphlets* (London: Chapman and Hall, 1987); John Stuart Mill, *Utilitarianism and Other Essays*, ed. Alan Ryder (New York and London: Penguin, 1987); Immanuel Kant, *Critique of Judgment*, tr. Werner S. Pluhar (Indianapolis: Hackett Publishing Company, 1987).

Wordsworth,1770—1850）的见地最为深刻，也最具有代表性。特里林（Lionel Trilling,1905—1975）曾经这样总结华氏的观点："对华兹华斯来说，愉悦是生命本身的关键属性"（Trilling 2000：430）。这一核心观点贯穿着他那著名的"《抒情歌谣集》序言"（Preface to Lyrical Ballads, 1802），其中有一段话引用率非常高：

> 诗人创作时只受一种约束，即必须给他人带来即时愉悦，这个他人有着你期望他拥有的知识。你不是期待他/她以律师、医生、水手、天文学家或自然哲学家这样的身份来读诗，而是作为一个人来读诗。（Trilling 2000：312）

此处可能让人困惑的是"即时愉悦"（immediate pleasure）一语：即时愉悦何以成为诗人/文学家创作的目的？这话看似肤浅，其实相当深刻。正如克默德所说，此处的精华在于愉悦跟"作为一个人"的关系（克默德 2009：12—13），也就是跟作为整体的人之间的关系。这一点已经被斯坦福大学的吉甘蒂（Denise Gigante）教授解释得非常清楚："诗歌给作为整体的人带来愉悦，而不是服务于某一门专业知识。事实上，愉悦使人振作，这是因为想象的愉悦本来就是综合性的"（Gigante 2010：xiii）。换言之，人的全面发展/身心健全有赖于愉悦的综合性力量。

事实上，英国浪漫主义诗人们大都跟华兹华斯一样，以创造愉悦为自己的宗旨。例如，柯勒律治（Samuel Taylor Coleridge, 1772—1834）就把诗歌界定为"与科学著作相对的文类，开诚布公地把愉悦作为直接目的"（Coleridge 1983：13）。又如，雪莱（Percy Bysshe Shelley, 1792—1822）有过一句名言："诗歌总被愉悦伴随着。当愉悦降临时，人就会敞开心扉，迎接智慧，而智慧总是交织着乐趣"（Shelley 2002：139）。言下之意：没有愉悦，人类恐怕难以抵达智慧，甚至不会去迎接智慧，而智慧就像生命一样，是任何单个专业/职业所无法囊括的，这也就是华兹华斯所说"作为一个人"的意思。关于此，吉甘蒂说得更到位："对浪漫主义诗人来说，审美愉悦对人有构成作用"（Gigante 2010：xiii）。除此之外，对浪漫主义诗人来说，审美愉悦还关乎人类的尊严。特里林在评论华兹华斯时这样说道："华兹华斯断言，愉悦这一重大基本原则构成了人类袒露的、与生俱来的尊严。人类的认知、生活、呼吸和运动都是基于这一原则的"（Trilling 2000：432）。从前文所提雪莱、柯勒律治等其他浪漫主义诗人的表述来看，他们也都信奉这一重大原则。

愉悦关乎人类尊严，关乎生命的奥秘。这还不仅是浪漫主义诗人奉行的原则，而且是古今中外许多优秀诗人/学人笃信的真谛。阿根廷诗人博尔赫斯（Jorge Luis Borges，1899—1986）曾经强调，"诗歌应该要有的样子，也就是热情与喜悦"（博尔赫斯 2008：2）。他说的就是愉悦（亦即"诗歌应该要有的样子"），而这愉悦又意味着"尝试人生"："我们尝试了诗；我们也尝试了人生。而我也可以很肯定地说，生命就是由诗篇组成的。诗并不是外来的——正如我们所见，诗就埋伏在街角那头。诗随时都可能扑向我们"（博尔赫斯 2008：3）。他的下面这段话说得更透彻：

> 事实上，诗与语言都不只是沟通的媒介，也可以是一种激情，一种喜悦——当理解到这个普通的道理的时候，我不认为我真的了解这几个字，不过却感受到内心起了一些变化。这不是知识上的变化，而是发生在我整个人身上的变化，发生在我这血肉之躯的变化。（博尔赫斯 2008：5）

此处，"发生在我这血肉之躯的变化"就是生命的升华，就是尊严所在。无独有偶，朱光潜在讨论诗人之乐并回答"子非鱼，安知鱼之乐"这一问题时，也谈到了"生命"和"变化"，而且境界更高一层：

> 诗人和艺术家都有"设身处地"和"体物入微"的本领。他们在描写一个人时，就要钻进那个人的心孔，在霎时间就要变成那个人，亲自享受他的生命，领略他的感情。所以我们读他们的作品时，觉得它深中情理。在这种心灵感通中我们可以见出宇宙生命的连贯。诗人和艺术家的心就是一个小宇宙。（朱光潜：2006：56）

博尔赫斯的"内心变化"也好，朱光潜的"变成那个人"也好，都体现了"一种喜悦",里面都"可以见出宇宙生命的连贯"。细心的人会发现,此处的话题已经跟"愉悦何为"发生了重合,因此正好跟下文相衔接。

3. 愉悦何为

愉悦有什么用呢?笔者前文中已经认可了"无所为而为"一说,但是这并不表明愉悦是无用的。恰恰相反,百无一用,则必有大用。概括地说,愉悦的深广功用主要体现在两个方面。其一,在个人层面,它有助于修身养性、陶冶情操。其二,在社会/国家层面,它有着不可小觑的文化功能,尤其是政治功能。

先说个人层面。前文在论证愉悦与真善美之间关系时,其实已经涉及这一话题。真善美就是愉悦的最高境界,是任何雅趣之士追求的境界。说到"雅趣",我们不能不提及发生在 17—18 世纪的西方启蒙运动。如吉甘蒂所说,"旨在趣味升华的课题"(the project of sublimating taste)是"启蒙运动的一个中心课题"(Gigante 2010: xi),因此 18 世纪常有"趣味世纪"(the Century of Taste)的美称。沙夫茨伯里(Anthony Ashley Cooper, 3rd Earl of Shaftesbury, 1671—1713)、艾迪生(Joseph Addison, 1672—1719)、哈奇森(Francis Hutcheson, 1694—1746)、休姆和伯克(Edmund Burke, 1729—1797)等人可谓前赴后继,把"愉悦"和"趣味"变成了一对孪生姐妹。且看艾迪生的如下言论:

> 带有雅趣从事想象的人士会收获诸多愉悦,而庸俗之人则跟这些愉悦无缘……文雅之士每读一段描述性文字,就会收获一份私密的喜悦;若有田野或草坪映入眼帘,他经常会获得比实际占有者更大的满足感。(Addison 1965: 63)

比艾迪生更进一步的沙夫茨伯里甚至把审美趣味与法律相提并论,提倡"趣味治人"(Shaftesbury 1999: 413)。言下之意:犹如法律从外部约束人那样,趣味则从内部约束人而威力丝毫不逊于前者。

愉悦贯穿其中的趣味还有许多具体的功用,如增进人的认知能力、想象力、鉴赏力、判断力、"内在感知力(internal sense)"和"反思性情感(reflective affection）"。鉴于何畅在这方面已经做了相当系统的梳理，此处不再赘述。① 不过，康德的一个相关观点不能不提——他认为人一旦实现了（与趣味密不可分的）审美愉悦与"单纯感官享受"的分离，就有了更多的思辨能力（康德 2017：162）。这种思辨能力与愉悦之间的关系，虽然在当代常常被不少人忽视，但是所幸总有另一些人会提及，比如奥尔特的论断：

> 文学给人愉悦，部分是因为它吸引我们更敏锐地去识破语言的智谋，或更深刻地去认识我们是谁，我们的世界是怎样的……不管文学的主题、心境和形式是什么，文学给人愉悦还因为在见证纯粹词语魔力的运用……的时候，我们也经历着喜悦与欢愉。（Alter 2004：12）

显然，一个人如若在直面"我们是谁""世界是怎样的"等形而上问题时，仍然能经历喜悦与欢愉，那他/她必然有一片高尚的心田。

再说社会/国家层面。在这一层面，愉悦的功用同样是多方面的，包括它在道德、政治、经济和教育等多个领域里发挥的作用，尤其是教化作用——贺拉斯"寓教于乐"的思想已绵延数千年，这本身就是一个典型例证（贺拉斯，1962：155）。上文讨论的真善美其实也不可能只局限于个人：个人（通过愉悦）的修养提高了，全民的文化素质也就提高了。由于篇幅有限，也由于流行于近几十年的"政治热"的缘故，我们以下将聚焦愉悦的政治功用。

如本文第一节末尾所暗示的那样，审美未必排斥政治。更进一步说，在处处有政治——政治有许多面向——的人类社会，审美不可能独步其外，它既受政治的影响，又为政治服务。那么，审美愉悦是怎样发挥政治功能的呢？不少学者已尝试对此作出回答，其中要数詹明信所论比较靠谱。他提出了"愉悦的恰当政治功用"（the proper political use of pleasure）这一主张：

> 要使愉悦的政治功用成为恰当，那就必须使它一直保持寓言性质，意思是……把某个特殊的"愉悦"主题化，用以指代某个政治问题，如为城

---

① 参考何畅《西方文论关键词：趣味》全文，载《外国文学》2022 年第 3 期。第 91—102 页。

市美容所作的斗争，或争取性解放的某些形式，或为某几种文化活动的途径所做出的努力，或美化社会关系的改造工程，或为身体政治做作的斗争。这样的政治寓言必须一直保持双重聚焦：局部问题的解决，这本身就是有意义的，是可取的，但是它同时又是比拟总体乌托邦目标的修辞格，用以比拟改造整个社会的系统性革命。（Jameson 1983：13）

詹氏所说的"总体乌托邦"是指全人类解放。他下面这句话说得更明白："归根结底，拥有某种具体愉悦的权利、某种具体的物质享受……必须用来比拟整个社会关系的改造，否则就不能成立"（Jameson 1983：14）。言下之意，优秀的文学作品必然在寓言层面发挥愉悦的政治功用。同为西方马克思主义者的伊格尔顿（Terry Eagleton, 1943— ）也强调愉悦的政治功用，他认为人身上有产生愉悦的不同机制（mechanisms），而"研究这些机制是值得的"，因为这种研究"能产生更具有政治效用的文化"，"还可以告诉我们关于政治社会本身的一些有用知识"（Eagleton 1983：65）。他跟詹明信一样，也致力于"把趣味提升到人类解放高度"（殷企平 2022：80），并坚信"了解人们喜爱什么，以及喜爱的原因，那是有裨益的，而艺术则是了解这些情况的好地方"（Eagleton 1983：65）。此处的"喜爱"，显然也是一种愉悦。

就愉悦政治功用的理论阐述而言，有一人比詹明信和伊格尔顿的贡献更大，那就是法兰克福学派的代表人物马尔库塞（Herbert Marcuse, 1898—1979）。《审美之维》可以看作他审美思想的集大成之作，其中有一段直接点明了愉悦/美感的特性：

> 美赋予理想以出自幸福的充满魅力、令人开怀、使人惬意的特性。……美的时刻一旦在艺术作品中获得形式，它就可能被持续重复地体验到，被永恒地化入艺术作品中。感受者在艺术的快感中，总能重新创作出这种幸福。（马尔库塞 2001：29—30）

马尔库塞所追求的愉悦和幸福感，跟他追求全人类解放的理想并行不悖——他跟詹明信和伊格尔顿一样，致力于人类社会的改造，即摆脱资本主义社会的桎桔，反抗物质-技术的"高度文明"给人带来的异化。在他看来，解放人的美感是抗拒异化的关键，就像李小兵所总结的那样："（对马尔库塞来说）艺术，蕴含着新的社会改造的生机。革命首先在于解放人的美感、快感、被压抑的追求愉悦的潜在本能"（李小兵 2001：10）。马尔库塞是从马克思那里得到灵感的，后者在《1844 年经济学-哲学手稿》里指出，人的感官结构中蕴藏着对美的追求。在这一思想的基础上，"马尔库塞改造了弗洛伊德的学说，认为只有在人性结构的深层——本能中，彻底改造人的攻击性-破坏性本能后，社会的变革才会有一个深厚的人性基础。而这一切，只有通过艺术-美学的方式才能达到"（李小兵 2001：10）。

以上分析表明，愉悦的功用极其深广，其表现形式也极其丰富。事实上，我们前面的讨论还隐含着一个非常重要的话题，即愉悦在建构人类共同体过程中的作用，而这离不开愉悦的一种特殊形式，即共享愉悦。下文就将从它说起。

（三）愉悦须共享

从广义上说，本节内容也可以作为愉悦的政治功用来讨论。在此处专辟一节，为的是彰显其重要性。

前文提到，启蒙运动的一个中心课题是提升趣味。事实上，这一课题可以具体表述为"共享愉悦"（communal pleasure），其背后有一个更高的追求，即建构人类共同体。关于这一点，伦敦大学国王学院的博伊森（Rowan Boyson）博士说得十分到位：

> 现代愉悦观主要具有个人主义色彩……启蒙哲学和华兹华斯诗歌中的一条思想脉络则与之相反，即主张愉悦的内在特质与其说是私密的、不为人知的，不如说是用来与人分享的。……愉悦可以彰显人与人互助互动的集体情感；与此相应地看，共同体情感也会产生愉悦。（Boyson 2012：1）

鉴于博伊森此处也谈到了华兹华斯，我们不妨再回顾一下本文第二节中引用的一段话，即诗人在创作时"必须给他人带来即时愉悦"。显然，华氏这里提倡的就是共享愉悦——诗人与读者共享的愉悦。克默德（Frank Kermode, 1919—2010）就曾这样解读华氏的观点：

> ……首先是诗歌与一位读者的交流，然后必然是诗歌和众多读者的交流。这些读者，用华兹华斯的话说，必须符合这样的条件——他们必须拥有我们期望他们作为人而拥有的知识，他似乎把拥有这种知识等同于拥有真正的人性。（克默德 2009：24）

上引文字见于《愉悦与变革：经典的美学》（Pleasure and Change: The Aesthetics of Canon, 2004）一书，其核心观点是：经典文学必须符合一个先决条件，即能够和读者交流，而且是"和众多读者的交流"，而这种交流必然是愉悦的。虽然克默德和华兹华斯都没有直接使用"共享愉悦"这一术语，但是他们所提倡的无疑是共享愉悦，一种可以与人分享的愉悦。克默德以下言论可以用来强化我们的论证：

> 从愉悦的本质来看，它需要某种形式的社会参与……愉悦来自和"文化享受及文化认同"的关联，而"欢愉"却打碎了这种认同，并且不能等同于享受。
> ……
> 个体的愉悦是同可以期望从一个普通公民（一个受教育的公众）那里得到的反应相关联的。华兹华斯急切地想把这种愉悦和其他任何一种从走钢丝或雪利酒那里获得的愉悦区分开来，他认为诗歌不仅仅是愉悦的源泉，它还是哲学的。（克默德 2009：12—13）

此处，"社会参与""文化认同"以及"期望从……受教育的公众……那里得到的反应"显然都属于共享愉悦的范畴。从表面上看，克默德讨论的只是经典生成/传播与共享愉悦的关系，但是其实质必然涉及共同体话题：经典的前提是作者与读者、作者与作者、读者与读者之间的愉快交流；这种交流实现了，共享愉悦就形成了，共同体也就形成了。

事实上，共享愉悦的思想种子早在康德那里就已埋下了。我们前面曾援引康德《判断力批判》中的一句话，即"鉴赏判断是想象力和知性这两种认识能力的自由协调活动或'游戏'，它所判定的是普遍可传达的愉快感"（参见本文第二节第一小节）。这里，"普遍可传达的愉快感"就是共享愉悦。类似的表述在《判断力批判》中反复出现，如下面这段话：

> ……如果他（笔者按：指任何人）宣布某物是美的，那么他就在期待别人有同样的愉悦：他不仅仅是为自己，也是为别人在下判断……所以他就说：这个事物是美的，而且并不是因为……他多次发现别人赞同他的愉悦判断，就指望别人在这方面赞同他，而是他要求别人赞同他。（康德 2017：37）

赞同他人的愉悦判断，这也属于共享愉悦的范畴。在康德看来，这种共享有一个前提，即人类的"共通感"，或者说"以一个共通感为前提的""普遍可传达性"（康德 2017：58）。康德对于"传达"的强调可谓影响深远。例如，朱光潜在比较"同赏共乐"与"自得其乐"时也使用了"传达"二字："艺术家见到一种意境或是感到一种情趣，自得其乐还不甘心，他还要旁人也能见到这种意境，感到这种情趣……因此艺术不像克罗齐派美学家所说的，只达到'表现'就可以了事，它还要能'传达'"（朱光潜 2006：48）。关于"传达"，朱光潜还谈道：

> 文艺要表现的正是这种不得不言而又不易为俗人言的秘密。你拿它向读者吐露时，就已经假定他是可与言的契友。……你这种假定，这种希望，是根据"人同此心，心同此理"这个基本原则。你传达你的情感思想，是要在许多"同此心"的人们中取得"同此理"的印证。这印证有如回响震荡，产生了读者的喜悦，也增加了作者的喜悦。（朱光潜 2006：173）

这段话中并未出现"共享愉悦"这一术语，可是用来阐释康德、华兹华斯等人的相关思想，似乎并不为过。

让我们再回到共享愉悦与共同体之间的关系。如前文所示，共享愉悦意味着一种共同体情感，甚至意味着融真善美于一体的至高境界（我们前面的讨论其实已经暗示了这一层意思）。不过，问题也就来了：是不是所有的审美愉悦都是共享愉悦呢？依笔者之见，审美愉悦是一个动态过程，它起于个人/私人层面，表现为（因认知、观赏、喜爱等而产生的）"独乐乐"状态，但是它必然具备"众乐乐"的潜质，一旦得以升华（也就是前文所说的"趣味"升华），就会促成共享愉悦，从而进入更高的境界。说到"境界"，朱光潜有一段极佳的描述：

> 无论是作者或是读者，在心领神会一首好诗时，都必有一幅画境或是一幕戏景，很新鲜生动地突现于眼前，使他神魂为之钩摄，若惊若喜，霎时无暇旁顾，仿佛这小天地中有独立自足之乐，此外偌大乾坤宇宙，以及个人生活中的一切憎爱悲喜，都像在这霎时间烟消云散了。纯粹的诗的心境是凝神注视，纯粹的心所观境是独立绝缘，心与其观境如鱼戏水，忻合无间……（朱光潜 2006：49—50）

这段描述本身可谓美轮美奂，很少有人能用更美的文字来描述愉悦了。然而，可能有人会问：此处的"独立绝缘"和"独立自足之乐"分明是一种"独乐乐"，它跟共享愉悦/共同体情感似无关系，因而又如何称得上"境界"的美誉呢？确实，就那个瞬间而言，作者/读者已"无暇旁顾"，"偌大乾坤宇宙"已让位于"小天地"。用朱光潜的另一句原话说，此时此境的个人"在刹那中见终古，在微尘中显大千，在有限中寓无限"（朱光潜 2006：50）。乍一看去，这是一个让人流连忘返的境界。然而，流连忘返，终归要返：有幸经历这等喜悦的人，其实是经历了博尔赫斯所说"血肉之躯的变化"（参见本文第二节第二小节），或者说经历了人格升华，完成了一次蜕变，这正是马尔库塞所说"人性""本能"和"感官结构"的彻底改造，也正是他和詹明信、伊格尔顿等人所追求的"全人类解放"——其中的喜悦和共同体含义不言自喻——所必需的。此外，并非所有人会在品读一首好诗时"神魂为之钩摄"，进入"独立绝缘"的"心所观境"；有福分进入这一境界的必然是有修养的人，也就是先前体验过共享愉悦的人。正如美国学者理查德·莎所说，"愉悦的体验并不全是'单独的'，也不仅仅关乎个人的趣味和自我身份的表达，而是文化修炼的反应"。① 我们不难想象，"文化修炼"（culturally learned and disciplined）必定是以无数次共享愉悦为前提的。

进一步说，有高尚品味/趣味的人，在经历上述审美愉悦之后，（只要有机会）就会与人分享。本文第二节中提到，审美愉悦是与趣味密不可分的。以此推论，愉悦跟共同体意识/精神也是密不可分的。除了艾迪生、沙夫茨伯里、康德和华兹华斯等人以外，当代人伊格尔顿也把（包含着共享愉悦的）审美趣味与精神共同体等量齐观。他在《美学意识形态》（*The Ideology of the Aesthetic*, 1991）一书中这样说道："审美趣味的全部意义在于，它作为精神共同体的模式，是不可能强加于人的"（Eagleton 1983: 63）。此处，"不可能强加于人"一语意味深长，它又让我们想起前文所提沙夫茨伯里的那句话，即"趣味治人"（taste governs men）：共同体的建构固然需要来自外部的约束力，如强加于人的法律，但是更需要来自人心内部的约束力，如审美趣味，或者说"对人有构成作用"的审美愉悦（参见本文第二节）。

以上分析隐含着这样一个观点：愉悦是共同体的一种精神纽带。共同体学说的集大成者滕尼斯（Ferdinand Tönnies, 1855—1936）认为，共同体有"三大支柱"（three pillars），即"血缘"（blood）、"地缘"（soil）和"心缘"（spirit），其中作为第三支柱的"心缘"包括"亲情、乡情和友谊"（Tönnies 2001: 204）。我们似乎可以加上一句：共享愉悦是这心缘的要素。没有愉悦，何谈亲情、乡情和友谊？何谈共同体？让我们再回到伊格尔顿的愉悦/趣味观，他在许多书中都把"趣味"一词与"公共领域"（the public sphere）、"精神共同体"（spiritual community）、"情感共同体"（community of sensibility）和"普遍共同的感觉"（universal common sense）这样一些词语相提并论。这分明是在告诉世人："对趣味的关注最终总要落实到公共精神"（殷企平 2022: 76）。同理，对愉悦的关注也要落实到公共精神，或者说共同体精神。

---

① 转引自 Michelle Faubert and Thomas H. Schmid, "Introduction", 载 *Romanticism and Pleasure*, ed. Michelle Faubert and Thomas H. Schmid (New York: Palgrave Macmillan, 2010, p. 7)。

三、结语

愉悦不再愉悦的现象,是社会历史使然,也是时髦理论兴风作浪所致。面对各种改造愉悦概念的努力,我们的举措应该一分为二,一方面正本清源,坚持区分美感和快感;另一方面正视现实,接受挑战,承认即便是巴特等人的激烈"革命行动",也有其可取的一面,即折射/揭示文学语言具有阶级局限性这一现实,以及晚期资本主义对人类精神领域——尤其是无意识领域——的侵蚀(导致"愉悦"沦为商品或虚假意识)。本文以上对"愉悦"异化原因的分析,以及对愉悦概念内涵外延的梳理,一方面是十分必要的,另一方面则有挂一漏万之虞。在过去一百多年里,"愉悦"概念变化之剧烈,解释之繁多,远非一篇短文所能囊括。不过,从已有的分析来看,"愉悦"外观虽千变万化,其核心内涵却不可撼动:审美、趣味、无为而为、小我利害的超脱、普遍的可传达性,这些特征为愉悦的共享奠定了坚实基础,也为人类共同体的建构提供了不可或缺的路径。愉悦亦真亦善亦美,它关乎个人修养,更关乎人类尊严和命运。

参考文献

[1] Addison J. *The Spectator*. Vol. 6 [M]. Oxford: Clarendon, 1965.

[2] Alter R. "Introduction" [A] //*Pleasure and Change*. By Frank Kermode [M]. Oxford: Oxford UP, 2004.

[3] Aristotle. *The Nicomachean Ethics* [M]. Trans. David Ross. Oxford: Oxford UP, 1998.

[4] Barthes R. *The Pleasure of the Text* [M]. Trans. Richard Miller. New York: Farra, Straus and Giroux, 1975.

[5] Boyson R. *Wordsworth and the Enlightenment Idea of Pleasure* [M]. Cambridge: Cambridge UP, 2012.

[6] Coleridge S T. *Biographia Literaria*. Eds. James Engell and W. Jackson Bate. Vol. 2 [M]. Princeton, NJ: Princeton UP, 1983.

[7] Eagleton T. "Poetry, Pleasure and Politics." [A] //Bennet T. et al.

(eds.) *Formations of Pleasure* [M]. London: Routledge & Kegan Paul, 1983.

[8] Eagleton T. *The Ideology of the Aesthetic* [M]. Oxford: Blackwell, 1990.

[9] Foucault M. *The History of Sexuality. Volume 1: An Introduction* [M]. Trans. Robert Hurley. New York: Vintage Books, 1990.

[10] Frost L. *The Problem with Pleasure: Modernism and Its Discontents* [M]. Columbia: Columbia UP, 2013.

[11] Gigante D. Foreword. *Romanticism and Pleasure*. Eds. Schmid T H & Faubert M [M]. New York: Palgrave Macmillan, 2010. ix–xv.

[12] Hume D. *Essays Moral, Political and Literary*. Ed. Miller E F [M]. Indianapolis: Liberty Claxssics, 1985.

[13] Jameson F. "PLEASURE: A Political Issue." [M] //Tony Bennet et al. eds. *Formations of Pleasure*. London: Routledge & Kegan Paul, 1983.

[14] Kant I. *The Critique of Aesthetic Judgement* [M]. Trans. James Creed Meredith. Oxford: Clarendon, 1952.

[15] Maugham W S. *Books and You* [M]. London: William Heinemann, 1940.

[16] Mizukoshi A. *Keats, Hunt and the Aesthetics of Pleasure* [M]. New York: Palgrave, 2001.

[17] Pearsall J. ed. *The Concise Oxford Dictionary* [M]. Oxford: Oxford UP, 1999.

[18] Roberts M M. Preface. *Pleasure in the Eighteenth Century*. Roy Porter and Marie Mulvey Roberts [M]. New York: New York UP, 1996.

[19] Shaftesbury A A C. *Characteristics of Men, Manners, Opinions, Times*. Ed. Lawrence E. Klein [M]. Cambridge: Cambridge UP, 1999.

[20] Shelley P B. *Shelley's Poetry and Prose* [M]. New York: W. W. Norton, 2002.

[21] Tönnies F. *Community and Civil Society* [M]. Trans. Jose Harris and Margaret Hollis. Cambridge: Cambridge UP, 2001.

[22] Trilling L. "The Fate of Pleasure" [M] // (ed.). Leon Wieseltier. *The*

Moral Obligation to Be Intelligent. New York: Farra, Straus and Giroux, 2000: 427 - 449.

[23] Wilde O. *The Picture of Dorian Gray* [M]. Oxford: Oxford UP, 2006.

[24] Wordsworth W. "Preface to *Lyrical Ballads*" [A] //Richter D H (ed.). *The Critical Tradition: Classic Texts and Contemporary Trends* [M]. Boston and New York: Bedford/St. Martins, 2007: 306 - 318.

[25] 奥尔特. 引言 [A] //克默德. 经典与变革：经典的美学 [M]. 张广奎, 译. 南京：译林出版社, 2009：1 - 12 页. [Alter, Robert. Introduction. *Pleasure and Change*. By Frank Kermode. Trans. Zhang Guangkui. Nanjing: Yilin P, 2009. 1 - 12.]

[26] 博尔赫斯. 博尔赫斯谈诗论艺术 [M]. 陈重仁, 译. 上海：上海文艺出版社, 2008. [Borges, Jorge Luis. *This Craft of Verse*. Trans. Chen Chongren. Shanghai: Shanghai Literature and Art, 2008.]

[27] 邓晓芒. 中译者序 [A] //康德. 判断力批判 [M]. 邓晓芒, 译. 北京：人民出版社, 2017. [Deng, Xiaomang. "Preface." *Kritik der Urteilskraft*. By Immanuel Kant. Trans. Deng Xiaomang. Beijing: People, 2017.]

[28] 贺拉斯. 诗艺 [M]. 杨周翰, 译. 北京：人民文学出版社, 1962. [Horace. *Ars Poetica*. Trans. Yang Zhouhan. Beijing: People, 1962.]

[29] 康德. 判断力批判 [M]. 邓晓芒, 译. 北京：人民出版社, 2017. [Kant, Immanuel. Kritik der Urteilskraft. Trans. Deng Xiaomang. Beijing: People, 2017.]

[30] 克默德. 愉悦与变革：经典的美学 [M]. 张广奎, 译. 南京：译林出版社, 2009. [Kermode, Frank. *Pleasure and Change*. Trans. Zhang Guangkui. Nanjing: Yilin P, 2009.]

[31] 李小兵. 译序 [A] //马尔库塞. 审美之维 [M]. 李小兵, 译. 桂林：广西师范大学出版社, 2001. [Li, Xiaobing. "Preface." *The Aesthetic Dimension*. By Herbert Marcuse. Trans. Li Xiaobing. Guilin: Guangxi Normal UP, 2001.]

[32] 马尔库塞. 审美之维 [M] 李小兵, 译. 桂林：广西师范大学出版社, 2001. [Marcuse, Herbert. *The Aesthetic Dimension*. Trans. Li Xiaobing. Guilin: Guangxi Normal UP, 2001.]

[33] 薛建成. 拉鲁斯法汉双解词典 [M]. 北京：外语教学与研究出版社，2001. [Xue, Jiancheng. *Dictionaire de la Langue Française avec Explications Bilingues*. Beijing: *Foreign Language Teaching and Research Press*, 2001.]

[34] 殷企平. 西方文论关键词：普通读者 [J]. 外国文学，2019，(6)：44-54. [Yin, Qiping. "The Common Reader: A Keyword in Critical Theory." *Foreign Literature* 6 (2019): 44-54.]

[35] 殷企平. 走向公共精神：伊格尔顿的趣味观 [J]. 外国文学，2022，(6)：71-80. [Yin, Qiping. "Towards the Public Spirit: Eagleton's View on Taste." *Foreign Literature* 6 (2022): 71-80.]

[36] 朱光潜. 谈美 [M]. 桂林：广西师范大学出版社，2006. [Zhu, Guangqian. *On Beauty*. Guilin: Guangxi Normal UP, 2006.]

（本文原载于《外国文学》2024年第3期）

文论讲座：概念与术语
含混

一、一句话概说

"含混"（Ambiguity）一词源于拉丁文"ambiguitas"，其原意为"双管齐下"（acting both ways）或"更易"（shifting）。自从英国批评家威廉·燕卜逊（William Empson，1906—1984）的名著《七种类型的含混》（*Seven Types of Ambiguity*，1930）问世以来，含混成了西方文论的重要术语之一。它既被用来表示一种文学创作的策略，又被用来指涉一种复杂的文学现象；既可以表示作者故意或无意造成的歧义，又可以表示读者心中的困惑（主要是语义、语法和逻辑等方面的困惑）。含混不仅是新批评派手中不可或缺的法宝，而且跟后现代主义文论中的"不确定性"这一理论概念有着千丝万缕的联系。

二、大背景解说

"含混"一词的普通用法往往带有贬义，它多指风格上的一种瑕疵，即在本该简洁明了的地方显得晦涩艰深，甚至含糊不清。经燕卜逊之手，它从遭人嫌的灰姑娘一跃而为备受青睐的王妃，一时间成了文学批评家们所簇拥的对象。作为一般的文学批评术语，含混通常带有褒义：它显示了一个诗人或其他文学体裁作者高超的技艺，即巧妙地运用单个词语或措辞来指涉两个或两个以上有差异的物体，或者表示两种或两种以上不同的态度、立场、思想或情感。当然，燕卜逊所说的含混远远超出了上述含义，他所做的工作的意义也远远超出了对含混类型的划分。假如没有燕卜逊及其对含混的研究，20世纪上半叶蔚为壮观的新批评运动本来会大为逊色。虽然人们通常把理查兹和艾略特称作新批评的首要代表人物，但是燕卜逊和他的含混实际上在新批评运动中有着举足轻重的地位，这一点曾经被周珏良先生道破："燕卜逊的分析方法……对于新批评派之注重对文本的细读和对语言特别是诗的语言的分析，可以说起了启蒙的作用"（王佐良等 1994：303）。

　　以燕卜逊为代表人物之一的新批评是在对传统文学批评的挑战中崛起的。20世纪初之前的文学批评大都以实证主义理论或浪漫主义的表现论为基石，前者把文学作为历史文献来研究，而后者则把研究的重心放在了作者的生平和心理上面。新批评针对传统批评忽视文学作品本身独特的审美价值这一缺陷，"在理论上把作品本文视为批评的出发点和归宿，认为文学研究的对象只应当是诗的'本体即诗的存在的现实'。这种把作品看成独立存在的实体的文学本体论，可以说就是新批评最根本的特点"（张隆溪 1986：39—40）。至于新批评的一般原则，特伦斯·霍克斯曾经做过如下简要的归纳：

> 　　它（新批评）提出，艺术作品，特别是文学的艺术作品应被看作是自主的，因而不应当参照作品的外在的标准或考虑来评判它。它只保证对自己细致入微的检查。与其说诗歌是由一系列关于外在"现实"世界的可供参考和可以证实的陈述组成，不如说它是以词语形式表现或精心组织一系列复杂的经验。批评家的目标就是追求那种复杂性。它服从封闭式的分析性阅读，不参照任何公认的"方法"或"体系"，不汲取作品之外的任何信息，不论它是传记的、社会的、心理的抑或历史的。（霍克斯 1987：157）

对复杂性的追求最终要落实到对文字的推敲，正是在这方面燕卜逊以他的含混研究开出了一条新路。下面就让我们以燕卜逊的具体工作为出发点，沿着含混的轨迹做一次旅行。

(一)"含混"的含混

如果说世上的许多概念都是含混的,那么"含混"这一概念就更加含混了。燕卜逊当年挑选含混作为自己的研究课题,这本身就显示了不小的学术勇气。

一些中外学者在评点《七种类型的含混》一书时,往往把其中的某一段话拣出来,说是燕卜逊给含混所下的定义。事实上,燕卜逊并没有明确地给出关于含混整体概念的定义,而是在给含混分门别类时才使用了"定义"(definition)一词。确实,燕卜逊在开篇处提议把"含混"一词的意义扩大引申,并强调字面意义的任何细微差异都跟他的主题有关,前提是这种差异"为同样的言语提供了意义变通的余地"(Empson 1947:1)。然而,这样的表述似乎还不足以作为含混的定义。书中的另一段话倒更像是一个定义:

> "含混"本身既可以指我们在追究意义时举棋不定的状态,又可以指同时表示多个事物的意图,也可以指两种意思要么二者必居其一、要么两者皆可的可能性,还可以指某种表述有多种意思的事实。(Empson 1947:5—6)

燕卜逊这里列举了含混意义的多种可能性,但是他远未穷尽含混意义的可能性。不无趣味的是,这段话中的"可以指"一词可以被视为作者本人"含混心态"的绝妙写照。

《七种类型的含混》1947年再版中的第一个注释颇耐人寻味:"什么是'含混'的最佳定义(手头上的例子是否应该被称为含混)?这一问题在全书的所有环节都会冒出来,让人始料不及"(Empson 1947:1)。也就是说,燕卜逊承认他自始至终都没有圆满地解决含混的定义问题。更令人回味的是,燕卜逊还在开篇不久后坦言自己"将经常利用'含混'的含混",以"避免引起与交流不相干的问题"(Empson 1947:6)。言外之意:假如要一味地追求含混的精确定义,反而会适得其反;不如还含混以本真状态,反倒能够顺藤摸瓜,逐个体悟其中的奥妙。

事实上,燕卜逊对个案研究的重视超过了他对理论概括的重视。他认为文学批评首先应该给人带来满足感,而这种满足感的第一要素与其说是作品印证了某某理论，不如说是找到了一种对作品的感觉。当然，就含混理论而言，燕卜逊居功至伟，但是他十分忌讳在理论领域里高驰而不顾，而是始终保持着对抽象理论的警惕性。他一方面不失时机地对含混现象进行理论梳理，一方面又时时提醒我们过于宽泛的理论免不了会捉襟见肘，这也是他一直在含混的总体定义问题上慎之又慎的原因。

虽然下定义十分困难，但是这并不意味着燕卜逊在总体思路上缺乏任何基本准则。他对含混的所有探索都基于两个鲜明的观点：其一，含混存在与否取决于读者是否产生了困惑。以双关语为例，假如一个作者用了双关语，但是他的实际用意一看/一听便知，那么这双关语还不属于含混的范畴；只有当读者不明白（至少是一时不明白）作者究竟取双关语中的哪一层意思时，这双关语才进入了含混的范畴。其二，语言文字的意义往往比乍一看去要复杂得多；一个词语的外延至少跟它的内涵同样丰富，而且在内涵与外延之间经常存在着逻辑上的冲突。了解了这两条基本准则，即使含混再含混，我们也算摸到了它的脉搏。

（二）含混的类型

根据词语内涵与外延在逻辑上混乱的程度轻重，燕卜逊把含混分成了以下 7 大类型：

1. 参照系的含混（ambiguity of reference）。这一类含混表示某一个细节同时在好几个方面发挥效力，亦即在好几个参照系里产生作用。燕卜逊所给的众多例子中要数关于莎剧《李尔王》中的那一段最能够说明问题：

Lear   This is nothing, fool.

Fool   Then 't is like the breath of an unfee'd Lawyer, you gave me nothing for't. Can you make no use of nothing, nuncle?

Lear   Why no, Boy.

Nothing can be made out of nothing.

Fool (to Kent)   Prithee tell him, so much the rent of his land comes to, he will not beleeve a Fool.

李尔　傻瓜，这些话一点意思也没有。

弄人　那么正像拿不到讼费的律师一样，我的话都白说了。老伯伯，你不能从没有意思的中间，探求出一点意思来吗？

李尔　啊，不，孩子。垃圾里是淘不出金子来的。

弄人（向肯特）　请你告诉他，他有那么多的土地，也就成为一堆垃圾了；他不肯相信一个傻瓜嘴里的话。（朱生豪译）

燕卜逊指出，如果孤立地看，以上细节仅仅传达了李尔王那痛苦的失落感，以及弄人的唠叨；但是上引细节应该跟当初李尔王对女儿考狄利娅的苛刻放在一起考察。考狄利娅拒绝用甜言蜜语来换取父亲的恩赐，而是直言自己"没有话说"，这引出了李尔王下面的一句话：

Lear　Nothing will come of nothing, speak again.

李尔　没有只能换到没有；重新说过。（朱生豪译）

由于多了后面这一参照系，nothing（没有）一词的意义陡然增殖：李尔王对弄人的一席话其实是百感交集的产物，其意思除了前面提到的之外还至少有四。其一，李尔王终于意识到考狄利娅当初"没有话说"是对的。其二，当初李尔王指望考狄利娅乞讨爱怜，然而真正需要乞讨爱怜的是他自己。其三，李尔王此时已经丧失了一切。其四，从本质上讲，李尔王是一无所有，因而任何从他那里得到什么的企图犹如从垃圾里淘金，最终将一无所得——他的另外两个女儿高纳里尔和里根虽然曾一时得逞，但是最终却赔上了性命。这一例子还体现了贯穿于《七种类型的含混》全书的一个观点：对含混的充分理解有赖于对上下文或语境（context）的全面把握。

2. 所指含混（ambiguity of referent）。用燕卜逊的原话说，"当两个或两个以上的意义合而为一的时候，词义或句法上的含混就产生了"。（Empson 1947: 48）下面是莎剧《麦克白》中的一个经典例子：

If it were done, when 'tis done, then 't were well

> It were done quickly; If th' Assassination
> Could trammel up the Consequence, and catch
> With his surcease, Success; that but ...

麦克白　要是干完了以后就完了，那么还是快一点干；要是凭着暗杀的手段，可以攫取美满的结果，又可以排除了一切后患；要是……（朱生豪译）

这一段独白表现麦克白在谋杀国王邓肯之前的矛盾心态，其复杂含义照常理会占用更多的句子和词语，但是此处却被浓缩在了一起。就句法而论，引文采用了"双重句法"（double syntax）形式——本来在"If it were done, when 'tis done, then 't were well/It were done quickly"后面应当画上句号，并另起一句。就词法而论，许多意思被糅进了单个词语。例如，consequence 一词既包含译文中的"结果"的意思，又暗含"登上王位"的意思——英语中有 a person of consequence（要人）的用法，而国王则是要人中的要人。trammel 同时有"用网捕鸟""用绳拴马腿""用钩子钩锅"以及"用杠杆推动轨道上的台车"等多层含义，用它来跟 consequence 搭配能够引发关于麦克白僭位手段方面的丰富联想。surcease 有"干完"的意思，也有"终止诉讼"或"推翻判决"的意思，这就暗喻了麦克白正在接受道德法庭的审判这一事实。燕卜逊还敏锐地指出，surcease 一词可以被看作"surfeit"（过度；过量）和 decease（死亡）这两个词的浓缩形式（Empson 1947：50），因而包含了麦克白贪心过度、邓肯将被杀死以及麦克白自己最终将走向灭亡等多层意思。引文中的另一些词语，如 assassination success catch 和 his 等，也都凝聚着多种含义。阅读以这类含混为特征的文本，即便读上几十遍，也不可能同时记住短短几行的蕴涵，这恰恰构成了一种独特的魅力。

　　3. **意味含混**（ambiguity of sense）。"当所说的内容有效地指涉好几种不同的话题、好几种话语体系、好几种判断模式或情感模式时，第三类含混就产生了"（Empson 1947：111）。这类含混跟前两类的最主要的区别在于它有一个后者所没有的前提，即同时出现的几种意义明显地不相关联，甚至互相抵触。属于这类含混的有双关语（puns）、暗喻（allusions）和讽寓（allegories），其中双关语和暗喻大多着眼于局部范围，而讽寓则大多以全部作品为范围。限于篇幅，

让我们只选择一个简单明了的例子。燕卜逊对弥尔顿的如下诗行赞不绝口:

> That specious monster, my accomplished snare.
> 那美丽而奸佞的妖怪,给我设下了高明的圈套。(笔者译)

这一行诗描写的是出卖参孙(Samson)的迪莉拉(Delilah)。燕卜逊指出,specious 一词既有"美丽的"意思,又有"奸佞的"意思;同样,accomplished 一词也有两层意思:它既指迪莉拉极尽阿谀奉承之能事,又指她陷害丈夫的阴谋得逞。在燕卜逊看来,specious 和 accomplished 是把两种大相径庭的意思巧妙地纳入一个单词的典范。它们分别提供了两种信息,分别属于叙述的两个部分。换言之,在原本需要两个单词的地方,弥尔顿只用了一个单词,并且不但没有使意义受损,而且还增添了无穷的趣味。这样的含混,堪称鬼斧神工之笔。

4. **意图含混**(ambiguity of intent)。燕卜逊为第四类含混下了这样的定义:"当某一表述中的两个或更多的意义之间发生龃龉,但是其合力却昭示了作者的矛盾心态时,第四类含混就产生了"(Empson 1947: 133)。这类含混的产生有 3 个前提:一是作者自己举棋不定;二是所表述的多层意义彼此不合;三是虽然这些不同的意义永远无法达到水乳交融的境界,但是它们那含混的并存却有一个不含混的功能,即明白无误地揭示了作者意图所处的模糊状态。英国玄学派诗人约翰·邓恩(John Donne, 1572—1631)的名诗《告别辞:关于哭泣》(A Valediction, of Weeping)中 Weep me not dead 一语可以被看作这方面的一个典型例子。它至少有以下 4 种解读:① 不要让我哭死过去;② 不要用你的眼泪使我悲痛得身亡;③ 不要哭得好像我已经死了那样,其实我还好好地躺在你的怀抱里(英语原文后面紧跟着短语 in thine arms);④ 不要对大海施展你的魔力,以致它用泪水般海浪把我淹死。需要特别指出的是,燕卜逊在分析这类含混时,与其说是抱着褒奖有关作家的目的,不如说是探索能够用来证明有关作家创作意图混乱的方法。从这一意义上说,第四类含混说的是作者的意图,但是燕卜逊真正关心的对象是读者——为他们提供解读作者意图的钥匙。

5. **过渡式含混**(ambiguity of transition)。燕卜逊把这一类含混称作"吉利的困惑"（Empson 1947：vi）。之所以吉利，是因为它的产生标志着新的发现："当作者在写作过程中发现了新的想法，或者说作者没有把这种想法封闭起来时，第五类含混就产生了"（Empson 1947：155）。跟第四类含混相似的是，文本中的某个比喻也有模棱两可的特征；不同的是，第五类含混指作者一开始并没有发现所用比喻同时还可以形容文本中的第二种事物。燕卜逊举了莎剧《一报还一报》中的一例：

> Our Natures do pursue
> Like Rats that ravyn downe their proper Bane
> A thirsty evil, and when we drink we die.
>
> 正像饥不择食的饿鼠吞咽毒饵一样，人为了满足他的天性中的欲念，也会饮鸩止渴，送了自己的性命。（朱生豪译）

按照燕卜逊的理解，莎士比亚最初选用 proper 一词时只是取其"对老鼠颇为合适"一义，但是在行文过程中发现该词的另外一个意思——"正确而自然的"（这一意义原本跟诗句无关）——跟人的贪欲正好吻合：欲念来自天性，因而是自然的；老天惩罚纵欲过度的人则是正确的。proper 还跟人类因亚当和夏娃偷吃禁果而遭天谴这一典故十分贴切。总之，用 proper 跟 Bane 搭配可谓一箭双雕：proper Bane 既形容杀鼠的毒饵，又比喻害人的毒鸩。这后一种寓意的获得是从前一种寓意过渡而来的，所以燕卜逊把整个情形称为过渡式含混。这种意外的双重效果其实有一个先决条件，即所用比喻本身本来跟两个被形容的事物之间都没有明显的联系（proper Bane 的原义分别跟毒饵和毒鸩都有一定的距离）。也正是有了距离，才使得从一个寓意到另一个寓意的过渡成为可能。

6. 矛盾式含混（ambiguity of contradiction）。第六类含混跟第五类最大的区别是它不像后者那样"吉利"。也就是说，第六类中的作者未能像第五类中的作者那样幸运地迎来令人欣喜的发现，而是自始至终解决不了因同义反复或牛头不对马嘴而引起的矛盾。事实上，最倒霉的要数读者：此时的他/她不得不捏造出一些理由，以解释文本中的矛盾。不难看出，第六类含混跟第四类（意图含混）有相当大的重合之处，不过第四类的标准主要侧重于心理（作者的意图），而第六类的标准则更注重文字本身。就第四类而言，读者可以通过含混的合力来解释作者意图的混沌状态，因而至少可以在总体上得到一个较为圆满的解释。相形之下，读者在处理第六类含混时就不那么走运，他/她必须依靠"含糊其词的表述模式"（Empson 1947：190）。换言之，读者此时只能仰仗含混来解释含混。《奥瑟罗》中一段独白就是一个典型的例子：

> It is the Cause, it is the Cause (my soul),
> Let me not name it to you, you chaste Starres,
> It is the Cause. Yet I'll not shed her blood,
> Nor scarre that white skin of hers, then Snow,
> And smooth as Monumental Alabaster：
> 只是为了这一个原因，只是为了这一个原因，我的灵魂！
> 纯洁的星星啊，不要让我向你们说出它的名字！
> 只是为了这一个原因……可是我不愿溅她的血，
> 也不愿毁伤她那比白雪更皎洁、比石膏更腻滑的肌肤。（朱生豪译）

这是奥瑟罗对苔丝狄蒙娜动了杀机之后的一段独白。它的首句（也是第五幕第二场的首句）中"只是为了这一个原因"一语令人困惑不解："这一个"是什么东西的"原因"？究竟是什么引起了奥瑟罗脑海中的轩然大波？人们可以拿出种种具有可能性的解释，燕卜逊在书中也作了许多不同的推测，同时表明他自己最倾向于把"血"（溅苔丝狄蒙娜的血这一决定）视为奥瑟罗情感波动的原因，但是他又坦言这毕竟是猜测而已。在这一类含混面前，读者（包括燕卜逊这样的批评家）最多的感受恐怕是无奈。

　　7. **意义含混**（ambiguity of meaning）。这类含混的先决条件是所选单词本身就含有两个截然相反的语义，如 let 一词既可以表示 allow（允许），又可以表示 hinder（阻碍），二者在意义上完全对立。又如，cleave 既有 split asunder（劈开）的意思，又有 stick fast to（黏合）或 embrace（拥抱）的意思。这种词义上潜在的对立往往会把文本意义上的矛盾推向极致。《一报还一报》中克劳狄奥关于他姐姐依莎贝拉的评论可以作为一例：

> In her youth
> There is a prone and speechless dialect
> Such as move men.
> 在她的青春的魅力里,有一种无言的辩才可以使男子为之心动。(朱生豪译)

引文中 prone 和 speechless 二词都孕育着互相对峙的内涵。prone 一方面有"积极的""倾向于"等含义,另一方面有"消极的"和"平躺着"等含义。speechless 既可作"害羞"解,又可作"狡猾"解。当然,孤立地看,克劳狄奥是在赞扬他姐姐,因而这两个形容词不应该发生歧义——读者应该分别取其"积极的"和"害羞"之义。然而,一旦我们把它们放在更大的语境中加以审视,就会产生这样的疑问:克劳狄奥只是在由衷地赞扬依莎贝拉吗?从下文中我们知道,克劳狄奥要求依莎贝拉用出卖贞操的方式向安哲鲁求情,以换取自己被赦免。由此我们发现,克劳狄奥在评论依莎贝拉时实际上受着一套肮脏的价值观的支配。在他看来,只要能换取自己的性命,让姐姐跟别人上床并算不了什么。从这一角度看,prone 还暗含"平躺着"(上床)的意思,因而也就折射出了克劳狄奥那阴暗的心理。同理,由于克劳狄奥是以小人之心度淑女之腹,他很可能会把依莎贝拉的 speechlessness(无言)看作狡猾的表现,而不会把它跟害羞的心理挂钩。不难看出,第七类含混不仅以完全矛盾的词语内涵为前提,而且还有赖于语境的巧妙设置。

细心人很快就会发现,燕卜逊在界定以上 7 种类型的含混时并未能把它们截然分开,事实上它们之间也不可能泾渭分明。界线的含混,这恐怕是含混的必然特征。对大部分读者来说,燕卜逊的最大魅力并不在于他划分出了 7 种类型的含混,而在于他凭借类型的划分,一而再再而三地让我们品尝到了文字不同内涵之间以及内涵与外延之间的微妙差别。

(三) 含混与不确定性

"含混"与"不确定性"同为 20 世纪西方文论中的关键性术语。从某种意义上说,不确定性是含混的延续和发展。贝尼特(Andrew Bennett)和罗依尔

(Nicholas Royle)在探讨后现代文论术语时就曾说过："在20世纪中叶新批评家们称作含混或悖论的东西,如今的批评家们总是从不确定性的角度加以考虑"(Bennett and Royle,1999:232)。至少有一点不容置疑:在过去人们特别关注含混的地方,如今人们特别关注不确定性。不过,尽管含混和不确定性在意义上有许多重合之处,但是两者之间存在着根本性的差别。这些差别主要表现在如下3个方面:

首先,含混纵然歧义丛生,也万变不离其宗——所有的变化都发生在有机统一的文本框架之内;而不确定性却倾向于打破框架。新批评派虽然注重文本的多义性和多价性,但是更着力于稳定文本的多义性和多价性,更关心怎样在保留多元性的同时保证统一性。不确定性则把对多义性的追求推向了极致:后现代批评家们似乎个个能上演撕裂文本的拿手好戏,而对文本的弥合却不那么感兴趣,或者干脆声称文本的裂缝永远不可能完全弥合。

其次,含混的基点在文本,而不确定性的基点在读者。虽然燕卜逊对读者的重视程度超过了其他新批评家,但是他并没有完成从文本向读者的重心转移。不确定性则把重心完全移向了读者。最早运用不确定性原则的批评家之一伊瑟曾大力主张读者建构文本的观点,并且强调每个读者都会"用自己的方法破译文本"(Iser,1978:93)。费希更直截了当地提出了"读者决定一切"的观点(张汝伦 1987:306),他认为文本的意义取决于读者的"批评观""阐释策略"或批评家所属的"解释界";"意义不是采集出来的,而是制造出来的——并不是由编码形式制造而成,而是由阐释策略生成形式,然后制作而成的……与其说意义产生阐释行为,不如说阐释行为产生意义"(Fish 1980:465)。

再次,不确定性不仅消解作者的权威和文本意义的稳定性,而且消解任何阐释立场的稳定性,甚至还威胁到读者的身份和资格本身(这其实是"读者决定一切论"走到极端的必然效应)。换言之,不确定性意味着任何读者迟早都会面临这样的问题:我是谁?我的解读能够成立吗?我有资格进行文本解读吗?对这些问题的回答最终也是无法确定的。用克尔凯郭尔的话说,"一旦确定了,疯狂也就开始了"(Bennett and Royle 1999:195)。对以阐释含混为主要目标的新批评家们来说,以上问题是用不着考虑的,甚至压根儿不会出现。

富有辩证意味的是,含混与不确定性之间的上述差异又在时刻提醒我们注意它们之间的联系。事实上,"不确定性"这一理论概念的开花结果离不开燕卜逊在含混土地上的开垦和耕耘。前文提到，对新批评派来说，文本的多元性不可能溢出其结构的严格限阈，然而燕卜逊的一只脚却跨出了这一限阈。塞尔登（Raman Selden）曾经颇具慧眼地指出，在新批评派中，"只有威廉·燕卜逊预示了后结构主义'多元'文本的观点"（塞尔登2000：307）。对于燕卜逊在含混问题上所做的开拓性工作，塞尔登予以恰如其分的评价：

> 他比任何其他新批评派都更理解语言总是"丰富和杂乱"的性质，必须依靠心智来赋予它以统一性，只有这样，才能将其限定在一定的范围内。他认为，把各不相关的意义聚拢在一起的"力"显然是读者的本能而非文本中的结构因素。读者在阅读过程中的阐释能力无疑动摇了稳定意义的观点，除非这种稳定的意义是读者强加其上的。
>
> （塞尔登2000：307）

由此可见，燕卜逊其实是一位过渡性人物：他既用含混为新批评派在文本细读方面作出了表率，又为含混向不确定性的过渡起了推波助澜的作用。

当然，除了燕卜逊、伊瑟、费希和克尔凯郭尔，还有许多学者为丰富"含混"和"不确定性"的理论内涵而作出了杰出的贡献。大家所熟悉的由德里达（Jacques Derrida）提出的"延异"（différance）概念其实就是"不确定性"概念的变体。非提不可的还有海德格尔（Martin Heidegger）、哈桑（Ihab Hassan）和德曼（Paul de Man）。海德格尔曾经把"多义含混"视为诗歌语言的特征，并肯定"语言的生命在于庞杂多义"。① 哈桑为了说明后现代文化内在的不确定性和不可把握性，索性把"不确定性"（indeterminacy）和"内向性"（immanence）这两个词合二为一，生造出一个新词："不确定的内向性"（indetermanence）。② 德曼从修辞学的角度切入，对意义的不确定性作了别开生面的探讨：

> 当我们一方面研究字面意义，另一方面又研究比喻意义时，我们的研究模式仍然停留在语法层面；但是当我们无法用语法或其他语言学手段来

---

① 详见赵一凡《欧美新学赏析》，第56页。
② 详见盛宁《人文困惑与反思——西方后现代主义思潮批判》，第5—7页。

确定两种意义（可能是完全不兼容的两种意义）中的哪一种占主导地位时，我们的研究模式就进入了修辞学层面。（参见 de Man 1979：10）

德曼的这段话其实是他给意义不确定性所下的一个独特的定义。

有一个现象值得一提：不少推崇含混和不确定性的学者在具体的批评实践中往往有意无意地追求清晰而确定的意义，甚至在理论表述上也前后矛盾。例如，燕卜逊的同道人理查兹虽然强调"含混……是语言行为不可避免的结果，是我们最重要的话语所必不可少的手段"（参见 Richards 1967：40）。但是他又把追求"不含混"（unambiguous）的意义视为读者的任务："事实上，就其直接效果而言，最好的诗歌的许多部分都是含混的。即便是最细心、最具感受力的读者也必须反复阅读，狠下功夫，直至全诗清晰地、毫不含混地从脑海里浮现出来。"（参见 Richards 1967：232）甚至连最早倡导不确定性原则的伊瑟也曾自相矛盾地主张寻求确定的意义："因此，阅读行为是这样一个过程，即致力于驯服摇摆不定的文本结构，从中找出某个具体的意义来"（Iser 1978：8）。"审美对象作为文本的对应物而产生于接受者的脑海中，因而它受到理解行为的检验。也正因为如此，阐释的任务是把审美对象转换成具体的意义"（Iser 1978：234）。

要解释这样的矛盾现象，恐怕得借用一下德里达的解构思想。按照德里达的观点，世上"没有什么纯粹的在场，一个在场总是伴随着'印迹'或某些别的东西，某些别的东西总是印在一个在场当中"（德里达 2003：156）。意义当然也是一种在场。既然没有什么纯粹的在场，也就没有什么纯粹的意义，而不纯粹的意义总是带有含混，总是带有不确定性。反之，纯粹的含混和不确定性也是不存在的。含混与不含混，确定性与不确定性，就像一对连体孪生姐妹。当其中的一个在向你眨眼睛的时候，另一个也在向你眨眼示意。在这种情况下，任何人陷入矛盾都在情理之中。

三、结语

不管人们情愿与否，"含混"和"不确定性"这两个概念已经在学术界扎根。离开了它们，20 世纪以来的文艺批评几乎是不可想象的。不可否认，含混研究极大地提高了人们的文学素养，增强了人们的敏感性，扩展了人们的学术视野，开拓了文学批评的疆域。然而，对含混——尤其是不确定性——的过度推崇很容易导致相对主义和虚无主义。事实上，在过去的几十年中，这一倾向始终存在。前文提到的费希等人的"读者决定论"就是一例。夸大意义含混或不确定性的人都忽视了一个简单的事实：大多数人对于大多数文本的感受和理解的趋同性实际上要大于其差异性。这一点已经由布思说得非常清楚：

> 就多数故事的阅读而言，我们大多数人共享的经历比我们在公开的争论中所承认的要多。当我们谈及任何故事时——如《堂吉诃德》《卡斯特桥市长》《傲慢与偏见》《奥列佛·特威斯特》——我们必然触及许多共同经历的核心部分："我们大家"（或者说我们大部分人）都会觉得桑丘·潘沙好笑，尽管我们对堂吉诃德的反应各自不同；我们都痛惜迈克尔·亨察得的悲惨命运，庆贺伊丽莎白和达西的婚姻，同情孤立无援的小男孩儿奥列佛。
>
> （Booth 1983：421）

当然，这些共同的反应中仍然有含混部分，仍然有细微的差别，但是后者不应该妨碍我们在从事阅读或阐释意义时遵循一定的标准和规则。

总之，含混就在我们的阅读当中，就在我们的生活当中。它将继续带给我们形形色色的困惑，同时又不断敦促我们寻求人类共同的意义。含混是一种悖论。

参考文献

[1] Abrams M H. *A Glossary of Literary Terms* [M]. Fort Worth: Harcourt Brace College Pubishers, 1999.

[2] Bennett A and Royle N. *Introduction to Literature, Criticism and Theory* [M]. London: Prentice Hall Europe, 1999.

[3] Booth W. *The Rhetoric of Fiction* [M]. Chicago and London: The University of Chicago Press, 1983.

[4] de Man P, *Allegories of Reading: Figural Language in Rousseau, Nietzsche, Rilke, and Proust* [M]. New Haven: Yale University Press, 1979.

[5] Empson W. *Seven Types of Ambiguity* [M]. London: A New Directions Book, 1947.

[6] Fish S. "Is There a Text in This Class?" *The Authority of Interpretive Communities* [M]. Cambridge: Harvard University Press, 1980.

[7] Iser W. *Prospecting: From Reader Response to Literary Anthropology* [M]. Baltimore: Johns Hopkins University Press.

[8] Iser W. *The Act of Reading* [M]. Baltimore and London: Johns Hopkins University Press.

[9] McArthur T. ed., *The Oxford Companion to English Language* [M]. Oxford and New York: Oxford University Press.

[10] Richards I A, *Principles of Literary Criticism* [M]. London: Oxford University Press, 1967.

[11] Richards I A. *The Philosophy of Rhetoric* [M]. London: Oxford University Press, 1936.

[12] 德里达. 德里达中国讲演录, 杜小真等编 [M]. 中央编译出版社, 2003.

[13] 塞尔登. 文学批评理论——从柏拉图到现在 [M]. 刘象愚等, 译. 北京: 北京大学出版社, 2000.

[14] 盛宁. 人文困惑与反思——西方后现代主义思潮批判 [M]. 北京: 三联书店, 1997.

[15] 特伦斯·霍克斯. 结构主义和符号学 [M]. 瞿铁鹏, 译. 上海: 上海译文出版社, 1987.

[16] 王佐良等. 英国二十世纪文学史 [M]. 北京: 外语教学与研究出版社, 1994.

[17] 张隆溪. 二十世纪西方文论述评 [M]. 北京: 三联书店, 1986.

[18] 张汝伦. 意义的探究 [M]. 沈阳: 辽宁人民出版社, 1987.

[19] 赵一凡. 欧美新学赏析 [M]. 北京: 中央编译出版社, 1996.

(本文原载于《外国文学》2004年第2期)

西方文论关键词：重复

一、一句话概说

"重复"（Repetition）是西方文论中的关键词之一；经弗洛伊德、本雅明、德鲁兹、米勒和鲍德里亚等人之手，它逐渐跟"怪异"（Uncanny）、"互文"（Intertext）和"类象"（Simulacra）等概念结下了不解之缘，发展成精神分析批评、解构主义批评和文化研究中必不可少的策略之一。

二、大背景解说

西方有关重复的思想可以追溯到前苏格拉底时期和《圣经》问世的前后。例如，在神学中，《新约全书》往往被阐释为《旧约全书》的一种重复。

近现代西方思想史中涉及重复的论述就更多，其中包括维柯、黑格尔、马克思、德国浪漫主义学派、克尔凯郭尔、尼采和弗洛伊德等人的论著。到了当代，以各种面目出现的重复理论几乎呈爆炸趋势——这些理论的集大成者米勒曾经承认，在不同程度和不同侧面对他自己的重复理论产生影响的当代学者就多达40来人，其中最负盛名的有德里达、詹明信、赛义德、德鲁兹、克莫德、卡勒和格拉夫等。

弗洛伊德的有关学说可以被看作重复理论史上的一个重要转折点。霍尔曼和哈蒙曾经这样说过:"自打弗洛伊德的论文《超越唯乐原则》(1920)问世,'重复'已经被承认为叙事作品中的一个要素。"(Holman and Harmon 1992: 402)其实,弗洛伊德的重复理论的意义远远超出了叙事学的范畴,它关系到了反映论和认识论等重大哲学问题。《超越唯乐原则》一文首次提出了"强迫重复"原则(意指人的本能要求重复以前的状态,要求回复到过去),进而为精神分析家追寻歇斯底里病症或"创伤性神经症"等重复现象背后的意义提供了理论依据。在此之前,弗洛伊德曾经对如何通过回忆来建构真实这一问题进行过探讨,而这种回忆和建构在本质上就是一种重复。在《幼儿期诱发性精神病史一例》(*Aus der Geschichte einer Infantilen Neurose*, 1919)中,弗氏提出了"初始场景"(the primal scene)这一概念,用以表示精神分析家根据病人的回忆而建构的有助于说明患者病因的场景或事件。① 在更早些时候的《癔病研究》(*Studies on Hysteria*, 1895)一书中,弗氏流露出了他对回忆的真实性的疑虑:

> 在病人们接受了他们曾经有过某某想法的事实之后,他们常常加上一句:"但是我记不得曾经有过这样的念头。"……或许我们应该假设我们其实在对付当时根本没有出现过的一些念头——这些思想只不过有存在的可能罢了?如果真是如此,我们在治疗过程中描述的只是一种当时并没有发生的心理行为。(弗洛伊德 1986: 346)

以上论述表明,弗洛伊德此时已经注意到了主体回忆和客体之间的差异,他意识到人们"回忆起来的东西"很可能与历史事实毫不相干。换言之,人们重新复制的事物很可能跟它的原型风马牛不相及。

弗洛伊德的贡献在于,他使人们对重复的形式及其含义的复杂性有了新的认识。在弗氏之前,人们对重复的认识和描述大都建筑在同一逻辑(the logic of identity)的基础上;而在弗氏之后,人们逐渐增加了对建立在差异逻辑(the logic of difference)基础上的重复形式的关注。这两大类重复形式之间的区别和相互之间的关系在米勒那儿得到了最为精彩的论述,而后者又离不开德鲁兹和

---

① 参见殷企平《走出批评话语的困境——从"初始场景"说起》,载《外国文学评论》1996 第 2 期。

本雅明的有关理论强有力的铺垫。本文下一小节将以此为中心展开讨论。

（一）米勒的假说

米勒的重复理论主要见于《小说与重复》（*Fiction and Repetition*，1982）一书。作者开宗明义地指出："一部像小说那样的长篇作品，不管它的读者属于哪一种类型，它的解读多半要通过对重复以及由重复所产生的意义的鉴定来完成。"（Miller 1982：1）可见，虽然该书主要讨论小说中的重复现象，但是其重复理论适用于小说领域以外的任何类似的长篇文本——事实上，米勒在第一章中曾经强调，他所提倡的工作原则既适用于文学文本，又适用于哲学文本（Miller 1982：17）。

开篇后不久，米勒便提出了至关全书命脉的"异质性假说"（the hypothesis of heterogeneity），即任何小说中都存在着两种互相矛盾的重复类型，而且它们总是以这样或那样的交织状态出现在一起；这种"异质性形式"（heterogeneity of form）还可能出现在其他文学体裁之中（Miller 1982：4—5）。

米勒所说的是哪两类基本的重复形式呢？这还要从法国学者德鲁兹的理论贡献说起。

德鲁兹在《意义逻辑》（*Logique du sens*，1969）中把重复划分成了意思迥异的两种类型：一类被称为"柏拉图式"重复，另一类被称为"尼采式"重复。

按照德鲁兹的解释，"柏拉图式"重复"邀请我们考虑以预设的相似原则或相同原则为基础的差异"（Deleuze 1969：302）。言下之意是，这类重复所产生的复制品虽然在严格意义上不同于它所模仿的原型，但是它的前提是尽可能地与后者接近乃至同化。我们知道，柏拉图认为世间万物皆是对理念世界的"摹仿"或"复制"，虽然柏氏曾把"诗"或艺术视为"拷贝的拷贝"，因而有"双倍地远离真实"的危险，但是究其本源，我们总能找到一个坚实的、恒定的、不受重复的影响的原型模子。长期以来，从亚里士多德一直到詹姆斯，西方文艺批评家们大都恪守了柏拉图的基本原则（尽管他们对"真实"或"理念"的理解不尽相同），即复制品的有效性取决于它所模仿的对象的真实性。

"尼采式"重复则要求我们"把相似甚至相同的事物视为本质差异的产物"，其前提是把人类现实"界定为类象的世界"，或者说"把世界本身作为幻影来呈现"（Deleuze 1969：302）。跟第一类重复不同的是，这第二类重复"缺乏某种范式或原型作基础"，因而它总"带有鬼魂般的效果"（Miller 1982：6）。米勒曾经以哈代的小说《卡斯特桥市长》为例来说明这种模式的重复：该书以亨察德卖妻的场景开局；在亨察德结束自己的生命之前，他又回到了当初卖妻的地点，然而实际上他是认错了地方。也就是说，在这类模式中，乙看似对甲的重复，但实际上并非如此。

米勒基本上沿用了德鲁兹的二分法，并在此基础上糅入了本雅明的观点。后者在《普鲁斯特的意象》（The Image of Proust）一文中区分了两类记忆："自觉记忆"（willed memory）和"非自觉记忆"（involuntary form of memory）。前者的工作方式是符合逻辑的，即每一次记忆/重复都有一个坚实的基础，而后者却缺乏任何坚实的基础，其特点就像梦幻——我们常常在梦中发现，本质上大相径庭的事物会以这样或那样的奇特方式呈现出一种模模糊糊的相似性。米勒认为，本雅明所说的"自觉记忆"正好相应于"柏拉图式"重复，而"非自觉记忆"则跟"尼采式"重复相对应。

米勒在阐释第二类重复时，进一步借用了本雅明的观点。后者在解读普鲁斯特时曾经关注过下列对应关系：记忆/遗忘、觉醒/梦幻、里面/外面、满/空、同/异、容器/容纳物。本雅明认为，这一组对应关系可以由"袜子"这一形象得到很好的说明：一只袜子可以被看作空袋子，同时又可以被看作一件礼物，当它被翻卷起来之后尤其如此——此时的"空"与"满"、"容器"与"容纳物"、"里面"与"外面"等概念不仅界线模糊，而且可以互相置换。本雅明认为，"觉醒"与"梦幻"、"记忆"与"遗忘"之间的关系也是如此。

受本雅明的启发，米勒发现袜子同样可以被用来贴切地比喻他所说的第二类重复形式，即"尼采式"重复。换言之，他发现这第二类重复的一个基本特点是能够产生"第三者"：空袋子和袋子里的礼物本来是两种不同的事物，可是它们之间的差别却由袜子这一形象——即第三者——而得到了弥补；同理，在第二类重复模式中，两种不同事物之间的呼应所产生的意义也带有第三者的特点。米勒用弗洛伊德关于歇斯底里病症的发现解释了上述关系：在幼年遭受过性攻击的歇斯底里病症患者往往对自己的病因及其性质缺乏理解，但是患者可能在很久以后的一个不起眼的事件中重复早先性攻击事件中的某个细节，这时医生就可以推断出疾病的真实原因。米勒强调，这两次事件有着上文所说的那种"模糊的相似性"，而作为第三者的歇斯底里病症既不存在于第一次事件中，又不存在于第二次事件中，而是存在于两者之间的关系之中。

米勒花大力气阐述第二类重复，并非要强调它比第一类重复更为重要，而是要强调这两类重复之间你中有我、我中有你的关系，进而确立他的"异质性假说"。在《小说与重复》中，米勒通过对 7 部英国小说的仔细解读，论证了以下观点：

> 每一种形式的重复以一种不可避免的强制力使人想起另一种形式的重复。第二种并非第一种的否定或者对立面，而是它的"对应物"。在这种奇怪的关系中，第二种是第一种的颠覆性幽灵，总是作为挖空它的可能性已经存在于它之中。①

这种犬牙交错的重复形式决定了有关文本的异质特性。

本小节开头处提到，米勒认为长篇文本的解读往往要借助于重复及其意义的鉴定。事实上，英美新批评学派——米勒早先深受该学派的影响——已经在鉴定文本中重复出现的细节方面作出了杰出的贡献。不过，米勒后来发现新批评有一个致命的弱点：它往往忽略那些与它所信奉的"有机整体"不相配的细节。也就是说，新批评关注的是重复的同一性，但是却忽视了它的差异性。从这一意义上说，米勒的"异质性假说"是对新批评的挑战。

（二）重复与怪异

"异质性假说"很容易让人联想到文学批评中的另一个术语，即"怪异"（the uncanny）。② "异质性假说"离不开怪异，也离不开重复，因为"怪异的首要形式是让人感到奇怪的重复"（Bennett and Royle 1999：37）。当然，重复本身并不构成怪异，真正构成怪异的是重复的方式。

---

① 该段的翻译部分参考了程锡麟和王晓路的译文，后者见于《当代美国小说理论》（外语教学与研究出版社，2001）。

② 一些学者在翻译"queer theories"时也用了"怪异"一词，其意思不同于本文中所说的"怪异"，应该特别指出。

英语"the uncanny"有多重含义,其中包括"陌生感""神秘感"以及"神秘而恐怖的感觉"。作为文学批评术语,它首先意味着一种双重的感觉,即"在熟悉事物的中心产生陌生感,或者在陌生事物的中心产生熟悉的感觉"(Bennett and Royle 1999:36)。也就是说,怪异并非仅仅意味着奇异乃至恐怖,而是更具体地表示对人们所熟悉的事物、思想和情感的震撼。

贝尼特和罗依尔曾经举过两个有关怪异的典型例子。

例一:你走进一个从未去过的房间,突然感到自己似乎曾经到过这里,甚至还预感到随后会发生些什么事情。

例二:你身处某个公共场所,突然有一个人闯入了你的眼帘,而且此人有一种让人不安的陌生感;定睛一看,你发现眼前站着的只是你自己——原来晃入你眼帘的是你在一面镜子或玻璃窗上的投影。

以上两个例子代表了两个极端:一是突如其来的似曾相识之感,二是突如其来的陌生感,两者都能产生强大的震撼力。一部好的文学作品也往往能产生类似的震撼力。正是出于这方面的考虑,一些学者干脆提出,"文学本身可以被界定为怪异的话语"(Bennett and Royle 1999:37)。确实,文学家们总是最不遗余力地揭示人类的经历、思想和情感中的怪异层面,因而也最能起到振聋发聩的作用。俄国形式主义者维克多·什克洛夫斯基曾经于20世纪20年代提出著名的"陌生化"原则,即文学作品必须变熟悉为陌生,必须向常人自以为是的信念和假设挑战。从这一意义上说,视文学为"怪异的话语"的观点跟形式主义理论是一脉相传的。

当然,怪异理论首先还要归功于弗洛伊德。1919年,弗氏发表了一篇常被后人称道的文章,其题目就是《怪异》。批评家们在该文中发现了"两个弗洛伊德":一个弗洛伊德相信文学和精神分析泾渭分明,而且精神分析有助于对文学作品作出客观而科学的解释;另一个弗洛伊德则时时流露出跟以上观点相悖的思想,即文学比精神分析家、科学家或信奉理性主义的人们通常所想象的要怪异得多、复杂得多。有意思的是,弗洛伊德自觉或不自觉地为怪异理论做了一场"现身说法"——我们熟知的那个把人类行为的一切动因都归之于利比多的弗洛伊德突然变得陌生起来。这种"双重人"现象可以被看作一种与同一逻辑相违背的重复,也就是米勒等人所说的"尼采式"重复。

总之，重复是怪异的形式，也是怪异的关键。由于有了重复或双重性，文学的怪异功能——其实也是一种教育功能——才得以发生效力：它能使人于平常中发现不平常，更能使人从误以为"熟"或自以为是的状态中醒悟。

（三）重复与互文

国内有学者曾经在评论米勒的《小说与重复》时指出，"在某种程度上，他的重复理论就是互文性理论的翻版"（程锡麟等 2001：152）。这一评论是切中肯綮的。

我们知道，"互文性"概念首先是由法国学者克里斯蒂娃提出来的。她给该术语下了这样一个定义：

> 互文性意味着任何单独文本都是许多其他文本的重新组合；在一个特定的文本空间里，来自其他文本的许多声音互相交叉，互相中和。（Kristeva 1980：145）

这里所说的"重新组合""互相交叉"和"互相中和"其实都是一种重复。当然，这种重复的痕迹有时候——尤其是在被"中和"以后——会变得难以辨认。这一点曾被巴特说得更为明白：

> 互文性是任何文本都无法摆脱的一种状况。当然，我们不能把互文性问题简单地还原成起源和影响的问题；互文是一片综合性的领域，它包容了各种几乎已经无法追溯其起源的无名程式，包容了各种不加引号的、在无意识状态或自动化状态中被引用的话语。（Barthes 1981：41）

"被引用的话语"和"程式"当然也是一种重复。尤其值得我们注意的是，巴特此处提到了"几乎无法追溯其起源"以及"无意识状态"中的互文/重复，这就使我们又想到了弗洛伊德及其"初始场景"一说。

本文"大背景解说"一节中已经给了如下暗示：对真实或起源的追寻构成了弗洛伊德所谓"初始场景"的中心思想。弗氏一方面承认回忆不等于真实，承认事物的本源或真相往往会随着时间的推移而被遮掩，另一方面又试图通过回忆来重构初始场景，从而接近真实。弗氏的这一思想先后经拉康和卢卡舍之手得到了进一步发展。

拉康把弗洛伊德重构初始场景的努力与海德格尔寻找"存在之家"的努力联系到了一起。拉康认为，弗洛伊德和海德格尔都为遗忘所困：弗氏发现自己的病人忘记了病因，而海氏则发现哲学史忘记了本真的源泉。拉康对海氏下面这段话表现出了浓厚的兴趣：

> 西方思想史并非以思考最引人深思的问题开始，而是以忘记这类问题开始。因此，西方思想的开端是一次遗漏，甚至是一次失败……西方思想的开端不同于它的起源。它的开端实际上是遮蔽起源的面纱……
> (Heidergger 1968: 152)

海德格尔此处所说的"起源"——即终极真理——已经超出了主体回忆的范围。拉康恰好从中看到了海德格尔与弗洛伊德的共同之处："弗洛伊德把'真理'置于主体回忆所及范围之外，因而从根本上改变了传统的真理观，这一思想跟海德格尔的看法极其相似。"(Lacan 181: 46) 事实上，拉康建立了弗洛伊德和海德格尔之间的互文关系，也就是建立了精神分析和哲学之间的互文关系，或者说建立了一种跨学科的重复关系。

卢卡舍在拉康所做工作的基础上，进一步扩展并丰富了"初始场景"的含义。他接过拉康的话头，强调弗洛伊德和海德格尔之间最具有意义的共同点是对起源问题的关注。跟拉康一样，卢卡舍认为，

> 弗洛伊德和海德格尔都要求我们以新的角度理解遗忘和回忆之间的关系。病人已经忘记了初始场景，而形而上学的历史则忘记了存在的历史。
> (Lukacher 1986: 42—43)

跟拉康不同的是，卢氏就"回忆是什么"这一问题提出了更明确、更简洁的说法。他对拉康下面这段话表示不满：

> 回忆不是柏拉图的回想——它不是理念的回归，不是天生烙印的回归，不是九霄云外真善美的理念向我们的回归。它是一种出于结构的必要性而向我们回归的东西，一种卑微的东西。
>
> （Lacan 1981：47）

卢氏指出，上述言论表明拉康跟弗洛伊德和海德格尔一样，能够毫不含糊地说出"回忆不是什么"，但是在"回忆是什么"这一问题上却含糊其词，故弄玄虚。回忆究竟是什么呢？卢氏明确地回答："它是一种阐释，一种构建，一种阅读。"（Lukacher 1986：43）既然回忆是一种阐释，那么它就有一个阐释时机和阐释角度的问题。卢氏提出阐释"首先要解决重复出现的东西"，进而"拖曳出病人言论和哲学史当中的存留之物"（Lukacher 1986：42）。有意思的是，卢氏强调阐释要从重复入手，这跟米勒的观点何其相似！

当然，在卢卡舍那里，从重复入手的阐释更明确地体现为连接文学、哲学和精神分析学的互文关系，而且是一种无法从本体论角度来确定的互文关系，这在他给"初始场景"所下的新定义中得到了清楚的说明：

> 由于文学、哲学和精神分析学的紧密联系，以及它们共同拥有的起源的揭示/遮蔽问题，我提议把初始场景的概念作为一种关于阅读和理解的比喻。为此目的，我不把"初始场景"限制在传统精神分析学对该术语的理解水平上……初始场景表示一种从本体论角度无法确定的互文性事件，一种介于史实性记忆和想象性建构之间的事件……（Lukacher 1986：24）

尽管卢卡舍和米勒都对"无法确定的互文性事件"，亦即重复，表现出了穷追不舍的劲头，然而我们还是要问：米勒是否会对卢卡舍的观点提出质疑？如前文所示，米勒的兴奋点集中于追寻纵横交错的重复关系中的异质性，并加以解释，而卢卡舍的热情却倾向于靠近真实，接近起源。对于这一本质上的区别，我们不可不察。

（四）重复与类象

重复不仅是现当代文学批评的基本策略之一，而且在文化理论中占有不可替代的地位。弗莱在谈论文化研究时，曾经对克尔凯郭尔的一本小册子颇为赞赏，这本小册子的题目就是《重复》。克尔凯郭尔用"重复"一语取代了传统的柏拉图的术语"回想"（anamnesis）或"回忆"（recollection），其用意是强调记忆——在某种意义上，文化是人类的记忆——不是一种经验的简单重复，而是对它的重新创造。弗莱接过克氏的话题，强调重复意识有助于研究人类的总体文化形态：

> 过去的文化并不仅仅是人类的记忆，而是我们自己已经埋葬了的生活。对它的研究导致一种认识，一种发现。通过它我们不但看到已往的生活，而且还看到当今生活的总体文化形态。
>
> （Frye 1990：346）

随着后现代主义文化理论的兴起，对弗莱所说的"总体文化形态"的研究越来越依赖于重复的一种特殊形式，即"类象"。上文中已经提到，米勒和德鲁兹都认为"尼采式"重复有一个前提，即把人类现实界定为"类象的世界"。那么，"类象"究竟是什么意思呢？这还要从首先提出该术语的法国学者让·鲍德里亚说起。

鲍德里亚认为人类在后现代陷入了"表征危机"（crisis of representation），因为此时人类现实的表征可以被系统地、无止境地同类复制。当某个表征生产出新的仿真复制品时，后者已经和原先的现实完全脱离，而这种仿真品还可以继续产生新的复制品，这样的循环往复当然离现实会越来越远。下面是一段鲍氏关于仿真（simulation）和类象的原话：

> 表征始于这样一个原则，即符号与现实是对等的（即便这种对等关系只是乌托邦精神的体现，它也仍然是一项基本准则）。相反，仿真始于上述对等原则的乌托邦形式，始于对符号价值的激烈的否定，始于符号的逆转以及对任何指涉物都宣判死刑。表征视仿真为伪表征，并借此吸纳仿真，而仿真却视表征本身为类象，进而吞没了整幢表征大厦。下面是形象的几个发展阶段：

1. 它反映了基本现实。
2. 它遮蔽并扭曲了基本现实。
3. 它遮蔽了基本现实的缺席。
4. 它断绝跟任何现实的关系；它只是自己的纯类象而已。

(Baudrilland 1988：170)

值得注意的是，鲍德里亚在上面这段话中提到了"形象"一词，并把类象界定成了形象发展诸阶段中的最后一个阶段。我们知道，"形象"（the image）一词不仅有着哲学上的背景，而且是 20 世纪以来备受系统分析的对象。萨特和詹明信①就都认为形象是很危险的东西，甚至认为它是"很隐秘地感染毒化现实的方法"（杰姆逊 1997：217）。言下之意是，形象之所以危险，是因为它有失去客观性或"他性"的倾向。詹明信对此做过这样的说明：电视机问世之前，媒介形象所表征的现实——如电影或报纸上的照片——或多或少地还保留着"他性"，即跟接受信息者仍然保留着一定的距离。然而，由于电视机完全地融入了我们的家庭生活，它所传递的形象也似乎完全属于我们自己，因此它便失去了他性，也就是失去了詹明信所说的"距离感"：

在电视这一媒介中，所有其他媒介中所含有的与另一现实的距离感完全消失了，这是个很奇特的过程，但这一过程可以说正是后现代主义的全部精粹。后现代主义的全部特征就是距离感的消失。（杰姆逊 1997：211）

距离感的消失意味着现实感的消失，这也就是类象引起后现代文化理论家们高度重视的原因。我们不妨再引用一段詹明信的原话：

形象、照片、摄影的复制、机械性的复制以及商品的复制和大规模生产，所有这一切都是类象。所以，我们的世界，起码从文化上来说是没有任何现实感的，因为我们无法确定现实从哪里开始，在哪里结束。正是在

---

① 即 Fredric Jameson，本文引用的汉译本译其为"杰姆逊"。

这里，有着后现代主义理论中最核心的道德、心理和政治的批判力量。……这一理论必须讨论类象的巨大作用力。（杰姆逊1997：219—220）

既然类象在后现代社会中有着"巨大作用力"，那么对社会的批判也必须从类象入手。事实上，许多后现代批评家在这方面已经做了许多工作。例如，萨达曾经指出了这样一种现象：西方跨国公司常常在非西方国家开辟新的市场，但是它们在那里推销的并不是用自己的生产线直接制造的产品，而是由当地某个承包公司制造的产品——这些子公司被允许使用跟母公司相同的品牌，同时又被默许使用不同的原料和配方。此举不但给母公司带来了低成本高利润的好处，而且还常被用来往西方国家脸上贴金，因为表面上它们是在帮助那些非西方国家的经济。萨达对这一现象作了如下批判：

> 在非西方国家出售的大多数西方产品只是类象而已：它们看上去货真价实，而且确实由真正的西方公司营销，但实际上却是伪劣的复制品。（Sardar 1998：56）

总之，当今世界可谓"类象环生"，其趋势一直有增无减，因而重复这一概念的内涵也必然会随之发生更多更微妙的变化。我们禁不住要问："重复"含义的膨胀是否也可以算作一种后现代现象？

三、结语

正因为"重复"概念的含义仍然在不断增殖，所以对其中的复杂原因及其变数的研究仍然有待于进一步地深入。关于这一研究工作的诸多意义，本文各小节其实都已有所暗示。我们没有必要在此逐一回顾这些意义，但是却有必要再次回到米勒的"异质性假说"上来：警惕异质性或各种奇异的"重复"，这不仅有助于我们比较清醒地阅读文学作品，而且还有助于我们比较清醒地面对更加广阔的学术领域乃至整个生活现实。米勒曾经从学术大背景的角度为"异质性假说"的意义作过说明，我们不妨以此作为本文的结束语，并以此作为今后

探索"重复"的一个理由:

20世纪思想史——无论是在语言学、心理学、生物学、人种学和社会学领域,还是在原子物理学和天体物理学领域——有这样一个特点,即人们认识到人类和自然领域比我们所想象的更奇异,因此人们正在作不懈的努力,以寻找这种奇异现象的规律,进而化陌生为熟悉。(Miller 1982: 18—19)

应该加上一句:米勒所说的仍然适用于21世纪。

参考文献

[1] Barthes R. *Untying the Text: A Poststructuralist Reader* [M]. London: Methuen, 1981.

[2] Baudrillard J. "Simulacra and Simulation" [A] // *Selected Writings*, ed. Mark Poster [M]. Oxford: Polity Press, 1988.

[3] Bennett A & N. *An Introduction to Literature, Criticism and Theory* [M]. London: Prentice Hall Europe, 1999.

[4] Deleuze G. *Logique du sens* [M]. Paris: Les Editions de Minuit, 1969.

[5] Freud S Breuer J. *Studies on Hysteria* [M]. trans. Stratchey. New York: Avon Books, 1966.

[6] Frye N. *Anatomy of Criticism* [M]. London: Penguin Books, 1990.

[7] Heidergger M. *What Is Called Thinking?* [M]. Trans. J. Glenn Gray [M]. New York: Harper and Row, 1968.

[8] Holman C H & Harmon [N]. *A Handbook to Literature* [M]. New York and London: Macmillan Publishing Company, 1992.

[9] Kristeva J. *Desire in Language* [M]. Oxford: Blackwell, 1980.

[10] Lacan J. *The Function and Field of Speech and Language in Psychoanalysis* [M]. trans. Alan Sheridan. New York: Norton, 1981.

[11] Lukacher N. *Primal Scenes* [M]. Ithaca and London: Cornell University

Press, 1986.

［12］Miller J H, *Fiction and Repetition* [M]. Oxford: Basil Blackwell, 1982.

［13］Sardar Z. *Postmodernism and the Other* [M] London: Pluto Press, 1998.

［14］程锡麟, 王晓路. 当代美国小说理论 [M]. 北京: 外语教学与研究出版社, 2001.

［15］弗·杰姆逊. 后现代主义与文化理论 [M]. 唐小兵, 译. 北京: 北京大学出版社, 1997.

［16］西格蒙德·弗洛伊德. 超越唯乐原则. 弗洛伊德后期著作选 [M]. 林尘等, 译. 上海: 上海译文出版社, 1986.

［17］殷企平. 走出批评话语的困境——从"初始场景"说起 [J]. 外国文学评论, 1996, (2).

(本文原载于《外国文学》2003年第2期)

说"顿悟"

就小说领域而言,"顿悟"(epiphany)一词源于詹姆斯·乔伊斯(James Joyce,1882—1941)之手,但是该词最初的意思是初生的耶稣在东方三贤(the three Magi)面前的突然显现。乔伊斯把该术语移入小说领域,并且在《艺术家青年时代画像》(*A Portrait of the Artist As a Young Man*,1916)的初稿中首次对该词作了如下界定:

"所谓顿悟,指的是突然的精神感悟。不管是通俗的言词,还是平常的手势,或是一种值得记忆的心境,都可以引发顿悟。他①认为文人应该极其小心地记录下这些顿悟现象,并且意识到这些现象虽然微妙,但是却稍纵即逝。他告诉克兰利,仓库办公室里的那座钟就有可能引发顿悟。"②

以上定义强调了两点:一是突发性的精神感悟,二是经由作者的生花妙笔的点缀,再普通的事物也能焕发出永恒之美的光辉。这正如斯蒂芬在另一处所说的那样,"最寻常的事物似乎辐射出了灵光。"③ 在乔伊斯之后,人们相继给"顿悟"一词下过不少定义,其中如《简明不列颠百科全书》中的说法:"指在文学里对一个人或情景的潜在真义的突然揭示。"另一个较为典型的定义出自著名英国小说家兼批评家戴维·洛奇:"顿悟这一术语适用于任何描写充满着超验

---

① 指斯蒂芬。
② J. A. Cuddon, *A Dictionary of Literary Terms*, André Deutsch Limited, 1979, p. 237.
③ 见 *The Portable James Joyce*, edited by Harry Levin, Penguin Books, 1979, p. 321.

性意义的外部现实的段落。"① 以上定义虽然大致勾勒了顿悟这一概念，但是笔者以为，对其含义的真正理解还有待于深入探讨如下两个问题：1）顿悟有哪些表现形式？2）实现顿悟的基本条件是什么？对这两个问题的回答构成了本文的主要内容。

概括地说，顿悟表现为低层次的顿悟和高层次的顿悟两种。低层次的顿悟是对个体经验或局部人生的一种突然领悟，而高层次的顿悟则是对整个人生真谛的领悟——是对真善美的纯粹观照。

低层次的顿悟至少还可以分为以下三种情况：

1. 对某段人生经历的猛然醒悟——包括对人物的生活方式、先前追求的生活目标等突然有了新的认识。以《艺术家青年时代画像》为例：斯蒂芬有一次看到写字台上乱涂着"胚胎"一词，平常人很可能会对此不屑一顾，可是斯蒂芬却突然从中看到了自己"怪胎般的生活方式"。这方面的例子在乔伊斯的短篇小说集《都柏林人》（Dubliners, 1914）中尤为集中。事实上，乔伊斯后来干脆把该书中所有十五个短篇都称为"顿悟篇"（Epiphanies）。这十五个短篇都以顿悟的方式反映了20世纪初都柏林市民生活的不同侧面——每一个短篇都是对某个生活片段的精神感悟。例如，在《阿拉比》（Araby）中，街市上"各种各样的喧嚣声"突然在主人公的想象中"汇聚成一种对生活的感觉：我想象着自己正捧着圣餐杯在一群敌人中穿行"。② 又如，在《死者》（The Dead）中，一首名叫《奥格里姆姑娘》的普通民歌引发了一连串的精神感悟，不仅使男主人公加布里埃尔和女主人公格丽塔悟到了他俩所谓爱情生活的肤浅和苍白，而且还使加布里埃尔意识到"自己的灵魂已接近那个住着大批死者的领域"。③ 再以《路遇》（An Encounter）为例：两个小孩儿在都柏林港口附近寻找一个"绿眼睛"的外国水手，以满足他们对一种新奇生活的向往，然而他们唯一找到的是一个眼睛绿得像酒瓶玻璃的性变态者。这就像侯维瑞先生分析的那样："正是在这个时候，他们经历了精神感悟的时刻。他们一心想在都柏林沉寂的生活之外寻求新奇而令人振奋的经历，到头来找到的却是乖戾、变态和堕落；一时间'绿眼

---

① David Lodge, *The Art of Fiction*, Secker and Warburg, 1992, pp. 146–147.
② James Joyce, *Araby*, 载 *The Portable James Joyce*, Penguin Books, 1979, pp. 41.
③ James Joyce, *The Dead*, 出处同上, pp. 241.

睛'成了他们幻想破灭和探索破产的标志。"① 需要在此一提的是，经历顿悟的并非一定是人物本身，而是可以单独由读者来感受作品所要揭示的生活真义。例如，《都柏林人》的第一篇《姐妹》（*The Sister*）主要描写一个孩子对一位神父去世的反应。一般评论者都把注意力集中于小孩儿在见过神父遗体后得到的所谓"启示"，即"牧师的圣职使他不堪忍受"。然而，那个小孩儿涉世未深，意识尚未成熟，因此不可能对神父之死有很深刻的认识。笔者以为，如果我们把注意力移向神父临死前打破圣餐杯这一幕，我们就会达到豁然开朗的境界：破碎的圣餐杯正好表明他那惨淡经营的宗教事业的破产——他苦心建筑的上帝与众生之间的桥梁已经断裂。

2. 对某个人物性格的突然领悟——人物的一举手、一投足、一种姿势或一种生理特点于一瞬间把人物性格的深处暴露在另一人物或读者面前。这方面的例子可以在许多小说中找到，而且可以在一部小说中就找到许多。例如，狄更斯的《大卫·科波菲尔》中尤利亚·希普那扭动的身躯使人一下子就想起他那毒蛇般的品格；《远大前程》中赫薇香小姐瘫伏在拐杖上凝视那块腐烂的婚礼蛋糕的姿态、贾格斯先生挥舞白手帕并且咬自己食指的动作、威密克先生那张像邮筒投信口的嘴巴以及乔太太围裙上插满的针都分别使匹普和读者猛然领悟到他们各自的性格，即赫薇香小姐的腐朽、贾格斯先生的愚蠢和邪恶、威密克先生的呆板和冷漠以及乔太太的泼辣。再以乔伊斯的《艺术家青年时代画像》中对科律根沐浴时的描写为例："他的肤色跟灰碳似的泥水一模一样……当他沿着浴池边往前走时，他的脚重重地拍打着潮湿的瓷砖；每前进一步，他那大腿上的肥肉就要抖动一番。"通过科律根那臃肿异常的体态，读者一下子就能领悟到他那愚钝拙劣的性格。

3. 对某传统价值观的顿悟——这方面的顿悟往往采用"陌生化"（defamiliarization）的表现方式。仅以夏洛特·勃朗蒂的小说《维列特》（*Villette*，1853）为例。女主人公露西有一次在艺术馆里参观画展，忽然有一幅题为"克娄巴特拉"的画吸引了她的注意力："画中表现的是一个女人。我想她的体积比现实中的人要大得多。……我们把她放在通常用来衡量重型货物的巨

---

① 侯维瑞，《现代英国小说史》，上海外语教育出版社，1985年版，第249页。

秤上过一过秤,就能够证明这一点。她确实饱食终日:她一定消费了不少从肉铺老板那儿买来的肉——至于面包、蔬菜和饮料,那就更不在话下了,要不然她根本不可能长到那样的宽度和高度,不可能长那么多的肌肉,也不可能长那么多的肥肉。她半倚半躺地靠在躺椅上……她看上去身体非常健康,完全能够胜任两个普通厨娘的工作——她没有理由躺在沙发上消磨掉整个中午。她还应该穿上得体的衣服;应该有一件袍裙合适地为她遮羞,可是画中明明画着一大堆衣料——足足有二十七码长,她却只用其中的一丁点儿来遮掩自己的身体……"[1] 这段精彩的描写是对传统审美观中荒谬之处的突然曝光——"克娄巴特拉"是一幅典型的传统绘画:近乎全裸的美女斜躺在那儿,身边拖着呈波浪形的衣物,或许还有随意搁置的酒杯、花瓶等。常人往往不假思索地把这类画称为"高雅艺术",可是作者却用"陌生化"的处理方法——即一反常规地描写这类画的内容及其表现手法——使露西连同读者一起突然领悟到所谓"高雅艺术"的低劣之处:藏匿于"艺术"光环中的原来是一个能吃会睡、无所事事、寡廉鲜耻的寄生虫!

与低层次的顿悟相比,高层次的顿悟的特点在于超越个体经验和局部人生,进而上升到对整个人生真谛的领悟。事实上,高层次的顿悟跟朱光潜先生所说的"诗的境界"极为相似:"每首诗都自成一种境界。无论是作者或是读者,在心领神会一首好诗时,都必有一幅画境或是一幕戏景,很新鲜生动地突现于眼前,使他神魂为之钩摄,若惊若喜,霎时无暇旁顾,仿佛这小天地中有独立自足之乐,此外偌大乾坤宇宙,以及个人生活中一切憎爱悲喜,都像在这霎时间烟消云散了。纯粹的诗的心境是凝神注视,纯粹的心所观境是独立绝缘。心与其所观境如鱼戏水,忻合无间……诗的境界在刹那中见终古,在微尘中显大千,在有限中寓无限。"[2] 虽然朱光潜先生这里谈的是诗的境界,可是小说的境界又何尝不是如此!一部好的小说应该能够把人导入孤立绝缘的心所观境,应该使人有豁然贯通的时刻,应该让人以一霎时的直觉突然看到普涵普盖的真善美——这就是我们所说的高层次顿悟。当然,小说和诗歌毕竟不同。诗的篇幅一般较小,因此容易形成朱光潜先生所说的那种有独立自足之乐的小天地,而

---

[1] Charlotte Brontë, *Villette*, Bantam Books, 1986, P. 191.
[2] 《朱光潜美学文集》第 2 卷,上海文艺出版社,1982 年版,第 49—50 页。

小说的篇幅较长，因此要使整个结构的含义突现于读者面前就相对难些。尽管如此，达到"境界"——即实现高层次顿悟——的小说还是不少。下面仅举三例。

先以《德伯家的苔丝》(*Tess of the D'urbervilles*, 1891)为例。该书快结尾处有关苔丝安睡于悬石坛的那一段描写就形成了高层次的顿悟：冉冉东升的旭日将其首束光辉仅仅献于苔丝一人，而那些石柱连同包围苔丝的警察仍然为黑夜所笼罩；这一强烈的反差不能不使读者的心为之震慑——悬石坛代表着人世间所有的苦难，那些包围者象征着人世间的所有不公正，而苔丝在饱经人世间的磨难以后又即将面对刑场的时刻却显得那样安详，那样泰然，那样美丽。顿时，我们不仅感受到了苔丝的人格力量，而且感受到了整个人类超越苦难的力量；我们对书中具体画面的观照霎时间变成了对绝对美的观照。可以说，这种具有高层次顿悟意味的画面必然是小说的总结性画面：小说的全部含义——即苔丝与苦难抗争的全部含义都浓缩在了这一画面之中，并且迸发出了足以使读者凝神观照的灵光。

另一个典型的例子可以在伍尔夫的《到灯塔去》(*To the Lighthouse*, 1972)中找到。书中布丽思科·莉莉临海作画的细节不可忽视。莉莉一共作了两幅画，第一幅在第一部分"窗口"中作成，第二幅在第三部分"灯塔"中作成。由于第一幅画不甚理想，所以莉莉力图通过第二幅画来获得成功。当她一边目送拉姆齐先生带领子女乘船驶向灯塔，一边苦心经营画境时，她眼前浮现出了拉姆齐太太的形象（这位集坚强、慈爱等众多美好品质于一身的女主人此时已经去世，但是她却比以往任何时刻都更牵动着书中所有人物的心）。后者的精神之光与灯塔的光芒互相辉映的情状顷刻间使莉莉来了灵感，帮助她捕捉到了新的意境："她眼前骤然一亮，心中一阵冲动，于是一笔画就了一条直线，正好落在画的中央。画好了，大功告成了。她疲乏地放下画笔，心里想：是的，我终于达到了我观察中的境界。"[①] 随着那一条直线的画就，莉莉经历了一次顿悟，读者也随之悟到了全书的精髓：这不是一条普通的直线，而是整部小说艺术结构和思想内容的脊梁。就其艺术结构而言，这条直线暗指小说的中间部分，即"时光飘

---

① Virginia Woolf, *To the Lighthouse*, New York: Harcourt Brace, 1927, P. 310.

逝"那一章——就像直线处在莉莉那幅画的中央那样,"时光飘逝"也处于小说叙事结构的中央(处于"窗口"和"灯塔"两章的中间),两者正好相映成趣。换言之,直线是莉莉那幅画成为整体的关键,而"时光飘逝"则是使小说连成一体的中枢。就小说的思想内容而言,直线象征着灯塔及其带来的光明和温暖,象征着拉姆齐太太那挺拔的精神,象征着一条精神航线——当拉姆齐先生携子女开始了去灯塔的航程时,他们也开始了一次精神上的航程,即追求拉姆齐太太毕生都在追求的理想:建立人与人之间的和谐与信任——这也是整个人类都应追求的理想,因而包含着整个人生的真谛。可见,莉莉那一条貌似普通的直线起到了使全书意义豁然贯通的作用。它妙不可言,令人回味无穷。

最后再以约翰·厄普代克的《兔子,跑吧》(*Rabbit Run*, 1960)为例。小说主人公哈利(绰号为"兔子")不甘忍受死水一潭的婚姻生活,于是就离家出走,并且投入了一个名叫露丝的女人的怀抱。当地牧师埃克里斯邀请他一起打高尔夫球,并借此机会劝他回到妻子身边去。下面是他俩的一段对话:

> "你为什么要离开她?很明显,你对她的感情很深。"
> "告诉过你了。就是那种东西,那里没有。"
> "什么东西?你见过啦?你敢肯定这东西存在?"①

接着,埃克里斯甚至嘲弄起哈利来了:"是什么?什么?硬的还是软的?哈利,蓝色的?红色的?有圆点儿花纹没有?"② 面对埃克里斯的追问和挖苦,哈利显得十分困窘和尴尬,可是又一时说不清自己的婚姻生活里究竟缺少了什么,于是就干脆抡起了高尔夫球棒——想趁早收场脱身,没料到就在他击球后的一刹那,他找到了答案:

> 他十分利索地把球棒挥过肩膀,然后朝球打下去。撞击的声音空灵,超凡脱俗。他还从来没听到过这样的声音。由于他双臂用力较猛,他的头也顺势抬得很高。只见那只球悬在老远的地方,其宛若月光的银灰色背后

---

① 参考李力、李欣译本,重庆出版社1987年版,第185页。
② 同上。

衬着一片片美丽的雨云,蓝幽幽的。那是他外祖父的颜色,浓浓地抹在东方的天际。球沿着一条笔直的线渐渐远去。一下打去,这球恰如流星赶月,眨眼间变成一个小白点。球迟疑了一下,"兔子"以为它要消失了,但是他上了当。那一迟疑只是一种依托,球在此基础上又做了最后一跳。就在它落下消失之前,那球分明是带着啜泣最后咬了太空一口。"就是这个!"他大叫起来,然后喜笑颜开地转过身来,对埃克里斯重复了一句:"就是这个。"①

打高尔夫球原本是一桩很普通的事情,但是就在那平平常常的一挥、一击、一看之间,哈利经历了一次顿悟:他生活中所缺少的正是那种流星赶月般的激情和壮美。读者也随之感悟到了小说的基本含义:"兔子"之所以要跑,要离家出走,是因为他想逃离人世间的平庸。高尔夫球虽小,但是它运行时的姿态、声响、色彩以及它与太空融为一体的情景却蔚为壮观。此时,哈利的心灵已经得到了升华——他的胸襟气韵分明已经贯注于天地万物之间。可以说,此时的哈利暂时超越了个体生命,而读者亦可通过对这一境界的观照而忘却小我,进入人和万物一体同仁的状态,形成物我的回响交流。

以上我们讨论了顿悟的表现形式。那么,实现顿悟的条件又是什么呢?依笔者所见,实现顿悟须有两个基本条件:一是形象的妙用,二是情感的积累。下面分别加以探讨。

顿悟的产生需要有一个"助产婆",即巧妙运用的形象。如前文已经暗示的那样,顿悟的突出特点之一就是用尽可能简洁的语言来表达尽可能丰富的含义,而这一任务非由经过精心选择的形象来承担不可。事实上,上举所有例子都是通过某个形象来实现顿悟的:无论是哈利一棒打出去的高尔夫球,还是莉莉一笔画就的直线,或是苔丝安然躺在悬石坛上的睡姿,都分别构成了有关顿悟现象的前提。这里再以《艺术家青年时代画像》为例。主人公斯蒂芬一生中曾经历过许多精神感悟的时刻,其中有两次最为重要:一次是他对"爱尔兰之魂"的顿悟,另一次是他对自己艺术家使命的顿悟,而这两次顿悟都以"鸟"的形象

---

① 参考李力、李欣译本,重庆出版社1987年版,第186—187页。

为依托。第一次他把整个爱尔兰的灵魂比作了蝙蝠："一个蝙蝠似的灵魂开始意识到自己正处于无人知晓的黑暗和孤独之中。"① 其后不久，斯蒂芬又感到"他所在种族的思想和欲望像蝙蝠那样掠过这一国家的黑暗胡同……"② 有关艺术家使命的顿悟则以"海鸟""鸽子"和"雄鹰"等形象为依托：在第四章中，斯蒂芬从一位涉水少女的形象中受到了启示，决心投身于艺术事业；在他的眼中，这位少女"好像被魔术点化成了一只美丽非凡的海鸟……"③ 就连她的胸脯也"宛若黑色羽毛的鸽子"。④ 在此之前，斯蒂芬其实已经从另一幅与鸟有关的景象中听到了艺术家使命的召唤："他似乎听到了海浪轻微的喧闹声，看见了一个长着翅膀的身影飞翔于海浪之上，并渐渐飞向天空……一位雄鹰般的男子跃出了水面，朝着太阳飞去。这不啻是一个启示：他生来就应该致力于这样的目标；他的童年和少年时代虽然云遮雾障，可是他一直梦寐以求的其实就是这样一个目标。眼前的景象又是一种象征：艺术家把地球上呆滞的物质锻造一新，创造出了一种能够展翅高飞的生物——它来去无踪，却永不陨灭……"⑤

顿悟的另一个基本条件是情感的积累。一般来说，顿悟的产生总是伴随着情感的迸发，而情感的迸发则须有情感的逐渐积累。上面一段中的最后一个例子就很能说明问题：从雄鹰般的鸟人到美丽的海鸟，斯蒂芬其实经历了一个感情递增的过程。随着情感活动的不断加剧，斯蒂芬对自己的使命感也不断加深。正是因为有了前面的情感积累和加剧，所以才有了后面斯蒂芬欣喜若狂的场面：斯蒂芬突然"两颊容光焕发，浑身火热如焚，四肢颤抖不已。他大步向前迈进，迈进，远远越过沙滩，向着大海引吭高歌。生活已经对他发出了召唤。斯蒂芬呼喊着迎接生活的到来。"⑥ 同样，前文所举《兔子，跑吧》中哈利打球一例也极能说明我们这里的观点：作者在描写哈利击球之前小心地作了许多铺垫工作，以暗示哈利此时复杂的情感活动——不美满的婚姻造成的积郁、因埃克里斯的挖苦而产生的恼怒、由于无法回答埃克里斯的追问而感到的窘迫、竭力想摆脱

---

① James Joyce, *A Portrait of the Artist As a Young Man.* 载 The Portable James Joyce, Penguin Books, 1979, pp. 446.
② 同上, pp. 494.
③ 同上, pp. 433。
④ 同上。
⑤ 同上, pp. 430—431。
⑥ 同上, pp. 434。

困境的焦急、对一种新生活的向往，所有这些情感都聚焦在了一起。事实上，前文引用的哈利击球那一段之前还有一个非常重要的细节：哈利和埃克里斯"走到发球座跟前，这是一座草皮垒成的平台，旁边一株弓腰驼背的果树，上面簇聚着一团团绷得很紧的浅色叶芽"。① 这里，"绷得很紧"一词恰如其分地渲染了当时的情感气氛，表现了哈利心头浓缩的情感急待迸发的情状，因此也为而后的顿悟作了有力的铺垫。

小说中的顿悟现象是一个非常复杂的现象。这方面值得研究的问题还有许多，如顿悟与叙事结构的关系、顿悟常用的修辞手段等。此外，顿悟的表现形式与基本条件很可能远远不止本文中提到的那么几种。本文只是想抛砖引玉，借此引发出更多的讨论而已。

（本文原载于《外国文学》1996 年第 3 期）

---

① 李力、李欣译本，第 186 页。

谈"互文性"

本文旨在探讨"互文性"（intertextuality）的基本含义及其具体表现形式。

一、"互文性"的基本含义

T. S. 艾略特曾经说过："稚嫩的诗人依样画葫芦，成熟的诗人偷梁换柱。"（Scholes et al. 1998）这句话其实蕴涵着后结构主义"互文性"思想的萌芽。所谓"偷梁换柱"，当然指的是对其他诗歌文本的利用或借用。那么，是不是所有诗人，乃至所有作家，都要从事这种"偷"与"换"的"勾当"呢？以"互文性"思想为中心的后结构主义文本批评的回答是肯定的。

"互文性"的定义很简单：最早提出这一术语的法国学者朱丽娅·克里斯特娃（Julia Kristeva）把它说成是"一文本与其他文本的相互关系"（Scholes et al. 1998: 131; 霍克斯 1987: 150; 李俊玉 1993）; 不过，这一貌似简单的定义包含着相当复杂的思想。其一，它是对结构主义文本理论的一种超越。结构主义是把现代结构语言学奠基者索绪尔（Ferdinand de Saussure）的方法和观点应用于文学领域的一种尝试。结构主义者力图阐明生成诗歌、小说等文艺作品的"诗学"，即关于文学规则的抽象系统。这种理论主要有三个特点：1）把文本当作一个独立自足的语言封闭体，一个由一系列符号/能指（signifiant）组成的明确的结构；2）只对文本作共时性的理解；3）试图通过对单一文本结构的关注而窥见统驭全人类作品的规则。互文性原则正是对具有以上特点的研究方法的否定：互文性强调文本结构的非确定性，强调任何文本都没有什么固定的界限，强调任何文本都不可能脱离其他文本而存在——每个文本的意义产生于它跟其他文本的相互作用之中。这种相互作用是永无止境的。因此，与其说文本是空间里的一个客体，不如说它是时间里的一次运动。在这种永恒的运动当中，若想通过对某一文本或文本系统的共时研究来抽象出左右全人类作品的规则，那只能是白费气力。

其二，虽然互文性思想是对结构主义文本理论的超越，但是它跟后者的关系首先是一种继承和发展的关系。和结构主义的观点一样，互文性的观点认为文本在语言之外没有起点，也没有终点，用解构主义代表人物德里达（Jacques Derrida）的话说，"文本应该被看作一股川流不息的能指"（Peck et al. 1984：166）。可见，结构主义强调能指而忽略所指的思想仍然是互文性原则的思想基础之一；互文性虽然强调任何词语乃至任何单独文本的意义超出自身所示，但是其意义指向仍然是其他文本及其词语，而不是文本之外的什么东西。

其三，互文性也成为后现代主义广义文化研究的一种武器。按照福柯（Michel Foucault）的观点，西方文学和文化研究已经从以人为中心的现代主义时期步入"第四知识共因时期"，即以多极综合阐释为特性的"后现代时期"（赵一凡 1989：531）。从贝尔（Daniel Bell）、斯金纳（Quentin Skinner）、波普尔（K. R. Popper）和罗尔斯（J. B. Rawls）到拉康（J. Lacan）、巴特（R. Barthes）、福柯（M. Foucault）和德里达（Jacques Derrida），一大批后现代主义学者都认为西方文化已经被科技理性和商业浪潮冲击得支离破碎，因而他们都提出要实现文化的全面整合与重建。这种"文化的整合"的前提之一就是打破学科与学科之间的严格界限，而互文性原则正好是对不同学科之间传统界限的超越：互文性不仅强调文学文本之间的相互作用，而且强调文学文本与其他学科领域内的文本之间的关系。爱德华·赛义德（Edward Said）曾经这样评论拉康、巴特、福柯和德里达等四人的研究方法："他们不拘泥于文学、文学批评、语文学、哲学、语言学、人类学、精神分析和政治学甚至理论与实践之间的区别——他们的共同方法是拼合。"（Bannet 1989：7）贝尼特说得更为明确："互文性……使拉康、巴特、福柯和德里达在不同类型的话语和不同类型的文本之间任意地漫游,并同时把它们结合在一起,对它们作出新的阐释,而对任何一个学科或任何一个文本的传统界线和规定则置之不顾。"(Bannet 1989:244)

二、对文本的改写

从作家的角度看,互文性表现为对文本的改写:任何作者在写作时都是在对别的文本进行有意或无意的改写。

有意识的改写包括诠注、翻译、典故的运用和反讽模仿等。这里仅以英国的两位反讽模仿大师亨利·菲尔丁和詹姆斯·乔伊斯的作品为例。先说菲尔丁的《约瑟·安特鲁和他的朋友亚伯拉罕·亚丹姆斯先生历险记》(1742,以下简称《约瑟·安特鲁传》)。这部小说对理查逊的著名小说《帕美拉》进行戏谑模仿。后者的主题是"贞洁得报":主人公帕美拉·安特鲁出身寒微,被迫给一家富人当女仆,但是她以自己的美和贞洁赢得了女主人之子 B 先生的真正爱情和尊敬,最终两人结为伉俪。为了讽刺这种用穷人的贞洁去换取富人的酬报的思想,菲尔丁对《帕美拉》的基本情节和结构稍加改造,写成了《约瑟·安特鲁传》。该书以帕美拉的兄弟约瑟为主人公;跟帕美拉一样,约瑟也去富人家当仆人;而且,就像 B 先生看上了帕美拉那样,孀居的女主人布比夫人也看上了约瑟。不过,约瑟的天真无邪并没有招来酬报,而是激怒了布比夫人。最后,约瑟被布比夫人赶了出去。

如果说《约瑟·安特鲁传》是对先前文本的戏仿,那么詹姆斯·乔伊斯的《尤利西斯》(1992)则是借古讽今。该书的书名直指荷马史诗《奥德赛》(尤利西斯即该史诗中的英雄奥德修斯)。此外,《尤利西斯》在情节和结构上也和后者形成了对应关系。《尤利西斯》的开头部分写斯蒂芬渴望在精神上重新找到一位父亲,因而和《奥德赛》第一部分相对应——该史诗的前四章主要描述奥德修斯之子特莱默克斯如何冲破阻力,外出寻找离散多年的父亲。《尤利西斯》的中间部分重点写布鲁姆在都柏林各处的奔波游荡,与《奥德赛》第二部分中奥德修斯的流浪漂泊相平行;《尤利西斯》的最后部分叙述布鲁姆和斯蒂芬"父子"深夜回家跟布鲁姆之妻莫莉"团聚",与《奥德赛》中奥德修斯跟妻子珀涅罗珀和儿子特莱默克斯大团圆的结局相对应。在人物刻画方面,渺小卑微的布鲁姆和顶天立地的奥德修斯相对应，内心空虚的斯蒂芬和勇敢无畏的特莱默克斯相对应，轻佻偷闲的莫莉和忠贞守节的珀涅罗珀相对应。正是这种平行对应关系，充分体现了英雄悲壮的历史和卑劣猥琐的现实之间的强烈反差。很明显，乔伊斯对现实的批判和反讽有赖于互文性原则：离开了《奥德赛》，《尤利西斯》本身的反讽意义也就荡然无存。

　　文本改写的另一种形式——而且是更普遍的形式——是作者对先前作品的无意识的改写。古往今来，不知有多少作品被誉为"石破天惊"之作。然而，即使是再独特的作品也是对其他作品进行改写的结果。不管一个作家有意与否，他写出来的东西都不能逃脱"互文"法则的制约——任何作品都是对以往某些作品的改写。诚然，许多作家（尤其是现实主义和自然主义作家）在写作时的唯一宗旨是客观地反映现实，但是他们用来观察现实的眼光不可避免地要受到以往文本的影响。也就是说，他们是用已经被以往文本所造就的眼光来直接观察自然、观察现实的。不仅如此，一个作家还要把他所观察到的事物和心得用这种或那种已经存在的文本形式写下来，而再"新"的文本形式也是从其他形式发展而来，不是凭空创造出来的。可见，再注重直接经验的作家也只能是用一只眼睛盯着现实，而用另一只眼睛盯着先前已经存在的文本。没有任何一部文本是在不了解其他文本的情况下写成的。这一点可以由社会语言学家威廉·拉波夫（William Labov）的研究成果得到证明。拉波夫在作了广泛而深入的研究之后发现，不管人们在文化程度、阶级出身、家庭背景等方面有多大的差异，只要他们叙述某一桩个人经历，他们就会有意无意地遵循一种结构，即由概括（abstract）、导向（orientation）、导致复杂情形的事件（complicating action）、评价（evaluation）、结果或解决办法（result or solution）和尾声（coda）等六个部分组成的结构——虽然这一结构依情况不同会有这样或那样的变体，但它们基本上都大同小异（Scholes et al. 1998）。在很多情况下，口述者并非有意模仿某一种叙事方式，但是他们在叙事以前曾经听到过许许多多的叙述，因而他们无形中已经掌握了某种叙述形式。同样，一个作家以前读过的文本必然会影响他的想象、眼光和手法；而他在写作过程中又反过来会对这些文本加以修正和改写，这就形成了"互文"。

　　为了说明"无意的文本改写"，我们不妨将瓦尔特·司各特的小说《密得洛西恩的监狱》(1818) 和莎士比亚的剧本《一报还一报》(1604) 作一番比较。这两部作品在主题和情节上有耐人寻味的相似之处。在莎剧中,伊莎贝拉的弟弟克芬狄奥因未婚便使别人怀孕而被判极刑;当伊莎贝拉向摄政大臣安哲鲁请求赦免时,后者答应了她的要求,但是要她以牺牲自己的贞操作为代价。伊莎贝拉凭着机智与安哲鲁巧作周旋,最后在公爵的协助下揭露并惩治了安哲鲁,救出了克芬狄奥。跟伊莎贝拉一样,司各特小说的女主人公珍妮也肩负着营救同胞手足的使命:她的妹妹爱菲受人引诱后生下的婴儿不久便神秘地失踪了,法庭误判她杀婴罪(值得一提的是,爱菲被判死刑也和未婚先孕有关)。根据当地一条奇怪的法律,只要爱菲曾经向任何人透露过自己怀孕这件事情,笼罩在整桩案件上的神秘气氛就会消失,爱菲也就会因此而被释放。珍妮本来完全可以借谎称爱菲曾经向自己吐露过真情而营救妹妹,但是她拒绝说谎。最后,她从爱丁堡一直走到伦敦,以自己的诚挚赢得了国王对爱菲的赦免。

由上所述,《密得洛西恩的监狱》和《一报还一报》至少在三点上如出一辙:1) 两个女主人公都面临着生命和原则孰轻孰重的问题;2) 两个女主人公要营救的都是自己的同胞手足;3) 虽然她们都极力营救自己的兄弟姐妹,但是她们都摒弃了用纯洁作交易的方法。那么,是不是司各特有意识地对莎翁的作品作了修改和借用呢?从一般评论者和司各特自己的叙述来看,当时司各特写这部小说主要是出于对海伦·沃克 (Helen Walker) 的钦佩——珍妮这一人物的形象是以现实生活中的海伦为原型的;司各特自己在小说的前言中还描述了他采访海伦的实况。可见,司各特的这部作品主要是受了现实生活的直接启发。然而,就像我们前面所说的那样,当司各特的一只眼睛有意识地盯着生活中的原型时,他的另一只眼睛很可能无意地盯住了莎士比亚的作品。凭莎翁在英国的影响和司各特本人的身份和阅历判断,司各特不大可能不熟悉《一报还一报》这部名篇。即使司各特对该剧不了解,他也必然会受到几百年来英国文化大语境的影响,而莎剧中所反映的思想及其表达方式则毋庸置疑地属于这一文化大语境。莎剧仍会通过文化语境(通过其他文本)对司各特产生作用。

以上分析告诉我们,有意识的文本改写体现了直接的互文关系,而无意识的文本改写则很可能体现间接的互文关系。

三、文本的完成

从读者的角度看，互文性又表现为文本的完成。大家知道，"由读者完成文本"是接受理论的一个核心观点。而接受理论的形成有许多历史渊源，其中包括俄国的形式主义、捷克的结构主义、法国的后结构主义以及以姚斯和伊瑟为代表的康士坦茨学派等。本文这里强调的是：文本的完成也离不开互文性知识的运用。意大利符号学家恩贝托·埃科曾经把阅读描述成一种协作行为：在这一行为中，"一个组织得很好的文本一方面以能力模式为前提（在某种意义上，这种能力模式来自文本之外）；另一方面，文本通过自身的手段造就这种能力"（Scholes et al. 1998）。埃科所说的"能力模式"是一种由读者的阅历、智力和审美情趣组成的综合物，它的形成在很大程度上有赖于互文性知识的积累。例如：当我们看到一个文本以"从前"或"很久很久以前"这样的字眼开头时，我们会立即知道眼前摆着的是一部神话故事，因而我们会期待着跟这类体裁有紧密联系的传统意象——如会说话的青蛙、邪恶的后妈和英俊的王子等——的出现。这是因为我们早已熟悉了属于这一传统体裁的其他文本。一旦我们辨认出某个文本是属于某种体裁，如神话故事、小说、戏剧和小品文等，我们就运用了互文性知识，运用了其他类似文本带给我们的知识。正如埃科所说的那样，"没有任何文本可以脱离其他文本而被阅读"（Scholes et al. 1998）。

艾琳·阿·费尔利曾经对美国某个大学一年级的一百多名英语专业学生进行调查，测试他们对著名美国女诗人西尔维娅·普拉斯（Silvia Plath）的诗歌《蘑菇》（Mushroom）的理解程度。根据研究结果，艾琳把这些学生大致分为两类：第一类死抠"蘑菇"的字面意思，结果对全诗的意义不甚了了，其中不少学生还抱怨该诗缺乏连贯性和整体性；第二类则能够挖掘出该诗的象征意义，其中的大多数通过"温顺的蘑菇"而看到了温顺的基督徒——这些基督徒虽然温顺、谦和，但是却能不断地"繁衍生息"，并试图"在明天接管全球"（Fairley 1988：295—307）。艾琳认为，第二类学生之所以能够较好地"完成"文本，是因为他们运用了互文性知识，尤其是运用了"基督教互文"（Christian intertext）（Fairley 1988：305）。艾琳所没有指出的是，上述第一类学生其实也用了互文性知识,至少那些寻求整体性和连贯性的学生是"参考"了传统诗歌表面结构比较连贯一致的特点。他们的问题在于缺乏较全面的互文性知识,尤其是缺乏对现代主义文本比较讲究深层结构和寓意系统等特点的了解,因而往往发现后者艰涩、难懂。

任何叙事的文本多多少少都会在时空上有所跳跃(现代主义文本当然更是如此),而这些跳跃后留下的"空缺"则需要读者去填补。这种凭借想象或推测而进行的填补工作是文本完成过程的一个重要组成部分。埃科把这类活动称为撰写"鬼魂章节":

> 在叙述一连串互为因果的、呈直线型关系的事件时,一个文本往往在向读者交代了事件甲之后就径直转入事件戊,这是因为作者认为读者理应想象到事件乙、丙、丁会是怎样一种情形(若以许多其他文本作为互文性参考框架,就可以推断出什么样的事件才能导致事件戊)。任何采用这类手法写就的文本都隐含着由读者试写"鬼魂章节"的合理性。(Scholes et al. 1998)

我们不妨举个简单的例子来说明上面这段话的意思。如果一个故事的第一句话是"史密斯在伦敦上了火车",而第二句是"史密斯到了曼彻斯特",那么我们很快就会推断出这样的结论:伦敦和曼彻斯特之间的这段旅行虽然平安,但却没有戏剧性变化。也就是说,读者在事件甲(史密斯上火车)和事件戊(史密斯到达曼城)之间"插写"的鬼魂章节很可能包括平淡无奇的事件乙(史密斯找到一个位子坐下)、事件丙(列车员前来检票)和事件丁(史密斯在车上打盹儿)。读者凭自己的直接经验和互文性知识就能知道上述事件是这类旅行中司空见惯的,所以作者不必一一细述。

当然,并不是所有的鬼魂章节都那么容易撰写。在许多情况下,读者需要根据作品的主题和人物性格等来决定鬼魂章节的细节和篇幅。以美国女作家凯特·肖邦(Kate Chopin)的著名短篇小说《吻》(The Kiss)为例。该故事的叙述在时间上有两大"断层",即哈维冒失地在布兰顿面前吻纳撒丽那一幕跟招待会之间的断层,以及招待会跟婚礼之间的断层。读者自然可以根据互文性知识来填补断层——如纳撒丽在招待会之前如何寻思引诱布兰顿上钩，招待会之后纳撒丽和布兰顿如何订婚、交换订婚戒指以及计划婚礼日期等等。不过有一定水平的读者（即具有较丰富的互文性知识的读者）决不会在鬼魂章节中花大量篇幅去安排纳撒丽的内心活动以及她跟布兰顿之间的感情交流：纳撒丽看中的只是布兰顿的万贯家财，所以她越快把后者钓上钩越好，其间不可能有丰富的情感活动和较多的踌躇犹豫。同时，高水平的读者会意识到时间上的跳跃正好符合纳撒丽的性格——她属于那种看上什么就立即采取行动而不愿瞻前顾后的女人。

根据互文性的观点，任何文本都永远不可能被彻底地完成，因为每个新的读者都会把自己独特的"能力模式"带入阅读过程，都会因自己的时代、社会、文化或家庭背景的不同而用不同的方法去填补文本的空缺。确切地说，任何读者只能相对地完成文本，而每一次文本的"相对完成"都是朝"绝对完成"这一目标的一次接近。不过，"相对完成"并不意味着读者可以漫无边际地凭想象来填补文本的空缺或撰写鬼魂章节。一部精心构建的文本固然可以产生无数"相对完成"后的文本，但是它不允许读者异想天开地去随意完成；相反，它引导读者朝一定的方向去完成文本（当然，在大方向一致的前提下仍然可能有无数细节上的差异）。这一点已经由佛克马和易布思指出过："并非所有的个人解释都构成审美客体。审美客体只是某一群接受者个人难免的主观解释的共同点，只要这些解释是根据艺术成品做出的。"（佛克马，伊布思 1988：37）艾琳在这方面说得更加明白："无论是阅读哪一个文本，人们总能够在若干问题上达成共识，总能够鉴定哪些读者的反应是恰当的或可取的。"（Fairley 1988：293）也就是说，我们在任何阅读过程中都要遵循一定的标准。不过，有限的阅读标准并不和无限的完成过程相矛盾，这些标准所限制的只是那些毫无逻辑、牵强附会的完成方式。

四、文本的阐释

从批评家的角度看，互文性还表现为文本的阐释。从广义上讲，文本的改写和完成也是一种阐释，但是它们都有自己的特点：文本的改写主要指由一种虚构形式向另一种虚构形式的转换,而文本的完成则主要指在脑海中"撰写"鬼魂章节等活动。这里谈的是狭义的阐释,即写评论文章对文本进行的阐释。

与文本的改写和文本的完成相比,文本的阐释要求阐释者更加自觉地并且是在更高的水平上运用互文性知识。一般来说,文本的阐释包括这样四个方面的工作:1) 说出作者的未尽之言;2) 变复杂为简单;3) 变暗示为明示;4) 从具体细节中抽象出普遍意义、原理和规则。这四个方面的阐释都需要互文性知识的运用。再以《尤利西斯》为例:阐释者只有运用了有关《奥德赛》的知识,才能挖掘出小说的未尽之言(如对西方社会由盛而衰的哀叹),才能点明小说中暗含的与《奥德赛》之间结构上复杂的对应关系。

在上述四个方面的阐释工作中,第四个方面——变具体为一般——对互文性知识的要求最高:这里,文本的具体细节被纳入了一个同时驾驭众多文本的观念体系和思想体系。苏珊·桑塔格(Susan Sontag)曾经这样描述这类阐释过程:"阐释者说:看,难道你没看见 X 其实就是——或者说意味着——A 吗?Y 其实不就是 B 吗?I 也不就是 C?"(Scholes et al. 1998)也就是说,X 和 A、Y 和 B 以及 I 和 C 本身都不重要,重要的是它们所代表的普遍精神和意义。要具备说"X 就是 A"的能力,就要掌握超越单独文本的价值体系和信仰体系,也就是要掌握足够的互文性知识。我们不妨以弥尔顿的《力士参孙》(1671)为例。虽然参孙这一原型取自《圣经》的《旧约》,但是西方一些有基督教思想的评论家常常把弥尔顿的作品与《新约》作类比。他们根据基督教的思想体系,得出了"参孙就是耶稣"的结论:跟耶稣一样,参孙也为拯救自己的人民而贡献了自己的生命;他在非利士人的神殿中的殉难相当于耶稣在罗马人的十字架上的殉难;同样,参孙和耶稣起先都是以被征服者的面目出现,但是他们都以自己的死征服了原先的征服者——参孙与征服者同归于尽,而耶稣则用鲜血换来整个罗马的基督化。显然,在这一类比过程当中,参孙和耶稣本人以及他们具体的活动形式和殉难方式都不重要,而他们所共同代表的价值体系和信仰体系则被越来越明确地放在了重要地位。

在互文性原则的基础上,西方一些文艺批评家在阐释文本时采用了文艺创作与文艺批评相结合的手法。这类手法的首倡者是法国的罗朗·巴特。按照巴特的观点,文艺批评与文艺创作在本质上是一回事情——那种把事实与虚构、真情与想象截然分开的传统做法忽略了一切文本的大前提，即所有经验的处理和组织（艺术领域和科学领域概莫能外）都要以语言作为媒介。基于这一想法，巴特发明了一种集评论、分析与艺术表现于一身的新型混合式小品文，其中最为著名的是《恋人絮语》。

《恋人絮语》包含了两条互相穿插交融的线索。第一条是创作型线索，即叙述一个爱情故事。整个故事的焦点集中在一场恋爱的紧要关头：主人公去一家咖啡馆赴约，可是对方却迟迟没有露面（事实上后者压根儿就不会出现）；等待期间，主人公借阅读歌德的小说《少年维特之烦恼》来消磨时间；他边读边把自己的不幸与维特的单相思做比较。最后，主人公选择了一条跟维特不同的解脱办法：他决定不像维特那样自寻短见，而是毅然地抛开往事。

《恋人絮语》的第二条线索是评论和分析。巴特对上述爱情故事的分析和评论在很大程度上表现在他对该故事的处理方式上：整个故事不是平铺直叙，而是被分成碎片散见于文本当中，或者说是曲折地反映在主人公的沉思中；这段爱情经历本来是带有强烈感情色彩的，但是巴特却像从事科学工作那样把这段经历的要素一一加以分类，然后围绕这些要素组织故事的情节和人物形象。由于这些要素同时也适用于所有爱情故事，所以围绕它们组织起来的言语以及人物的思维方式和行动方式常常给人以似曾相识的感觉（当然是对有互文性知识的读者而言）。更明确地说，每个要素都有一段与之相对应的话语片段。巴特用了一个修辞学术语"辞格"（figure）来形容他的话语片段：每个片段就是一个辞格，而全书则是诸辞格的不同形式的变奏。巴特的用意是：每个恋爱故事的叙述者都会有意无意地遵循某种辞格，而这种辞格的形成则是古往今来无数文本互相碰撞的结果。

《恋人絮语》的结构是精心设计的：每一段聚合都有一个正题和一个副题，紧接着是一小段"开场白"，解释正题或副题的意义，即点明其适用于同类文本的普遍意义。例如，正题为"告诉我应该爱谁"的片段以"归纳"为副题，然后紧跟着是这样一段开场白："热恋者在堕入情网之前已经参照了其他人，因此才觉得自己的意中人值得爱慕。无论爱的方式如何特殊，爱的欲望总是产生于归纳。"（Scholes et al. 1998）显然，这段开场白也适用于其他涉及爱的欲望的文本。每个片段的正文也都是自觉运用互文性原则的结果：作者叙述故事就像电台播送体育实况那样，不断地插入几句颇具互文意味的评论和分析（如主人公和维特之间的类比）；同时，作者在每页的空白边角处不时地写上一些名作家（如夏多布里昂和司汤达）以及一些著名作品中的主要人物（如维特）的名字，以提醒读者注意所读文本跟其他文本间的相互关系。

《恋人絮语》也好，前文提及的《力士参孙》和《新约》之间的类比也好，它们都代表了一种旨在探索文本的普遍意义的努力，而这种努力的立足点则始终是互文。

五、结束语

互文性原则无疑为文艺创作和文艺批评提供了新的视角，开拓了新的思路。就作者而言，互文性知识的妙用能够加深并丰富所写作品的内涵。就批评家乃至一般读者而言，互文性知识的自觉运用能够提高他们的审美情趣。同时，互文性原则还有助于打破文学创作和文学批评之间的界限，甚至有助于打破不同学科之间的界限。

互文性的最大功能恐怕是对传统的权威式批评的消解。我国青年学者徐岱曾经指出："从一代美学大师黑格尔、谢林、施莱格尔兄弟，到俄国批评家三巨头别林斯基、车尔尼雪夫斯基、杜波罗留波夫，批评家一直被要求站在作者与读者之上，成为能够主宰作品命运、叱咤文坛风云的拿破仑式的人物。在这些人的身旁足下，站着感激涕零的陀思妥耶夫斯基和果戈理，匍匐着屠格涅夫和涅克拉索夫。"（徐岱 1993：83）这种权威式批评有一个认识误区，认为少数权威掌握着通向文本终极意义的钥匙。与此相反，互文性原则却强调文本的非确定性，强调后人可以无数次地对文本进行改写，不断地加以完成和阐释，这正是对权威式批评的釜底抽薪。在我国，权威式批评至今仍有一定的市场：时常听到有人对某某作家或某某作品作盖棺定论，殊不知任何一种批评都只是"一种局限和片面的'出场'"（徐岱 1993：84）。当然，我们无意贬低这种片面"出场"的重要意义——每一次认真的片面性"出场"都朝绝对真理接近了一步。我们只是提倡对话式的文艺批评，而互文性思想对弘扬批评的对话精神有不可忽视的作用。

当然，互文性原则也有它的局限性。我们前面已经谈到，虽然互文性是对结构主义拘泥于共时性研究以及对文本的封闭式研究等思想的超越，但它强调的仍然只是文本，即文本之外的文本。将这种思想推向极端，必然导致文本与现实的割裂、意识与物质的割裂。伊格尔顿在批判结构主义思想时这样说："在列举文学文本潜在的规则系统的特征之后，结构主义者只能是坐在一边，不知道下一步该做什么。把作品与所写的现实联系起来，与产生它的条件联系起来，或者与实际研究它的读者联系起来，统统都谈不上……"（Eagleton 1983：109）尽管相形之下，互文性思想确实比结构主义思想前进了一步，它把作品与研究它的读者联系了起来，同时还把作品与产生它的部分不可或缺的条件（即此前此后、古往今来的其他文本）联系了起来，然而它仍忽略了产生作品的另一部分同样也相当重要的条件，即作者所处的社会、历史、文化语境和直接的个人生活经验。诚然，作者、读者观察思考社会历史、文化的现实时的眼光以及写作、阅读时的思想和方法必然要受到先前文本的制约与影响，但是社会、历史、文化的现实同时也在不断地影响、调整、修正并改变着作者与读者的互文性结构，其间的关系只能是辩证的关系。

参考文献

[1] Bannet E T. Structuralism and the Logic of Dissent [M]. London: Macmillan Press, 1989.

[2] Eagleton T. Literary Theory: An Introduction [M]. Minneapolis: University of Minnesota Press, 1983.

[3] Fairley I R. The reader's need for convention [A] //Willie Van Peer (ed.) The Taming of the Text [M]. London and New York: Routledge, 1988.

[4] Peck J and Coyle M. Literary Terms and Criticism [M]. London: Macmillan Education Ltd, 1984.

[5] Scholes R, Comley N R and Ulmer G L. Text Book [M]. New York: st. Martin's Press, 1998.

[6] 佛马克，马布思. 二十世纪文学理论 [M]. 北京：三联书店，1988.

[7] 李俊玉. 当代文论中的文本理论研究 [J]. 外国文学评论，1993，(2).

[8] 特伦斯·霍克斯. 结构主义和符号学 [M]. 上海：上海译文出版社, 1987.

[9] 徐岱. 论批评的复调特性 [J]. 浙江社会科学, 1993, (3).

[10] 赵一凡. 后现代主义探幽 [J]. 外国文学评论, 1989, (1): 53.

（本文原载于《外国文学评论》1994 年第 2 期）

实验的结果是写实

——布洛克-罗斯的小说创作和理论

英国女作家克里斯廷·布洛克-罗斯（Christine Brook-Rose, 1926— ）常常被当作小说实验的极端例子。批评家们几乎不约而同地把她的作品归在后现代主义小说之列，并且常用"反现实主义"或"非现实主义"来形容她的理论立场。凯瑟里奥（Robert Caserio）就曾经说过："布洛克-罗斯偏爱后现代主义小说，而不喜欢现实主义小说的那种排除歧义、追求确定性意义的程式。"（Caserio 1990：312）更有意思的是，一些学者曾经当着布洛克-罗斯的面把她定性为非现实主义作家。例如，弗里德曼（Ellen G. Friedman）和弗克斯（Miriam Fuchs）在1987年采访她时这样问道："你在创作生涯中的某个关头确实有意识地决定撰写意义不确定的小说，而不撰写现实主义小说，对吧？"（Friedman & Fuchs 1989：2）希德（David Seed）在1992年的采访中又提出了同样的问题："是什么使你于60年代背离了现实主义？"（Seed 1993：250）在后来发表的采访录前言中，希德坚持认为"布洛克-罗斯的非现实主义小说始于《外出》发表之时"（Seed 1993：247）。

布洛克-罗斯真的背离或反对了现实主义吗？

首先，我们应该承认她是个热衷于实验的小说家。从《外出》（*Out*, 1964）到《穿过》（*Thru*, 1975），从《阿麦尔格门农》（*Amalgamemnon*, 1984）到《下一个》（*Next*, 1998），她的每一部小说在手法上都有所创新。然而，实验并不一定意味着对现实主义的否定。不少评论家把实验和写实看作两个截然对立的概念，这其实有很大的问题。比这问题更大的是把"实验小说"看成一种既定的模式，一种可以跟"科幻小说""鬼怪小说"和"现实主义小说"等相类比的体裁。布洛克-罗斯自己就说过："实验其实意味着你不知道要走向何方，意味着发现这一过程本身"（Friedman & Fuchs 1989：3）。

那么，布洛克-罗斯发现了什么呢？

她发现自己离不开写实，离不开现实主义。下面是她自己的几个结论：《外出》是"一部非常注重模仿现实的小说"；《如此》（*Such*, 1966）的特点之一是"对现实的缓慢回归"；《阿麦尔格门农》有一个"现实主义的框架"，而《索兰达》（*Xorandor*, 1986）甚至要比前面几部小说还"有着多得多的现实主义色彩"（Friedman & Fuchs 1989：2—7）。至于以凸显小说的虚构性为特征的《穿过》，布氏承认她在写作时就料到自己会因此而受到猛烈抨击，不过当时她曾一度痴迷于结构主义和后结构主义理论，事后她"确实感到自己走得太远了"（Tredell 1990：30）。如果一定要为该书找一个合理的依据，那就是"它其实是为一小撮叙事学家而写的"（Jredell 1990：30）。换言之，《穿过》的对象已经不是普通意义上的小说读者，因此它不应该算作真正意义上的小说。

在进一步审视布洛克-罗斯的小说之前，我们不妨先来看一下她对现实主义的理解。就在她回答希德（见本文第一段）的问题时，她对后者的概念作了这样的限定："我想您所说的'现实主义'指的是20世纪中叶通行的、现实主义小说中某些已经疲乏的成规，而不是指十九世纪的现实主义吧？"（Seed 1993：250）这句话有两层意思。其一，布氏对整个现实主义传统并无异议；即使有所反对，其矛头也只指向该传统中某些已经落入俗套的常规。其二，布氏对19世纪以来的现实主义小说传统本身持积极肯定的态度。当弗里德曼和弗克斯把现实主义小说和所谓的"意义不确定的小说"描绘成水火不相容的两极时（见本文第一段），布洛克-罗斯当即反唇相讥："这是一种多么奇怪的两极观！现实主义小说有它自己的不确定因素。"（Friedman & Fuchs 1989：2）

在她的两部专著《虚幻修辞学》（*A Rhetoric of the Unreal*, 1981）和《故事、理论和物体》（*Stories, theories and things*, 1991）中，布洛克-罗斯曾经提出了一

个大胆而独特的见解：所有小说都是现实主义的。她尤其反对那种把现实主义小说和所谓"后现代主义小说"视为两个极端的观点。虽然她多次使用过"后现代主义"这一术语，但是她毫不客气地称之为"缺乏想象力的、空洞的、体现懒散精神的名词"（Brooke-Rose 1981：344—345）。她还强调，"后现代主义"恰恰是一种"现实主义的再现"："许多'后现代主义'小说展现的是令人难以置信的图景，但是它们（在技巧层面上）用现实主义的手段再现了当代人类的状况。"（Brooke-Rose 1981：364）她的下面一句话其实把"后现代主义"小说也包括在内："所有的荒诞叙事作品都有一个现实主义的基础，甚至连神话故事也要在现实中找到某种依托，因为只有在现实的衬托下才能显出虚幻。"（Brooke-Rose 1981：81）

布洛克-罗斯的现实主义观还体现于她对"反现实主义"这一术语的质疑。在她看来，至少有两个重要的事实能够提醒人们尽量地避免"反现实主义"这种提法。其一，"反对现实主义的潮流存在于所有时期"（Brooke-Rose 1991：206）。其二，"最极端、最荒诞、最自足自律的文本世界也指涉现实世界，否则读者就无法想象它们的存在"（Brooke-Rose 1991：208）。据此，她认为把"反现实主义"看成一个历史分期的概念是错误的。更重要的是，她还提出了这样一个问题：那些热衷于"反现实主义"的小说家和批评家们究竟是在反对现实主义呢，还是在反对那些被称为"反现实主义"的小说创作成规？布氏认定是后一种情况。那么有哪些成规被错误地等同于现实主义了呢？她认为主要有四：1）客观世界是先于小说而存在的，是可以确定的；2）客观世界受制于一些连贯清晰的规则；3）有关客观世界的数据是可以证明的；4）客观世界的物质形态是可以描述的（Brooke-Rose 1991：209）。这些所谓的"现实主义"成规并不代表布氏心目中确切意义上的现实主义，而只是"现实主义在某一个历史阶段的形态"（Brooke-Rose 1991：221）。

正是基于以上考虑，布洛克-罗斯提出了一个十分重要的概念，即"现实主义复数"（realisms）。如上文所说，那些被称作"现实主义"的成规只是现实主义的某一种形态，因此还应该有其他许多并未"疲惫"甚至还未产生的形态。有鉴于此，布氏发出了以下倡议："我们可以用丰富的方式来探索呈复数形式的现实主义，而不是一味地攻击那些已经疲竭的成规本身。"（Brooke-Rose

1991：222）也就是说，布氏提倡的是一种动态的、不断在生长发展的现实主义概念。这一生长的过程其实也是对原有现实主义成规进行改造、加工和更新的过程。

为了更好地理解布洛克-罗斯的观点，我们不妨对她最近出版的至今还鲜有人问津的小说《下一个》（Next）略做分析，进而探讨她在继承并发展现实主义传统方面的具体实践及其意义。

《下一个》讲述的是一群无家可归者的故事。

从表面上看，该书的形式确实跟人们通常所说的"现实主义小说"大相径庭。除了旋转式的叙述角度和大段大段的意识流之外，小说的文字拼写和文字排列也显得稀奇古怪。最让人困惑甚至让人望而生畏的是书中的某些对话：为了模仿伦敦底层社会中流行的方言，布洛克-罗斯在文字拼写上做了大胆的更动。虽然这一手法本身早就有人使用（如狄更斯和奥威尔等），但是布氏所作的更动在幅度和难度上大大超过了前人——有时候整句乃至整段中几乎每个词的拼写都有变动，读者需要读上好几遍才能辨认。仅以埃尔西劝外号为"沙喉咙"的昆廷少抽烟那一句为例：

"Yer ough'er seey to tha' corf, Craoakey, daon i 'keeyp yer awike a' nah's?"（"你应该对咳嗽多加注意，沙喉咙。晚上你会因此睡不安稳吧？"正规拼写应该为：You ought to see to that cough, Croaky, doesn't it keep you awake at night?）（Brooke-Rose 1998：16）

顺便提一句，布氏采用的特殊拼写跟以往狄更斯等人的完全不同，而且反映不同人物的拼写方法也不尽相同，以表现他们在发音之间的微妙差异。因此，我们完全可以说布氏在这方面做了一次新的实验，一次拼写方法的陌生化处理。具有辩证意味的是，这种陌生化处理最终起到了拉近我们与作者笔下那个现实世界之间的距离：一旦我们辨认出这些"古怪"文字的意思，捉摸出它们的独特发音，我们就会产生身临其境的感觉，产生跟有关人物的亲近感——这种亲近感是任何现实主义小说家都孜孜以求的移情效果的可靠基础。

布洛克-罗斯在文字排列上也作了多种实验。全书文字的排列格式有阶梯式的，有半圆形的，有树形的，还有菱形的。小说第一段的文字排列就颇具特色：

> 近期故事梗概：黛丽卡早就嫁给了石油大王布莱德。多年以来，她替后者管理牧场，并且照料着她俩生下的一对双胞胎——雷克斯和丽贾纳。然而，黛丽卡从来无法掩饰她对特里克斯的深情，因为后者是她跟旧情人杰西的私生子。杰西是布莱德生意上的对手，后来跟蒂娜结了婚，可是眼下他正在追求基娜。道格是雷克斯新结交的朋友。这一天，他带着辛蒂去雷格斯那儿串门，碰巧布莱德也在家。布莱德一下子迷上了辛蒂，而道格却迷上了基娜，可是基娜却正和里克打得火热——里克眼下正帮着黛丽卡管理产业。有一次，黛丽卡跟萨尔大吵了一场。余怒未消，她又吩咐丹思对布雷德里的行为进行干预。
>
> （Brooke-Rose 1998：1）

即使我们不理会上面这段文字本身的意思，它们所组成的图形也有着强烈的象征意义：这幅图形看上去正好像一架电视机，而中间的那一处空白既可看作电视机的屏幕，又可被理解为媒体内容的空洞。如果我们结合文字本身，就更加能够理解其中的含义：原来这是一段电视肥皂剧的故事梗概，其内容不但空泛，而且极其无聊，品味极其低劣。

把这样一段空洞的文字及其空心的图形摆在小说的开头，布洛克-罗斯的用意究竟何在？乍一看去，这段文字似乎游离于全书结构之外：它里面的故事和人物跟小说本身的故事和人物毫不搭介。难道这纯粹是一种标新立异的"实验"？若果真如此，那岂不是一大败笔？至少可以算作对现实主义传统的背离？

在仔细阅读小说的过程中，我们发现这段开头其实跟小说描写的现实有着千丝万缕的联系。从小说的第二段中，我们得知流浪汉泰克把载有那段"故事梗概"的电视节目周刊当作了枕头（他穷极潦倒，连枕头都买不起）。随着故事的推进，我们经常看到不同人物在贫民收容所看电视的镜头。跟"看电视"有关的是两组反复出现的"主旋律"。其一，书中人物常常对电视/媒体的内容进行评论。例如，外号"雅皮"的杰西曾经对电视节目的商业性以及节目内容的贫乏表示不满："每次预报下一个节目时，总是先来一点儿该节目的片段，可是紧接着播音员就会说'先休息一下'。可是这一休息就没完没了:先是广告,再是促销剪辑,然后又是广告,接着是信息宣传,再接下去又是促销剪辑。"(Brooke-Rose 1998:11)比节目贫乏更可恶的是虚假,这一点多次在不同人物的对话中被提及。雷奥纳多就曾经对斯特拉这样说:"可笑的是电视台……拍摄的总是大街上浩浩荡荡的就业大军。可是那些人都属于幸运儿。这世上还有许多人在流浪,在沿街乞讨。他们累了只能在公园的长凳上歇歇脚,困了只能在屋檐下宿上一宿。"(Brooke-Rose 1998:29)同样,从昆廷跟奥利弗的一次对话中,我们了解到媒体上的"失业率上个月几乎降到了零,可是实际上却什么都没有改变"(Brooke-Rose 1998:184)。可见,小说篇首的那段"象形文字"为这些人物的对话埋下了伏笔:英国媒体乃至整个资本主义制度的实质是虚假,就像那个文字图形中的"空心"一样。

其二,书中反复出现电视播音员的一句节目结束语:"不要离开我们!"如果我们结合以上的分析,就会发现这句话极具讽刺意味:成千上万个无家可归者仍然过着饥寒交迫的生活,可是媒体对这一严酷的现实却视而不见;电视上播送的不是虚假的新闻,就是无聊空洞的肥皂剧,而播音员们还不厌其烦地要求观众继续观看("不要离开我们!")。正是看到了其中的荒唐之处,布洛克-罗斯把这句话用作全书的结束语,但是却作了微妙的更动:"不要离开他们!"(Brooke-Rose 1998:210)虽然只有一词之差,但是起到的效果却异常深刻。如果说前面反复出现的播音员的结束语是一种含蓄的讽刺,那么这最后一句是对虚假媒体的顺势一击和盖棺定论:任何有良知的人都应该远离媒体所营造的虚拟现实,而把目光和同情心投向"他们"——现实生活中成千上万个饥寒交迫的人。当然,这最后一句分明是作者本人的声音。很可能会有人对这种"作者介入"的手法提出批评。然而,依笔者之见,布氏在小说最后关头的突然介入不仅无损于作品的真实感和艺术效果,而且巧妙地把她所虚构的世界跟我们所处的现实世界结合在了一起,因为在"不要离开我们"和"不要离开他们"之间有着平稳的过渡和精心的铺垫。

简而言之,小说的开头以其独特的方式跟上述两组"主旋律"形成了呼应,从而有力地烘托了小说所描写的现实。

还须进一步指出的是,在上述实验手法的背后,还有着一层坚实的依托,即逼真的细节描写。这种真实的细节描写不仅表现在小说的时间、地点和人物方面，而且还表现在个人和社会之间的关系方面。

首先，小说的时间、地点和人物都具有典型的现实意义。

就时间而言，小说有一个扎实的现实基础。故事发生的年代不在过去，也不在将来，而就在我们的眼前。"经济全球化""控制全球化""贸易全球化""高科技""信息技术""国际互联网"和"历史的终结"等词语在书中比比皆是，这些分明是当今时代才有的标志。

就地点而言，小说也有一个扎实的现实基础。书中所有人物的活动地点都局限于伦敦之内。更值得注意的是，书中人物常常出没的地段包括"海德公园""大理石拱门"和"肯辛顿花园"这样一些实实在在、为常人所熟悉的地点，这就又给小说增添了一层现实色彩。

就人物而言，小说依然有一个扎实的现实基础。书中的主要人物不仅拥有无家可归者的普通特点，如衣衫褴褛、忍冻挨饿等，而且还拥有经济全球化浪潮冲击下社会最底层者的特点——随着经济全球化的加速，沦落街头者的成分也发生了变化：以往的那些街头流浪者——如狄更斯笔下的奥利弗——大都与良好的教育无缘，可是布洛克-罗斯笔下的奥利弗却在英国最好的伊顿公学受过教育，然后又在牛津大学拿到过学位。而且，类似的现象还相当普遍，如泰克在里丁大学历史系拿到过学位，埃尔西和昆廷曾经在很好的商业学院受过教育（埃尔西的英语成绩以及计算机等科目的成绩都是优秀，而昆廷还在一家生产电子门的公司当过经理），等等。经济全球化意味着剧烈而无情的竞争，即使拥有高学历者也随时面临着失业并沦落街头的危险。

因此，《下一个》在本质上刚好与恩格斯有关现实主义的著名定义——典型环境下的典型人物——相吻合：泰克、埃尔西、昆廷和奥利弗等人是典型的当代经济全球化背景下最富有的资本主义社会中典型的底层人物。

细节的真实还体现于书中个人与社会之间的关系。威廉斯（Raymond Williams，1921—1988）曾经不无道理地指出，现实主义小说最重要的成就在于取得社会和个人之间的平衡。他认为乔治·爱略特和托尔斯泰的小说代表了现实主义的最高境界，"这类小说评判了人类的全部生活方式，呈现了广阔的社会图景——这一社会比它的任何成员都大得多。与此同时，这类小说又评判了人类个体——虽然这些个体从属于社会，受到社会的影响，并且常常被用来界定整个社会的生活方式，但是他们本身又绝对具有存在的理由。社会也好，个人也好，都不能单独构成优先考虑的理由。社会并不仅仅是研究个人关系所需要的背景；反之，个人也不仅仅是社会生活方式的某些方面的例证"（Williams 1961：278）。《下一个》与威氏所说的现实主义标准正好并行不悖。可以说，它从某个特定的角度评判了人类的全部生活方式。虽然它的主要焦点是在伦敦的最底层社会，但是作者的眼光并没有仅仅停留于泰克等个人的悲惨遭遇，而是始终凭借这些无家可归者的生活来透视资本主义生产方式全球性扩张带来的一些恶果。世界经济全球化的依托是技术革命，如今人们常常夸耀的也是技术革命，可是几乎影响了地球上每个人的高科技对社会正义和人类的生存起到了多大的作用呢？在布洛克-罗斯笔下的世界里，我们看到昆廷原来所在的公司因技术落后而倒闭，他本人也因此过上了颠沛流离的生活。泰克所学的历史知识不能直接给任何企业带来利润，因而他也只能在街头风餐露宿。埃西既漂亮又聪明，还受过良好的教育，可是却惨遭强奸并谋杀，而高科技既没能保障她的安全，又无法替她报仇申冤——凶手直到小说结束时还逍遥法外。难怪书中泰克在听到埃尔西谈论"科技进步"时立即加以纠正："你所说的不是进步，而是科技的发展。"（Brooke-Rose 1998：34）在一个高度富有、科技高度发展的社会里居然还有成群的无家可归者，这种触目惊心的社会现实正是布氏关注的焦点，可是假如没有上述有关个人细节的真实描写作依靠，对社会的判断就会苍白无力。

同样，《下一个》在评判人物个体方面也毫不逊色。书中不少人物不仅仅是当代英国某些社会问题的例证，而且具有他们自身存在的价值。他们不仅仅是无家可归者这一群体的代表，而且有着自己的独特个性。他们同属于一个类型，但是彼此之间又有着微妙的差异，几乎每个人都有着鲜明的个性：泰克整天耽于沉思；尤利西斯为人憨厚；里奇喜欢逗能；杰西（外号"雅皮"）过于俗气；帕芙罗娃性情开朗，却略显轻浮；奥利弗虽然多情，却不乏自尊，等等。性格刻画最为成功的恐怕要数昆廷。他在公司破产后感到无颜面对家人，居然连招呼都不打一声就离家出走，开始了长达七年的流浪生活。此举既反映了他自尊的一面，又反映了他对家庭不负责任的一面。随着故事情节的逐渐展开，我们发现昆廷的善良多于他的自私。在七年的漂泊生涯中,他一直盼望并试图重新找到工作,以便和家人重新团聚——他不愿意在成为妻子的累赘的情况下回去。后来,他跟希拉里重新取得了联系,后者出于地位尊卑方面的考虑而禁止他跟孩子们见面(他其实渴望着见上他们一面),可是他却毫无怨言,这体现了他能够为他人着想的优点。希拉里借给了他一套住房,同时开了一个附加条件:不许再与任何无家可归者来往。然而,他在跟奥利弗邂逅以后,仍然热情地邀请后者去自己的住所做客。这一细节看似平常,可是对昆廷来说却是价值取向上的一次重大抉择——他不仅冒了失去住房的风险,而且还冒了永远失业的风险(希拉里借给他房子是为了帮助他找工作,因为没有住址的人找工作非常困难)。昆廷这一人物使人想起乔伊斯笔下的布鲁姆,虽然平时形象委琐,但是却富有同情心;虽然没有任何英雄之举,但是常在细微之处显示出可爱的一面。这一点还可以在他与埃尔西的对比中得到印证:有一次他俩去同一家公司参加招工面试;出来以后,昆廷不假思索地去找埃尔西交流面试的情况,不料后者已经不辞而别。这一细节反映出埃尔西工于心计,而昆廷却比较厚道,即使在涉及自身重大利益时也不对旁人设防。这类耐人寻味的细节描写在书中俯拾皆是。通过它们,作者揭示了隐藏在一个备受忽视和歧视的社会阶层背后的丰富的性格世界,从而为书中每一个作为个体的人物的存在提供了充足的理由。

正是因为有了这些真实的细节描写作为基础,上文所说的那些实验才有了生命力。至此,我们已经可以从布洛克-罗斯那儿得到这样的启示:一旦小说家对人类现实加以真诚的关注,无论他/她从事怎样新奇的实验,其效果——如果这实验成功的话——最终仍然是现实主义的。换言之,不用写实作为依托,任何实验都不会成功。

参考文献

[1] Brooke-Rose C. *A Rhetoric of the Unreal* [M]. Cambridge:Cambridge University Press,1981.

[2] Brooke-Rose C. *Next* [M]. London:Carcanet,1998.

[3] Brooke-Rose C. *Stories, Theories and Things* [M]. Cambridge:Cambridge University Press,1991.

[4] Caserio R L. Mobility and Masochism: Brooke-Rose and J. G. Ballard. In Spilka & McCracken-Lesher C (eds.) [C]. *Why the Novel Matters: A Postmodern Perplex*. Bloomington And Indianapolis: Indiana University Press, 1990.

[5] Friedman E G and Fuchs M. An Interview with Christine Brooke-Rose [J]. *Review of Contemporary Fiction*, Fall 1989, Volume 9.

[6] Seed D. Christine Brooke-Rose Interviewed by David Seed [J]. *Textual Practice*, Spring 1993, Volume 7.

[7] Tredell N. Christine Brooke-Rose in Conversation [J]. *Poetry National Review*, September/October 1990.

[8] Williams R. *The Long Revolution* [M]. London: Chatto & Windus, 1961.

(本文原载于《外国文学研究》2002年第1期)

节奏即境界:从福斯特的小说观说起[*]

若论对于小说节奏研究的贡献,当首推福斯特(E. M. Forster,1879—1970),无人能出其右。之所以这么说,是因为他的"节奏论"超出了技巧层面。

迄今为止,大部分相关论述都把小说节奏看成叙事功能或表现形式,如邓颖琳和蒋翃遐的如下论述:"小说节奏是指小说艺术各要素有秩序、可衡量、有一定节律的交替变化过程,反映小说人物、事件、场面等整体向前运动变化的速度。小说节奏在小说创作中已成为一个独立的叙事要素,发挥着自己的功能性作用"(邓颖琳,蒋翃遐 2012:91)。邓的论文是过去二、三十年相关论文中较为典型、较为出色的研究成果,类似的还有我国蒋虹教授的论文《俄罗斯芭蕾与伍尔夫小说中的色彩元素》(2012),以及新西兰奥塔戈大学马丁博士的《乔伊斯与节奏学》(*Joyce and the Science of Rhythm*,2012)。蒋的论文强调"(伍尔夫的)小说创作始终在追寻新的表现形式,其核心概念是'变化的节奏'"(蒋虹 2015:55),而马丁则侧重研究了"《都柏林人》中作为姿态的节奏""《尤利西斯》中作为动作的节奏"和"《青年艺术家画像》中作为延展的节奏"(Martin 2012:201)。可以说,这些研究基本上沿袭了美国学者苏姗·朗格(Susanne Langer,1895—1985)的思路,后者在《艺术的问题:哲学十讲》

---

[*] 本论文系浙江省哲学社会科学重点研究基地"文艺批评研究院"资助项目【项目批号:wypp2020001】的成果。

(*Problems of Art: Ten Philosophical Lectures*, 1957) 一书中论述了小说节奏的本质，称其为"某种与功能有关的东西，而非与时间有关的东西"（Langer 1957：50）。

问题也就因此而产生：小说节奏的本质只跟功能有关吗？若果真如此，学界关于小说节奏的探讨只能在技巧层面上打转转，且很难达成共识。纵观现实，这方面的争论已陷入僵局，这在英国爱丁堡大学的达彦教授和圣安德鲁斯大学的埃文斯博士关于"文学节奏"（也包括小说节奏）的自问自答中可见一斑："何谓节奏？能否有笼统的理论？对这后一个问题，当代显然还没有答案"（Dayan & Evans 2010：147）。我们认为，要走出这一困境，不妨从福斯特那里汲取灵感。本文就从他的"节奏论"谈起。

一、"更大的存在"

福斯特在其名著《小说面面观》（*Aspects of the Novel*, 1927）中对小说的方方面面有过论述，而"节奏"（rhythm）在他心目中的小说价值体系中占据了最高等级。他认为节奏只能在阅读（读完整本小说）之后才得以辨认，其效果足以与交响乐的整体感相类比：

> 小说产生的效果是否能与贝多芬第五交响乐的整个效果相媲美呢？在演奏这支交响乐时，乐曲一停，为什么我们的耳畔仍然萦回着旋律，一种从未演奏过的旋律？从第一乐章到慢板，又从慢板到包括诙谐曲和终曲在内的第三乐章，顷刻间全部涌进了心窝，然后又互相交织，汇合成一个整体。这个整体，这一新的感受，就是交响乐本身。这种效果的获得主要（不是全部）在于三大乐章中各种乐器之间形成的音响关系。我把这种关系称为"节奏性"。
>
> （Forster 1927：168）[①]

福氏的意思是，在听完一部交响曲以后，我们耳际仍然盘旋着一种从未演奏过

[①] 部分文字参考苏炳文中译本，广州：花城出版社，1984年版。

的乐曲；与此相仿，我们在读完一部小说以后，也应该有一种从未见诸笔墨的东西萦绕于脑际。这种东西，他称为"节奏"，并且命名为"更大的存在"（a larger existence）（Foster 1927: 169）。此处，福斯特则把节奏的地位提升到了精神/形而上层面，而这正是其高明之处。

依笔者之见，福氏所说的"节奏"和"更大的存在"，与中国文论中的"境界"有异曲同工之妙。就中国文论而言，王国维、朱光潜、钱钟书和王佐良都专门讨论过境界，其中以朱光潜的"境界说"与福氏的"节奏论"最为契合。在《谈美》一书中，朱光潜下过这样一个定义："境界就是情景交融事理相契的独立自足的世界"（朱光潜 2006: 193）。这一简洁的定义包含三个要素，即"情景交融""事理相契"和"独立自足"，而福氏笔下的"节奏"其实恰恰隐含了这三层意思。所谓"更大的存在"，必然是独立自足的世界，而要进入这世界/存在，既非情景交融不可，又非事理相契不可，否则就不可能如福氏所说，在读完小说以后会有一种从未见诸笔墨的东西萦绕于脑际。换言之，福氏笔下"更大的存在"颇像朱光潜在下文中所描绘的"心所观境"：

> 无论是作者还是读者，在心领神会一首好诗时，都必有一幅画境或是一幕戏景，很新鲜生动地突现于眼前，使他神魂为之钩摄，若惊若喜，霎时无暇旁顾，仿佛这小天地中有独立自足之乐，此外偌大乾坤宇宙，以及个人生活中的一切憎爱悲喜，都像在这霎时间烟消云散了。纯粹的诗的心境是凝神注视，纯粹的心所观境是独立绝缘，心与其观境如鱼戏水，忻合无间〔……〕（朱光潜 1982: 49—50）

此处所论虽是诗的境界，但是小说境界何尝非此？福氏所说"更大的存在"，就是朱光潜的"心所观境"，二者都意味着一种"独立绝缘"的境界，都能（使作者/读者）"在刹那中见终古，在微尘中显大千，在有限中寓无限"（朱光潜 1982: 50）。确实，我们在阅读一部优秀小说时，会情不自禁地忘却自我，也就是进入了福氏所说的节奏，以致在掩卷之后，仍然沉浸于那虚构世界之中，这就如朱光潜所说的"无暇旁顾，仿佛这小天地中有独立自足之乐，此外偌大乾坤宇宙，以及个人生活中的一切憎爱悲喜，都像在这霎时间烟消云散了"。境界也好，节奏也好，都能把人导入与万物一体的状态，形成物我的回响交流。一言以蔽之，节奏和境界都意味着物我两忘的状态。

需要留心的是，这种物我两忘的状态并非一蹴而就，而是必有积累的过程，有一个前提条件。那么，该怎样积累呢？其前提又是什么呢？福斯特对此有过两处重要的议论。一处可以在前面的引文中找到：小说各章犹如乐章，不同的乐章需要"互相交织"，进而"汇合成一个整体"，这分明是在暗示节奏/物我两忘状态的形成过程——"交织"与"汇合"显然是动态的，是一个过程，而且在同一段引文中还出现了"音响关系"一词，用来比喻"节奏性"。另一处关于节奏形成前提的论述见于福氏对普鲁斯特（Marcel Proust，1871—1922）的评论，后者的小说《追忆逝水年华》（*À la recherche du temps perdu*，1912）中有一个反复出现的曲调，即文特义尔所作小提琴奏鸣曲中的一个小片段。小说主人公史旺起先对此并未太留意，但是最后突然从中得到了一种精神感悟："主人公倾听着——他仿佛置身于一个陌生而恐怖的宇宙，目睹一道不祥的曙光把海水照得通红。突然，那一奏鸣曲的小片段重新奏响，不但他听见了，而且读者也听见了——乐曲半隐半现，还出现了变奏，但是完全起着主导作用〔……〕"（Forster 1927: 166）福斯特进而指出，那个乐曲片段虽小，却有神奇的力量，或者说"具有自身的力量"（Forster 167）。他还指出，普鲁斯特的作品本来显得混乱，但是那小小的音乐片段却有"从内部缝合普鲁斯特之书的力量，使它产生美感，勾起回忆，让读者为之销魂"（Forster 1927: 167）。此处，来自小说内部的"缝合之力"甚为关键，它的表现形式可以是《追忆逝水年华》中的那段奏鸣曲，也可以是任何能令读者"销魂"——"销魂"即节奏，即境界，即物我两忘，即"更大的存在"——的重复+变奏。用福斯特的原话说，小说节奏"可以被界定为重复加变化（repetition plus variation）"（Forster 1927: 168）。这一观点后来在克莫德（Frank Kermode，1919—2010）那里得到发展，被重新界定为"微妙的重复"（Kermode 55）。按照克莫德的阐述，"节奏具有发射信号（暗示秘密）的功能〔……〕它暗示的是一种更大的存在。乍一看去，节奏的表现形式可能是一些琐碎而无关紧要的细节，可是一旦高水平的读者把握住这些细节的积累或组合方式，就会发现它们的意义陡然增值，并且成为一种超越故事、具有震撼力的象征"（殷企平等 2001: 239—240）。克莫德和福斯特的阐述有一个共同点，即视重复为导向"更大存在"的"缝合之力"。当然，这种重复必须讲究"细节的积累或组合方式"，否则就难以实现意义的增值。

接下来的问题是：上述"重复"／"缝合之力"是导向"更大存在"的唯一必要前提吗？在这一问题上，福斯特语焉不详，克莫德亦是如此。因此，我们有必要追问："更大存在"还有别的前提吗？这将是本文下一小节的话题。

二、节奏的第一环节：起念

本文以上的论述，其实隐含着福斯特"节奏论"的一个缺陷：他未能阐发小说节奏的原初动力。诚然，"更大存在"的形成有赖于"重复"这一"缝合之力"，但后者又源于何处呢？不回答这一问题，就无法认识节奏的全部环节。依笔者之见，小说节奏的环节主要有三：除了"缝合之力"和"更大存在"（亦即物我两忘的状态）这两大环节以外，应该还有一个最初的环节，也就是形成"更大存在"的前提，我们不妨把它称为"起念"。鉴于福氏对此并无阐述，所以有必要加以探讨。

所谓"起念"（the moment of conception），即小说家开始构思的那一片刻，英国小说家兼批评家洛奇（David Lodge, 1935）称其为"受孕的片刻"（Lodge 2007：109）。不难想见，如果那一刻出现了问题，整部小说就不可能正常地发育，因而也就无所谓节奏了。在詹姆斯（Henry James, 1843—1916）那里，"起念"又被称为"萌芽"（germ），如他自己在《淑女画像》（*The Portrait of a Lady*, 1881）的前言中所说：

> 我构思的萌芽〔……〕不在于任何"情节"的构想〔……〕而完全在于对某个单一人物的感想，对一位动人的特定年轻女子的感想，对她性格和神态的感想。随后需要做的只是添加所有通常的"主题"要素，当然还需添加背景要素。（James 1962：42）

根据詹姆斯自己的描述，"萌芽"表现为他的最初"所见"，这在他关于俄国作家屠格涅夫（Ivan Turgenieff, 1818—1883）对自己影响的论述中可见一斑：

> 我总是怀着眷恋，回忆起多年以前伊凡·屠格涅夫亲口讲述的一段话，那是关于他通常如何开始构思小说画面的经验之谈。他开始写作时，几乎总会先在脑海里浮现出某个或某些人，后者主动或被动地在他眼前徘徊，恳求着他，吸引着他，吁请他给予关注〔……〕(James 1962: 42)

此处，"在脑海里浮现"的原文是 vision，也就是我们上文中论及的"所见"、"萌芽"或"起念"。詹姆斯跟屠格涅夫一样，十分注重这"所见"，并以《淑女画像》为例，强调该书就起念于他（在脑海里）见到了"一位挑战自己命运的年轻女子"，而这"单块小小的基石"却足以构成"小说大厦所有材料的起源"(James 1962: 48)。可能有人要问：那小小的"基石"或"萌芽"真的那么有力量吗？

詹姆斯的回答是肯定的。他曾经通过一个真实的故事，演绎自己的观点：一位英国女作家塑造了一个作为法国青年的新教教徒形象，她把后者的性格刻画得十分深刻，可是她在这方面的直接经验仅仅是短暂的一瞥（也就是稍纵即逝的"所见"）——她有一次访问巴黎，偶然经过一位牧师的家门口，瞥见里面的餐桌前围坐着几位年轻的新教教徒，看那样子是刚吃完了饭。詹姆斯认为那短短的一瞥已足以起念：

> 那一瞥产生了一幅图画；它只持续了一刹那，但是这一刹那就是经验。她获得了一个印象，并借此创造了一个典型人物。她了解青年的特点，也了解新教教义，又有机会看到当法国人是怎么回事情，所以她把这些概念融合在一起，转化成一个具体的形象，创造出一个现实。然而，最重要的是，她得天独厚地具有得寸进尺的能力。这种才能跟居住地点或社会地位等偶然因素相比，是一种大得多的力量源泉〔……〕(James 1980: 718—719)

此处最精妙的是"得寸进尺的能力"一说。小说家一旦有这种能力，他/她的"萌芽"就能够生长成"判断整体的能力"和"全面感受生活的条件"：

（这是一种）由所见之物揣测未见之物的能力，揭示事物内在含义的能力，根据模式判断整体的能力；这种能力是全面感受生活的条件。有了这一条件，你就能够很好地了解生活的任何一个特殊的角落。（James 1980：719）

这段话有两个关键词，即"整体"和"全面"，这正好与福斯特的"节奏论"相契合。我们在上一小节里已经提到，福氏曾经把小说节奏跟交响乐的整体感相类比，并强调这种"整体"是一种"新的感受"。也就是说，福斯特和詹姆斯都追求整体感，而且都是从"起念"的那一刻起就进行追求了。

福斯特和詹姆斯的上述相关论述其实折射了英国小说批评史上的"音乐"与"图画"之争。前文提到，詹姆斯和屠格涅夫的小说都起念于 vision，这说明他们都注重从绘画艺术中汲取灵感。持有相同主张的还有不少小说家，如康拉德（Joseph Conrad 1857—1924）。他在《"水仙号"上的黑家伙》（*The Nigger of the "Narcissus"*, 1897）的序言中就强调"关键的关键是看见"："我正致力于完成的任务是通过文学的力量使你听到，使你感到——最关键的是使你看到。除此以外，再无任何目的——看见就是一切"（Conrad 1923：52）。康拉德虽然也提到了"听到"和"感到"的重要性，但是他显然把"看到"放在了最高位置。正是在这一点上，福斯特表达了不同的观点，他一方面以《奉使记》（*The Ambassadors*, 1903）为例，肯定了詹姆斯"图式小说"的整体感和"匀称性"（symmetry），并称詹氏用细节"创造出的匀称性是永恒的"（Forster 1927：153）；另一方面又坚持认为"音乐"比"图画"更胜一筹，理由是"在音乐中，小说很可能找到与它最近似的东西"（Forster 1927：168），而这种东西就是他心心念念的节奏。

对于本文来说，"音乐"与"图画"孰优孰劣，这并不重要。从以上的比较和分析来看，二者其实是殊途同归——都以追求整体感为最高境界。本文所要强调的是，假如福斯特的"节奏论"当初吸收了詹姆斯的理论，即加强节奏在起念这一环节的论述，它本来是可以更加完善的。假如我们承认"节奏"只是一种喻说，一种比方，那么它不但适用于福斯特的"音乐"，而且也应适用于詹姆斯的"图画"。谁说图画就不能有节奏呢？也就是说，福氏跟詹氏本来是有相通之处的，无非用了不同的比喻而已。不仅如此，他们的相通之处还表现在节奏的另一环节，即"重复"／"缝合之力"。福斯特虽然如本文上一小节所示，在《小说面面观》中对它有较多的阐述，但是实际上挖掘空间还很大。有鉴于此，我们将在下一小节作更深入的探讨。

三、"重复"与境界

如前文所示，福斯特所说的节奏若要呈现为境界，就要满足一个先决条件，即通过（某细节的）重复从内部把作品缝合起来。事实上，福斯特的"重复+变奏"说（详见本文第一小节后半部分）还有待于完善，而且可以向詹姆斯借鉴。如果我们仔细地观察福氏和詹氏的具体阐述，而不纠缠于关于"音乐"或"图画"的不同比喻，就会发现他们都十分注重小说各个部分/细节之间的内在联系。前文提到，福氏论述"重复"时曾经用了"音响关系"这一喻说，而詹氏也多次用"关系"（relations）一词来阐发他的小说观，并提出了"连续性原则"（the principle of continuity），还强调小说家应该像画家那样通过展现"关系"来处理主题思想：

> 画家的主题显然在于某些人物和事物彼此之间的相关状态。一旦这些关系得以辨认，画家展现它们，就是在"处理"主题思想〔……〕（James 1962：5）

詹氏在作上述阐发时，特别强调"关系在哪里都不会停止"，"这种延续性绝不会中断，哪怕是一瞬间，哪怕是一英寸"（James 1962：5）。对他来说，"关系"是动态的，是一种"过程"（process），或者说永远处于"多重推进状态"（developments），而小说家在推进"关系"方面还须严格把握分寸，时时关注以下两个问题："如此这般的推进在多大程度上对抓住读者兴趣是必不可少的？超过了何种程度就不能算作严谨的推进了？"（James 1962：4—5）从这些论述中，我们可以得到这样的启发：难道这种对"关系"的描述不正可以用在节奏及其"重复"环节上吗？难道福氏的"重复+变奏"不是一种"推进"吗？换言之，假如福氏当初吸收了詹氏的有关思想，而不为"音乐"与"图画"的孰高孰低而纠结，那么他的"节奏论"本来会变得更为丰富。

从今天的角度来看，我们还可以从美国学者米勒（J. Hillis Miller 1928—2021）那里汲取养料，以期进一步完善福氏的"重复"一说。米勒在《小说与重复》（*Fiction and Repetition: Seven English Novels*, 1982）中提出了一个著名观点："一部像小说那样的长篇作品，不管它的读者属于哪一种类型，它的解读多半要通过对重复以及由重复所产生的意义的鉴定来完成"（Miller 1982：1）。米勒还指出，任何小说中都存在着两种互相矛盾的重复类型，而且它们总是呈"异质性形态"（heterogeneity of form），即以这样或那样的交织状态出现（Miller 1982：1—6）。米勒的观点有助于我们发现福斯特有关论述中的一个缺陷：福氏的"重复"虽然有"变奏"，但是两者应是同质的，后来克莫德所说的"微妙的重复"也属于同一范畴。鉴于米勒的研究成果，我们有必要提问：同质的重复可以导向"境界"，亦即完成"节奏"，那么异质的重复呢？如果某个细节——如事件、（人物）形象、举止和行为等——的重复呈"异质性形态"，那么这重复会不会失去缝合之力，从而破坏小说的节奏，亦即无法达到境界呢？

为回答上述问题，我们不妨审视一下詹姆斯的《淑女画像》、哈代（Thomas Hardy, 1840—1928）的《德伯家的苔丝》（*Tess of the d'Urbervilles*, 1891）、乔治·艾略特（George Eliot, 1819—1880）的《弗洛斯河上的磨坊》（*The Mill on the Floss*, 1860）和《米德尔马契》（*Middlemarch*, 1871—1872）等四部小说。它们有一个共同点，即都起念于一个"弱女子"形象，但是我们在读完故事之后，所有这些"弱女子"的形象都挥之不去，也就是把我们带入了"更大的存在"，带入了境界，而作为境界前奏部分的"缝合之力"不仅呈同质性的重复，而且呈异质性重复。

先以詹姆斯的《淑女画像》为例。前文提到，该小说起念/萌发于作者的最初"所见"，即伊莎贝尔·阿切尔。她的故事由许多重复出现的事件、意象等缝合而成，如"求爱"事件的重复：古德伍德和沃伯顿分别向伊莎贝尔求爱，而拉尔夫虽然（因明知自己患了不治之症）没有正式求爱，却也通过让她继承遗产等方式而表明了心迹，因此也算是一种重复。最重要的重复表现为伊莎贝尔与奥斯蒙德的两次聚合：奥斯蒙德与情人默尔夫人做局，致使伊莎贝尔误嫁奥斯蒙德；伊莎贝尔后来有机会走出不幸的婚姻，而且事实上离开了奥斯蒙德一段时间，可是她最后却选择回到婚姻中去，也就是"重复"了那段婚姻。可以说，伊莎贝尔与奥斯蒙德的"重聚"是一种重复，但绝不是同质性重复，而是异质性重复。换言之，伊莎贝尔与奥斯蒙德"聚"了两次，第一次是怀着爱慕（奥斯蒙德貌似高雅，加以默尔夫人助其巧妙伪装），而第二次则是一种自我牺牲的行为，两者显然不同性质。伊莎贝尔为什么选择回到婚姻中呢？因为她觉得有义务照看继女潘茜。后者是奥斯蒙德和默尔夫人的私生女，但是在生父和生母那里都得不到真爱和照料，后者只是利用她来掩盖自己的暧昧关系。伊莎贝尔做出抉择之前，有理由、有机会接受古德伍德或沃伯顿的求爱（他俩都真心地爱着她），但是她发现假如自己选择新的生活，潘茜的处境会更加糟糕。下面这段对话折射了她的心理活动和崇高品质（伊莎贝尔在前）：

"你害怕什么呢？"
"害怕爸爸——有点儿。还怕默尔夫人。她刚来看过我。"
"你千万别对他们那样说哦，"伊莎贝尔说道。
"唉，他们要我怎么做，我都愿意。只是你在的话，我会好受些。"
伊莎贝尔考虑了一会儿。"我不会抛弃你，"她最后说道。"再见，我的孩子！"（James 1947: 608）

此处的语言十分含蓄、简练而传神。"考虑""不会抛弃"和"我的孩子"等，用词简单，寥寥数语，却生动地传递了激烈的思想斗争、庄严的承诺，以及她的善良和爱心——她把潘茜视为"我的孩子"，这是一种大爱，她为此牺牲了小爱，从而升华至崇高境界，也把读者带入了同样的境界/节奏。

再以哈代小说《德伯家的苔丝》为例。女主人公苔丝跟亚历克和克莱尔都有"两聚两散"的经历：她跟亚历克第一次的"聚"是因为受其诱奸，不得已与其同居，而第二次则是走投无路（克莱尔无法接受她的过去，于新婚之夜离家出走），为资助家境窘迫的父母弟妹而再次与亚历克"相聚"；她与克莱尔的第一次"聚"（恋爱+结婚）是在与亚历克的"散"之后，而第二次则是在克莱尔回心转意，又去找她并当面忏悔之后（这也导致了她与亚历克的第二次

"散"——她痛恨亚历克再次毁掉了她跟克莱尔结合的可能性，因此杀死了亚历克）。这两聚两散是一种双重"重复"，每次的性质显然不同，但是每一次都在逐渐加深"弱女子不弱"的含义。小说中最后的一聚一散伴随着警察的追捕：苔丝跟克莱尔短暂相聚，但是很快被警察围捕，随后被处以极刑。在被捕前的最后一刻，她只平静地说了一句："我准备好了"（Hardy 1975：418）。这淡淡的一句话足以构成交响乐节奏的高潮，让人久久不能忘怀。与之配合——或者说"交响"——的是苔丝在被捕前安睡于悬石坛的画面：冉冉东升的旭日将首束光辉仅献于苔丝一人，而那些柱石连同围捕她的警察依然为黑夜所笼罩；这一强烈的反差使读者的心为之震慑——悬石坛代表着人世间所有的苦难，围捕者象征着人世间所有的不公，而苔丝在饱经人世间的苦难以后，又即将面临死神毒手，却显得那样安详，那样泰然，那样美丽。顿时，我们不仅从中感受到了苔丝的人格力量，而且感受到了整个人类超越苦难的力量；我们对书中具体画面的观照瞬时间变成了对绝对美的观照。可以说，小说的全部含义——即苔丝与苦难抗争的全部含义——都浓缩在这一稍纵即逝的画面中，并且迸发出足以使读者凝神观照的灵光，终至物我两忘。

最后再以乔治·艾略特的《弗洛斯河上的磨坊》和《米德尔马契》两部小说为例。《弗洛斯河上的磨坊》围绕玛吉和哥哥汤姆之间的无数次"聚散"而展开：玛吉纯真善良，从小就处处为哥哥着想；可是汤姆私心较重，每次相聚——不管是玩耍，还是议事——都对妹妹过于严苛，包括粗暴干涉其爱情生活，以至总是不欢而散。这种重复性场景在最后一次却发生了质变：弗洛斯河突然洪水泛滥，汤姆身处险境，玛吉不计前嫌，义无反顾地单身划船，救出了哥哥，随后又带他一起去救助他人，但是不幸翻船，他俩溺水身亡。这最后一次重聚/重复跟以往不同：以往都是不欢而散，可是这一次汤姆经历了精神上的升华，被妹妹的勇敢和爱心深深打动，从心底里升起"某种敬畏之情和羞耻心"（George Eliot 1995：458）。跟以往形成更强烈对照的是，兄妹俩这一次不离不弃，死后也紧紧相拥："小船重新露出水面，但是兄妹俩却离去了，死后两人仍然拥抱着，从此不再分离"（George Eliot 1995：459）。小说最后以他俩的墓志铭收束："死亡也没有把他们分开"（George Eliot 1995：459）。从无数次不欢而散，到最后的不离不弃，玛吉的故事完成了异质性重复，自然而然地把读者带入了情感升华的节奏，这难道不也是一种境界？

类似的情形还可以在《米德尔马契》中找到。该书中重复出现的意象很多，其中两次人物形象的"重叠"最引人注目，一次在小说的序曲（Prelude），另一次在尾声（Finale）。序曲第一句就暗示女主人公多萝西娅像16世纪西班牙圣女德雷莎（Saint Theresa），并且在第二段中为两者之间的差异埋下了伏笔："许多德雷莎降生到了人间，但没有找到自己的史诗，无法把心头的抱负不断转化为引起深远共鸣的行动。她们得到的也许只是一种充满谬误的生活，那种庄严的理想与平庸的际遇格格不入的后果，或者只是一场失败的悲剧，得不到神圣的诗人的歌咏，只能在凄凉寂寞中湮没无闻"（艾略特 1987：1—2）。此处二人形象的重叠本身就是一种重复，而它又跟尾声部分的类似重叠形成了另一种重复——在尾声倒数第二段中，多萝西娅与德雷莎的形象再次重叠："一个新德雷莎几乎没有机会去改革修道院的生活〔……〕那些轰轰烈烈的业绩得以成型的条件已经一去不复返了"（George Eliot 2000：688）。乍一看去，上述重复似乎属于同一种性质，尾声中的"重叠"似乎只是呼应了序曲定下的"基调"，或者说重复了这样一种假设：新德雷莎/多萝西娅已无用武之地，成就英雄事业的社会条件已不复存在。事实上，这只是一种异质性重复，它所重复的假设已经被发生在序曲与尾声之间的故事推翻了——全书呈现了一个"平民英雄"的故事：多萝西娅一辈子乐于做好事，不以善小而不为，其事迹看似平淡，没有德雷莎的显眼，却更加令人尊敬。也就是说，在讲了多萝西娅的故事之后，尾声中重提上述假设，其实是予以否定。作者为防止这种重复的异质性被误读，还在尾声最后一段洒下了如下赞美多萝西娅的精彩文字：

> 她那高尚纯洁的精神不虞后继无人，只是不一定到处都能见到罢了。她的完整性格，正如那条给居鲁士堵决的大河，化成了许多渠道，从此不在世上享有盛誉了。但是她对她周围人的影响，仍然不绝如缕，未可等闲视之，因为世上善的增长，一部分也依赖于那些微不足道的行为，而你我的遭遇之所以不致如此悲惨，一半也得力于那些不求闻达、忠诚地度过一生然后安息在无人凭吊的坟墓里的人们。（艾略特 1987：980—981）

这是一段摄魂震魄的文字，丝毫不逊于交响乐的力量。随着交响乐般的节奏，多萝西娅的高尚品质蔓延、浸润于我们的全部心境，我们的情趣和她的姿态交感共鸣，往复回环，仿佛进入了一个孤立绝缘的意象世界，一个纯洁高尚的意象世界，一个让人流连忘返的境界。

参考文献

［1］Conrad J. Preface to *The Nigger of the "Narcissus"*, *Conrad's Prefaces to His Works*. Ed. David Garnett［M］. London：J. M. Dent & Sons Ltd, 1923.

［2］Dayan P & Evans D. Rhythm in literature after the crisis in verse.［J］. *Paragraph* 2010, 33（2）（July 2010）：147－157.

［3］Eliot G. *Middlemarch*［M］. Hertfordshire：Wordsworth Editions Ltd, 2000.

［4］Eliot G. *The Mill on the Floss*［M］. Hertfordshire：Wordsworth Editions Ltd, 1995.

［5］Forster E M. *Aspects of the Novel*［M］. San Diego：Harcourt, Inc., 1927.

［6］Hardy T. *Tess of the d'Urbervilles: A Pure Woman*［M］. London：Macmillan London Ltd, 1975.

［7］James H. The Art of Fiction. In *Anthology of American Literature*, Vol. II. Ed. George McMichael［M］. New York：Macmillan Publishing Co., Inc., 1980.

［8］James H. *The Art of the Novel*［M］. New York：Charles Scribner's Sons, 1962.

［9］James H. *The Portrait of a Lady*［M］. Oxford：Oxford UP, 1947.

［10］Kermode F. *The Genesis of Secrecy*［M］. Cambridge, Massachusetts and London：Harvard UP, 1979.

［11］Langer S. *Problems of Art: Ten Philosophical Lectures*［M］. New York：Charles Scribner's Sons, 1957.

［12］Lodge D. *The Year of Henry*［M］. *James* London：Penguin Books, 2007.

［13］Martin W. *Joyce and the Science of Rhythm*［M］. New York：Palgrave Macmillan, 2012.

[14] Miller J. *Fiction and Repetition* [M]. Oxford: Basil Blackwell, 1982.

[15] 艾略特. 米德尔马契 [M]. 项星耀译, 北京: 人民文学出版社, 1987. [Eliot, George. *Middlemarch*. Trans. Xiang Xingyao. Beijing: P of People's Literature, 1987.]

[16] 邓颖琳, 蒋翃遐. 论小说节奏的叙事功能 [J]. 外语与外语教学, 2012, (1): 91-94. [Deng Yinglin and Jiang Hongxia. "On the Narrative Function of Rhythm in a Novel." *Foreign Languages and the Teaching of Foreign Languages* 1 (2012): 91-94.]

[17] 蒋虹. 俄罗斯芭蕾与伍尔夫小说中的色彩元素 [J]. 外国文学, 2015, (2): 55-62. [Jiang Hong. "The Russian Ballet and the Pigmentation of Virginia Woolf's Novels." *Foreign Literature* 2 (2015): 55-62.]

[18] 殷企平等. 英国小说批评史 [M]. 上海: 外语教育出版社, 2001. [Yin Qiping et al. *A History of Criticism of English Fiction*. Shanghai: P of Shanghai Foreign Languages Education, 2001.]

[19] 朱光潜. 谈美 [M]. 桂林: 广西师范大学出版社, 2006. [Zhu Guangqian. *On Beauty*. Guilin: P of Guangxi Normal U, 2006.]

[20] 朱光潜. 朱光潜美学文集. 第2卷 [M]. 上海: 上海文艺出版社, 1982. [—. *Zhu Guangqian's Aesthetic Works*, Vol. II. Shanghai: P of Shanghai Art and Literature, 1982.]

(本文原载于 Interdisciplinary Studies of Literature, Vol. 5, No. 1, 2021)

New Possibilities Brought About by Hypertext

IS THE NOVEL DEAD?

There has been no lack of prophecies of the death of the novel since the beginning of the 20th century. Many prestigious critics, such as T. S. Eliot, Ortega Y. Gasset, Alberto Moravia and Cyril Connolly, have relentlessly pronounced death sentence on the novel. Although thousands of novels are still being written and millions are being sold today, Leslie Fiedler's following view is still quite prevalent:

> ... the novel is dying if not dead .... To be sure, some writers ... continue to write as if that death had not occurred, but so do certain men and women continue to attend church services despite the well-advertised Death of God (Fiedler 1974).

Is the novel really dead? If yes, in what sense has it died? A typical answer is that all the traditional or "realistic" attributes of the novel (characters, story, atmosphere) no longer exist. In Ronald Sukenick's words:

> The contemporary writer ... is forced to start from scratch: Reality doesn't exist, time doesn't exist, personality doesn't exist (Sukenick 1969).

All these elements no longer exist not because they cannot be found in contemporary novels, but because they are no longer new. In other words, all the possibilities of the novel have been exhausted. Christine Brooke-Rose has written cogently about this problem: "All then has been said, there is nothing new under the sun ... And even scenes are labeled, the happiness sequence, the chase sequence, the scene of violence, the marital scene, the love-scene, the high society scene, the scene of diplomatic intrigue, the office sequence, the work sequence, with its appropriate music and lighting" (Brooke-Rose 1991). Brooke-Rose here has actually echoed the views of Ian Watt, Anthony Burgess and Bernard Bergonzi, who have argued on various occasions that one of the defining elements of the generic identity of the novel lies in its being "new" (Yin 1999). Bergonzi's following statement is another way of announcing the novel as dead: "If the novel is truly no longer novel, then many of our critical procedures for discussing it will need revision; perhaps, even, we shall do well to think of another name for it" (Bergonzi 1972).

The death of the novel, however, does not exclude the possibility of its rebirth. On the contrary, it has to die in order to be reborn. Quite a few people have drawn blueprints for the renaissance of the novel, but most of them turn out to be more or less vague. Brooke-Rose, for instance, pins her hope on the electronic revolution which she believes will "enable us to create new dimensions in the deep-down logic of characters" (Brooke-Rose 1991). The weakness in Brooke-Rose's argument is that she fails to specify the exact meaning of that "computer logic" and the sense in which it is different from the old logic underlying novel writing. The present paper, therefore, proposes to explore the specificities of the above-said new logic and the extent to which the renewal of the novel might benefit from such a logic.

NEW POSSIBITIES BROUGHT ABOUT BY HYPERTEXT

What Brooke-Rose has left undone can be done by drawing inspiration from Stuart Moulthrop's theory on hypertext. In his seminal article "Rhizome and Resistance: Hypertext and the Dreams of a New Culture", which is acclaimed as "a moment of critical transition in the nature of discourse" (Davis and Schleifer 1998), Moulthrop surveys the emerging nonlinear discourses of electronic texts and sees in hypertext the dawn of a new age. Although his purpose is to shed light on epistemological changes brought about by technologies of computer hypertext, the distinctions he makes between the printed text and the electronic text provide a context for exploring new possibilities for the novel.

Moulthrop's contribution lies in his effort to relate Michael Joyce's conceptions of electronic writing space, which he calls "constructive hypertext", to the distinction Deleuze and Guattari draw between smooth and striated cultural spaces (Joyce 1998). As Moulthrop aptly sums up, striated space manifests itself in hierarchical and rule-intensive cultures, whereas smooth space is mediated by discontinuities. In striated space, which is defined or supported by books of the print-based text, the overriding principles are best characterized as routine, specification, sequence and causality, and those who follow the logic of striated space are "the champions of order, purpose and control — defenders of logos, or the law" (Moulthrop 1998). Smooth space, by contrast, is defined in terms of transformation instead of essence, and it "propagates in a matrix of breaks, jumps, and implied or contingent connections" (Moulthrop 1998). Ulmer's age of video and Mcluhan's electronically mediated global village constitute two good examples for Moulthrop, for they "both operate in smooth space, which is best served not by the linearizing faculties of print but by the parataxis and bricolage of broadcasting" (Moulthrop 1998).

What Moulthrop has said can be regarded as a concrete complement to Brooke-Rose's "computer logic". The novel in a traditional sense, of course, is essentially based on the logic of striated space. But can it draw impetus from the logic of smooth space so as to be reborn? Does hypertext represent an entirely new textual model for the novel? Those who deny this possibility might rest their argument on the truism that nonlinearizing faculties are no novelty, for they are exactly the characteristics of postmodernist fiction, which has been active for several decades. It is interesting to notice that even people like Brooke-Rose, who themselves are often put under the name of "postmodernists", can see nothing new in such works as represented by Samuel Beckett's *The Unnamable*. The so-called postmodernist writings, in Brooke-Rose's opinion, are all "subject to a discursive expansion rule, almost a rule of proliferation" which is chaotic, cancerous, that is, obsessional, reflexive, autophagous (Brooke-Rose 1991).

A close-up look at the transition from printbased literacy to hypertext, however, does reveal new implications for discourse technologies. By "new implications" I do not mean a total disruption of the established power of publishing institutions and a complete transformation of the traditional book-based novel into the form of an electronic text. It is true that we can now read a novel on the computer, but it is a common sense that the print-based novel is still in many ways easier to handle and enables us to read in a more comfortable posture. What I mean is, rather, that the novel may absorb new nourishment from the way of thinking and discourse technologies suggested by electronic texts and electronic literacy, while still remaining in a book form. As Moulthrop points out, current thinking about hypertext systems relates strongly to the idea of a discourse system founded on nomos as opposed to logos (Moulthrop 1998). The writing system founded on logos follows the logic of the above-said striated space which is ordered, controlled, teleological, temporal and hierarchical, whereas the discourse system based on nomos, by contrast, suggests the logic of smooth space, which is dynamic, spatial and anti-hierarchical. What Moulthrop has in mind is Deleuze's and Guattari's concepts of "Arbor" and "Rhizome". An arborescent book is assumed to have roots (hidden meanings) and a hierarchical structure that resembles a tree. It is founded on logos, namely, logocentric, hierarchically grounded truth. A rhizomatic book simply resembles grass, whose underlying logic is nomos or nomadism or nomadology, i. e. , continuing movement, lines of flight and deterritorialization. Niall Lucy has once given us a lucid summary of the above-mentioned distinction: "Unlike a tree, grass is always on the move, always forming alliances with the world outside itself as it keeps on spreading across and across the surfaces of things. Grass doesn't grow up; it spreads out. Trees settle; grass roams" (Lucy 2000). Is it possible for a novel, then, to appear rhizomatic or grasslike?

If a novel is to be rhizomatic, according to Deleuze and Guattari, it has to contain within itself heterogeneous traits and should have "neither beginning nor end" (Deleuze and Guattari 1987). But the novel, print-based as it is, is bound to have a beginning and an end. Besides, one of the great charms of novels is that they have to end. Frank Kermode, in his classic *The Sense of an Ending*, rightly points out that we human beings need fictive concords with origins and ends so as to make sense of our lives. The greatest function of the novel is perhaps to provide "a concord of imaginatively recorded past and imaginatively predicted future, achieved on behalf of us, who remain 'in the middest' " (Kermode 1996).

In a metaphorical sense, however, the novel can appear grass-like and keep spreading across its own boundaries. This is where the notion of intertextuality comes in. As we all know, intertextuality means the collapse of boundaries — textual or even generic crossovers. Although intertextuality is intertwined in the roots of the novel and can be regarded as the very condition of the latter, most traditional novelists tend to hide or suppress — they may even fail to know — the fact that their works are actually woven from tissues of other texts. Since James Joyce there has been an increasing tendency among novelists to openly exploit the principle of intertextuality, freely recycling earlier novels or works in other literary genres. Typical examples are James Joyce who tip off his readers by entitling his epic of modern Dublin life *Ulysses*, Jean Rhys whose remarkable Wide Sargasso Sea explores the "hidden" story of *Jane Eyre*, and David Lodge who begins his *Small World* with a prologue that is facetiously reminiscent of Geoffrey Chaucer's *Canterbury Tales*. This sort of intertextual play at least resembles operations in the above-mentioned smooth space, for these books openly reach beyond their own boundaries and claim kindred with other texts or, more precisely, form an integral part of a "super-text." In other words, the novel can appear grass-like even without any impetus from electronic hypertextuality.

But the rhizomatic propensities of the novel can be and have been proliferated and made pervasive by the impact of the age of hypertext. Brian McHale has actually touched upon the extended possibilities of the novel as a whole while depicting the rhizomatic process of postmodern novels' borrowings from and overlappings with each other. In his "POSTcyberMODERNpunkISM", McHale manages to build a picture of cyberpunk that can be described as interactive or hypertextual. He sees in the 1980s the emergence of what he calls "postmodernist fiction of the cybernetic interface" or "texts which register the first, often traumatic encounters between 'literary' culture (high culture generally) and the transformative possibilities of computer technology" (McHale 1991). Interestingly, he considers Christine Brooke-Rose's "computer trilogy" *Amalgamemnon* (1984), *Xorandor* (1986) and *Verbivore* (1990) to be exemplary in this regard. Although Brooke-Rose herself has failed to specify, as we have observed in the first section of the present paper, what she calls "the computer logic", McHale comes closer to what it specifically means by pointing out that in Brooke-Rose's novels "the literary repertoire has been reconfigured so as to begin to accommodate — right down to the 'micro' level of verbal detail — the realia of computer technology" (McHale 1991). Brooke-Rose is of course not the only one who has responded to the advent of hypertext. Among the most directly responsive to the changes in technology of writing are such texts as Russell Hoban's *The Medusa Frequency* (1987), James McConkey's *Kayo* (1987), William Vollman's *You Bright and Risen Angels* (1987) and Umberto Eco's *Pendolo di Foucault* (1988). In all these novels, as McHale notes, there is "an obvious extension of the topos to adapt it so as to reflect the newest writing technology, that of personal computers and word-processing" (McHale 1991). So hypertext does have an important role to play in renewing writing technologies of the novel. It does not follow that the novel has to be turned into a hypertext but, rather, its operational logic can be made to approximate that of a web of hypertext links.

A good example can be found in the complex architectonics of Peter Ackroyd's *Hawksmoor*, in which the reader is confronted with six 18th century endings, each of which is qualified by a 20th century perspective, as well as six 20th century endings, each of which is contextualized by an 18th century vignette, and each of which anticipates the "future" development of the 18th century plot. The high number of endings naturally entails the multiplication of beginnings. Thus the novel is designed in such a way as to resemble a matrix of independent but cross-referential discourses which the reader is invited to enter more or less at random, regardless of the fact that the text itself arrives as a print artifact.

There should be many other ways of making a novel operate like a web of hypertext links, but the above-mentioned example alone sufficiently suggests that possibilities of the novel can be greatly increased by gesturing towards "an incunabular hypertext."

LIMITATIONS AND CONSTRAINTS

It should be emphasized that what has been advocated above is a mere approximation towards or "borrowing" from hypertext. In a book-based novel, words are necessarily contained between covers. Moreover, we should not lose sight of the fact that hypertext systems themselves, after all, are essentially routinized. As Moulthrop observes, vastness and randomness are not particularly valuable *per se*. Even in a nomadic hypertextual culture some principles of regulation and constraints are indispensable. While reflecting upon the "hidden unity" underlying any discursive practice that is dedicated to multiplicity and flexible articulation, Moulthrop arrives at the following thoughts:

> That which purports to be a true multiple — a rhizome, a nomadology, a smooth space — may in fact be only a little world made cunningly, some

deterministic system passing itself off as a structure for what does not yet exist. It may even be the case ... that we are hopelessly bound to determinism as a consequence of our engagement with technologies of writing (Moulthrop 1998).

Moulthrop has in fact been influenced by Martin Rosenberg who, in his "Physics and Hypertext: Liberation and Complicity in Art and Pedagogy", argues against the celebratory treatment of hypertext and its cultural possibilities. Both Moulthrop and Rosenberg hold the view that "anything produced out of a systemic relationship between lexias and links, cards, buttons, and fields also participates in the same geometrical episteme that produced Newton's laws and classical stasis theory, Freynman diagrams of subatomic particle interactions, formal logic, computer languages, and the fractal scaling of sea coasts, black holes, and chess" (Moulthrop 1998).

By "anything produced out of a systemic relationship between lexias and links, cards, buttons, and fields", Moulthrop and Rosenberg actually mean hypertext which is characterized by the principles of "vastness and randomness." Indeed vastness and randomness cannot completely liberate us from geometry, rationalist method, or the logocentric thought.

The example set by Hawksmoor can again be used to illustrate our point: The nomadic play of the text does not really liberate Ackroyd's novel from the constraints of logos. To be sure, randomness, excess and short circuit are all in some way or other visible in Hawksmoor. As some critics have pointed out, the novel is in fact composed according to a circular logic, a logic which transcends the barriers of time and space. Cynthia J. Wheaton, for instance, states that "the novel lacks a focus that would make a point beyond the wealth of detail. As it is, tantalizing symmetries, provocative discussions of architecture, debates on ancient and modern lead nowhere and frustrate the reader" (Wheaton 1986). But despite the randomness that creates such a strong sense of discontinuity, Ackroy paradoxically also succeeds in subtly creating a sense of continuity by weaving into his novel numerous symmetrical and parallel patterns. The multiplication of beginnings and endings, as observed in our second section, does create a sense of circularity and discontinuity, but a sensitive reader will not fail to perceive the symmetrical relationship between the twentieth-century chapters of the novel and the eighteenth-century chapters of the novel. In other words, smooth space, characterized by the discontinuity principle, actually depends on striated space dominated by the continuity principle. The paradox lies in the fact that the very possibility of giving full play to smooth space presupposes the existence of striated space. The tension has to be there, or both spaces will vanish.

All this does not mean, however, that the age of hypertext has only brought a false dawn on the revival of the novel. Although the alternation between or mixture of striated and smooth spaces may have long been one of the fundamental conditions of the novel, the emergence of computer technologies is bound to increase the speed of the alternation between smooth space and striated space. In the technologically enhanced speed of the traffic in models between smooth space and striated space, in short, lies the hope of the renaissance of the novel.

References

[1] Ackroyd P. *Hawksmoor* [M]. London: Penguin Books Ltd., 1993.

[2] Bergonzi B. *The Situation of the Novel* [M]. Pittsburgh: University of Pittsburgh Press, 34.

[3] Brooke-Rose C. *Stories, Theories and Things* [M]. Cambridge: Cambridge University Press, 1991.

[4] Davis R C and Schleifer R. *Literary Criticism* [M]. Longman, New York: Longman, 1998.

[5] Deleuze G, Guattari F. Introduction: Rhizome [A] //A Thousand Plateaus: Capitalism and Schizophrenia. Trans. by Massumi B. [M]. Minneapolis: University Minnesota Press, 20.

[6] Fiedler L A. The Death and Rebirth of the Novel [A] //The Theory of the Novel. John Halperin (ed.). New York: Oxford University Press, 1974: 194 – 195.

[7] Kermode F. *The Sense of an Ending* [M]. London: Oxford University Press, 1966: 8.

[8] Lucy N. *Postmodern Theory* [M]. Oxford: Blackwell Publishers, 2000: 140.

[9] McHale B. POSTcyberMODERNpunkISM [A] //McCaffery L. (ed.) *Storming the Reality Studio: A Case Book of Cyberpunk and Postmodern Science Fiction* [M]. London: Durham and Duke University Press, 1991: 317, 318, 318.

[10] Michael J. Siren shapes: Exploratory and constructive hypertext [J]. *Academic Computing*, 1988, (11).

[11] Moulthrop S. Rhizome and Resistance: Hypertext and the Dreams of a New Culture [A] //Robert Con Davis and Ronald Schleifer (eds.) *Literary Criticism* [M]. New York, Longman, 1998: 240, 240, 240, 239.

[12] Sukenick R. *The Death of the Novel* [M]. New York: The Dial Press, INC., 1969: 41.

[13] Wheaton C J. Ackroyd, Peter: Hawksmoor [J]. *Library Journal*, 1986, 111: 98.

[14] Yin Qiping. The Novel No Longer Novel and Bergonzi's Narrative Theory [J]. *Contemporary Foreign Literatures*, 1999, 2 (76): 134–141.

(本文原载于 Journal of Zhejiang University Science 2001 年第 4 期)

第三编

作品评论

文化的物质性

——哈代小说中的哥特式建筑*

一、哥特式建筑引出的话题

尽管我国已有学者关注到哈代（Thomas Hardy, 1840—1928）小说中的哥特式建筑书写，但是他们只把它看作一种与观念相一致的质料，并未真正聚焦于哥特式建筑本身，未从物质文化层面探究其物质性内涵与价值。相较之下，国外有学者在这方面已走得很远，例如美国俄勒冈大学教授普莱（Forrest Pyle）指出，《无名的裘德》（*Jude the Obscure*, 1895）中缺乏对历史的叙述，而是代之以对幸存古建筑的描述，旨在通过对实物的考古来恢复被资本主义破坏的历史传统（Plye 1995: 367—368）；又如美国加州大学伯克利分校的卡农（Benjamin Cannon）指出，修复古物实际上对建筑材料构成了破坏（Cannon 2014: 210）。他还指出，哈代认为历史建筑的潜能就在于它"笨拙的物质性"（unwieldy materiality）（同上，203）。这种言论背后的美学思想是将历史视为物质的过程，具有不可重复性。此中涉及的建筑物质性及其重要性成为本文笔者思考的起点。

围绕文化观念中的物质性（materiality）所展开的争论由来已久。例如，伍尔

---

* 本文是殷企平和张琰合写的。

夫将爱德华时代的 3 位作家威尔斯（H. G. Wells）、贝内特（Arnold Bennett）和高尔斯华绥（John Galsworthy）斥为"物质主义者（materialists）"（Woolf 1925：60）。同样，她也批评哈代，认为后者虽然已经意识到"精确再现物质性事实之真实在艺术中已不再具有重要意义"（引自 Woolf 1978：68），虽然已对"物质主义"有所反思，但在她看来，哈代的这"一半"被他现实主义的另一半"压抑了"（同上，67）。换言之，哈代的矛盾就在于，他在作品中无法处理好物质与非物质部分的和谐统一。而这恰好反映出他对社会转型时期物质与心灵关系的分离感到焦虑。笔者认为，关于上述矛盾现象，恐怕还要从当时哥特式建筑出现的问题说起。

哈代在书信中提到了他的艺术观念："'艺术'是一种不成比例（disproportioning）（即扭曲，抛弃比例）的现实……'现实主义'不是艺术"（Hardy 1962：229）。其中"比例"等语词的使用，让人联想到他早年哥特建筑制图员的生活经历。作为一名训练有素的建筑师，哈代十分熟悉同世纪前辈罗斯金（John Ruskin，1819—1900）的建筑-文学理论，并在信件中多次提到罗斯金[①]，后者反对古典主义建筑的"比例/均衡"（proportion）原则，并且批评古希腊建筑"无想象力，无宗教性……唯有精确测量的比例而已"（Ruskin 1854：94）。罗斯金在 19 世纪中叶还提出一个极具影响力的论点，即哥特艺术是疏离现代意识的最佳方式，也即通过扭曲和不规则发挥艺术作用（Vuohelainen 2018：10）。然而，哈代在学习罗斯金的同时，又常与后者意见相左。例如，他在威尼斯参观圣马可教堂（St. Marks）时，在书信中反驳了罗斯金关于该建筑的溢美之词：

> 当这个教堂被视为一个整体时，它照例会产生某种狂喜、夸张［的感觉］，——罗斯金这样说，莫不是言不由衷吧？……它的一个建筑缺陷是无法克服的，从自然角度可［明显地］看出它的矮胖……另一个缺陷是它那脆弱、呈波浪形的构造线条。……尽管它非常优美，但东方式的古怪细节特征使其给人的总体印象变得野蛮。
>
> （Hardy 1962：193）

[①] 见 Hardy, Florence Emily. *The Life of Thomas Hardy 1840-1928*. London & Basingstoke：Palgrave Macmillan UK, 1962：38, 172, 193-195, 235, 293, 353。

事实上，哈代小说中的哥特式建筑也具有扭曲、残缺的特征，它除了折射维多利亚时期哥特式建筑复兴的盛况，还反映了复兴背后哈代与罗斯金等人文主义者对于19世纪英国社会转型时期物质与心灵相分离产生的焦虑。但是，相较于罗斯金，哈代关注的焦点不在于探究哥特式艺术的本质，而在于探讨建筑环境中人与物之间复杂的关联，其中人与建筑的联系在很大程度上又依赖于建筑的物质属性。本文将结合罗斯金的建筑批评，探讨哈代小说中与哥特建筑相关的修补、坠落和倒置情节，以及建筑师角色背后所可能包含的历史遗迹毁灭者、牧师等隐性人物身份。具有"小说家-建筑师"身份的哈代，从历史、宗教、艺术等角度全面思考了哥特式建筑所包含的人与物、物与社会的辩证关系，由此揭示了文化观念中物质性的重要意义。

然而，目前学界对文化观念中"物质性"的内涵仍存有较多争议，不少学者将其与物性（thingness）一词混用，以此强调物质的能动性。米勒（Daniel Miller）认为，物质性一词包含了通俗与哲学两种用法：前者主要指人造的物（artifact），而后者超越了主客二元论，它指的是相对于前者简单定义之外的思想。换言之，它是"物质性的广域"，包含了诸如"瞬息的、虚构的、生物有机的、理论编造的"物质（Miller 2005: 4）；米勒认为物质性的理论"是最包罗万象的，还把物质文化置于更大的文化概念化之中"，但同时它的通俗用法不应被忽略（同上，4）。本文中使用的"物质性"一词更符合米勒的主张，强调哥特式建筑所体现的物质性，涵盖了从物理层面到历史、宗教、艺术等层面上的意义。

二、历史之物——修补的挽歌

哈代小说中存在关于哥特式建筑修复的大量描写，如短篇小说《湛蓝的眼睛》（*A Pair of Blue Eyes*, 1873）和《冷漠的人》（*A Laodicean*, 1881）。实际上，建筑本身就具有叙事功能，可以说是"叙事场所"和"故事式物质"（a storied matter）（Iovino and Oppermann 2012: 83）。用哈代自己的话说，历史建筑是"石质的编年史"（chronicles in stone）（Hardy 1990: 204）。哈代特别关注现在与过去的连续性，哀叹其断裂，这体现在《无名的裘德》中一段关于中世纪精神与现代性冲突的描述，我们不妨称它为"修补"的挽歌：

> 在他看来，这儿的活儿，顶多不过是复制、修补、模仿。他认为，这也许是由于暂时性或者地方性的原因。其实他没看出来，那是因为中世纪的精神已经和煤块里面羊齿植物的叶子一样，早就没有生命了；在他四围那个世界里，另有新的发展演变，在这种发展里，哥特式的建筑以及和哥特式建筑有关的事物是没有地位的。现代的逻辑和想象，对于他那样敬仰的事物，有解不开的仇恨，那时候他还不知道呢。
>
> （哈代. 哈代文集⑥. 2004：110）

此段采用了反讽，除了表现裘德的天真，还点明了新旧更迭之下哥特式建筑的遭遇。首先，联系前文可知，裘德凭石匠手艺在基督寺勉强安身，徜徉于中世纪建筑，犹如流浪的骑士，满眼都是"伤感的魂灵"与"缥缈的形体"（哈代.哈代文集⑥. 2004：100—101）。相比于基督寺的居民，裘德更有感于窗花格里的贤人先知、美术馆里的绘画雕像以及走廊方庭等历史遗迹，因此更具有历史想象和中世纪情结。如比尔·布朗所说，物的能动性与施事功能体现在"能影响主体的焦虑以及喜好，使主体感到恐惧或者充满想象"（Brown 2003：3—4）。这些无生命的物体成为基督寺中亡故之人提喻式的存在，获得了幽灵般的生命，裘德也随之逐渐成为一个脱离"现代逻辑"的主体，此处主客体的界限被磨灭。继裘德与建筑物相互融合之后，物的不幸遭遇成为主人公悲剧命运的转喻。裘德对命运之"仇恨"的一无所知，暗合世人对中古建筑遭遇的后知与后觉。然而，这些建筑究竟遭遇了什么？现代生活为什么会对它有"解不开的仇恨"？在哥特式复兴期间，中世纪建筑作为石匠热衷模仿的对象为何"没有地位"？其关键在于对建筑进行修复。"修复"其实包含了一种德里达称为"哀悼"（mourning）（Derrida 1995：52）的悖论逻辑，可视为现在对过去的哀悼。一方面，出于对古物废墟的忧思，意在通过修复延续亡灵的存在；另一方面，现代材料对古物来说是异质的他物，致使"修复"成为一种亵渎与篡改。哈代指出，这种隐蔽的侵犯是长久广泛的危害，与拆毁一样，能造成过去与现在的断裂（Hardy 1990：215）；从宏观角度看，现代性神话就体现在与过去完全决裂的态度，它总与"创造性破坏"（creative destruction）有关（Harvey 2003：1），而哈代小说中现代对过去"解不开的仇恨"正是那些"顶多不过是复制、修补、模仿"的石匠活儿。

其实，早在该书"在玛丽格伦"这一章中，哈代就揭示了"修复"悖论。他通过描写古村遭受的暴力，从古树、教堂被"铲平""伐倒""拆掉"和"碾成"，到"找不出痕迹"和"已湮灭无踪"，塑造了一个来自伦敦的"历史遗迹毁灭者"的建筑师角色（《哈代文集》⑥，6），或者说"建筑师-毁灭者"的悖论身份。历史遗物的缺席唤醒了历史记忆的在场，怀旧情绪由此产生；同时，历史的物质性得到前景化，表现为建筑并非凝固的形式，而是能动且变化的物质现实。对于历史的物质性，哈代的表达是跨艺术且具诗意的。例如，同样的花纹图案，石场"是用近代散文表现的"，而学院内中世纪建筑苔藓斑驳的墙面则是"用古诗表现的"。哈代还辩证地写道："即便那些现在成了古董的石活儿，当年还新的时候，或许也只是散文。他们只是在那儿一无所为地等候，就熬成诗了。"（同上，109）建筑物从新到旧，被比作从散文到诗的艺术，物质变化与文学体裁流变相类比，由此充满了符号、意义与想象。换言之，物质的历时性及其文化价值能赋予物本身以厚重的情感内核，而"复制、修补、模仿"则破坏了历史的延续性，使人类的情感结构和价值体系难以维系。

物质性之重要就在于，它反对抽象观念对物质经验的宰制。物质不是也不应被"贬低成一种为了某些另外的抽象'生活'目的而实施的、仅仅具有技术性的手段一样的"社会过程（威廉斯2008：67—68）。相反，意义与物质是融合且不可分离的，"物质性与话语性相互牵扯，同处于动态的内在互动（intra-activity）中"（Barad 2007：336）。哈代预见性地认为，建筑不是沉默的存在，它本身就成了一种话语建构。例如，建筑物常常因扮演备忘录角色而发挥作用，如"保留了回忆、故事、手足之情以及仁爱"（Hardy 1990：205）。同样，罗斯金称建筑为"记忆之灯"，并认为它作为人类一种更生动形象的历史应被保存，建筑的"辉煌在于其年龄，在于其有话要说的深邃感，在于其严厉的观察，在于其神秘的同情之心"（Ruskin 1903：234）。虽然哈代与罗斯金都关注历史的物质性，但两者的感情色彩不同：罗斯金从哥特式建筑中看到的是理想愿景，而哈代关注的是物质现实。这两种情感就好比白天观物和夜晚观物所产生的不同观感："在夜里看起来完美无疵、合于理想的东西，到了白天，就变成了或多或少带有缺陷的现实之物了"（哈代.哈代文集⑥.2004：108）。当然，罗斯金也批判建筑修复,只是哈代更能体会到那些辉煌建筑"和时光、风霜、人类等作过生死斗争",终难逃"遍体鳞伤,肢体残缺,失掉了原来的外形"这一残酷命运(同上,108)。一言以蔽之,哈代强调历史的物质基础十分脆弱,若不加保护,过去与现在的延续性就难以维系。

三、宗教之物——坠落的寓言

哥特式教堂的相关描写常见于哈代早期哥特小说中。有学者指出,哥特建筑与哥特小说都是人类思想的载体,中世纪对于 18 世纪以来哥特复兴的影响,"主要通过建筑,而不是文学作品",后人从中世纪"获得的神秘与奇幻的刺激感,主要来自哥特建筑,而不是《亚瑟王之死》"(转引自苏耕欣 2010:13)。苏耕欣认为,哥特小说可被理解为社会转型期的矛盾文学,小说中哥特式建筑的塑造很大程度上也表现了转型社会中人们的矛盾情感(同上,13)。这种复杂情感同样存在于哈代的哥特小说中,如《非常手段》(*Desperate Remedies*,1871)中女主人目睹建筑师父亲从塔尖坠落身亡前的情景。我们不妨称该建筑叙事为"坠落"的寓言:

> 塔尖约有一百二十英尺高。在上面干活儿,五个人似乎完全脱离了一般人的生活范围和生活体验。他们看上去比鸽子大不了多少,这使他们微小的举动带着一种轻柔,一种精灵般的沉静。他们的举止给地面上的人最深的印象就是对目标的全神贯注,而对下面纷乱的世界漠不关心,甚至根本没意识到它的存在。
>
> (哈代.哈代文集①.2004:9—10)

坠落前的建筑师如"鸽子"般依附于教堂塔尖,高空之中有一种神性,此时建筑师与宗教建筑仿佛融为一体。哈代将教堂塔尖观念化,成为一种精神象征,建筑师的精神空间随塔尖向上延伸,获得片刻的崇高感。类似的描述还见于哈代其他小说,如《裘德》中的"大教堂的尖阁",主人公常常"用这些东西来激发自己"(哈代.哈代文集⑥.2004:113)。值得注意的是,哥特式塔尖之所以能体现建筑师当时的一种扩张性心理状态,是因为该建筑风格自身蕴含的物质力量。如德勒兹与加塔利称哥特式对罗马式的超越就在于前者"征服了一个光滑空间"(Deleuze and Guattari 1987:364),即包含了一种不断变化、生成的哲学意味;又如布朗所说,"偶然的干扰"反而可以揭示物的"在场和威力的顿时性",而"当客体不再为我们工作时……我们已经开始面对客体的物性"(Brown 2001:3—4)。换言之,陡峭的塔尖因拥有让人坠落的威胁力使其自身不再停留于一种静态观念的投射,而成为一种与人相交的经历,在这种给人造成生命威胁的瞬间,它完成了对人与物主客体关系的挑战,即德里达所说"物不是一个客体,不可能成为一个客体"(Derrida 1984:126)。同时,坠落行为还体现了身体"物"的一面:身体本身属于物质界,也就具有一定意义上的物性与自主性。总之,从坠落前的神性到坠落时的物性,坠落的建筑师体现了精神的肉体化过程,即精神不是对立于身体的知性,而是在一定程度上体现了物质与观念的融合与统一。

当然,坠落情节设计的用意显然在于表现小说的主题,身体向下运动与塔尖向上耸立方向相反,即灵与肉矛盾冲突的线性表征。"坠落"的建筑师生前"跟他的朋友亨特威同一年考进剑桥大学,同一年毕业,而后亨特威去担任神职工作"(哈代.哈代文集①.2004:1),哈代似乎有意在建筑师与神职工作之间建立某种联系。哥特教堂的尖耸不但让观者望而生畏,而且让建造者身临死亡,却又超越对死亡的恐惧。可以说,"建筑师—牧师"身份的关联,一定程度上象征宗教与世俗的关系;纯真的建筑师"坠落"之死,似乎佐证了哈代情感中对上帝的怀疑和犹豫。

从建筑批评转向文化批评,强调物质与观念和谐统一的远不止哈代。罗斯金在《威尼斯的石头》中就提出了一砖一瓦皆俗物的整体观。他在谈论哥特式本质时说,"尖拱顶、圆屋顶、飞檐和怪异的雕塑并不是哥特式建筑的组成部分",但"组合在一起时,就重新有了生机"(罗斯金 2014:140),即哥特式的本质在于整体性,在于建立组合关系,产生共同作用。不过,哈代和罗斯金在整体观上仍有区别:罗斯金强调的是外在形式与内在精神的依存关系,而哈代则强调宗教与世俗的紧密联系;后者偏重物性,而前者却更看重德性。罗斯金主张"首先要明确什么是哥特式建筑的精神力量,其次明确什么是哥特式建筑的物质形式"（罗斯金 2014：141），而哈代则强调"看四周那些无数建筑，与其说用的是艺术家的眼光""不如说用的是匠人的眼光"，去琢磨它们"是怎样用气力使那些设计实现的"（哈代. 哈代文集⑥. 2004：108）。所有这一切，都可以看作哈代与罗斯金在文化层面的对话。

四、艺术之物——倒置的隐喻

在英国，哥特式建筑传统悠久，从教堂到乡间别墅乃至普通民居，都广泛采用。哈代在《远离尘嚣》（*Far from the Madding Crowd*, 1874）中有一段关于女主人公芭斯谢芭所住宅邸的描写，不妨称作"倒置"的隐喻：

> 这种情景（房屋前面），以及这儿到处弥漫着的那种令人昏昏欲睡的气氛，和房屋背面那种生机盎然的景象截然相反。这不禁会使人想到，当初为了办农场改修这所建筑物，就把主体部分转了个身，弄成背朝前、面朝后了。许多高楼大厦——无论是独立的还是位于街道和市镇建筑群里——本来只是为了娱乐而设计的，现在用来经营买卖，往往都被弄得这么颠三倒四，畸异残缺，严重地瘫痪了。

（哈代. 哈代文集②. 2004：82）

从该引文的上文可知，女主人公的哥特式邸宅位于城镇与乡村的交界，"碎石小径从前门一直通到公路"，体现了城市化的一面，而后面"庄园的广阔土地汇成一片"，保留了乡村田园的一面；至于建筑内部的结构，前面是主人的厅堂，"没有铺地毯，木板表面的虫蛀痕迹历历在目"，"每一扇门的开关都要引起一扇窗户发出哐当的回响"，以至于给人一种"无论你在房子里走到哪儿，都有嘎嘎的声音像鬼魂一样跟随"的感觉（哈代. 哈代文集②. 2004：82—88）。哈代将建筑物改造后所体现的城市化的"前面"描述为"昏昏欲睡"，其未被改造的"背面"反而"生机盎然"，而且农场劳动者都充满了生命力。这段描写与罗斯金的如下评论形成了呼应："19 世纪人们从一部书中享受的乐趣来自图画、雕塑和中世纪建筑的小型物品，主要是因为它们都生动美丽。任何现代建筑都不能给予我们这样的乐趣。"（罗斯金 2014：147）同样，哈代认为乡村建筑依托自然，建筑设计多体现追求审美趣味的一面，而城市建筑出于商业考虑，沦为资本的一种炫耀方式。由此，扭曲的哥特艺术"仅仅表达着肆意开支和金钱算术"（Ruskin 1907：250），畸形而丑陋。芭斯谢芭的宅邸被改得"颠三倒四，畸异残缺"，这其实折射了资本控制下城市居民的畸形生活方式。传统建筑遭遇颠覆性的改造，体现了传统社会经济结构被瓦解，成为现代性对传统社会的倒置隐喻。

哈代擅长描写谷仓，后者是一种融审美与功用为一体的哥特式建筑，其典型特征是肋拱、尖顶与窄窗。这跟罗斯金的如下主张十分契合："哥特式不是骑士或贵族所专有的艺术，而是人民大众的艺术；它不是教堂或避难所独享的艺术，而是住宅与家庭所共有的艺术……最重要的是，它不是形式或传统的艺术，而是拥有生动的实践和永久的自我更新能力的艺术。"（同上，251）此处的"大众""共有"和"实践"等词凸显了罗斯金艺术观的精髓，即把物质的生产生活方式作为艺术的出发点。仿佛与此呼应，哈代写道，古老的谷仓"无关于任何已被推翻的防御艺术或陈腐的宗教信条。每天用面包来保护和拯救肉体仍然是一项课题、一个信念、一种愿望"（哈代. 哈代文集②. 2004：170—171）。言下之意，谷仓"不仅在形式上可以和位于它附近的一所教区教堂相匹敌"（同上，170），而且能通过拯救肉体满足人类的物质需要，从而给予人类一定的精神慰藉，如"信念"和"愿望"等。

谷仓与教堂形状与功能的暗合体现了艺术的物质性一面，即恩格斯所说的"首先必须吃、喝、住、穿，然后才能从事政治、科学、艺术、宗教，等等"（恩格斯 2009：601）。换言之，物质的生活资料生产是艺术生产的基础。哈代笔下的谷仓也体现了艺术以物质生产为基础的观念。有学者认为，芭斯谢芭的谷仓其实是一个共享知识并且基于共同价值观的"共同体"（community），它不仅生产了公共的社会空间，还体现了公社的理想（Griffith 2016：1—2），这更说明哈代与罗斯金不谋而合。

总之，哈代跟罗斯金一样，强调艺术的物质性和实践性。他小说中的"倒置"隐喻彰显了他的艺术观和文化观，即追求审美与功用的有机统一，强调大众与艺术之间不可分割的关系。这样的艺术观和文化观在当今世界仍有重要的现实意义。

五、文化：观念与物质的共生

哈代的建筑书写预示了威廉斯（Raymond Williams）提倡的文化观念。后者在《文化与社会》一书中提到了文化观念发展中的一个基本假设，即"一个时期的艺术与当时普遍盛行的'生活方式'存在密切的必然联系"（威廉斯 2018：201）。18 世纪中叶至 20 世纪初英国漫长的哥特式复兴折射了英国社会"文化"观念的演变。普金（A. W. N. Pugin，1812—1852）首先阐明艺术与时代的必然关系，他的思想得到了罗斯金的呼应，后者强调"良好的气质与道德修养是造就优美建筑的神奇力量"（Ruskin 1903：xlii）。其后，莫里斯（William Morris, 1834—1896）引领了工艺美术运动。这一波又一波的文化思潮根植于维多利亚时代的人对社会贫富悬殊、环境污染等工业革命造成的社会问题的忧虑，以及对工具理性的怀疑，而"文化"观念及其演变就源于这"现代性焦虑"（殷企平 2013：3）。上述人物之所以把目光投向中世纪，是因为渴求从中找到应对之策。

迄今为止，学术史上存在一个盲点，即未意识到哈代也以建筑书写的方式介入了上述文化思潮，其宗旨就是威廉斯所说的"整体生活方式"。哈代通过建筑书写表现财富和道德之间的摩擦、灵魂与肉体的搏击，以及旧传统与现代化之间的角逐，其复杂情感和人文观念与前辈一脉相承，反映了哥特式建筑复兴背后人文主义者对工业文明中物质与心灵割裂的忧虑。罗斯金将哥特式建筑与文艺复兴时期的建筑进行对比，诊断出文艺复兴时期建筑的"不道德的因素"，或者说"傲慢"因素，即一种对劳动者灵魂的不尊重。罗斯金旨在从哥特式建筑中提取艺术的道德标准，进而从艺术批评转向社会/道德批评。同样，哈代笔下的哥特式建筑也脱离了浪漫化的状态，转而成为对社会文化变革理想的艺术表达。他通过建筑书写，将物与人之间的联系转化为物与社会秩序、时代精神之间的紧要关系。然而，威廉斯在撰写《文化与社会》时竟将哈代等作家遗漏，这委实是一种遗憾。相较于罗斯金，哈代的焦点不在于整体地探讨哥特艺术的本质，而在于具体地发掘建筑中人与物的关联。不无巧合的是，"关联"（relation）一词是 T. S. 艾略特文化批评的核心观念之一。艾略特认为文化与宗教紧密关联，英国文化本质上是其宗教的道成肉身（incarnation）（Eliot 1960：

101；105），是民族精神的具体化过程，是一种物质与观念同存、共生的状态，体现了文化的物质性，而这也正是哈代的核心文化观。

哈代的建筑书写还反映了他建筑师与小说家结合的身份，呈现出一种物质与观念的和谐统一。通过梳理其生平可知，哈代知行合一的风格也体现在其小说文本之外。建筑师哈代加入由莫里斯创立的古建筑保护协会后，在题为《回忆教堂的修复》（"Memories of Church Restoration"，1906）的致辞中强调建筑对建立和谐社会关系的重要性，提出建筑是"人际关系"（human associations）之仓库的观点（Cannon 2014：203）。哈代似乎比普金与罗斯金看得更细致入微，除了强调"记忆之灯"的功能，他还强调对建筑的物质性体验影响人的认知活动，从而将人的感受从时间维度转为物质化的空间维度，如其病榻诗作《未致命的疾病》将人生的体验比作穿越肋拱结构的哥特建筑："我穿过疼痛之拱/此拱以阴森可怖的肋骨构筑/衣着怪异的无常将我押送/打入极端的痛苦"（哈代．哈代文集⑧．2004：87）。此外，哈代还将"哥特"概念从建筑的视觉维度延伸到诗歌的语言维度以及审美与道德范畴，提出"去虚饰（veneer）存实质（texture）"的哥特艺术原则（Robins and Wolfreys 2000：64）。总之，哈代以建筑绘制文学，借建筑思考了生活。

可以说，哈代的哥特式建筑书写早于威廉斯参与了"整体生活方式"这一文化观念的建构。早年"文化唯物主义者"威廉斯视文化为表意系统，但对表意的强调并不意味着对物质的否定。正如T. S. 艾略特所说，"文化"一词"包含了一个民族所有的特色活动与兴趣爱好"，其中包括"19世纪哥特式教堂和埃尔加音乐"（Eliot 1960：103—104）。换言之，"文化"是一种关于全部生活的、有机的统一体，其载体除了非物质性的语言文字部分，还包括物质性的建筑、雕塑、服饰乃至日常用品，而其中非人的物质对人的文化建构有重要作用，体现在物本身的能动性与施事功能。如今多学科领域的"物转向"已成为趋势，在"新物质主义"（new materialism）等"客体导向哲学"（object-oriented philosophy）的推动下，"物"业已成为西方人文社科领域近10年的热门话题之一（韩启群 2017：89）。物质文化赋予了文化大观念更丰富的视角和研究空间。作为文化观念重要内涵的物质性，值得学界进一步挖掘探讨。

参考文献

[1] Barad K. *Meeting the Universe Halfway: Quantum Physics and the Entanglement of Matter and Meaning* [M]. Durham: Duke UP, 2007: 336.

[2] Benjamin W. The Work of Art in the Age of Mechanical Reproduction [A] //*Illuminations* [M]. New York: Schocken, 1969: 687.

[3] Brown B. *A Sense of Things: The Object Matter of American Literature* [M]. Chicago: U of Chicago P, 2003: 3-4.

[4] Brown B. Thing Theory [J]. *Critical Inquiry*, 2001, 28 (1): 3-4.

[5] Cannon B. The true meaning of the word restoration: Architecture and obsolescence in *Jude the Obscure* [J]. *Victorian Studies*, 2014, 56 (2): 203, 210.

[6] Deleuze G and Guattarif F. *A Thousand Plateaus: Capitalism and Schizophrenia.* Trans. Brian Massumi [M]. Minneapolis: U of Minnesota P, 1987: 364.

[7] Derrida J. "Ja, or the faux-bond II." [A] //Trans. Peggy Kamuf. *Points…: Interviews, 1974-1994.* Ed. Elisabeth Weber [M]. Stanford: Stanford UP, 1995: 52.

[8] Derrida J. *Signéponge/Signsponge.* Trans. Richard Rand [M]. New York: Colombia UP, 1984: 126.

[9] Eliot T S. *Christianity and Culture: The Idea of a Christian Society and Notes towards the Definition of Culture* [M]. New York: Harcourt Brace & Company, 1960: 101-105.

[10] Griffith J D. *All Men Are Builders: Architectural Structures in the Victorian Novel* [M]. Temple UP, 2016: 1-2.

[11] Hardy F E. *The Life of Thomas Hardy 1840-1928* [M]. London and Basingstoke: Macmillan, 1962: 193-229.

[12] Hardy T. "Memories of Church Restoration." *Thomas Hardy's Personal Writings.* Ed. Harold Orel [M]. Basingstoke: Macmillan, 1990: 204-205, 215.

[13] Harvey D. *Paris, Capital of Modernity* [M]. New York: Routledge, 2003: 1.

［14］Iovino S and Oppermann S. Material ecocriticism: Materiality, agency, and models of narrativity［J］. *Ecozone*, 2012, 3（1）: 83.

［15］Miller D. "Introduction." *Materality*［M］. Durham and London: Duke UP, 2005: 4.

［16］Pyle F. The demands of history: Narrative crisis in Jude the Obscure［J］. *New Literary History*, 1995, 26（2）: 367–368.

［17］Robbins R and Wolfreys J. *Victorian Gothic: Literary and Cultural Manifestations in the Nineteenth Century*［M］. Basingstoke, UK: Palgrave Publishers Ltd., 2000: 64.

［18］Ruskin J. *"A Joy for Ever." The Two Paths*［M］. London: George Allen & Son, 1907: 250–351.

［19］Ruskin J. *Lectures on Architecture and Painting*［M］. London: George Routledge Sons Limited, 1854: 94.

［20］Ruskin J. *The Seven Lamps of Architecture*［M］. New York: Longmans, Green, and Co., 1903: xlii, 234.

［21］Vuohelainen M. 'Deeds of Darkness': Thomas Hardy and Murder［J］. *Humanities*, 2018, 66（7）: 10.

［22］Woolf V. "Half of Thomas Hardy." In: *The Captain's Death Bed and Other Essays*［M］. London: Harcourt Brace Jovanovich, Inc., 1978: 67–68.

［23］Woolf V. "Modern Fiction." *The Common Reader: First Series*［M］. London: Harcourt Brace Jovanovich, Inc., 1925: 60.

［24］恩格斯. 马克思恩格斯文集: 第10卷［M］. 北京: 人民出版社, 2009: 601.

［25］哈代, 托马斯. 哈代文集① 非常手段［M］. 王振昌, 刘春芳, 译. 北京: 人民文学出版社, 2004: 1, 6—14.

［26］哈代, 托马斯. 哈代文集⑧ 诗选［M］. 刘新民, 译. 北京: 人民文学出版社, 2004: 87.

［27］哈代, 托马斯. 哈代文集⑥ 无名的裘德［M］. 张谷若, 译. 北京: 人民文学出版社, 2004: 6, 100—110, 113.

[28] 哈代,托马斯.哈代文集② 远离尘嚣[M].傅霁等,译.北京:人民文学出版社,2004:82,170—171,320.

[29] 韩启群.西方文论关键词:物转向[J].外国文学,2017,(6):89.

[30] 罗斯金,约翰.威尼斯的石头[M].孙静,译.济南:山东画报出版社,2014:140—147.

[31] 苏耕欣.哥特小说——社会转型时期的矛盾文学[M].北京:北京大学出版社,2010:13.

[32] 威廉斯,雷蒙.马克思主义与文学[M].王尔勃,周莉,译.郑州:河南大学出版社.2008:67—68.

[33] 威廉斯,雷蒙.文化与社会[M].高晓玲,译.北京:商务印书馆,2018:3,201,203.

[34] 殷企平."文化辩护书":19世纪英国文化批评[M].上海:上海外语教育出版社,2013:3,162.

(本文原载于《复旦外国语言文学论丛》2019年秋季号)

夜尽了，昼将至：
《多佛海滩》的文化命题*

在马修·阿诺德（Matthew Arnold，1822—1888）的诗歌作品中，《多佛海滩》（"Dover Beach"，1867）是流传最广影响最深的一首。国内外对该诗的研究热情似乎从未消退过。以我国为例，过去十年里涉及该诗的研究成果就不下十余种，大都把兴奋点集中在"阿诺德的悲观"这一话题上，而对《多佛海滩》的文化命题未能深究。可以说，新近的研究依然沿袭了当年吴宓先生如下评论所遵循的思路："安诺德深罹忧患而坚抱悲观，然生平奉行古学派之旨训，以自暴其郁愁为耻，故为文时深自敛抑，含蓄不露。所作者光明俊爽，多怡悦自得之意，无激切悲伤之音。惟作诗时，则情不自制，忧思劳愁，倾泻以出。"① 当今学界大都沿着这条思路，认定阿诺德是借《多佛海滩》倾泻悲情，可以说是形成了一种思维定式。例如，《英国19世纪文学史》对《多佛海滩》作了这样的解读："信仰和怀疑、希望和绝望之间的斗争是阿诺德忧郁的源头，也是他对他的时代做出极端悲观的描述的原因。"②

《多佛海滩》仅仅是倾泻悲情吗？依笔者之见，如果我们细细揣摩该诗的两

---

* 本文为国家"十一五"规划社会科学基金资助项目《"文化辩护书"——文化主义传统中的19世纪英国文化批评》（06BWW021）阶段性成果。
① 吴宓：《吴宓诗集》，上海：中华书局，1935年，第65页。
② 钱青：《英国19世纪文学史》，北京：外语教学与研究出版社，2006年，第179页。

组中心意象,即"海潮"意象和"夜战"意象,并顺势挖出其背后的文化命题,就不会简单地给阿诺德贴上"绝望"的标签。

在分析"海潮"意象和"夜战"这两个意象之前,我们有必要澄清一下"悲观主义"这个概念。在西方文学中,"悲观主义"并不是一个简单的、消极的概念,因而不能简单地跟"沮丧绝望"和"灰暗色调"画等号。尼采就曾经这样发问:"悲观主义一定是衰退和堕落的标志吗?一定是失败的标志吗?一定是疲惫而羸弱的本能的标志吗?"① 他还提倡"一种有力量的悲观主义(pessimism of strength)"。② 我们不妨借用尼采的口吻提问:《多佛海滩》是否也传达了一种有力量的悲观主义呢?当它与文化命题交织在一起的时候,是否尤其如此?

一、潮起潮落为哪般?

"绝望论"往往依据诗中关于海潮的描写,引用得最多的是下面这一诗节:

> 信仰之海
> 也曾有过满潮,像一根灿烂的腰带
> 把全球的海岸围绕。
> 但如今我只听得
> 它那忧伤的退潮的咆哮久久不息,
> 它退向夜风的呼吸,
> 退过世界广阔阴沉的边界,
> 只留下一滩光秃秃的卵石。③

---

① Friedrich Nietzsche, "An Attempt at Self-Criticism", in Oscar Levy, ed., *The Birth of Tagedy or Hellenism and Pessimism*, *The Complete Works of Friedrich Nietzsche*, Vol. 3, translated by WM. A. Haussmann (Edinburgh: T. N. Foulis, 1910) 1–19, 2.

② Friedrich Nietzsche, "An Attempt at Self-Criticism", in Oscar Levy, ed., *The Birth of Tragedy or Hellenism and Pessimism*, *The Complete Works of Friedrich Nietzsche*, Vol. 3, translated by WM. A. Haussmann, 2.

③ 阿诺德:《多佛海滩》,载《英国维多利亚时代诗选》,飞白译,长沙:湖南人民出版社,1985年,第184页。

确实，此处"信仰的海洋已经退潮"，① 使得许多学者都从中找到了阿诺德"悲观"的原因。安德森（Warren D. Anderson）就曾经根据诗中"潮水起伏循环的意象"，强调"这首诗因其悲观主义而独步一时"，② 而对其"悲观主义"的内涵则未作深入的分析，对"海潮"意象的其他含义更没有顾及。伊莎贝尔·阿姆斯特朗（Isobel Armstrong）也认为，阿诺德"哀叹基督教神话的消失，就像《多佛海滩》中'信仰之海'退潮那样"。③ 今年刚问世的《剑桥英国文学指南：1830—1914》（*The Cambridge Companion to English Literature, 1830–1914*, 2010）中的一篇文章，也仅仅指出"《多佛海滩》讨论的是退潮的'信仰之海'"。④ 不能否认，诗中的"海潮"意象的确是指涉"信仰之海"的退潮，指涉达尔文的"进化论"以及科技发展给宗教信仰带来的打击，但是众所周知，文学意象的意蕴远非一对一的指涉关系所能涵盖的，这里的海潮也不例外。

"海潮"意象在诗中出现过多次。除了上举引文以外，它还分别出现在第二和第三小节。在第三小节中，我们看到（同时也听到）"索福克勒斯很久以前/在爱琴海边听到的/引起他内心共鸣的人类苦难的/浑浊的潮落潮起……"（Sophocles long ago/Heard it on the Aegean, and it brought/Into his mind the turbid ebb and flow/Of human misery …）⑤ 在第二小节中，我们看到海浪"涌起，停息，再涌起"（Begin, and cease, and then again begin）。以笔者之见，这反复出现的潮起潮落，不光在哀叹"信仰之海"的退潮，更重要的是意味着维多利亚思想史上的一次范式转换。

这次范式转换的端倪表现为隐喻转换，即从"钟摆"或"车轮"的隐喻向"潮汐"的隐喻转换——先前用"钟摆"或"车轮"来形容人类社会的总体进程，此时则改为用"潮汐"来形容。奥尔悌克（Richard D. Altick）曾经对此有过这样的叙述：在维多利亚时期，一些有识之士（包括阿诺德）开始

---

① 钱青：《英国 19 世纪文学史》，第 179 页。
② Warren D. Anderson, *Matthew Arnold and the Classical Tradition* (Ann Arbor: The University of Michigan Press, 1971) 70.
③ Isobel Armstrong, *Victorian Poetry: Poetry, Poetics and Politics* (London and New York: Routledge, 1993) 173.
④ Andrew Sanders, "Writing and religion", in Joanne Shattock, ed., *The Cambridge Companion to English Literature, 1830–1914* (Cambridge: Cambridge University Press, 2010) 205–221, 217.
⑤ Matthew Arnold, "Dover Beach", *in Beverly Lawn, ed., Literature: 150 Masterpieces of Fiction, Poetry and Drama* (New York: St. Martin's Press, 1990) 392–393, 392.

把社会历史的变迁比作"潮落与潮涨、命题与反题、腐败—死亡—新生的循环轮回,而这在先前则被比作钟摆或车轮,后者的运行方向非左即右,非上即下,因而用以判断人事时,其寓意总是非好即坏,两者只能取其一"。① 笔者认为,这一隐喻的转换,其实意味着向当时"进步"话语的挑战:19世纪,流行着一种令无数英国人陶醉的进步观;英国因其工业、科技和军事上的实力而成为世界霸主,麦考莱(Thomas Babington Macaulay,1800—1859)等人大肆传播"进步"学说,致使许多人抱有一种"认进步为不绝的和必然的事情之信仰",② 尤其是许多资本家"把自己的好运气看作自然规律,并且认为这种好运气会永远延续下去"。③ 支撑这种进步观的就是以"钟摆"——更确切地说,是以"直线"——为核心隐喻的思维范式。英国举国上下,无不痴迷于一种宏伟的构想,即人类社会因财富的无限增长而直线式地、无止境地朝着幸福状态进步。当此之际,阿诺德的"潮汐"隐喻对所有做着这一美梦的人来说,不啻为当头棒喝。

在当时社会,在"潮汐"隐喻崛起的背后,还有一个重要的"历史大发现":通过对出土文物和史前洞穴的研究,当时的考古学家们发现,以往几千年的人类文明并非遵循了一个由低级到高级的直线发展轨道,而是在历史的长河中,众多文明几度兴盛,几度衰亡,就像海潮的起伏波动。这一发现,对当时踌躇满志的英国人来说,几乎是颠覆性的,因为他们引以为荣的"古希腊和古罗马文明远非最早的伟大文明,无论是在此之前,还是在此同时,都出现过成就堪与比肩的其他文明,出现的地点不仅在地中海周围和近东,而且在亚洲和中美洲。这些文明个个都一落千丈了"。④ 这一史实对把英国吹嘘为"有史以来最伟大最高度文明的民族"⑤ 的麦考莱等人构成了极大的讽刺,也使阿诺德的"海潮"意象具备了深厚的意蕴。对此,奥尔悌克有过如下评论:"阿诺德的

---

① Richard D. Altick, *Victorian People and Ideas* (New York and London: W. W. Norton and Company, 1973) 110 - 111.
② 罗伯特·路威:《文明与野蛮》,吕叔湘译,北京:三联书店,1984年,第73页。
③ A. L. Morton, *A People's History of England* (London: Lawrence & Wishart and International Publishers, 1979) 398 - 406.
④ Richard D. Altick, *Victorian People and Ideas*, 111.
⑤ 转引自 Walter E. Houghton, *The Victorian Frame of Mind: 1830 - 1870* (New Haven and London: Yale University Press, 1957) 39。

《多佛海滩》中的'潮落潮起'意象是一个特别合适的象征,它象征着那些较为敏感的维多利亚人的一种意识,即每一英里的进步,都很可能会有一英里的退步来抵消它。"① 当然,我们不必完全同意奥尔悌克的说法,因为凡是象征,都具有多义性,"海潮"意象完全可以不局限于"进步"和"退步"相抵消的含义。然而,向"进步"话语提出质疑,这无疑是"海潮"意象的蕴涵中极其重要的部分。

《多佛海滩》全诗的内容和行文节奏都可以用一涨一落的海潮来形容。仅以诗歌的首节和末节为例:两者之间的互动和对比恰似潮水的涌起和低落。首节是宁静而甜美的梦幻开局:

> 今夜大海平静,
> 潮水正满,月色朗朗,
> 临照海峡,——法国海岸上
> 微光渐隐,而英国的峭壁高竖,
> 在宁静的海湾里显出巨大模糊的身影。
> 到窗边来吧,晚风多么甜!②

末节则揭示这一切全是虚幻的表象:

> 啊,爱人,愿我们
> 彼此真诚!因为世界虽然
> 展开在我们面前如梦幻的国度,
> 那么多彩、美丽而新鲜,
> 实际上却没有欢乐,没有爱和光明,
> 没有肯定,没有和平,没有对痛苦的救助;
> ……③

---

① Richard D. Altick, *Victorian People and Ideas*, 111.
② 阿诺德:《多佛海滩》,第183页。
③ 同上,第184页。

两相对比,分明是潮水的一涨一落:首节中是朗朗的月色、宁静的海湾、甜美的晚风和满满的潮水,其美妙已经不言自喻;可是末节笔锋突转,指出在"多彩、美丽而新鲜"的背后,实际上"没有爱和光明",甚至连"对痛苦的救助"都没有,这跟潮水的低落又十分合拍。

在这潮涨潮落的节奏中,我们似乎可以听到对如下文化命题的追问:什么是进步?什么是幸福?什么叫有质量的生活?奥尔悌克曾经指出,人民大众的生活质量问题,在维多利亚时代首次成了"文化"命题:

> 在维多利亚时代,人民大众的生活质量第一次成了紧迫的社会问题,引起了关注。由工业化及其相关的社会发展造成的巨变促人思考这样一个问题:社会该怎样改造并装备自己,才能给社会成员带来最大的内心满足,帮助他们充分发挥自己的才能?
>
> 有人认识到,英格兰希望建成的美好社会有赖于某种叫做"文化"的东西。"文化"一词在19世纪上半叶经历的这种意义上的演变,表明社会思想领域出现了一种新的观念。①

《多佛海滩》中的潮汐似乎正好跟这生活质量有关:首节中貌似甜美的海景恰好与维多利亚社会的表面繁荣暗合,而末节潮水的低落则表明维多利亚式的文明并非真正的进步,并没有带来真正的幸福,并没有提供品质良好的生活。诚然,得益于工业革命和军事掠夺,19世纪中期英国的国内生产总值(GDP)和贸易总量远在其他国家之上:它的工业生产约占世界的三分之一,铁和煤的产量占世界的二分之一,贸易总额占世界的四分之一;而且,"英国商船的吨位高居各国首位。伦敦成为世界唯一的金融中心"。② 然而,这一切只是《多佛海滩》首节中表面的甜美,其本身不能构成欢乐、爱和光明,因而不能给人民大众带来内心的满足,不能让他们全面施展自己的才能并展示自己的禀赋,也就是不能提高他们的生活质量。当然,把上述一切当作进步、幸福和高品质生活的维多利亚时代的人不在少数,他们自信满满,就像《多佛海滩》首节中的"潮水正

---

① Richard D. Altick, *Victorian People and Ideas*, 238.
② 余开祥:《西欧各国经济》,上海:复旦大学出版社,1987年,第187页。

满"。正因为如此，阿诺德要用末节中的无情潮水冲走那表面的繁荣。这潮水卷走了"多彩、美丽而新鲜"的"梦幻国度"，同时也卷走了那自欺欺人的"进步"话语。从这一角度看，"海潮"意象何尝不具有积极意义？

"海潮"意象的积极意义还由索福克勒斯这一形象得到了加强。我们在前文中已经引用以下诗行："索福克勒斯很久以前/在爱琴海边听到的/引起他内心共鸣的人类苦难的/浑浊的潮落潮起……"此处，我们在字面上看到和听到的虽然只是"人类苦难"，但是海潮的旋律把索福克勒斯所代表的希腊精神①烘托到了全诗的顶点。就在阿诺德和索福克勒斯一起聆听的那一刻，时空的超越得以完成，世界的完整图景得以观照，就像尼采在谈论"悲剧文化"时所说：

> 这种文化最重要的标志是，智慧取代科学成为最高目的，它不受科学的引诱干扰，以坚定的目光凝视世界的完整图景，以亲切的爱意努力把世界的永恒痛苦当作自己的痛苦来把握。②

除了把握痛苦以外，索福克勒斯及其希腊与悲剧精神还强烈地暗示着一种形而上的慰藉以及坚不可摧的生命和欢乐。这一点也不妨用尼采的话来说明："每部真正的悲剧都用一种形而上的慰藉来解脱我们：不管现象如何变化，事物基础之中的生命仍是坚不可摧和充满欢乐的。"③ 这生命，这欢乐，是否也奏响在海浪与索福克勒斯组成的交响曲中呢？

二、夜尽了，昼将始

"绝望论"的另一个重要依据是诗中的"夜战"意象。"夜战"的伏笔早在首节中就已埋下："……那一条长长的浪花线/传来磨牙般的喧声。"在本文上一小节开端处所引的那几行诗句中，"退潮的咆哮""夜风的呼吸"和"广阔阴沉的边界"也都预示着一场"夜战"的来临。终于，在诗歌的最后三行里，"夜

---

① 阿诺德十分推崇希腊精神（Hellenism），他在《文化与无政府状态》中曾专辟一章来阐述希腊精神和希伯来精神。
② 尼采：《悲剧的诞生》，周国平译，北京：三联书店，1986年，第78页。
③ 同上，第28页。

战"意象达到了高潮：

> 我们犹如处在黑暗的旷野，
> 斗争和逃跑构成一片混乱与惊怖，
> 无知的军队在黑夜中互相冲突。①

全诗在"混乱"与"惊怖"的夜战中结束，这在一些人看来，似乎印证了阿诺德的"悲观绝望"。然而，问题没有那么简单。本文上一小节的分析已经表明，《多佛海滩》的背后有一个文化批评的语境。所以诗中"夜战"的意象，也必须放在这一语境中来审视，必须结合"海潮"意象来审视，还必须结合该诗与阿诺德其他作品的互文关系来审视。

要理解"夜战"意象的含义，首先要弄明白上引诗行中"无知的军队"的意思。对此，中外评论界仁者见仁，智者见智，不过最典型的要数下面这一解释："'无知的军队'是指1848年的欧洲革命和法国军队1849年对罗马城的围攻，但是它也指意识形态的冲突。"② 跟这种解释相比，阿姆斯特朗的解释更令人信服。她认为此处的掌故至少有二：一指修昔底德笔下的埃皮波莱战役（the battle of Epipolae），二指纽曼（John Henry Newman，1801—1890）于1839年的一次布道中提及的当时思想界的论战。在修昔底德所记载的那场战役中，雅典人因黑夜而分不清敌我，结果互相厮杀，不过这对《多佛海滩》来说，只起到了形容作用。跟本文所说的文化命题更加相关的是纽曼的那段话：

> ……论战没有在天国主人们……和邪恶势力之间进行……而是变成了一种**夜战**（按：黑体为笔者所加），敌友无法分辨，人人只为自己而战。③

令阿姆斯特朗特别感兴趣的是，纽曼此处"惊人地搬用了经济学那咄咄逼人的

---

① 阿诺德：《多佛海滩》，第184页。
② 钱青：《英国19世纪文学史》，第177页。
③ 转引自 Isobel Armstrong, *Victorian Poetry: Poetry, Poetics and Politics*, 175。

语言以及热衷于自由竞争的个人主义者惯用的语言,来描述他所处时代的精神生活"。① 阿姆斯特朗的观察确实非常敏锐:阿诺德笔下"无知的军队"原来是以当时走红的政治经济学("进步"话语的一部分)为武器、狂热地从事自由竞争的个人主义者和自由主义者。

值得注意的是,纽曼和他所批判的自由主义同样出现于阿诺德的另一经典之作《文化与无政府状态》中:

> 纽曼博士所看到的自由主义、这个让牛津运动折损的自由主义究竟为何物?它其实是伟大的中产阶级自由主义。这自由主义所信奉的基本信条,从政治上说是1832年的国会选举改革以及地方自治;在社会领域,是自由贸易、无制约的竞争、办工业发大财;在宗教上,就是"力陈异见,固守新教"。②

在《文化与无政府状态》中,阿诺德明确地把自由主义者称为文化的"敌人",因为后者只专注于"办工业发大财",这种"某一种能力过度发展而其他能力则停滞不前的状况,不符合文化所构想的完美"③。

跟《多佛海滩》末节海潮低落和远退一样,《文化与无政府状态》中的"无知大军"及其"自由主义蔚为大观了",而"牛津运动夭折了,败阵了,四处的海面都漂浮着我们的残骸"④。问题是:阿诺德沮丧了吗?绝望了吗?我们的回答是——

在《文化与无政府状态》中,他没有。反而,他认为牛津运动虽败犹荣:

> 我们对优美温雅的热爱,对丑陋粗鄙的憎恶,我们的这般情怀,才是我们靠拢许多失败了的事业,也是我们反对那么多成功了的运动的根本原

---

① Isobel Armstrong, *Victorian Poetry: Poetry, Poetics and Politics*, 175.
② 阿诺德:《文化与无政府状态:政治与社会批评》,韩敏中译,北京:三联书店,2002年,第24页。
③ 同上,第11页。
④ 同上,第24页。

因。这感情是虔诚的，它从来没有被整个地摧垮，它虽败犹荣……我们已于不知不觉中对国人的思想产生了影响，我们培育起的感情洪流冲蚀和削弱了对手们似已占领的阵地，我们保持着同未来的沟通联系。①

而且确信最终会取得胜利：

> 纽曼博士的牛津运动培育的感情洪流，这运动所滋养的追求美与雅的愿望，它所表露的对中产阶级自由主义之苛刻庸俗的反感、厌恶，它那照得中产阶级新教教义的丑恶怪诞无处遁迹的强光——在引发秘密的不满大潮，从而暗中损毁30年来自信的自由主义的地基、为之突然崩塌和被取而代之铺平道路的过程中，所有这些起了多大的作用，谁可以予以评说？牛津的美与雅的情操正是以这样的方式取胜的，而且还会继续长期地取胜！②

在《多佛海滩》中，他也没有。虽然全诗在"混乱"与"惊怖"的夜战中结束，但是海潮背后的文化洪流，是否也跟《文化与无政府状态》中的"感情洪流"一样，"于不知不觉中……冲蚀和削弱了""无知大军""似已占领的阵地"呢？我们前面的分析已经表明，《多佛海滩》末节中的潮水象征着对表面繁华的冲击，对"进步"话语——也就是"无知大军"所信奉的话语——的冲击。我们前面还提到，无论从诗歌的内容来看，还是从节奏形式来看，首节和末节的互动都宛若海潮的一涨一落：首节如潮涨，末节如潮落。"无知的军队"，还有那"混乱""惊怖"的夜战，都将随着落潮被卷走，其中岂无深意？

诗歌中还有一个细节不能不提：全诗最后以"黑夜"（night）一词结尾——"无知的军队在黑夜中互相冲突"这一诗行的原文为"Where ignorant armies clash by night"。乍一看去，用"黑夜"来压轴，这好像是悲凉到了极点，然而，我们似乎可以从中读出另一层意思：night一词放在诗的尽头，难道这不意味着黑夜已经走到了尽头？

---

① 阿诺德：《文化与无政府状态：政治与社会批评》，第24—25页。
② 同上，第25页。

借用语言学中的概念，我们可以把"黑夜"及其所占的位置看成一种"型式化"（patterning）。它是语篇凸显的部分，是语篇前景化的部分，用以突出语篇要传达的主要信息，或者说为我们探索主题提供基础。① 那么，"黑夜"的"型式化"究竟为我们提供了怎样的信息呢？依笔者之见，它提供了积极的信息。黑夜被推向极致，这恰恰反衬了对光明的呼唤。在诗中，光明的确还未到来——"光明"（light）一词分别出现在首节和末节（我们前面已经引用了译文），第一次它微微闪动，便渐渐隐退：... on the French coast the light/Gleams and is gone ...；第二次干脆以缺席的身份出现：Hath really neither joy, nor love, nor light。惟其如此，更显诗中对它的期盼。应该说，"光明"在诗中也构成了一种"型式化"，它与"黑夜"的型式化两相呼应，似乎在传递着这样的信息：黑夜到头了，光明还会远吗？由此，我们不由得会想到雪莱当年洒下的诗句："冬天来了，春天还会远吗？"当然，我们也不能简单地在两者之间画等号——阿诺德不是雪莱那种类型的乐观主义者。在一篇专论中，阿诺德曾经称雪莱为"美丽而无效的天使，徒劳地在虚无中拍打着发光的翅膀"。② 也许，我们可以把阿诺德划入悲观主义的范畴，但是他所信奉的至少是尼采所说的"有力量的悲观主义"。（参见本文的引言部分）这种力量来自他的执着和勇敢。在另一篇文章中，他曾经把海涅跟雪莱和拜伦等人相比较，并指出海涅比后者的高明之处，在于他能真正地融入歌德所代表的"现代精神"（the modern spirit），即"跟非利士主义③展开生死搏斗"。④ 海涅也许没有像雪莱那样乐观，甚至有些悲观，但是在阿诺德的眼里，他是一位真正意义上的"人类解放战争中的勇敢战士"。⑤ 阿诺德之所以赞扬海涅，是因为他身处茫茫黑夜，却永不放弃对光明的追求。在《多佛海滩》中，阿诺德呼唤的也是这种精神。

在《文化与无政府状态》中，光明与黑夜之间的关系也极其相似。该书的

---

① 任绍曾：《语篇中语言型式化的意义》，载《外国语》，2000年第2期，第110—116页。
② Matthew Arnold, "Shelley", in S. R. Littlewood, ed., *Essays in Criticism: Second Series* (London: Macmillan & Co. Limited, 1951) 121 – 147.
③ 阿诺德在许多作品中都用了"非利士人"（Philistines）一语来指称中产阶级，并且把后者的信念、主张和价值观统称为"非利士主义"（Philistinism）。
④ Matthew Arnold, "Heinrich Heine", in R. H. Super, ed., *Lectures and Essays in Criticism* (Ann Arbor: The University of Michigan Press, 1962) 107 – 132, 111.
⑤ Matthew Arnold, "Heinrich Heine", in R. H. Super, ed., *Lectures and Essays in Criticism*, 107.

第一章以"美好与光明"为题,其呼唤光明的热情跃然纸上,但是它同时又承认光明的缺席:"长期以来,光明无以穿越,我们头上无光,于是也就无从谈起使行动适应于光明了。"① 不过,光明尚未来到,并不意味着不会来到。"美好与光明"的结束语借用了圣奥古斯丁的语录,来点明"夜"与"昼"之间的辩证关系:

> 我们不会让你独自保留创世的秘密,如你在开辟天地、分出光暗之前所做的那样;让你的放置天空的神灵之子发出光来,普照大地,分出昼与夜,宣告时光的流转;因为旧的秩序过去了,新的秩序已出现;夜尽了,昼将始;你派耕者去收获他人播种的庄稼;你派出新的耕者劳作在新的播种季节,而收获时节尚未到来;你这样做的时候,是为岁月赐大福了。②

这段话中最让人回味的是"夜尽了,昼将始"这一句。这难道不是与《多佛海滩》中的"潮落潮起""黑夜"与"光明"形成了呼应吗?

还须说明的是,阿诺德追求"文化之光",但是并不过于急切。他在《文化与无政府状态》中对"文化"和"行善的热情"作了如下区别:

> 行善的热情很容易过于急切……它迫不及待地要披挂上阵;这种热情又很容易将自己的构想和计划当成行动的基础,而因为这些构想是当前发展阶段的产物,故具有与此相适应的一切不完善、不成熟之处。文化同行善的热情之区别,就在于文化既具有行善的热情,也具有科学的热情……因此即便是为了纠错解惑和排忧解难的伟大目标,它也不会急于在思考之前就采取行动、着手规划;它会牢记,如果我们不了解该做什么以及怎样做,那么行动和规划就没有多大用处。③

---

① 阿诺德:《文化与无政府状态:政治与社会批评》,韩敏中译,北京:三联书店,2002年,第8—9页。
② 同上,第32页。
③ 同上,第8页。

这也许是《多佛海滩》中没有出现"披挂上阵"的"光明战士"的原因。为此阿诺德曾备受指责，被说成"选择了逃避和哀叹"。① 不仅如此，"阿诺德的诗歌……作为一个病态社会的病态心灵的记录，的确反映了维多利亚社会的心绪走向和发展主线。……但是，作为一个诗人，他仅仅反映这个现实，并没有试图为这个病态寻求一个良方。他把这个任务和使命推迟到了后期，推迟到了他完全放下了诗歌创作的笔之后。"② 这种说法不那么准确。如前文所说，《多佛海滩》的潮水意味着对"进步"话语的冲击，这显然是寻求良方的努力的一部分。诗中没有匆忙披挂上阵的战士，却不乏催人深思的浪潮，这未尝不是采取行动、着手规划前的准备。阿诺德的其他不少诗歌也是如此。在《海涅之墓》中，他奉劝国人不要"整天愚蠢地奔忙，／全为那机械的商务，却让／荣誉、天赋和欢乐／逐渐从生命中消亡"。③ 在《吉卜赛学者》中，主人公虽然暂时远离尘嚣，却有一个远大的抱负，即"在学成之后，向世人传授艺术的奥秘"。④ 这一切都反映了阿诺德一以贯之的文化思想：在行动之前，先要有思想的高扬；可以不要惊天动地的业绩，却不可以不期待"在未来结出果实"。⑤

让我们再回到前面有关牛津运动的那段引文：阿诺德于失败的牛津运动中看到了一种"照得……丑恶怪诞无处遁迹的强光"，这是一种文化之光，它正在"引发秘密的不满大潮"。这强光，这大潮，是否也孕育在《多佛海滩》中呢？

潮落了，潮将起。夜尽了，昼将至。

（本文原载于《外国文学评论》2010 年第 4 期）

附：论文撰写个案解析

我写《夜尽了，昼将至：〈多佛海滩〉的文化命题》（下文简称《多佛》），因循了古人"起承转合"的笔法。元代范德机在《诗法》中说："作诗有四法：

---

① 钱青：《英国 19 世纪文学史》，第 180 页。
② 同上，第 181 页。
③ Matthew Arnold, "Heine's Grave", in Kenneth Allott, ed., *The Poems of Matthew Arnold* (London: Longmans, 1965) 472–473.
④ Matthew Arnold, "The Scholar-Gipsy", in Kenneth Allott, ed., *The Poems of Matthew Arnold*, 339.
⑤ 刘意青：《评阿诺德"去个人好恶"的文学批评原则》，载《英美文学研究论丛》第 11 辑，上海外语教育出版社，2009 年，第 313 页。

起要率直,承要舂容,转要变化,合要渊永。"学术论文与写诗不同,但不外乎起笔、承接、转折和结尾这四大要素。

学术论文的"起",有其特殊性,即必须做好选题,而选题的前提有二:1)一手资料的完备;2)二手资料的穷尽。就《多佛》一文而言,一手资料是阿诺德的名诗《多佛海滩》(主要研究对象),而二手资料则指有助于研究《多佛海滩》的任何文献,尤指前人的相关研究成果。要写好学术论文,一手资料是根本,二手资料是关键。此话怎讲?所谓"根本",您若不对一手资料烂熟于胸,那就根本写不好文章。所谓"关键",文章题目的选定取决于您对二手资料的把握。很多新手往往错把"一手"当"二手",结果栽了跟斗。以《多佛海滩》为例,您或许能倒背如流,而且颇有心得,但是这不足以作为您选题的依据,原因是您的选题可能已经被人做过了——即使再有心得,也可能是重复劳动。因此,选题要从二手资料中去找,也就是要从 the on-going debates(当下有关热点的争论)中去找,这样才能形成跟学界的对话,才有可能发人之所未发,见人之所未见。一言以蔽之,别人的研究终点,是您的研究起点。《多佛》一文的起因,是我发现先前研究大都沿袭了当年吴宓先生的思路,即认定阿诺德是借《多佛海滩》倾泻悲情。这跟我阅读一手资料的心得不符,因此产生了对话的动机,也有了对话的必要性。

接下来就是"承"了,即承接"起笔",指出"悲观绝望"论应予修正,提出自己的看法。要写好驳论,最好的办法是从对方的论据着手,即所谓釜底抽薪。纵观"悲观绝望"论的依据是"海潮"意象和"夜战"意象,二者组成了《多佛海滩》的中心意象。先说"海潮"意象:它的确指涉"信仰之海"的退潮,但是我通过文本细读,指出文学意象的意蕴远非一对一的表象所能涵盖,进而举例说明潮水卷走的是"进步"话语。从这一角度看,"海潮"意象具有积极意义,绝不只是宣泄悲观绝望情绪。再说"夜战"意象:全诗在"无知的军队""混乱"与"惊怖"的夜战中结束,这似乎可以印证阿诺德的"悲观绝望",可是我通过文本细读,证明诗歌的节奏形式意味着"黑夜"/"夜战"将随着落潮被卷走,而这也显然具有积极意义。

再就是"转"了。就《多佛》而言,"转"与"承"不能截然分开,而是互相交织的。上文提到了"细读",后者并非像很多人误解的那样,仅是仔细阅读而已，而是指运用新批评 close reading 的理论和方法。换言之，是要关注文本的"张力"（tension）、"反讽"（irony）、"含混"（ambiguity）、"悖论"（paradox）和意义的"多元性"（multiplicity）等。《多佛》全文虽未出现这些术语，但是体现于实际行文过程中。例如，文中把诗歌首节和末节作对比，意在彰显诗歌的张力：首节潮水满满，末节潮水消退，正好形成了一种张力，其中既有反讽的力量，又有含混的力量，还有悖论的力量；这些力量在那里"缠斗"，呈现出一个硕大的阐释空间。更具体地说，首节是宁静而甜美的梦幻开局，而末节却指出在"多彩、美丽而新鲜"的背后，实际上"没有爱和光明"，甚至连"对痛苦的救助"都没有，这其实是一种戏剧反讽（dramatic irony）——笃信"进步"话语的维多利亚时代的人满以为自己活在一个繁荣进步的国度/时代，殊不知这只是表面的繁荣。如此看来，诗中的"多彩""美丽"和"新鲜"等许多词语都具有歧义，因而含义颇为含混。至于悖论，《多佛》中对"黑夜"（night）一词在诗中位置的分析就是一例：night 一词放在诗的尽头，恰恰意味着黑夜已经走到了尽头；黑夜被推向极致，恰恰隐含着对光明的强烈呼唤。可见，"细读"过程充满了转折，至少是语义的转折。

不仅如此，《多佛》除了需要在"细读"层面讲求"转折"之外，还在另一层面的"转折"上颇为着力，即所谓做"语境化处理"（contextualization），也就是把所有的文本细节放在文化语境（包括政治、经济、社会和历史语境）中加以审视，然后加以阐释。这种处理要求把一手资料和二手资料结合起来，要求把《多佛海滩》跟阿诺德的其他作品（如《文化与无政府状态》），以及同时代人的相关言论（如纽曼对自由主义的批判）和前人的研究成果（如奥尔悌克对维多利亚文化思想史的研究、阿姆斯特朗对维多利亚诗歌的研究）结合起来解读。通过这样的交叉/转折式阅读，我们可以于"黑夜"/"夜战"中看到维多利亚思想范式的转换，可以于潮涨潮落中听到阿诺德对如下文化命题的追问：什么是进步？什么是幸福？什么叫有质量的生活？

最后自然是"合"了。合即结尾，即总结。《多佛》以十二字合之："潮落了，潮将起。夜尽了，昼将至。"在我发表的论文里，这篇的结尾是我最满意的，而且似乎"得来全不费工夫"，其实是水到渠成。回想起来，当时是顺势而为：文章自发端始，就咬住主旨不放，虽行文迂回曲折，却不离文化命题，且都顺着潮起潮落、昼夜交替的节奏，于是功到自然成——打字的键盘响至尾声处，那十二个字自然涌现，恰好与文章的题目形成了围合。这让我想到朱光潜先生说过的一句话，大意是写作者应把重点完全摆在主旨上，在这上面鞭辟入里，烘染尽致，这样便能攻坚破锐。

（本文原载于《英美文学研究论文写作》，上海大学出版社，2021年）

走向生物共同体:《阿弗小传》的意义[*]

一、引言

《阿弗小传》(*Flush: A Biography*, 1933)是弗吉尼亚·伍尔夫(Virginia Woolf, 1882—1941)继《奥兰多》(*Orlando: A Biography*, 1928)之后创作的又一部传记,出版后迅速成为畅销书,但由于内容貌似缺乏严肃性,因此长久以来未受到学界重视,甚至被评价为"根本不值得一读"(Snaith 2002: 615)。例如,我国著名学者瞿世镜就曾认为"这部轻松的小说使人愉悦"(瞿世镜 2015: 198),但对其思想内容的深刻性却未给予关注。实际上,伍尔夫生活在一个共同体观念空前生发的年代,而她为共同体观念的演变增添了生态维度,这是一种独特的贡献。《阿弗小传》就是这方面的明证。

《阿弗小传》的主角弗勒希是维多利亚时代女作家勃朗宁夫人(即巴雷特小姐)养的一条宠物狗。关于巴雷特小姐与弗勒希的第一次见面,书中的描写意味深长:"他俩之间隔着再宽不过的鸿沟,足以分离两种不同的生物。她会说话;他却不能。她是个女人;他是条狗。"[①](伍尔夫著,唐嘉慧译,2009: 18)这段描述常被看作伍尔夫为打破人类中心主义所作的尝试。例如,伍尔夫的侄

---

[*] 本文由殷企平和王婉莹合写。
[①] 该作品的引文均参考唐嘉慧的译文,其原标题为《弗勒希——一条狗的传记》(上海:上海译文出版社,2009),但是本文选择借用郑佰青和张中载所译的标题。

子兼其传记作者贝尔就曾指出，伍尔夫"从狗的视角描述温珀尔大街、白教堂和意大利，创造一个由气味、忠诚和欲望构成的犬类世界"（Bell 1972：409）。还有学者指出，伍尔夫赋予非人类以主体形式，跨越了人类与非人类的鸿沟，并促进了二者关系的理解，这（对人类思想史）是一种实质性的贡献（Smith 2002：360）。这些评价虽已指出伍尔夫跨越了人类与非人类的鸿沟，但是还未从生物共同体的高度来审视上述作品。

在我国，已有学者陆续从环境美学、生态伦理、生态女性主义等角度解读《阿弗小传》。例如，郑佰青和张中载在《为动物立传：〈阿弗小传〉的生态伦理解读》一文中，从非人类中心主义生态伦理批评视角解读该传记，认为对动物的描述投射了伍尔夫重建和谐生态的理想（郑佰青，张中载 2015：131）。又如，在《跨向鸿沟 走向和谐——〈弗勒希——一条狗的传记〉的生态女性主义解读》一文中，沈渭菊从生态女性主义视角，通过分析小说中女性与动物的独特关系，揭示伍尔夫强烈的女性关怀和生态意识（沈渭菊 2013：110）。不过，上述学者尚未关注传记中的嗅觉描写，只有唐岫敏在《从环境美学看〈弗拉狮传〉》一文中涉及了书中多元的审美手段，并把目光投向"伍尔夫对弗勒希嗅觉的直接而生动的描写"（唐岫敏 2007：105），但其论述的侧重点仍在环境，而未关注故事背后的生态意识，更未把这种关注上升到生物共同体的高度。

本文所说的"生物共同体（biotic community）"，意指生活在一定生态环境内、相互作用着的动植物种群的总体（孙宏 2009：79）。须在此强调的是，本文中"生物共同体"这一概念不同于学界常见的"生态意识"一说："生态意识"泛指人类与其他生物之间的关联性，所强调的关联度可大可小，甚至可以非常模糊；而"生物共同体"强调以生物为中心，物种之间无优劣之分，这一点在《阿弗小传》中尤其明显。简而言之，"生物共同体"比"生态意识"更具有"完整性、稳定性和美感"（Leopold 1989：224—225）。在伍尔夫之前，德国社会学家、哲学家滕尼斯曾经在与"社会"相对的意义上，给"共同体"下了一个经典性定义："共同体意味着人类真正的、持久的共同生活，而社会不过是一种暂时的、表面的东西。因此，共同体本身必须被理解为一种生机勃勃的有机体，而社会则是一种机械的聚合和人工制品。"（Tönnies 2001：19）滕尼斯此处讲的是"人类真正的、持久的共同生活"，尚未把目光投向人类与其他生物的共同生活，而人类若不跟其他生物和平共处，就很难想象人类内部真正而持久的共同生活。正是在这一意义上，伍尔夫的贡献显得十分重要——她虽然未直接给生物共同体下过定义，但是她用生动的故事和诗性语言演绎了建构生物共同体的可能性。

鉴于上述伍尔夫所作贡献的特殊性，本文拟从嗅觉、理性和情感三个维度来探讨《阿弗小传》中人与动物、人与自然的关系，并阐释作品中强烈的生物共同体意识。

二、嗅觉审美

前文提到，国内已有学者注意到《阿弗小传》中的嗅觉描写，但是未能指出后者所体现的生物共同体意识。

传统的维多利亚时代传记是清一色的英雄伟人式传记，小人物不可能担任传记的主角，遑论动物。然而，《阿弗小传》打破了禁忌，不但以一条狗为传主，而且以它的"嗅觉"为重心。弗勒希"活在嗅觉的世界里"；"爱情主要是味道，形状与颜色也是味道，音乐、建筑、法律、政治及科学全是味道"（伍尔夫著，唐嘉慧译，2009：97）。这段描述的上文中有一段令人回味的文字："'美'若想碰触到弗勒希的感官，至少必须先结晶为绿色或蓝紫色的粉末，再由某位神仙以针筒注射进弗勒希的鼻孔，渗入鼻孔后面的网状管道才行"（伍尔夫 2009：96）。此处的中心词"美"颇为关键，它自然而然地把故事引向审美范畴。更值得留心的是上引文字中的联觉和通感："味道"整合了"形状"与"颜色"，因而极富审美价值，而这种审美思维还囊括了人类的精神世界，如爱情、音乐、建筑、法律、政治和科学。不仅如此，在这审美/精神世界里还生活着弗勒希这样的非人类生物，这分明是提出了一个文化命题，一个以共同体为核心的文化命题——跟先前文人学者不同的是，伍尔夫的文化/共同体想象包括了非人类生物，甚至把后者当作主角。换言之，在伍尔夫笔下，看似普通乃至戏谑的审美活动蕴藏着强烈的生物共同体情怀。

嗅觉在《阿弗小传》中的重要性，就连一般的意识流小说都不能相比。我们知道，意识流小说作者大都喜欢描写"人们通常忽视的嗅觉气味"，而这正是

"意识流小说人物心理活动的生理诱因之一"（张世君 2012：59）。伍尔夫曾在小说《海浪》（*The Waves*，1931）中将小说人物珍妮比作"一只凭着嗅觉追逐猎物的猎犬"（伍尔夫 2012：113），而在《阿弗小传》中，她干脆从一只狗的视角出发，从嗅觉入手，书写弗勒希一连串的"意识流活动"。全书一共六章，其中四章以地名命名，而每经历一次空间的位移，都伴随着有关弗勒希嗅觉的翔实描述。如下面这段描写："土的浓重，花的香甜；树叶和荆蔓无名的味道；穿过小路时闻到的酸味儿；踏入豆田时闻到的刺鼻味儿……"（伍尔夫著，唐嘉慧译，2009：8）再如弗勒希在温珀尔街 50 号的"新发现"："每一个房间——餐厅、起居室、图书室、卧室——都飘出一种特别的味道，再集合成仿佛大锅汤的味道"（伍尔夫著，唐嘉慧译，2009：14）。又如，白教堂令弗勒希记起了他非常厌恶的古龙水的味道，"令他头脑昏聩，丧失一切欲望"（伍尔夫著，唐嘉慧译，2009：63）。当然，也有令他愉快的味道："在弗勒希最充实、最自由、最快乐的那几年里，意大利对他而言，主要是一连串的味道。"（伍尔夫著，唐嘉慧译，2009：97）正如瞿世镜先生所说，"当弗勒希由农村迁入城市，由女主人的卧室走到伦敦的街头，由英国迁往意大利，它首先注意到各种东西的气味和质地的变化，然后才注意到它周围的景色"（瞿世镜 2015：197）。美国学者哈维·理查德·施夫曼也曾在其心理学著作中提出，嗅觉记忆对当时环境的检索具有很大的帮助（转引自吴仕乾 2017：132）。根据伍尔夫对弗勒希嗅觉记忆的描述，我们可以清晰地了解到弗勒希对某些环境的喜好：他爱意大利甚于伦敦，爱阳光甚于阴暗；而隐藏在嗅觉喜好背后的则是弗勒希想要回归自然、与大自然联结的渴望。在意大利，弗勒希连"昔日桎梏他的最后一条铁链也断了"（伍尔夫著，唐嘉慧译，2009：87）；他驰骋于乡间与街道，"享受味道所带来的狂喜"（伍尔夫著，唐嘉慧译，2009：98）。可以说，弗勒希用嗅觉拥抱意大利，其实是拥抱阳光下的大自然，原因在于意大利有"杂种狗""骆驼"和"松树林"等（伍尔夫著，唐嘉慧译，2009：84），是相对理想的生物共同体。与此同时，巴雷特小姐也在用她的方式拥抱意大利："穿上那双厚皮靴，手脚并用地去攀岩"；"坐上一辆破烂的出租马车，一路摇摇晃晃地到湖边欣赏山景"，累了就"坐在石头上看蜥蜴"（伍尔夫著，唐嘉慧译，2009：83）。此时，伦敦那个与世隔绝的"阁楼"早已成为往事，而意大利的大自然才是让巴雷特小姐魂牵梦萦的地方:这里没有人类社会中的尔虞我诈,更没有物种之间的优劣之分。透过这一幅幅人与自然水乳交融的图景,以及人与其他生物不分高低的图景,我们可以听见伍尔夫对生物共同体的呼唤。

对生物共同体的呼唤还回响在伍尔夫的其他作品中。在《到灯塔去》(*To the Lighthouse*, 1927)中,"树木、溪流、花朵"都和人"化为了一体"(伍尔夫著,瞿世镜译,2009:77)。同样,在《海浪》中,伯纳德曾感到自己就是"这田野""这谷仓""这一棵棵的树"(伍尔夫 2012:84)。在《达洛维夫人》(*Mrs. Dalloway*, 1925)中,达洛维夫人也感觉到"乡村的天空,威斯敏斯特上面的天空,都与她的一部分生命交融",产生一种"与万物为一"的念头(伍尔夫 2007:177)。总之,在伍尔夫的世界里,人类与其他生物紧密联系,组成了一个和谐统一的整体,即生物共同体。

还须一提的是,《阿弗小传》中关于人类嗅觉的描述只有寥寥数笔,而且还带有讽刺意味,如下面这段描述:"世界上最伟大的诗人,也不过只闻得到玫瑰和粪便的味道而已"(伍尔夫著,唐嘉慧译,2009:97)。尽管有这种对人类迟钝嗅觉的嘲讽,但是如果我们细读文本,就不难发现,伍尔夫对人类嗅觉的态度经历了从失望到乐观的转变。起初的失望在巴雷特先生与弗勒希的对照中尤其明显:虽然弗勒希能在房间每个角落都闻到布朗宁先生的味道,但是巴雷特先生的嗅觉却格外迟钝,他坐在布朗宁先生"刚坐过的椅子里","头靠在那个男人刚靠过的枕头上,却浑然不觉"(伍尔夫著,唐嘉慧译,2009:42)。不过,后来的情形有所转变:当地点从伦敦变换到了意大利时,伍尔夫第一次真正写到了人类嗅觉:"出大太阳她高兴,天气冷她也高兴。炉火将熄,她会把从公爵森林捡来的松枝丢进火里,然后他们一起坐在噼啪响的烈火前,用力闻那股辛辣浓郁的松香味儿"(伍尔夫著,唐嘉慧译,2009:83)。这里的"他们"指巴雷特小姐和弗勒希,此时已没有动物和人类之分,而只有相互陪伴的好朋友,分明是一幅和谐的生物共同体图景!这幅图景的来龙去脉传递了如下信息:正是弗勒希让巴雷特重新感受到了嗅觉带来的幸福,因此人类应该向动物学习,不但用感官体验世界,而且"也用感官认识世界,从而使他所感触到的环境……转换成对另外一种环境的认识"(唐岫敏 2007:106)。在美学史上,人们普遍认为眼睛和耳朵才是审美器官,唯有视觉、听觉能产生美感，而嗅觉不能产生美感。然而，嗅觉经验含有去功利成分。借用康德的"审美判断力"一说，我们不妨把《阿弗小传》中的嗅觉也看作"人精神和心理上的巨大审美体会"（吴仕乾 2017：132）。一言以蔽之，伍尔夫通过《阿弗小传》揭示了人类与动物交往的必要性，以及人类（通过这种交往）重拾嗅觉审美的可能性，而这正是构建生物共同体的意义之一。

三、动物的理性

伍尔夫的生物共同体思想还体现为她对"理性动物"的描绘。

17 世纪法国哲学家笛卡尔（Rene Descartes，1596—1650）有一个著名观点，即动物与"我思故我在"的人类不同，是一台"缺乏理性"的"自动机"（宋斌 2012：212—213）。海德格尔（Martin Heidegger，1889—1976）在《存在与时间》（*Being and Time*，1927）和《形而上学的基本概念》（*Introduction to Metaphysics*，1935）中也谈论到了人与动物的差异，他断言石头不拥有世界（worldless），动物贫乏于世（poverty in world），而人则建构世界（world-forming）（Heidegger 1995：211）。海德格尔还认为动物完全受制于环境，其活动也仅仅是出于本能，不能通达存在本身，因此被剥夺了世界；相反，人能够接近周围的存在，能够通达存在本身，能够向世界敞开，因此他建构着世界（丁林棚 2014：113）。针对这一人类中心论，伍尔夫在《阿弗小传》中刻画了一个有理性、会思忖的动物。随着故事的展开，我们惊奇地发现：弗勒希也在不断地经历着身份危机。在温珀尔街的卧房里，弗勒希在镜子前思忖："什么才是'自我'呢？那是别人看见的东西？还是真正的'自我'？"（伍尔夫著，唐嘉慧译，2009：33）尽管问题无疾而终，但从弗勒希开始发问"我是谁"的那一刻起，他就不再只是笛卡尔所说的一台机器了。

在佛罗伦萨的夏天，弗勒希饱受跳蚤之苦，而这竟让他找到了身份问题的答案。剪去了一身的"西班牙猎犬的勋章"后，弗勒希"觉得自己仿佛遭到阉割，变得垂头丧气，羞愧得无地自容"（伍尔夫 2009：101）。这难道不是自我意识的体现吗？当他再次照镜子时，他又一次发问：我是谁？然而这一次，镜子给出了既残酷又诚实的答案："你什么都不是！"（伍尔夫 2009：101）顷刻间，弗勒希从一只西班牙猎犬变成了一个无名小卒！然而，做个无名小卒，真的就一点儿都不快乐吗？弗勒希又开始陷入沉思：

> 毕竟，做个无名小卒，不正是世界上最令人满足的状态吗？他再看看镜中的自己：那是他的环状颈毛，用他模仿、解嘲那些自以为了不起的家伙，不也是种极有潜力的事业吗？而且无论如何，他肯定再也不必为跳蚤烦恼了。他甩甩自己的颈毛，抖抖他无毛而瘦弱的脚，跳起舞来，精神随之大振。（伍尔夫著，唐嘉慧译，2009：101）

可见，弗勒希已具备理性思考的能力：失去了毛皮也就意味着摆脱了跳蚤；成了无名小卒也就更有资格嘲讽那些自大狂。弗勒希有着老子般的智慧，深知"祸兮，福之所倚；福兮，祸之所伏"的道理（老子 2017：120）。巴雷特小姐还称赞弗勒希是"真正的哲学家"（伍尔夫著，唐嘉慧译，2009：102），而哲学家必然具备理性思辨的能力。

此外，弗勒希还会像人类一样从事理性判断，而判断的依据则是（生物）共同体原则。在第三章《神秘客》中，布朗宁先生的出现令弗勒希再次感到危机——此时的弗勒希视布朗宁先生为"情敌"，决定采取强烈的手段夺回巴雷特小姐的宠爱。接连遭遇两次失败后，弗勒希陷入了沉思，并面临着一种艰难的选择：

> 遭放逐的他躺在地毯上，情绪起伏有如陷身澎湃汹涌的漩涡，灵魂随水势在岩石间冲撞、碎裂，终于找到一小块立足点，艰难无比、痛苦万状地将自己拉出水面，爬回陆地上，终于得以站在浩劫之后的宇宙边缘，俯瞰一个根据全新计划所建构出来的世界。问题是：该选择哪一种呢？——是毁灭，还是重建？
>
> （伍尔夫著，唐嘉慧译，2009：50）

此处的弗勒希"闪烁着思想的光辉，最后这句哈姆莱特式的内心独白蕴含深刻的哲学内涵"（郑佰青，张中载 2015：133），但弗勒希似乎比哈姆莱特更胜一筹。哈姆莱特只是思想上的巨人，而弗勒希经过反思后认识到"爱即是恨，恨即是爱"（伍尔夫著，唐嘉慧译，2009：51），于是决定以后要像爱巴雷特小姐一样好好爱布朗宁先生，从此他们三个人"一起同情，一起恨，一起反抗黑色的独裁暴政，一起爱"（伍尔夫著，唐嘉慧译，2009：54）。这难道不是一种共同体？不仅是，而且是生物共同体。弗勒希把共同利益放在个体利益前面，接纳布朗宁先生也就等于选择了团结，选择了共同体。正如雷蒙·威廉斯所说："团结观念把共同利益定义为真正的自我利益，认为个体的发展只有在共同体中才能得到检验，因此这种观念是社会潜在的真正基础。"（威廉斯 2011：343）伍尔夫显然是赞同威廉斯的这一观点的，不过她笔下的共同体还包括了非人类生物，这突出表现为巴雷特小姐对弗勒希的不离不弃。弗勒希在温珀尔街被绑架后，巴雷特先生和布朗宁先生都竭力反对将弗勒希赎回，但巴雷特小姐把后者的生命看得比自己的安全更为重要。她在信里向布朗宁先生袒露心声："我不能没有弗勒希，你知道吗？"（伍尔夫著，唐嘉慧译，2009：63）伍尔夫笔下很多人物都和巴雷特小姐一样，十分同情并爱惜动物。比如，在另一本传记《奥兰多》中，奥兰多就是一个不折不扣的动物保护主义者，他有一次发现未婚妻斐薇拉用鞭子抽打小狗，便认定斐薇拉"性情残忍"（伍尔夫 2003：13），于是立马终止了与她的婚约。事实上，伍尔夫本人从十岁起就发誓再也不佩戴野生鸟类的羽毛，而且刻画了一个个酷爱动物的人物形象，这一切显然跟她的生物共同体意识有关（Alt 2010：127）。

四、动物的情感

在伍尔夫的生物共同体想象中，关于动物情感的描绘也举足轻重。

笛卡尔在区分人类与动物时提出，动物无法感知痛苦，因为痛苦是作为"亚当之罪"而存在的（引自郑佰青等 2015：135）。言下之意，动物缺乏情感。在人类认识动物及其情感的历史进程中，达尔文的进化论是一个里程碑，被恩格斯列为 19 世纪自然科学的三大发现之一（其他两个是细胞学说和能量守恒与转化定律）。1871 年，达尔文发表了《人类起源和性选择》（*The Descent of Man, and Selection in Relation to Sex*），指出人由古猿进化而来，人和动物有着共同的起源。第二年，在《人与动物的情绪表达》（*The Expression of the Emotions in Man and Animals*, 1872）一文中，达尔文还宣称人类和动物的情感高度相似。伍尔夫深受达尔文的影响，这可从她的小说创作中得到验证。比如，在《达洛维夫人》（*Mrs. Dalloway*, 1925）中，伍尔夫将达尔文与希腊人、罗马人和莎士比亚相提并论，认为他们为人类文明做出了极其艰辛的努力（伍尔夫 2007：62）。在达洛维夫人的意识流里，甚至出现了有关达尔文对缅甸花的言论，可见伍尔夫对达尔文的生物研究颇为熟悉（伍尔夫 2007：169）。在另一部小说《到灯塔去》中，伍尔夫再次表达了对达尔文的赞赏与敬佩："我们不可能个个都是提香，我们也不可能人人都成为达尔文。"（伍尔夫著，瞿世镜译，2009：87）此外，我们在伍尔夫的日记中还可发现这样一个细节：二战期间，她那位于塔斯托克广场的住房被炸毁后，她从残骸中搜救出来的物品除了日记、银器、玻璃制品和瓷器外，还有达尔文的著作（Woolf 1985：331）。因此，我们有理由推断，达尔文对伍尔夫的生物观产生了深远的影响。

《阿弗小传》的首页开宗明义："西班牙猎犬天生通人性，接下来关于弗勒希的故事，亦证实他对人类情绪的感知能力分外敏锐。"（转引自伍尔夫著，唐嘉慧译，2009：8）更具体地说，弗勒希具备同情/移情的能力，是一条"身为犬类却十分通晓人性"（伍尔夫著，唐嘉慧译，2009：39）的狗。通过与巴雷特小姐的相处，弗勒希"愈来愈能感觉在他俩之间存在某种紧密的联结，虽然令他不舒服，同时却令他因兴奋而战栗；因为如此，倘若他的快乐便是她的痛苦，那么他的快乐也就不再是快乐，反而变成三倍的痛苦"（伍尔夫著，唐嘉慧译，2009：25）。这种"紧密的联结"，我们可以用"同情"乃至"移情"一词来定位。斯宾诺莎（Baruch de Spinoza, 1632—1677）在《伦理学》里对"同情"有过这样一段描述："当我们想象着我们的同类感到痛苦时，我们必将感到痛苦，反之，假如我们想象着我们的同类感到快乐时，则我们必定喜欢。"（高晓玲 2008：13）跟斯宾诺莎不同，伍尔夫使"同情"超越了物种的界限，因而一条狗也能感知人类的快乐与痛苦，甚至与人类同情共感："弗勒希睡过人类的膝盖头，听过人类的声音，他的体内充满属于人类的热情；他懂得各种层次的嫉妒、愤怒与绝望，因而也必须承受苦难"（伍尔夫著，唐嘉慧译，2009：99）。巴雷特小姐与弗勒希之间的关系，不仅仅只是"单纯在空间意义上的分享"（但汉松

2018：29），两者还存在着精神上的相互分担与给养，这与哈洛维（Donna Haraway）提出的"同伴物种"十分相似。哈洛维在 2003 年发表的《同伴物种宣言》一文中提到，"同伴物种"是生物共生关系（symbiosis）的必然结果，"生物体"是由"基因组、同伴、共同体、没消化干净的晚餐、死亡边界（mortality boundary）的构建所组成的众多生态系统"（Haraway 2003：7）。伍尔夫笔下的人类与动物其实也是"同伴物种"，而且人作为"复杂的生命形式"，有必要跟其他生物发生"更紧密、更多向的联结活动"（Haraway 2003：7）。《达洛维夫人》中就曾暗示未来科学有把狗变成人的可能（伍尔夫 2007：62）。不仅如此，伍尔夫笔下的几乎每一个人物都曾被比作某种动物。例如，《海浪》中罗达将珍妮比作一只"乘风破浪"的"海鸥"（伍尔夫 2012：92），《到灯塔去》中的詹姆斯把拉姆齐先生看成了一头"展开黑色的翅膀突然猛扑过来的狰狞的怪鹰"（伍尔夫著，瞿世镜译，2009：226）。这些无不体现了伍尔夫认为人与动物生来平等的生物共同体思想。

  国内学者高奋曾经指出，伍尔夫小说理论的精髓在于强调"小说是记录人的生命的艺术形式"（高奋 2016：363）。确实，伍尔夫小说艺术洋溢着一种大生命观，而"爱"则是这种大生命观的支撑点。《海浪》中的奈维尔就曾这样说道："我们这不堪入目的平庸生活，只有在爱的目光下，才会变得有光彩，有意义"（伍尔夫 2012：159）。这代表了伍尔夫作品中一以贯之的思想，即每种生物（包括人类）都免不了要走向死亡，但是爱能赋予生命以意义。在《阿弗小传》中，引导巴雷特小姐走向爱之巅峰的正是弗勒希，他让巴雷特小姐发现了"纯粹的爱，简单的爱，彻底的爱，毫无负担的爱，不知羞惭、悔恨为何物的爱，如同采花的蜜蜂才懂得的、当下此刻的爱……"（伍尔夫 2009：89）弗勒希的爱不计对象，不计得失，分明是一种博爱，一种大爱。书中还有诗为证（弗勒希被比作了古希腊神话中的潘神）：

> 起先我惊讶，仿佛阿卡迪亚人，
> 乍见朦胧树丛间半人半羊的神仙
> 然而，当虬髯的脸庞更贴近
> 我的泪已干，我知道那是弗勒希。

超越惊讶与哀伤,我感谢真正的潘

透过低等动物,带我登上爱的巅峰。

(伍尔夫 2009:119—120)

伍尔夫让弗勒希带领巴雷特小姐走向了"爱的巅峰",也就是让低等动物帮助人类找到了真正的爱。换言之,动物不仅与人类情感相似,还可以看作人类的情感导师。这难道仅仅是一般的生态意识?分明是一种独特的生物共同体想象!可以说,伍尔夫用一本动物传记更生动地表达了后来德里达(Jacques Derrida,1930—2004)想要表达的思想,打破了他所批判的"大写人类(Man)和大写动物(Animal)之间的界限"(Derrida 2002:397)。

五、结论

综上所述,《阿弗小传》所体现的生物共同体思想具有强烈的前瞻意识,可谓与阿尔贝特·施韦泽(Albert Schweitzer,1875—1965)的生命伦理观不谋而合:"绝不允许个人放弃对世界的关怀。敬畏生命始终促使个人同其周围的所有生命交往,并感受到对他们负有责任。"(施韦泽 2003:32)21 世纪的人类依然面临着生态危机(包括自然、社会、人际、精神等方面),因此有必要重温伍尔夫,继续构建生物共同体。

参考文献

[1] Alt C. *Virginia Woolf and the Study of Nature* [M]. Cambridge: CUP, 2010.

[2] Bell Q. *Virginia Woolf: A Biography* [M]. New York: Harcourt, 1972.

[3] Derrida J. The animal that therefore I am [J]. David Wills (trans.). *Critical Inquiry* 28, 2002 (2): 369–418.

[4] Ferdinand T. *Community and Civil Society* [M]. Jose Harris & Margaret Hollis (trans.). Cambridge: Cambridge University Press, 2001.

[5] Haraway D. *The Companion Species Manifesto: Dogs, People, and Significant*

Otherness [M]. Chicago: Prickly Paradigm Press, 2003.

[6] Heidegger M. *The Fundamental Concepts of Metaphysics: World, Finitude, Solitude* [M]. William McNeill & Nicholas Walker (trans.). Bloomington: Indiana University Press, 1995.

[7] Leopold, A. *A Sand County Almanc* [M]. Oxford: Oxford University Press, 1989.

[8] Smith C. Across the widest gulf: Nonhuman subjectivity in Virginia Woolf's "Flush" [J]. *Twentieth Century Literature*, 2002 (48): 348–361.

[9] Snaith A. Of fanciers, footnotes and Fascism: Virginia Woolf's "Flush" [J]. *Modern Fiction Studies*, 2002 (48): 614–636.

[10] Woolf V. *The Diary of Virginia Woolf* [M]. Vol. 5. Anne Olivier Bell and Andrew McNeillie (eds.). London: Penguin, 1985.

[11] 但汉松."同伴物种"的后人类批判及其限度 [J]. 文艺研究, 2018 (1): 27–37.

[12] 丁林棚. 论《羚羊-5秧鸡》中人性与动物性的共生思想 [J]. 当代外国文学, 2014 (2): 110–118.

[13] 高奋. 走向生命诗学: 弗吉尼亚·伍尔夫小说理论 [M]. 北京: 人民出版社, 2016.

[14] 高晓玲."感受就是一种知识!"——乔治·艾略特作品中"感受"的认知作用 [J]. 外国文学评论, 2008 (3): 5–16.

[15] 瞿世镜. 意识流小说家伍尔夫 [M]. 上海: 上海译文出版社, 2015.

[16] 老子. 老子 [M]. 冯国超, 译注. 北京: 华夏出版社, 2017.

[17] 雷蒙·威廉斯. 文化与社会: 1780—1950 [M]. 高晓玲, 译. 长春: 吉林出版集团有限责任公司, 2011.

[18] 庞红蕊. 海德格尔的动物问题 [J]. 中国图书评论, 2013 (1): 44–49.

[19] 沈渭菊. 跨越鸿沟走向和谐——《弗勒希——一条狗的传记》的生态女性主义解读 [J]. 英美文学研究论丛, 2013: 110–119.

[20] 施韦泽. 敬畏生命 [M]. 陈泽环, 译. 上海: 上海社会科学院出版社, 2003.

[21] 宋斌.论笛卡尔的机械论哲学[M].北京:中国社会科学出版社,2012.

[22] 孙宏.薇拉·凯瑟作品中的生物共同体意识[J].外国文学研究,2009(2):71-80.

[23] 唐岫敏.从环境美学看《弗拉狮传》[J].外语研究,2007(3):103-107.

[24] 吴仕乾.嗅觉美感剖析[J].北方文学,2017(10):131-133.

[25] 伍尔夫.奥兰多[M].北京:人民文学出版社,2003.

[26] 伍尔夫.达洛卫夫人[M].孙梁,苏美,译.上海:上海译文出版社,2007.

[27] 伍尔夫.到灯塔去[M].瞿世镜,译.上海:上海译文出版社,2009.

[28] 伍尔夫.弗勒希——一条狗的传记[M].唐嘉慧,译.上海:上海译文出版社,2009.

[29] 伍尔夫.海浪[M].曹元勇,译.上海:上海译文出版社,2012.

[30] 张世君.意识流小说的嗅觉叙事[J].国外文学,2012(2):59-66.

[31] 郑佰青,张中载.为动物立传:《阿弗小传》的生态伦理解读[J].外国文学,2015(2):131-137.

(本文原载于《英语研究》2019年第1期)

劳伦斯笔下的彩虹[*]

彩虹是劳伦斯（D. H. Lawrence, 1885—1930）名著《虹》（*The Rainbow*, 1915）的中心意象，然而国内有关研究在涉及彩虹意象时往往是一笔带过，而且大都给人以一种错觉，好像彩虹只是在小说结尾处才出现似的。下面仅举三例：

侯维瑞先生有过这样的评论："小说结尾凌空而起的彩虹象征着对未来新生活的憧憬，但这种未来像虹一样，也是远不可及、虚无缥缈的。"（侯维瑞 1985：213）

王佐良先生和周珏良先生主编的《英国二十世纪文学史》中有关彩虹的论述也只有寥寥数行："……大病以后的厄秀拉坐在窗前，看见在丑恶的工矿城市上空伸展的一条斑斓的彩虹：'她在这条彩虹身上看到了地球上的新建筑，那陈旧、脆弱、朽烂的房屋和工厂被扫除了，世界按上帝的生机勃勃的结构建造起来，和头顶的苍穹相配。'"（王佐良，周珏良 1994：325）

罗婷女士是在彩虹意象上着墨最多的一位，但是她的视线同样集中在小说的结尾："小说结尾出现的那道彩虹，象征着她（笔者按：指厄秀拉）所憧憬的美好未来。……彩虹象征在整个宇宙之间人类争取男女之间的完美关系，从而创造一个理想世界的展望。……厄秀拉抛弃了许多假彩虹，终于见到了那拱架在碧空中的真彩虹。它虽然有点神秘主义的色彩，仍不失为一个鲜明的艺术形

---

[*] 基金项目：国家社科基金项目（s10101）。

象。"(罗婷 1996:84—85)

以上几位学者的见解都不无道理,然而由于他们忽略了小说结尾处彩虹意象与书中先前彩虹意象的联系和呼应,因此未能更加深入地发掘该意象的丰富内涵。针对这一缺憾,本文拟从彩虹意象的结构性作用入手,进而分析它背后蕴藏着的深刻含义。

(一)

彩虹是统驭小说全局的结构性意象。劳伦斯用它作为小说的题目,显然有其画龙点睛的意图。假如只是把它跟小说结尾处厄秀拉的憧憬相联系,那就无法恰当地把握它在全书中的地位。

厄秀拉并非直到小说结尾处才看到彩虹,而是在婴儿时期就和彩虹结下了缘分:在第6章中,初为人母的安娜怀抱厄秀拉站在窗前,观看几只蓝山雀在雪地里打架;看着看着,她突然神游起来。朦胧中,她仿佛来到了毗斯迦山①巅,眼前浮现出"一条凌空飞架的彩虹"(Lawrence 1949:195)。从彩虹那里,安娜得到了满足,看到了希望:"黎明与黄昏是彩虹跨越白天的双足,她从这儿看到了希望,看到了许诺。她何必要到更远的地方去旅行呢?"(劳伦斯 1956:263)安娜曾经有过出门远游、探索未知世界的向往,但是她从彩虹那里得到启示,发现"即便她不是未知世界的旅行者……彩虹下面仍然敞开着她的大门"(Lawrence 1949:196)。

安娜看彩虹,而且是怀里揣着婴儿厄秀拉看彩虹,这显然是为后来厄秀拉独自看彩虹埋下了伏笔。换言之,两次看彩虹跟母女俩分别所选择的生活方式有关。安娜的选择意味着对外面的未知世界(其实是工业社会——详见下文分析)的拒绝,而厄秀拉的选择意味着她盲目闯入"外面的世界"、继而遭受挫折、最终有所觉醒这一过程。

让我们先来看一下母女俩各自对"外面的世界"所作的具体反应。

安娜是跟着继父汤姆·布朗文在乡村里长大的。虽然当时的农村已经受到

---

① 毗斯迦山(Pisgah Mount)位于约旦河东。

工业文明的种种威胁，乡民们也受到了城市生活的种种诱惑，但是安娜跟父母居住的马什农庄却基本上保持着与世隔绝的自然状态：

> 马什农庄的生活确实有某种自由，也比较随便。那儿没有金钱的烦恼，没有人为琐事的斤斤计较，也无须注意别人有什么想法，因为无论是布朗文还是布朗文太太都无法察觉到外界的人对他们的评价。他们的生活与外边太隔绝了。
>
> 因此，安娜只有在家里才感到心情舒畅。……（译文稍作更动）（劳伦斯 1956：131）

安娜曾经有过离家远游的冲动，但是彩虹给了她这样的启迪："有些东西她先前未尝占有，现在也没占有，而且无法占有。有些东西是遥不可及的。她又何必为这些东西而远行呢？她站在毗斯迦山上不是很安全吗？"（Lawrence 1949：195）在彩虹的启示下，安娜最终决定留在家乡这片宁静的土地上。

长大以后的厄秀拉对母亲所选择的生活方式感到不满，因此于 17 岁那年就离家出走，开始在外面的世界寻求她心目中的高尚生活。她在圣菲力普小学谋到了教师职位，满以为这下可以过起天高任鸟飞的生活，不料很快就发现自己原来是"身陷囹圄"；孩子们在那里学到的净是些机械僵硬的知识，就连教员们（如布伦特先生）的声音也"总是像机器那样生硬、刺耳、缺乏人性"（Lawrence 1949：372—376）。更糟糕的是，孩子们还频频遭受体罚，恐怖的气氛让人窒息。后来，厄秀拉进了一所高校求学，满心希望在知识的海洋里畅游，然而她又经历了一次幻灭——不仅校舍处于"肮脏的工业城镇"之中，而且学校本身也成了工厂的附庸：

> 这里就像一家二手货商店，人们不过是为了考试在那儿买点装饰而已。学校之于镇上的工厂，犹如杂耍之于正戏。她渐渐地、不知不觉地形成了对它的认识。它绝不是宗教修身之地，也不是学子的净土。它是一个学徒作坊，人们为了赚钱来这里装潢门面。学院本身只不过是工厂的一个邋遢的小实验室。（Lawrence 1949：434—435）

只是在接二连三地经历幻灭之后，厄秀拉才看到了她母亲当初看到的彩虹。

也就是说，上述两次出现的彩虹之间形成了一种具有反讽意味的张力：安娜"足不出户"便看到了彩虹，而厄秀拉偏要在外面的世界闯荡并撞得"头破血流"之后才看见彩虹；既然不出远门也能看见彩虹，那又何必去招惹外面那陌生的世界呢？厄秀拉把自己的理想彩虹寄托在外面的世界，可是她去外面闯荡的每一步都是事与愿违、适得其反，到头来还得回到她母亲当初的立场上，才能真正看见彩虹——小说最后一章（其标题就是《彩虹》）中，也就是彩虹意象即将再度出现之前，有一个常被评论家们忽视的细节：厄秀拉"突然从公正和实事求是的角度认识了母亲。她的母亲朴素无华，实实在在，因此能够随遇而安，而她自己却未能如此——她傲慢自负，执意让生活适应自己。她的母亲是正确的，是非常正确的，而她自己却是错误的，有的净是些想入非非的低劣念头"（Lawrence 1949：485）。

由彩虹意象烘托的反讽基调在小说中有一种结构性的象征意义：在两次关键时刻出现的彩虹之间，厄秀拉刚好完成了一次圆圈似的历程——以跟母亲分道扬镳始，又以回到母亲的立场终。

厄秀拉的历程又象征着一个范围更大的历程：人类在工业化进程中走过的历程。在厄秀拉的历程背后，隐含着这样一个问题：人们盲目投入"外面的世界"——即工业革命的洪流——是否得不偿失？从这一角度看，小说中的彩虹就不像许多评论家所说的那样，只象征着带有神秘主义色彩的、通向未来美好世界的出路，而是主要象征着对人类是否应该匆匆赶奔工业化"康庄大道"这一问题的反思。

（二）

透过劳伦斯笔下的彩虹，我们看到的是这样一种焦虑和疑问："外面的世界"真的像彩虹那样美好吗？劳伦斯所关心的与其说是为工业社会寻找出路，不如说是怎样从工业潮流中抽身。雷蒙德·威廉斯在《文化与社会》一书中曾经指出："劳伦斯一直忙于挣脱工业社会制度，因而从来就无暇认真考虑如何改变它的问题……"（Williams 1959：204）然而，我们不能因此就贬低劳伦斯作品在回应工业革命方面的价值。尽管劳伦斯没有开出治疗时弊的良方，但是他在捕捉工业社会的情感结构方面功不可没。①

更具体地说，劳伦斯敏锐地捕捉到了工业社会中普遍存在的一种失落感，一种失去原有的、已知的社会群体的感受。威廉斯在他的另一本专著《英国小说——从狄更斯到劳伦斯》中强调，"劳伦斯比本世纪其他任何英国小说家都更加有力地描写了对失去社群的体验"（Williams 1973：182）。按照威廉斯的解释，"社群"（community）意味着"某种跟个人的感受密切相关的东西：一个人和其他人气息相通；彼此间话题投机，所用的语言也十分融洽"（Williams 1973：172）。确实，人类这种对社群的归属感在工业革命进程中逐渐消失了。劳伦斯是怎样表述这种失落感的呢？他在表现这种失落感时究竟有哪些出色的地方？威廉斯在这方面却语焉不详。有鉴于此，我们有必要顺着威氏的话题作进一步的挖掘。

劳伦斯所捕捉的失落感伴随着心灵的震撼，即工业革命前后的巨大变化所引起的空前的震撼。《虹》的第一章展现的是前工业时期的景象——安娜的继父汤姆·布朗文的祖辈们生活在一个物我回响交流的世界：他们能感受到"天地间的交融"和"土地的脉搏"，甚至能"意识到世界长着嘴唇，富有思想，在那儿诉说着"（Lawrence 1949：8）。然而，这种景象和人们的归属感突然一去不复返了。小说第二章记载了1840年以后运河的开凿、煤矿的兴起、铁路的铺设和城市的扩张。比外部的纷乱和喧嚣更加可怕的是一种普遍的内心体验：人们"竟在自己的家乡成了陌生人"（Lawrence 1949：12）。这是一种前所未有的心灵震撼。问题也就来了：该怎样表达这种新的内心体验呢？现成的语言形式能够充分揭示新形成的情感结构吗？

劳伦斯在《小说与情感》（*The Novel and the Feelings*，1925）一文中曾经抱怨英国人"没有表达情感的语言"（Lawrence 1936：757）。这句话常常被误读，其实我们不妨把它理解为劳伦斯认定现成的语言形式已经无法传递上述新的情感体验。要传递新的体验，就要用新的语言形式。劳伦斯笔下的彩虹就是表达

---

① "情感结构"（structures of feelings）是威廉斯提出的重要术语，意指"流动中的社会体验"。详细介绍见笔者和胡玲玲合著论文《论〈我们如今的生活方式〉中的情感结构》，《外语教学》2003年第1期，第87页。

新体验的新奇比喻——它的驱动力来自作者那颗受到强烈震撼的心灵。

前文提到，彩虹是统驭小说《虹》全局的结构性意象。由于劳伦斯所描写的疑问、困惑、焦虑和失落感是一种极其复杂的内心体验，因此彩虹必然不会是简单地比况单一事物的断金碎玉，而是具有磁性的、关系到小说整体结构的象征。除了我们在前一小节中已经作出的分析以外，彩虹的结构性象征意义还必须被放在它跟书中其他诸多意象、事件和细节的错综复杂的关系中加以体会。在审视这种关系之前，我们不妨先引用一段伯齐托有关象征的精彩论述：

> 哪里有象征，哪里就建立起了一个由事件、象征和细节组成的磁场。这一磁场把无数纷杂的含义吸引在它的周围。当然，在象征主义作品里，不同含义之间的逻辑关系的纽带并没有丧失殆尽。不过，意象和节奏已经不再是缠绕着逻辑主干的芜蔓枝藤。它们的作用不仅仅是装点主干，使它勉强呈现生机。相反，意象和意象之间、场景和场景之间以及节奏和节奏之间都首尾呼应，互映成趣，就像在图画中相同或相反的颜色都互相对应一样。那些看来是必要的对应关系并非仅仅是出于逻辑上的需要才建立起来的。松散的逻辑关系呈线条形状，而象征关系则呈圆弧形状。后者暗示着一种往返穿梭、四通八达的关系。一部作品的全部象征意义"总是在趋于完成"，然而却永远有待于完成，因为它总是在不断地产生新意，并将其统一在自己的有机体中。（普伯托齐 1995：150）

劳伦斯笔下的彩虹可以被看作上述"磁场"的中心，在它的周围团聚着许多其他意象，而且彼此之间有着一种往返穿梭、四通八达的关系。

在书中，最跟彩虹相映成趣的是小鸟意象。

紧挨着安娜第一次看彩虹的那个段落之前，有八个段落都被用来描写安娜抱着厄秀拉在窗前观看小鸟打雪仗的情景：光是"鸟"（birds）或"蓝山雀"（blue-caps/blue-tits）一词就连续出现过八次；安娜边看边对着这些小鸟和怀中的婴儿自言自语，并且把厄秀拉称呼为"我的小鸟儿"，甚至还恍恍惚惚地感到"她自己也是属于那鸟儿世界的，她跟鸟类已经同化了"（Lawrence 1949：194—195）。也就是说，安娜是在融入鸟的世界以后才看到彩虹的。

同样，厄秀拉在看到彩虹不久之前也有融入鸟类世界的经历。《彩虹》一章中有一段关于厄秀拉在森林中寻找躲雨之处的描写：她一会儿觉得自己是"如飞的小鸟"，一会儿又像"驭风而行的小鸟"（Lawrence 1949：487）。

母女俩都是先与鸟类化为一体，然后再跟彩虹结下缘分，这恐怕不是作者笔下无意促成的巧合。小鸟是大自然的一部分（彩虹也是大自然的一部分），它跟书中工业城市里种种龌龊、丑陋和机械呆板的景象（关于劳伦斯对这种景象的描绘，前人已经做了很多的评价，此处不再赘言）形成了对抗，这一含义是不言而喻的。

"鸟"还有另一层意思：它其实就象征着厄秀拉本人。除了母亲安娜把她称作"小鸟"以及她自己觉得像小鸟之外，安索尼也曾经这样对厄秀拉说："你在那边就像一只小鸟。"（Lawrence 1949：415）厄秀拉这只小鸟飞出了她母亲所依恋的家园，其实就意味着她失去了原本可以依托的社群，而且她在"外面的世界"更无法找到可以归属的新社群。她在外面闯荡时曾经接触过不少人，但是没有一个跟她真正建立起具有精神价值的关系。她的初恋情人斯克里本斯基和她的叔叔小汤姆本来应该成为她最亲近的人，可是她痛苦地发现这两个人都只是行尸走肉：斯克里本斯基的"灵魂埋在了坟墓里"（Lawrence 1949：328）；小汤姆的"所作所为都毁于他那死了的灵魂"（Lawrence 1949：344）。灵魂的丧失跟他俩所处的相似的工业背景不无关系：斯克里本斯基是军队里的工程师，而小汤姆在成为一个精明的矿主前曾经是一位工程师的得意门生。这种相似的情形恐怕不是巧合，而是工业狂潮摧残人的灵魂这一普遍现实的写照。厄秀拉在工业世界里与没有灵魂的"机器人"苦苦周旋，其中的辛酸、困惑乃至震惊就像前文所说的那样，无法用现成的语言来描绘，因此劳伦斯让她"变成"了一只孤立无援、居无定所的小鸟，以此表达他对社群消失这一历史进程的体验。

我们如果做进一步的推敲，就会发现"鸟"还跟彩虹一样，有着结构性象征意义：厄秀拉展翅飞翔，最终归于平静。第十章《圈子的扩大》中有一个细节不容忽视：布朗文一家去教堂做完礼拜后回到家里，那"宁静的气氛就像一只奇特的小鸟在呼吸"（Lawrence 1949：273）。这里的鸟儿意象又多了"宁静"的意思，这不能不让人联想到当初安娜留在家乡那片宁静的土地上的决定，以及厄秀拉向母亲所持立场的回归。

前文提到，厄秀拉在圣菲力普小学谋到教师职位以后，曾经以为这下可以过上一种天高任鸟飞的生活；这时的她其实处于浮躁的幻觉当中。她甚至直截了当地把自己定位成"一个旅行者"（Lawrence 1949：417），这就更显出了她那"鸟"的本色。下面这段描写把厄秀拉的旅行者形象和小鸟意象结合得天衣无缝：

> 她看见自己沿着一个圆圈旅行，现在只剩下一段弧线还未完成了。接着，她腾空而起，像一只小鸟一样飞到半空。她已经是一只初步学会飞翔本领的小鸟了。（Lawrence 1949：417）

这段话中的两个词尤其值得深究："圆圈"（circle）和"弧线"（arc）。彩虹不也是呈弧圈形的吗？

彩虹和其他弧圈形意象之间的联系还见于第七章《大教堂》。这一章讲安娜跟随威尔参观林肯大教堂，在那里她又一次"看见"了彩虹：

> 在这里她体会到了摆脱时间、逃离时间的感受。那教堂犹如一粒生命的种子默默地躺在东方与西方之间，躺在黎明与黄昏之间，躺在萌芽前的黑暗里，躺在死亡之后的寂静中。……那阴暗中充满了五颜六色，看上去好像有彩虹在移动，它使静寂中有音乐，黑暗中有光明，死亡中有丰收；犹如层层叶子之上的种子和笼罩在根基和花瓣之上的寂静，它在死亡、生命和永恒之间严守着秘密。（劳伦斯 1956：274）

安娜是在教堂里产生顿悟而与彩虹邂逅的，而教堂里的拱形——即弧圈形——结构恰好跟彩虹形成了呼应。在上引段落接下去的几段中，"arch"（拱门/拱形构造）一词连续出现了三次，其中的一次特别耐人寻味："使她敬畏和沉默的是那延伸得很远的、一个连着一个的拱形结构，和飞起插入高空、托着巨大屋顶的石头。"（劳伦斯 1956：275）这里的"拱形结构"跟当初毗斯迦山上空的那条彩虹可谓异曲同工：它们都在安娜心中唤起了敬畏之情，使她陷入了关于生命意义的沉思。从安娜思考的内容来看，她那超越时间的感受以及对生命和死亡之间辩证关系的洞察都跟厄秀拉后来的盲目"飞行"形成了反差。

彩虹、小鸟（包括它飞翔时划出的弧线）、教堂里的拱形结构、厄秀拉所作的圆圈式旅行，这一切拧成了一股合力，强烈地烘托出小说的反讽基调：厄秀拉奋勇飞向"外面的世界"，结果却事与愿违，迎来的只是幻灭。换言之，"天高任鸟飞"这一理想不可能在一个失落了社群、丧失了灵魂的工业世界里实现。

当然，小说中与彩虹相关的意象远不止小鸟、教堂和旅行者。凡是读过《虹》的人都会发现许多关于山川、森林、花草、星星、太阳和月亮（顺便提一句，太阳和月亮也都是弧圈形的）的描写。从广义上说，它们都和彩虹有着前勾后连的关系。就连小说的谋篇布局都突出了圆弧形状的地位：除了第十六章的标题直接用了"彩虹"一词外，第十章和第十四章还意味深长地用了同样的标题（这种重复方式实在罕见），即《扩展中的圆圈》（*The Widening Circle*）。限于篇幅，本文就不一一细究。

总之，劳伦斯用彩虹及其相关的意象唱出了一首关于社群失落的哀歌。弗格森曾经赞扬劳伦斯即兴创造比喻的能力，并把他所创造的比喻称作情感的"客观对应物"（objective equivalents），他说："他比任何人都更加明白，我们的感情或道德和宗教情感只有通过'客观对应物'才能得到共同的体验。"（Fergusson 1959：74）。确实，彩虹以及以它为中心的意象群可以被看作工业浪潮下人间悲情的一组客观对应物。

参考文献

[1] Fergusson F. D. H. Lawrence's Sensibility [A] //William Van O'connor (ed.). *Forms of Modern Fiction* [C]. Bloomington：Indiana University Press，1959：72-79.

[2] Lawrence D H. The Novel and the Feelings [A] //Edward McDonald (ed.). *Phoenix: The Posthumous Papers of D. H. Lawrence* [C]. New York：Viking Press，1936：756-758.

[3] Lawrence D H. *The Rainbow* [M]. Harmondsworth：Penguin Books Ltd，1949.

[4] Williams R. *Culture and Society: 1780-1950* [M]. London：Chatto &

Windus, 1959: 199-215.

[5] Williams R. *The English Novel: From Dickens to Lawrence* [M]. London: Chatto & Windus, 1973: 169-184.

[6] 安吉洛·普伯托齐.《恋爱中的妇女》中的象征手法 [A] //蒋炳贤.劳伦斯评论集 [C].上海：上海文艺出版社，1995：145-172.

[7] 侯维瑞.现代英国小说史 [M].上海：上海外语教育出版社，1985：208-217.

[8] 劳伦斯.虹 [M].漆以凯，译.天津：百花文艺出版社，1956.

[9] 罗婷.劳伦斯研究——劳伦斯的生平、著作和思想 [M].长沙：湖南文艺出版社，1996：74-85.

[10] 王佐良，周珏良.英国二十世纪文学史 [M].北京：外语教学与研究出版社，1994：316-342.

（本文原载于《外国语》2005年第1期）

《黑暗的心脏》解读中的四个误区

康拉德发表《黑暗的心脏》以来，评论文章和著作可谓汗牛充栋，可是在对以下几个关键问题的回答上，评论家们的分歧之大，几乎达到了不可调和的程度。如：

《黑暗的心脏》这一书名的含义是什么？

马洛的非洲腹地之旅的实质是什么？

库尔茨临死前的呼喊——"可怕呀！可怕呀！"——究竟是什么意思？

康拉德是个种族主义者吗？

等等。

究其原因，笔者以为在解读《黑暗的心脏》中存在着若干个认识的误区。本文举四例，就教于方家。

误区一：抽象地谈论人性

在评论《黑暗的心脏》时，许多中外学者都认同了一个观点，即马洛/库尔茨的非洲之行是探索人类本质的历程。

王佐良先生主编的《英国二十世纪文学史》就曾这样写道："库尔茨的非洲之行实质上是对人类的本质的探寻……从马洛这个角度进行叙述惟妙惟肖地体现了这个时期在康拉德创作思想中占主导地位的怀疑主义，反映了他对人的本

质的揣测和疑问。"（王佐良，周珏良 1994：209—210）

郁青也坚持认为，《黑暗的心脏》是"对自我精神和潜意识世界的探索"，而"主人公马洛的刚果之行，不仅是进入非洲腹地的航程，同时也是一个探索自我、发现人内心黑暗世界的历程"（郁青 1997：93）。

赖辉在不久前的一篇文章中谈道："他（马洛）叙述的重点在于从库尔茨的堕落上找到对人类灵魂深处黑暗本质的认识。"（赖辉 1999：25）

彼得·蔡尔茨（Peter Childs）最近的一段评论也颇具代表性："康拉德……精心讲述的故事意在指明人类探索自我的行程，指明人类发现自我的心理历程。就像弗洛伊德当年所做的一样，康拉德也通过自己的故事向维多利亚时期的读者传递了这样一个信息：狂暴的欲望构成了每个文明人的核心——黑暗的心脏里跳动着狂暴的欲望。"（Childs P. 1999：189）

以上四段引文里的"人类的本质""人内心黑暗世界""人类灵魂深处黑暗本质"和"每个文明人的核心——黑暗的心脏"等说法都有欠确切，因为这里所说的"人"都只是抽象意义上的人，好像真有为全人类所共有的永恒人性似的。

上述评论家是在讨论康拉德作品的象征意义时提出自己的观点的。值得注意的是，在文艺评论中，有一种抽象地谈论作品的象征意义的倾向，即置作品所描写的大量有关历史、地理、社会和政治的细节不顾，却对作品的意义作出了结论。这种倾向恰恰助长了抽象人性论的蔓延。

看来，问题的关键是怎样分析《黑暗的心脏》的象征意义。我们认为，任何作品的象征意义都必须有两个基本前提：1）抽象必须以具体为基础；2）作品细节本身的意义不应该受到忽视。正如劳·坡林所说，"象征意味着既是它所说的同时又超过它所说的"（劳·坡林 1981：56）。也就是说，象征必须首先是它所说的，然后才能超过它所说的。

因此，我们有必要先对《黑暗的心脏》中的细节加以分析。

首先，这些细节是对西方殖民主义的揭露。马洛从非洲之行的开头到结尾，看到的都是欧洲殖民主义者对非洲土著的欺压、掠夺、奴役，乃至残害。作品中，这类细节比比皆是。甚至连马洛成行的先决条件也跟殖民主义者的"光荣业绩"有关：原来的白人船长因毒打土著而遭到后者的反抗，最终在冲突中丧了命,所以马洛才得到了船长的头衔。在启程之后,他看到了无数类似于下文引用的种种情形:瘦骨嶙峋的黑人劳工脖子上套着锁链(其中有的还是孩子),被无情地驱使着,直至"在生病丧失工作能力以后,才被允许爬离工作场地,慢慢地死去"(Conrad 1994:22—25)。这类惨象在马洛快要结束整个航程时还有增无减:他惊讶地发现库尔茨窗前的立柱上放着一颗颗人头——土著在惨遭杀戮之后,其人头还要遭受凌辱。所有这些细节揭露的对象不首先是殖民主义,又能是什么呢?

其次,这些细节是对殖民主义者内心世界的揭露。它们象征着有关人物内心的贪婪、傲慢和残暴,象征着他们内心的黑暗世界,但这绝不是所有人——或像蔡尔茨所说的"每个文明人"——的内心世界,而是在特定环境下特定人物的内心世界,即以库尔茨为代表的殖民主义者的内心世界。

以上观点可以由书中两类细节得到印证。

第一类有助于区别土著黑人和入侵白人(外来移民)。在康拉德的笔下,那些外来移民大都面目可憎。且不说嗜血成性的库尔茨,即使其他许多外来移民,也都像马洛遇到的埃尔多拉多探险队队员们那样,其"唯一的欲望便是从这块土地里抢走所有的宝藏"(Conrad 1994:44)。他们不仅对黑人如凶神恶煞,而且彼此之间也尔虞我诈,钩心斗角。相形之下,那些黑人的形象要可爱得多。仅以划桨的黑人为例:他们"像沿着他们的海岸激起的浪涛一样自然、真实……看着他们真使人感到莫大的安慰",而且马洛只有跟他们在一起时才"觉得自己仍然属于一个让人感到踏实的世界"(Conrad 1994:20)。显然,马洛褒谁贬谁,爱谁恨谁,已经不容争辩了。

第二类有助于区别马洛和库尔茨。不少学者认为,马洛在发现库尔茨的同时,也发现了另一个自我,即"人类本质"(这也是马洛非洲之行被说成"对自我精神和潜意识世界的探索"的主要论据)。诚然,马、库二人先后遵循了同一条线路,去了同一个地方"探险"。然而,库尔茨的初衷是征服和掠夺,而马洛的初衷却是旅游和观光。库尔茨把土著当成"畜生",并叫嚣要"把这些畜生统统消灭掉"(Conrad 1994:72),而马洛则用激烈的言辞表明了截然相反的立场和态度:"苍天作证!这些拿人——我说的是人——当牲畜一般使唤的恶人,都是些强大的、贪婪的、红眼睛的魔鬼"(Conrad 1994:23)。库尔茨最终让贪欲的黑色浊流吞噬了自己的灵魂，只剩下了一个"空心的身子"（Conrad 1994：83）；而马洛则以一个带有大慈大悲含义的姿势告别了自己的探险经历——当他讲完自己的那段经历以后，他看上去"像一尊正在打坐的菩萨"（Conrad 1994：111）。还有一个细节不容忽视：马洛曾经用鲜明的态度向那位俄国水手表明"库尔茨先生并不是我的崇拜偶像"（Conrad 1994：84）。

如果我们对这两类细节给予足够的重视，就不可能简单地说马洛的非洲腹地之旅的实质是探索所谓的人类的共同本质，而应该说是探索殖民主义者的罪恶本质。换言之，马洛探索了人的精神世界不假，但是这里的"人"绝不是抽象意义上的人。

误区二：过分突出作品的语言层面

过分突出作品的语言/叙事层面，把社会、政治和历史等层面贬至次要或从属的地位，这是《黑暗的心脏》解读中的另一个误区。

这方面的主要代表有希利斯·米勒（J. Hillis Miller）和彼得·布鲁克斯（Peter Brooks）。根据他们的观点，马洛的非洲之行的实质是对语言指涉功能的探索，《黑暗的心脏》的真实含义是语言或叙事作品在揭示真实/意义方面的失败，因而该书书名中的"黑暗"实指叙事层面上的黑暗（narratological darkness）——语言无法照亮现实或作品的意义。

米勒解读的主要基础是小说第一叙述者"我"的一段话：

> 海员们信口诌成的故事，都是那样直截了当，简单明了，其中的寓言就包含在打开的外壳之中。不过，马洛却属例外（如果把他喜欢讲故事的癖好除外的话）。在他看来，一个故事的含义，并不像果仁那样藏在外壳里面，而是在故事本身之外，围在故事的外层，让故事像白热的光所放出的辉雾一般显现出它的含义来，那情景倒有点像人们在月夜的幽光之下，偶尔看到的一种雾蒙蒙的月晕。（Conrad 1994：8）

在米勒看来，上面这段话的中心思想和德里达解读索绪尔语言学理论时提出的观点如出一辙。按照德里达对索绪尔理论的解释，一个符号的意义不在于符号内部，而在于符号外部，在于它所属的整个符号/能指系统。巧得很，"故事的含义，并不像果仁那样藏在外壳里面"这一句似乎也表达了同一种思想。米勒把康拉德的作品跟传统的寓言故事（the parable）做了比较：传统寓言中故事和意义之间的关系就像外壳和内核，故事犹如"不能食用的外壳，必须被层层剥离，以便故事的含义被读者吸收"（Miller 1989：211—212）；在马洛讲述的故事里，米勒却找不到像果仁那样简单明了的寓意。因此，米勒把马洛的非洲之行比作"圣杯不在场的探索"（grailless quest）——我们知道，对传统叙事作品的解读常常被喻为"圣杯的探索"（grail quest），因为只要这些作品的读者锲而不舍，最后总能豁然开朗，犹如圣杯闪现在圣洁骑士加拉哈面前一般。米勒认为，我们跟随马洛经历了千辛万苦，一心指望在库尔茨身上找到一个对全部事件的圆满答案，可是库尔茨只给我们留下了两句临死前令人纳闷的呼喊："可怕呀！可怕呀！"这两句呼喊的所指究竟何在？它们似乎维系着故事的全部意义，可是它们却像一团迷始终被笼罩在黑暗之中。总之，米勒认为我们只是跟随马洛进行了一场圣杯不在场的探索，就像德里达笔下"所指不在场"的文字游戏和探索一样。这就是米勒的结论。

布鲁克斯也曾经发表过跟米勒极为相似的观点。他认为马洛的叙述实质上是对库尔茨故事的一种复述，然而马洛最终未能成功地再现有关库尔茨的真实故事，因此整部作品充其量意味着"语言的失落"（Brooks 1985：252）。

我们必须承认，米勒和布鲁克斯并非毫无道理。康拉德确实在作品中用了一些渲染神秘气氛的语句。除了前文中有关果仁和故事含义的那段话以外，他还使用了不少诸如"深不可测的奥秘""不可名状的仪式"和"不可思议的秘密"之类的词语。然而，如本文第一小节所述，书中更多的是控诉殖民主义罪行、刻画库尔茨那扭曲灵魂的生动细节描写。这些细节构成的意义不言自明，而绝不是"语言的失落"。

即便是库尔茨临死前发出的那两句呼喊也并非深不可测。虽然库尔茨本人没有道破"可怕"的实际含义，但是我们只要结合上下文的具体描述，就不难窥见那闪光的"圣杯"。就在库尔茨发出叫喊之前，马洛在他脸上"看见一种由忧郁的傲慢、无情的权势、怯懦的恐怖——一种强烈的无可奈何的绝望——所构成的复杂表情"（Conrad 1994：99）。库尔茨死后，马洛紧接着有一句评论："他对自己的灵魂在这个地球上所从事的冒险事业作出了结论"（Conrad 1994：100）。在相隔一页左右的地方，马洛又做了更为详细的评论："他作出了总结——他作出了判断，'真可怕呀！'……无论怎么说，这话表达了他的某种深信不疑的认识。在他临终时所发出的耳语般的声音里，含有坦白、坚信、颤动的反抗语气。它现出了真相被窥破后的狰狞面目——一种贪婪和痛恨的奇特的混合"（Conrad 1994：101）。至此，让库尔茨感到可怕的原因已经十分明白：贪婪和绝望交织而成的痛苦是他一生冒险事业带给他的唯一收获，这怎能不让他感到恐惧？

如果我们把视线推得更远一些，就会发现库尔茨的叫喊还暗示着一种更加可怕的图景：库尔茨之流不仅把殖民地的人民推入了苦难的深渊，而且还把宗主国本土的许多人投入了可怕的精神状态——许多不明真相者不但不痛恨那些血债累累的罪人，反而把他们当成英雄来崇拜。库尔茨的未婚妻就是如此。当马洛去看望她时，她急切地想知道库尔茨的临终遗言，以便"有点东西伴着"她"活下去"（Conrad 1994：110）。为了让她免遭幻想破灭之苦，马洛撒谎说库尔茨最后喊的是她的名字，因此引起了她"一声欢喜若狂的可怕的喊叫"（Conrad 1994：111）。这一声喊叫确实可怕，因为它意味着她将继续对殖民主义者盲目崇拜下去。这一声喊叫与库尔茨临终前的喊叫形成了呼应：确实，再没有什么比殖民主义对人的肉体和精神的双重奴役更为可怕的了。

简而言之，《黑暗的心脏》的语言至少清楚地指明了两大寓意：一是殖民主义扩张行为，二是殖民主义思想对人的灵魂的侵蚀。这些寓意也就是该书书名的基本含义。利维斯曾经对库尔茨临死前状态的细节描写——尤其是他那骷髅般的身躯在草地上爬行的丑态——大加赞赏，认为这些细节"成功地揭示了库尔茨的怙恶不悛以及他那怪诞而可怕的灵魂"（Leavis 1954：218）。这就是说，利维斯也肯定康拉德的语言对故事寓意的指涉作用。不过，利维斯同时批评康拉德犯了画蛇添足的忌讳——后者坚持使用"深不可测的奥秘"等词语，这实际上"削弱了库尔茨临终前那呼喊的效果"（Leavis 1954：220）。

借助利维斯的启示，我们可以发现康拉德的一个自相矛盾之处：一方面，他巧妙地通过生动的细节本身传递了作品的寓意；另一方面，他又多此一举地故弄玄虚。米勒等人只看到了这一矛盾中的后一个方面，因此作出了那样的结论。对我们来说，康拉德的作品固然有自相矛盾之处，但是那些成功地揭示故事寓意的语言毕竟是主要方面。换言之，《黑暗的心脏》虽然在某些地方凸显了语言的自我关涉层面，但是它在更多的情况下超越了这一层面，出色地指向了真实。

误区三：生搬后殖民主义批评

从后殖民主义批评的角度切入，是近年来解读《黑暗的心脏》的时髦做法。

后殖民主义批评的一个主要观点是，许多西方小说家在文化层面上对殖民地国家和地区的历史重新建构，而其实质是剥夺、歪曲或篡改这些国家和地区的文化。在所有后殖民主义批评家中，创始人赛义德（Edward W. Said）倒算是对康拉德最公允的一个——他承认《黑暗的心脏》的主题是"欧洲人在非洲实施帝国主义统治，推行帝国主义的意志"（Said 1994：25），这至少没有让康拉德背上篡改殖民地国家文化的罪名。尽管如此，赛义德还认为"马洛是帝国主义宗主国话语的代表"（Said 1994：32）。至于其他一些后殖民主义批评家，则把康拉德说成了故意歪曲非洲人民形象的罪人。持这类观点的典型代表有阿齐贝（Chinua Achebe）和布兰特林格（Patrick Brantlinger）。

阿齐贝把康拉德叫作"该死的种族主义者"，其理由是他在《黑暗的心脏》中"突出了作为'他者世界'的非洲形象；非洲成了欧洲以及文明的对立面，成了人在兽性的嘲弄下斯文扫地的地方"（Achebe 1980：113）。

布兰特林格跟阿齐贝的观点相呼应，认为康拉德虽然"描写了帝国主义道德的崩溃"，但是其手法却是"把欧洲人的动机和行为等同于非洲人的偶像崇拜和野蛮。在他的笔下，非洲和库尔茨同样被抹了黑"（Brantlinger 1999：197）。据此，布兰特林得出了这样的结论："阿齐贝把康拉德对非洲人的描写说成种族主义的产物，这是完全正确的。"（Brantlinger 1999：197）

康拉德真的是个种族主义者吗？他真的是把非洲人民跟库尔茨之流一同抹了黑吗？

本文第一小节已经指出，《黑暗的心脏》的许多细节都足以证明土著黑人与入侵白人之间的区别。我们不妨重复一下马洛的一段肺腑之言："苍天作证！这些拿人——我说的是人——当牲畜一般使唤的恶人,都是些强大的、贪婪的、红眼睛的魔鬼。"这里,马洛明明白白地把那些黑人说成真正的人,而欺压他们的白人侵略者才是恶人,甚至是魔鬼。马洛的——更不用说是康拉德的——是非观念在此是不容置疑的。假若阿齐贝的话还有一些合理的成分,那是因为在当时的非洲,人的尊严确实受到了兽性的嘲弄和践踏,但是这些兽性并非来自那些被当成牲畜的非洲人,而恰恰是来自那些"文明的"欧洲人。

布兰特林格批评康拉德把非洲人民与库尔茨等量齐观的主要论据有二。

其一,当地土著把库尔茨奉为偶像,就像库尔茨"崇拜自己那没有约束的权力和欲望"一样(Brantlinger 1999:197)。

其二,"康拉德把同类相食描绘成刚果人民的日常习俗"。(Brantlinger 1999:198)

上述第一个论据一点不假:书中确实有一些土著对库尔茨顶礼膜拜,甚至跟着他打家劫舍,滥杀无辜。然而,我们是否能换一个角度来看一下这一事实呢?它是否正好说明了西方殖民主义者对非洲人民在精神上的侵略、压迫和麻痹呢?此外,书中并非所有的土著都愚昧地对库尔茨敬若神灵。前文提到,库尔茨窗前的立柱上摆着一颗颗人头;根据书中那位俄国水手的介绍,"这些都是叛乱分子的人头"(Conrad 1994:84)。这恰恰说明,有许多勇敢的土著不惜以生命为代价来反抗殖民主义统治;他们才是非洲土著的真正代表。可见,康拉德笔下的非洲人及其心灵并非一团漆黑。

至于那第二个论据的真假,我们最好先来看一下马洛本人对那些所谓的"食人生番"的评价:"汽艇曾不止一次地搁浅,全靠二十个食人生番溅着水花推动它前进。这一路上,我们从他们中间录用了一些作为水手。真是些好人——那些食人生番们——个个都规规矩矩。他们都是些可以共事的人,我对他们心存感激。更何况,我毕竟没有亲眼看见过他们谁把谁生吃掉了。"(Conrad 1994:49—50)这番话明白无误地告诉人们,所谓的"食人生番"只不过是道听途说罢了,马洛的所见所闻所说正好提供了反面的证词。布兰特林格等人对这样一个重要的细节居然视而不见,大概不仅仅是粗心大意的缘故吧?

以上分析表明,谁简单地把马洛/康拉德看成帝国主义宗主国话语的代表,谁就是青红不分,皂白不辨。《黑暗的心脏》的可贵之处恰恰在于它超越了当时占主流地位的宗主国话语体系。抹杀了这一点，也就抹杀了该作品的基本价值。

误区四：硬套女权主义批评

一些中外学者从女权主义批评的立场出发，"发现"《黑暗的心脏》充满了男权意识，进而断定马洛的非洲之行是对女性的殖民过程，而小说名字本身则象征着女性世界。

在我国，杜维平是这一观点的典型代表。他在《非洲、黑色与女人》一文中提出："小说的叙述者马洛的非洲腹地之旅，实质上无异于一次性经历探索。通过他对这一航程的叙述，我们可以发现其中潜埋的浓厚的男权意识和他无意识中对女性历史的记录——女性无历史。"（杜维平 1998：34）

在西方，斯特劳斯（Nina Pelican Straus）可以被看作这方面的典型代表。她批评康拉德把性别问题排除在叙事问题之外，并且把康拉德看成了马洛（在排斥女性方面）的同谋："在《黑暗的心脏》中，马洛虽然也谈论女人，但是他的话语对象是其他男人。没有任何迹象表明女人也可以被包括在他的听众之内，也没有迹象表明他所赖以生存的'人类'包括了女性。康拉德在故事的外围故意增添了一层框架，以便把读者也包括在马洛的听众之内。正是这一框架泄露了全书叙事话语那秘而不宣的实质——康拉德似乎跟马洛共同密谋了一段排斥女性的叙事话语。《黑暗的心脏》出奇地晦涩艰深，其原因很可能在于它把历史极端地男性化，在于它坚持把女性排除在读者圈之外。"（Straus 1996：50）

对《黑暗的心脏》作女权主义批评者大都有这样一个共同点：专拣有利于自己的观点的细节加以阐发，而把与自己意见相左的细节忽略不计。

杜维平似乎也未能例外。他的论据之一是马洛的下面这一段话：

> 女人！什么？我刚才提到女人了吗？哦，她和这个没有关系，一点儿关系也没有。她们——我是说女人们——都和这事无关，——不应该参与这事。我们必须帮助她们，让她们停留在自己美丽的世界中，免得她们把我们的世界变得更糟。（杜维平 1998：35）

杜维平认为上面这段话反映了马洛的男权意识，说明马洛是"不想让女人进入他的故事"（杜维平 1998：35）。

马洛究竟是不想让女人进入他的故事，还是不想让她们卷进殖民主义者的罪恶勾当呢？

我们只消看一下马洛那段话的上下文，就会得出跟杜维平不同的结论。马洛是在提及库尔茨的未婚妻时说那段话的。他在那段话之前承认自己"用一句谎言驱散了库尔茨的'鬼魂'"（指隐瞒库尔茨临终前叫喊真相一事），然后在那段话之后紧接着说："你们真应该知道，她那时完完全全跟这事儿不沾边儿。"（Conrad 1994：69）显而易见的是，马洛是在强调库尔茨的未婚妻与库尔茨本人的罪行无关，同时也强调不应该让妇女们受到牵连。库尔茨之流干了太多的坏事，假如再牵连他们的妻女，那世界可就会变得更糟，这恐怕是马洛的真实意思。顺便提一下，杜维平的误读跟他对原文的误译有关："should be out of it"（杜译："不应该参与这事"）应该译为"不应该受到牵连"，而"lest ours gets worse"（杜译："免得她们把我们的世界变得更糟"）应该译为"以免我们的世界变得更糟"。

常被女权主义批评家们用作例子的还有库尔茨在刚果的那个情妇。在这一方面，杜维平的评论依然具有代表性："女人无论如何不能离开家庭，否则，她就会从天使堕落为魔鬼。库尔茨的情人野女人就是离开家庭的女人。正因为她没有待在家里，所以她为马洛和他所代表的男权观念所不齿。"（杜维平 1998：36）

诚然，马洛笔下的这位女子有着狂野的形象。马洛至少有三次用了"凶猛"和"凶蛮"等词语来修饰她，但是我们从马洛的叙述中更多地看到了她的悲伤和痛苦。当马洛首次与她相遇时，"她的脸上有一种悲伤而凶猛的表情，内中显示出狂野的悲愤和无告的痛苦"（Conrad 1994：87）。当马洛的汽艇最后载着行将就木的库尔茨离去时，她又"悲伤地张开赤裸的双臂跟在我们后面"（Conrad 1994：97）。

她的悲伤从何而来呢？

从上下文中我们得知，库尔茨只是把她当成了一种商品（杜文也承认这一点）；库尔茨占有了她，却又在宗主国有着一个未婚妻，这不可能不引起她的怨恨（我们从另一个人物的口中得知，她曾经跟库尔茨"大吵大闹了一场"）

(Conrad 1994：88)；当库尔茨最终离她而去时，竟然没有一丝一毫对她表示牵挂的反应。从所有这些细节中我们看到的分明是一个殖民主义者一手制造的对殖民地的女人始乱终弃的悲剧。恰恰跟杜文的结论相反，马洛的笔端蘸满了对那位备受欺凌的弱女子的同情。假如她真的为马洛所不齿，马洛怎么会对她那痛苦的表情和姿态表现出那种挥之不去的关切呢？

马洛对库尔茨的未婚妻撒谎一事也是女权主义批评的热点之一。让我们再来看一下杜维平先生的评论："通过撒谎，马洛把库尔茨未婚妻的名字和库尔茨临死前的最后一句话'可怕呀！可怕呀！'联系到了一起。这样，我们就可以从他的叙事语法中得到这样一个结论：女性是可怕的。根深蒂固的男权意识使马洛好像得了厌女症一般对女性望而生畏。"（杜维平 1998：36）对此我们实在无法苟同。假如马洛真的得了厌女症，那么他为什么还要不辞辛苦地看望库尔茨的未婚妻呢？假如他真的厌恶后者，他完全可以告诉她真相，又何必动恻隐之心，情愿委屈了自己（如杜文所说，马洛一向痛恨谎言），而不愿看到她遭受精神上的打击呢？

当然，我们并不能完全排除康拉德受男权意识影响的可能。诚如杜文所说，马洛叙述中提到的几个女子都处在故事边缘"他者"的位置上，他甚至没有告诉我们其中任何一个女性的名字。亦如斯特劳斯所说，马洛当时的听众是清一色的男性。

然而，造成上述现象的是两个显而易见的原因。

首先，康拉德本人不可避免地受到了时代和他个人生活经历的限制。在他所处的时代，女性的自觉意识远远没有今天这样强烈。指望他用当今的标准来反映女性问题，这显然是一种苛求。而且，他多年生活在清一色的男性水手中间，自然对女性知之甚少，因此他在刻画人物方面扬长避短，这也是势所难免，情有可原。

其次，故事的题材本身决定了男性要唱主角。当时从事殖民主义侵略活动的主要是男人，这是不争的历史事实。至于马洛的听众的性别问题，那就更在情理之中：讲故事的场所是在内利号巡航艇上；当时在恶劣的自然环境下冒险远航的都是男性，即使有女性，那也是绝少的，如果硬要往他们中间塞一两个女子，那只能会使故事的真实性受损。此外，马洛的听众的性别跟康拉德的读者的性别之间没有必然的联系——斯特劳斯硬要在两者之间画等号，除了她的主观臆想之外，实在看不出还有什么理由。

即便康拉德受到了男权意识的影响，我们也不能以偏概全。如前文所述，《黑暗的心脏》中占压倒多数的细节都指向了殖民主义者在非洲犯下的罪行，指向了既殃及女人又殃及男人的黑暗势力。假如非要把马洛的非洲之行说成是对女性的殖民过程，那至少是冲淡了康拉德对殖民主义的控诉。

参考文献

[1] Achebe C. Viewpoint [J]. *Times Literary Supplement*, 1980, Feb. 1: 113.

[2] Brantlinger P. Kurtz's "Darkness" and *Heart of Darkness* [A] //Childs P. (ed.). *Post-Colonial Theory and English Literature: A Reader* [C]. Edinburg: Edinburg University Press, 1999.

[3] Brooks P. *Reading for the Plot: Design and Intention in Narrative* [M]. New York: Vintage, 1985: 252.

[4] Childs P. *Post-Colonial Theory and English Literature* [M]. Edinburgh: Edinburgh University Press, 1999.

[5] Conrad J. *Heart of Darkness* [M]. London: Penguin Books, 1994.

[6] Leavis F R. *The Great Tradition* [M]. New York: Doubleday and Company, 1954.

[7] Miller J H. Heart of Darkness Revisited [A] //Murfin R. (ed.) *Heart of Darkness: A Case Study in Contemporary Criticism* [C]. New York: St Martin's Press, 1989.

[8] Said E. *Culture and Imperialism* [M]. London: Vintage, 1994.

[9] Straus N P. The Exclusion of the Intended from Secret Sharing [A] // Elaine Jordan (ed.) *Contemporary Critical Essays: Joseph Conrad* [C]. London: Macmillan, 1996.

[10] 杜维平. 非洲、黑色与女人——《黑暗的中心》的叙事话语批判 [J]. 外国文学评论, 1998, (4).

[11] 赖辉. 论《黑暗的心》的叙述者、叙述接受者和"陌生化" [J]. 外国

文学研究(人大报刊复印资料), 1999 (10): 25.

[12] 劳·坡林. 诗的象征 [J]. 世界文学, 1981 (5): 56.

[13] 王佐良, 周珏良. 英国二十世纪文学史 [M]. 北京: 外语教学与研究出版社, 1994.

[14] 郁青.《雨王汗德森》与《黑暗的心》 [J]. 外国文学评论, 1997 (3): 93.

(本文原载于《外国文学评论》2001年第2期)

Communal Pleasure in Jean Rhys's Fiction

Introduction

For more than half a century there has been a tendency among critics to place Jean Rhys's work in relation to modernism. While most studies concerned have focused either on the issue of how "Rhys's Caribbean background strongly informs her modernism" (Savory 2009: 14), or on the question of how Rhys's texts show "that female modernism takes up female subjectivity at precisely the point that Freud abandoned it" (Moran 2007: 17), Laura Frost's *The Problem with Pleasure: Modernism and Its Discontents* has blazed a new trail and annexed the concept of pleasure to the notion of modernism in her reading of Rhys's fiction. More specifically, she uses Rhys's texts as typical examples of "modernism's dismissal of accessible pleasure as facile and trite, and its valorization of that which requires effort and training" (Frost 2013: 9). Underpinning all Frost's analysis of Rhys's fiction is a central argument, namely that "the fundamental goal of modernism is the redefinition of pleasure: specifically, exposing easily achieved and primarily somatic pleasures as facile, hollow, and false, and cultivating those that require more ambitious analytical work" (Frost 2013: 3). Such a view, obviously, presupposes a hierarchy of pleasures ranging from the highest, such as a purified or refined kind of pleasure, to the lowest, which suggests crudity and debasement. What makes Laura Frost's work remarkable is her emphasis on "modernism's contribution to the genealogy of pleasure", which she describes as "the declared substitution of one set of pleasures (refined, acquired, and cognitive) for another (embodied, accessible), in which the disavowal of the latter is promoted as an aesthetic principle" (Frost 2013: 22). It seems logical that Jean Rhys has made a similar contribution, otherwise she would not have caught Frost's close attention.

There is a problem, however, with *The problem with pleasure.* For all its meticulously traced genealogy of pleasure, one particular type of pleasure, namely communal pleasure by which I mean the aesthetic pleasure that implies a sense of communal well-being and a yearning for communal feelings, is conspicuously absent. In Frost's analysis, Rhys's protagonists are hardly presented as capable of sharing their pleasure with others. Frost also argues that Rhys tends to position her down-and-out protagonists as more sympathetic than her upperclass characters, "but this sympathy is earned by individuals through their inability or refusal to take part in collective pleasure", and it is because of this inability that her "characters are drawn to obliteration, repetition, debasement, and self-destruction" (Frost 2013: 164). Admittedly, almost all Rhys's female protagonists "have been diagnosed by critics as depressed, melancholic, schizophrenic, borderline personality, and, perhaps most commonly, masochistic" (Frost 2013: 189), but are these symptoms innate and inborn? If not, what has given rise to such psychological traits? My own reading of Rhys's stories cautions against a simplistic generalization of her treatment of various kinds of pleasure. If her characters' lives are by and large overcast pleasure-wise, the clouds do give way to sunshine sometimes, however brief such happy moments may be. How should one then explain such complications?

I

The basic premise of Laura Frost's argument is that Jean Rhys, like other modernist writers, aims at the reconceptualization of pleasure. In order to specify the way modernist writers reconceptualize pleasure, Frost comes up with the term "unpleasure" which she defines as follows:

> ... unpleasure is not the opposite of pleasure, but rather its modification. The concept of unpleasure breaks with the conventional separation of human experience into two tendencies, as expressed in Bentham's ominous opening of *The principles of morals and legislation:* "Nature has placed mankind under the governance of two sovereign masters, *pain and pleasure* ... " (Frost 2013: 6)

Frost seems quite satisfied with her use of the term, as revealed in the following claim: "More than any other term, 'unpleasure' is able to encompass both the complex, dialectical representations of pleasure and the readerly affects modernism puts into play" (Frost 2013: 25). What is particularly worthy of attention here is the word "dialectical", which shows that Frost's approach is informed by Lionel Trilling, who in his essay "The fate of pleasure" pinpoints a "dialectic of pleasure which is the characteristic intellectual activity of Keats's poetry" (Trilling 2000: 433). The following is Trilling's own explanation of that "dialectic":

> Keats, then, may be thought of as the poet who made the boldest affirmation of the principle of pleasure and also as the poet who brought the principle of pleasure into the greatest and sincerest doubt. He therefore has for us a peculiar cultural interest, for it would seem to be true that at some point in modern history the principle of pleasure came to be regarded with just such ambivalence. (Trilling 2000: 434)

Frost bases her views on the above-said "dialectic" and moves on to argue that "Trilling points to Romanticism as a contrast" (Frost 2013: 4), namely a contrast to modernism.

It is true that Keats' discourse of pleasure is a legitimate context for examining such modernist writings as those by Jean Rhys, but another Romantic poet, namely William Wordsworth, seems to be a more relevant context. As pointed out by Rowan Boyson in her monumental work *Wordsworth and the Enlightenment idea of pleasure*, "the modern idea of pleasure" could have benefited more from Wordsworth's poetry:

> The modern idea of pleasure is primarily individualistic; indeed, modernity is often characterized (and criticized) as the moment, which legitimized individual pleasures, rather than transcendent ends, such as God, family or society. The argument of this book, however, is that there is a counter-strain in Enlightenment philosophy and in Wordsworth's poetry, in which pleasure is considered as inherently communal rather than private and solipsistic. The book seeks to retrieve this almost-forgotten idea about how pleasure might register a feeling of collective dependence and interaction, and might be generated from a feeling of community. (Boyson 2012: 1)

What merits our special attention here is Boyson's endeavour "to retrieve this almost-forgotten idea about how pleasure might register a feeling of collective dependence and interaction, and might be generated from a feeling of community." Here comes, then, an interesting question: Is "this almost-forgotten idea" also forgotten by Laura Frost? Does her concept of unpleasure contain any feeling of collective dependence and interaction? Does she take into account any feeling of community at all when she theorizes about unpleasure and applies it to the interpretation of Rhys's fiction?

The "almost-forgotten idea" of communal pleasure is at least ignored, if not forgotten, by Frost. She does mention Wordsworth once in *The problem with pleasure*: "Trilling points to Romanticism as a contrast, exemplified by ... Wordsworth's praise in his preface to *Lyrical Ballads* for 'the naked and native dignity of man' that is found in 'the grand elementary principle of pleasure'" (Frost 2013: 4). But she seems to have overlooked a frequently quoted argument which is at the core of Wordsworth's idea of pleasure: "The poet writes under one restriction only, the necessity of giving immediate pleasure to a human being possessed of that information which may be expected of him, not as a lawyer, a physician, a mariner, an astronomer or a natural philosopher, but as a man." (Wordsworth 2007a: 312) This argument for "the necessity of giving immediate pleasure" is in a way an appeal for the sharing of aesthetic pleasure. It would be a pity if this aspect of Romantic discourses on pleasure went unnoticed, when any attempt is made to refer to Romanticism as a contrast to modernist writings like those by Rhys.

Let me hasten to add that it would be an even greater pity to leave unnoticed such writers as Walter Pater, John Ruskin and William Morris, whose fin de siècle British discourses of pleasure can actually provide an even more relevant context, both spatially and temporally, for the works of Jean Rhys who resided and was educated in Britain from 1906. Like Wordsworth, who maintains that a pleasure/joy is "imperfect while unshared" (Wordsworth 2007b: 292), Pater, Ruskin and Morris all set much store by the collectivity of pleasurable experiences — they not only advocate aesthetic pleasure, but also see in it the possibility of community. Pater, for example, calls for a "life of refined pleasure", in his preface to *Renaissance*, which implies "eras of more favorable conditions, in which the thoughts of men draw nearer together than is their wont, and the many interests of the intellectual world combine in one complete type of general culture" (Pater 1873: xxx). Herein lies a clear indicator of the communal nature of his proposed pleasure, i. e., the one that is conducive to the thoughts of men drawing nearer together. While emphasizing that "there is a certain number of artists who have a distinct faculty of their own by which they convey to us a peculiar quality of pleasure which we cannot get elsewhere", Pater believes that these artists "have their place in general culture, and must be interpreted to it by those who have felt their charm strongly" (Pater 1873: 50). Here his emphasis on the need to "convey ... pleasure" and on "general culture" clearly indicates a type of pleasure which is to be shared and will contribute to a culture in a communal sense. To him, all refined pursuits tend to yield a pleasure which ought to be shared in as broad a sense as possible. As observed by Kurt Lampe, Pater simply aims at some sort of "music, in that wider Platonic sense", which "includes all the arts — dancing, singing, playing instruments, civic and religious rituals, military exercises, mathematics, and philosophy — by which a society attempts to create a beautiful orderliness in its individual and collective life" (Lampe 2015: 183). In short, Pater has left to the twentieth century Britain a cultural heritage which hinges on beauty, order and communal pleasure.

No less influential on fin de siècle British discourses of pleasure is John Ruskin, whose most noteworthy contribution in this connection is his book *The pleasures of England* which consists of four lectures, given in Oxford in 1883 – 1885, all under the rubric of "pleasures", namely "The pleasures of learning", "The pleasures of faith", "The pleasures of deed", and "The pleasures of fancy." "Of these pleasures," he argues, "the leading one was that of Learning", "a pleasure totally separate from that of finding out things for yourself" (Ruskin 1988: 12). In other words, the issue of pleasure does not interest him in the slightest unless it goes beyond one's self interest. While explaining the overall sketch of his above-said lectures, he chooses not to mince the following truth: "I have approached every question from the people's side, and examined the nature, not of the special faculties by which the work was produced, but of the general instinct by which it was asked for, and enjoyed." (Ruskin 1988: 12) Like Pater, Ruskin sees an urgent need for conveying the pleasure perceived by whoever engages in refined pursuits. For instance, he praises "the drawings in Saxon manuscripts" for the "rapid endeavours to express for themselves, and convey to others" the pleasure felt by the artists themselves (Ruskin 1988: 26). Many similar examples can also be found in his *Sesame and Lilies*, where he insists on the importance of pursuing "wholesome pleasure" (Ruskin 2002: 17), and the need for a "writer's delight" to "become in turn a source of pleasure for readers" (Helsinger 2002: 113). Another typical example of his proposed wholesome pleasure is his comment on the source of aesthetic pleasure on the part of Alpine excursionists: he refutes the claim that Alpine excursionists "should attribute their pleasure to some true and increased apprehension of the nobleness of natural scenery", and contends that the "real beauty of the Alps is to be seen, and seen only, where all may see it, the child, the cripple, and the man of grey hairs" (Ruskin 2002: 6). Such pleasure, accessible to and shareable by old and young, healthy and disabled, is wholesome indeed and cannot but be a valuable object of study for anyone who is interested in discourses of pleasure, especially the ones in the late 19th-century and the early 20th-century Britain.

Equally influential, if not even more so, is William Morris who, in many of his essays, relates aesthetic pleasure to the happiness of the whole mankind. In "The aims of art", for instance, he claims that "the aim of art is to increase the happiness of men, by giving them ... hope and bodily pleasure in their work; or, shortly, to make man's work happy and his rest fruitful. Consequently, genuine art is an unmixed blessing to the race of man" (Morris 1948a: 591). Even in appreciating the beauty of an old building, he would like people to think about "all the generations of men": "How we please ourselves with an old building by thinking of all the generations of men that have passed through it ... we should feel a pleasure in thinking how he who had built it had left a piece of his soul behind him to greet the new-comers one after another long and long after he was gone" (Morris 1948b: 560). Similarly, he offers to share with his fellow countrymen his responses to "lesser arts", along with "the men who wrought this kind of art": "I believe I am not thinking only of my own pleasure, but of the pleasure of many people, when I praise the usefulness of the lives of these men, whose names are long forgotten, but whose works we still wonder at" (Morris 1915a: 112). Seeing that lesser arts are often rejected in his own country, he points out that this is "to the injury of the community" and then declares himself to be "a professed pleader and advocate for them ... since it is through them that I am the servant of the public, and earn my living with abundant pleasure" (Morris 1915b: 235). A more intriguing example is his definition of "wealth":

> Wealth is what Nature gives us and what a reasonable man can make out of the gifts of Nature for his reasonable use. The sunlight, the fresh air, the unspoiled face of the earth, food, raiment and housing necessary and decent; the

storing up of knowledge of all kinds, and the power of disseminating it; means of free communication between man and man; works of art, the beauty which man creates when he is most a man, most aspiring and thoughtful — all things which serve the pleasure of people, free, manly, and uncorrupted. This is wealth. (Morris 1948c: 608)

Morris here is evidently pleading in favour of communal pleasure, indicated by such expressions as "serve the pleasure of people", "the power of disseminating it", "free communication", etc. The fact that he, together with Ruskin and Pater, helps shape the powerful fin de siècle British discourses of pleasure is indisputable.

However, one question remains unanswered, namely the question of whether Jean Rhys has read Pater, Ruskin and Morris, albeit their powerful influence. No solid evidence seems to have been produced which can point to the direct impact of their ideas on Rhys. It does not matter, however, whether she once came under their direct influence. What matters is that she did live in an era when their discourses of pleasure had been among the shaping forces of British literature. Given their status and the cultural climate at that time, their ideas concerned could not have gone unheeded for a novelist, like Rhys, who is also deeply interested in the issue of pleasure. It is legitimate, therefore, to assume that Rhys has at least benefited indirectly from Pater, Ruskin and Morris who have left their imprints on modern discourses of pleasure, the idea of communal pleasure not the least among them.

Has Laura Frost paid due attention, then, to the above-said discourses of pleasure? As already mentioned in the introductory part of the present paper, Frost sees in Rhys's protagonists a mere "inability or refusal to take part in collective pleasure." To be sure, Frost's concept of unpleasure does throw insight into the complexity of the nature and the causes of pleasure, and the way modernist writers redefine pleasure. Her chief merit lies in her meticulous analysis of different types of pleasure on the basis of a close reading of modernist writings, including those by Jean Rhys. More praiseworthy is her attempt to avoid simplification and to distinguish between the various kinds of pleasure/unpleasure that she examines in the works of various authors even if these works are categorized under the same rubric of "modernism." Frost writes as follows in this regard:

> While Joyce's masochism and Lawrence's female submission, for example, are impulses towards unpleasure, those authors both maintain the horizon of conventional (easy, simplistic, somatic) as well as valorized (analytical, aesthetic, transformative) pleasure. For Hamilton and Rhys, by contrast, unpleasure is a spectrum ranging from ennui to *jouissance* that is shadowed by anhedonia. (Frost 2013: 164)

Frost's comparative studies on Joyce, Lawrence, Hamilton and Rhys have shed light on their respective characteristics, for which she has provided ample textual evidence indeed. Unfortunately, however, she has failed to ponder over the possibility of incorporating into her notion of unpleasure any strand of collective, or communal, pleasure. Whatever kind of pleasure she examines, be it a broad "horizon of conventional (easy, simplistic, somatic) as well as valorized (analytical, aesthetic, transformative) pleasure", or "a spectrum ranging from ennui to *jouissance* that is shadowed by anhedonia", it is treated as private, solipsistic and individualistic. It seems that, to her, communal pleasure is simply out of sight, if not out of mind.

But does Jean Rhys, too, merely focus on individualistic pleasure? Are her characters capable of affecting which induces feelings of community, which in turn generate pleasure at all? To answer these questions, one needs to have a close-up look at Rhys's texts proper, which constitutes the main content of the following passages.

II

It is true that Rhys's fiction often paints a bleak picture. More often than not, her female protagonists get bogged down in a somatic world characterized by sex and alcohol. "Critics", therefore, "regularly refer to 'the Rhys woman': a narcissistic, self-defeating, financially dependent victim who makes dubious decisions and declares the world a hostile conspirator against her" (Frost 2013: 187). All this being acknowledged, it still remains to be found out if Rhys's characters are utterly unable to take part in collective pleasure. Do they always indulge themselves in crude pleasure or false amusements?

A close examination of Rhys's texts reveals that her protagonists ARE capable of feelings which can by no means be put into the category of low, passive and corporeal pleasures. Almost all her female protagonists, to a greater or less extent, show genuine love for the pleasure or joy afforded to them either in nature, or in music, dancing and fine arts whose appreciation is achieved through taste. In other words, they are capable of deriving pleasures that are associated with taste rather than the gratification of appetite. Furthermore, when they experience such pleasures, they often feel an impulse to share them, not only with their loved ones, but also with strangers. It does not go too far to say that, in such circumstances, their pleasure gives rise to communal feelings.

A typical example can be found in *Good Morning, Midnight*, which is considered by many to be Rhys's bleakest novel. Sasha, the heroine and the first-person narrator, reminds one of Baudelaire's flâneur or, more appropriately, flâneuse. She is often found wandering in streets, noticing people and things, shopping and meeting strangers, and then going back to her cheap rented room for eating and drinking. But she is not without happy moments. Before her baby dies, she has enjoyed a happy life with Enno (whose true nature has not been revealed at that time), and we see her "tuned up to top pitch" by love, which makes her notice the lovely colours in the sky or of lights on water (Rhys 2020: 111). Herein, obviously, lies a joy not only derived from beautiful colours and lights offered in nature, but also a joy coupled with communal feeling, love being a kind of feeling which is meant to be shared. Sasha is appreciative of beauty not only in nature, but also in art. There is a description in the novel of her memory of the room where she was happy with Enno, even many years afterwards, which had "rose-patterned wallpaper" (Rhys 2020: 110). This time the pleasurable experience is associated with the beauty of art, instead of the beautiful sky and water. Nonetheless it registers communal feeling. A more convincing case is Sasha's encounter with Serge, a Russian painter, from whom she manages to purchase a picture. The whole scene involves music, dancing and fine arts. A third person involved is Delmar, who helps display Serge's finished pictures to Sasha by arranging them around Serge's room:

> When he has finished pictures are propped up on the floor round three sides of the room.
> "Now you can see them", he says.
> "Yes, now I can see them."
> I am surrounded by the pictures. It is astonishing how vivid they are in this dim light... Now the room expands and the iron band round my heart loosens. The miracle has happened. I am happy. (Rhys 2020: 93)

Sasha is happy because she is elevated by those pictures. And her pleasure is in fact gradually built up — before she gets to see those pictures, she has already had a pleasant time talking with both Delmar and Serge who, in addition, plays "some beguine music, Martinique music" and then "holds the mask over his face and dances" (Rhys 2020: 86). Here the pleasure produced by the music and dance is shared: Sasha feels that Serge "dances very well" and Delmar "claps his hands in time to the music" (Rhys 2020: 86). What is more touching is that Serge, seeing that Sasha is deeply moved by the music and has burst into tears, convinces her that she is "with friends" (Rhys 2020: 87). This friendship, developed in the atmosphere of music and dance, is certainly a pleasant feeling of community, which can be further proved by Serge's generosity — when Sasha discovers that she is not able to pay him on the spot for the purchase of a picture, Serge makes a generous offer: "But have it, take it, all the same. I like you. I'll give it to you as a present." (Rhys 2020: 94) The whole scene ends in still another meaningful interaction between Serge and Sasha:

> ... He rolls up the picture in tissue-paper, ties it round with a bit of string and I take it under my arm. Then he gives my hand a long, hard shake and says "Amis." When he shakes my hand like that and says "Amis" I feel very happy ... (Rhys 2020: 94)

It should be added that Sasha does not know Serge and Delmar until the picture-purchase-scene, which is an undeniable testimony to her capacity for affection and her willingness to share her pleasure even with strangers. Moreover, the detail in Sasha's reiteration of her pleasure — "I am happy", and then "I feel very happy" — serves to reinforce her willingness and capability to take part in collective pleasure, given right and proper circumstances.

A similar case can be found in *Quartet*, where there is a description of how the heroine Marya is attracted and even uplifted by music. Although she has to live in a sordid hotel, being poor, she enjoys waking in the mornings to the sound of a "man with a flock of goats who passed under her window every morning about half-past ten, playing a frail little tune on a pipe" (Rhys 1929: 111). His music "enchanted her", because it is "thin, high, sweet", "like water running in the sun" (Rhys 1929: 111). The pleasurable feelings that Marya is going through here are evidently emotions of taste, which are different from other feelings such as sexual desire and acquisitiveness, and which call for imagination. In other words, Marya is capable of "the pleasures of imagination" as specified by Mark Akenside, whose prestigious philosophical poem, *The pleasures of imagination*, "popularized Addison's ideas" advocated in his "famous essays on the imagination from the *Spectator*" (Brewer 2013: 82). More interestingly, Marya here is spiritually attached to a friend who she has never really met, namely the pipe-playing man, who "is like an ancient shepherd giving the world unintentional poetry, in a twist on the pastoral tradition" (Savory 2009: 33), for "the man played, not to attract customers, but to keep his flock in order" (Rhys 1929: 111). Marya feels spiritually attached to the man because he not only plays sweet music but also, by playing the music, manages to keep the sheep in order, the sense of order being another factor which contributes to her pleasure. Although she does not know the pipe-playing man in person, her spiritual attachment to him and her sense of order, deriving from the enchanting music, register nonetheless feelings of community. In a way, she has participated in some sort of collective pleasure, which almost has a lasting effect — we are told that, even when the music starts to fade, she thinks the pipe-playing man's music "persistent as the hope of happiness" (Rhys 1929: 112). To say the least, Marya yearns for communal pleasure.

There is a similar case in *After Leaving Mr. Mackenzie*, whose female protagonist Julia also has the potential for emotions of taste that may give rise to the impulse to communicate and to share one's pleasurable experiences or happy memories. Although the adult Julia lives "the life of a dog" (Rhys 1931: 11), she is sensitive to beautiful things, such as flowers and trees, or to places where she has had fond memories. In one of her conversations with Horsfield, she tries to share with him her memories of Ostend where she has spent her childhood — her face "brightened up" while doing so: "I like Ostend. I like it very much. I was happy there, and I always remember places I was happy in. I mean, I remember them so that I can shut my eyes and be there . . . " (Rhys 1931: 50) Despite the fact that she gets increasingly unhappy as she grows up, she always cherishes the memories of her happy childhood:

> The last time you were really happy — happy about nothing? When you were happy about nothing you had to jump up and down. "Can't you keep still, child, for one moment?" No, of course you couldn't keep still. You were too happy, bursting with happiness. You ran as if you were flying, without feeling your feet. And all the time you ran, you were thinking, with a tight feeling in your throat: "I'm happy — happy — happy. . . " (Rhys 1931: 159)

When she is happy, Julia is likely to become highly imaginative and her imaginative empathy even extends to a tree: "When you were a child, you put your hand on the trunk of a tree and you were comforted, because you knew that the tree was alive — you felt its life when you touched it — and you knew that it was friendly to you ..." (Rhys 1931: 158) On another occasion we find Julia "thinking of the words 'orange-trees', remembering the time when she had woven innumerable romances about her mother's childhood in South America" (Rhys 1931: 105). The image of orange-trees here is evocative in the sense that it brings forth pleasant memories which forge a link between Julia and her mother, a link which is in a way communal. An equally evocative bond can be found in flowers, which reflect Julia's strong emotional attachment to her mother: she once spends more than she can afford for her mother on some red roses, for which "she took her last ten-shilling note from her bag" (Rhys 1931: 127). All these details testify to Julia's capacity for emotions of taste.

Still another example can be found in *Voyage in the Dark*, whose heroin Anna is not without pleasures of imagination and emotions of taste. Shortly after the beginning of the novel, she is found "reading *Nana*", a novel by Zola (Rhys 1982: 9). In addition to reading, she also enjoys going to the theatre or the cinema, and a most significant detail in her experience of a film is an unattributed line from Coleridge's "Kubla Khan": "Through caverns measureless to man down to a sunless sea ..." (Rhys 1982: 107) Admittedly, her story is by and large a sad one: she is forced to move from her Caribbean home to England together with an uncaring stepmother, after the death of her father; almost alone in England, she has to support herself by working as a chorus girl, which marks the beginning of an unhappy life. But she always cherishes memories of her home in the West Indies which, when compared with England, is a poignant reminder of "a difference in the way I was frightened and the way I was happy" (Rhys 1982: 7). Of all her happy memories, the most touching one is that of her close emotional tie to a black servant called Francine, whom she finds endearing because of her kindness, diligence, simple-heartedness, and her singing and even her complexion: "I was happy because Francine was there ... Being black is warm and gay, being white is cold and sad." (Rhys 1982: 31) By describing "being black" as "warm and gay", the narrator here drives home the message regarding the connection between pleasure and communal feelings. Even the way Francine eats mangoes brings pleasure to Anna:

> The thing about Francine was that when I was with her I was happy. She was small and plump and blacker than most of the people out there, and she had a pretty face. What I liked was watching her eat mangoes. Her teeth would bite into the mango and her lips fasten on either side of it, and while she sucked you saw that she was perfectly happy. When she had finished she always smacked her lips twice, very loud — louder than you could believe possible. It was a ritual. (Rhys 1982: 67 - 68)

It would be hard to find a more touching and more vivid depiction of pleasurable experiences tinged with warmth, ingenuousness, and feelings of community.

No less similar is *Wide Sargasso Sea* in terms of communal pleasure. Antoinette, the heroine, first impresses us as a daughter of Nature. In her early days, "she is full of life, but wild, like the nature that surrounds her" (Savory 2009: 81). Like almost all the other female protagonists under the pen of Jean Rhys, Antoinette is sensitive and responsive to the beauty of Mother Nature. Her friendship with Tia, the daughter of a black slave, is formed in the midst of natural surroundings which are aesthetically appealing to her: she meets Tia "nearly every morning at the turn of the road to the river" and they have such fun together that they sometimes even "stayed till late afternoon", and she enjoys "looking at the pool deep and dark green under the trees, brown-green if it had rained, but a bright sparkling green in the sun" (Rhys 1999: 13). She is so observant that she is able to capture the nuances of the depths, light, and colours of the water: "The water was so clear that you could see the pebbles at the bottom of the shallow part. Blue and white and striped red. Very pretty." (Rhys 1999: 13) There are in fact many descriptions of how Antoinette responds with pleasure to plants/flowers, especially those in the garden in her own house. For instance, she is particularly drawn to an octopus orchid which, when flowering, "was a bell-shaped mass of white, mauve, deep purples, wonderful to see. The scent was very sweet and strong" (Rhys 1999: 11). The plants that attract her include roses, coralita, jasmines, orchids, ferns, ginger lilies and honeysuckles, to name only a few. The significance of her delight in those plants goes beyond her private feelings, as aptly pointed out by Elaine Savory:

> For Antoinette, the pleasure of home inheres in whatever grows at home: orchids, roses, tree ferns and honeysuckle... She learns in her convent school that Theophilus received a rose which never died and later became a Christian and a martyr... so a rose becomes more than just a flower: it is an emblem of faith, but one associated with self-sacrifice and martyrdom. Significantly, the association of flowers with self-sacrifice emerges in the context of her honeymoon, where the honeymoon house is strewn with flowers, with coralita on the dining table and roses on a serving tray. (Savory 2015: 95)

Indeed the association of flowers with self-sacrifice indicates the extent to which Antoinette is willing to share her pleasure/happiness with her loved ones. A most telling piece of evidence can be found in the honeymoon house, which is "strewn with flowers" as already observed by Savory, where the happy Antoinette offers her unnamed husband — although we all know that he is none other than Mr. Rochester — "soft light kisses" when he is asleep and even tries to cover him up with her own body against "the land breeze" which she thinks "can be cold" (Rhys 1999: 55). That is to say, Antoinette is willing to share her happiness even at the cost of her own health and, in such a case, self-sacrifice is part of communal pleasure.

The above-analyzed cases show that all Rhys's female protagonists have in fact the capacity or potential for sharing their own pleasure, even to the extent of self-sacrifice. But why are they all eventually drawn to obliteration, debasement and even self-destruction? The answer to this question lies in the socio-historical circumstances in which they live; these circumstances constitute the main content of the third section of the present paper.

III

Although Rhys's female characters are capable of taking part in collective or communal pleasure, they are rendered unable to do so in one way or another, the ultimate reason being the influence of socio-historical conditions on their life. More specifically, they are all "denied socially valued places of belonging" (Lopoukhine et al. 2020: 133). They have all lost their voices, so to speak, which would have given expression to their communal pleasure. To be more precise, their voices are "silenced" or "obstructed", in the words of Juliana Lopoukhine, Frédéric Regard and Kerry-Jane Wallart, by "the power structures of organized society" that "depend on a complex interaction of economic, class, racial, national and gender privilege" (Lopoukhine et al. 2020: 133). It should be added that, in Rhys's fiction, these power structures are invariably embodied in some mercenary and treacherous men.

On the face of it, Rhys's characters often base their action on their own choices, but are their choices purely voluntary? Laura Frost maintains that "her characters do exercise choice; however, they make choices that steer them away from pleasure and happiness" (Frost 2013: 206). Nevertheless, a close-up look at the sociohistorical contexts of the lives of Rhys's characters shows that they are often forced to make such choices rather than doing so of their own accord. A revealing circumstance is that they do not have a permanent place of residence, thus having to move from one hotel to another, often a sordid one, with the exception of Antoinette who ends up in a "madhouse" which is even worse. As soon as the novel *After Leaving Mr. Mackenzie* opens, for instance, Julia is found living in "a cheap hotel on the Quai des Grands Augustins", which "looked a lowdown sort of place and the staircase smelt of the landlady's cats" (Rhys 1931: 9). The heroine of *Quartet*, similarly, is forced to live in "Montmartre hotel" which "cannot possibly be called a solid background" (Rhys

1929: 8). In the opening part of *Good Morning, Midnight*, too, the female protagonist Sasha is found staying temporarily in "a large room, the smell of cheap hotels faint, almost imperceptible", trapped in a "narrow, cobble stoned" street, which the first-person narrator calls "an impasse" (Rhys 2020: 3). Actually, throughout the story, Sasha is recurrently trapped in anonymous and uncanny hotel rooms, as indicated by one of her interior monologues: "Back to the hotel without a name in the street without a name. You press the button and the door opens... You go up the stairs. Always the same stairs, always the same room." (Rhys 2020: 138) Equally uncanny are some of the hotels in which Anna, the heroine of *Voyage in the Dark*, finds herself. In one summer, she has to stay in "the chorus-girls' hostel in Maple Street" which gets on her nerves (Rhys 1982: 21) and later she stays in a hotel where some "stags' heads stuck up all over the dining-room... The one over our table was as big as a cow's. Its enormous glass eyes stared past us" (Rhys 1982: 77). All these hotel-scenes suggest that their dwellers are constantly on the move, roaming about for safety, jobs, food, etc. What is it, then, that causes them to be out of their elements?

  If one unreservedly applies Laura Frost's theory of "unpleasure" to the analysis of the above-mentioned dislocations, he/she is likely to look upon the homelessness of Rhys's characters as something they do of their own free will. True, it is in those hotels, with the exception of the case of Antoinette, that Rhys's female protagonists eventually abandon themselves to alcohol or loveless sex which places them under the governance of both pain and pleasure, or rather "unpleasure" which Frost sees as "not so much a by-product of political disenfranchisement or personal trauma as it is a chosen attraction" (Frost 2013: 164). But is it really a chosen attraction? At least they do not choose to live in those places, but are actually forced to live there. Julia, for instance, once tells Mr. Horsfield that she is from Ostend and she "was happy there" (Rhys 1931: 50). However, she has to leave Ostend and seeks living, together with her mother, in England. The loss of their former happiness is reflected in her mother's sighing which strikes a sympathetic chord in Julia's heart: "This is a cold, grey country. This isn't a country to be really happy in." (Rhys 1931: 105)

The story of Marya, too, opens up with Stephan and herself boarding in a cheap hotel in Paris which is foreign to her. After Stephan is thrown into jail, she is utterly impoverished and compelled by Heidler and Lois to become part of a ménage à trois. No less peripatetic is Anna's life, as she is forced to leave her Caribbean home and taken to England by her stepmother Hester, who cuts her off financially after she leaves school. Stranded and alone, Anna has to support herself as a chorus girl and then is seduced by Walter who does not really love her. Like Anna, Sasha is also financially unstable, having had an unhappy marriage and a traumatic experience of her child's death, which leaves her adrift in streets. Unlike Sasha, Julia, Anna and Marya, Antoinette does not have to board at a hotel, but she is isolated from the rest of the world in the mansion she calls the "cardboard house" (Rhys 1999: 107), after she is taken by her husband from Jamaica to England. Being thought mad and confined, she leads a more miserable life than a peripatetic one. In brief, Rhys's female protagonists all end up in lodgings that they would not have chosen if there had been any alternative, which means that they are bound to be out of their elements.

That is to say, Rhys's characters are rendered increasingly incapable of higher pursuits by their miserable lodgings, which eventually force them to succumb to what Frost calls "unpleasure". For the Rhys heroine, a more appropriate term than "unpleasure" would be "manic pleasure", a term that Mary Lou Emery has used to describe Maria's state of mind which is in fact a "self-deception that accompanies her social displacement" (Emery 1990: 108). What Emery says about Maria actually applies to all Rhys's female protagonists, whose life experiences have one thing in common: vulnerability to social dislocations. This is probably one of the reasons why Nancy R. Harrison contends that, in Rhys's five novels, seemingly "only the name of the heroine is changed" (Harrison 1988: 61). Viewed from a broader perspective, the dislocations suffered by Rhys's characters are caused by deep, complex social and historical factors, such as industrialization, increasingly large-scale wars and globalized colonization that has gone rampant. The rootlessness of Julia, Marya and Sasha reflects the phenomenon of polarization which is part of the capitalist industrialization, whereas

Anna and Antoinette are simply wrenched from their Caribbean homes, which refracts the sufferings wrought by globalized colonization. Rhys aptly responds to such sociohistorical phenomena as a modernist writer, for "modernism ... is said to represent dislocations caused by intense industrialization, world war, collapsing or changing belief systems and the enormous impact of globalized colonization" (Savory 2009: 14). Rhys's fiction sheds light on such a turbulent world by depicting her characters as outsiders. Indeed, "Rhys's great theme in her fiction is the outsider", which has to do with "modernism developed in Europe" (Savory 2009: 116).

It should be further pointed out that the term *modernism* has a wide range of implications and is capable of several levels of interpretation. Frost's focus on modernism's reconceptualization of pleasure is quite legitimate, but her approach would have been more holistic if she had taken into account communal pleasure. A related problem is that she mentions "conventional pleasure" in the same breath with "the dumb happiness of beasts" while discussing the "hallmarks of modernism": "Conventional pleasure is dismissed precisely because it is too easy and seems to pander to the dumb happiness of beasts. " (Frost 2013: 20) This simplistic juxtaposition of conventional pleasure with somatic pleasure is repeated several times in Frost's book. For example, she argues that Rhys is "highly attuned to vernacular culture as the main force of conventional, bodily pleasure" (Frost 2013: 31). The problem with this juxtaposition is twofold. First, conventional pleasure is not necessarily confined to corporeal pleasure, but should also include communal or collective pleasure, because the word "conventional" really means "following what is traditional" (Hornby et al. 2010: 332) and there has been a long tradition of regarding pleasure as inherently communal ever since the forming of "a counter-strain in Enlightenment philosophy and in Wordsworth's poetry", even more so in fin de siècle British discourses of pleasure, as already discussed in the first section of the present paper. Second, Rhys's characters ARE capable of higher pleasures, although in the end they are all fallen in one way or another. However, as implied in the foregoing analysis, they would have chosen in the first place a kind of pleasure that is far beyond the dumb happiness of beasts.

To be sure, Rhys uses the metaphor of animals for all her female protagonists to a greater or less extent, but the animal images often suggest that they are at bay because of outward circumstances rather than their inborn animal desire. In *Quartet*, where references to animals are most frequent, Marya is described as "a strayed animal" (Rhys 1929: 11). A suggestive detail in the text is her response to Heidler's amorous advances: as he pushes her bedroom door open and moves towards her, she is seized with the "Fright of an animal caught in a trap" (Rhys 1929: 90). An even more suggestive detail is the depiction of Marya lying in Heidler's arms "quivering and abject" "like some unfortunate dog abasing itself before its master" (Rhys 1929: 131). Obviously, Marya's sexual relationship with Heidler does not bring her any pleasure or even what Frost calls "unpleasure", but sheer pain and fear. Admittedly, she has desire for pleasure, spiritual as well as physical, and she does have such pleasure, though briefly, which can be seen in her reflections on Stephan: "This was the only human being with whom she had ever felt safe or happy." (Rhys 1929: 134) But her happiness is soon gone after she falls into Heidler's clutches, even if she still keeps longing for pleasure:

> And her longing for joy, for any joy, for any pleasure was a mad thing in her heart. It was sharp like pain and she clenched her teeth. It was like some splendid caged animal roused and fighting to get out. (Rhys 1929: 74)

The analogy between a caged animal and Marya's longing for joy brings out in sharp relief the root-cause of Marya's sufferings — all her accesses to pleasure, communal pleasure in particular, are blocked just as an animal is caged and cornered.

The metaphor of animals is also used in all the other novels we have discussed so far. In *Good Morning, Midnight*, for example, the hungry Sasha becomes "so animal-conscious" that she compares herself to a mare fearing that unknown people around "would let gates bang on my hindquarters", thus triggering "the bright idea of drinking myself to death" (Rhys 2020: 37). In *After Leaving Mr. Mackenzie*, the animal images become more specific. We are told that Julia lives "the life of a dog" (Rhys 1931: 11), and that she doesn't have "a dog's chance" against "the combination of Mr. Mackenzie and Maitre Legros", the former having sexually exploited her whereas the latter serving as Mackenzie's lawyer (Rhys 1931: 22). In *Voyage in the Dark*, too, occurs a dog image — Anna's relationship with Walter so disgusts Vincent that he calls Walter a "dirty dog" (Rhys 1982: 86). A more sinister animal image crops up in *Wide Sargasso Sea*: on the wedding night, Antoinette tells "Rochester" about her childhood memory of how she "saw two enormous rats, as big as cats, on the sill staring at me" (Rhys 1999: 48). The metaphor of animals here is actually an innuendo to the Creole madwoman who is locked by Mr. Rochester like a caged howling animal, which Rhys has made clear in one of her own letters:

> The Creole in Charlotte Bronte's novel is a lay figure ... She's necessary to the plot, but always she shrieks, howls, laughs horribly, attacks all and sundry — *off stage*. For me (and for you I hope) she must be right on stage. She must be at least plausible with a past, the reason why Mr. Rochester treats her so abominably and feels justified, the reason why he thinks she is mad and why of course she goes mad, even the reason why she tries to set everything on fire, and eventually succeeds. (Personally, I think that one is simple. She is cold — and fire is the only warmth she knows in England.) (Rhys 1984: 156 – 157)

Antoinette feels cold indeed. But, before she moves to England, she has warmth and warming pleasure which she will willingly share with her loved ones, including black servants, and her newly-wed husband in particular. I have already shown, in the second section of the present paper, how Antoinette tries to share her pleasure, after they make love, by offering to "Rochester" "soft light kisses" and even to protect him with her own body against the cold breeze. What I have withheld is her husband's behaviour in the same intimate scene, which is narrated through his own mouth: "One afternoon the sight of a dress which she'd left lying on her bedroom floor made me breathless and savage with desire. When I was exhausted I turned away from her and slept, still without a word or a caress." (Rhys 1999: 513) From this revealing spot we can see the whole leopard, namely "Rochester", who has no love but only savage desire for Antoinette. In other words, she is misused by a man who should have provided her with security which would have enabled her to enjoy and share a happy life.

Like Antoinette, Rhys's other female protagonists are also essentially affectionate and capable of warmth, as already analyzed above, but are abominably exploited and betrayed by the men whom they either mistakenly love or would have loved. Marya is first disappointed by Stephan and then is mistreated by Heidler. Julia is successively cheated by Mr. Mackenzie, Mr. Horsfield and Mr. James, who invariably dismiss her with some money after taking advantage of her. Anna is first seduced and then jilted by Walter. And Sasha is abandoned by Enno, who cast her off unfeelingly after the death of their baby. One commonality of all these relationships is that they are corrupted in one way or another by money or what Thomas Carlyle calls the principle of "cash-payment nexus" (Carlyle 1965: 38). What makes things worst is that this cash nexus is internationalized, as reflected in Sue Thomas' analysis of *Good Morning, Midnight*, in which even music, together with Sasha, is reduced to "part of an international commercialized pleasure industry" (Thomas 2022: 98). Given such an international climate, there is really no escape, for the Rhys heroine, from becoming "commodities to be bought and hostages who must pay their way" (Harrison 1988: 63). The most typical case here is the arranged marriage between Antoinette and "Rochester" whose precondition for marrying Antoinette is "thirty thousand pounds ... paid to me without question or condition" (Rhys 1999: 41). Although Antoinette tries to build up a mutually affectionate relationship with him, he is primarily interested in financial security, since all his father's property will go to his elder brother through primogeniture. The same logic underpins Julia's relationships with MacKenzie, Horsfield and James, who all give Julia money as if that would clear their consciences.

For instance, Horsfield feels "powerful and dominant" when he has given Julia "the five hundred and one of the thousand notes" (Rhys 1931: 47). In the case of *Quartet*, the root-cause of the tragedy lies in Stephan's being a fly-by-night art dealer whose dishonesty in financial transactions not only lands him in jail but also renders Marya extremely vulnerable. A similar case is found in *Good Morning, Midnight*: the break-up of Sasha's marriage is mainly caused by the irresponsible Enno who, while in their financial difficulty, tells her that she "mustn't talk about love" (Rhys 2020: 111) and never returns to her after he finds a job and then leaves home, having made an empty promise to send money. A worse case is Anna's relationship with Walter who, treating her as a plaything purchased by money, simply dismisses her with a "cheque for £20" for her "immediate expenses" at the moment of deserting her (Rhys 1982: 58). All this shows that Rhys's female protagonists are betrayed into the hands of treacherous men who render them unable to lead a normal life, let alone a happy life which they would otherwise share with others.

In a nutshell, Rhys's downtrodden female protagonists deserve sympathy indeed, but this sympathy is not earned through their refusal to take part in collective pleasure, as Frost has claimed, but by their sufferings caused by mercenary men who take advantage of their poverty and dislocations, which reflect or refract such sociohistorical factors as intense industrialization and globalized colonization. True, they are ultimately drawn to obliteration, debasement and even self-destruction, but they do not choose such "attractions". Rather, they are compelled to deaden the hurt by what Frost sees as "unpleasure". A close analysis of Rhys's texts reveals that her characters do have capacity and potential for feelings which can by no means be categorized as easy, low, passive and corporeal pleasures. Like plants they all love, they would bloom with luxuriant foliage, given proper soil and climate. Unfortunately, however, they are deprived of wholesome soil and are left adrift in a hostile world. Each of Rhys's novels contains some moments, however brief, that throw insight into her female protagonist's genuine love for the pleasure afforded either in nature or in art whose appreciation cannot be achieved unless through taste. And they are capable of sharing such pleasure with people around, and even with strangers, which implies a sense of communal well-being and a yearning for communal feelings. Admittedly, part of Rhys's contribution to modernism is her redefinition of pleasure. Notwithstanding, an integral part of that reconceptualization is her reshaping of communal pleasure.

Funding This paper is sponsored by National Social Science Fund of China (Project Number 21ZD&274).

References

[1] Boyson R. *Wordsworth and the Enlightenment Idea of Pleasure* [M]. Cambridge: Cambridge University Press, 2012.

[2] Brewer J. *The Pleasures of the Imagination: English Culture in the Eighteenth Century* [M]. London: Routledge, 2013.

[3] Carlyle T. *Past and Present* (Riverside Editions) [M]. New York: New York University Press, 1965.

[4] Emery M L. *Jean Rhys at "World's End": Novels of Colonial and Sexual Exile* [M]. Austin: The University of Texas Press, 1990.

[5] Frost L. *The Problem with Pleasure: Modernism and Its Discontents* [M]. New York: Columbia University Press, 2013.

[6] Harrison N R. *Jean Rhys and the Novel as Women's Text* [M]. Chapel Hill: The University of North Carolina Press, 1988.

[7] Helsinger E. Rethinking *Sesame and lilies*: Authority, desire and the pleasures of reading [A] //D. E. Nord (Ed.), *John Ruskin, Sesame and Lilies with Essays by Elizabeth Helsinger, Seth Koven and Jan Marsh* [C]. New Haven: Yale University Press.

[8] Hornby A S, Turnbull J, Lea D, Parkinson D, et al. (Eds.) *Oxford Advanced Learner's Dictionary of Current English* [M]. Oxford: Oxford University Press, 2010.

[9] Lampe K. *The Birth of Hedonism: The Cyrenaic Philosophers and Pleasure as a Way of Life* [M]. Princeton: Pinceton University Press, 2015.

[10] Lopoukhine J, Regard F. & Wallart K. Introduction: Jean Rhys: Writing precariously [J]. *Women-A Cultural Review*, 2020, 31 (2): 131-137.

[11] Moran P. *Virginia Woolf, Jean Rhys, and the Aesthetics of Trauma* [M]. Palgrave Macmillan, 2007.

[12] Morris W. Making the best of it [A] // *The Collected Works of William Morris XXII* (pp. 81-118) [M]. London: Longmans Green and Company, 1915a.

[13] Morris W. The aims of art [A] // Cole GD. (ed.) *Stories in Prose, Stories in Verse, Short Poems, Lectures and Essays* [M]. London: Nonesuch Press, 1948a.

[14] Morris W. The beauty of life [A] // Cole GD. (ed.) *Stories in Prose, Stories in Verse, Short Poems, Lectures and Essays* [M]. London: Nonesuch Press, 1948b.

[15] Morris W. The lesser arts of life [A] // *The Collected Works of William Morris XXII* [M]. London: Longmans Green and Company, 1915b.

[16] Morris W. Useful work versu useless toil [A] // Cole GD. (ed.) *Stories in Prose, Stories in Verse, Short Poems, Lectures and Essays* [M]. London: Nonesuch Press, 1948c.

[17] Pater W. *Studies in the History of the Renaissance* [M]. New York: Modern Library, 1873.

[18] Rhys J. *After Leaving Mr. Mackenzie* [M]. New York: W. W. Norton & Company, 1931.

[19] Rhys J. *Good Morning* [M]. New York: W. W. Norton & Company, 2020.

[20] Rhys J. *Quartet* [M]. New York: W. W. Norton & Company, 1929.

[21] Rhys J. *The Letters of Jean Rhys*. Eds., F. Wyndham & D. Melly [M]. New York: Viking, 1984.

[22] Rhys J. *Voyage in the Dark* [M]. New York: W. W. Norton & Company, 1982.

[23] Rhys J. *Wide Sargasso Sea* [M]. New York: W. W. Norton & Company, 1999.

[24] Ruskin J. Sesame and Lilies [A] //Nord DE. (ed.) *John Ruskin, Sesame and Lilies with Essays by Elizabeth Helsinger, Seth Koven and Jan Marsh* [M]. (pp. 1 – 93). New Haven: Yale University Press, 2002.

[25] Ruskin J. *The Pleasures of England* [M]. Exetes: Dodo Press, 1988.

[26] Savory E. *Cambridge Introduction to Jean Rhys* [M]. Cambridge: Cambridge University Press, 2009.

[27] Savory E. Jean Rhys's environmental language: Oppositions, dialogues and silences [A] //Johnson E L. & Moran P (Eds.). *Jean Rhys: Twenty-first-century Approaches* (pp. 85 – 106) [M]. Edinburgh: Edinburgh University Press, 2015.

[28] Thomas S. *Jean Rhys's Modernist Bearings and Experimental Aesthetics* [M]. London: Bloomesbury Academic, 2022.

[29] Trilling L. *The Moral Obligation to Be Intelligent: Selected Essays* [M]. New York: Farrar, Straus. and Giroux, 2000.

[30] Wordsworth W. Preface to *Lyrical Ballads* [A] //In Richter D. H. (ed.) *The Critical Tradition: Classic Texts and Contemporary Trends* [M]. Boston, New York: Bedford/St. Martin's, 2007a.

[31] Wordsworth W. *The Excursion* [M]. Ithaca: Cornell University Press, 2007b.

(本文原载于 Neohelicon, Vol. 51, No. 1, 2024)

The Meaning of Community under the Pen of Wordsworth

I

The meaning of "community" in William Wordsworth's poems deserves further exploration. Recent studies have shown an increasing interest in Wordsworth's thoughts and feelings regarding community. Of all the ongoing debates, the most interesting is the one between Lucy Newlyn and Simon J. White. In an article whose subtitle is "Community in *The Prelude*", Newlyn argues that in writing *The Prelude* Wordsworth's "aim was nothing less than to show how the foundations of a benevolent society might be laid using 'the growth of the poet's mind' as the starting point. Self, as he understood it, was best seen in terms of its responsibilities to community" (Newlyn 2003: 59). This view is challenged by White who, on the one hand, acknowledges that "the poem is about the role of community in the development of the individual" and, on the other hand, insists that Wordsworth's sense of community can only be found in "suppressed interstices of the narrative" (White 2013: 59), or "tempered by the suppressed accounts" (White 2013: 66). "In general," White proceeds to argue, "representations of work and the working community are absent from *The Prelude*. Instead the speaker employs suggestive rustic imagery in the quasi-philosophical response to the working countryside. In so doing he satisfies the expectations of a polite reading audience conditioned by the absence of close-up images of work from eighteenth-century pastoral and *Georgic* poetry" (White 2013: 64).

White further claims that, by the time Wordsworth had completed *The Excursion*, his thoughts had undergone a fundamental change and "he had become less concerned with individual human agency ... and more concerned with local social structures ... and rather than condemn 'those responsible' for human suffering, he asks what makes for properly functioning human communities that are mutually supportive and self-sustaining" (White 2013: 67). In other words, "Wordsworth's poetics had moved on from one rooted in the representation of heroic individuals to one that acknowledged the importance of connections between people" (White 2013: 79). Both White and Newlyn have made a praiseworthy contribution to shedding light on a sense of community in Wordsworth's poems, but their views are both biased in their respective ways: Newlyn has laid an exclusive emphasis on the role of the individual in a community, whereas White has put the notion of individual in antithesis with that of community, thus losing sight of their dialectical relationship. Wordsworth's views on community are, in fact, multidimensional and developed from different perspectives. We must therefore approach the issues concerned by examining them in a broader context.

One framework in which we can benefit by examining Wordsworth's "communitarian" poetics is the ongoing theoretical debate between modern communitarian thinkers, like Raymond Williams and Alasdair MacIntyre, and such liberal theorists as Stephen Holmes. As Valerie Wainwright has aptly summarized, communitarian thinkers firmly believe that "the community model provides its members not only with essential life goods (security, solidarity, fraternity) but also ... with a robust sense of personal identity, with a 'thick' self that is firmly rooted in his or her environment and capable of affection and empathy", whereas "liberals translate 'embeddedness' into restriction and restraint and find that the liberal goals of personal freedom and individuality are ditched in the cause of belonging" (Wainwright 2007: 110). Holmes's interpretation of "embeddedness" can be traced to Martin Heidegger, who has developed "a set of formulations that sum up the distinction ... between being in a community, that is, lost in the 'they', and detaching oneself from the community for the sake of becoming what one already secretly potentially is, that is, authentic *Dasein*" (Miller 2015: 13). Is it true, then, that being in a community will inevitably lead to the loss of one's authentic Dasein? Or, in Holmes's terms, the loss of personal freedom and individuality? A close-up look at Wordsworth's poems will help throw insight into the intricate, and yet dialectical, relationship between the individual and community.

In order to have an adequate understanding of Wordsworth's thoughts on community, we must start with the basic meaning of the concept of community. A definition of community will therefore be my next starting point.

II

Any history of community studies would be impoverished by the absence of Ferdinand Tönnies, whose classic definition of "community" (gemeinschaft) is developed in opposition to the meaning of "society" (gesellschaft): "Community means genuine, enduring life together, whereas Society is a transient and superficial thing. Thus Gemeinschaft must be understood as a living organism in its own right, while Gesellschaft is a mechanical aggregate and artefact." (Tönnies 2001: 19) This definition dovetails with Wordsworth's views on community.

Wordsworth lived in an age that witnessed the disintegration, under the impact of unprecedented industrialization, of traditional rural communities. Such a situation bears close resemblance to what Matthew Arnold describes, with reference to the social transition in which he found himself, as "wandering between two worlds, one dead, / the other powerless to be born" (Arnold 1965: 288). The new communities in Wordsworth's time were too powerless to be born. The spiritual vacuum created by such social transition naturally compels thoughts on how a new world/community should be built, and it gives rise to a great anxiety that finds expression in *The Prelude*:

> If these thoughts
> Be a gratuitous emblazonry
> That does mock this recreant age, at least
> Let Folly and False-seeming, we might say,
> Be free to affect whatever formal gait
> Of moral or scholastic discipline
> Let them parade, among the Schools, at will;
> But spare the House of God. Was ever known
> The witless Shepherd who would drive his Flock
> With serious repetition to a pool
> Of which 'tis plain to sight they never taste? (Wordsworth 1969: 45)

Implied in these lines is a mockery on rationalism and mechanism, which pervaded British society at that time, and the thrust of criticism is toward such Enlightenment thinkers as William Godwin. Wordsworth was once one of Godwin's followers, having been inspired by the social vision in *An Enquiry Concerning Political Justice*.

With time, however, Wordsworth discovered that society as envisaged by Godwin was one dominated by mechanistic principles, namely what Tönnies would call "a mechanical aggregate". This aspect of Wordsworth's thinking should be given priority when we study his views on community. As a matter of fact, Wordsworth makes numerous challenges to mechanism, a typical example of which can be found in "The Tables Turned": "Our meddling intellect/Mis-shapes the beauteous forms of things: —/We murder to dissect." (Wordsworth 1986: 151) Similar thoughts are also expressed in *The Prelude*, in which Wordsworth describes how he himself had once been "a bigot to a new idolatry", namely to Godwin's mechanical theories:

> Thus strangely did I war against myself;
> A Bigot to a new Idolatry ...
> And, as by simple waving of a wand
> The wizard instantaneously dissolves
> Palace or grove, even so could I unsoul
> As readily by syllogistic words
> Some charm of Logic, ever within reach,
> Those mysteries of passion which have made,
> And shall continue evermore to make,
> (In spite of all that Reason has perform'd
> And shall perform to exalt and to refine)
> One brotherhood of all the whole human race. (Wordsworth 1969: 208)

Here "one brotherhood of all the whole human race" is obviously a vision of community, with which both "syllogistic words" that "unsoul ... mysteries of passion" and the "meddling intellect" that "mis-shapes the beauteous forms of things" are completely out of tune. In other words, Wordsworth was already aware, while envisaging the future of humanity, that community building should start with abolishing the idolatry of instrumental reason and mechanism.

Wordsworth's thoughts on community, regarding how to abolish this idolatry, touch upon various aspects and layers. In addition to the role of the individual in a community and the role of local social structures, which Newlyn and White have respectively pinpointed, Wordsworth's views take into account such factors as the bonds of a community, shared faiths and creeds, the interaction and dialectical relationship between the individual and society, interpersonal communication (including that between the living, the dead, and the unborn), the communication between humans and Nature, etc. His descriptions of those factors may or may not involve direct use of the word "communication", but they all point to what he regards as prerequisites for the depth of communication. For instance, communal beliefs constitute a basis for communication. What I would like to emphasize is that all the types of communication under Wordsworth's consideration have one common element, namely, feeling — not merely personal feeling but the structure of feeling, pervading a whole society — which is exactly what we find lacking in rationalist and mechanistic thought. Although Wordsworth never uses the term "the structure of feeling", his views coincide with those of Williams, who invented the term: by the structure of feeling Williams means "the deep community" that makes "communication possible" (Williams 1961: 65). What concerns Wordsworth in his imagined communities is exactly how to make this communication possible, so his ideal community is nothing short of a deep community.

That is to say, Wordsworth attaches great importance to the depth of communication in his pursuit of the depth of community. In order to guarantee such a depth, he would not confine himself to a narrow concept of communication. Instead he takes into consideration the cornerstone of communication — such as the cultivation of the mind when advocating for interpersonal communication, for example. The cultivation of the mind, as we know, presupposes the scenes where an individual thinks things out for him/herself, especially the scenes where he/she can draw nourishment, inspiration, and intimations from Nature. This is where Wordsworth often gets misinterpreted and comes under fire — such as from White who, as mentioned above, has blamed him for indulging for a period of time "in the representation of heroic individuals". Another example can be found in the critique from Timothy Clark, who accuses *The Prelude* of "promulgating an individual ethos of continuous self-development" (Clark 1997: 94).

These accusations are grounded in the fact that Wordsworth has devoted a lot of space in *The Prelude* to the passages in which the poet-speaker thinks and moves all by himself: those of his communing with Nature in particular. But are these accusations fair? Does solitude necessarily mean singularity or, in Heidegger's terms, "detaching oneself from the community"? If we take an all-inclusive view of *The Prelude*, we will find a large amount of evidence pointing to the fact that Wordsworth was far from indulging in representing heroic individuals who seek to escape from communitarian life. The following lines from *The Prelude* merit our attention and suggest what an ideal university should be:

> A habitation sober and demure
> For ruminating creatures; a domain
> For quiet things to wander in; a haunt
> In which the Heron might delight to feed
> By the shy rivers, and the Pelican
> Upon the cypress spire in lonely thought
> Might sit and sun himself. (Wordsworth 1969: 46)

It is true that such expressions as "ruminating creatures", "a domain for quiet things to wander in", and "in lonely thought" suggest solitude. However, it is erroneous to mention solitude and singularity in the same breath. On many occasions, the image of a "solitary" under the pen of Wordsworth does not signify severing ties and communications with others. In the case of *The Prelude*, the poet-speaker often appears to be a solitary figure, but he actually opts for solitude not for its own sake. Rather, his solitude is for the sake of getting on more harmoniously with others.

I make my argument above on the strength of two observations.

First, what the poet-speaker thinks about, though in solitude, mostly has to do with the common destiny of mankind. When he is in school, he is found pondering alone over the ways in which a human being, even from early childhood, can become "an inmate of this active universe" (Wordsworth 1969: 27). He has also described Coleridge as, starting from their youth, "In many things my brother", "For thou hast sought/The truth in solitude" (Wordsworth 1969: 33). During summer vacations (in book 4), we find him often wandering alone in "rural solitude", just as we find him in "The Daffodils", but

> A freshness also found I at this time

> In human Life, the life I mean of those
> Whose occupations really I lov'd.
> The prospect often touch'd me with surprize,
> Crowded and full, and Chang'd, as seem'd to me,
> Even as a garden in the heat of Spring,
> After an eight-days' absence. For (to omit
> The things which were the same and yet appear'd
> So different) amid this solitude,
> The little Vale where was my chief abode ... (Wordsworth 1969: 58)

Here the community sentiments, as couched in "whose occupations really I loved", stand vividly revealed on the paper. In book 12 the poet-speaker is found in self-reflection:

> Such meditations bred an anxious wish
> To ascertain how much of real worth
> And genuine knowledge, and true power of mind
> Did at this day exist in those who liv'd
> By bodily labour, labour far exceeding
> Their due proportion, under all the weight
> Of that injustice which upon ourselves
> By composition entail. To frame such estimate
> I chiefly look'd (what need to look beyond?)
> Among the natural abodes of men,
> Fields with their rural works ...
> And tumult of the world's to me could yield,
> How far soe'er transported and possessed,
> Full measure of content; but still I craved
> An intermingling of distinct regards

And truths of individual sympathy

Nearer ourselves... (Wordsworth 1969: 220 – 221)

While interpreting these poetic lines, critics tend to focus on the debate between Wordsworth and Godwin. Godwin holds that rural laborers are deficient in virtue because they are deficient in learning, which is the basis of virtue, whereas Wordsworth sees in rural laborers mental power and genuine virtue. I would like to add that Wordsworth here voices his deep concern for the depth of community, for these lines touch upon such issues as the social basis of community, the main community members the rest should rely on, and the community ethics that are significantly represented by ordinary, rural laborers who are hardworking and of a piece with Nature. Equally significant in the lines above is the emphasis on "truths of individual sympathy nearer ourselves", which later on finds an echo in George Eliot's views on sympathy (it is well-known that Wordsworth had a tremendous influence on Eliot). Gao Xiaolin has given an apt exposition of Eliot's concept of sympathy: "Sympathy can sometimes be understood as fellow-feeling with an emphasis on communal emotional experiences, thus differentiating itself from condescending pity ... Sympathy lays emphasis on the experience of a subject who identifies his own feeling with those of others, or on the exchange of feelings between one subject and another. This kind of sympathy often shows a greater power of social cohesion than cool intellect, and is therefore an important bond of social harmony." (Gao 2008: 11) Such a comment also applies to Wordsworth.

Second, the poet-speaker in *The Prelude* often rests himself, only to receive intimations and inspirations regarding the true meanings of community. In book 1 he emphasizes that "Fair seed-time had my soul, and I grew up/Foster'd alike by beauty and by fear." (Wordsworth 1969: 9) The significance of these lines goes beyond the cultivation of an individual soul, for community building is unthinkable without the cultivation of the individual mind. Since the shaping of a community should begin, as mentioned above, with abolishing the idolatry of instrumental reason and mechanism, the poet-speaker needs to turn to Nature from time to time, for that is where he can draw inspiration as to the ways in which such idolatry can be abolished. Here is an example of what he "sought" from Nature:

> I hasten on to tell
> How Nature, intervenient till this time,
> And secondary, now at length was sought
> For her own sake. But who shall parcel out
> His intellect by geometric rules,
> Split, like a province, into round and square?
> Who knows the individual hour in which
> His habits were first sown, even as a seed?
> Who that shall point, as with a wand, and say,
> This portion of the river of my mind
> Came from yon fountain? (Wordsworth 1969: 25 – 26)

Similar examples abound. In books 6 and 13, for instance, there is no lack of "episodes that defeat rational control — moments of surprise, shock, accident, chance, and mischance" (Wolfson 1984: 922). In opposition to rationalist modes of thinking, the poet-speaker is well versed in living Nature:

> My inner knowledge,
> (This barely will I note) was oft in depth
> And delicacy like another mind
> ... for being vers'd
> In living Nature, I had there a guide
> Which open'd frequently my eyes, else shut,
> A standard, which was usefully applied,
> Even when unconsciously, to things

Which less I understood ... (Wordsworth 1969: 88)

This sort of aesthetic pursuit is foregrounded in books 11 and 13, which are both entitled "Imagination and Taste, How Impaired and Restored." What restores imagination and taste is Nature, as realized by the poet-speaker:

> [Nature]... early tutored me
> To look with feelings of fraternal love
> Upon the unassuming things, that hold
> A silent station in this beauteous world.
> Thus moderated, thus composed, I found
> Once more in Man an object of delight,
> Of pure imagination, and of love ... (Wordsworth 1969: 219)

One cannot but read into these lines a strong sense of community. In the same book the poet-speaker makes it clear that Nature has helped him see

> With settling judgments now of what would last,
> And what would disappear, prepared to find
> Ambition, folly, madness, in the men
> Who thrust themselves upon the passive world
> As Rulers of the world, to see in these,
> Even when the public welfare is their aim,
> Plans without thought, or bottom'd on false thought
> And false philosophy: having brought to test
> Of solid life and true result the Books
> Of modern Statists, and thereby perceiv'd
> The utter hollowness of what we name
> "The Wealth of Nations." (Wordsworth 1969: 220)

Here "the public welfare", "solid life", and "the wealth of nations" all indicate a solicitude for community. More important in these lines is "the utter hollowness of what we name/ 'The Wealth of Nations' ", which obviously refers to Adam Smith's *The Wealth of Nations*. Wordsworth's satirical description of Smith's theories as "Plans without thought, or bottom'd on false thought", and even "madness", is consistent with his criticism of rationalist/mechanical modes of thinking as represented by Godwin. Such a criticism on one hand is based on taste, imaginative and aesthetic criteria drawn from Nature, and, on the other hand, is impregnated with a deep concern for community life.

The above analysis shows that Wordsworth, in his thoughts on community, views the individual and society as two inseparable concepts. He in fact anticipates Williams, whose well-known cultural theory is built upon the following dialectical way of thinking: "In the case of the individual and society we need to learn ways of thinking and feeling which will enable us genuinely to know each in the other's terms." (Wordsworth 1869: 118) In other words, those who wrongly accuse Wordsworth of promulgating individualism have lost sight of the fact that he has a deep understanding of the dialectical relationship between the individual and society, and of the truth that there can be no depth of community without a deep inquiry into the individual.

III

The depth of a community can also be measured by its members' attitudes toward strangers. A community would have no depth whatsoever if strangers could not find a foothold or feel rebuffed by it. One important aspect of Wordsworth's thoughts on community is the way he thinks strangers should be treated. Jon Mee has pointed out that the encounter with strangers is Wordsworth's favorite subject. "In the Wordsworthian encounter poem", he argues, "there is often dialogue in formal terms, at least two speakers are often represented in the text, but mutual comprehension is rarely its outcome. Interiorities resist disclosure" (Mee 2011: 192). Mee's remarks are in fact an echo of a conclusion made by David Bromwich, who claims that Wordsworth's poems contain an overwhelming implication that "the motives of every moral agent are special to that agent, and we can never enter into them sufficiently to judge them" (Bromwich 1998: 65). If this were true, the community under the pen of Wordsworth would be deficient in depth, for the "dialogue" that seldom leads to mutual comprehension is no in-depth communication and therefore cannot lead to a deep community.

What is mystifying in Mee's above-mentioned studies is the conspicuous absence of *The Prelude*, which contains no lack of in-depth communication, especially among strangers, even though it is often criticized for its so-called "individual heroism". Moreover, throughout the poem, wherever communication is found lacking, there is an implication of criticism and an indication of wishes for wholesome communication. In book 7, for instance, the criticism is spearheaded against the phenomenon of alienation during the poet-speaker's residence in London: "... one thought/Baffled my understanding, how men lived/Even next-door neighbours, as we say, yet still/Strangers, and knowing not each the other's names" (Wordsworth 1969: 108). In contrast to such alienation, many episodes or scenes are symbolic of in-depth communication and a vision of the deep community. In book 2 the poet-speaker addresses his aspirations to Coleridge:

> Thou, my Friend! wert reared
> In the great City, 'mid far other scenes;
> But we, by different roads at length have gained
> The selfsame bourne. And for this cause to Thee
> I speak, unapprehensive of contempt,
> The insinuated scoff of coward tongues,
> And all that silent language which so oft
> In conversation betwixt man and man
> Blots from the human countenance all trace

Of beauty and of love ... (Wordsworth 1969: 33)

Obviously, the "conversation betwixt man and man", which is indicative "of beauty and of love" and which has "gained the selfsame bourne" "by different roads", is an in-depth sort of communication. A more specific episode with the same message is in book 4, where the poet-speaker has a chance encounter with a veteran soldier/traveler who is held up by illness. Their initial conversation is marked by "a strange half-absence" on the part of the veteran, but the ice is broken after the poet-speaker helps him find a cottage where he can rest:

> Assur'd that now my comrade would repose
> In comfort, I entreated that henceforth
> He would not linger in the public ways
> But ask for timely furtherance and help
> Such as his state required. At this reproof,
> With the same ghastly mildness in his look,
> He said, "My trust is in the God of Heaven,
> And in the eye of him that passes me!" (Wordsworth 1969: 66)

Such words as "trust" and "mildness in his look" (with "ghastly" meaning "ethereal") make it clear that the stranger is now no longer strange and that estrangement can be overcome by in-depth communication.

In book 9 the poet-speaker has another encounter with a stranger, an officer "With harder fate, /Though like ambition"; "many a long discourse, /With like persuasion honour'd we maintained" (Wordsworth 1969: 162). Their long and many conversations touch upon some "dearest themes," and they both have the ambition of "making social life, /Through knowledge spreading and imperishable, /As just in regulation, and as pure/As individual in the wise and good" (Wordsworth 1969: 161). It is not hard to perceive in such conversations a deep concern for the depth of community. Almost half of book 9 is devoted to their conversations which, moreover, unfold progressive thoughts and feelings regarding community. The following lines are but one of the many examples:

> We summon'd up the honourable deeds
> Of ancient Story...
> And how the multitudes of men will feed
> And fan each other...
> How quickly mighty Nations have been form'd
> From least beginnings; how, together lock'd
> By new opinions, scatter'd tribes have made
> One body spreading wide as clouds in heaven...
> To ruminate with interchange of talk
> On rational liberty, and hope in man,
> Justice and peace... (Wordsworth 1969: 161 – 162)

In these lines the solicitude for community transcends territory and nationhood, thus attaining the realm of great harmony of mankind as a whole. What is particularly worthy of attention here is how "scatter'd tribes" can be "together lock'd by new opinions", which raises the issue of the roots of communal identity. Over the past three centuries in the history of Britain, debate has occurred, on and off, as to whether a community has to be rooted in a particular place or in a particular world-view. White sees Robert Burns as a representative of "the world-view camp", for "he does represent a cohesive world-view that transcends place and social or class distinctions", and "his poetry represents a commonalty and mutuality rooted in a very particular world-view" (White 2013: 152, 177).

In my view Wordsworth is a more typical and more sophisticated representative of those who would like a community to strike its roots in a worldview, namely what he calls "new opinions". More important, Wordsworth's poetry raises the questions of whether and how a stranger can identify himself with a community, or how each community member should treat a stranger. The cohesiveness of a community depends on how each of its members imagines their own community including strangers therein, simply "because the members of even the smallest nation will never know most of their fellow-members, meet them, or even hear of them, yet in the minds of each lives the image of their communion" (Anderson 1991: 6). In other words, for each member of a community, most of his/her fellow members are actually strangers. Is there any way, then, in which strangers can be integrated into a cohesive force? A brilliant answer is given by such Wordsworthian lines as "together lock'd/By new opinions."

As a matter of fact, scenes of encounter and communication with strangers are numerous in *The Prelude*. In book 13, for instance, the poet-speaker gives an account of his "dear delight" in conversing with rural laborers whom he has never met before but speaks of as if he were meeting friends:

> Oh! next to such enjoyment of our youth,
> In my esteem, next to such dear delight,
> Was that of wandering on from day to day
> Where I could meditate in peace, and find
> The knowledge which I love, and teach the sound
> Of Poet's music to strange fields and groves,
> Converse with men, where if we meet a face
> We almost meet a friend, on naked Moors
> With long, long ways before, by Cottage Bench,
> Or Well-spring where the weary traveller rests. (Wordsworth 1969: 221 – 222)

The scene in which one can "Converse with men, where if we meet a face/We almost meet a friend" is little short of a hallmark of the deep community. What is more thought-provoking here is the consistency between the poet-speaker's seemingly solitary "wandering on from day to day" and the actual realm of the deep community he has attained. The poet "could meditate in peace, and find/The knowledge which I love, and teach the sound/Of Poet's music to strange fields and groves", which indicates that he is an integral part of Nature. Only in an organically developed community, which is in the meantime in perfect harmony with Nature, can one meet a stranger as if he/she were meeting a friend. These implied meanings have unfortunately been overlooked by people like White and Mee.

I offer one more example of the extent to which, in Wordsworth's eyes, strangers should communicate with each other:

> ... When I began to enquire,
> To watch and question those I met, and held
> Familiar talk with them, the lonely roads
> Were schools to me in which I daily read
> With most delight the passions of mankind,
> There saw into the depth of human souls,
> Souls that appear to have no depth at all
> To vulgar eyes ... (Wordsworth 1969: 222)

Here "familiar talk", "daily read ... the passions of mankind" and "saw into the depth of human souls" all point to the depth of communication. In such a deep community, the phenomenon of interiorities resisting disclosure, as Mee claims, can only last temporarily even if it does exist.

In contrast to the scenes analyzed above, some episodes in *The Prelude* are of a completely different kind, such as the social occasions that the poet-speaker experiences at Cambridge: "Our eyes are cross'd by Butterflies, our ears/Hear chattering popinjays; the inner heart/Is trivial, and the impresses without/Are of a gaudy region." (Wordsworth 1969: 46) What is depicted here forms part of the poet-speaker's self-reflection — part of his university life is spent in "unprofitable talk":

"We saunter'd, play'd, or riot'd; we talk'd/Unprofitable talk at morning hours." (Wordsworth 1969: 41) This sort of talk is unprofitable, the poet-speaker realizes in his reflections, because it does not aim at "seeking those who might participate/My deeper pleasures..." (Wordsworth 1969: 40). By offsetting scenes of encounter with strangers that involve the depth of communication against unprofitable talk, Wordsworth drives home the message that shared values will lead to in-depth communication even among strangers, whereas acquaintances will feel estranged from each other if they share no beliefs and ideals.

By "strangers" Wordsworth also means those who are dead. Many of his poems give prominence to images of graveyards and funeral processions, as in the second book of *The Excursion*: The poet-speaker and the Wanderer, while traveling together, come across a funeral procession and are deeply touched by the mourners' dirge: "Shall in the grave thy love be known." (Wordsworth 1850: 63) To the poet-speaker and the Wanderer the one lying in the coffin is surely a stranger, but a bond is forged between them by the words of the dirge, which gives expression to Wordsworth's ideal that a true community should include those who have passed away, no matter how long ago they died. While watching the mourners lift the corpse and move it toward its final home on earth, the Wanderer is seized with an impulse and blurts out: "What traveller — who —/ (How far soe'er a *stranger*) does not own/The bond of brotherhood, when he sees them go ... ?" (Wordsworth 1850: 63, 69; emphasis added).

A strong sense of community is here revealed in the bond of brotherhood that brings together the living and the dead. A more thought-provoking example is found in a dialogue between the Wanderer and the Solitary. The Wanderer, seeing the graves in a churchyard, describes the dead as "blest": "Oh! blest are they who live and die like these, /Loved with such love, and with such sorrow mourned!" The Solitary, however, replies "with a faint sarcastic smile": "That poor Man taken hence today ... must be deemed, I fear, /Of the unblest...." The poet-speaker, who is also present, makes it clear that the Solitary's reply "did not please me" (*EP*, p. 70). In the whole dialogue is couched Wordsworth's own critique of the views represented by the Solitary. To Wordsworth, in other words, the dead constitute an indispensable part of a family and a society/community. Of all his poems that give expression to the same thoughts, "We Are Seven" is perhaps the most touching one. The poem revolves around a dialogue between the poet-speaker and a little cottage girl, who insists that her family still contains seven children despite the fact that two of them, John and Jane, have passed away:

"How many of you, then", said I,
"If they two are in heaven?"
Quick was the little Maid's reply,
"O Master! We are seven."

"But they are dead; those two are dead!
Their spirits are in heaven!"
'Twas throwing words away; for still
The little Maid would have her will,
And said, "Nay, we are seven!" (Wordsworth 1986: 148)

This is indeed a deeply touching dialogue, which, in addition to conveying the little maid's genuine love for her siblings, drives home a message that enables the poet-speaker to undergo an emotional transformation. Although Jane and John are out-and-out strangers to the poet-speaker, a bond is forged between him and the two dead children under the impact of the little maid's spontaneous overflow of feelings. Furthermore, he develops a new cognition of and affection for the deceased, whom he has never met. Between such lines as "Quick was the little Maid's reply", "'Twas throwing words away" and "The little Maid would have her will" we can read into the poet-speaker's admiration for, appreciation of, and identification with the little cottage girl, and his culturally significant reflections on the implications of a deep community.

Reading Wordsworth's poems is reminiscent of T. S. Eliot, who forges a direct link between the fate of a community and the attitude toward strangers, including the deceased. In his *Notes Towards the Definition of Culture*, Eliot queries the notion of the family that consists of merely living members and of no more than three generations. Against such a concept, then prevalent among his contemporaries, Eliot develops his own definition of the family in line with his thoughts on culture, of which the idea of the community is an integral part: "When I speak of the family, I have in mind a bond which embraces a longer period of time than this: a piety towards the dead, however obscure, and a solicitude for the unborn, however remote. Unless this reverence for past and future is cultivated in the home, it can never be more than a verbal convention in the community. " (Elliot 1948: 44) What deserves our particular attention here is the direct use of the word "community" and the direct link between the fate of a community and its attitudes toward strangers, inclusive of its deceased members. I point out here that Wordsworth anticipated Eliot by over one hundred years and that their thoughts, though similar, were rendered more poetic under the pen of Wordsworth.

In a nutshell, Wordsworth's poems envision and often dramatize the practice of "community" values that have significant implications for the current debate over the following theoretical issues: What is the meaning or nature of community? Is there such a thing as a genuine community? Can the ideal of communitarian life be realized at all? If yes, in what ways? Does the pursuit of community life necessarily lead to the loss of personal freedom and individuality? Or, on the other hand, does solitude necessarily mean singularity? If not, what is the proper relationship between the individual and community? My analysis in the foregoing passages shows that Wordsworth's poems prove to be rich resources into which we can tap while dealing with the issues above.

More specifically, at least three basic features of Wordsworth's theoretical assumptions about community emerge in his poems. One is the assumption that humanity can fulfill its dreams of an ideal community and that the ideal model is none other than what Williams would call "the deep community", which presupposes shared faiths and creeds and, above all, the "truths of individual sympathy nearer ourselves" that bear great resemblance to what Williams would describe as "the structure of feeling".

The second assumption, which is fundamental to Wordsworth's thinking about community, is that great importance should be attached to the depth of communication in humanity's pursuit of the depth of community. In order to guarantee such a depth, he lays emphasis on the cultivation of the mind, which he looks upon as the cornerstone of communication. A key to the successful cultivation of the mind, to Wordsworth, lies in communing with Nature, which eventually inspires an individual in such a way as to achieve deep and successful interpersonal communication.

Last but not least, Wordsworth's vision of an ideal community is, by and large, determined by his assumption about the dialectical relationship between the individual and community. For him, individuality and community need not be contradictory, one being inseparable from the other and vice versa. In his imagined communities, each member has a strong sense of belonging and a robust sense of personal identity and, on the other hand, the community model is made possible and forever enriched by various individuals whose minds are cultivated, hence capable of love and empathy. Even strangers can find a firm foothold in Wordsworth's community where, contrary to the theoretical claims made by Mee and Heidegger, interiorities need not resist disclosure and where the authentic Dasein need not get lost in the "they". Furthermore, Wordsworth's notion of strangers includes the deceased members of a community, which not only anticipates Eliot but also has far-reaching theoretical implications for many community-building generations to come.

References

[1] Anderson B. *Imagined Communities: Reflections on the Origin and Spread of Nationalism* [M]. London: Verso, 1991: 6.

[2] Arnold. Stanzas from the Grande Chartreuse [A] //Allott K. (ed.) *The Poems of Matthew Arnold*. London: Longmans, 1965: 288.

[3] Bromwich D. *Disowned by Memory: Wordsworth's Poetry of the 1790s* [M].

Chicago: University of Chicago Press, 1998: 65.

[4] Clark T. *The Theory of Inspiration: Composition as a Crisis of Subjectivity in Romantic and Post-Romantic Writing* [M]. Manchester: Manchester University Press, 1997: 94.

[5] Eliot T S. *Notes Towards the Definition of Culture* [M]. Croydon: Faber and Faber, 1948: 44.

[6] Gao X L. Sensibility Is Knowledge! — The Cognitive Role of 'Sensibility' in George Eliot's Works [J]. Foreign Literature Review, 2008 (3): 11.

[7] Mee J. *Conversable Worlds: Literature, Contention, and Community, 1762 to 1830* [M]. Oxford: Oxford University Press, 2011: 192.

[8] Miller J H. *Communities in Fiction* [M]. New York: Fordham University Press, 2015: 13.

[9] Newlyn L. 'The Noble Living and the Noble Dead': Community in *The Prelude* [A] //Gill S. (ed). *The Cambridge Companion to Wordsworth* [C]. Cambridge: Cambridge University Press, 2003: 59.

[10] Tönnies F. *Community and Civil Society* [M]. Harris J, Hollis M (trans.) Cambridge: Cambridge University Press, 2001: 19.

[11] Wainwright V. *Ethics and the English Novel from Austen to Forster* [M]. Aldershot: Ashgate Publishing Ltd., 2007: 110.

[12] White S J. *Romanticism and the Rural Community* [M]. Hampshire: Palgrave Macmillan, 2013: 59.

[13] Williams R. *The Long Revolution* [M]. Harmondsworth: Penguin Books, 1961: 65.

[14] Wolfson S. The illusion of mastery: Wordsworth's revisions of 'the drowned man of Esthwaite,' 1799, 1805, 1850 [J]. PMLA, 1984, 99 (5): 922.

[15] Wordsworth W. *The Complete Poetical Works of William Wordsworth* [M]. London: Edward Moxon, Son and Co., 1869: 118.

[16] Wordsworth W. *The Excursion: A Poem* [M]. New York: C. S. Francis and Co., 1850: 63.

[17] Wordsworth W. *The Prelude or Growth of a Poet's Mind*, ed. Ernest de Selincourt [M]. London: Oxford University Press, 1969: 45.

[18] Wordsworth W. The Tables Turned [A] //Abrams M (ed.) *The Norton Anthology of English Literature*, vol. 2 [M]. New York: W. W. Norton and Co., 1986: 151.

[19] Wordsworth W. We Are Seven [A] //Abrams (ed.) *The Norton Anthology of English Literature* [M]. New York: W. W. Norton & Company, 1986: 148.

(本文原载于 Philosophy and Literature, Vol. 44, No. 1, 2020)

Where Is the West-Running Brook Flowing? Robert Frost in Taoist Perspective[*]

Quite a few scholars have touched upon the affinity between Robert Frost (1874 – 1963) and Taoism. Cheng Aimin, for instance, once maintained that Frost "had been influenced, directly or indirectly, by the philosophical thinking of Lao Tzu and Zhuang Tzu" (Cheng Aiming 1996: 80). Few people, however, with the exception of Hong Qi, have taken an in-depth look at the similarities between the themes of Frost and such philosophical ideas as proposed by either Lao Tzu or Zhuang Tzu. In an article on the resemblance between the themes of Frost's poems and Zhuang Tzu's philosophical vision, Hong Qi argues that their commonality lies in "a quest for a thorough freedom", namely, freeing oneself from the bonds of nature, society and the self (Hong Qi 2004: 164 – 166). Although there is validity in Hong Qi's views, her interpretation seems a bit simplistic. She gives too much emphasis to the tendency, in both Frost's and Taoist philosophy, to *Chu Shi* (to renounce the world), and neglects the fact that this tendency is subtly balanced by a readiness for *Ru Shi* (to accept the world). It is the aim of the present paper, therefore, to analyze the way in which Robert Frost bears

---

[*] 本文由殷企平和何畅合写。

affinities to Taoism in both the aspect of *Ru Shi* and that of *Chu Shi*.

The notions of *Chu Shi* and *Ru Shi* are closely related to the key concept of Taoism, namely, the Tao. According to Lao Tzu, the Tao is a universal, irresistible and all-inclusive law which determines the motion of all the substances in the universe, and this belief is expressed in Chapter 51 of *Tao Te Ching*, in which Lao Tzu describes the Tao as the mother of everything, or the origin of all the things in the universe, for "Tao gave them birth", and "[t]he 'power' of Tao reared them, shaped them according to their kinds, perfected them, giving to each its strength" (Lao Tzu 1997: 109; 道生之；道畜之，物形成，势成之). Therefore, "of the ten thousand things there is not one that does not worship Tao and do homage to its 'power'" (Lao Tzu 1997: 109; 是以万物莫不尊道而贵德). Chapter 25 contains an interesting attempt to categorize the nameless Tao or "Way":

> There was something formless yet complete, that existed before heaven and earth [...]. Its true name we do not know; 'Way' is the by-name that we give it. Were I forced to say to what class of things it belongs I should call it Great. (Lao Tzu 1997: 53; 有物混成，先天地生. 吾不知其名，字之曰"道"，强为之名曰"大")

Interestingly, Robert Frost's poetic philosophy reveals a similar preoccupation with the nameless 'Way' which falls into the category of "by-names", as we shall see in the analysis below.

One stumbling block to a comparative study of Frost and Taoism is the difficulty of tracing the genealogy of influences. Only vague speculative thinking has hitherto been done as to how Frost came under the influence of Taoism. No solid evidence seems to have been produced which can point to the direct impact of the ancient Chinese philosophy on Frost. Is then an approach to Frost from a Taoist perspective legitimate? It is our argument that the legitimacy of such an approach is twofold. First, Robert Frost lived in an era when ancient Chinese philosophy had long been one of the shaping forces of western literatures, and there is plenty of evidence with regard to the influences of Taoist thinking on a number of western writers who have in turn influenced Frost in one way or another. It is now universally acknowledged that transcendentalists have left their imprints on Frost, who once praised Emerson's "Uriel" as the "best western poem yet" (Parini & Miller 2005: 99). Chang Yaoxin has pointed out that "Frost did write very much in the Wordsworthian tradition, and there is a good deal of Emerson in him" (Chang Yaoxin 2002: 268). Huang Zongying has also affirmed this conclusion by suggesting that "Emerson's doctrine lies behind Frost's continuous and instinctive sense of correspondences between his 'outer' and 'inner' weather" (Huang Zongying 2000: 149). And traces of Chinese culture are visible in the works of Emerson, who "copied aphorisms from Confucius in his *Journals*, [and] mentioned Confucius in his translation of selected sayings of Confucius (such as from *The Analects*) in *The Dial*" (Toming 2002: 90). Furthermore, the period of Emerson's lifetime witnessed an increasing interest in and passion towards Taoism. The first English translation of *Tao Te Ching* appeared in 1868, followed by the publication of almost a hundred versions of its kind in the West (Zhao Yiheng 2003: 315). Such an important cultural trend, for such a sensitive and erudite scholar as Emerson, could not have gone unheeded. The hypothesis seems legitimate, therefore, that Frost's similarity with Taoism emanates indirectly from the influence of transcendentalism which is synthesized from several cultural sources, the Taoist philosophy not the least among them.

Second, Frost's poems abound in details that seem inspired by those in Taoist works such as *Tao Te Ching*. Of all the striking similarities, two images are worthy of particular attention, namely, the images of "road/way" and "water." Just as these two images form part and parcel of the Taoist philosophy, so do they occupy a predominant position in Frost's poetics. The surprisingly similar ramifications centering round the images above, in both Frost's poems and Taoist works, compel close examination and legitimize a meticulous comparative study.

"West-Running Brook", with its central image of a brook which is at once water and road, offers itself as a good point of entry into this investigation. The brook, being both a metaphor and a synecdoche, is nothing short of a key to the true understanding of Frost, who preferred to call himself a "synecdochist" and once gave the following definition of poetry: "Poetry is simply made of metaphor [...]. Every poem is a new metaphor inside or it is nothing." (Frost 1995, 786) For him, metaphor is "the height of poetry, the height of all thinking, the height of all poetic thinking, that attempt to say matter in terms of spirit and spirit in terms of matter" (Cox & Lathem 1968: 41). All this is reminiscent of a saying in ancient Chinese philosophy, namely, "to set up an image to make the most of the significance" （立象以尽意）. This is no mere coincidence, and we are thus once more justified in concentrating on the meandering brook of Frost.

1. *Chu Shi*: Frost as a "Terrifying" Poet

"West-Running Brook", like many other poems, confirms Lionel Trilling's well-known claim that Frost's universe is "a terrifying one" and that Frost himself is "a terrifying poet" (Trilling 1959: 445). The "terrifying" tone begins right with the title in itself and the opening scene: the brook that Fred and his bride are contemplating runs west, contrary to the direction of "all the other country brooks" flowing "east to the ocean" (Frost 1995: 236). Throughout the poem a sense of fear and helplessness can be detected, and a seemingly sinister aspect looms large, particularly in the following lines:

> It is from that in water we were from
> Long, long before we were from any creature.
> Here we, in our impatience of the steps,
> Get back to the beginning of beginnings,
> The stream of everything that runs away.
> Some say existence like a Pirouot

> And Pirouette, forever in one place,
> Stands still and dances, but it runs away,
> It seriously, sadly, runs away
> To fill the abyss' void with emptiness.
> It flows beside us in this water brook,
> But it flows over us. It flows between us
> To separate us for a panic moment.
> It flows between us, over us, and *with* us.
> And it is time, strength, tone, light, life, and love —
> And even substance lapsing unsubstantial;
> The universal cataract of death
> That spends to nothingness — and unresisted,
> Save by some strange resistance in itself,
> [...]
> ("West-Running Brook," ll. 45 – 63)

Here the destructive power of water could not be more obvious, what with "The universal cataract of death/That spends to nothingness — and unresisted" and "existence" that "seriously, sadly, runs away/To fill the abyss' void with emptiness".

On a personal level, the brook/water provides the platform on which Fred and his bride can communicate with each other. A brook is a road on which human beings can travel. In the case of our poem, the brook implies a new road of life for a newly married couple and symbolizes a quest that would presumably result in their marital relationship growing to maturity and harmony. Unfortunately, however, their communication fails. What should be a moment of mutual understanding is revealed as the physical conjunction of two people whose thoughts are running on different tracks. The wife's thoughts are characterized by wishful thinking:

> As you and I are married to each other,

> We'll both be married to the brook. We'll build
> Our bridge across it, and the bridge shall be
> Our arm thrown over it asleep beside it.
> Look, look, it's waving to us with a wave,
> To let us know it hears us.
> ("West-Running Brook," ll. 16 – 21)

But Fred the husband sees just the opposite:

> That wave's been standing off this jut of shore
> Ever since rivers, I was going to say,
> Were made in heaven. It wasn't waved to us.
> ("West-Running Brook," ll. 32 – 34)

Whereas the wife holds on to her views, Fred remains uninfluenced and even becomes ironical:

> Oh, if you take it off to lady-land,
> As't were the country of the Amazons
> We men must see you to the confines of
> And leave you there, ourselves forbid to enter, —
> It is your brook! I have no more to say.
> ("West-Running Brook," ll. 37 – 41)

The failure of communication is obviously a sign of alienation which is made poignant by the foregrounded image of the brook, suggesting both the unruliness of water and the perils of travel on a road, be it a road of marriage or life. In a word, there is something "terrifying" here indeed.

As a matter of fact, the "terrifying" image of Frost appears time and again in many of his poems. The opening part of "Mending Wall" is another typical example:

> Something there is that doesn't love a wall,
> That sends the frozen-ground-swell under it
> And spills the upper boulders in the sun,
> And makes gaps even two can pass abreast.
> ("Mending Wall," ll. 1 – 4)

Undoubtedly this "something" refers to the fearful and formidable natural force which defies mankind's violation of its fixed rules to such an extent that it forthrightly overthrows the symbol of this intrusion, the wall, by "spilling" it with a gap as big as "two can pass abreast".

A close-up look at this "something" will reveal its similarity with the Tao in ancient Chinese philosophy since both of them emphasize the indomitable power of the natural law which governs the whole universe. Han Feizi (ca. 280 – 233 BC) explains the Tao as "the origin and the fundamental essence of the universe" ("道者，万物之所然也，万物之所稽也。……道者，万物之所以成也"),[①] which is as objective as the existing "something" in Frost's poetry. Literally speaking, the Chinese character "道" (Tao) reminds us first and foremost of the image of road, as defined in *The Related Associations* or *Shuo Wen Jie Zi* (《说文解字》): "Tao, the road one takes" (Su Baorong 2003, 72; "道，所行道也"). One of the predominant images in Frost's poetry is the road, and this road is as "irretrievable" and "irresistible" as the law in Taoism. In "Stopping by Woods on a Snowy Evening", Frost talks about the destined road we have to take even if we want to make a "death-wish" choice and to abandon the obligation of our life. Similarly, "The Road Not Taken" embodies an everlasting sigh about the "irretrievability" of the road: "I doubted if I should ever

---

[①] This definition comes from Han Feizi's analysis of Lao Tzu's philosophy in *Han Feizi* (《韩非子》). For further consultation, please refer to *Han Feizi* (《韩非子译著》) translated by Liu Qianxian (Harbin: People's Press of Hei Longjiang, 2002).

come back" ("The Road Not Taken," l. 16).

The fearfulness of the road also lies in its namelessness, shapelessness and formlessness, as suggested by something that "makes gaps even two can pass abreast" in "Mending Wall", and by a more "terrifying" something that causes "even substance lapsing unsubstantial" in "West-Running Brook". It is exactly this namelessness that many readers of Frost fail to name. Even Trilling's thought-provoking description of Frost as "terrifying" often renders the reader hopelessly aware of the indescribable terror of his nature. Here a Taoist perspective may help shed light on the significance of this nameless road or Tao. Tao, in Lao Tzu's words, is characterized by "shapeless shapes" and "forms without form", and is overwhelmingly everywhere but beyond senses of smelling, seeing and touching (Lao Tzu 1997: 29; 无状之状，无物之象). In his *Tao Te Ching*, Lao Tzu begins with the following famous lines: "The Way that can be told of is not an Unvarying Way. The names that can be named are not unvarying names" (Lao Tzu 1997: 3; "道可道，非常道；名可名，非常名"). In other words, the Eternal Way and the Eternal Name simply defy naming, just as Frost's defiant brook runs west rather than east. The west-running brook carries along all the things in this universe, either sensible or insensible. So it is "time, strength, tone, light, life and love —/And even substance lapsing unsubstantial" ("The West-Running Brook", ll. 59 - 60). It contains "death," changes itself into "unresisted" nothingness, and combines not only man and woman but also mankind and nature. In short, it "flows between us, over us, and *with* us" (*ibid.*, l. 58) as an all-inclusive law which shares similarity with the Tao. As mentioned in the beginning of the present paper, the Tao is a universal, irresistible and all-inclusive law which determines the motion of all the substances in the universe, and this all-inclusiveness steeps, in its transcendental splendour, heaven and earth alike. Rather than succumbing to human efforts to categorize it into a clear shape and definite name, the Tao has an irresistable power to shape and form everything humanly imaginable, hence "terrifying" in a way. It is this "terrifying" aspect that forges a link between Taoism and the poetic philosophy of Frost. Just as Lao Tzu can only give a by-name to his Tao, so does Robert Frost find himself wrestling and grappling with a nameless west-running brook. No matter how we name Frost's "brook" or "road" or "universal cataract of death", they are bound to be "by-names".

The call for eternal naming results from a yearning for transcending time and space. That is why critics like Hong Qi, as mentioned in the introductory part of the present paper, have found in Frost an escapist. It is true that the escapist vision is there. In the lines quoted above, we find Frost indicating a wish to "Get back to the beginning of beginnings" ("The West-Running Brook," I. 48) and contemplating "The stream of everything that runs away" (*ibid.*, I. 52). Here is undoubtedly a longing for *Chu Shi*, the desire to renounce the world and to transcend mundane affairs. Another example can be found in these lines: "Some say existence like a Pirouot/and Pirouette, forever in one place, /Stands still and dances, but it runs away, /It seriously, sadly, runs away" (*ibid.*, II. 50-52). As two ideal characters in French dumb show, Pirouot and Pirouette stand for the beautified fixed existence of life which defies any progress. All this is reminiscent of "Wu-wei" (无为), a key notion of Taoism, which means "non-action" or quietism, very much in line with the philosophy of *Chu Shi*.

2. *Ru Shi*: Frost as a Positive Poet

But does *Chu Shi* constitute the only aspect in which Robert Frost bears affinities to Taoism? In Frost's poetic philosophy, *Chu Shi* is offset by *Ru Shi*. In other words, the poet's desire to renounce the world is offset by his desire to accept the world.

By way of illustration, let us turn once more to "West-Running Brook". Although "the brook runs west", which seems to suggest a drift to nothingness ("West-Running Brook," I. 3), there exists a counter drift toward renewal — Fred in the poem has observed "contraries" and urges his bride to "see how the brook/In that white wave runs counter to itself" (*ibid.*, II. 43-44). The poem in fact abounds with contraries and contrasts. Sadly running away as it is towards the end, the brook is at the same time going back to the beginning. There is unmistakably a "throwing backward":

> It has this throwing backward on itself
> So that the fall of most of it is always
> Raising a little, sending up a little.
> Our life runs down in sending up the clock.
> The brook runs down in sending up our life.
> The sun runs down in sending up the brook.
> And there is something sending up the sun.
> It is backward motion toward the source,
> Against the stream, that most we see ourselves in,
> The tribute of the current to the source.
> It is from this in nature we are from.
> It is most us.
> ("West-Running Brook," Ⅱ. 66 – 77)

For all the "death", "nothingness", "void" and "emptiness" that we have discussed above, the brook carries with it a confident belief that "being downstream" is equivalent to "being upstream", since the whole process runs in endless circles. In this sense, the west-running brook is an integral part of all those brooks flowing east. To "fall" is actually to "raise", while to head for the west is the same as heading for the east.

All the contraries are, therefore, solved and harmonized with the west-running brook's flowing "by contraries". What is more, Frost regards the west-running brook's "backward motion toward the source" as a "tribute" of the current to the source of the water, which explicitly shows his admiring attitude towards "going back", and it cannot but remind us of Lao Tzu's appraisal of "returning" (反). In Chapter 40 of *Tao Te Ching*, Lao Tzu clearly says that "[i]n Tao the only motion is returning" (Lao Tzu 1997: 87; "反者道之动"). And Tao being "Great", as analyzed in the previous section, it "also means passing on/And passing on means going Far Away/And going far away means returning" (Lao Tzu 1997: 53; "大曰逝, 逝曰远, 远曰反"). In a way, the west-running brook could be regarded as a symbol of this returning Tao, or a unifying principle, which combines all the oppositions into a unity with its endless circulation. Apparently, both the Tao and the philosophical west-running brook stem from an objective observation regarding the law of the universe. And this objectivity might lead to the "affinity" in a certain way.

As we have already observed, all the contraries in "West-Running Brook" revolve around the central image of water which has one particularly significant property, i.e., the propensity to run down. But it runs down only to send up, as indicated in the line "The brook runs down in sending up our life" ("The West-Running Brook," I. 70). For all its perils and destructive power, which is likely to breed a desire for *Chu Shi*, the water in question is nonetheless a sign of restoration and resuscitation reaffirming the need for *Ru Shi*. A striking similarity can be found in *Tao Te Ching*, where water also flows down (and keeps "staying in the lowly place") but in the meantime symbolizes "the highest good":

> The highest good is like water
> Water benefits all things generously without striving with them.
> Staying in the lowly place that men disdain, it is close to the Tao.
> It knows to keep to the ground in choosing the dwelling.
> It knows to hide in the hidden deep in cultivating the mind.
> It knows to be gentle and kind in dealing with others.
> It knows to keep its words in speaking.
> It knows to maintain order in governing.
> It knows to be efficient in handling business.
> It knows to choose the right moment in making a move.
> Since it does not strive with others,
> It is free from blame.

(qtd. in Zhou Yi/Liang Yihua 1993: 59 - 60)

Lao Tzu's philosophy is often misunderstood as purely characterized by *Chu Shi*. In the quotation above, however, we can clearly see a paradoxical eagerness to act, to govern, to handle business and to achieve the highest good. That is to say, Taoism does not object to *Ru Shi* at all, only it prefers to "choose the right moment in making a move" and "does not strive with others".

Similarly, Frost's poetic philosophy is apt to be misinterpreted as having focused on an escapist vision which we have already seen emphasized by such critics as Hong Qi. It is true that Frost does indicate from time to time a wish for standing off and being far from the madding crowd, just as the wave of the west-running brook has been "standing off this jut of shore" ("The West-Running Brook", I. 23). Even a wish for death can be spotted every now and then. The reasons are not hard to come by. Frost lived in a period which witnessed the unchecked spreading of materialism and the spiritual emptiness caused by wars. It is quite natural that such a social reality would spur him to get away from it all and to find some way to "be whole again beyond confusion" ("Directive", l. 62). Hence his weariness of life, as indicated in the line "I am overtired/of the great harvest I myself desired" in "After Apple-Picking" (II. 28 - 29); or, as confessed in "Birches", his wish to be "a swinger of birches" again because he was "weary of consideration" and because "life is too much like a pathless wood" (II. 43 - 45); or his momentary impulse to stay forever in the woods that "are lovely, dark and deep," as strongly expressed in "Stopping by Woods on a Snowy Evening" (I. 10). All this, however, is counterbalanced by a strong sense of mission for one's own world, which is equally, if not more emphatically, prevalent in Frost's poems. As we have seen in "West-Running Brook", even in the very nature of the drift to "the abyss' void with emptiness", there exists a counter drift toward fullness and "something sending up the sun". Frost's dialectical thoughts on "emptiness" ring a bell again, for we are once more reminded of Lao Tzu who has, in his *Tao Te Ching*, given the following remarks: "What is most full seems empty" (Lao Tzu 1997: 97;

"大盈若冲").

"The counter drift" is not confined merely to "West-Running Brook", but asserts itself repeatedly in Frost's poetry with a diversity of forms. Barry Ahearn, in a recent article on Frost's sonnets, has rightly pointed out that he "wants to maintain humanity's exceptional status" and that "Frost prefers to believe in an essential, crucial distinction between humankind and the rest of nature, a distinction he wishes to retrieve" (Ahearn 2007: 45). The wish to retrieve the distinction between humankind and the rest of nature is undoubtedly a wish to *Ru Shi*, which dovetails the above-mentioned image of "the counter drift." Similar instances abound. In "Stopping by Woods on a Snowy Evening", for instance, the poet finally refuses the call of the "lovely" woods, and is determined to accomplish his journey, although it means "miles" of arduous journey (Ⅱ. 15 – 16). He has "promises to keep" (Ⅰ. 14), and those promises have nothing to do with *Chu Shi*, and have everything to do with *Ru Shi*. In "The Road Not Taken", the poet eventually comes to terms with the fate coming from his previous choice of "the one less traveled by" although he knows that "that has made all the difference" (Ⅱ. 15 – 16). And in "Birches", Frost makes it clear that his wish to be away from the "earth" will last only "awhile", and then he would like to "come back to it" again since "Earth's the right place for love:/I don't know where it's likely to go better" (Ⅱ. 49 – 54). He even indicates a fear that fate might misunderstand him:

> May no fate willfully misunderstand me
> And half grant what I wish and snatch me away
> Not to return...
> ("Birches," Ⅱ. 51 – 53)

So the poet here does want to return, i.e., to *Ru Shi* in Taoist terms. It would be wrong then to look upon Frost merely as an escapist. "Birches" is one of the poems which most vividly and adequately display the philosophical attitude of Frost towards reality, and that attitude is most aptly embedded in the image of "a swinger of birches":

> I'd like to go by climbing a birch tree —
> And climb black branches up a snow-white trunk
> Toward heaven, till the tree could bear no more,
> But dipped its top and set me down again.
> That would be good both going and coming back.
> One could do worse than be a swinger of birches.
> ("Birches," II. 55 – 60)

For all his fantasy about "climbing" toward heaven, toward *Chu Shi* in a sense, the poet never fails to see the restricted ability of the birch tree which, having struck roots deeply in the earth, will eventually send him down to the earth again. *Ru Shi*, or accepting the world, is therefore Frost's ultimate choice or, in his own opinion, "man's sacred duty".① In the swinging of birches, we can see a curve or rather two curves similar to the waves in "West-Running Brook": a drift and a counter drift.

It should be further pointed out that the image of water, with its drift and counter drift, is like a pervading thread running through the whole career of Robert Frost. It appears in his earliest poems and in his last one. In "The Pasture", which is among the first three poems he published, water pops up in the form of a "spring": "I am going out to clean the pasture spring" (I . 1). Then the water runs down through Frost's poetry just like the "confident" west-running brook, and finally shows up in his last poem "Directive", which contains another philosophical statement: "Here are your waters and watering place, /Drink and be whole again beyond confusion" (II. 61 – 62). The act of "drinking" symbolically implies the attitude of acceptance. With the publication of "Directive", the west-running brook of Frost's poetic career seems to

---

① This idea comes from Radcliffe Squires's introduction to *The Major Themes of Robert Frost*, which says: "His [Frost's] life has spanned the violent and war-torn years of the 20th century, yet his poetry is dominated by a belief in man's sacred duty to endure" (s. the front cover of Squires 1963).

have completed a full cycle and to have definitely flown into a place of acceptance rather than a place of refusal. His sincere acceptance of reality is fully consistent with the Taoist philosophy of *Ru Shi*, which means, in Chuang Tzu's words, to "bear the doomed fate with equanimity" ("安之若命") and to "be content with what you have" ("安时处顺").① Just as the Taoist "water" (the highest good) always presupposes "having tranquility in the hustle and bustle" ("结庐在人境，而无车马喧"),② so is Frost's west-running brook eternally returning to its origin.

3. Conclusion

Thanks to the west-running brook, we have come to see a closer link between the poetic philosophy of Frost and ancient Chinese philosophy. A cross-reading of Frost and Taoist works confirms Radcliffe Squires's view that "West-Running Brook" is "the summit of Frost's poetry" (Squires 1963: 104). A summit it is, for it contributes to bridging the gap between the philosophical thoughts of the East and the West. Although they are remote from each other in time and space, the poetic philosophy of Frost and Taoism bear striking affinities that call for a meticulous comparative study.

Reading Frost in Taoist perspective, as shown by our analysis above, is conducive to exploring the undercurrents of and counter drifts in his poetry, which will lead to an understanding of Frost not as a mere escapist, nor as a merely "terrifying" poet, but as a sage with more balanced philosophical attitudes toward life. True, the poetic lines of Frost often betray an impulse to renounce the world, but it is always offset by a willingness to accept and even embrace the world. The west-running brook may head for

---

① Both of the ideas come from *Chuang Tzu* (《庄子》). "安之若命" comes from 《庄子·人间世》, and "安时处顺" comes from 《庄子·养生主》. For further consultation, please refer to *Chuang Tzu* (《庄子今注今译》) translated by Cheng Guying and edited by Wang Yungwu (Taibei: The Commercial Press of Taiwan, 1983).

② This saying is adapted form Wang Rongpei's translation of the fifth poem of Tao Yuanming's poetry series, "Drinking Wine". The original poetic line is "结庐在人境，而无车马喧", and translated by Wang Rongpei as "My house is built amid the world of men/Yet with no sound and fury do I keen." For further consultation, please refer to Wang Rongpei's *The Complete Poetic Works of Tao Yuanming* (《英译陶诗》, Beijing: Foreign Language Teaching and Research Press, 1999).

Chu Shi, but it will eventually end up in *Ru Shi*.

References

[1] Ahearn, Barry. Frost's Sonnets, In and Out of Bounds [A] //Viorca Patea and Paul Scott Derrick, eds. *Modernism Revisited: Transgressing Boundaries and Strategies of Renewal in American Poetry* [C]. Amsterdam and New York: Rodopi, 2007: 35 – 52.

[2] Chang Yaoxin. *A Survey of American Literature* [M]. Tianjin: Nankai University Press, 2002.

[3] Cheng Aimin. The consanguineous cultivation of a fictitious land of peace: A comparative study of Tao Yuanming's and Frost's poems on nature [J]. *Journal of PLA University of Foreign Language* 1996 (2): 75 – 81.

[4] Cox, Hyde, and Edward C. Lathem. Introduction [A] //Hyde Cox and Edward C. Lathem, eds. *Selected Prose of Robert Frost* [M]. New York: Macmillan, 1968: 3 – 50.

[5] Frost, Robert. *The Collected Poems, Prose and Plays* [M]. Eds. Richard Poirier and Mark Richards. New York: Library of America, 1995.

[6] Hong Qi. An extrication transcending time and space: The theme of Frost in Chuang Tzu's perspective [J]. *Theory Horizon*, 2004 (4): 164 – 166.

[7] Huang Zongying. *A Road Less Traveled By: On the Deceptive Simplicity in the Poetry of Robert Frost* [M]. Beijing: Peking University Press, 2000.

[8] Lao Tzu. *Tao Te Ching* [M]. Trans. Arthur Waley. Beijing: Foreign Language Teaching and Reserach Press & Cumberland House, 1997.

[9] Parini, Jay and Miller B C. *The Columbia History of American Poetry* [M]. Beijing: Foreign Language Teaching and Researching Press & Columbia University Press, 2005.

[10] Squires, Radcliffe. *The Major Themes of Robert Frost* [M]. Ann Arbor, MI: The University of Michigan Press, 1963.

[11] Su Baorong. *Shuo Wen Jie Zi* [M]. Xi'an: People's Publishing House of Shanxi, 2003.

［12］ Toming, Liu. *A History of American Literature* ［M］. Nanjing: Yilin Press, 2002.

［13］ Trilling, Lionel. A speech on Robert Frost: A cultural episode ［J］. *Partisan Review* 1959 (26): 445 – 452.

［14］ Zhao Yiheng. *The Goddess of Poetry Traveling Faraway: How the Modern American Poetry Has Undergone a Metamorphosis in China* ［M］. Shanghai: Shanghai Translation Publishing House, 2003.

［15］ Zhou Yi, and Liang Yihua. *Chinese Culture* ［M］. Nanning: Guangxi Education Press, 1993.

(本文原载于 Zeitchrift für Anglistik und Amerikanistik, Volume 58, Issue 2, 2010)

第四编

教育思想

外国文学的"新"与"旧":
新文科浪潮下的思考[*]

一、引言

近几年来,"新文科"浪潮可谓波涛汹涌,在外国文学领域也是如此。许多有关外国文学教学/研究的文章和研讨会,都被冠以时髦的"新文科"名号。然而,越是热浪滚滚,越需冷静思考。从现有的论述来看,有不少对"新文科"的理解停留在表层,尤其是对其历史由来不甚了了,既然不谙由来,就无从展望走向。可知在当今的热潮之下,潜藏着暗礁险滩,最危险的是对"新文科"之"新"缺乏价值考量。有鉴于此,有必要力求对"新文科"的含义进行深入探讨,求得真知。我们认为,"新文科"重在跨学科,即讲求一个"跨"字。那么何为"跨"?怎么"跨"?这些都值得深究。

"新文科"建设势在必行,人们对此的创新热情也无可厚非,但是不以冷静思考和研讨为前提的热潮是难以为继的,甚至会导致触礁沉船。历史上不乏在"新""旧"转换中胎死腹中的教训,我们必须审慎汲取。对此,本文将从"新文科"最早的定义及其含义说起。

---

* 本文系浙江省哲学社会科学重点研究基地"文艺批评研究院"资助项目(编号wypp2020001)的成果。

二、"新文科"的由来及其含义

关于"新文科"（the new humanities）这一术语最早出现的日期，有不同的说法，但是似乎都还缺少准星。从笔者找到的资料来看，下面这段考证中的日期比较可靠：

> 什么是"新文科"？就我们所知，这一术语最早被用于1991年的一次研讨会中，那次会议由澳大利亚人文研究院在堪培拉举办，其名称就是"超越学科：新文科"。（Fuery & Mansfield 1997：X）

关于当时与会者心目中"新文科"的含义，澳大利亚学者Fuery和Mansfield（1997：x）教授给出了如下解释："这一用法显然强调人文学科新近发展所带来的可能性，即打破传统学科领域的界线，催生多个领域工作者之间交流的新形态和新进程。"对照这一解释，我们会发现如今关于"新文科"的表述基本上与30年前那次会议所主张的并无二致。在当今众多倡导"新文科"的表述中，下面这段出自《中国社会科学报》的言论比较典型：

> 新文科是相对于传统文科而言的，是以全球新科技革命、新经济发展、中国特色社会主义进入新时代为背景，突破传统文科的思维模式，以继承与创新、交叉与融合、协同与共享为主要途径，促进多学科交叉与深度融合，推动传统文科的更新升级，从学科导向转向以需求为导向，从专业分割转向交叉融合，从适应服务转向支撑引领。（王铭玉，张涛2019：004）

此处，"突破传统文科的思维模式"跟前面引文中"超越学科"以及"打破传统学科领域的界线"等说法并行不悖。也就是说，上面这段表述除去增加了"以全球新科技革命、新经济发展、中国特色社会主义进入新时代为背景"等话语之外，基本上延续了30年前"新文科"的说法。

此外，我们还应看到，即便是 30 年前的"新文科"，也已经不那么"新"了。20 世纪 90 年代的堪培拉大会其实是 50 年代和 60 年代"两种文化"之争的延续。1959 年，英国小说家兼科学家查尔斯·珀西·斯诺（Charles Percy Snow）在剑桥大学发表了题为《两种文化与科学革命》（*Two Cultures and the Scientific Revolution*）的演讲，其主题是文理之间日趋扩大的鸿沟——学文科的和学理科的互相缺乏了解，甚至彼此怀有敌意，就好像代表了"两种文化"似的，"学文的知识分子为一个极端，而科学家则为另一个极端……这两种人互相缺乏了解，形成了一个鸿沟——有时候（尤其是在年轻人中间）还互相抱有敌意和厌恶情绪，但是最多的是相互间缺少了解"（Snow 1959：3）。由于斯诺在演讲中还流露出对理工科的偏爱，因此激怒了当时英国的文坛巨人弗兰克·雷蒙德·利维斯（Frank Raymond Leavis），后者足足准备了三年，也在剑桥大学发表了演讲，题目是《两种文化？查·珀·斯诺的意义》（*Two Cultures? The Significance of C. P. Snow*，1962），其中针对斯诺主张用科学学科——斯诺认为"科学家们骨子里就代表着将来"（Snow 1959：12）——带动其他学科的观点，提出了另一种跨越文化鸿沟的办法，即在大学建立一个中心，而"这个中心应该设立于富有生命力的英文学院"（Leavis 1962：29）。其理由是英文学院最有助于人脑的基本活动（包括智力活动和情感活动），"没有这种基本活动，科学大厦的巍峨耸立是不可能的"（同上：27）。利维斯和斯诺之间尽管是唇枪舌剑，其实他俩都赞成打破不同学科之间的壁垒，跨越不同系科的界线，也就是跨越文化鸿沟。也就是说，他们争吵的细节并不重要，重要的是他们引起了一场波及大西洋两岸的、旷日持久的大辩论，并激发了许多国家在跨学科方面的高等教育改革。这在斯诺本人五年之后的一次回顾中可见一斑："在耶鲁、普林斯顿、密西根和加利福尼亚，世界级的科学家在向非理工科学生授课；在麻省理工学院和加州理工学院，理科学生正在认真学习人文学科"（Snow 1964：69）。从 20 世纪 60 年代到 90 年代，这类跨越学科界线/文化鸿沟的改革不仅风行于美国，而且在英国也得到了广泛的实践。例如，英国苏塞克斯大学从 1963 年起就推出了"文理渗透项目"（Arts/Science Programme），而时任剑桥大学克莱尔学院院长的埃里克·阿什比（Eric Ashby）教授则设计了"博雅教育课程"（liberal education courses），即一种以专业为核心并不断向外"辐射"的课程结构；伦敦大学的罗纳德·巴尼特

(Ronald Barnett)教授也设计了一个类似的课程，称其为"思辨型交叉课程"（Critical Interdisciplinarity）（殷企平 1995：125—140）。由此可见，"新文科"有其历史由来。我们有必要借鉴历史上的经验教训，从而确保"新文科"建设走上健康发展的轨道。

诚然，当今世界可谓日新月异，可是就跨/超越学科这一理念而言，如今的"新文科"跟30乃至60年前的情形大致相仿，这就需要我们充分参照前人的做法，避免前人走过的弯路，尤其是在对于指导性原则的具体表述上要慎之又慎。就以前面引自《中国社会科学报》的那段话为例，其中"从学科导向转向以需求为导向，从专业分割转向交叉融合，从适应服务转向支撑引领"这几句就值得商榷。试想："新文科"难道就该仅仅以需求为导向吗？在"新文科"口号响彻云天之前，我们就没有交叉融合吗？"支撑引领"这样的提法很好，但是它跟"以需求为导向"是否有矛盾之处呢？倘若那篇文章的作者充分借鉴了"两种文化"之争，以及随后各国高等教育的改革实践，就可能意识到"以需求为导向"这样的提法过于简单。在"两种文化"之争以后，世界上许多高校其实都遵循了如下常识：高校办学依赖三条"力"之合，即学科内在逻辑（the inner logic of a discipline）、学生/家长的需求和用人单位的需求这三方力量的平衡。在"新文科"建设中，这三条"力"同样缺一不可，否则会导致办学体系的崩溃。同此，"从专业分割转向交叉融合"这一句也值得斟酌。须知在"新文科"术语问世之前，学科/专业的交叉融合就已经存在了，而且许多交叉融合是自然形成的，或者说是自下而上形成的。上引文字给人以一种只靠自上而下的力量来形成交叉融合的感觉，并且忽视了学科内在逻辑的力量，这不能不说是一种缺憾。就拿文学学科来说，其学科发展的内在逻辑必然会导致它跟周边学科的交叉和融合，中国文学和外国文学皆是如此。正因为如此，"两种文化"之争的主角之一利维斯主张让英文学院作为大学的中心（参见本文上一小段），其理由是文学学科最接近人类意识的中心：

> ……大学不仅仅是一些不同专业系科的搭配——它也应该成为人类意识的中心：洞察力、知识、判断力和责任感都构成了人类的意识。（Leavis 1962：29）

确实,"洞察力、知识、判断力和责任感"构成了人类意识的要素,而文学学科最能体现这些要素。更重要的是,文学在体现这些要素时,已经或必然会融入其他许多学科的视角,或者说跨入其他多个学科。文学就是人学,而人学——包括对洞察力、知识、判断力和责任感这些人类意识的研究——本身就涵盖着跨学科的视野,以及多学科的融合(本文第三小节还会就此做进一步的探讨)。

因此,要吃透"新文科"的含义,还须对"新文科"之"新"做一番推敲,这将是我们在下一小节中的主要任务。

三、对于"新"的价值考量

"新文科"带着"新"字,这是否意味着只要创新,就万事大吉了呢?"新"是否一定就比"旧"好呢?在外国文学领域里,我们经常要面对"旧"作家、"旧"作品,难道这就违背"新文科"精神了吗?

要回答上述问题,我们不妨从特里·伊格尔顿关于"新"与"旧"的论述说起。他在《如何读文学》(*How to Read Literature*,2013)一书中曾经这样说道:

> 对一些文学批评家来说,创意举足轻重。一件作品越是与传统和惯例决裂,越是真的有新意,我们就越有可能给予高度评价……然而,片刻的反思就足以让我们对此产生怀疑。(Eagleton 2013: 175)

伊氏此处指出了一个文学研究中的陷阱,或者说很多研究者的一个通病,即一味求新。事实上,不仅文学研究,而且在生活中的许多方面,"新"与"旧"之间的关系往往是辩证的。"新"并非绝对好,"旧"也并非绝对坏。就像伊氏所说的那样,"并非每样新东西都是珍贵的。化学武器是晚近的产物,但为之欢欣鼓舞的人却不多。反之,传统的东西也并非都是沉闷乏味的"(同上)。在文学领域,我们研究对象中的大部分都带有文化遗产性质。一谈到遗产,人们首先想到的很可能是"传统""往昔"和"回顾"这样一些概念,可是正如伊氏所说，"遗产既意味着向后看，又可能引起未来的巨变。习俗也并非总是僵硬或违背自然的。'习俗'一词最干脆的意思是'走在一起'，而如果没有这样的汇集，就不可能有社会存在，遑论艺术作品"（同上：175—176）。此处的"习俗"在英文原文中是"convention"，它还有"常规""惯例"的意思，更有"正式会议"的意思，两者都意味着"汇聚"和"融合"。换言之，习俗/遗产不仅意味着古今沟通，更意味着与未来沟通。

对于"新"的价值考量，曾经是18世纪英国文坛上的熟悉话题。根据伊格尔顿的考证，当时的英国文人们在这方面有个共识，即"求新是一种怪癖"，而且"道德真理无所谓新旧"，"数百万男女在过去数百年里都认定的真理，必定比某些新奇的概念更值得尊敬"（Eagleton 2013：175—176）。依笔者之见，这也应该是整个人类社会的共识。当今社会，以"新"标榜的事物层出不穷，却往往不如一些"老话"和常识，这是因为后者经过了千百年的淬砺，积淀着数代乃至几十代人的智慧。用伊氏的话说，"某个两眼发直的天才可能会在凌晨两点凭空想出什么主意，但是它不可能胜过人类的普通智慧。不管在何处，人性总是相像的，总会像荷马和索福克勒斯描述的那样，不会有真正的改进"（同上：176）。言下之意，智慧是不能用"新"与"旧"的标签来衡量的，而讲求智慧，或体现智慧，往往是艺术的特性，文学艺术尤其如此。在这一点上，我们还可以找到艺术与科学的区别："科学会进步，但是艺术不会。契合之处比分歧更值得关注，共性比个性更有分量。艺术的任务是为我们提供生动的形象，以揭示我们已经熟悉的东西"（同上）。也就是说，揭示"旧"东西——即伊氏所说"我们已经熟悉的东西"——是文学艺术的任务，无非揭示的手法比较生动/新颖罢了。用詹姆斯·乔伊斯（James Joyce）的《为芬尼根们守灵》（*Finnegans Wake*, 1939）来说明这一点，恐怕再有力不过了：

> 很难想象比《为芬尼根们守灵》更加新得惊人的作品了。确实，我们很难一眼就看出它是用什么语言写成的。事实上，《守灵》这部书汲取了全部被摸熟了的文字。它新就新在组合这些文字的古怪方式。就这一意义而言，它只不过更张扬地做了所有文学作品一直在做的事情。（Eagleton 2013：179）

上引文字也出自伊格尔顿的手笔,他用令人信服的例证表明,一部文学作品的价值并不取决于它是"新"还是"旧"。伊氏(Eagleton 2013:181)的下面这段文字说得更为明白:"假如优秀文学永远只是开拓性文学,那么我们就会被迫否定许多伟大文学作品的价值;从古代田园诗和中世纪神秘剧,到十四行诗和民间歌谣,莫不如此。"当然,具有开拓性,或者说具有新意,也应该是评价文学作品的一项参照依据,但是不应作为唯一的依据,更不应作为永远的依据。

在"新文科"建设中,上文所涉话题也是每位外国文学教师必须面对的问题。事实上,在"新文科"热潮兴起之前,我们已经面临类似的问题——常常有人这样质疑:在当今世界,在高校课堂讲授莎士比亚还有价值吗?笔者本人也曾多次收到来自一些学生、学生家长乃至部分高校领导的建议,要求在课堂上只教授"鲜活的语言",而把莎士比亚留给少数专家去研究,其理由是后者已经老朽,跟社会的现实需求相去甚远。可以想见,类似的主张会在"新文科"浪潮中再次出现。即便还未出现,我们也要做好回应上述质疑的准备,至少要准备回答如下问题:在强调需求导向的今天,传授/阅读较古老的外国文学作品,是否违背了"新文科"的精神呢?回答自然应该是否定的。以莎士比亚英语为例,它不仅没有死去,而且鲜活地存在于当今日常英语的方方面面,或者说已经渗入日常英语的角角落落。一个特别有趣的现象是,如今许多英国人、美国人并不知道他们所说的英语中有许多是来自莎士比亚的。例如,"It is Greek to me"(这对我来说是一本天书)这一句话常挂在人们的嘴边,可是很少有人知道它起源于莎剧《裘力斯·恺撒》(*The Tragedy of Julius Caesar*, 1599);剧中人物凯斯卡和凯歇斯有一段对话,后者询问有关西塞罗言谈的主旨,而凯斯卡干脆用了"it was Greek to me"这一表述(西塞罗说希腊语,所以凯斯卡犹如听天书)。(Shakespeare 1987:1094)又如,很多英美人喜欢使用"the better part of valor is discretion"(谨慎即大勇)这一成语,却不知道它也是来自莎士比亚,即出自《亨利四世上篇》(*Henry IV, Part 1*, 1598)人物福斯塔夫之口(Shakespeare 1987:294)。这些例子从一个侧面说明了文学经典的当代性,其重要意义不言而喻。

就文学而言,"新"与"旧"之间很难划出一条界线,皆因两者常常你中有我，我中有你。看似"旧"的作品，却能对当代的新人言说，这本来就是文学的奥秘所在，外国文学也不例外。关于一个国家学习他国文学的意义，19世纪英国文豪马修·阿诺德（Matthew Arnold）曾经这样说道："知彼才能知己，知己才能改错，才能获得拯救"（Stone 1997：1）。此处的"彼"，也应包括古代外国文学。对于这一点，对阿诺德推崇备至的美国学者唐纳德·斯通（Donald Stone）有过十分出色的阐释。他认为"文学是一个过去和现在之间永不完结的对话，它应该不断接受考验，在代代相传中新意迭出。像阿诺德和伽德玛一样，斯通在希腊文化中——尽管那是古老的异国文明——看到了最永恒的'现代'观"（转引自殷企平、陈姝波 2002：104）。斯通为此提出的理由是："过去文化作品中对真理的主张和公共价值观永远具有现代性"（Stone 1997：117）。当然，昔日的主张和公共价值观并不都是正确的，甚至还会有不少谬误，但是它们至少能激发我们的思考，并与我们形成一种对话关系，而这种对话历久弥新。

总之，"新文科"之"新"并非一味排"旧"，而往往是"新"中有"旧"，"旧"中有"新"，这在外国文学领域会表现得更为明显。

四、何为"跨"？怎么"跨"？

前文提到，"新文科"讲求一个"跨"字，那么何为"跨"？怎么"跨"？我们还须进而提问：在外国文学领域中，"新文科"建设中的"跨"又该如何落实？

关于"跨"的旨趣，很少有人比金衡山教授表述得更为生动，更富有哲理。他在最近的一篇文章中写道：

> 跨学科之"跨"乃是一种存在的必然，是世界构成的本源，是文化的底色，是生活的原味。作为"人学"的文学……在"跨"行为的过程中，其丰富性、饱满度和真实素会自动绽放。（金衡山 2021：88）

此处的关键词是"必然""本源""底色""原味"和"自动"。也就是说，文学——包括外国文学——必然会跨入其他学科。"跨"乃学科内在逻辑使然，无须太多来自外部的推动,或者说"跨"首先是"自动"的行为。

那么,"新文科"建设是否就不需要了呢?当然需要,可是得讲究"跨"的方式。上文其实有个"潜台词",即传统文科建设并非不"跨"。既然都得"跨",那么"新文科"之"跨"就必须从传统文科之"跨"推陈出新,否则"新"就无从谈起。更确切地说,"新文科"建设必须吸取以往跨学科举措中的经验教训,尤其要祛除原先一些顶着"改革"之名的弊端。事实上,在过去三十多年里,我国高校试行过不少带有跨学科性质的课程改革,一个典型的特点是开设各种各样的通识课程。然而,在很多情况下,所谓的"通识课程"相互之间缺少有机联系,更谈不上与专业课程之间的联系——在理论上自然会有联系,但是在实际操作层面没有确保它们互动的机制。更具体地说,很多学校只是开出了五花八门的"通识课程",而任课教师间缺少沟通,各开各的课,很少顾及所开课程与专业课程的联系。这种做法与其说是开设通识课程,不如说是"摆学摊";摊子越摆越大,而帮助学生融会贯通的实际环节却越来越少,更何况在如今这个知识爆炸的年代,摊子再大也无济于事,因为学生的有限精力和有限学时绝不允许他们修那么多的课程,因而无法实现(学科之间)真正的跨越。

要实现真正的跨越,我们可以借鉴国外的一些经验。前文提到的阿什比及其"辐射型课程"就值得借鉴。他这样描述这类课程:

> 我认为可以把专业学习(无论什么专业:冶金学也好,牙科学也好,挪威语也好,全都一样)作为核心,在其周围簇拥着与专业学习有关的博雅教育课程。但是这些课程必须和专业有关;通向文化的道路应该贯穿一个人的专业,而不是绕过专业。(Ashby 1966:84)

此处的"文化"特指博雅教育,或者说一个人在接受博雅教育后的修养。阿什比用"贯穿专业"和"绕过专业"的两相对比,精辟地点明了他的"辐射"理念。那么,在具体的操作层面,这种"贯穿"或"辐射"是怎样实现的呢?巴尼特设计的"思辨型交叉课程"(见本文第一小节)为阿什比的理念做了很好的脚注。按照巴尼特的课程设计,任何学科首先要有一个凸显本学科属性的专业课程计划及其核心知识和技能,而"别的学科"——即核心课程之外的学科——都可以发挥"审问者"(interrogators)的作用:

> 这些学科就像审问者——历史学、美学、伦理学、经验科学、数学或任何学科都可作为审问者;它们被选来做真正的批判工作或照明工作。它们的批判力量不是来自学科内部固有的特点,因为任何学科在原则上都可以被召来做这种工作。它们的力量来自这样一个事实,即作为批判的武器,它们显示了接受批判的学科的局限性。它们的力量来自批判本身。(Barnet 1990:186)

根据上述理念,我们可以为(外国)文学学科勾勒一个"思辨型交叉课程"结构图(虽然巴尼特并没有这样专门勾画文学学科,但是这一构图体现了他的思想)。

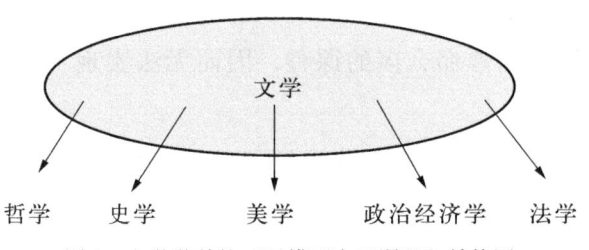

图1 文学学科的"思辨型交叉课程"结构图

图1表明,文学学科牢牢占据着核心课程的地位,但是它随时会受到来自其他学科的"审问"。例如,文学课堂上会自然出现这样一个问题:文学是什么?该问题自然而然地导入哲学领域——在探究某个东西是什么的时候,其实就涉及了本体论话题,而本体论是哲学学科的支柱之一。又如,教师在课堂上讲解某部作品时,必然会涉及相关历史时期的特征等,这就会引导学生把目光投入史学领域。再如,当课堂讨论围绕文学家的审美趣味而展开时,势必需要借用美学领域的原理、方法和视角。教师还可以用类似的方法引导学生跨入政治经济学、伦理学、法学、地理学和生态学,等等。这好比随时打开专业核心课程的窗户,从邻近学科借助光线,照亮自身学科,弥补自己学科的不足。

除上述方法之外，跨学科研究/教学还须注重每次跨越过程中的愉悦（pleasure）乃至游戏性（playfulness）。诚然，知识的开拓和传承有其严肃性（尤其是严谨的治学态度），但是也离不开研究/教学者愉悦的身心状态，离不开愉悦所发挥的作用。美国加州伯克利分校的罗伯特·奥尔特（Robert Alter）教授曾经就全球知识环境做过如下评论："对游戏性的忽略是一种症状，它表明我们的知识氛围过于沉闷。例如，在哈罗德·布鲁姆的《西方正典》里面就没有游戏性的立足之处……"（Alter 2004：11），奥尔特是在将近20年前说这番话的，可是他所指出的症状仍然存在。那么，我们是否能借"新文科"东风，来改变上述症状呢？

依笔者之见，"新文科"之"跨"正好能带来愉悦的春风。更确切地说，愉悦是"跨越"之道，是"跨越"的必要前提。此话怎讲？我们不妨借助莱昂内尔·特里林（Lionel Trilling）评价华兹华斯（William Wordsworth）的一句话来做铺垫：对华兹华斯来说，"愉悦是生命本身的关键属性"（Trilling 1963：77）。探究生命的奥秘，这是每个学科直接或间接的使命，而要完成这一使命，非依靠学科的交叉与融合不可，也就是要跨越尽可能多的学科。如果这一逻辑成立，那么愉悦就是学科交叉/跨越的必由之路——既然愉悦是生命的关键属性，那么旨在通向大生命观的学科交叉又怎能忽略这一属性呢？忽略了愉悦，就会导致知识氛围的沉闷，也就会导致视野的狭窄，而这正是与"新文科"之"跨"背道而驰的。

还须强调的是，"跨越"有赖于愉悦的判断最能体现于文学的教学与研究。美国斯坦福大学的丹尼斯·吉甘蒂（Denise Gigante 2010：xiii）教授说得好："诗歌给作为整体的人带来愉悦，而不是服务于某一门专业知识。事实上，愉悦使人振作，这是因为想象的愉悦本来就是综合性的。"（Gigante 2010：xiii）吉甘蒂此处所强调的"综合性""作为整体的人"以及"不是服务于某一门专业知识"都渗透着跨学科意识，渗透着整体意识，而这些又都得益于愉悦。"愉悦使人振作"（Pleasure pulls man together）这句话尤为精辟，因为"振作"意味着调动人身上所有的精神力量，以及所有的知识和技能，这显然超越了任何单个学科所能提供的力量。换言之，愉悦所调动的力量远远超过某个学科的知识。不仅如此，愉悦还能导向比知识更重要的东西，即智慧。雪莱（Shelley 2002：

139)有过一句名言:"诗歌总被愉悦伴随着。当愉悦降临时,人就会敞开心扉,迎接智慧,而智慧总是交织着乐趣。"此言可谓切中肯綮。没有愉悦,人类恐怕难以抵达智慧,甚至不会去迎接智慧,而智慧就像生命一样,是任何单个学科都无法囊括的。

五、结语

从以上分析中,我们可以看到一条有助于反思"新文科"浪潮的历史脉络。它提醒我们冷静思索,谨慎探索,从而少走弯路。最需谨慎的是对于"新"的价值考量,最需探索的是"跨越"之道,最需提倡的是作为"跨越"之道的愉悦。还得加上一句:"新文科"建设必须依靠两个积极性——既要有自上而下的积极性(如发文件、开大会等),又要有自下而上的积极性(如基层组织乃至教师个体自发的、扎扎实实的研究和教学实践),而愉悦是后一种积极性的根本保证。

参考文献

[1] Alter, R. Introduction [A] //F. Kermode. *Pleasure and Change* [M]. Oxford: Oxford University Press, 2004: 3 – 14.

[2] Ashby, E. *Technology and the Academics* [M]. New York: St. Martin's Press, 1966.

[3] Barnett, R. *The Idea of Higher Education* [M]. Milton Keynes: Open University Press, 1990.

[4] Eagleton, T. *How to Read Literature* [M]. New Haven & London: Yale University Press, 2013.

[5] Fuery, P. & N. Mansfield. *Cultural Studies and New Humanities: Concepts and Controversies* [M]. Melbourne: Oxford University Press, 1997.

[6] Gigante, D. Foreword [A] //T. H. Schmid & M. Faubert (eds.). *Romanticism and Pleasure* [C]. New York: Palgrave Macmillan, 2010: ix – xv.

[7] Leavis, F. R. *Two Cultures? The Significance of C. P. Snow* [M]. London: Chatto & Windus, 1962.

[8] Shakespeare W. The History of Henry the Fourth（I Henry Fourth）[A] //S. Wells & G. Taylor（eds.）. *The Complete Oxford Shakespeare* [C]. New York: Oxford University Press, 1987: 263-295.

[9] Shakespeare, W. The Tragedy of Julius Caesar [A] //S. Wells & G. Taylor（eds.）. *The Complete Oxford Shakespeare* [C]. New York: Oxford University Press, 1987: 1089-1119.

[10] Shelley P. B. *Shelley's Poetry and Prose* [M]. New York: W. W. Norton, 2002.

[11] Snow C P. *The Two Cultures and a Second Look* [M]. Cambridge: Cambridge University Press, 1964.

[12] Snow C. P. *The Two Cultures and the Scientific Revolution* [M]. New York: Cambridge University Press, 1959.

[13] Stone, D. *Communications with the Future: Matthew Arnold in Dialogue* [M]. Ann Arbor: The University of Michigan Press, 1997.

[14] Trilling, L. The fate of pleasure: Wordsworth to Dostoevsky [A] // N. Frye（ed.）. *Romanticism Reconsidered: Selected Papers from the English Institute* [C]. New York: Columbia University Press, 1963: 73-106.

[15] 金衡山.外国文学研究的跨学科方式及其缘由——从美国文学研究谈起[J].四川大学学报（哲学社会科学版），2021（6）：83-92.

[16] 王铭玉，张涛.高校"新文科"建设：概念与行动[J].中国社会科学报，2019，3（21）：4.

[17] 殷企平，陈姝波.为英语"文学道路"正名[J].浙江大学学报（人文社会科学版），2002（6）：102-107.

[18] 殷企平.英国高等科技教育[M].杭州：杭州大学出版社，1995.

（本文原载于《当代外语研究》2022年第2期）

阐释三境界：外国文学教学的艺术之路

在过去的十年里，有关外国文学教学的论文数量以加速度的态势激增。仅以"浙江网络图书馆"的期刊文献库为例，键入"英美文学教学"这一关键词，就可以查到382篇（2000—2006年共80篇；2007—2010年共302篇），而在1990年至1999年之间，相关论文数总共才5篇。

然而，数字的繁荣遮不住一个严重的缺憾：如何切实帮助学生理解文本/文字的论文寥若晨星，而外国文学教学的最大难题正在于此，其中"理解"二字是问题的核心。诚然，许多从教材、课堂活动模式和网络技术等角度探讨文学教学的文章，多多少少有助于对文学作品的理解，但是这些文章大都停留在技术操作的层面，或者停留在教育学和心理学的层面，而对文学艺术的学科特点关注不够。例如，近年来遭到热捧的"建构主义"教学模式①主张学生的自主性，探讨以学生为中心、以"任务驱动"为特点的教学活动形态。从表面上看，这些话题固然重要，可是它们并没有涉及以下最根本的问题：学生成为中心（其实对绝大多数老师来说，是否应该注重学生的自主学习，已经不是问题）以后，仍然面临着一个"难"字——理解文学作品难，理解外国文学作品更难。没有

---

① 在过去的六年中，平均每年至少有一篇论文的题目直接把"建构主义"和外国文学教学挂钩。

涉及造成这些困难的根本原因是什么，该怎样去克服困难。

以上所述热衷于"模式"的文章，往往忽视一个重要的事实，即理解首先是一门艺术，而艺术不是用简单的模式或纯粹的概念就能囊括的。关于理解的艺术，阐释学（hermeneutics，又译"诠释学"）研究领域的前辈们已经留下了丰富的论述。我们何不从中汲取营养，为外国文学的教学另辟蹊径呢？

一、常恨言语浅，不如人意深

文学理解的困难，首先来自语言的固有特性，即它的隐喻性（metaphoricity），以及随之而来的语言与思想/现实之间产生脱节的情形。正是由于语言的隐喻性，文学创作者常常会有词不达意的感受和经历，而读者必然会因之感到费解，甚至会误解作品的意思。张隆溪先生在把施莱尔马赫（Friedrich Schleiermacher）对阐释学所作的基本假设①跟钱锺书的有关思想做比较的时候，专门提到后者从刘禹锡那里引用的两行诗句："常恨言语浅，不如人意深。"

古往今来，发出类似感叹的，在中国有老子、孔子、庄子、陆机、苏轼和钱锺书等人，在西方有柏拉图、莎士比亚、席勒、施莱尔马赫、黑格尔、谢林、马拉美、T. S. 艾略特、海德格尔和伽达默尔等人。鉴于张隆溪在《道与逻各斯》（*The Tao and the Logos*, 1992）一书中已经对此做过详尽的梳理，我们只需强调一点：由于语言有其固有的局限性和不足，语言的使用者也有其主观上的局限和不足，因此人类的思维跟语言/文字的表达之间永远都不可能有百分之百的一致性。正是这种差异性，使上文所说的语言的隐喻性应运而生。

语言的隐喻性既是一种缺陷，又是一种生机。说它是缺陷，是因为它千百年来始终伴随着文学作者"词不达意"和"言不尽意"的困境。说它是生机，是因为它为世人克服这一缺陷提供了无限的可能性——创作和阐释都是如此。

先说语言的缺陷，或者说它的局限性。思维跟言说/书写之间永远都有一条沟。前者要转化为后者，就要实现跨越。跨越得不好，自然是一条鸿沟。跨越得好，会显得天衣无缝；不过，仅仅是"显得"而已，因为既然是转化，就会

---

① 这一假设是："误解是理所当然的，正是它使阐释成为绝对必要的事情。"（Zhang：55—56）

产生差异。用伽达默尔的话来说，思维一旦进入了言说和书写状态，就形成了一种"自我异化"。伽达默尔的观点源自施莱尔马赫，后者把转化为物质形式——他称之为"固定的外在言语"——之前的思想称作"内在言语"（internal speech）。

> 一旦思想者试图……用作为外在言语的语言来进行表述和传达，他的思想便不得不依靠那用于传达的语言。此时内在的言语便变成某种和自己迥然不同的东西，变得不足以实现其传达的目的——这样，语言在发挥其作为交流手段的作用时，便似乎总是使自己遭受挫折。（张隆溪，《道与逻各斯》，2006：16—17）

这种"挫折"，被张隆溪称为"思想在语言中的异化，即内在言语转化为语言符号，尤其是固定的、外在的书写形式"（Zhang：12）。历史上言说这种挫折和异化的例子举不胜举。席勒的这两行诗就是一例："活生生的精神为何不对另一个精神显现？／当灵魂发言时，唉！灵魂已经不再发言。"（Zhang 1992：52）

比这更精彩、更贴近常人感受的表述见于雪莱的《为诗一辩》（*A Defence of Poetry*，1840）："写作一旦开始，灵感便衰退了。迄今流传于人世的诗歌中，即便是最璀璨的，也恐怕是诗人原初构思的乏力的影子而已。"（Shelley 1986：788）假如还有比这更动情的感慨，那就只能从莎士比亚那里去寻找了。且看他的十四行诗第76首中的前八行：

> 为什么我的诗那么缺新光彩，
> 赶不上现代善变多姿的风尚？
> 为什么我不学时人旁征博采
> 那竞奇斗艳、穷妍极巧的新腔？
> 为什么我写的始终别无二致，
> 寓情思旨趣于一些老调陈言，
> 几乎每一句都说出我的名字，
> 透露它们的身世，它们的来源？（梁宗岱译文）

在十四行诗第 85 首中，莎士比亚还有过这样的抱怨："我那拴住了舌头的缪斯悄然无语。"（Shakespeare 1978：67）关于语言局限性的抱怨，在现代诗人那里，发展成一个迫在眉睫的难题。对此张隆溪做过对比和分析：

> 如果说在莎士比亚那里我们发现了"拴住了舌头的缪斯"，那么在马拉美那里，我们看到的却是丧失了力量的缪斯，是充满焦虑的"虚弱无力的现代缪斯"（Muse moderne de l'Impuissance）。如果说在莎士比亚那里，抱怨自己语言的软弱无力还更多的是一种姿态，那么在现代诗人这里，这种抱怨似乎已更为真实，并且显示出更为紧迫的问题。（《道与逻各斯》：88—89）

在张隆溪所举的诸多例子里，艾略特的几行诗句尤其夺目：

> 文字辛艰，
> 因重负而裂开，乃至破碎，
> 因紧张而滑跤，开溜，夭折，
> 因破绽而衰朽，不再各安其位，
> 不再气定神闲。①（Zhang 1992：65）

这里，艾略特分明画出了一幅文字异化的文字画。它再一次强化了横亘在人类面前的永恒难题：思想必然会在语言中异化。

在这种异化面前，人类难道就束手无策了吗？

前文其实已经暗示：语言的隐喻性是一种二律背反。它既是一种缺陷，又是一种生机；既意味着异化，又为克服异化提出了要求，提供了可能性。事实上，自古以来，人类从未停止过努力，以克服上述异化。文学家们是如此，阐释者也是如此。就如伽达默尔所说，"书面文本提供了真正的阐释学任务。书写是自我异化。因此，克服这种异化，解读文本，就是理解的最高使命"（Gadamer

---

① 此处诗行为笔者所译。

2004：392）。那么，该怎样克服异化呢？这不仅是文学家要解决的问题，也不仅是阐释者/批评家要解决的问题，而且是外国文学教师要解决的问题。① 这就是本文下一小节要回答的问题。

二、言有尽而意无穷

要克服异化，克服语言的局限性，同样要着眼于语言的隐喻性。在《道与逻各斯》的前言里，张隆溪直言该书的主旨是"重新思考语言的隐喻性质，思考文字作为符号和象征使用时所固有的局限性和暗示功能（suggestiveness）"（Zhang 1992：x）。也就是说，语言的局限性和暗示功能构成了它固有特性的两个方面。在《道与逻各斯》的正文中说得更为明白："语言的局限性和暗示力不应该被视为相互冲突而应该被视为彼此补充，因为它们是同一符号作用的两面。"（张隆溪 2006：181）正是这其中的一面，即语言那无穷的暗示功能，为克服语言的局限性提供了渠道和保障。更确切地说，局限性和暗示力是语言特性中相生相克的一对矛盾，形成了上一小节中所说的二律背反。

熟谙这二律背反的道理，并加以巧用，是古今中外杰出文学家的必由之路。他们一方面抱怨乃至哀叹文字/言语的软弱无力，另一方面又极尽寓言假物、譬喻拟象之能事，也就是凭借暗示谋求出路。根据张隆溪的梳理，我国的钟嵘、司空图、严羽、梅圣俞和苏轼都把"言/文有尽而意无穷"看作诗学的理想境界，或者说发挥语言暗示功能的理想境界（Zhang 1992：170—173）。在外国文学领域里，"言有尽而意无穷"何尝不也是文人们追求的境界？自然，外国文学的教学，必须关注这种境界的追求方式，必须关注使语言局限性得以克服的种种技艺，否则仍旧是缘木求鱼。

更通俗地说，优秀的文学作品总是以暗示性语言取胜的。暗示的艺术手法多种多样，其中最主要的要数象征（Symbol）和讽寓（Allegory）。依笔者之见，从事外国文学的教学，首先要教会学生如何去捕捉一部作品的象征意义。我国的外国文学课堂，常常陷入一个误区，即把象征和讽寓混为一谈，甚至把象征

---

① 当然也是本国文学教师要解决的问题。此处强调外国文学，只因本文是针对外国文学教学的问题而写的。

和隐喻/明喻混为一谈。以"自主学习"或"建构主义模式"著称的课堂尤其如此。因此，我们有必要先强调一下这些术语的区别：隐喻/明喻指的是在一对一的基础上不同事物之间的类比，而象征则不可避免地带有多义性和歧义性；隐喻/明喻把 A 比作 B，而象征则用 A 来暗示 Bs（B 的复数）。比这更难把握的是象征和讽寓之间的区别。张隆溪在一篇文章中曾经这样说过："就其在形象之外另有寓意这一点说来，象征和讽寓并没有本质的区别。"（张隆溪 2006，《讽寓》：129）可能正是这一缘故，许多教师和学生往往把两者等量齐观，然而它们之间其实是有很大的区别的。就在同一篇文章里，张隆溪有过这样的描述：

> 到 18 世纪末，讽寓的重要性越来越低落，似乎它本身是没有意义的外壳，只指向自身之外的某种意义。与此同时，象征则被视为与讽寓完全相反的另一个范畴，它自身既是具体的形象，又有形象以外的象征意义，但其具体形象本身又是实在的，而非仅仅是寄托意义的外壳。（张隆溪 2006，《讽寓》：128）

换言之，任何人物、事件或其他事物在获得多义性或象征性之前，应该首先具有真实性，而讽寓往往只注重形象以外的象征意义。关于这一点，坡林（Laurence Perrine，1915—1995）说得更为明白："象征意味着既是它所说的，同时又超过它所说的。"（殷企平，1995：55—56）以劳伦斯为例，他在用玫瑰来暗示深邃的意境时，不会像有些作家那样，把它表现得跟现实中的花朵迥然不同，而会首先从花朵的现实特征入手，因为他知道"只有那些亲眼看见过玫瑰的人，才能在看到玫瑰花瓣儿和闻到它的香味儿时激起对整朵玫瑰的联想"（殷企平，1995：56）。假如我们不指导学生细察象征的这些特点和前提，而让他们"自主"地"建构"作品的象征意义，势必会导致让人啼笑皆非的结果。

在捕捉象征意义时，我们的学生最难把握的，恐怕要数整个作品的结构性意象。一部优秀的作品，其象征意义不会简单地寄托于比况单一事物的断金碎玉，而会栖身于具有磁性的、文本的整体结构。象征犹如一个磁场，整个作品的各个部分、各个细节都要在这个磁场的不断"运动"中不断地产生出新的意义。伯齐托在这方面有过精彩的论述：

> 哪里有象征，哪里就建立起了一个由事件、象征和细节组成的磁场。这一磁场把无数纷杂的含义吸引在它的周围……意象和节奏已经不再是缠绕着逻辑主干的芜蔓枝藤。它们的作用不仅仅是装点主干，使它勉强呈现生机。相反，意象和意象之间、场景和场景之间以及节奏和节奏之间都首尾呼应，互映成趣，就像在图画中相同或相反的颜色都互相对应一样。那些看来是必要的对应关系并非仅仅是出于逻辑上的需要才建立起来的。松散的逻辑关系呈线条形状，而象征关系则呈圆弧形状。后者暗示着一种往返穿梭、四通八达的关系。一部作品的全部象征意义"总是在趋于完成"，然而却永远有待于完成，因为它总是在不断地产生新意，并将其统一在自己的有机体中。（伯托齐 1995：150）

我们不妨以劳伦斯的小说《虹》（*The Rainbow*，1915）为例。在分别伴随安娜和厄秀拉出现的彩虹之间，形成了一种具有反讽意味的张力：安娜"足不出户"便看到了彩虹，而厄秀拉偏要在外面的世界闯荡并撞得"头破血流"之后才看见彩虹；厄秀拉把自己的理想彩虹寄托在外面的世界，可是她去外面闯荡的每一步都是事与愿违、适得其反。也就是说，彩虹意象烘托了全书的反讽基调，具有结构性的象征意义。在两次关键时刻出现的彩虹之间，厄秀拉刚好完成了一次圆圈似的历程——以跟母亲分道扬镳始，又以回到母亲的立场终。这历程又象征着一个范围更大的历程，即人类的工业化进程。在厄秀拉的历程背后，隐含着这样一个问题：人们盲目投入"外面的世界"（工业革命的洪流），是否得不偿失？劳伦斯笔下的彩虹可以被看作上述"磁场"的中心，在它的周围团聚着许多其他意象，彼此之间形成了一种往返穿梭、四通八达的关系。小鸟儿（包括它飞翔时划出的弧线）、教堂里的拱形结构、厄秀拉所作的圆圈式旅行，它们都和彩虹前勾后连。书中还有许多描写涉及山川、森林、花草、星星、太阳和月亮，后者往往呈弧圈形。就连小说的谋篇布局都突出了圆弧形状的地位：不仅小说第十六章的标题直接使用了"彩虹"一词，而且第十章和第十四章意味深长地用了同样的标题，即"扩展中的圆圈"（The Widening Circle）。这一切拧成了一股合力，强烈地烘托出小说的反讽基调，即厄秀拉奋勇飞向"外面的世界"，迎来的却只是幻灭。换言之，"天高任鸟飞"这一理想不可能在一个失落了社群、丧失了灵魂的工业世界里实现。（殷企平 2005：66—71）

诸如此类的象征意义，要加以把握，绝非一朝一夕之功。对绝大多数本科生乃至硕士生来说，没有教师的悉心指导，是很难"自主"地心领神会的。当然，我们鼓励并欣赏学生的自主性，但是他们首先得对相关文字/文本烂熟于胸，才谈得上自主性。在当今世界，主张以读者为中心的"读者反应批评"理论占着主导地位，但是我们不妨重温一下维多利亚圣人罗斯金（John Ruskin，1819—1900）对此的不同主张。他在把每一部经典文学作品比作历史的宫廷后，以宫殿主人（作者）的口吻对读者提出了以下忠告：

> 你渴望与智者交谈吗？学会理解，你就能聆听高论了。还有另外的条件吗？——没有。假如你不努力上升到我们的境界，我们是不会屈尊于你的。活着的君主也许会礼仪有加，活着的哲人也许会不厌其烦地为你答疑解惑，但是在历史的宫廷里，我们既不装腔作势，也不加任何解释。倘若你想要从我们的思想中汲取快乐，就必须把自己提高到这些思想的水平；倘若你想要体认我们的存在，就必须分享我们的情感。（Ruskin 1921：62）

罗斯金所说的理解和提高，意味着读者/学员须放低自己的身段，摆正自己的位置，保持谦虚的态度。至于具体的操作，罗斯金也有话说："你必须养成密切关注文字的习惯，确保自己理解它们的意思，要精读每一个音节——不，要精读每一个字母。"（Ruskin 1921：64）同理，对象征意义的把握，也必须精细到每一个意象才行，而其间的奥妙，只有在博学的教师的搀扶下，我们的学生才能逐个参悟。

三、静故了群动，空故纳万境

克服语言的局限性，发挥它的启示性，还可以达到一个更高的境界，即"此处无声胜有声"的境界，也就是中西诗学都常常提到的"沉默"或"无言"境界。写作的艺术如此，阐释的艺术同样如此。张隆溪在对比中西诗学时引用过苏轼的诗句："欲令诗语妙，／无厌空且静。／静故了群动，／空故纳万境。"（张隆溪 2006，《道与逻各斯》：233—234）对此，张隆溪作了这样的评价：

> 虚空和寂静中蕴含着丰富的想象与可能。中国诗人对"禅"的运用，其方式并非不能在西方找到相似或相等的情形。例如，中世纪的审美体验就"默默地采用了保罗关于上帝恩典的说法：tamquam nihil habentes, et omnia possidentes（《哥林多后书》第六章：'似乎一无所有，却是样样都有'）"。（张隆溪 2006，《道与逻各斯》：234）

这里所说的，其实就是中西哲人为走出言不尽意这一困境而采取的策略。不管是庄子所说的"非言"（non-words），还是龙树（Nagarjuna）所说的"假名"（provisional names），或是埃克哈特（Meister Eckhart）所说的"沉默的文字"（silent words），其实都可以看作同一种策略，即言说不可言说之事物的策略，都可以归结为里尔克用诗句表述的"沉默诗学"：

> 沉默吧。谁在内心保持沉默，
> 谁就触到了言说之根。
> 那时生出的每一音节，
> 对于他都是一次胜利。（Zhang 2006：91—92，冯川译文）

沉默本来是一种无奈，但若是运用得当，恰恰能触及"言说之根"，起到"空故纳万境"的效果，即容纳自然界的万千气象，以及人们内心的千言万语。

既然写作艺术可以达到上述境界，那么阐释艺术也应该如此。我们的外国文学教学，就是要帮助学生掌握这种阐释艺术，帮助他们于无声处听"惊雷"，于无言处品万境。当然，问题也就随之而来了：该怎样贴近沉默？沉默在哪里？什么时候的沉默最有意味？

如前文所示，暗示性沉默，相对于直接表达，可以是一种更高级的传意方式。既然是传意方式,那就有一定的理路、轨道和原则可循。在如今的外国文学课堂上,以及学生的作业里,不乏"在沉默处做文章"的例子,然而这些"自主性"的发挥往往不着边际,犹如天马行空。对这种情形,做教师的应该负主要责任,因为我们平时大都注重文字的显性表达方式,而容易忽略文字的负面表达方式(negative mode of expression),即沉默的方式。

该怎样去寻找并体验沉默的方式呢?我们不妨再次从张隆溪的阐释思想中寻求启示:

> 恰恰是在言说的中央,沉默可以比言说更具表现力。也许正因为如此,我们在伟大的文学作品中——如同在伟大的乐曲中——便往往发现:高潮瞬间恰恰是无言的停顿。唐代著名诗人白居易便这样描述过停顿的技巧:"此时无声胜有声。"这里,状语"此时"极为重要,因为它把沉默放在了乐曲或言说的框架中。(张隆溪 2006,《道与逻各斯》:180—181)

这段话的关键词是"此时""框架""停顿""高潮瞬间"和"言说的中央"。它们也应该是外国文学课堂上的关键词。也就是说,体悟沉默仍然要以文本为基础,以语境为框架。离开了文本/语境的沉默,必然是无力的,因而是不值得阐释的。

在优秀的文学作品中,往往埋伏着各种特殊的信号,好像在提醒着读者:此处的停顿、空白或沉默意味深长,非下大力气琢磨不可。让我们以英国女作家布洛克-罗斯(Christine Brook-Rose, 1926—)的小说《下一个》(*Next*, 1998)的第一段文字为例:

> 近期故事梗概:黛丽卡早就嫁给了石油大王布莱德。多年以来,她替后者管理牧场,并且照料着她俩生下的一对双胞胎——雷克斯和丽贾纳。然而,黛丽卡从来无法掩饰她对特里克斯的深情,因为后者是她跟旧情人杰西的私生子。杰西是布莱德生意上的对手,后来跟蒂娜结了婚,可是眼下他正在追求基娜。道格是雷克斯新结交的朋友。这一天,他带着辛蒂去雷克斯那儿串门,碰巧布莱德也在家。布莱德一下子迷上了辛蒂,而道格却

迷上了基娜，可是基娜正和里克打得火热，里克眼下正帮着黛丽卡管理产业。有一次，黛丽卡跟萨尔大吵了一场。余怒未消，她又吩咐丹思对布雷德里的行为进行干预。（Brooke-Rose 1998：1）

乍一看去，这段文字似乎游离于全书结构之外：它里面的故事和人物跟小说本身的故事和人物毫不搭界。为何在小说最醒目的地方安插这样一个不相关联的段落？叙述者对此始终缄默不语，不做直接的解释。更让人费解的是，整段文字逃不出一个"空"字：空洞的文字和空心的图形。然而，这正是一个强烈的信号：此中有真意，空白纳万言。如果我们引导学生结合文本及其语境加以分析，至少可以读出以下几层意思。

首先，空心的文字图形分明是一架电视机的形状，而中间的那一处空白既可看作电视机的屏幕，又可理解为媒体内容的空洞。如果我们结合文字本身，就更加能够理解其中的含义：原来这是一段电视肥皂剧的故事梗概，其内容不但空泛，而且极其无聊，品味极其低劣。小说《下一个》的内容跟媒体及其作用有着千丝万缕的关系，因而在全书的开头安放一段空洞而无趣的文字，实在是一种有趣的讽刺。

其次，它跟小说描写的贫穷现象有关。在小说的第二段，有这样一个细节：流浪汉泰克把载有那段"故事梗概"的电视节目周刊当作了枕头（他穷极潦倒，连枕头都买不起）。从空心的文字中领悟贫苦大众的囊空如洗，未尝不是一种审美体验。

第三层意思更为重要——随着故事的推进，我们经常看到不同人物在贫民收容所看电视的镜头，同时听到他们收看时的评论。例如，外号"雅皮"的杰西曾经对电视节目的商业性以及节目内容的贫乏表示不满："每次预报下一个节目时，总是先来一点儿该节目的片段，可是紧接着播音员就会说'先休息一下'。可是这一休息就没完没了：先是广告，再是促销剪辑，然后又是广告，接着是信息宣传，再接下去又是促销剪辑。"（Brooke-Rose 1998：11）比节目贫乏更可恶的是虚假，这一点多次在不同人物的对话中被提及。雷奥纳多就曾经对斯特拉这样说："可笑的是电视台……拍摄的总是大街上浩浩荡荡的就业大军。可是那些人都属于幸运儿。这世上还有许多人在流浪，在沿街乞讨。他们累了只能在公园的长凳上歇歇脚,困了只能在屋檐下宿上一宿。"(Brooke-Rose 1998:29)同样,从昆廷跟奥利弗的一次对话中,我们了解到媒体上的"失业率上个月几乎降到了零,可是实际上什么都没有改变"(Brooke-Rose 1998:184)。可见,小说篇首的那段"空心文字"为这些人物的对话埋下了伏笔:英国媒体乃至整个资本主义制度的实质是虚假,就像那个文字图形中的"空心"一样。

第四层意思同样重要——书中反复出现了电视播音员的一句节目结束语:"不要离开我们!"这句话极具讽刺意味:成千上万个无家可归者过着饥寒交迫的生活,可是媒体对这一严酷的现实视而不见;电视上播送的不是虚假的新闻,就是无聊空洞的肥皂剧,而播音员们还不厌其烦地要求观众继续观看("不要离开我们!")。正是看到了其中的荒唐之处,布洛克-罗斯把这句话用作了全书的结束语,不过作了微妙的更动:"不要离开他们!"(Brooke-Rose 1998:210)虽然只有一词之差,但是产生了异常深刻的效果:前面反复出现的"不要离开我们!"是一种含蓄的讽刺,而"不要离开他们!"是对虚假媒体的顺势一击和盖棺定论。换言之,作者的心声在这一瞬间达到了高潮:任何有良知的人,都应该远离媒体所营造的虚拟现实,而把目光和同情心投向"他们"——现实生活中成千上万个饥寒交迫的人们。

只有像上面那样去领略沉默的含义,捕捉言外之意,我们的学生才谈得上登堂入室,进入了阐释艺术的殿堂。

四、结语

本文实际上论证了阐释艺术的三个境界,它们也应该是外国文学教学的三个境界。"常恨言语浅,不如人意深"是其中的第一个境界,它意味着对言不尽意这一道理的深刻体会,以及克服文字异化的强烈愿望。第二个境界,即"言有尽而意无穷",要求学生体悟语言的启示性,熟谙语言的局限性和暗示力相生相克、二律背反的道理,并通过细读来掌握作品的结构性意象。而"静故了群动,空故纳万境"则标志着阐释艺术的第三个境界,也是最高境界。凡是达到了这一境界的学生,必能从空无/沉默中读出意义的深邃与丰饶。

参考文献

［1］Brooke-Rose C. *Next*［M］. London：Carcanet，1998.

［2］Gadamer H. *Truth and Method*［M］. London：Continuum，2004.

［3］Lawrence D. H. *The Rainbow*［M］. Harmondsworth：Penguin，1949.

［4］Ruskin J. *Sesame and Lilies*［M］. New York：Metropolitan Publishing，1921.

［5］Shakespeare W. *Shakespeare's Sonnets*. Ed. Stephen Booth［M］. New Haven：Yale UP，1977.

［6］Shelley P B. A Defence of Poetry［A］// *The Norton Anthology of English Literature*. Ed. M. H. Abrams［M］. New York：Norton，1986.

［7］Zhang, Longxi. *The Tao and the Logos*［M］. Durham：Duke UP，1992.

［8］伯托齐.《恋爱中的妇女》中的象征手法［A］//载蒋炳贤编.劳伦斯评论集［M］.上海：上海文艺出版社，1995.

［9］莎士比亚.十四行诗［A］//莎士比亚全集［M］.第11卷.北京：人民文学出版社，1978.

［10］殷企平.劳伦斯笔下的彩虹［J］.外国语，2005（1）.

［11］殷企平.小说艺术管窥［M］.天津：百花文艺出版社，1995.

［12］张隆溪.道与逻各斯［M］.冯川，译.南京：江苏教育出版社，2006.

［13］张隆溪.讽寓［A］//赵一凡等，编.西方文论关键词［C］.北京：外语教学与研究出版社，2006.

（本文原载于《外国文学》2012年第1期）

两种文化和英国高等教育（上）

第二次世界大战以后，英国高等教育思想界曾经发生过一场著名的争论，即"两种文化"之争。这场争论不仅牵涉到英国高等教育的根本思想，而且对当今英国高等教育的改革仍然产生着重大的影响。本文旨在探讨这场争论的来龙去脉以及由此所引起的具体改革措施。

两种文化

"两种文化"之争是因著名小说家兼科学家查尔斯·珀西·思诺（Charles Peroy Snow, 1905—1980）的一篇演讲而起的。就是这篇后来以小册子形式发表的《两种文化》演讲稿（Two Cultures），造成了英国历史上一场罕见的大辩论，因此，"两种文化"常常被用作那场争论的代名词。由于思诺的主要论敌是弗·阿·李维斯（F. R. Leavis, 1895—1978），这场争论又被叫作"思诺-李维斯之争"（Snow - Leavis Controversy），或者干脆被叫作"思诺之争"（Snow Conflict）。

1959年，思诺在剑桥大学发表了题为《两种文化》的长篇演说，其主题是文理之间日趋扩大的鸿沟——学文科的和学理科的相互缺乏了解，甚至彼此怀有敌意，好像代表了"两种文化"似的；除非采取必要措施，这种现象将产生危险的后果。思诺这样说："我认为整个西方社会的精神生活已经日益分裂成两个极端……学文的知识分子为一个极端，而科学家则为另一个极端，其中以物理科学家最具有代表性。这两种人互相缺乏了解,形成了一个鸿沟——有时候(尤其是在年轻人中间)还互相抱有敌意和厌恶情绪,但是最多的是相互缺少了解。"(Snow 1959:3)至于"两种文化"的产生原因,思诺认为:"这种文化的鸿沟不仅仅是英国独有的现象,它存在于整个西方世界。但是它似乎在英国最为明显。其原因有二:一是因为我们狂热地相信教育专业化——无论是在西方还是在东方,没有一个国家比我们更对此深信不疑了;二是因为我们倾向于让社会形式固定化……一旦任何像文化鸿沟之类的东西得以产生,所有社会力量都会起来使它更加僵化,而不是使它具有一些可塑性。"(Snow 1959:4)

在谈到克服文化鸿沟的办法时,思诺说:"走出这一难关的办法只有一个:重新考虑我们的教育。"(Snow 1959:19)5年后他写了《对两种文化的回顾》(The Two Cultures: and a Second Look),明确提出要向美国的一些大学学习:"在美国,这种鸿沟就不那么难以逾越……在耶鲁、普林斯顿、密歇根和加利福尼亚,世界级的科学家在向非理科学生授课;在麻省理工学院和加州理工学院,理科学生正在认真学习人文学科。"(Snow 1964:69)

思诺在强调知识的专门化会带来的危险的同时,还流露了他对理科的偏爱:"科学家们骨子里就代表着将来,而传统文化(笔者按:此处指文科知识分子)则希望将来并不存在。"(Snow 1959:12)正是思诺这种对理科和科学家的偏爱,激怒了当时英国文坛巨人之一——首屈一指的文学批评家弗·阿·李维斯。他在经过长达3年的充分准备之后,于1962年也在剑桥大学发表了演说,题目是《两种文化?查·珀·思诺的意义》(Two Cultures? The Significance of C. P. Snow)。这篇演讲措辞之激烈,几乎达到了人身攻击和谩骂的程度。

李维斯这样谈论他和思诺的分歧:"和思诺一样,我也关心大学的情况。跟他不同的是,我想要使它成为一个名副其实的大学;这种大学不仅仅是一些不同专业系科的搭配——它也应该成为人类意识的中心:洞察力、知识、判断力和责任感都构成了人类的意识。"(Leavis 1962)事实上,李维斯和思诺都反对知识过分专门化,都赞成要加强不同知识领域之间的联系。所不同的是,他们在如何实现这种联系的问题上各执己见。思诺想要用他那"代表着将来"的科学学科来带动其他学科,而李维斯则认为跨越文化鸿沟的办法是在大学建立一个中心:"这个中心应该设在一个富有生命力的英文学院。"(Leavis 1962)李维斯这样主张的理由是：英文学院最有助于人脑的基本活动（这种活动包括智力活动和情感活动），"没有这种基本活动，科学大厦的巍峨耸立是不可能的。"（Leavis 1962）在他的另一本专著《教育和大学》（Education and the University, 1948）中，李维斯对如何通过"英文学院"来沟通不同专业学科的设想有过更加详细的阐述。他首先承认："当然，专业化是不可避免的（虽然一些学科的专业化不如另一些学科那样具有明显的必要性）；问题是如何在不同专门学科及其学习之间建立起一种有意义的联系——去发现如何训练一种中心智力，并通过它把所有不同的学科联系在一起。"（Leavis 1948）李维斯强调，简单地同时学习多门学科丝毫不解决问题："对六七门专业的一知半解，甚至是多得多的了解，并不能产生一个受过教育的人。"（Leavis 1948）他接着援引美国学者奥蒂斯（Otis）的话说："教育旨在提供能表达我们时代文明的基本思想。这种教育必须是真正从哲学和历史的角度把不同知识融为一体的结果——这种知识整合的过程将显示不同思想、不同影响和不同力量之间的真实的相互作用，并且在一定程度上标出它们整体运动的方向，使它们闪出意义之光。"（Leavis 1948）

李维斯的演讲发表之后，立即在英国高教界掀起了一场轩然大波。许多同情、支持思诺的人纷纷撰文驳斥李维斯的观点，并且谴责他对思诺的"残酷攻击"。然而，支持和响应李维斯的也不乏其人。于是，双方展开了一场英国历史上罕见的、旷日持久的大辩论。由于篇幅有限，我们不可能一一介绍他们的观点，但是其中有一个人却是非提不可：他就是理查德·沃莱姆（Richard Wollheim）。在众多支持思诺的人当中，沃莱姆从理论上为他的观点作出了实质性的补充，因而在当时颇受重视。沃莱姆认为，思诺关于科技教育应该在高等学府中占主导地位的观点十分正确，但是他没能够提供有力的理论依据。因此，沃莱姆为这一观点提供了他认为十分重要的理论依据。第一条依据和"平等"这一社会价值观有关："我们正在进入一个机会均等的社会，换言之，在这样的社会里，社会差别将取决于能力……而鉴别能力的最好方法是整个教育过程。因此，我们所需要的是一个能够非常明显地区分不同能力的教育系统。科学教育所提供的正是这一鉴别过程。所以，教育系统的主要性质应该是科学教育。有前途的艺术必须有广泛的吸引力；要获得这种吸引力的唯一途径是采用具有广泛吸引力的内容，而这种内容则只能在科学及其应用中找到。"（Wollheim

1959：168）

沃莱姆的第二条理论依据和"文化的性质"有关："文化是一种有机的整体；它之所以能够成为整体，是因为它所有部分都流动着共同的血液，并因此而得到净化。在任何现代文化中，占主导地位的精神必定是科学精神，因为正是这一方面，人类的智力和创造力在过去的一百年当中得到了充分的显示。所以，任何不体现这一时代主流精神的诗歌或绘画形式是一种时代错误。这种诗和画也许能一时美得出奇，但是它们终究缺乏生机，是一种垂死而无味的东西"（Wollheim 1959：168）。

在很大程度上，"两种文化"之争是 19 世纪"文实之争"的延续：当时以纽曼和阿诺德等人为一方、以赫胥黎等人为另一方的英国高等教育界就文科和理科孰轻孰重的问题发生过激烈的争论。从思想源流上看，思诺和沃莱姆、赫胥黎等人有许多相通之处，而李维斯的思想则跟纽曼等人的思想一脉相承。先说李维斯和纽曼之间的共同点：两人都十分强调"智力的训练"，都对"哲学"一词有特殊的偏爱——纽曼把他的"自由知识"说成是"哲理性知识"（提倡这种知识是纽曼自由教育思想的核心），而李维斯则主张"从哲学的角度"整合知识。所不同的是，李维斯进一步明确地提出了"中心论"，即大学生应该以"英文学院"为中心——这种中心不仅训练"中心智力"，而且还培养、雅化情感："英文学院的基本学科应该是文学和文学批评……它以其他任何学科都无法具备的方法同时训练智力和情感，培养人的敏感性、对事物反应的精确性以及智力的灵敏性和完整性——这种智力不仅能够分析事物，而且能够综合事物……"（Leavis 1948）不过，李维斯强调以上主张"绝不意味着文学教育本身就使人满意了……学习文学的好处之一是它能不断地把人引向其他学科的学习"（Leavis 1948）。

再说思诺、沃莱姆和赫胥黎等人的共同之处：他们都把科学看作文化的不可分割的一部分，而且是主要部分。赫胥黎的一个著名观点是"科学应该成为教育大厦的基石"（Huxley 1971：105），而思诺及其支持者则在褒实贬文方面比赫胥黎走得更远——前面已经提到，思诺强调科学代表着将来，而文科往往代表着过去。思诺的这种观点似乎是更多地受了伯特伦·罗素（Bertrand Russell）的影响。罗素曾经在他著名的论文"作为文化—要素的科学"（Science as an

Element in Culture）中这样谈论文科的"缺陷"："在学习文学或艺术时，我们的注意力总是固定在过去；古希腊或文艺复兴时期的人比现在的任何人都强；昔日的成就根本没有促进我们自己这个时代的新成就，相反，它们实际上增加了创造新成就的难度——要独辟蹊径总是难上加难。"（Russell 1913：234）罗素认为，学理科的不会像学文科的那样受到以往成就的羁绊，而是往往能够利用过去的成就创造出更高的成就，因此他们代表着未来："在科学领域里，人们找到了具有最高价值的活动；艺术领域非得依靠不断涌现出一个比一个更伟大的天才才能取得进步，而在科学领域里，后来者总是能够站在前辈的肩上———旦一个出类拔萃的天才发明了一种方法，成千上万个普通人都能运用它。"（Russell 1913：235）

和思诺等人不同的是，罗素十分强调"科学的固有价值"。他认为科学知识有它的内在目的。根据罗素的观点，这种固有价值或内在目的是由科学的教育功能所决定的。他把"教育"界定为"通过教育手段，形成某种思维习惯和某种对人生和世界的态度"，而这种思维习惯和人生观的形成"一定得有科学的贡献"（Russell 1913：203）。罗素的这一观点曾经得到另一名英国学者约翰·阿·贝克（John R. Baker）的响应。他在1945年发表了一篇题为"科学本身即目的之欣赏"（The Appreciation of Science as an End in Itself）的文章。在这篇文章中，他除了提出和罗素相似的观点之外，还提出科学也能诉诸人的情感，给人以美的享受。我们前面提到，李维斯认为文科应该作为"中心"的理由之一是它能培养人的情感。可是，贝克早就曾强调科学能够给先前杂乱无章的世界带来秩序与和谐，从而给人以美感。贝克坚持认为，科学家能够"因一种对自然环境的特殊感受而得到激励，他们有一种与大自然彼此交流的感觉，并且为大自然的瑰丽而感到欢乐；这种感受和诗人以及画家在他们各自的领域中所感受到的没有什么两样"（Baker 1945：31）。

以上的各种观点都有一定的道理，但是也都带有片面性：李维斯及其拥护者所提倡的"英文学院"固然能够训练人的智力，培养人的情感，但是其他学科的学习只要得法，似乎也能得到相同的效果。同样，思诺等人的"科学"固然代表着未来，但是如果理科专业的人能够学一些文科，在想象力和创造性方面会更加丰富完美，也就是说，适当的文科训练有助于培养出更好的科学家，有助于"代表将来的科学"的发展。文理本来应该相通，何必把它们对立起来？当然，不同的时期，不同的环境，对不同的学科有所侧重那是完全自然的。那么，在当今这个高科技社会里，是不是应该侧重理科和工科呢？这就引出了我们下面的话题：当今高等教育的核心问题是什么？

作为"两种文化"的续音，英国高教界在20世纪60年代后期和70年代围绕"高等教育的核心问题是什么"这一话题展开过激烈的争论。这一问题其实又牵涉到下面三个问题：高等教育的根本理想是什么？高等教育怎样为社会服务？科技社会中人类面临的最大问题是什么？尽管关于这些问题的争论至今仍在进行，但人们在两个方面基本上达成了共识。其一，科学教育和职业教育肯定要加强。其二，高等教育的最终目标是培养能够适应科技社会的公民，而不仅仅是满足科技以及相应职业培训方面的需求。依笔者拙见，70年代前后英国高等教育思想要数下列三人最有影响：埃里克·阿什比（Eric Ashby）、罗依·尼布列特（W. Roy Niblelt）和赫尔巴特·布特菲尔德（Herbert Butterfield）。这三人有一个共同点：他们都承认知识的分化、职业的专门化和科技教育的发展是历史的必然，但是他们又都同时为过度专业化以及科学社会所隐含的其他危险而担忧。

阿什比是积极主张大学教育要适应科技社会的倡导人之一，但是他仍然把培养公民的需要放在首位。他说："毫无疑问，社会对受过教育的公民的需求甚至要超过对职业培训的需求。"（Ashby 1974）在阿什比看来，"教育"和"职业培训"是两个不可混淆的概念，而当今高等教育的"核心问题是教育和职业培训之间的矛盾"（Ashby 1974）。阿什比认为，科技社会中人类面临的最大问题不是来自科技本身，而是来自掌握科技的人以及科技知识和其他各种知识结合的情况。他不无明智地说："科学的进步不仅有赖于对职业科学家的培训，而且还有赖于科学在公众中的形象——它产生于把科学织入当代文化的机器，即科技新闻学、科幻小说以及传播科学思想的收音机、电影和电视等。"（Ashby 1974）阿什比所谓"把科学织入当代文化"的过程实际上就是我们前面讨论的"知识整合"的过程，也就是"两种文化"互相沟通的过程。

和阿什比一样，尼布列特也不反对职业培训，而是把它看作"高等教育最明显的传统功能"（Niblett 1969：243）。他所关心的问题是如何在大力发展职业教育的同时把握它的方向。他提出，在为社会服务的过程中，有必要区分社会的近期需要和长期需要。他为那种只顾眼前利益的功利主义态度感到担忧："危险不在于大学会对科技时代的近期需要响应不力；危险的恰恰是与此相反的情形：大学对这些需求的响应是如此积极，如此有效，以致它们会遇上自我解体的风险……"（Niblett 1969：247—248）尼布列特的意思是，如果大学为了社会的一些近期目标而忙于兜售一鳞半爪的知识，它必然会随着知识的分崩离析而瓦解。换言之，高等教育的根本目标和理想应该是为社会的长期需要服务。那么，什么是社会的长期需要呢？在尼布列特的眼中，社会最终需要的是全面发展的人，而高等教育的目标也就是要培养这样的人。尼布列特强调，这种培养目标在现代社会中正受到严重的威胁，因为"在高科技社会中，个人很容易随波逐流——接受培训只不过是为了找一个能够带来可观收入的工作……然而，随波逐流本身就是一种异化，是把人的价值隶属于稍纵即逝的时尚"（Niblett 1969：250）。为了抗拒这种异化，尼布列特也寄希望于"知识的整合"。他尤其赞赏"近几年建立的许多交叉学科的中心……如城市研究中心、人口研究中心、交通研究中心……这些中心有助于抵消过度的知识分化"（Niblett 1969：251）。

布特菲尔德在他的《大学和当今教育》（*The Universities and Education Today*）一书中也着重谈了大学的理想以及大学应该如何适应社会需求的问题。他首先指出，知识专业化是自古有之的现象，比如中世纪的布洛哥纳大学就是一个法律专业的中心；因此，专业学习本身无可非议。然而，不管是什么专业，都应该"把人放在首位"（Butterfield 1961：72）。布特菲尔德这样看待社会的需求："如果我们认为教育和社会生活的需求之间有任何联系，我们就应该正视这样一个事实：世界上的大量问题在本质上仍然是人的问题。这样说的原因是，这些问题的解决需要对人的性格、人类的矛盾以及人与人之间的关系具有洞察力，并且需要这方面的经历。"（Butterfield 1961：70）正因为如此，布特菲尔德直言不讳地把自己的教育理想称之为"人文主义的理想"。事实上，布特菲尔德的"人本位"跟尼布列特的"全面发展的人"以及阿什比的"公民"都没有多大的区别。

在谈论如何对付知识过度分化这一问题时，布特菲尔德把更多的希望寄托于课外活动的有效组织上："正是因为正规课程已经变得如此专业化，以致我们的传统知识中只有一小部分传授给了任何个别学生,所以我们比以往更有必要强调课外活动在传播我们文化遗产方面所发挥的重要作用……体育运动、戏剧的排练、俱乐部和学生会的组织、刊物的发表、报纸的阅读、辩论的开展——所有这些非正规活动形式使我们文化中的主要部分得以流传下来。这些活动还可以通过阅读当代小说、从事慈善事业和崇拜各种艺术而得到加强。所有活动中最有价值的也许是不同专业人员的交流——当科学家、历史学家、美学家和工程师经常碰在一起时,这种交流就会产生"(Butterfield 1961:75)。布特菲尔德这里提倡的所有这些活动也都是为了一个目的,即重新整合已经被分割了的"文化"。

在知识激增的当今社会,高等教育面临的已不再是"两种文化",而是"多种文化"。由于知识的不断分化,隔行如隔山的现象不仅存在于文科和理科之间,而且还存在于所有不同学科之间,甚至存在于同一学科内不同的分支之间。在这些日益增多并扩大的"文化鸿沟"面前,人类究竟应该采取什么对策?除了以上介绍的一些主张之外,还有哪些具体的办法?有哪些具体的经验和教训可循?事实上,英国高校自50年代以来在跨越文化鸿沟方面有过不少具体的实践。本文的第二部分将对这些具体的改革措施做一些探讨。

参考文献

[1] Ashby E. *Adapting Universities to A Technological Society* [M]. London: Jossey-Bass Publishers, 1974.

[2] Baker J R. *The Appreciation of Science as an End in Itself* [A] // *Science and the Planned State* [M]. New York: The Macmillan Company, 1945.

[3] Butterfield H. *The Universities and Education Today* [M]. London: Routledge and Kegan Panl, 1961.

[4] Huxley T H. *Scientific Education* [A] // *T. H. Huxley on Education* [M]. Cambridge: Cambridge University Press, 1971.

[5] Leavis F R. *Education and the University* [M]. London: Chatto and Windus, 1948.

[6] Leavis F R. *Two Cultures? The Significance of C. P. Snow* [M]. London:

Chatto and Windus, 1962.

[7] Newman J H. *The Idea of a University* [M]. Indiana: University of Notre Dame Press, 1982.

[8] Niblett W R. *Higher Education: Demand and Response* [M]. London: Travistock Publications, 1969.

[9] Russell B. Science as an element in culture [J]. The New Statesman, 1913, May 24.

[10] Snow C P. *The Two Cultures: and A Second Look* [M]. Cambridge: Cambridge Univerity Press, 1964.

[11] Snow C P. *The Two Cultures and the Scientific Revolution* [M]. New York, Cambridge University Press, 1959.

[12] Wollheim R. Grounds for approval [J]. The Spectator, 1959 (8): 168.

(本文原载于《高等教育研究》1994年第2期)

两种文化与英国高等教育（下）

跨越文化鸿沟的努力

从 20 世纪 50 年代开始，英国不少高校在课程设置方面尝试了跨越文化鸿沟的各种办法，其中以苏塞克斯大学的文理渗透项目以及工科类院校中的"自由教育科目"最为典型。下面让我们来看一下这些具体的办法。

1. 苏塞克斯大学 1991—1992 学年文理渗透项目

（1）背景与目的

苏塞克斯大学文理渗透项目始于 1963 年。起初，该项目适用于所有文理科的学生，即所有理科学生都必须修一门人文学科或社会学科的课程，而文科学生则必须修一门理科课程。由于财政等原因，该项目从 1972 年起对文科学生已不再适用，但是在理科学院中一直坚持至今。

文理渗透项目主席麦克尔·布朗（Michael Brown）在接受笔者的采访时，曾经这样强调该项目的目的："从'思诺之争'以来，文理隔阂的现象非但没有缓减，而且日趋严重。我们的目的之一是要消除这种隔阂。我们的目的之二是要适应现代科技社会的特点。学习理工科的学生往往忽视这样一个重要事实：高科技社会的发展不但给人类带来了物质文明，而且还给人类带来了许多问题，如生态环境的破坏和污染等。这些问题的解决不能依靠科学本身，而是要依靠掌握科学的人。让理科学生选修一些人文学科或社会学科的课程，这关系到我们未来的科学家是否能负起对社会乃至整个人类的责任的重大问题。"

（2）特点与课程设计

文理渗透项目所包含的课程很多，但是所有这些课程都着眼于把学生引向一些共同的问题。用该项目学生手册中的话说："本项目并不是一连串互不相干的课程……每门课程确实有它自己的侧重点或特殊的授课方法，但是它们都要审视这样一些问题：我们怎样才能表达自己的思想和想象力？我们是怎样获取现有知识的？我们怎样才能预见未来？我们生活的局限性何在？我们该怎样决定自己的未来？"①

除了用一些共同的问题连接诸多课程以外，这个项目还包括"跨学科"以及"以人为中心"的特点："总的来说，这些课程是'跨学科'性质的，因为它们都'以人为中心'。它们都从问题入手——都关心人类的问题，并且对解决这些问题的现有方法以及各种建议进行评论和批判。"②

文理渗透项目开设的课程涉及范围很广，大致可以分为八类：（1）技术/文化/社会学；（2）管理学；（3）政治/经济/历史学；（4）哲学；（5）自我研究；（6）文学；（7）艺术/电影/音乐学；（8）外语。以第一类为例，属于该类课程的有："地球的自然资源：一种系统观""技术社会学""家庭技术：设计、表现和性别""动物的权力和科学实验""机器人的形象""电子计算机控制下的怪物机器和可怕的技术""科学革命"。

显然，以上所举的课程就带有"跨学科"性质——它们需要从多学科的角度来探讨，这样就自然地跨越了不同学科之间的"鸿沟"。

（3）效果与问题

笔者曾经对选修 1991—1992 学年文理渗透项目课程的学生进行了随意抽样调查。调查的方式为"半框架式交谈"，即事先准备好一些特定的问题，但是并不拘泥于这些问题，而是根据交谈过程中出现的一些疑问临时提问，在所有 220 个参加该项目的学生中，有 40 个同笔者进行了交谈。所提问题主要有这么四个：（1）你为什么修该项目的课程？（2）你是否感到这门课程帮助你增强了知识

---

①② University of Sussex, Arts/Science Programme 1991-1992, p. 4.

的整体观，即对不同学科之间相互关系的认识？（3）你认为该项目能够帮助你成为一个更好的专家呢，还是分散了你的精力，使你不能集中时间学好专业？（4）除了上课以外，你和该课程老师的个别接触是否足够？你和老师的关系如何？在回答以上第 1 个问题时，29 个学生说他们修这些课是出于无奈——迫于学校的规定，但是其中有 18 人承认他们已经从"不喜欢"转变为"喜欢"这些课程，因为他们从中受益匪浅，尤其是拓宽了知识面；在其他 11 个人中，6 个人声称本来就觉得有必要开阔自己的视野，这些课程有助于全面发展；而另外 5 个则说本来就无所谓，但是修课以后也觉得很有意思，有帮助。从以上情况看，认为自己在不同程度上得益于该项目的学生共有 29 人，占 72.5%。

对于第二个问题，25 人（占 62.5%）给了肯定的回答，11 人（占 27.5%）给了否定的回答；其余 4 人（占 10%）似乎自己也不太清楚。

对第三个问题，28 人（占 70%）给了肯定的回答，11 人（占 27.5%）给了否定的回答，另外 1 人（占 2.5%）认为既没有浪费时间，也没有感到"增加知识面"和"成为更好的专家"之间有必然的联系。

在回答第四个问题时，18 人（占 45%）表示有关教师跟自己的接触令人满意，22 人（占 55%）表示接触时间不足，师生关系不甚理想。

从以上调查情况看，多数学生在不同程度上感到受益于文理渗透项目，尤其是 62.5% 的学生明确表示有关课程增强了自己对不同学科之间相互联系的认识，这说明该项目还是相当成功的。但是，从对第四个问题的回答情况看，希望有关教师跟自己有更多接触的学生比例高达 55%。这一问题看似和我们讨论的中心——跨越文化鸿沟——关系不大，其实不然：课程的巧妙设计和安排只是跨越不同学科之间鸿沟的手段之一；任何课程的作用的充分发挥都有赖于良好的师生关系以及师生之间经常不断的接触。关于这一点，我们在下文中还要继续讨论。

2. 工科类院校中的"自由教育科目"

1957 年 5 月，英国教育部第 323 号通函（这是英国历史上有关如何实施自由教育的第一个官方文件）提出了以下五条关于在高等技术学院等院校内加强自由教育的具体措施（Davies 1965）：（1）增加额外的科目；（2）理工科课程本身的面要加宽；（3）增加学院图书馆的使用率；增加研讨课、小组讨论、个别辅导和课外自修等活动；在教员和学生中间培养大学中常见的那种导师制下形成的关系；（4）鼓励学院中的社团生活，开展各种课外活动；（5）跟国外院校建立联系。

第323号通函还特别强调工科院校要加强四个领域的学习，即人际关系、英语和交流艺术、经济学、工业的演变（Davies 1965）。它还推荐了一大串选修科目，其中包括艺术、法律、外交事务、外语、政治学和体育（Davies 1965）。虽然该通函推荐的科目很多，但是它强调在组织这些科目的学习时要注意两点。第一，要区分必修科目和选修科目；第二，重点要放在研究工业中"人的问题"，尤其是如何建立不同工业集团之间的良好关系的问题，以及如何实现人与人之间更有效的交流的问题（Davies 1965）。在第323号通函以及其他政府文件的敦促下，所有当时的高级技术学院都先后设置了所谓的"自由教育课程"，即跨越文化鸿沟的课程。下面以波洛夫多科技学院的自由教育课程大纲为例：

第一年
技术和社会Ⅰ：
西方文明史
英语语言学
经济学原理
选修科目

第二年
技术和社会Ⅱ：
文化面面观
有效的口语
报告的撰写
选修科目

第三年
技术和社会Ⅲ：
科学史和科学哲学
社会和政治哲学
现代英国的社会经济发展
选修科目

第四年
工业管理
工业组织
工业中的人际关系
选修科目

以上的"选修科目"涉及更多的领域，包括考古学、社会人类学、人种学、教育学、社会心理学和工业设计等（Davies 1965）。波洛夫多科技学院的这个自由教育课程大纲通过"技术和社会"这一主题,把诸多课程结合在了一起。不过,跟其他多科技术学院的自由教育课程一样,这些课程在很大程度上只是一种附加物,即在原来的专业课程之外加上一些课程而已;而且,这些课程的设置虽然体现了广度,但是由于学生的时间有限,很可能因广度而牺牲了深度。也就是说,专与博的关系究竟如何解决,这在以上大纲中并没有得到真正体现。关于专与博如何有机结合的问题,阿什比和英国高等教育界新秀巴尼特先后有过较精辟的论述。下面分别加以介绍。

3. 形成"辐射圈"

为了既跨越文化鸿沟,又不因此牺牲专业的深度,阿什比在《技术与学术》一书中提出了以专业为核心,并且不断向外"辐射"的办法:"我认为可以把专业学习(无论什么专业,冶金学也好,牙科学也好,挪威语也好,全都一样)作为核心,在其周围团聚着与专业学习有关的自由教育课程。但是这些课程必须和专业有关;通向文化的道路应该贯穿一个人的专业,而不是绕过专业"(Davies 1965)。阿什比这里所说的"文化"也就是消除了鸿沟之后的文化整体。

关于如何"辐射"的具体问题,在罗纳尔德·巴尼特的《高等教育思想》一书中得到了更加深入的讨论。

和阿什比一样,巴尼特也设计了一个以专业为核心的课程结构。他把它称作"批判性交叉学科课程"并为自己的课程结构设计了一套理论,其主要观点是:高等教育的一个基本理想和特征是培养学生的批判能力(Ashby 1966:84)——这种"批判"不但指学生的独立思考和判断,而且指用一学科对另一学科进行评价的方法和过程。巴尼特认为,任何专业学科既有它的长处和合理性,又有它的短处和局限性。因此,"在高等教育中,我们希望学生们不仅仅勤奋地攻读专业——如果只是局限于所选学科或职业,再勤奋的学习都是不够的。我们还希望,在课程结束时,学生们已经能够往后退一步,以便在更广阔的情境下审视他们的核心科目,了解它的发展过程以及它和其他科目的联系,并且基本认识它对世界的贡献"(Barnett 1990)。巴尼特这里所说的"往后退"以及"在更广阔的情境下审视核心科目"也就是一种"批判"。既然是批判,就要涉及批判的标准问题。巴尼特认为,应该把批判的标准分为两类:一类是"内部标准"，即学科内部传统的理论和观念等；另一类是"外部标准"，即其他学科的原理和方法等。巴尼特说，人们在评论和判断某种理论、事物或人类的行为时，大部分用的是自己所在学科内的标准。巴尼特认为这是自然和正常的，但是仅仅有内部标准还不够，还需要有外部标准来帮助学生对自己的专业进行反思。"进行这种反思的可以是土木工程学的学生，他可能会考虑一个新建筑的社会效应——换而言之，他会使用社会学的观点和方法；进行反思的也可以是英语专业的学生，他可能会问：'什么是文学？我们为什么认为它是一种好东西？'——这里就包含了伦理哲学的思想；进行反思的还可以是一个学习艺术的；他可能试图了解一种特定传统是怎样形成的，以及为什么形成——这样就开始了史学研究；再以化学专业的学生为例，他可能被要求考虑工业或农业化学品对自然环境的影响——这样就多了一种从生物学角度研究化学的方法……"（Barnett 1990）。

正是这种从外部对核心学科的批判，构成了巴尼特心中的高等教育的要旨——他把"教育"和"培训"作了这样的区别："核心学科以及它们的内部评价形式构成了学生课程的大部分，这是可以理解的。但是一个只让学生从内部探索一个或多个学科的课程不能算作高等教育课程；它只能算是那些学科领域里的培训。不管是怎样高水平的培训，只有在学生具有下列能力以后才算是转化成了高等教育：他们必须能够对自己所学或所掌握的东西进行独立的评价，能够把它置入和其他事物的关系之中，能够既看到它的优点，又看到它的局限性"（Barnett 1990）。巴尼特的这种观点是非常正确的。对于任何一个高等院校来说，如果它培养出来的学生只能用自己学科的内部标准去判断事物，那它提供的就不是真正的高等教育。

基于"批判"这一原则，巴尼特提出了他的"批判性交叉学科课程"，并且用了以下图形（见下页图1）来表示它的结构（Barnett 1990）。

巴尼特认为图1所示的结构是一种开放型结构，它可以无止境地从知识的总体领域里吸收养料。由于它的开放性特点，"别的学科的光线可以射入这一结构"（Barnett 1990）。巴尼特还把这种"别的学科"——即核心课程之外的学科——称为"审问者"，"这些学科就像审问者——历史学、美学、伦理学、经验科学、数学或任何学科——它们被选来做真正的批判工作或照明工作。它们

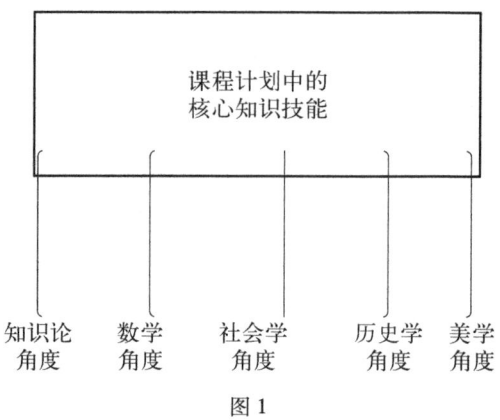

图 1

的批判性力量不是来自学科内部固有的特点,因为任何学科在原则上都可以被召来做这种工作。它们的力量来自这样一个事实,即作为批判武器,它们显示了接受批判的学科的局限性。它们的力量来自批判本身"(Barnett 1990)。

巴尼特和阿什比各自设计的课程虽然还只是"纸上谈兵",但是它们代表了一种旨在提出跨越文化鸿沟的实际方案的努力。然而,光从课程入手究竟能起到多大作用?这将是下一小节的中心话题。

4. 师生关系的重要性

光从课程入手是否能解决问题?我们只要稍微思考一下就会发现,设计得再好的课程也都无法避免两个问题。其一,无论一种课程的知识面有多宽,它仍然是"挑选后的知识"——从知识总体中挑出来的一小块而已。其二,即使人们可以设计出"完美"的课程,任何法定或成文的课程计划都很可能跟教师和学生头脑中的实际知识相去甚远。第一个问题的原因显而易见,无须赘言。第二个问题的原因有二:一是跟教师的教学态度和能力有关,二是跟学生的学习动机和态度有关。如果一个教师因本身素质较差或其他原因而未能有效地贯彻法定课程的意图,那就等于推翻了原来的课程。因此,在加强课程改革的同时,必须加强师资队伍的建设(包括对教师职业道德的教育、业务的培训——尤其是实施交叉学科教育的技能培训等)。至于学生的学习动机和态度,这又牵涉到学业的评定方法问题。爱丁堡大学社会学教授麦克佛森在分析苏格兰高等教育时认为,在19世纪中叶引进了考试制度以后,苏格兰的自由教育传统日益受到了威胁,"教学和学业评定开始脱节"(Barnett 1990),学生们"只把注意力集中在课程中某些可能考到的知识领域"(Mcpherson 1972)。麦克佛森不无道理地指出:"频繁的系科考试可能不仅会影响学生的知识取向,而且会影响他在联系不同知识领域方面的态度和能力。"(Mcpherson 1972)麦克佛森分析的这种情况不仅存在于苏格兰,而且还存在于整个英国,甚至存在于整个世界。就在中国的高等学府里,"六十分万岁"的口号至今仍不绝于耳。必须承认,考试在督促学生和评定学业成绩方面确有一定的作用,但是它在肢解知识方面的危害性也不可低估。

如何解决上面这个难题?笔者曾经于1992年带着这个问题走访了麦克佛森教授。他的回答是:跨越文化鸿沟的主要出路在于培养良好的师生关系。我们完全同意麦克佛森的观点。师生之间一旦建立了良好的关系,我们前面分析到的两个问题——教师的教学态度和能力以及学生的动机和态度——就有了解决的希望:教师可以在跟学生的真正接触中发现并同情后者的困难和问题,并且因此而激发对教学的热情;而学生则可以在自然、轻松、和谐的气氛中从教师那儿获得知识并了解不同知识之间的相互关系——这种潜移默化比为了考试而死记硬背支离破碎的知识要强得多。从我们前面分析的情况看,苏塞克斯大学文理渗透项目那种对课程的精心设计,如果辅之以在培养师生关系方面的具体措施,可能会取得更好的效果。

总之,消除文化鸿沟不仅需要加强课程改革,而且需要加强良好的师生关系。从某种意义上说,后者比前者更重要,而且更困难。可惜的是,几乎没有人对这一问题进行过学术性探讨。但是,在高等教育需要大发展的今天,这一问题亟待人们的重视。

参考文献

[1] Ashby E. *Technology and the Academics* [M]. New York: St. Martin's Press, 1966.

[2] Barnett R. *The Ideal of Higher Education* [M]. SRHE: Open University Press, 1990.

[3] Davies L. *Liberal Studies and Higher Technology* [M]. Cardiff: University of

Wales Press, 1965.

［4］Mcpherson A F. *An Old Ideal in a Changing University Structure* ［M］. The Open University Press, 1972.

［5］University of Sussex, Arts/Science Programme 1991－1992: 4.

（本文原载于《高等教育研究》1994 年第 3 期）

纽曼大学观探微

在西方高等教育史上，约翰·亨利·纽曼（John Henry Newman，1801—1890）是一个颇有争议的人物，也是一个不容忽视的人物。他的重要地位和影响用当代英国学者艾·梯·科尔的一句话来形容最合适："在纽曼以后的所有关于大学教育的论著都是对他的演讲和论文的脚注。"（Ker 1974）这些"脚注"毁誉参半，甚至贬多于褒，但是它们都说明了一点：不了解纽曼，就无法了解整个西方高等教育思想的源流。

纽曼当过牛津大学的教堂牧师，青年时期曾经受过新教思想的影响，后来经过"牛津运动"中的争论和思考，放弃了英国国教，皈依了罗马天主教，最后成了红衣主教。除了宗教之外，教育是他终生关注的问题。他在加入天主教以后，曾经应邀接受了都柏林大学校长的职位，在那里作了若干次演讲，后来集为一书，题名《大学的理想》（*The Idea of a University*，1852）。这部书后来成了自由教育思想的代表作。这里需要指出的是，"自由教育"一词并非纽曼首创。它早在"经院哲学派或者亚里士多德的词汇里就已存在了"（Rothblatt 1976：13）。不过，不同的时代，不同的人，对它的解释不尽相同，甚至大相径庭。比如，它在古代可以指"文科教育"（Liberal arts），也可以指"三艺"（Trivium）和"四艺"（Quadrivium）（Rothblatt 1976：14）。"在乔治王朝的英国，整段自由教育的历史……是社会道德行为的历史"（Rothblatt 1976：15）。根据罗斯布赖特（Sheldon Rothblatt）的考证，"在整个近代史的大部分时期内，自由教育都带有功利性质"（Rothblatt 1976：9）。在纽曼那里，自由教育则又有其独特的含义。搞清纽曼的真实思想，这就是本文的目的。

让我们首先来看一下《大学的理想》赖以产生的时代背景：

在欧洲，以夸美纽斯、杜瑞、哈特布利为开端的注重普及、实用和科学的教育改革运动始于17世纪。到了19世纪，这场运动仍然方兴未艾。就英国高等教育而言，其最明显的动向是以伦敦大学为首的一批新型高等学府的崛起和发展。它们高举"学以致用"的大旗，径直向踞守正统的牛津、剑桥大学挑战——后者因其传统课程而广受抨击诘难。随着新型院校势力的壮大，科学技术开始在高等学府登堂入室，和宗教以及古典的人文学科分庭抗礼。可以说，这场教育改革的进程也是教育不断现代化的过程，其主要标志之一是教育的专业化或职业化。纽曼所处的时代是崇尚工具理性或实用主义的时代。当时最流行的是以杰律米·边沁（Jeremy Bentham）、詹姆斯·密尔（James Mill）和理查德·洛弗尔·埃奇沃思（Richard Lovell Edgeworth）等为代表的实用主义思潮。其中的埃奇沃思曾经在《爱丁堡评论》（*Edinburgh Review*）上连续发表题为"论专业教育"（"Essays on Professional Education"）的文章，猛烈抨击了传统大学的课程。在实用主义思潮的影响下，伦敦大学和曼彻斯特学院等高校实行了一系列的课程改革和教学法改革。这场改革亦称"新教育"运动，其信奉者的座右铭就是"实用"。他们在攻击牛津、剑桥大学的陈旧课程时不无道理，然而他们中的许多人同时又走向了另一个极端——他们片面地强调知识的实用性，在编排课程时急功近利，满足于一鳞半爪的肤浅知识而忽视知识的系统性、连贯性和全面性。正是针对这一点，纽曼用他的《大学的理想》向世人提出了警告。

《大学的理想》共分两大部分。第一部分由九篇演讲稿组成，第二部分由十篇论文组成。第二部分的主要思想精华均已包括在第一部分之中，而第一部分的主要精华则又集中在该部分的后五章（即后五篇演讲稿）——它们的轴心线是自由教育的实质和用途。人们常常指责纽曼在《大学的理想》中花了太多的篇幅谈论神学问题（主要局限于前四章），可是他们往往忽视了纽曼当时的处境：纽曼其时受聘于天主教大学，不得不考虑来自各方面的压力。根据他和亲友的书信，他自己也认为前几篇演讲稿"枯燥无味——然而（此话不可外传）这几篇演讲稿都是按上司的意图写的，我想应付他们一下罢了……"（Ker 1988：

379），只是在应付了差使之后，纽曼才认为自己"接下去要正常地阐述大学的理想"（Ker 1988：379）。可见，纽曼花大量篇幅谈神学自有他的苦衷，只是在后五篇讲稿中他才"正常地"探讨了"正常的思想"。

纵观全书，《大学的理想》贯穿着这样一个中心思想："所有的知识都交融合一"（Newman 1982：XXXVII）；而大学则是"传授天下一切知识的地方"（Newman 1982：XXXVIII）。纽曼的所有观点都是以这一思想为前提、为基础的。在他的众多主张中，至少有两大观点值得详细介绍：

第一，纽曼主张把教学和科研截然分开。他认为大学应该只保留教学的职能，而把科研的职能留给科学院，提出："发现和教学是两种迥然不同的职能，而且它们也是迥然不同的天赋。同一个人兼备这两种天赋的情形并不常见。而且，整天忙于向所有求学者灌输自己现有知识的人不可能有闲暇和精力去掌握新知识。探寻真理的人往往是离群索居，心无旁骛，这是人类的常识。最伟大的思想家们在研究某一课题时总是专心致志，不允许自己的工作被打断。他们在做别的事情时总是神不守舍，行为怪僻，并且对课堂教育和公开讲课都多少有些忌讳。'大希腊之光'毕达哥拉斯曾经一度穴居。'爱奥尼亚之光'泰勒斯终身未娶，深居简出，并多次拒绝王公贵族们的邀请。柏拉图离弃雅典，去阿卡德漠斯园林居住。亚里士多德负笈师事于柏拉图达二十年之久。修士培根在伊希斯塔隐居一生。牛顿终日冥思苦想，几乎因此丧失了理性。化学和电学方面的伟大发现不是在大学内取得的……教学需要和外界打交道，而实验和思辨的自然条件则是隐居。"（Newman 1982：XL—XLI）正是基于以上理由，纽曼认为"要在科学院和大学之间进行智力分工"（Newman 1982：XL）。

第二，纽曼反对过早地分专业。他认为大学是学习所有知识的地方，所以不应该在那儿细分专业。有人曾因此而把纽曼说成是职业教育的反对者。不错，纽曼确实反对把职业教育简单地作为大学教育的目的，但是他并非不考虑为大学生将来的职业做准备，而是想从根本上解决这一问题。关于这一点，我们将在下文中详细探讨。在纽曼眼里，大学教育的主要功能之一是智力训练，也就是用天下一切知识来锻炼智力。然而，一个学生不可能修习大学里的全部课程。怎样才能解决这一矛盾呢？纽曼提出了师生同住校园的办法："虽然学生们不可能学习每一个向他们开放的科目，但是只要他们生活在那些代表全部知识的人群中间，并受到后者的指点，他们就能够有所收获。这就是我所说的在高等学府住读的好处……学者们云集大学，虽然各自都热衷于自己的学科，虽然彼此都是竞争的对手，但是他们为了创造和谐的学术环境而走到了一起——他们亲密地互相接触，互相调整各自学科的主张以及彼此之间的关系。他们学会了互相尊重，互相商量，互相帮助。这样就形成了一种纯洁清澈的思想空气。每个学生也都呼吸这种空气，尽管他只修习众多学科中的少数几门。"（Newman 1982：76）显然，纽曼把思想氛围和学术空气放在比课程更为重要的地位。学生们只要沉潜浸润于这种空气之中，通过耳濡目染和相互交流就能自然而然地找到掌握"天下一切知识"的途径。当然，纽曼并没有否定具体课程的作用。他主张所有的课程都为智力培训服务。不过，虽然他认为每一门课程都是知识总体中不可分割的一部分，但是他实际上强调最多的还是文法、古典文学和哲学等传统大学课程。比如，他把文法放在相当突出的位置。他说："我非常坚决地认为，智力训练的第一步是在孩子的脑子里印上科学、方法、秩序、原则、系统、规则、例外、丰富、和谐等概念。让孩子首先修习文法通常是收到这一效果的极好办法"。（Newman 1982：XLIV）

必须指出，以上两大观点都有其缺陷和谬误，甚至是严重的谬误。比如，教学和科研分家的观点显然过于极端。实践已经证明，教学和科研不可能截然分开；只要处理得当，它们应该是相辅相成的。不过，这一观点未必全错，它至少提醒我们要重视这样一个事实：如果处理不当，教学和科研也会发生矛盾，发生冲突。只讲教学和科研互相补充的一面，而不讲它们互相矛盾的一面，实际上是要出乱子的。纽曼的第二个观点，即反对在大学里细分专业的观点，也失之偏颇。然而，这一观点中含有重视智力训练、主张住读教育等思想成分。这些思想成分应该说是合理的。

由此可见，纽曼的思想观点包含着许多复杂的成分，其中既有消极的一面，也有积极的一面。

前面提到的两个观点只是纽曼整个自由教育思想中的一部分。其实，纽曼的自由教育思想十分丰富，也十分复杂。任何简单的概括和归纳都只能挂一漏万。本文限于篇幅，自然不可能面面俱到。但是，笔者以为，要正确理解纽曼的自由教育思想，必须抓住一把钥匙，即对他的一句著名口号——"为知识而知识"——加以正确理解。下面我们就来试用一下这把钥匙。

《大学的理想》第五章的标题就是"知识本身即目的"。后人常常片面地、断章取义地解释这句话的意思，殊不知这句话具有深刻的含义和哲理。首先，这句话是针对功利主义者的论调而提出来的。前文已经提到，当时埃奇沃思等人曾经在《爱丁堡评论》上连篇累牍地攻击传统大学的课程；他们同时还鼓吹洛克的功利主义，认为"凡是不以功利主义原则为基础的教育系统都产生不出什么好东西"（Newman 1982：121）。纽曼针锋相对地提出："如果自由教育是好的，那它也一定是有用的"（Newman 1982：124）。功利主义者认为只有有用的东西才是好的，而纽曼则坚持只有好的东西才是有用的。"为知识而知识"这句话本身即使有它的片面性，也不失为对功利主义的一种有力的制约。

其次，纽曼所说的"知识"有它特定的含义。他要追求的是"自由知识"。世人常常对"自由知识"的意思有这样或那样的误解，不少人简单地把它看成是和实际知识截然相反的东西，进而把传播"自由知识"的自由教育视作与职业教育势不两立的东西。一些人甚至把英国工业的衰退归咎于纽曼的"自由知识"。比如，科雷里·尼特就曾经认为英国工业落后的重要原因之一是"纽曼所谓的'自由知识'的信奉者赢得了胜利"，而"'自由知识'是一种跟'具体知识和实际知识'毫不相干的知识"（Barnett 1986）。纽曼真的对具体的、实际的知识毫不关心吗？恰恰相反，他在书中曾经这样强调："不要以为我否认注重具体知识和实际知识的必要性，也不要以为我否认这些知识的益处……没有它们，生活就无法持续下去。我们日常的幸福归功于它们。运用它们是许多人的职责——对承担这一责任的人我们应该由衷地表示感谢。我只不过是说当知识分得越来越细时，它将不再成其为知识"（Newman 1982：124）。那么，纽曼为什么没有使用"实际知识"来作为口号，而是采用了"自由知识"一词呢？"自由知识"究竟是何物呢？让我们先来看一下纽曼对"自由"的解释："'自由'一词的含义究竟是什么呢？就它的语义而言，它首先是和'受奴役'相对立的"（Newman 1982：80）。显然，纽曼提倡的是知识的融会贯通和它的灵活运用。记得曾经有人把"为知识而知识"理解成"死读书"，殊不知纽曼反对的恰恰是"死读书"，恰恰是受知识的束缚或"奴役"。关于这一点，他说得很清楚："你必须驾驭你的知识，而不是让它压迫你，否则它就会使你窒息"（Newman 1982：

105）。既然知识是由人驾驭的，那它就带有工具性。所以，纽曼下了这样一个定义："本身既是工具又是结果的知识叫作自由知识"（Newman 1982：163）。可见，纽曼并不反对知识的工具性，并不反对把知识运用于实践，而是反对纯粹把知识当作工具的态度。事实上，纽曼从来没有反对过知识的实用性。他只是把知识的目的分成了内在目的和外在目的。他在强调知识的内在目的时并不否认它具有外在目的："本身好的东西不可避免地要发挥多种外在的用途……它必然会给社会带来好处。这种好处的大小和多少跟它本身的优秀程度成正比"（Newman 1982：137）。诸如此类的话在《大学的理想》一书中比比皆是。比如："凡是优秀的、美丽的、完美的、自身可取的东西不可避免地要外溢，它会把自身的美好向四处散发"（Newman 1982：124）。又如："只要大海潮水汹涌，我们将毫不怀疑它会灌满每一条海峡，每一道海湾，每一个港口"（Newman 1982：142）。我们可以这样来理解纽曼的话：他不是不要有用的知识，而是想确保有用的知识，因为只有可以作为目的自身的知识才是真正有用的知识。这里，我们不妨参考一下西方学者库尔梯斯和布尔特沃德的一段话："纽曼并不反对有用的教育本身。他承认这种教育不但具有价值，而且必不可少；如果他今天还活着的话，他可能会率先出来指出：这种培训本身包含的文化因素和那些通常跟人文学科相联系的文化因素同样重要"（Curtis & Boultwood 1965：433）。

为了防止别人误解他的意思，纽曼曾经把"作为目的自身的知识"比作人体健康：健康本身就是一种好东西；虽然人们很难说它有哪一种特定的用处，可是伴随着它的好处是如此之多，如此之大，以致人们一想到健康，不仅会把它看作一种好东西，而且也会把它看作一种有用的东西。"自由知识"也是一样：它虽然不是为了哪一种特殊用途而存在，但是却能让人终身受用。

一个高明的医生在治病救人时，总是着眼于治本，而不是治标。同样，纽曼是一个始终关心如何"治本"的教育家。他所用来"治本"的方法就是智力训练。这种训练的目的是要人们从天下万事万物而学之：一个从大学出来的人"已经审视了所有的知识"（Newman 1982：126）。当然，人脑毕竟是有限的，但是"有限的人脑应该尽可能地去囊括所有的事物，并力求对它们有一个清楚而准确的认识和理解"（Newman 1982：105）。智力训练的关键是掌握事物与事物之间的关系。经过了训练的人"不仅掌握了有关事物本身的知识，而且掌握了有关它们相互之间真实关系的知识；这种知识不但可以被看作一种占有物，而且可以被看作一种哲学"（Newman 1982：101）。纽曼这里所说的"哲学"指的是"理解一学科和另一学科之间的联系。每门学科对其他任何学科的用处，以及所有学科的位置、缺陷和变化"（Newman 1982：38）。换言之，纽曼眼中的智力乃是一种"哲学思辨"的能力。他曾经这样描述人的智力："它能够从不同的现象中找出普遍规律，能够找出事物的特性，能够按照原则行动，并且能够发现事物的因果关系。总之，它能够进行哲学思辨"（Newman 1982：56）。不难看出，纽曼之所以对"作为目的本身的知识"孜孜以求，是因为他想探寻事物的本质和普遍规律。这也就是他又把"自由知识"称作"哲理性知识"（Philosophical Knowledge）的原因（Newman 1982：94）。

纽曼在强调智力训练时，并没有忘记它的外在用途："智力训练是大有用处的"，因为受训练者"将来会处于这样一种智力状态，即能够从事任何学科的研究或从事任何职业"（Newman 1982：125）。这也就是说，纽曼要通过智力训练来培养一种通才。不过，他并没有把通才的培养跟职业的培训或科技知识的学习对立起来。他曾经毫不犹豫地指出："没有什么比在教育中忽视一个孩子将来的职业所必需的那些东西更加荒谬的了"（Newman 1982：121）。纽曼要培养通才，是因为"智力的全面培养是对职业学习和科技学习最好的帮助"（Newman 1982：125）。可见，纽曼对教育的职业培训功能和实用性是非常注意的。当然，他对"实用"的理解和当时流行的看法相去甚远。

除了上面谈到的"智力的全面培养"以外，纽曼所说的"实用性"还有另一层意思：

"如果必须给大学课程一个实用的目的，那么我说它是训练社会的良好成员。它的艺术是社会生活的艺术，它的目的是适应世界。……大学训练是达到一个伟大而又平凡的目的的伟大而又平凡的手段，它首先在于提高社会的精神格调，培养公众的智慧，纯洁民族的趣味，为群众所喜提供真正的原则，为群众所望提供确切的目标，对时代的思想能扩大其内容，冷静其情绪；也旨在推进政治权力的运用，雅化个人之间的交往。这种教育使人对所持的意见和判断有清楚的自觉，能用真理去发展它们，雄辩地说明它们，有力地提倡它们。它训练他看清事实，抓住要点，理出思想头绪，发现似是而非的东西，摒弃无关紧要的枝节。它使他作好准备，能胜任任何职务，掌握任何学问。它指引他去适应别人，能了解别人的心情，同时使别人了解自己，能影响他们，能同他们达成谅解，与之善处。他能在任何社会安身，同任何阶级找到共同之处……"（Newman 1982：134—135）。①

纽曼在上面这段话中既提到了智育，又提到了德育。耐人寻味的是，德育——培养优秀的公民——被放在了比智育更重要的位置，成了"最实用的目的"。纽曼所处的时代正是英国工商业日趋繁荣的时代，可是他最强调的是提高社会的精神格调以及纯洁民族的趣味，这说明他透过经济的繁荣看到了道德上和文化上的危机。正是基于这一忧患意识，他对"实用"的认识和理解比普通人高出了一个层次：本身优秀的人（即品学兼优者）才是真正的"实用"之材。

综上所述，纽曼的"为知识而知识"是和普通人理解的"为知识而知识"大相异趣的。他的"知识本身即目的"实际上是一大悖论：他苦心孤诣地追求作为目的自身的知识，实际上正是为了最大限度地发挥它的外在用途。

诚然，纽曼的某些观点已经过时了。比如，他虽然想用自由教育包括职业教育的内容，但是对单独使用"职业教育"这一名称却十分忌讳。他大概没有想到，在一百多年以后的今天，职业教育不仅堂而皇之地成了大学教育的目标之一，而且已经成了整个高等教育的主体（至少在西方是如此）。根据本·戴维的调查，"在欧洲先进国家的所有高校以及美国研究生院的毕业生中，大约有百分之七十到八十的人最终进入专门职业或管理职业，而且，他们学习的目的也很可能仅仅是为了找一个职业而已"（Ben-David 1977：30）。本·戴维在分析德、英、法、美等四国的高等教育时甚至把"职业教育"这一术语用来"表示所有专业化的或非专业化的高等教育"（Ben-David 1977：30）。然而，职业教育的蓬勃发展并不意味着与它相伴而行的危机已不复存在。从某种意义上说，纽曼当年指出的危险，尤其是过分追求专业人才所带来的危险，如今变得更大了。必须承认，由于现代社会已经进入了高科技时代，社会发展的节奏比纽曼时代大大加快，所以需要大力并迅速地培养专门人才。然而，正因为科学技术的高速发展，社会瞬息万变，过分追求专业人才往往会效果适得其反——一旦原有的

---

① 参考王佐良译文，见《外国文学》1990年第6期第48页。

社会需求改变，专门人才的应变能力可能远不及通才的应变能力。打个简单的比方：桌子形成以后很难改成他用，而作为原料的木头就比较容易应变。美国加州大学贝克莱分校的副校长田长霖曾经指出过这样一个矛盾："一方面，社会潮流一定要把职业教育变得很重，另一方面，职业性一强，就愈来愈不能适应周期性转换日益变短的趋势。所以，一方面应该加强基础课目，另一方面又需要有职业性的教育。这是一种矛盾，一种冲突，大家认为这是一个危机，如果弄得不好，整个高等教育的思想就会变掉"（田长霖 1986：338—339）。田教授这里所说的危机不正是纽曼当年预见到的危机吗？

总之，纽曼的大学观虽然有这样或那样的偏颇之处，但是仍瑕不掩瑜，给后人留下了许许多多值得细细咀嚼的东西。

参考文献

［1］ Barnett C. *The Audit of War* ［M］. London：Macmillan London Limited，1986.

［2］ Ben-David J. *Centres of Learning* ［M］. New York：McGraw-Hill Book Company，1977：30.

［3］ Curtis S J & Boultwood, ME. *A Short History of Educational Ideas* ［M］. London：University Tutorial Press Ltd.，1965：433.

［4］ Ker I. Introduction ［A］// *The Idea of a University* ［M］. Clarendon Press，1974.

［5］ Ker I. *John Henry Newman: A Biography* ［M］. Oxford：Oxford University Press，1988：379.

［6］ Newman J H. *The Idea of a University* ［M］. Indiana：University of Notre Dame Press，1982：XXXVII.

［7］ Rothblatt S. *Tradition and Change in English Liberal Education* ［M］. Faber and Faber Limited，1976.

［8］ 田长霖. 美国高等教育发展趋势 ［A］// 余立编. 现代教育思想引论 ［C］. 上海：华东师范大学出版社，1986：338-339.

（本文原载于《杭州大学学报》1992年第3期）

Teaching English Literature in China: Importance, Problems and Countermeasures*

The past two decades have been a difficult time for many teachers of English literature in Chinese universities. English departments have come under increasing pressure to bring their teaching into line with the "practical" needs of society. The denial or belittling of the value of English literature displays itself at almost all levels: in the various forms of official documents; in curriculum manuals; in the prefaces of multifarious functionally-oriented textbooks; in the "reform manifestos" of some avant-garde advocates of "pragmatic English" who celebrate "The End of the Literary Road";[1] in the ever-rising outcry among the students who would like to banish Shakespeare, if not all literature, from their English courses; in the pressing demands from the parents whose primary concern is that their children should get a ticket to a good job; in the recruiting policies of employers who often give preference to those who have taken "pragmatic courses" such as "Scientific English" and "Foreign Trade English" which impress employers with their apparent practical utility (see also Cheng; Pang, Zhou and Zheng this issue).

---

* 本文由殷企平和陈姝波合写。

One most recent trend is illustrated by the fashionable slogan: "Cultivate multi-talented foreign language majors!" (*Pei yang fu he xing wai yu ren cai!*). Although its definition is still subject to controversy, this slogan has become a guiding principle for the newly-amended national teaching program for English majors in institutions of higher education.[2] According to the program, less than 10 percent of the total teaching hours are devoted to courses in literature (The English Section of the Guiding Committee for Specialized Foreign Language Teaching in Institutions of Higher Education 2000: 3-5). The real problem, however, does not lie in the proportion of time assigned to the courses in literature, which are usually not offered until the third year. What really does harm is that such a program, by putting courses like "basic English" and "advanced English" (formerly called "intensive reading") into the category of "the curricula of special techniques", gives the green light to the currently prevalent curricula that tend to completely squeeze literature out of the first two years of English studies. We know that literature used to take a considerable share of the course in intensive reading. The most popular textbook used in that course, from the 1960s to the early 1980s, was *English*, compiled by Xu Guozhang. This course consists of four books designed respectively for the first four semesters. Book I introduces such literary genres as fables, legends and short poems, while in Book II just under half of the volume is devoted to various forms of literature, including "The Golden Touch" (from Greek mythology), "A Devoted Friend" (a short story by Oscar Wilde) and "A Service of Love" (a short story by O. Henry). In Book III and Book IV literary genres account for an even higher percentage of the text. By contrast, Li Guanyi's *New English Course*, which has been most widely used by our first- and second-year English majors since 1986, hardly contains any purely literary texts. The evident implication of this is that our students are no longer as well-prepared as they used to be, for the courses in literature by the time they move onto their third year.

Even worse, many of our English majors are never offered any course in literature during their undergraduate years. As a recent investigation survey of five prestigious Chinese universities indicates, 13 percent of their foreign language majors during the period of 1993 – 1997 had no access whatsoever to any course in literature even when they became third- and fourth-year students (North Project Group 1998: 4). To be sure, there are different factors underlying this deficiency, one possible explanation being the shortage of teachers. But the fact that the so-called "departments of pragmatic English" have actually mushroomed in many regions of our country reveals a more disconcerting cause: the deliberate blocking of access to creative literature in English. Behind all this current tendency lurks a prevalent assumption: that English education is a matter of ingesting information, of mastering techniques, of acquiring facts and know-how, whereas literature is a soft option, an indulgence or a mere trimming to decorate the hard center of the market-oriented syllabus. "Pragmatic", in a nutshell, has become a buzz word.

Seductive as it is, however, the concept of pragmatism in this context, we believe, is fallacious, and acts as a poison in our educational system. The first and foremost danger of the so-called "pragmatic English programs" lies in their corrosive influence on the fundamental ideals of a university. While such programs at their best do provide good training in practical skills and useful knowledge, their achievements are made at the expense of such fundamental principles of education as a breadth of horizon, and the rounded development of individuals. Abbs (1994: 14), in a book published eight years ago, criticizes the tendency in Britain to amalgamate the two terms "to train" and "to educate", "to make them slide into each other, to make them referentially synonymous". The same criticism applies to pragmatic English programs in China, which have turned some of our institutions of higher education into mere training centers. In such training institutes, Abbs (1974: 2) asserts, "the individual is reduced to the status of a passive vessel moving on a conveyor belt and being filled, at the same time, with useful knowledge and necessary techniques. The result ... is a deep inertia among the students: a mindless torpor — or what might be described as a pathology of boredom." How can anyone in a mindless torpor be really useful?

If training is narrow, exclusive and aims at fragmented knowledge, education is ideally expansive and all-embracing. In other words, a well-trained person may not be well-educated, whereas a well-educated person will by definition be well-trained. As early as the mid-nineteenth century John Henry Newman (1982: 134) aptly pointed out that the only practical end of a university is "training good members of society". According to Newman (1982: 137), "what was good in itself could not but have a number of external uses, though it did not promise them, it was good; and that it was necessarily the source of benefits to society, great and diversified in proportion to its own intrinsic excellence." If literature contributes to cultivating good members of society, it should then also be considered useful and it would be wrong, as contemporary pragmatists typically do, to think of literature and useful knowledge in antagonistic terms. Our view is that literature is absolutely good and by definition useful.

But why and how? Being a discipline of the imagination, creative literature has a crucial role to play in making the student more imaginative and more creative. F. R. Leavis's views in this respect, for all their flaws, can be used to support our argument:

> Literature was important not only in itself, but because it encapsulated creative energies which were everywhere on the defensive in modern "commercial" society. In literature, and perhaps in literature alone, a vital feel for the creative uses of language was still manifest, in contrast to the philistine devaluing of language and traditional culture blatantly apparent in "mass society". The quality of a society's language was the most telling index of the quality of its personal and social life: a society which had ceased to value literature was one lethally closed to the impulses which had created and sustained the best of human civilization. (Eagleton, 1994: 50)

Although what Leavis means by "the best of human civilization" is questionable, few people would disagree with him in that the language of commercial society tends to be abstract and anaemic. Over the past few decades a great many countries, China being no exception, have witnessed the increasing trend towards the commodification of many areas of social life, and therefore they face the arduous task of reinvigorating their languages. One of the indispensable sources of invigoration is literature, for it is here that a people have done most creative writing and best express themselves.

But why should a Chinese student major in English literature? What profit is there in reading, say, Chaucer and Shakespeare, in hearkening to any non-Chinese and, "worse", non-modern non-Chinese voices? In his *Communications with the Future*, Donald Stone provides us with an excellent answer to the question of the value of studying a foreign literature. In a fashion similar to Matthew Arnold in "A Speech at Eton", Stone (1997: 1) pins his hope for man's intellectual, as well as moral, "deliverance" on a dialogical principle "in favor of finding ourselves in that other world". Among the remarks by Arnold the following is Stone's favorite one and it should also be our favorite: "To know how others stand, that we may know how we ourselves stand; and to know how we ourselves stand, that we may correct our mistakes and achieve our deliverance — that is our problem" (quoted from Stone 1997: 2). Arnold's problem is no less a problem for us in twenty-first-century China. China is now increasingly and irreversibly involved in all sorts of international affairs. How can it afford not to know how others stand?

As to the question of the value of *classical* foreign literature, we may again turn to Stone for an answer. To him literature is a never-ending dialogue between past and present, and it should be ever tested and responded to anew from generation to generation. Like Arnold and Gadamer, Stone (1997: 117) sees in Greek culture — ancient and foreign as it is — the most enduringly "modern" of perspectives, because the "truth-claim and communal values" of the works of past cultures "are always contemporary to us". Although we may not fully accept some past truth-claims and communal values, they are contemporary to us in the sense that they stimulate our thoughts and form a dialogical relationship with us. An English program that does not look to the past and the cultural heritages embodied in the past works of literature in particular, is a severe truncation of the English language and deprives our students of the opportunity to participate in the ongoing, cross-cultural and life-enriching dialogue between past and present.

It is of vital importance, therefore, for our English departments to expose their students to a polyphony of voices and to help them develop multi-cultured perspectives, no matter what they will do in the future. If literature is severed from our English programs, our students can in no way develop a coherent multi-cultured perspective. One may argue that language is part of culture and that in many of our language courses cross-cultural communication *is* given due emphasis — and it can be easily observed that courses in the name of "cross-cultural communication" have fared much better than literature courses recently. But language and literature, after all, cannot be separated without doing violence to the organic structure of language itself. Just as no single literature is adequately comprehended except in its relationship to other literatures, so no language is adequately understood unless literature retains its right and proper status. Furthermore, literature is the richest reservoir of a society's culture. Without literature any so-called "cross-cultural communication" is bound to be shallow, to say the least. As Donald Stone (1997: 109) has said, when we study a foreign literature, "we go out of ourselves in order to come *home*." An English program without literature is thus a program without a homecoming.

It should be further pointed out that a true "literary roader" is, more often than not, better equipped with practical skills and knowledge than one who has been confined to those narrow and fragmented "useful" courses. The reason is quite simple: Although a well-designed literature course does not merely aim at a specific set of skills matching a specific set of operations, it presupposes the internalization of various skills and techniques. Just as education does not exclude training, so an education-oriented literature course does not exclude language skills and communication techniques. Literature is mediated by language, and one of the hallmarks of a good literary work is the high quality of language and the skilful use of rhetorical devices, without which human communication in most cases would be unthinkable. A good literature course therefore is bound to be conducive to the student's ability to use language and to communicate in whatever circumstances. As a matter of fact, a large number of people with an educational background in foreign literatures now hold various key positions in the "pragmatic" areas of foreign trade, international economics, international banking and tourism in China. In 1996, we conducted an investigation, in the form of semi-structured interviews (all the respondents were the leaders of various units concerned), with regards to the job performance of the graduates from English departments who were working in the economic sectors of Zhejiang Province. The result showed that about 76 percent of those who could be grouped under the category of "literary roaders" compared favorably with the graduates from foreign trade departments, tourist departments and all sorts of newfangled departments. It was true, they said, that English majors often found themselves at a disadvantage during the first two years of employment, but they soon showed a greater potential for development and eventually caught up with those armed with a whole list of certificates from various "pragmatic courses".

That is not to say that a background in literature will automatically make a person well-educated and welcomed into society. The teaching of English literature, especially for a Chinese teacher, is a demanding job and, if not handled well, could be self-defeating and kill the student's interest forever. In fact, one of the factors underlying the loss of interest in literature, especially on the part of our English majors, is the deplorable way in which many of our teachers, foreign teachers hired by Chinese universities being no exception, approach a text and conduct a class. According to a questionnaire we conducted by sampling ten Chinese institutions of higher education two years ago, about 34 percent of the teachers of English literature were found by their students to conduct "boring" classes, mainly because the teaching tended to be in the form of a monologue rather than a dialogue. Most teachers do ask questions, but their questions often go unanswered, so they often end up talking only to themselves. Many foreign teachers as well as Chinese teachers blame this tendency on "the oriental shyness" of their students, but we feel this is a fallacy, and that the real problem lies in the lack of adequate preparation, in two broad respects.

First, no adequate measures are taken to make sure that our students acquaint themselves with the text properly before they come to class. True, students are in most cases given reading assignments, even coupled with questions. Find out the theme, students are told; prepare yourselves for a discussion on its plot, characterization, imagery, style, etc. Such assignments are usually more paralyzing than heuristic, because they simply ignore the students' cultural backgrounds. If a student is not convinced of the cultural relevance of what she or he is supposed to read, hardly any real interest can be aroused. Questions should therefore be designed in such a way as to help students realize the relationship between the voices in the text concerned and their own personal and social lives.

Second, as mentioned in the opening section of this paper, no preparatory courses are offered to iron out typical obstacles for Chinese students. In the West, English majors will have had considerable exposure to Western literatures by the time they enter university. Many of them will have already encountered such tales as "The Prodigal Son", "Beauty and the Beast", and popularized versions such as Lamb's *Tales from Shakespeare*. In contrast, their Chinese counterparts often have to start from scratch. Most of them do not begin to read English literature in the original until they become third-year students and, once they start, they are usually overwhelmed with a great number of works in their original forms, which often appear too unfamiliar and too daunting for them. All inundation and no initiation, that is what nips in the bud a prospective lover of English literature.

How can we then arouse students' interest in English literature? How can their interest, if aroused, be sustained and channeled into an educational experience? These issues are vitally important, not only because a teacher should always try to improve his/her teaching methodology, but also because they are related to the question of how to combat those current "pragmatic" trends which are hostile to the very existence of programs of English literature. As teachers of English, we may not be able to persuade government officials, employers and parents to attach importance to the teaching of English literature, but we can at least win back some of our students by teaching them to love what we love. In other words, our most feasible and effective countermeasures should begin with our efforts to upgrade the quality of teaching.

We should, first and foremost, focus our energies on awakening in our students a heart-felt engagement with what they are reading. The earlier we try to elicit their response, the more likely we are to succeed, for younger people are more impressionable and more responsive than adults. Vendler (1994: 30) makes the following comment on American universities: "If our students, in their first acquaintance with departments of English and foreign languages, experience too little of that delight at the access of knowledge, it is because the best delights we have to offer — those of literature — have somehow not been included in our first courses for students — courses that are often our last chance to reach them." She therefore proposes that all freshman English courses "should devote at least half their time to the reading of myth, legend, and parable; and beginning language courses should do the same" (Vendler 1994: 35). If American students are deprived of "the best delights" in their first acquaintance with English departments, ours are even more so, and perhaps need more hours devoted to the reading of literature. And it is also a good idea to lead our first- and second-year students to the reading of myth, legend and parable, so that they will encounter fewer obstacles, language ones in particular, at a preparatory stage which will eventually launch them into a wider range of literary experience in greater depth.

This emphasis on "delights" also relates to the role that emotion plays in an English program. One serious problem in our English programs is that some teachers of literature, as well as the advocates of "pragmatic courses", tend to overemphasize intellectual cultivation at the expense of emotional transformation. While it is quite natural for pragmatists to lose sight of the importance of emotional education (and even mistake the "functional" for the "intellectual"), it is a pity that too many of our teachers of literature treat their own courses as a means for mere intellectual exercise and abstract speculation. What they tend to forget is that intellect without emotion often results in apathy and inertia. Literature is where we are most likely to find affective elements of consciousness, and to overlook these elements is nothing short of castration.

We do not of course advocate feeling against thought. What we advocate is thought as felt and feeling as thought.

But how can we achieve that? In what way can we make sure that intellect and emotion do not part company? Vendler (1994: 28) has emphasized that a literature course should lead a student to a "state of intense engagement". But what concrete measures can we take to ensure this state of intense attention and self-forgetfulness? Here we may again turn to Abbs, whose concept of "physical engagement" goes a long way in helping us to "lure" students into intense exploratory engagement with literature, and in anchoring students' thoughts in the aesthetic and emotional response. In *The Educational Imperative*, Abbs elaborates on a whole range of strategies, including "oral recreation", "auditory imagination", "attention articulately sounded", "critical evaluation" and "creative amplification", etc, which aim to "bring the students' feelings, sense-perceptions, imagination — and the intelligence active in all of these — inside the pattern of the words" (Vendler 1994: 151 – 154). What merits our attention most is Abbs's call for "including the practical experience of making literature in any course on English studies", so that students can develop "an acute awareness of the medium and its formal possibilities". Abbs would like students to try "not just writing in the analytical mode (though that would have its place), but in all the main forms of expressive utterance" (Abbs 1994: 153). This may sound radical, but we cannot help finding Abbs's proposal thought-provoking: if our students have learned not to be afraid of wrestling and grappling with various forms of literature, what other forms of writing would prove to be too intimidating for them in the future? What experience can be more practical in its true sense?

Another problem that has been hampering the teaching of English literature in China is that a considerable number of teachers are strongly opposed to the spread of theory. By "the spread of theory" here we mean the teaching of theories of literary criticism. In a national conference on English literature held in Xiamen in May, 1999, for instance, there was a fierce debate on whether theory should be taught to our English majors. Quite a few scholars maintained that literature teaching was a matter of "embracing the concrete", as suggested by F. R. Leavis, while the teaching of theories was "corrupting". From our own teaching experience, however, we find that exposure to ongoing critical debates on literary works often works to arouse students' interest and to enliven the classroom atmosphere. Gerald Graff once told a story about himself: When he was a university student, he found literature boring until one day when his instructor introduced a theoretical debate on whether *The Adventures of Huckleberry Finn* should end where the Afro-American Jim is stolen by the boys. And this experience made him realize that many students, just like himself, "had to be corrupted first in order to experience innocence" (Graff 1994: 38-40). The following is his explanation of why students are apt to be tongue-tied in a literature class:

> Again, the problem is that what students are able to say about a text depends not just on the text but on their relation to a critical community of readers, which over time has developed an agenda of problems, issues, and questions with respect to specific authors and texts and to culture generally. When students are screened from this critical community and its debates, or when they experience only the fragmentary and disconnected versions of it represented by a series of courses, they are likely to either be tongue-tied in the face of the text or to respond in a limited personal idiom ... (Graff 1994: 42)

What Graff sees as a problem for American students is no less a handicap for Chinese students. It should be further pointed out that relation to a critical community need not corrupt innocence. Let us, too, take *The Adventures of Huckleberry Finn* for example. A teacher may start by confining himself to some focused insight on the ending alone, while withholding the rest of the information about the debate on the novel as a whole, so that the student can still gain the fresh experience of reading insofar as the bulk of the book is concerned. Afterwards the student can be introduced to the rest of the debate so as to gain further intimacy of literary experience.

To conclude, the teaching of English literature in China not only has its educational value, but also has its cultural and economic relevance to our contemporary life. By exposing our students to a critical community, and by linking literary texts physically to their memories, feelings and imagination, we can in our modest way breathe new life into our English teaching programs.

NOTES

1. The old conventional way of organizing English teaching, which gives great emphasis to literature, is often defined as "the literary road" in China.

2. See *The English Teaching Program for English Majors in Institutions of Higher Education* (p. 17), compiled by The English Section of the Guiding Committee for Specialized Foreign Language Teaching in Institutions of Higher Education (2000), full reference below.

References

[1] Abbs P. *Autobiography in Education* [M]. London: Heinemann Educational Books, 1974.

[2] Abbs P. *The Educational Imperative: A Defense of Socratic and Aesthetic Learning* [M]. London: The Falmer Press, 1994.

[3] Eagleton T. The Rise of English [A] //In Richter D H (ed.). *Falling into Theory: Conflicting Views on Reading Literature* [C]. Boston: Bedford Books of St. Martin's Press, 1994: 44-54.

[4] Graff G. Disliking books at an early age [A] //In Richter D H (ed.). *Falling into Theory: Conflicting Views on Reading Literature*. Boston: Bedford Books of St. Martin's Press, 1994: 36-43.

[5] Newman J H. *The Idea of a University* [M]. Notre Dame: University of Notre Dame Press, 1982.

[6] North Project Group [Bei fang ke ti zu] A survey of foreign language graduates in five Chinese universities [J]. Foreign Language Teaching and Research, 1998: 1-4.

[7] Stone D. *Communications with the Future* [M]. Ann Arbor: The University of Michigan Press, 1997.

[8] The English Section of the Guiding Committee for Specialized Foreign Language Teaching in Institutions of Higher Education. *The English Teaching Program for English Majors in Institutions of Higher Education* [M]. Shanghai: Shanghai Foreign Languages Education Press, 2000.

[9] Vendler H. What we have loved, others will love [A] //In Richter D H (ed.). *Falling into Theory: Conflicting Views on Reading Literature* [C]. Boston: Bedford Books of St. Martin's Press: 27–36.

(本文原载于 World Englishes, Vol. 21, No. 20, 2002)

第五编

对话访谈

文化观念流变中的英国文学典籍研究：殷企平教授访谈录[*]

一、文化观念的孕育与发展

李云锦（以下简称李）：殷老师，首先祝贺您和您的团队出版了系列丛书"文化观念流变中的英国文学典籍研究"。作为国家社科基金重大招标项目成果，该丛书已经引起了较大反响，今天就让我们继续谈谈这套丛书。在访谈开始之前，我想请教您一个问题：在您看来，什么是"文化"？"文化"从何而来？

殷企平（以下简称殷）：在西方思想语境中，"文化"一词的含义有一个逐渐展开与深化的过程，其基本脉络是从物质走向精神、从个体走向社会这两种向度的延伸和转变。早在18世纪，欧洲启蒙思想家就从社会变迁和历史发展的角度，直接或间接地论述了"文化"与"文明"这两个概念，以及它们在语义上既紧密相连又相互抵牾的关系。19世纪英国文学和思想领域的代表人物托马斯·卡莱尔（Thomas Carlyle, 1795—1881）和马修·阿诺德（Matthew Arnold, 1822—1888），将社会道德批评与人文主义式的文化理想结合起来，对工业资本主义时代的英国社会做出了深刻的批判。卡莱尔是在对工业主义的批判中提出

---

[*] 本文由李云锦与殷企平合写。本文作者李云锦，杭州师范大学外国语学院英语语言文学专业硕士研究生，主要从事英美文学方向的研究。

并完善自己的文化观的,他的文化思想不仅表现为对精神与物质失衡现象的批判,也表现为寻求平衡之路的努力。在阿诺德眼中,文化则被描述为一种"和谐的完美",它应具有追求纯粹知识的理性力量,也更应具有追求善的道德和社会激情。随后的约翰·罗斯金(John Ruskin,1819—1900)和威廉·莫里斯(William Morris,1834—1896)又给文化概念注入了较多的艺术元素。换句话说,从卡莱尔开始,"文化"一词越来越具有针对现代文明的批判内涵。当代英国批评家雷蒙德·威廉斯(Raymond Williams,1921—1988)运用历史语义学的方法,从社会变革的角度追溯并辨析了"文化""文明""民主""艺术"等众多文化关键词的历史源头、文化衍射和语义演进。文化既是人类完善自身的一种状态或过程,也是记录人类思想和经验的知性想象作品的整体,更可以视为一种对个体和社会大众生活方式的描述。

李: 不少学者认为,"文明"是"文化"的高等形式。文明是在文字出现、城市形成和社会分工之后形成的。尤其是在历史学与考古学界,文明时常被认为是较高的文化发展阶段。但在特里·伊格尔顿(Terry Eagleton,1943—)看来,早在19世纪初,"文化"就开始从"文明"的同义词转变成了它的反义词。发展到今天,"文明"与"文化"呈现出极大的观念差异。面对这两种不同的见解,您如何看待"文化"与"文明"之间的关系呢?

殷: 我赞同伊格尔顿的观点。伊格尔顿主要是在《文化观念》(*The Idea of Culture*,2000)和《文化》(*Culture*,2016)这两本书中阐发上述观点的。他认为"文明"一词本来"集事实与价值于一身"(Eagleton 2000:10),它既描述某种社会生活形态,又隐含价值判断。例如,"文明"一词起先可以用来颂扬某种生活方式/形态及其精神诉求,也可以用来标明个人的全面发展、人际关系的和谐,以及国家的繁荣昌盛,等等。也就是说,"文明"的语义原来有两个基本层面,一个是关乎事实的描述层面,另一个是关乎价值的规范层面。然而,由于以"机械崛起"为特征的工业革命走入歧途,因此"文明"原有的两个语义层面产生了断裂:它的描述/物质层面得以保留,而它的规范/精神层面却丢失了。关于这一点,伊格尔顿在他后来出版的《文化》中又做了精辟的论述,他说"文明如今只关乎事实,而文化却追问价值"(Eagleton 2016:10)。说得更通俗一点:"文明"和"文化"原本是一家,后来分家了,分家的结果是"文明"

不再承担原有的价值使命,而"文化"则承担了这一使命。你前面曾问"文化"从何而来,我觉得刚才所说已经部分回答了你的问题。换句话说,"文化"是从"文明"那里分家而来的,而造成分家的最大原因是工业革命。用伊格尔顿的话说,"是工业革命助产了文化观念"(Eagleton 2016:10)。不过,这样的回答还不够全面。更全面的说法应该是:英国文学家们在对工业革命以及驱动工业革命的启蒙思想的回应中催生并发展了文化观念,或者说他们因工业革命引起的转型焦虑催生了文化观念,这从美国学者杰弗里·哈特曼(Geoffrey Hartman,1929—2016)一个著名论断中可见一斑:"到了穆勒、阿诺德和罗斯金的时代,对于文明的肤浅及其悖逆自然的效应的焦虑开始赋予'文化'一词新的价值含义"(Hartman 207)。这里所说的"焦虑"自然是指由农业文明向工业文明转型而带来的焦虑。当然,给"文化"观念注入转型焦虑等新含义的远远不止穆勒、阿诺德和罗斯金,还包括许许多多的优秀英国文学家,尤其是以卡莱尔为代表的维多利亚文学家。

李:文化观念是一种动态的观念,会随着时代的变迁而变化。您刚才主要谈了19世纪以及之前的情形,那么此后的情形呢?两次世界大战带来的全球性变化,以及后现代主义思潮和经济全球化浪潮的兴起,必然会对文化观念形成强烈的冲击,因此新一代作家也会予以回应,而这种冲击和回应又将导致文化观念的进一步流变。或者说,从爱德华时期以来,英国的文化观念有了新的发展。您能谈谈这一发展中的文化观念吗?

殷:你说得很对。文化观念在不同历史时期会有不同的内涵。我们先来看一下从爱德华时期到二战结束之前的情形。这一时期,由于英国社会的思想格局经历了世纪末的转变,而且两次世界大战更是对英国民族的文化心理与身份意识产生了深远的影响,因此文学家们与文化观念之间产生了新的互动,其结果是文化观念的内涵和外延更为丰富了,而且有了一些新的特点。更具体地说,新一代作家在上一时期文学家们所做工作的基础上,继续拓展文化观念的内涵,包括对转型焦虑、共同体意识、文化身份和审美趣味的深度探索等。例如,伊丽莎白·鲍温(Elizabeth Bowen,1899—1973)的《心之死》(*The Death of the Heart*,1938)所呈现的转型焦虑,包含了趣味和伦理两个层面,因而是对转型焦虑的深度挖掘。

再来看一下二战以后的情形：这一时期的文化观念受到了后现代主义思潮和经济全球化浪潮的强烈冲击，以致新一代作家必须做出回应，而这种冲击和回应导致了文化观念的裂变。例如，关于"共同体"和"英格兰特性"的观念出现了多样化和多重性的趋向，甚至出现了"反文化"这样一些术语。此时文学家们的文化诉求和道德关注呈现出有别于上一时期的新特点。也就是说，文化观念的新变迁影响了当代的英国文学典籍，同时又得到了后者的反映和折射。当代英国文学家们面临着如下一些新课题：怎样在经济高速发展的形势下营造共同文化？英国特性究竟存在与否？英国文学如何再现英国特性？值得关注的是，得益于众多文学家的努力，一种更加包容、富有弹性的英国特性得以形成，而原来以种族为文化身份或英国特性的标识这一观念越来越不得人心。例如，彼得·阿克罗伊德（Peter Ackroyd，1949— ）等当代作家用出色的创作向世人传递了这样一种观念：杂糅拼贴并非"后现代"的专利，而是英国文化遗产的一部分；正视多元化/多样性未必意味着混沌，而杂糅/包容可以成为一种绵延不绝的民族传统。更值得称道的是，不少当代作家——包括阿克罗伊德和 V. S. 奈保尔（V. S. Naipaul, 1932—2018）——比以往更重视语言的建构性，但是在他们的笔下，语言的建构性不但没有解构传统，反而因其本身的稳定性成为维护与更新传统的力量。对所有面临建设多民族共同体任务的国家来说，当代英国文学家的上述努力都具有深刻的借鉴意义。

二、关于"文化观念流变中的英国文学典籍研究"丛书

李：前一部分的访谈是为今天核心话题所做的铺垫。您和您的团队不久前出版了系列丛书"文化观念流变中的英国文学典籍研究"。请问你们当初为什么选择做这项研究？

殷：我们这项研究是针对当前文学典籍研究和文化观念研究相脱节的状况而展开的。作为一种新型的外国文学研究项目，它旨在服务中国文化建设。它既有助于说明文化观念的发展对于文学典籍生成的作用，又有助于发掘文学典籍在文化观念意义上的深层价值，从而说明文学典籍在引领文化走向、塑造共同体意识等方面的积极作用。通过研究英国社会转型期的文学和文化建设，我们

希望能够为中国本土的核心价值观和公共文化建设提供借鉴。文化观念制约着共同体中的人对生活的全面理解，而文学典籍是表达并交流这种理解的关键性媒介。文化观念的变化和发展直接影响着文学典籍的生成方式，而文学典籍又反过来对文化观念的走向施加重要影响。就文学研究而言，只有将这种在历史进程中互为表里的关系纳入视野，才能拥有对作品的透彻把握，进而将文学研究提升至文化研究的高度。随着文化批评理论在20世纪下半叶的兴起，文学研究中的文化意识逐渐增强，但是在我们从事这项课题以前，还没有一项研究工作以上述思路对一种民族文学进行过大规模的系统研究，没有以全面、具体、细致的方式阐释文化观念与文学典籍究竟如何在漫长的进程中相辅相成，从而在各个历史关头对民族共同体的形成、巩固和发展发挥作用。

李：这很有意思。我注意到项目的研究焦点是英国文学。在我国的外国文学研究领域中，英国文学的研究成果占据了很高的比例，您会不会觉得你们的研究可能会与先前的研究有重合的风险？

殷：英国文学典籍研究是我国世界文学研究的一个重要组成部分，成果丰硕。然而，由于此前的工作不够重视文化观念及其相关问题，因此典籍研究常常局限于审美愉悦的层次，缺乏文化价值方面的深度探讨。此外，文化研究虽仍方兴未艾，却较少系统、细致地介入文学典籍的研究，因而缺乏文学研究所能提供的对文化状况细腻、丰满的把握，也未能充分阐释文学典籍在引领文化走向、塑造共同价值方面的具体机制。如何将这两方面的研究融合为一个有机的整体，使文学典籍研究与文化观念研究真正做到相辅相成、忻合无间，以推进英国文学研究，并为中国当前的文化建设工作服务呢？这是摆在我们面前的一项任务，它既是学术发展的要求，也是社会现实的要求。中国的英国文学研究是在现代化转型困境的激发下诞生的，它为中国人了解西方、融入现代世界做出了巨大贡献。一个世纪过去了，中国的转型尚未完成，只是问题的重心落到了更深的文化层次，即随着现代化转型的深入，传统价值观念、民族凝聚力和个体生活的品质都在经受严峻考验。因此，英国文学研究被时代赋予了新的使命。当中国在现代化进程中处于重大历史转折的时刻，习近平总书记强调指出："文化是一个国家、一个民族的灵魂"，"文运同国运相牵，文脉同国脉相连。"如今，建成文化强国这一目标已经上升为我国的国策。在这样的时代背景下,对文化观念流变中的英国文学典籍进行充分的梳理、阐释和评价,以期提供借鉴,已经成为他山之石的当然之选。

李: 可以介绍一下你们这套丛书的核心观点吗?

殷: 当然可以。我们在书中提出了以下四个核心观点:

第一,先前文学典籍研究和文化观念研究相脱节,因此我们需要一个新型的、旨在服务于中国文化建设的外国文学研究课题。我们丛书所说的"文化"既起因于(社会)转型焦虑,又必须提供走出焦虑的途径,如描述各种愿景,包括共同体愿景、乌托邦愿景,或者关于美好社会秩序的愿景,而后者又离不开心智的培育、民族良心的锻造和民族特性的构建,以及提倡理想的工作/生活方式等。对于所有这些文化内涵的关联性、复杂性和丰富性,非文学典籍不足以充分表达。就最主要的文化命题而言,英国文学家们在不同时期给出了相同的答案,即生活质量不在于发达的工业、诱人的科技经济指标,而在于共同体的和谐,在于精神与物质的互补和平衡。

第二,英国文化观念的流变经历了中世纪后期到17世纪的萌芽、18世纪的生长、19世纪的成熟、20世纪上半叶的拓展,直至二战后到21世纪的裂变,其含义显示出一个逐渐展开与深化的过程,其基本脉络是从物质走向精神、从个体走向社会两种向度的延伸和转变。从中世纪后期开始,英国文学伴随着近代社会的转型而演变;几个世纪以来的英国文学既是这一社会转型进程的产物,又积极影响着这个进程。从《乌托邦》(*Utopia*, 1551)到《来自乌有乡的消息》(*News from Nowhere*, 1890),从威廉·莎士比亚(William Shakespeare, 1564—1616)到石黑一雄(Kazuo Ishiguro, 1954—),英国文学不断对侧重物质文明的现代价值体系发出质疑,通过展望理想的共同体生活,逐渐形成了一个强大的文化主义传统。大量的文学典籍在争论与创新中以丰富多彩的文学意象不断地影响着民族的想象,打造着英国的公共文化,成为民族核心价值体系的建设者与守望者,帮助英国在世界各民族中相对顺利地完成了社会转型。

第三,"共同体"文化实践始于莎士比亚乃至更早时期的乔叟(Geoffrey Chaucer, 1342/43—1400)。无论是马克思主义哲学家,还是优秀的文学家,他们在倡导/想象共同体时并不仅仅把它看作一个形而上的概念,而是更多地把它看作一种文化实践。这种实践作为一种社会活动乃至运动,在19世纪已经蔚为壮观。参与这种实践的除卡尔·马克思（Karl Marx，1818—1883）和弗里德里希·恩格斯（Friedrich Engels，1820—1895）之外，还有英国的威廉·华兹华斯（William Wordsworth，1770—1850）、卡莱尔、查尔斯·狄更斯（Charles Dickens，1812—1870）、乔治·爱略特（George Eliot，1819—1880）、托马斯·哈代（Thomas Hardy，1840—1928）、阿尔弗雷德·丁尼生（Alfred Tennyson，1809—1892）、罗斯金和莫里斯等作家，他们想象共同体的出发点跟马克思的一样，是为了改造整个世界。可见，"共同体"概念最重要的属性是文化实践。这种实践始于莎士比亚乃至更早时期的乔叟，并一直延续至今。

第四，文化观念、文学的发展与社会变迁存在着一种共生互释的学理关系。在中世纪后期的英国，由某些关键词所代表的文化内涵已有不少开始萌发。例如，因田园文明向商业文明过渡而产生的"转型焦虑"，早在威廉·兰格伦（William Langland，1330—1400）的作品里就已经初现端倪，而"心智培育"和"共同体"等术语所指涉的文化内涵也在这一时期渐现雏形。18世纪，英国文化的砥砺和磨合过程为伟大作家和艺术家的存在提供了广阔、丰富的土壤和空间，使他们创作出不朽的经典作品。19世纪英国目睹了"文化"与"文明"的决裂，而这就是文化观念成熟的标志。就"文化"和"文明"的观念而言，必须有众多文人学者致力于它们的语义区分，才能确保其成熟。恰恰是在维多利亚这一时期，几乎所有优秀的文学家都承担起了给"文化"和"文明"分家的工作，都奋起批判独尊"事实"的文明，都表达了一种蕴含价值诉求的文化思想。这一时期的文学家们对文化的多重观照，已经更自觉地表现为对秩序/共同体的理想诉求、对人类生活总体方式的精神审视、对人的全面发展状况（各种禀赋和潜能的协调发展）的文化反思，也表现为对追求单向度发展的"进步"话语的一种强烈质疑。英国文化观念在20世纪上半叶的拓展与变化可以理解为进一步反思"进步"话语的思想史，而同期的文学则与其形成了互动。二战以后，英国文化观念受到了后现代主义思潮和经济全球化浪潮的强烈冲击，因此文学家们奋起回应，一方面他们要坚持文化诉求，另一方面又要顺应时代潮流，结果导致了文化观念的裂变。他们所表达的文化诉求呈现出有别于上一时期的文化新特质。例如，在他们的书写中，作为文化重要内涵之一的"英国特性"变得更加包容，更富有弹性，更凸显多民族（包括外来移民）在共同体中的参与和平等地位。

李：我们注意到这套丛书在构思和撰写方面有不少新意和特色。例如，丛书揭示了社会转型过程中文化变迁与文学再现之间的内在逻辑，为认识并解读文化和文学开辟了新的路径。

殷：确实，揭示你所说的"内在逻辑"是我和团队成员们所追求的目标。我们的丛书以"点""线""面"的立体维度展开，构建文化观念与文学典籍对接与对话的经纬之图，从文本细察出发，爬梳文化观念流变过程，以勾勒作家作品的"点"、文学思潮和社会思潮的"线"，以及英国社会变迁的"面"；同时，我们力求具体文学作品的解读与文化理论深度融合，从而在宏观感知与微观"厚描"之间始终保持思想的张力，呈现一种学科互涉的知识学新景观。以往文学史著作的主旨多在描述文学的进程，而我们的思路则是在文学中追溯文化观的变迁，这一思路更有益于探寻文学经典在传承民族共同体价值观中的作用。

李：您刚才谈到了"厚描"，这本身是一种文化实践，对吗？

殷：对。我和团队成员们尝试"厚描"式地论证文化观念史在诸多文学文本中的复现，力求展现文学典籍所具有的文化史和思想史的坐标原点价值和研究意义。换句话说，我们力求突破单纯的文学作品范围，拓展到与文化观念相关联的文学领域，包括文学批评著作、文学刊物中的特写和文学传记等。

李：这种较宽的研究范围一经划定，就会增加你们的研究难度。这样不畏艰难的学术勇气实在令人叹服！我还想问一个连带的问题：你们的研究不仅聚焦文学，也聚焦文化观念史，关于文化，您前面已经谈了许多，但是对于观念史，您又是怎样理解的呢？

殷：广义的观念史，常常也被称为思想史，与西文 the history of ideas 或 the intellectual history 相对应，而狭义的观念史则类似范畴史或概念史。我们的课题取其折中，在宏观层面上力求通过对文学典籍文本的整理与阐释，辨梳文化观念的关键词如何借由文学典籍文本意义的衍射，来反映其思想内涵和发展过程的复杂性、多样性和矛盾性，同时也在微观层面着力于描述文化观念及其范畴，以及它们对文学典籍生成的潜在规定和形塑影响。

李：您这里提到了"文化观念的关键词"。可否请您更详细地介绍一下？

殷：好。为做好上述课题，我们提炼了凸显文化观念内涵的 10 个核心概念，它们分别是"转型焦虑""共同体形塑""秩序诉求""审美趣味""心智培育""文学语言的创造""民族良心""道德伦理传统""工作/生活方式"和"愿景描述"。我们这样做，是为了彰显中国学者的关怀，既在理论上找到植根于英国文化的内在特性，又在实践上体现出新时代中国外国文学研究者的特色。我们通过聚焦关键词，以英国文学家针对现代性——与现代化相匹配的现代价值体系——的文学表达和思想质询为审视对象，尝试为中国本土核心价值观和公共文化建设提供积极借鉴。例如，我们的丛书对共同体观念的界定、对幸福伦理和共同体形塑的探究不仅呈现英国共同体书写的景观，更是回应了莫里斯·布朗肖（Maurice Blanchot, 1907—2003）、让-吕克·南希（Jean-Luc Nancy, 1940—2021）和 J. 希里斯·米勒（J. Hillis Miller, 1928—2021）等西方学者对共同体有机/内在属性的质疑，这其实暗含了关于中国乃至人类命运共同体的思考。最后，我还得提一下上述各个关键词的关联性。我在前面介绍丛书核心观点时其实已经谈到"转型焦虑""愿景描述""共同体形塑""秩序诉求""心智培育""民族良心"和"工作/生活方式"之间的内在联系。让我再举一个例子："道德伦理传统"和"转型焦虑"之间也存在密切的逻辑关系——对于社会转型的焦虑除了是对"文明"／"进步"话语的回应之外，还意味着人类的工作/生活方式（因转型）出了问题，或者说"礼崩乐坏"（社会秩序混乱，伦理道德败坏）。通过文学典籍来透视这些文化内涵的关联性、复杂性和丰富性，是我们丛书的题目赖以立足的理由。

李：我还发现了丛书的另一个特色，即开辟了文学批评写作的新路径。更具体地说，您和您的同事们开辟了有别于国外常见的文学通史、文学选读或文学经典传统研究的新路径，也有别于国内的专题型学术专著，既站在英国文学与文化的内部考察分析，又立足于中国历史与社会现实来构思写作，着眼之处是文学的民族特性所承载的跨越时空和超越国界的文化精神价值。

殷：谢谢你的夸奖！我们确实尝试这样做了。至于做得怎么样，还得留待后人评说。

李：非常感谢您接受这次访谈！

参考文献

[1] Eagleton T. *Culture* [M]. New Haven and London: Yale UP, 2016.

[2] Eagleton T. *The Idea of Culture* [M]. Oxford: Blackwell, 2000.

[3] Hartman G. *The Fateful Question of Culture* [M]. New York: Columbia UP, 1997.

（本文原载于《英美文学研究论丛》2022年第1期）

"普通读者"与外国文学研究：殷企平教授访谈录[*]

一、"普通读者"话题的前情

张琰：殷老师好，非常感谢您接受我的访谈。您是国内最早对"普通读者"（the common reader）这一概念进行学术研究的学者。2018年11月17日至18日，《外国文学》编辑部牵头的《西方文论关键词》新书发布会在北京举行，会上您做了题为"普通读者"的主旨发言，从文学批评中的"普通读者"传统出发，探讨当下中国外国文学研究中存在的问题，呼吁学界搭建专业读者与普通读者之间的桥梁。您的发言引发了全场最为激烈的争论。当时有学者就您对文学批评去审美化、泛政治化现象的严厉指责表示不满。随后，您的论文《西方文论关键词：普通读者》刊载于《外国文学》2019年第6期，这成了学术圈内一次"黑天鹅"事件，引发不少国内学界同仁的反思。例如，但汉松教授就在最近出版的《文学之用》封面引用的推荐语以及《文学为什么重要》的中译版序中，将"普通读者"作为关键词，来介绍国外学者的基本观点[①]。周星月与王

---

* 基金项目：浙江省哲学社会科学重点研究基地杭州师范大学文艺批评研究院资助项目（wypp2020001）。
本文由张琰与殷企平合写。张琰，杭州师范大学外国语学院英国文学方向硕士研究生。

敖在近期引进出版的《看不见的倾听者》的译序中称，诗歌批评家文德勒（2019：3）想象的"看不见的倾听者"有两类，即诗人与"普通读者"。叶丽贤（2020：34）在《萨缪尔·约翰逊〈诗人传〉对英诗经典的建构》的绪论中，探讨了约翰逊笔下"普通读者的真实与虚构"等问题。由此可见，无论是在文学批评理论中，还是在文学作品的经验性研究中，如今都出现了您所说的"普通读者的身影"。尽管存在偶然与巧合，但上述情况足以说明，"普通读者"可被称为西方文论的一个关键词。

作为一位文学批评家，您总能从社会问题出发，关照现实生活。如今中国的外国文学研究领域，存在理论先行、批判先行的思维方式，然而，理论与读者本身的阅读体验没有多大联系，理论的专业术语往往在普通读者与专业读者之间设下障碍。以上问题，是否就是您文章中提到的"文学批评的异化"？（殷企平 2019：46）②您还提出，文学批评变异的根源在于"去经典化浪潮"（殷企平 2019：48）。当前中国的文化研究高歌猛进，文学系似乎也逐渐变为文化研究系。而您对审美的辩护，对经典的守护，让我想起了大洋彼岸捍卫正典的大批评家布鲁姆。您的《普通读者》一文，能否看作您对布鲁姆-詹姆逊之争的遥远回响？

殷企平：与其说我呼应了布鲁姆-詹姆逊之争，不如说我呼应了克莫德-卡勒之争，那场争论事关文学批评的宗旨。我在那篇文章中提到，文学批评的宗旨之一是为普通读者服务，这意味着批评家有义务就文学经典价值与普通读者达成共识；背离了这一宗旨，就意味着文学批评的异化，而异化的根源在于去经典化思潮（殷企平 2019：48）。这一思潮在过去几十年已经泛滥成灾，其背后有许多推手，但是最大的推手要数卡勒（Jonathan Culler）（殷企平 2019：45）。在他的诸多奇葩理论中，最有害的是主张文学批评应有"新型的研究对象"，即以晦涩为共同特点的文学文本，为此他推崇所谓"晦涩的长处"（the virtues of obscurity），同时又猛烈抨击所谓"奉清晰为圭臬的意识形态"（the ideology of lucidity）（殷企平 2019：48—49）。换句话说，晦涩成了正道，而清晰则成了邪道。既然晦涩是正道，那么普通读者自然就被拒之门外了（殷企平 2019：49）。克莫德奋起反击卡勒，不仅仅是维护普通读者的正当权益，而且是捍卫文学批评的根本宗旨，正是这一点深深吸引了我。当然，卷入"普通读者之争"的远不止克莫德和卡勒，还有很多著名的文人学者，其中包括了您提到的布鲁姆和詹姆逊。关于布鲁姆-詹姆逊之争，我还未做深入研究，但是希望有人来研究，尤其是像您这样的青年学者。

二、"普通读者"的内涵与外延

张琰：首先我注意到，"普通读者"作为一种术语，出现在您与其他评论家的批评话语中，而未得到严格的界定。例如，布鲁姆（Harold Bloom）称自己对约翰逊的爱促使他离开学术论争，"转向颂扬我不断遇到的众多孤独的读者"（Bloom 2000：23）；同时，他还在《西方正典》（*The Western Canon*，1994）中指出，"约翰逊和他之后的伍尔夫称为'普通读者'的人仍然存在着"（Bloom 1994：518）。这里的"普通读者"被视为一位"孤独的读者"，通过阅读来扩大自身的存在，从而获得一种崇高，一种世俗超越，以消减孤独。然而，这样浪漫的"普通读者"，显然与您文章引用的《正典与普通读者》（*The Canon and the Common Reader*，1990）中那种具有民粹力量的"普通读者"全然不同。此外，布鲁姆本人大概会把该书的两位作者打入"憎恶学派"，理由是这两位把"普通读者"归入（在文学经典建构中）与文化精英对立的阶层，或是权力斗争中的"他者"——这类"他者"在不同时期表现为"约翰逊的普通读者、阿诺德的非利士人、美国贫民窟的黑人小孩，以及大批被剥夺权利的妇女"（Kaplan, *et al.* 1990：11）。当然，《正典与普通读者》的那两位作者恐怕也会生气地大喊，"普通读者"应该是真实的生命，而不是神秘主义者的空想，更不该沦为一种修辞术，成为布鲁姆自白的传声筒。

殷企平：布鲁姆所说"孤独的读者"有多种含义。除了您刚才指出的"浪漫"色彩以外，他所说的"普通读者"之所以孤独，主要是因为讨论、评价文学经典/正典的正当途径越来越少，或者说越来越多的文学批评/理论已经不对非专业人士言说。就像我前面提到的那样，越来越多的专业人士不以"晦涩"为耻，反以为荣。用克莫德（Frank Kermode）的话说，过去四五十年可以视作"文学理论全盛期"，而这恰恰意味着对文学本身的冷漠乃至敌视，或者说"理论正在淹没文学"（Kermode 1989：7）。面对这一潮流，重提"普通读者"，其意义在于恢复文学应有的地位，同时保持专业/职业批评家与普通读者的良性互动，促进文学与文学批评的共同繁荣。正是在这一点上，布鲁姆与克莫德是并行不悖的。尽管他们所说的"普通读者"成分不尽相同，但是也不乏重合之处，至少他俩借"普通读者"话题发出了共同的心声，即反对任何"淹没文学"的理论。

张琰：关于"普通读者"的说法，您援引了伍尔夫（Virginia Woolf）与约翰逊（Samuel Johnson）的观点，但我发现，他们的观点也彼此冲突。伍尔夫称，普通读者不为传授知识，不为纠正他人观点，仅为愉悦自我而读书；但在约翰逊笔下，普通读者能够凭借出色的常识来决定诗人地位，光荣地参与公共领域的文学经典建构。关于"普通读者是谁"，这一问题在您那里仍然悬而未决。在您眼里，"普通读者"会是真实存在者吗？或许只是"理想读者"的语义反复？

殷企平：伍尔夫并非只把普通读者看作"为愉悦自我而读书"的群体，而是跟约翰逊一样，认为普通读者"在最终裁定诗坛荣耀方面有某种发言权"，而且"值得写下自己的思想和见解"，理由是尽管这些思想和见解"本身微不足道，却能促成一种巨大的效果"（Woolf 2010：4）。关于"普通读者是谁"这一问题，您问得很好。在我看来，普通读者既可以是现实存在者，又可以是理想读者，但首先是现实存在者，他们是广大的受众。古今中外，都有志存高远却被挡在学府以外的"寒门学子"，就像托马斯·哈代笔下的裘德那样——裘德尽管是艺术虚构的人物，却是千千万万受众的缩影。随着生活水平的普遍提高，越来越多的普通读者不再"寒门"，但是能进入文学专业的读者总是少数。也就是说，不是文学专业却又热爱文学的读者总占多数，他们就是实实在在的普通读者。至于您所说的"理想读者"，无论是当年的约翰逊和伍尔夫，还是后来的克莫德，他们心目中的普通读者可能跟现实中的不完全相符，很可能会在品味、志向和毅力方面高出现实中的普通读者，但是理想总是基于现实的，而且对现实起着形塑或引领作用。换句话说，即便理想读者暂时很难在现实中找到，也会对现实中的普通读者起到感召作用，从而催生出新的、接近理想水平的读者。

张琰：在"普通读者"文化史的细察者中，有人称 18 世纪之前没有"普通读者"，只有"文雅的读者"，前者实际上是一种精神建构，由作家、出版商、评论者、读者的交流配合构成（Engell 1989：160）；但也有人说，"普通读者"

指的不是社会底层的平民百姓，而是新古典主义下具有普遍人性的人，或者说是批评者用来掩饰自己身份的一种方法（Wellek 1955：95）。当然，除了被虚构的那一类，还有被视为真实的"普通读者"。例如，有人相信"普通读者"有客观实指，但指的不是当时全体的书籍消费者，而是（伴随印刷品大量涌现而产生的新兴读者中）被约翰逊塑造的那种读者共同体，不过约翰逊本人并没有明确赋予该群体阶层、职业、教育等内涵（Kernan 1989：232）。此外，还有人认为，"普通读者"其实指代约翰逊本人的血肉之躯，以及他的"经验自我"（Damrosch 1977：41）。

然而，上述引发"多与一""在场与缺席"之争的"普通读者"，被克莫德、伊格尔顿和哈特曼等理论家简约为"公众"这一建制性观念，并与"公共领域"等具有启蒙内涵的话语挂钩③，最终成为语用工具。可见，"普通读者"在给学者带来灵感的同时，也被时代赋能。例如，上述三位理论家就将"普通读者"这一概念移植到理论的时代，他们借助"普通读者"的前理论视角，审视批评制度的变化，反思"理论热"。然而，在对"普通读者"的呼唤中，这三位都偏好公众而非大众。换句话说，当专业读者占据了底层读者的发声立场时，前者却回避了后者的心声。例如，最讽刺是，当学院派利维斯哀叹"普通读者已死"④时，自称"平民"⑤的伍尔夫刚好完成了《普通读者》第二集。当您把"普通读者"阐发为文论关键词时，您会有什么顾虑吗？我的意思是，我们该如何关照那些沉默的底层读者呢？

殷企平：当今世界，"建构"理论盛行。在不少学者眼中，几乎天下万物都是由人脑建构出来的。阶级、性别、种族、主体/自我和客体/他者，统统都可以冠以"建构"之名。在某些学者的论述中，就连男女性别之分也因"建构"一说而被彻底"消解"了。当然，上述概念确实是建构出来的，但是它们能够完全脱离现实的物质基础而得以建构吗？显然不能。任何概念多多少少带有建构/虚构的成分，这一点不假，但是把"建构"论推向极致，否定任何概念的现实/物质基础，那就会陷入虚无主义的泥淖。"普通读者"这一概念也可以有不同的建构，可以有不同阶层、职业、教育背景等内涵，可以有约翰逊那样的血肉之躯，也可以是在利维斯所在时期"已经死去"的——因而也只是他理想中的——普通读者，还可以是"公众"/"公共领域"中的一员，当然更可以是您所说的"平民""大众"或"底层读者"。所有这些内涵都可以因"建构者"而异，在不同时期、不同场合以及因不同目的而被植入"普通读者"这一大概念，但是它们应该有一个最大公分母，即文学专业/职业之外的所有读者，而后者是客观存在的。我前面提到了裘德，他是哈代建构出来的，可是假如哈代身边没有成千上万普通读者，他就不可能建构出裘德这一生动的人物形象。一个更实际的例子可以从狄更斯那里找到：他在一次演讲中谈到，他所创作的《老古玩店》引起了无数普通劳动者浓厚的兴趣，他们纷纷给狄更斯写信：

> 写信者都居住在沼泽地带和密林深处的那些小木屋里。许多被斧头和铁锹磨炼得非常坚定的手，许多被夏日骄阳晒黑了的手，拿起了笔杆子，向我叙述一个个有关普通人家悲欢离合的小故事。（狄更斯 2015：18）

狄更斯这里讲述的显然是您所说的"底层读者"，不过这些普通读者并没有沉默。倒是在当今世界，越来越多的普通读者不得不沉默了，这是因为在他们和文学作家之间隔着"理论家"。某些"理论家"把文学作品阐释得越来越晦涩，这自然会吓跑一大批受众，至少会让他们沉默。让我们再回到您提的问题：我们该如何关照那些沉默的底层读者呢？最好的关照就是还他们应有的地位。重塑普通读者（包括底层读者），重申他们在经典化过程中的重要性，维护他们对于经典化的参与权，承认他们是检验经典性的最高标准，这既是对他们的关照，也是对我们自己（专业读者）的关照，是对文学/文学批评性质的关照。

三、"普通读者"与共同体

张琰：您将普通读者纳入共同体研究，这让我想到您文中提到的意图将公共生活与私人创造结合起来的罗蒂（Richard Rorty）。罗蒂在《偶然、反讽与团结》（*Contingency, Irony, and Solidarity*, 1990）中提出，小说能促使读者想象他人的痛苦，产生情感共鸣，从而加强各个时代读者的"协同性"。他认为文学批评的功能不在于解释意图或评估价值，而在于梳理脉络、建立人物关系；他所垂青的批评家有阿诺德、佩特、利维斯、艾略特、克莫德以及美国的威尔逊、特里林和布鲁姆（Rorty 1989：80）。其中，利维斯以《细察》（*Security*）为阵地，塑造了一批有"共同追求"的学生读者团体（Leavis 1956：105）；特里林通过散文、书评培养了一群美国中产阶级读者，"这些散文构成了一种理想的亲密的共同体"（West 1989：170）。在我看来，您与罗蒂也十分相似：你们都捍卫文学经典，回避意识形态行话，欣赏具有对话意识的批评家，重视文化实践。简而言之，你们的核心诉求都是发展文学文化，防止让科学文化、哲学文化占绝对优势。

殷企平：我很高兴您捕捉到了我那篇文章的潜台词之一，即普通读者应该纳入共同体研究，或者说共同体研究离不开对普通读者的关注。我欣赏罗蒂把公共生活与私人的创造性活动结合起来的主张，但是我不同意文学批评的功能"不在于评估价值"这样的说法。文学之所以重要，文学批评之所以重要，多半是因为文学阅读能帮助人类甄别价值，从事价值判断。共同体需要共同的价值观来维系，正是在这一点上，普通读者大有可为。没有他们的积极参与，没有他们的文化实践（文学作品的阅读、鉴别和讨论就是一种文化实践），共同体的价值纽带就难以形成，形成了也会消失。我赞同您把罗蒂放在由阿诺德、利维斯、艾略特、克莫德和特里林等人形成的传统中加以审视。作为中国学人，我们有必要借鉴他们在建设阅读共同体方面的经验，但是我们还有另一个使命，即超越他们。我们要构建的阅读共同体，不能局限于利维斯所塑造的学生读者团体，也不能局限于特里林所培养的中产阶级读者，而是服务于习近平主席所倡导的"人类命运共同体"的阅读共同体。另外，我还要就您所说的"文学文化""科学文化"和"哲学文化"多说几句。把"文化"这样细分的做法多见于西方，我更喜欢中国文化中"文史哲不分家"的传统。当然，这一传统多多少少受到了现代化浪潮的冲击。我们在这里谈论普通读者，应该考虑到随着教育的普及及文化程度的普遍提高，如今现实生活中有文化诉求的人不仅会阅读文学作品，而且会尽可能地阅读其他学科/专业的书籍。也就是说，如今普通读者在挑选读物时，变得越来越具有跨学科视野，他们的文学知识往往跟其他学科的知识相互交融。这又把我们带回到您刚才所说的"科学文化"：真的有纯粹的"科学文化"吗？我不禁想起了19世纪英国科学家兼教育家赫胥黎（Thomas Henry Huxley）和诗人兼教育家阿诺德（Matthew Arnold）之间关于"文化"的争论，后者可以看作 20 世纪利维斯（F. R. Leavis）和斯诺（C. P. Snow）关于"两种文化"之争的先声。赫胥黎通常被视为科技教育的倡导者，但是他在批判所谓"人文主义者"拘泥于古典教育的同时，还提出了如下著名观点：科学技术是整个文化中不可分割的一部分。更值得注意的是，他在强调科学技术的重要性时，并不贬低文科教育的作用。他说：

> 我比任何人都深信真正的文科教育的重要性……单一的科技培训只会扭曲人的心智，就像单一的文科训练一样。如果一艘货船的形状十分难看，它装的货物即使再有价值也弥补不了它的丑陋。如果我们的理工学院造就出来的尽是一些畸形的人才，那会使我十分遗憾……（Huxley 1898：153—154）

赫胥黎还呼应过古希腊亚里士多德的相关思想，提出了"哲学即科学"的主张："哲学和科学……是全体与部分、一般与特殊的关系"⑥。我引用赫胥黎的话，是想说明科学是不能单独成为文化的，因而也是无法跟文学截然分开的，而普通读者往往会穿梭于两者之间，这是我们建构阅读共同体时必须考虑的重要因素之一。

张琰：您没有遵循"普通读者是谁"这一本质主义的思考方式，而是提供叙事和形象，从而不断塑造多文化的、跨国的读者社群；您还试图重新描述一种以约翰逊、伍尔夫、克莫德为代表的具有读者共同体意识的英国文学批评传统，由此重申人文主义的立场。例如，您提到，伍尔夫建议读者不要听从什么指点，要独立判断（Woolf 2010：46）。这听上去有些独断，但她绝没有以自我为中心的意思；相反，伍尔夫比学院派批评家更擅长倾听，她经常通过做比较，接受不同观点，考虑它们的复杂性，然后做出经验判断，而非纯理性批判；在此过程中，她还习惯称呼她的读者为"我们"。这种"倾听的共同体"与费什的"阐释的共同体"，在某种意义上形成了对照，即以普通读者群为一方，以专业读者群为另一方。但在我看来，他们似乎只能在学科之外的文化荒野中相遇。以上观点，您同意吗？另外，我们前面已经谈到普通读者与共同体的关系，这与您研究过的文化观念之间有什么联系吗？

殷企平：恕我不敢苟同"文化荒野"这样的说法。学科之内就一定没有荒芜之地吗？学科之外就一定是文化荒野吗？不过，您确实提出了一个很有趣的话题。这要看我们如何界定"文化"一词。根据威廉斯（Raymond Williams）的考证，"文化"一词如今有三种常见的用法：1）用来形容思想、精神和审美演变的总体过程；2）表示一个群体、一个时期、一个民族乃至全人类的某种特定生活方式；3）指涉思想艺术领域的实践和成果（Williams 1983：87—90）。这三种定义无一把"文化"局限于学科之内，第二种定义尤其如此——如果"文化"指人类社会的总体生活方式，那么它远远超出了学科的范围。也就是说，在学科之外，文化可谓"芳草碧连天"。说得更明白一点，对普通读者来说，天涯何处无（文化）芳草？专业读者若把这碧连天的芳草关在学科高墙之外，那就只能陷入孤芳自赏的局面。在此，我还想进一步引用威廉斯的观点，他在《文化与社会》（*Culture and Society*，1958）一书中说道：

> 文化一词的演变记录了人们对历史性变化的反应，即对我们的社会、经济和政治生活中的重大历史性变化做出的重要而持续的反应。该词的演变本身好比一种特殊的地图，从中我们可以探索那些变化的性质。（Williams 1958：xvi—xvii）

威廉斯这里所说的重大历史性变化，指的是社会转型，即农业文明向工业文明的转型。正是这一转型，造成了社会、经济和政治乃至总体生活方式的空前变化，而这一转型带来的焦虑，是我们所说"文化"观念的最主要内涵。这就把我们带回到您刚才提到的问题：普通读者/共同体与我研究过的文化观念之间有什么联系吗？联系可大了！2012年以来，我有幸跟国内40来位学者一起，从事一项国家社科重大课题研究，题目是"文化观念流变中的英国文学典籍研究"（最终成果已经由上海外语教育出版社以6卷本丛书的形式出版）。在这套丛书中，我们用了10个关键词来勾勒文化观念的主要内涵，分别是"转型焦虑""愿景描述""共同体形塑""秩序诉求""审美趣味""心智培育""文学语言的创造""民族良心""道德伦理传统"和"工作/生活方式"。这些关键词之间都有着内在的联系，或者说你中有我，我中有你。例如，对于社会转型的焦虑意味着人类的工作/生活方式（因转型）出了问题，或者说"礼崩乐坏"（社会秩序混乱，伦理道德败坏）。既然"文化"由"转型焦虑"而生，那它就必须提供走出焦虑的途径，如描述各种愿景，包括共同体愿景、乌托邦愿景，或者关于美好社会秩序的愿景，而后者的实现离不开心智的培育、民族良心的锻造和民族特性的构建，以及提倡理想的工作/生活方式，等等。不妨对"共同体"做这样的归纳：它是一种人类生存和相处的结合机制，主要由血缘、地缘、精神或利益关系构成。"共同体"本身极具复杂性、矛盾性，它和历史上各种思潮进行着复杂互动，这是它的迷人之处，考验着人们的经验、智慧、思辨能力和批评意识，这也是它成为历代英国作家文学想象的重要客体的原因之一（姜仁凤，李维屏 2021：6）。我们在那套丛书里所要证明的观点之一就是：英国文学家们在拓展上述文化观念内涵方面作出了不可磨灭的贡献。应该承认，我们在丛书中没有直接用"普通读者"一词，但是每一卷都有不少篇幅讨论"共同体形塑"话题，其中多多少少隐含了普通读者的作用。例如，由杭州师范大学欧荣教授牵头的第 6 卷中提到，利维斯对"共同体"的想象体现为"少数人"与"心智成熟的民众"之间的创造性合作（欧荣等 2021：8）。这里，"心智成熟的民众"就是普通读者。利维斯的"少数人文化"常常遭到误解，其实他只是想解决"大众文明"时代的"文化困境"，并且十分清楚光靠"少数人"的突围是不够的，只有得到"心智成熟的民众"的回应和支持，文化传承才有希望，为此他提出了"共同语言"（Leavis 1956：109）一说。普通读者当然也是这"共同语言"的使用者。

张琰：我还注意到，您和您的同事们不仅在理论层面讨论"普通读者"的重要性，不仅视其为一种文化实践，而且身体力行。在您的带领下，杭州师范大学外国语学院创办了外国文学经典读书会——敦雅书社。可否请您简单介绍一下敦雅书社的经典阅读、"普通读者"等系列活动？

殷企平："敦雅书社"是浙江省社科联下属"阅读联盟"的集体会员之一，旨在推进全民阅读，以期在作品和读者之间建立起一种天然而健康的关系。书社开展的活动大致有三类：1）经典作品分享会，每月一次，每次安排一位专业读者做读书报告，而对象既包括专业读者，又包括普通读者；2）经典作品进校园，可以进高校，也可以进中学和小学，以期待培养不同层次的普通读者；

3）经典作品进公共图书馆，如浙江省图书馆等。2020年6月10日，我们书社"普通读者"系列活动正式拉开序幕，并邀请中国社科院外文所陈众议研究员以腾讯会议形式作了题为"时代的需要与文学的问题"的开幕讲座。2020年11月1日晚，我们还把读书活动移到杭州宝石山上的纯真年代书吧，与诗刊《诗建设》、浙江图书馆文澜朗诵团共同举办了2020诺贝尔文学奖得主美国女诗人露易丝·格丽克诗歌双语品读会。这类线上线下的读书活动已经得到不少普通读者的热烈响应。如您所说，我们从事的是一种文化实践，或者说是一种文化话语实践。说到这里，我不由地想起中国北宋文学家苏洵在《管仲论》中的一句话："夫功之成，非成于成之日，盖必有所由起；祸之作，不作于作之日，亦必有所由兆"。我们不妨试问："建造共同体之功"成于何时呢？我想这样作答：成于文学/话语介入之日，成于普通读者热烈参与之时。

张琰：殷老师，非常感谢您接受这次访谈，期待您更多学术成果问世！

注释：

① 关于外国学者对"普通读者与专业读者良性互动"的主张，参见：菲尔斯基. 2019. 文学之用［M］. 刘洋，译. 南京：南京大学出版社：9；伊戈尔斯通. 2020. 文学为什么重要［M］. 修佳明，译. 北京：北京大学出版社：6。

② 下文凡引自殷企平. 2019. 西方文论关键词：普通读者［J］. 外国文学（6），只标注页码。

③ 关于将"普通读者"化约为"公众"的观点，参见：Kermode F. 1989. *An Appetite for Poetry*［M］. Cambridge：Harvard University Press：49；Eagleton T. 2005. *The Function of Criticism*［M］. London：Verso：9；Hartman G H. 1991. *Minor Prophecies: The Literary Essay in the Culture Wars*［M］. Cambridge：Harvard University Press：15–16。

④ 关于"普通读者的传统已死"的观点，详见：Leavis F R. 1932. *How to Teach Reading: A Primer for Ezra Pound*［M］. Cambridge：G. Fraser, The Minority Press：4。

⑤ 关于伍尔夫自称"平民"的观点，详见：Woolf V. 1947. "The Leaning Tower"［C］//The Moment and Other Essays. Woolf L（ed.）. London：Hogarth

Press: 125; 关于《普通读者》第二集的出版时间，参见: Woolf V. 1932. *The Common Reader-Second Series* [M]. London: Hogarth Press。

⑥ 详见: 殷企平. 1995. 英国高等科技教育 [M]. 杭州: 杭州大学出版社: 41。

参考文献

[1] Bloom H. *How to Read and Why* [M]. New York: Simon & Schuster, 2000.

[2] Bloom H. *The Western Canon: The Books and School of the Ages* [M]. New York: Harcourt Brace & Company, 1994.

[3] Damrosch L. *The Uses of Johnson's Criticism* [M]. Charlottesville: University Press of Virginia, 1977.

[4] Engell J. *Forming the Critical Mind: Dryden to Coleridge* [M]. Cambridge: Harvard University Press, 1989.

[5] Huxley T H. Science and Education [A] //Collected Essays (Vol. Ⅲ). New York: D. Appleton & Company, 1898: 153 – 154.

[6] Kaplan C, Rose E C. *The Canon and the Common Reader* [M]. Knoxville: University of Tennessee Press, 1990.

[7] Kermode F. *An Appetite for Poetry* [M]. Cambridge: Harvard University Press, 1989.

[8] Kernan A B. *Samuel Johnson and the Impact of Print* [M]. Princeton: Princeton University Press, 1989.

[9] Leavis F R. *The Common Pursuit* [M]. London: Chatto & Windus, 1956.

[10] Rorty R. *Contingency, Irony, and Solidarity* [M]. Cambridge: Cambridge University Press, 1989.

[11] Wellek R. A History of Modern Criticism 1750 – 1950 (Vol. 1), *The Later English Century* [M]. New Haven: Yale University Press, 1955.

[12] West C. *The American Evasion of Philosophy: A Genealogy of Pragmatism* [M]. Madison: The University of Wisconsin Press, 1989.

[13] Williams R. *Culture and Society* [M]. London: Chatto & Windus, 1958.

[14] Williams R. *Keywords: A Vocabulary of Culture and Society* [M]. Flamingo: Fontana Press, 1983.

[15] Woolf V. *The Common Reader* [M]. Shanghai: Shanghai World, 2010.

[16] 狄更斯. 狄更斯演讲集 [M]. 殷企平, 丁建民, 徐伟彬, 译. 上海: 上海三联书店, 2015.

[17] 姜仁凤, 李维屏. 英国文学中的命运共同体跨学科研究——李维屏教授访谈录 [J]. 广东外语外贸大学学报, 2021 (4): 5-13.

[18] 欧荣, 等. 文化观念流变中的英国文学典籍研究（卷六）: 文化观念裂变时期的英国文学典籍研究 [M]. 上海: 上海外语教育出版社, 2021.

[19] 文德勒. 看不见的倾听者 [M]. 周星月, 王敖, 译. 桂林: 广西师范大学出版社, 2019.

[20] 叶丽贤. 萨缪尔·约翰逊《诗人传》对英诗经典的建构 [M]. 厦门: 厦门大学出版社, 2020.

[21] 殷企平. 西方文论关键词: 普通读者 [J]. 外国文学, 2019 (6): 44-54.

（本文原载于《广东外语外贸大学学报》2022年第3期）

"共同体"与外国文学研究

——殷企平教授访谈录*

一、我的外国文学研究之路

李睿（以下简称李）：殷老师，您好！非常感谢您能在百忙之中接受这次访谈。从1980年代起，您就一直在高校从事外国文学的教学与研究工作，至今已经有40年，可以说是直接见证、参与和推动了改革开放以来我国的外国文学研究。您能否先简单分享一下您最初为何选择了外国文学研究这条道路？

殷企平（以下简称殷）：小李好！上中学时，我读了《大卫·科波菲尔》的译著，很快就爱上了狄更斯（Charles Dickens），萌发了读原著的愿望。上大学后，对比原著和译著，我发现翻译的"文化亏损"在所难免。回想起来，这一意念其实已经产生了些许进行研究的意向。在大学三年级时，有一位美国教授介绍了阿诺德（Matthew Arnold）的文化思想，其中的一项重要命题打动了我：文化从何开始？这个问题伴随了我好久，促使我不断地寻找阿诺德的作品。阿诺德认为，文化只在一种情况下才开始，即当人们开始了解并学习其他文化，并用以反思或修正自己的行为方式时，文化才真正开始。他在许多场合都发表

---

* 本文由李睿与殷企平合写。本文系国家社科基金项目"英国文化研究的谱系学和现代转型研究"（编号：18BWW015）的阶段性成果。

过类似的观点，其中要数在伊顿公学演讲时的一句话最为典型："知彼才能知己，知己才能改错，才能获得拯救。"（Stone 1997：2）我十分认同这一观点。作为中国文化的传人和建设者，我们理应研究文学，因为文学是讨论重大文化问题的领域。不仅要研究本国文学，而且要研究外国文学，否则就不能知己知彼。

李：不管是中国还是中国的外国文学研究，这40多年间都可以说是发生了翻天覆地的变化。在您看来，外国文学研究这些年间取得的主要成绩有哪些，是否也存在一些不足之处？外国文学研究未来的发展方向有哪些？

殷：在过去40多年里，我国的外国文学研究取得了许多显著成绩，但是如果仓促列举成绩，肯定会挂一漏万，因此请允许我略过不谈，只谈一个我认为急需解决的问题，即如何尊重普通读者的问题。在过去的四五十年中，我国外国文学领域多多少少受到了一股国际不良潮流的影响，即轻视乃至敌视普通读者的倾向。文学批评应有的宗旨是要为所有文学爱好者服务（既为专业读者，也为普通读者），但是它如今很少为普通读者服务了。就像英国学者雅尔丁（Lisa A. Jardine）所指出的那样，"普通读者不复存在了"（Kaplan, Rose 1990：377）。为什么会这样呢？问题的根子在于"理论"被无限拔高了。英国著名学者克莫德（Frank Kermode）曾经哀叹："能够指望普通读者听懂理论教授们高谈阔论的时代早已过去了；假如理论家们跟普通读者扯上了关系，就会觉得自己的尊严被冒犯，这就是我们所面临的奇情怪状。那些理论家自诩为专家，不再对普通读者负有义务……许多书籍被划入文学批评类别，其供应量日益增多，可是文学爱好者中很少有人能读懂这些书，就连专业读者也不都懂。"（Kermode 1989：8）另一位英国文坛翘楚布雷德伯里（Malcolm Bradbury）也发出过类似的哀叹："文学批评已经远离公共领域，躲进了大学的象牙塔，在那里变成了另一种东西。它不喜欢原先意义上的评判工作，结果变成了现在的文学理论：作为文学的一种变体，它一味迎合各种时髦的意识形态，热衷于拉山头、占地盘，充斥着专业话语。"（Bradbury 1999：52）美国学者奈特（Christopher J. Knight, 2003）也曾批评美国文学教授/批评家们常常醉心于学术特技表演，而全然不顾跟普通读者沟通的必要性。这种现象在我国的高校和研究机构可能不那么严重，但是至少应该反省，应该引以为戒。这就自然地引向了您提的一个问题：外国文学研究未来的发展方向有哪些？我觉得至少应该有一个"重塑普通读者"的发展方向，而这首先要求我们彻底揭露"去经典化"思潮的谬误，因为普通读者的消失，是"去经典化"思潮作祟所致。普通读者是检验经典性的最高标准，因此我们应该探索与普通读者良性沟通的新渠道，这将是摆在众多外国文学工作者面前的重要课题。

李：您的学术成果丰硕，其中19世纪英国文学和文化始终是您关注的一个重点。在您看来，这一时期的文学作品和文化观点具有怎样的特殊价值？

殷：19世纪英国文学作品和文化观点的特殊价值在于它们对现代性的反思。所谓现代性，是以科学主义、工具理性、客观知识主体论，以及鼓吹"无限进步"的宏大叙述为特征的现代价值体系，是启蒙思想家在变革激情下提出的理想蓝图和哲理设计，这一价值体系/哲理设计最早在英国赢得了实践的土壤——英国工业革命是在19世纪达到高潮的。也就是说，世界意义上的现代化最早发生于英国，与之相匹配的现代价值体系也最早成熟于英国。19世纪的英国文学家们针对（因工业革命的胜利而形成的）举世颂歌滔滔的局面，提出了一个个发人深思的文化命题：什么是进步？什么是幸福？什么是高品质的生活？美好的社会究竟依赖什么？是依赖诱人的科技经济指标，还是别的、更重要的东西？如阿尔梯克（Richard D. Altick）所说，19世纪已经"有人认识到，英格兰希望建成的美好社会有赖于某种叫作'文化'的东西"（Altick 1973：238）。换言之，19世纪英国的优秀文学家们做了一项有特殊价值的工作，即在语义层面对"文化"和"文明"观念作了区分。无论是卡莱尔（Thomas Carlyle）那样的散文家，还是华兹华斯（William Wordsworth）那样的诗人，或是狄更斯那样的小说家，都奋起批判独尊"事实"的文明，都表达了含有价值诉求的文化思想，也就是承担起给"文化"和"文明"分家的工作。他们以生动的故事、诗性的语言和熠熠生辉的人物形象来传达自己的文化思想，也就是构建了文化观念的内涵。他们的话语有一个共同点，即鲜明地采取了与"文明"决裂的战斗性姿态，其人数之多，影响之广，言辞之激烈，前所未有。可以说，到了19世纪末，"文化"与"文明"的决裂已经完成，它标志着文化观念的成熟，而这一伟业要归功于19世纪英国那些优秀文学家们的前仆后继。

李：在19世纪的英国小说家中，您对狄更斯的研究尤为深入。您通过一系列文章解析了狄更斯等作家所开创的"质疑'进步'话语的传统"（殷企平 2006）。在您看来，以狄更斯为代表的这些作家在"质疑"的同时，是否也在文学作品中描摹了他们眼中的理想社会形象？这样的理想社会又具备怎样的共同特征？

殷：肯定是的。他们都描绘了美好的共同体愿景，而与此紧密相关的是"英格兰特性"（Englishness）的建构，即描述或凝练英格兰民族的特色，其用意是促进民族身份的认同。对共同体的憧憬，离不开对财富的思考。更具体地说，离不开对下列问题的思考：财富是什么？财富意味着什么？应该由谁来掌管财富？该怎样掌管？在 19 世纪英国，无论是小说家，还是诗人，或是散文家，都对以上问题提交过精彩的答卷。狄更斯、阿诺德和罗斯金（John Ruskin）分别是这 3 方面的杰出代表。对财富的关注，必然会导向对生活方式的关注，包括对工作方式的关注。把工作视为生活方式，并且以崇敬的态度对待它，这是 19 世纪出现的一种新动态，其背后的主要推手是卡莱尔、金斯利（Charles Kingsley）、阿诺德、罗斯金和莫里斯（William Morris）——我在《"文化辩护书"》中曾经描述过文化观念从"工作福音"向"艺术福音"的嬗变。需要补充的是，推动这一观念的还有许多小说家。例如，乔治·艾略特（George Eliot）笔下的亚当（Adam）就是"工作福音"的化身。要重塑生活/工作方式，就得从心智的培育做起。从奥斯汀（Jane Austen）起，尤其是进入维多利亚时期之后，英国文学家比以往更注重心智培育。再以艾略特为例：她的所有小说都涉及如何培育心智的问题；虽然故事情节会比较复杂，可道理却很简单，即心智培育有两个基本前提：爱心和知识，两者还必须融合。我特别喜欢《丹尼尔·德隆达》（Daniel Deronda）中的一句话："在高尚的生活里，爱心穿戴着知识。"（Eliot 1984：421）19 世纪英国文学中理想社会的另一个共同特征是秩序诉求，尤其是关于秩序基础的责任意识。秩序主题在金斯利的《向西去啊！》（Westward Ho!）、康拉德（Joseph Conrad）的《"水仙号"上的黑家伙》（The Nigger of the "Narcissus"）等海洋文学作品中尤为突出。还须提一提吉辛（George Gissing）的《失去归属者》（The Unclassed）。该书围绕主人公魏玛克的写作目标，引人入胜地把小说创作与治国理政相提并论，这非常值得借鉴。在上述愿景描述中，都有一种"乌托邦冲动"（the utopian impulse）。"乌托邦冲动"自古有之,但是就 19 世纪英国文学而言,这种冲动烙上了一种特殊的(社会转型旋涡越转越快的)时代印记,这在金斯利和莫里斯的作品中尤为明显。在金斯利的小说《奥尔顿·洛克》(Alton Locke)中,主人公奥尔顿的"绅士理想"代表了一种乌托邦梦想,它既蕴含着破除阶级/等级藩篱的愿望,又含有强烈的共同体诉求。这部小说的玄妙之处在于贯穿其中的一个张力,即个体乌托邦和共同体理想之间的互动。当然,"乌托邦之最"非莫里斯的《乌有乡消息》(News from Nowhere)莫属。该书呈现了关于人类总体生活方式的文化蓝图,并提出了实现这一蓝图的具体路径,即打破工作与休闲的界限,把普通劳动者的日常工作提升到艺术化的境界,这跟马克思(Karl Marx)、恩格斯(Friedrich Engels)描绘的共产主义社会蓝图十分契合。

二、"进步"话语与英国文化批评

李:在《推敲"进步"话语》中,您从 19 世纪的英国小说出发探讨了彼时英国盛行的"进步"议题,揭示了作品与社会转型引发的思想和情感危机的内在联系。这是否体现了您的文学研究观?作为人文研究的重要组成部分,文学研究在当下应扮演怎样的角色?

殷:可以这么说吧:我在《推敲"进步"话语》的开篇处曾坦言该书受到了黄梅博士的启发。她在《推敲"自我"——小说在 18 世纪的英国》一书中指出,当年我国学术界有关处于从农业文明向工业文明转型时期的英国研究中存在着一种失衡现象:探讨在"强国之路"上英国政治体制、科技振兴计划和经济运行方式的专著和论文频频问世,而关注同一时期英国人的困惑、痛苦以及思想/感情危机方面的作品却如凤毛麟角(黄梅,2015)。我们国家如今仍然处于社会转型时期,当然有必要参照当年英国在经济腾飞道路上的诸多经验,但是更有必要聆听许多英国有识之士在快速发展的旋涡中所发出的心声,而聆听的最好场所莫过于在相应时代写就的文学作品。如怀特海(Alfred North Whitehead)所说,"如果我们希望发现某代人的内心思想,我们必须求助于文学"(Whitehead 1948:76)。我对 19 世纪英国小说的研究,可以看作对黄梅博士所做工作的一种延续:我所选择的历史时期有所不同,但是研究宗旨跟她相仿，意在揭示作品与社会转型引发的思想和情感危机的内在联系。我想补充说明的是，19世纪的英国比18世纪的英国更加具有"转型"的特点，因为只是到了19世纪，人们的普遍意识里才形成了"社会转型"这一概念，这在19世纪英国文学中可以得到印证。

李：在《"文化辩护书"》这本书中，您提出了"19世纪英国文化批评"这一概念，主张将文化观念的流变与文学典籍相互参照进行研究。请问您如何看待文学研究和文化研究这两者间的关系？如何在把握好外国文学研究底色的同时开展文化研究？

殷：我想，您是要我谈一谈文化批评和文学之间的关系吧？我一直抱持这样一个观点：最有影响力的文化批评工作，其实是由优秀的文学家们来完成的。应该承认，如今许多以"文化批评"名义开展的活动都发生在非文学领域，但是在诸多领域中，是否有一个中心呢？我认为中心是存在的，这个中心仍然是，并且应该是文学。我特别喜欢美国杰出文化批评家特里林（Lionel Trilling）的一段话，大致意思是这样的：文学情景就是文化情景，文化情景就是围绕道德问题而展开的战斗；道德问题跟私人形象不无关系，而私人形象则跟文学风格不无关系。不仅在道德领域，而且在政治、经济等诸多领域，人类发现自己面临的困惑越来越多，越来越大，这就越需要我们学会审时度势，而要做到这一点，就要依靠文学。用特里林的原话说，"文学这一人类活动，能给予事务的复杂性最充分、最精确的考量，既敏锐感知于世间万千气象，又明察人生百味千状，因而最能应对扑朔迷离的情形"（Trilling 1950：ix—xv）。我去年底在《英语研究》（第12辑）上发表了《文化批评的来龙去脉》一文，借此提出了以下观点："文化批评即针对'文明'弊端的批评活动。它反对'分离'，抗拒异化，关注人类社会的整体性与和谐性。对整体性/和谐性的诉求离不开想象力，而文学是最具想象力的学科。因此，文化批评的手段尽管是跨学科、多学科和超学科的，却需要以文学为中心，否则有可能流于肤浅。"（殷企平 2020：48）我这里所说的"中心"，可能就是您所说的"底色"。

李：与19世纪的英国境况相仿，我国当前正处在社会急剧转型的阶段，文化问题、文化现象层见叠出，其中很多都可以被概括为"转型的焦虑"。以"消费主义"问题为例，阿诺德曾因维多利亚时代显现的"消费主义"倾向痛心疾首，并提出通过"提高社会文化素质"，即"了解世界上最优秀的思想和言论""保存过去的精神遗产"（殷企平 2013：103）等方式来应对这一问题。在您看来，阿诺德的这一论断对当下的我们是否具有借鉴意义？当代社会中的个人又可以从英国文化批评中获得何种启示来帮助我们应对因时代巨变而产生的焦虑？

殷：阿诺德仍然对我们言说着。他不仅把消费文化诊断为一种现代疾病，而且提出了医治它的药方，可是这些药方未能广为传播。我在《"文化辩护书"》里专辟一章，写阿诺德对消费文化的回应，就是想为上述药方的传播起一些推动作用。确如您所说，阿诺德认为医治"消费疾病"的关键在于提高人的文化素质，也就是敦促世人"了解世界上最优秀的思想和言论"——大家都知道这是阿诺德给"文化"下的定义。也就是说，有文化作保障，人类就不至于被消费浪潮给淹没。阿诺德的药方有其鲜明的特色，我们只有在把他的诗歌作品和文化理论联系起来时，才能真正得以领悟。您刚才提到如何"应对因时代巨变而产生的焦虑"这一问题，阿诺德正是在这方面能给我们许多启示。例如，他在《吉卜赛学者》（*The Scholar Gypsy*）中这样赞扬主人公："你只有一个目标、一个事业、一个愿望。"（Arnold 1965：339）与这一句形成鲜明对照的是诗中的另一句："这现代生活的怪病，/带着它病态的匆忙，带着因目标过多而产生的迷茫……"（Arnold 1965：342）阿诺德通过这种对比，或者说通过吉卜赛学者这一形象，提醒现代人要目标专一，避免因"病态的匆忙"或"目标过多"而产生迷茫。值得留意的是，"病态的匆忙"和"目标过多"还有另一层含义，即现代人匆匆消费，盲目消费，因而分散了生活目标，这就跟诗中对消费文化的批评形成了相互映照的关系。换一句话说，吉卜赛学者这一形象是阿诺德为现代人——或者是您所说的"当代社会中的个人"——树立的榜样，是他为医治消费文化开出的一剂良方。

李：在《文化》（*Culture*）一书中，伊格尔顿（Terry Eagleton）对"文化"概念进行了考察，并在该书的结尾部分指出："事实上，人类在走入新千年时所面对的核心问题根本与文化无关。它们比文化世俗、物质得多。战争、饥荒、毒品、军备竞赛、种族屠杀、疾病、生态灾难，这一切都是文化层面，但文化并不是问题的核心。"（Eagleton 2016：162）在他看来，文化并非解决很多重大问题的"良药"，您是否同意伊格尔顿的观点？

殷：伊格尔顿那本书的结语部分有一个小标题，叫作"文化的傲慢"（The Hubris of Culture）。这个标题有歧义：是文化本身的傲慢呢，还是（通过文学）教授文化知识的文学批评家（这里主要指大学教师）的傲慢？该书的第一句就说："文学批评家们一直对自己的重要性存疑。"（Eagleton 2016：149）在第二句中，伊格尔顿承认"文学应对的是人类现实中最根本的问题，这是不可否认的"。（Eagleton 2016：149）在第三句中，他又讲了事情的另一个方面："自从文学作品的研究抛弃了公共领域，躲进了学术界，它就成了次要活动，这种边缘化的程度使人不难想象大学文学系正在成为明日黄花（确实，整个艺术人文学科都如此）。"（Eagleton 2016：149）此处的"公共领域"一说让人想起伊格尔顿在《批评的功能》（*The Function of Criticism*，2005）中提出的一个著名观点，即在 18 世纪，文学批评的正当性是由当时存在的公共领域得以确立的，但是到了 19 世纪，这种公共领域消失了，文学批评家也随之陷入了孤立。我想补充的是，这里所说的"公共领域"跟我前面说的"普通读者"有关：一旦文学批评脱离了由普通读者组成的公共领域，那么它就无法在人类社会的根本性事务中发挥重要作用，只能被边缘化，成为伊格尔顿所说的"次要诉求"（a peripheral pursuit）。在这一意义上，我同意伊格尔顿的观点。然而，对他的"人类在走入新千年时所面对的核心问题根本与文化无关"一说，我实在不敢苟同。关键在于：他所说的"文化"究竟是什么？如果他指的是躲在象牙塔里、无视普通读者、不屑于构建公共领域的某些傲慢的大学教授/学者，那么他是对的，但是我们还得看一下他自己也认同的"文化"定义——就在您所说的《文化》一书中，他还认同了自己前几年在《文化观念》（*The Idea of Culture*，2000）中所做的有关界定，即"文化"和"文明"原本好比一家人，但是自 19 世纪初以降，"文化观念开始从'文明'的同义词转变成了它的反义词"（Eagleton 2000：14）。为什么会这样呢？按照伊氏的说法，"文明"一词本来"集事实与价值于一身"，即既标明某种社会生活形态，又隐含价值判断，如颂扬相关的生活形态及其精神诉求，或个人的全面发展、人际关系的和谐，以及国家的治理和昌盛，等等。换言之，"文明"的语义原有两个基本层面：一是描述层面，二是规范层面；前者关乎事实，后者关乎价值。随着工业革命的兴起，"文明"的上述两个语义层面产生了分裂：它的描述/物质层面犹在，而它的规范/精神层面则丢失了，这一点在《文化》中说得很明白:"文明如今只关乎事实,而文化却追问价值。"(Eagleton 2016: 10)也就是说,"文明"原有的价值使命,如今只能由"文化"来承担了。不但如此,"文化"还负起了反思/质疑"文明"的使命。19世纪英国优秀文学家们所承担的就是这一使命,而这一使命还要由当代各国的优秀文学家们来继续承担。当今世界,(伊格尔顿所说的)"战争、饥荒、毒品、军备竞赛、种族屠杀、疾病、生态灾难"等问题大都是以"文明"的名义造成的。例如,某些西方"文明"政客不知给人类带来了多少痛苦和灾难,其根本原因就是他们没有文化。优秀的文学作品就是用文化来与"文明"抗争,优秀的文学批评家自然也要奋起抗争,岂能把"保持沉默"作为明智之举?

三、文学中的共同体

李: 就外国文学研究领域而言,您是国内最早进行"共同体"研究的学者之一,早在2013年您就发表了《"朋友"意象与共同体形塑》。近年来,您针对"共同体"这一主题发表了十余篇学术论文。请问是什么促使您关注外国文学中的共同体这一话题的?

殷: 我先前在阅读英国小说时,发现经常会跳出"community"这个单词来,从狄更斯到拜厄特(A. S. Byatt)都是如此,这就自然而然地激发了我的兴趣。后来我在从事文学批评工作中,发现文学典籍研究和文化观念研究之间存在着脱节状况,因而萌发了一个念头,即做一个旨在服务于中国文化建设的外国文学研究项目,既说明文化观念的发展对于文学典籍生成的作用,又说明文学典籍在引领文化走向、塑造共同体意识等方面的积极作用。文化观念制约着共同体中人们对生活的全面理解;而文学典籍是表达并交流这种理解的关键性媒介。文化观念的变化和发展直接影响着文学典籍的生成方式,而文学典籍又反过来对文化观念的走向施加重要影响。就文学研究而言,只有将这种在历史进程中互为表里的关系纳入视野,才能拥有对作品的透彻把握,进而将文学研究提升至文化研究的高度。我想再回到您前面提的问题,即文学研究和文化研究这两者之间的关系问题。在我看来,文化研究虽然是目前方兴未艾的盛事,却较少系统地、细致地介入文学典籍的研究,因而缺乏文学研究所能提供的对文化状况的细腻、丰满的把握，也未能充分阐释文学典籍在引领文化走向、塑造共同价值方面发挥作用的具体机制。如何将这两方面的研究融合为一个有机的整体，使文学典籍研究与文化观念研究——尤其是共同体观念的研究——真正做到相辅相成、欣合无间，以推进外国文学研究，并为中国当前的文化建设工作服务，既是学术发展的要求，也是社会现实的要求。

李：您在《共同体》一文中对共同体理论的演变、发展进行了梳理，并多次谈到了共同体的"有机/内在属性"，认为"共同体概念最重要的属性是文化实践，意在改造世界"（殷企平 2016：79）。可以说，进行文化实践是共同体建构的重要途径，由此也为当今的文化实践提出了新的要求。您认为这些讨论可以为我们从事外国文学研究提供怎样的启示？

殷：这方面的讨论可以大大拓宽外国文学研究的思路。例如，如果我们把目光投向文学作品中的会话，那就能发现一个广阔的空间，或者说有一片广阔的土地在等待着我们去开垦。以英国文学为例，近三百年的英国文学史都可以看作一部会话和共同体的交融史——文学家们对于共同体的构想从来都是充分运用会话元素的。作为一般概念，"会话"与"共同体"在语义上有着血缘关系，但是这一关系还须从文化层面上来理解。会话与共同体的亲缘关系不仅体现于小说，而且体现于诗歌、戏剧和随笔等文类，甚至有一种"会话体随笔"，里面的许多共同体元素还未被发掘。会话的共同体精神体现在对于会话分寸的拿捏方面，取决于会话者的态度、语气和措辞是否得体，这方面的素材实在太多。我曾经在这方面做过初步研究，但是做得很不够。优秀的文学家对共同体的想象，实际上是对现实生活中共同体的塑造，而共同体的建构与其说依赖启蒙运动提倡的那种理性设计，不如说是一种文化/话语实践和探索，会话就是一种文化/话语实践。威廉斯（Raymond Williams）曾经说过，文化探索在很大程度上是一种无意识或未知的体验，而未知的体验不可能有铁定的方案、计划和公式。正因为如此，他认为"一个美好的共同体，一种鲜活的文化，都会促进人们在公共需求方面的意识，不仅会为此提供空间，而且会鼓励所有的人都为此努力"（Williams 1960：354）。这种鲜活的文化就存在于文学作品中，存在于文学批评（批评应该是一种会话）活动中。我想借苏洵《管仲论》中的一句话来结束我的回答："夫功之成，非成于成之日，盖必有所由起；祸之作，不作于作之日，亦必有所由兆。"那么,"建造共同体之功"成于何时呢?我的答复是:成于文学/话语介入之日,成于会话分寸拿捏得体之时。

李:如您所言,"共同体"这一概念其实牵涉到很多的维度,但是目前在国内学界还未充分展开,如雷蒙·威廉斯在讨论"可知共同体"时就论及其中的权力问题。威廉斯认为,"可知共同体"既是"显在事实,有自然赋予的成分,但也是有意的选择和构建,体现了叙述者的立场",而"话语本身就是一种对权力的主张"(何卫华 2017:178)。可以说,对共同体的理解受制于作家、批评家的个人立场。这一论断同时也集中反映在您的《共同体》一文中。在您看来,从建构共同体的角度出发,共同体研究今后还可以向哪些方面推进?

殷:可以推进的角度还有很多。我前面讲的"普通读者"就可以看作共同体研究方向的一个重要子方向。当然从严格意义上讲,它是"元批评"(批评之批评)层面的话题,但是归根结底,"元批评"仍然属于文学范畴。我们前面提到的愿景描述、秩序诉求、乌托邦形态、民族身份(如"英格兰特性")、财富的归属和掌管、生活/工作方式、会话的诸多形态等,都可以作为共同体研究的推进方向。我前面忘记提"民族良心"了,这也是一个和共同体息息相关的话题。在英国文学中,萨克雷(William Thackeray)与乔伊斯(James Joyce)都为锻造民族良心留下了许多动人的文字。探究民族良心,就是想象共同体。再就是"音乐"——我曾经在《外国文学研究》(2016年第5期)上发表《英国文学中的音乐与共同体形塑》一文(这只是初步的探讨,欢迎大家对我提出批评),并在此基础上往前推进。值得切入的角度实在很多。上海外国语大学李维屏教授目前正主持国家社科基金重大课题"英国文学的命运共同体表征与审美研究",这是一个十分有意义的课题。

李:2020年是历史上极不平凡的一年,我们遭遇了中美两国贸易摩擦、科技争端、新冠疫情,过去看似稳定的世界秩序被彻底打破,"独体"倾向愈发显现。在此背景下,您觉得共同体研究能否为我们提供一些启示?

殷:当然能。在国际政治领域,共同体研究能为我们在跟"独体"论的拥趸们进行论战时提供思想武器。西方的一些学者和政客不认可共同体理想,这是因为他们深受自由主义思想的影响。例如,美国学者霍姆斯(Stephen Holmes, 1989)在《反自由思想的永久性结构》("The Permanent Structure of

Anti-liberal Thought")一文中把"个人扎根于自己所在环境"的共同体模式定性为"镶嵌性模式"(embeddedness),而这种"镶嵌"又无异于"限制"(restriction)或"遏制"(restraint)。言下之意,共同体/秩序诉求必然意味着个人自由的丢失。我们不能认同这样的观点。从马克思主义的观点看,个人自由和共同体互为依存,两者相辅相成,彼此之间是一种辩证的关系。这本来是一种常识,可是到了那些高深的西方哲学家/批评家手里,却成了水火不相容的东西。这种非此即彼的思维方式,究其根源,与启蒙现代性不无关系——启蒙思想家们过度依赖工具理性,过度热衷于个人对福祉的主观感受,因而使个人自由/幸福与共同体/秩序诉求截然对立,导致现代幸福观念中认知维度和伦理维度的分裂。用麦金泰尔(Alasdair MacIntyre)的话说,"责任和幸福的纽带逐渐被撕裂了"(MacIntyre 1998:107)。责任本来应该是幸福伦理的核心要素,可是如今它已游离了许多现代西方人的幸福观念;在启蒙现代性语境下,自由主义者往往无视个人对社会的责任,无视本人所在国家对全世界、全人类的责任。在跟自由主义者交流乃至论战时,我们该怎样坚持人类命运共同体的理想呢?我认为最好的办法是"以子之矛,攻子之盾",这"矛"就是外国文学作品中呈现的一幅幅共同体图景。例如,从19世纪至今,英国文学家们在想象共同体时,已经对如何保持"秩序"与"自由"之间的平衡这一问题有过深入的思考。无论是19世纪的奥斯汀、狄更斯、乔治·艾略特和乔治·吉辛,还是当代的斯威夫特(Graham Swift)、麦克尤恩(Ian McEwan)、阿克罗伊德(Peter Ackroyd)和拜厄特,英国文学家们描绘的共同体图景足以对"独体"论形成解构作用。自由主义者是不会愿意读奥斯汀、狄更斯的,但是总会有不少西方人愿意读,这应该是我们建构人类命运共同体的一块基石。

李:非常感谢您接受这次的访谈!

参考文献

[1] Altick, R. D. *Victorian People and Ideas* [M]. New York: W. W. Norton and Company, 1973.

[2] Bradbury, M. A stern and righteous reader [J]. Ed. Wood J. *New Statesman*. 1999 Feb, 12: 52-53.

[3] Eagleton T. *Culture* [M]. New Haven: Yale University Press, 2016.

[4] Eagleton T. *The Function of Criticism from 'The Spectator' to Poststructuralism* [M]. London: Verso Press, 2005.

[5] Eagleton T. *The Idea of Culture* [M]. Oxford: Blackwell Press, 2000.

[6] Eliot G. *Daniel Deronda* [M]. Oxford: Clarendon Press, 1984.

[7] Holmes S. The Permanent Structure of Antiliberal Thought [A] // Rosenblum N L (ed.) *Liberalism and the Moral Life* [C]. Cambridge, MA: Harvard University Press, 1989. 227-253.

[8] Kaplan C. and Rose E C. *The Canon and the Common Reader* [M]. Knoxville: University of Tennessee Press, 1990.

[9] Kermode F. *An Appetite for Poetry* [M]. Cambridge, MA: Harvard University Press, 1989.

[10] Knight C J. *Uncommon Readers: Denis Donoghue, Frank Kermode, George Steiner, and the Tradition of the Common Reader* [M]. Toronto: University of Toronto Press, 2003.

[11] MacIntyre A C. *A Short History of Ethics: A History of Moral Philosophy from the Homeric Age to the Twentieth Century* [M]. Psychology Press, 1998.

[12] Stone D. *Communications with the Future* [M]. Ann Arbor: The University of Michigan Press, 1997.

[13] Trilling L. *The Liberal Imagination* [M]. New York: The Viking Press, 1950.

[14] Whitehead A N. *Science and the Modern World* [M]. New York: New American Library, 1948.

[15] Williams W. *Culture and Society* [M]. New York: Anchor Books, 1960.

[16] 何卫华. 雷蒙·威廉斯: 文化研究与"希望的资源"[M]. 北京: 商务印书馆, 2017.

[17] 黄梅. 推敲"自我"——小说在18世纪的英国 [M]. 北京: 生活·读书·新知三联书店, 2015.

[18] 殷企平. 文化辩护书 [M]. 上海: 上海外语教育出版社, 2013.

[19] 殷企平.文化批评的来龙去脉[J].英语研究,2020(12):39—49.

[20] 殷企平.西方文论关键词:共同体[J].外国文学,2016(2):70—79.

[21] 殷企平.质疑"进步"话语:三部英国小说简析[J].浙江师范大学学报(社会科学版),2006(2):12—19.

(本文原载于《复旦外国语言文学论丛》2021年秋季号)

悖论文化：文学中的文化反思

——殷企平教授访谈录*

笔者受委托专程采访浙江大学博士生导师、杭州师范大学外国语学院院长殷企平教授。

访谈时间：2012 年 5 月 18 日。

访谈地点：杭州师范大学下沙校区 D 楼。

廖昌胤（以下简称"廖"）：殷老师，我受《英美文学研究论丛》编辑部的委派，专程前来拜访您。非常感谢您百忙中接受访谈。

殷企平（以下简称"殷"）：非常高兴接受贵刊的访谈。

廖：您的《英国小说批评史》在我国关于英国小说理论的研究中，无论是在系统性，还是在深度方面，都是开山之作。我读这部著作的时候，注意到戴维·洛奇说，百年来的英国文学在现代主义与反现代主义之间摇摆。但他没有说，百年来的英国文学同样在现实主义与反现实主义之间摇摆。如果探究其原因，是不是可以说，任何小说都存在着现实主义与反现实主义的悖论因素，从而给这个问题带来无休止的纷争？

---

* 本文由廖昌胤与殷企平合写。廖昌胤，上海外国语大学文学研究院教授，主要从事悖论诗学研究。

殷：应该说，在我们国家，关于戴维·洛奇的研究还是不够的。关于这个钟摆论，上海外国语大学的侯维瑞先生在《现代英国小说史》这部书里也有过饶有趣味的介绍。关于现实主义……

廖：和反现实主义……

殷：你是说关于现实主义小说、现代主义小说和后现代主义小说，它们之间的一些悖论？我觉得我在那本书中提到一些。我体会得比较深的，或者是我比较喜欢的，是克里斯廷·布洛克-罗斯，在我那本书里有这一节。她提到现实主义复数这个概念。在她看来，即便是当代的所谓"后现代主义小说"，其实也是现实主义中的一种，因为它模仿世界的不可阐释性，而这种不可阐释性正是当今人类的现实。它只是说明人类现在的认知有限，暂时无法说明当下的现实。现实的这种不可阐释性和复杂性，是困惑，也是一种现实。所以你说现实主义也好，现代主义也好，后现代主义也好，都含有现实主义的因素。她说得挺概括的，我觉得非常 witty。这是一方面。

廖：你能否谈一下传统意义上的现实主义？

殷：传统意义上的现实主义主张反映现实，或者批判现实，它有一套成规。现代主义作家、后现代主义作家，对现实主义的一些写作成规抱有质疑的态度，或者批判的态度。但是呢，现代主义和后现代主义作家更多地表现出一种元意识（meta-consciousness）。就传统意义上的现实主义小说而言，从整体上来说，这种元意识还没普遍表现出来——当然，并不是说没有表现，如在 18 世纪斯特恩的《项狄传》中就表现得相当明显。

廖：后现代主义小说更强调这一点。

殷：对。刚才提到的戴维·洛奇，他在对语言的关注、对语言的敏感性方面，超过了以前的作家。但是，他对语言关注，并不等于他对现实不关注。

廖：您这本《英国小说批评史》对这个解释得非常透彻，视野非常宏大。后来，我又读了您的《推敲"进步"话语》这部新著，感觉它有"小说经济学"的新理论思考，里面的许多视角与思考比有些经济学家更 witty，更 sensible。我感觉印象深刻的一点，就是萨克雷《名利场》"第六十五章中谈到了利蓓加的'堕落的经过'（the history of her downward progress）"（殷企平 2009: 157）这个 downward progress，是个矛盾修辞，所揭示的堕落式进步的概念，与亚里士多德所说的"与期望相冲突"式悖论的概念有些相似的地方。从复句的结构上看，这是一个悖论结构。本来，进步是朝着预想的、好的方面发展，但是实际的"进步"过程呢，是向着堕落的方向发展。这启发我们需要审视现代化文化的一个巨大的悖论：进步欲望的现代化过程恰恰是人类倒退的过程，在某些人所标榜的"文明"进程中，人类的"进步"恰恰走向充分的堕落。我们所遇到的问题是，当代知识分子是否能够提出一个解决这个悖论的方法，或者是进行有益的思考？

殷：你提出的这个问题确实是非常有趣的。downward progress，它的确就是这样一种悖论。从我们文学作品来说，它是一种 irony。可以说，《名利场》整部小说都可以放在这种情境中来思考，来解释。

廖：对。放在反讽的情境中来思考。

殷：它追求一种进步，但是这种所谓的进步，其实是一种堕落。它只追求物质方面，或者说社会地位方面的进步，它往往是单向度的。它的单向度的进步，仅仅在一个方面，而在其他方面，恰恰是与进步背道而驰的。所以说我的《推敲"进步"话语》是放在进步的宏大叙事这样一个背景下的。我们应该看到，英国19世纪小说家笔下所描述的这种所谓的"进步"现象，都是跟这样一个大背景分不开的，即工具理性，即启蒙主义思想提供的一种进步的宏伟蓝图，企图建构一个理性的世界。这种背景或者可以称为文明化的背景。我刚刚写的一部新书，提到这种"宏伟文明"的工具理性，而这种工具理性与文化是不一样的。再回到《名利场》这部小说，它其实是对当下现实的一种非常精炼的勾勒。一方面，人们追求进步；另一方面，事情总是事与愿违，适得其反。这就是我们所说的情境反讽。你追求的目标是一种进步，但是结果呢，恰恰是相反。

廖：您刚才提到，最近写了一部文化批评的新书？

殷：是关于19世纪的文化批评。

廖：关于文化批评，这非常及时，您能否大概地透露一点儿？

殷：那本书里面的部分内容，我已经以文章的形式发表了。其中，就有关于文化的概念问题。文化作为一种概念，或者作为一种观念，其内涵在19世纪经历了十分重要的演变。我这本书可以看成《推敲"进步"话语》的一个姐妹篇。因为我在研究英国19世纪这些小说家时发现，对于"进步"话语的批判或质疑不仅仅局限于小说领域。一些诗人和散文家也对"进步"话语进行了批评，如卡莱尔、阿诺德、罗斯金和威廉·莫里斯这些重要的文人堪称文化批评家，他们对文化概念的内涵进行了一番梳理，并进行了充实。这是一个很有趣的现象，文化的概念因为他们而成熟起来。从卡莱尔开始，到马修·阿诺德，再到查尔斯·金斯利，然后再到约翰·罗斯金，再到莫里斯，这样一步一步地发展，使得文化的内容比以前要充实得多。

廖：您对他们的观点梳理以后呢，能不能形成一个他们对文化的界定——从总体上说，他们观念中的文化是什么样子的？

殷：关于文化的定义，可以找出几百种。但是，在这本新书中，我提出了一个观点，就是文化在不同的时期，在不同的背景下，它有好多意思。比如说，在17世纪，在文艺复兴的时候，培根与他同时代的霍布斯等人已经用了拉丁词cultura。这个词开始指的是心智培育，而后来有很多意思。雷蒙德·威廉斯在《文化与社会》里面已经说得很清楚，它除了指心智培育以外，还有价值体系等意思。我感兴趣的是工业化，因为在过去三百多年的历史过程中，人类生活中发生的最重大的事情就是工业化。在过去的三百多年中，人类社会的头号变化，非工业文明的崛起莫属。由它引起的社会转型以及随之而来的一系列现代性问题，自然激发了文人学者们的回应，其内容和性质恰恰在文化概念的演变轨迹中得到了生动的体现。从这一意义上说，文化概念的最重要内涵是对社会转型的回应；虽然它还有许多其他内涵，但是上述内涵跟人类社会最重大的变化密切相关，因而我们的文化之旅应该从社会转型开始。更具体地说，文化概念的内涵首先意味着"现代性焦虑"，即农业文明向工业文明转型而引起的焦虑。

廖：大多数人对这种转型不适应所产生的焦虑。

殷：工业革命的兴起，所谓的工业文明，带来了我们刚才说的单向度"进步"，对财富的追求，特别是追求速度。但是，精神层面的，比如说，道德良心啊，也就是我们当今所说的文化软实力的建设，在当时就是顾不上了。用我们现在的话说，导致精神文明与物质文明之间的脱节，或者说，两个价值体系之间发生了断裂。很有意思的是，席勒就对工业文明造成的断裂非常担心。由于社会的分工和劳动的分工，人的智力其实是越来越畸形化。智力非常发达，可以把某一个部件造得非常精细，但是人的全面发展受到了遏制。

廖：只是在某一方面突出。

殷：某一方面突出，另一方面就萎缩。席勒对此表示过高度的担心，即焦虑。到了卡莱尔，就表达得更加充分了。

廖：这是不是可以看成，一方面，社会也好，个人也好，都期望一种美好的生活，期望能够通过工业化的推进来实现美好的生活，却又发现愿望与现实/结果之间形成了巨大的反差。我们是不是可以把这看成 anxiety paradox？

殷：对。这里面也是一种 paradox。我知道，你对现代性悖论这个概念感兴趣。童明（刘军的笔名）在书中也讲到现代性的悖论。这其实也是一种反讽。启蒙学者提出了宏伟目标，一个非常诱人的、激动人心的宏伟蓝图，但是，人们为了达到这种目标所采取的一些手段，与目标渐行渐远了。因为人们过分强调物质的建设，强调工具理性，强调设计的能力。如今的"全球化"也是一样——资本主义在全球实现扩张，它的逻辑是竞争，继续剥削。在这种逻辑下，"现代性"的宏伟目标是无法实现的。所以，到了卡莱尔和阿诺德的时代，civilization 的问题就凸显了。与"文明"针锋相对，"文化"强调一种更全面的发展，也就是卡莱尔和阿诺德等人强调的平衡以及过去、现在与将来的衔接。不仅强调对物质的追求，而且从文化层面更强调了一种与自己的对话，与自己心灵的对话。

廖：这是不是对原先所谓 civilization paradox 的一种反思？特别是阿诺德提出了 perfection 这个概念，似乎是想为前面出现的文明悖论提供一种解决方案。从19世纪到雷蒙德·威廉斯，文化概念是不断变化的。我觉得，威廉斯的文化概念似乎有些需要探讨的地方。他在《漫长的革命》中认为文化既不是一套理想（"ideals"），也不是一套历史（"records"），更不是"social by-products"（Williams 1961：43），可能在他之前有这么三种代表性的对文化的理解，而不是"a way of life"（Williams 1961：46）。那么什么是 a way of life 呢，他强调要研究特定时空里的"felt sense of the quality of life"（Williams 1961：46）。他又用一个 organization 来解释，并说关键词是"pattern"。为了说清楚这个"范式"，他发明了一个术语 structure of feelings，并强调 structure 以及"all the elements"（Williams 1961：48）。在《马克思主义与文学》中，他再次阐述 structure of feelings，认为"feeling"这个词是用来区别"world-view"和"ideology"的

(Williams 1977：132），随后又说情感结构可以定义为"social experiences in solution"（Williams 1977：133）。这样，感觉他想用情感结构来强调某种范式，a way of life 中的 way，他可能理解为组织范式。这样就可能引起种种不同的理解。比如说，某种生活方式，如果把它看成文化的话，那么是不是与 19 世纪阿诺德他们提出的文化概念不一样？

殷：总体上来说，威廉斯对卡莱尔、阿诺德、金斯利、罗斯金以及后来的莫里斯所梳理的文化概念是持肯定态度的，但并不是说他没有一定的批评。比如说，他认为阿诺德有一种精英倾向，因为阿诺德把文化定义为"世界上最精彩的言论与思想"。那么，怎样界定"最精彩的言论与思想"呢？由谁来提出或界定呢？可能会是精英阶层。所以他提出的 a way of life，其实是暗地里跟阿诺德进行对话。但是，从卡莱尔，一直到莫里斯，文化有丰富的内涵。前面提到的转型焦虑这一内涵，就是因工业化进程中人类生活方式出现了问题而产生的焦虑。除了焦虑，文化概念的内涵还包括关于美好生活方式的愿景。这些都在 19 世纪的诗歌、散文和小说里得到了呈现。事实上，威廉斯是在 19 世纪文化批评家们所奠定的基础上提出"culture is ordinary"这一观点的。他是说，文化不能只包括精英阶层的阳春白雪，不只包括人们通常所说的经典，而且应当包括各个层面，如流行音乐、通俗艺术等。但是，对人类总体生活方式的关注，其实是从卡莱尔就已经开始了；后来越来越明确，到莫里斯那里就再明确不过了。莫里斯在他的散文里面，把通俗艺术与高雅艺术之间的关系讲得最好。我觉得，直到现在仍然没有人超过他。他说，高雅艺术需要通俗艺术的支撑，而通俗艺术须靠高雅艺术的引领。如果离开了通俗艺术，高雅艺术就变成了一种没有土壤、没有根的东西。反之，没有高雅艺术的引领，通俗艺术就没有办法提升。这两者是一种相互依存的关系。

廖：我觉得他提得很好。但是，难道威廉斯片面强调了通俗文化吗？

殷：威廉斯对高雅艺术绝对是有研究的！不过，我觉得，就高雅艺术与通俗艺术之间关系而言，威廉斯的阐述还不如莫利斯的。话又要说回来，威廉斯在《文化与社会》里曾经强调，在莫里斯那里，文化的概念经历了一个非常关键性的转折，他对莫里斯还是高度肯定的。

廖：如果仅仅研究个人的生活方式的话，有可能消解莫里斯所说的那种精品的内涵。

殷：威廉斯在他的书中，不仅关注个人的生活方式，而且关注全社会的生活方式，他对社会与个人之间的关系的阐述也是比较辩证的。他对马克思主义的辩证法的领悟是相当深刻的。我在《英国小说批评史》里，说到对可知社群（the knowable community）的讨论，关于个人与社会之间的关系，强调个人中有社会，社会中有个人。这样一种互动关系，威廉斯描述得非常充分。再回到你刚才说到的 structure of feelings。我觉得，威廉斯提出这个情感结构的概念，是一大贡献。从怎么样去评价小说，特别是以往的小说来看，我比较喜欢他这个概念。就是把小说看成一种珍贵的史料。当然，我并不是说小说就是历史，但是，马克思指出：小说在某种程度上，尤其是在 19 世纪的英国，实际上比一些御用的所谓历史学家更好地记录了历史的真实。马克思只说到这里。但是威廉斯提出了一个更适合文学批评的方法。我们可以去看看，19 世纪的英国小说怎么对历史的真实进行记录。那么怎么样来解读这些作品呢？其实，它们并不是记录了一些官方的话语。官方对现实的解释跟普通人民对现实的感受是脱节的。所以威廉斯认为，普通人的情感结构才是真正的现实。官方对现实的解释，往往沉浸在臆测上。

廖：是为了既得利益集团。

殷：对，是服务于既得利益集团的解释。官方的解释跟真正的现实是两回事情。例如，我们再回到对"进步"话语的解释——当时官方的解释是，大英帝国代表了最伟大的、最先进的、可以说是最进步的国家。但是，从狄更斯、萨克雷、乔治·爱略特的小说里感到的是另一种感情。这种情感结构跟官方的主观现实是不一样的。你官方说是进步，但事实上明明是堕落的进步。官方所说的进步，从情感方面、伦理方面、道德方面看，它是在<u>堕落</u>。

廖：其实这种情况，这种看法，一直延续到丹尼尔·贝尔，他也提到文化悖论——"品格结构的不一致和各种领域的脱节"（丹尼尔131），这些矛盾"与来自现代社会本质的一个更为普遍的问题相关。工业社会的特有品格有赖于经济与节俭原则，即追求效率，讲究低成本、高利润、最优选择和功能合理性。然而，就是这种品格与西方世界领先的文化潮流发生冲突，因为现代主义文化强调反认知和反智模式。它们都渴望回到表现最初的本能，一方强调功能理性，专家决策，奖勤罚懒；另一方强调天启情绪和反理性行为方式。正是这种脱节现象构成了西方所有资产阶级社会的历史性文化危机。这种文化矛盾使作为关系到社会存亡的最重大分歧长期存在下去"（丹尼尔 1989：132）。他似乎启发我们认识到这样一个资本主义悖论：要求自由谋财、自由消费的自由市场经济的生产却是在铁笼似的法规和限制中的资本主义生产线中生产物质文化产品，形成的"自由"价值观体系越完美，人越不自由。我们应当怎样去看待这个悖论？其实，前面阿诺德他们实际上是提出了方案，试图来解决这些问题。但是，这里面有一个技术层面的东西，就是强调人的本能，而官方提出的宏伟蓝图其实也是一种个人的本能或欲望的体现。那么，这个悖论该怎么去理解呢？

殷：关于丹尼尔·贝尔的一些观点，我在《推敲"进步"话语》中也提到了。资本主义文化矛盾，在我看来，是不可解决的。只要资本主义还存在，只要剥削还存在，最主要的是对工具理性的盲目崇拜还存在，就不可解决。你刚才说的这种悖论就会存在，全是因为工具理性在作祟。我想最好的一个悖论表述就是：irrationality of rationality。无论奖勤罚懒也好，制度完善也好，再精细、再科学的算计也好，都无法逃脱这种悖论，因为正是在这种工具理性被推向极致的时候，非理性显得越发疯狂。这种悖论社会学家丹尼尔·贝尔分析得不如文学家（如狄更斯）那样深刻，后者是用感性与理性交融的手法来表现的，而丹尼尔·贝尔则用比较理性的手法。

廖：他用一种理性来规范这种表述。

殷：对，用规范的方式来描述。

廖：另外，关于资本主义的文化悖论，还有一个詹明信的总结。詹明信的原著似乎比较难懂。比如说政治无意识，比如说所涉及的一些社会冲突，即社会的范式与个人的意识形态之间形成不可调和的矛盾，阅读起来还是比较拗口。

殷：我对 Friedrich Jameson 的研究欠深入，但是欣赏他的"政治无意识"一说以及他对后现代主义的解释——他把后现代主义解释为资本主义在全球的扩张，这还是很有见地的。另外，他为人们对文学作品的理解提供了一些方法论，他的认识产生了较大的影响。例如，至少在把文学作品 politicize 这一潮流中起了推波助澜的作用。

廖：您说的这个 politicize 是一个新方法。

殷：其实这种阐释的政治化也不仅仅是詹明信一个人在推动。像福柯，像一些西方马克思主义、新历史主义以及后来的文化研究理论，都对文学的经典进行政治化解读。关于经典的争论都是跟这有关系的。对原来的经典，对经典生成的原因，尤其是政治原因进行了质疑。其实特里·伊格尔顿跟詹明信相似，都是采取这种政治视角的。但是，我觉得，伊格尔顿对文学的审美比较敏感，是很有研究的。詹明信更多地从宏观方面切入文学，而对微观方面的研究比较欠缺——Friedrich Jameson is not my cup of tea. 他在对文学的细读方面没有给我带来多少震撼，倒是伊格尔顿在这方面——对文学作品的细读方面——使我非常钦佩。他对狄更斯等许多人的细读，都有非常独到的见解。

廖：伊格尔顿的细读的确引人入胜。另外，在讨论文化的时候，现在有一个比较热门的概念，就是文化软实力。文化软实力其实也是在理性悖论中生产出来的，原来称作"文化硬实力"，现在又变成软实力，这种文化硬实力与软实力的关系不知应该怎么看？

殷："文化"与"硬实力"这样的搭配似乎没有见到过。文化软实力这个概念产生的背景值得我们深思。这个背景就是我们刚才所说的精神文明与物质文明脱节。我们以前强调四个现代化——农业现代化、工业现代化、国防现代化、科学技术现代化，强调经济建设和制度建设。现在来反观我们走过的路子，虽然政府一直强调两手抓，物质文明与精神文明一起抓，但是各个具体部门在具体操作的时候，总是着力在硬的方面。当然，这并不是说制度建设不重要，其实我们的制度建设（如法律制度的建设）还很不足；况且制度建设永远是滞后的，总要对它的裂隙方面进行不断修改和完善。问题是我们实际上把经济建设放在了第一位，把制度建设放在了第二位，而对于心灵的改变、人的精神方面的建设，重视得还很不够，远远落后于制度建设——糟糕就糟糕在这一方面。

廖：按理说，应该首先是个人观念的改变。文化的发展，应该走在前面，随之才能产生新的物质文化，然后制度才能跟进。所以我觉得，文化软实力的建设来源于借鉴。1954 年，美国总统艾逊豪威尔派艺术家出国表演，把它当作一种外交策略，称作"文化外交"。哈佛大学教授约瑟夫·奈（Joseph Nye）把这称作"软实力"，即"思想吸引力，文化的普遍性"（Lewis 1999：6）。从此，美国实施"文化软实力"战略。开始时，把文化艺术作为外交的一种策略。凯思·休特认为"硬实力,是这样一种诸如叫某人做某事的能力,否则,你会开枪。软实力是一种吸引力,是一种把人们吸引到你身边来的能力。"(Suter 2011: 163)但是,半个世纪以来,美国的文化软实力与武力硬实力两手都搞,却招致 9·11 的灾难,这说明他们的文化软实力并没有收到预期的效果。分析其中的原因,也许在于,将文化软实力当成一种辅助手段,配合硬实力来征服世界,这形成了一种软实力悖论:"软实力"从美好的策略愿望出发,却获得了格林沃尔德所指出的"软实力悖谬"的结果。(Greenwald 2010: 77)美国的文化软实力战略,本身就是一个巨大的悖论:以"软"的方式去实现"硬"的侵略性目标,把文化当成了实现其霸权的工具,让别人接受自己的思想观念,按照自己的意志行动。这就背离了文化的内涵。总结美国文化软实力战略的教训,是不是可以认为,文化软实力之所以软,从目标上它软在利他,而不是软在利己;在表现上,它是无形的,而不是无力的;在方式上,它是软的,但不是弱的;在策略上,它软在灵活性,而不是软在无效性。总之,它软在"人性美、品质美、思想美、观念美、技术美"。"文化软实力"事实上是指这样一种能力:创造具有吸引力的思想、观念、策略,形成人类共同发展的向心力。从国际事务上来看,文化作为一种战略,形成一种"不战而屈人之兵"的文化力量。这种文化软实力是不是有可能形成起来?

殷:我觉得你刚才提到的美国的文化软实力战略,跟 19 世纪阿诺德、金斯利、莫里斯他们提到的文化观念,或者说我说的这种软实力,不是一回事情。我觉得美国人二战以后提出的文化软实力,恰恰是带有工具理性成分的东西。一些美国人所谓的文化建设,旨在增强自身的竞争能力,旨在称霸,也就是侵略,就是扩张。军事上达不到目的,就想靠所谓的"文化"来实现,这是假文化之名,行反文化之实,带有工具理性。这也是一种 irraionality of rationality。他们无非是把这种非理性的理性更扩大了,并不强调人的修养,仍然强调一种外在的东西。而真正的文化,则是一种心灵的改革。艾逊豪威尔等人所谓的"文化"其实就是霸权的概念,就是让你认同,让其他国家来认同美国这样一个帝国,一个用文化伪装得很巧妙的帝国;企图让其他国家来认同他所谓的价值观,把你吸引过去;标榜他有所谓的民主、自由,但这仍然是浅薄的东西。正确的文化价值观,应当是人与人、国与国之间平等的。所以,美国当权者如今吹嘘的"文化软实力"其实是带有霸权的。这是一种恶劣的文明，包含着一种资本主义恶劣的因素在里面，与我前面提到的我所向往的文化是背道而驰的。这就是我为什么更喜欢金斯利所说人的"心灵的变化"（the change of the heart）。我在尚未出版的那部新书里强调：改革必须始于心灵的改革。

廖：金斯利提出这种心灵的改革，他到底想怎么实现呢？

殷：心灵的改革有多个层面。我觉得从阿诺德到莫里斯，他们对精神文明与物质文明之间相互关系的主张都值得研究。金斯利在他的小说里讲到，工人要自己组织起来，进行互助，生产组织靠的不是雇佣与被雇佣的关系，而是呈现一种互助组的形式。金斯利强调劳动致富，强调人与人之间的相互尊重。金斯利、莫里斯他们的笔下的社会，存在于实实在在的社会建设、经济建设当中，他们消除了阶级。莫里斯与阿诺德有本质的区别。在莫里斯的乌有乡里，政府是不需要的。劳动只是一种艺术；人类在艺术化地生活。人可以自由从事各种各样的工作，他可以有各种各样的追求：上午可以去做船夫，或者做排字工，或者到工厂里面去劳动，去割草打禾，等等；下午他可以去打鱼，去运动。晚上可以谈谈文学批评。就像马克思在《德意志意识形态》里提到的 labor 与 leisure 的关系。莫里斯跟马克思一样，把休闲看成发展式的休闲，是劳动的一种延伸。在这种消灭阶级、消灭三大差别的情况下，消灭了严格的劳动分工的状态。人们的劳动是修身。所以这不是抽象的精神建设。这样才能真正体现人与人之间的同情、人与人之间的爱。

廖：那么他们提到的这种理想化的模式，理想化的心灵改变，能不能实现呢？

殷：实现起来当然很困难，但是，即使现在不能实现，人类也需要这种文学作品。这种文学艺术作品，它的最根本的意义是代表了一种乌托邦的精神。尽管有人把它看成虚幻的东西，但是人类是需要乌托邦精神的。

廖：我觉得 Utopia 这个词让人感觉它是虚无缥缈的东西。Utopia 是莫尔构造的一个词，如果我们把它译成"优道邦"，正像有人解释的那样，其中有一个字母代表"好"的意思，然后 top 具有明显的词根意思："冠"和"顶端"。这样，是不是可以理解为社会优化的道路。要是译成乌托邦，在中国容易造成子虚乌有的误解。

殷：我也觉得是这样。我非常欣赏你关于乌托邦的思考和理解。你至少是看到了翻译中存在的缺陷。但是，这里有些词已经是约定俗成了，要改变是非常难的，至少人们得先有一个接受的过程，需要像你这样的年轻学者对乌托邦的内涵加以梳理，加以深化。

廖：它是提出了对现存的社会悖论的一种可能的解决方案。

殷：关键就是看对社会现实有没有反思。

廖：它提出的东西虽然可能不太完善，但是它对解决社会的文化悖论提出了一种可能。其实我觉得对乌托邦的研究还需要进一步深入。虽然乌有乡在名义上像是"无"，事实上它还是有。用追求心灵的改变来校正工具理性。

殷：应该是这样。乌托邦意味着一种反思，一种思想表述。我相信，真正对乌托邦了解的学者，会有这样一种 awareness 在里面。乌托邦的真正意义、真正内涵，它的社会价值和政治价值，学者们都充分地意识到了。但是，对于普通读者而言，由于阅读不够，就会简单地把乌托邦与虚无缥缈的幻想联系起来。我相信，经过学者们——尤其是年轻学者们——的不断努力，这种"乌有"的看法会慢慢改变，至少可以让这个 paradox 从贬义发展为褒义。当然，我们现在也不能就说它是贬义的。

廖：非常感谢殷老师抽出了这么长的时间来接受访谈。我想，今天提到的一些观点，虽然有些是您以前发表过的，但是经过您的即兴发挥，形成了一些画龙点睛的表述，对我们有很多启发。

殷：谢谢你的来访。

参考文献

[1] Greenwald A. The Soft-Power Fallacy [J]. *Commentary*, 2010, 130 (1): 75–80.

[2] Lewis M B. Soft Power [J]. *American Theatre*, 1999, 16 (3): 6–7.

[3] Raymond W. *Marxism and Literature* [M]. Oxford: Oxford University Press, 1977.

[4] Raymond W. *The Long Revolution. Revised Edition* [M]. New York: Harper & Row, Publishers, 1961.

[5] Suter K. The end of the American century? [J]. *Contemporary Review* 2011, Vol. 283 Issue 1701: 158–165.

[6] 丹尼尔·贝尔. 资本主义的文化矛盾 [M]. 赵一凡等, 译. 北京: 生活·读书·新知三联书店, 1989.

[7] 殷企平. 推敲"进步"话语——新型小说在19世纪的英国 [M]. 北京: 商务印书馆, 2009.

(本文原载于《英美文学研究论丛》2013年第1期)

"英语专业与人文教育"二人谈[*]

阮炜：今天这个话题基于两个社会背景，第一是机器翻译和人工智能发展迅猛，似乎在抢我们的饭碗。我的一个学生开了一家翻译公司，按传统方法操作，起码得雇十个人，但实际上她只雇了三四个人，大量工作由机器完成。公司业务，包括学术性较强的文章，首先用翻译软件过一遍，正确率大约在百分之五十左右，某些情况下甚至高达百分之八九十。之后只需人工对它作少量修订，便是较好的译文了，非常省力。第二个大背景，就是汉语的崛起，现在越来越多外国人学汉语而且学得越来越好，这对英语的重要性已构成了不小的挑战。我们先要讨论中国大学的英文教育是什么性质的教育，是人文教育还是技能性的语言教育？这个问题意义深远，因为它牵涉到从业者今后怎么规划生活，甚至牵涉到下一代到底要不要选择英语专业。去年，复旦大学外文学院蔡基刚教授的一些观点和论断引发了热论，借此机会想跟殷企平教授作一个对谈，看能否产生一些思想火花，把问题的讨论推向深入。

首先得搞清楚什么是人文教育。它包含两个概念，一是"人文"，二是"教育"。"教育"是什么？Education 用英语讲清楚，不会有太大的歧义。"人文"翻译成英文就麻烦了。Humanities? Humanism? 所谓"人文教育"，翻译成

---

[*] 本文由阮炜和殷企平合写。阮炜，湖南师范大学潇湘学者特聘教授、博士生导师，深圳大学西方文化研究中心主任。研究方向：现当代英国文学、比较文明与文化、西方古典学研究及时评。电子邮箱：2639742395@qq.com。

Humanistic Education? Humanities Education? 确实很难译，谁也没说清楚过。但我直接的感受就是它代表了文科教育的一种理想。教育部早在2005年就已经批准设立"人文教育专业"了，指导性意见中指出："人文教育本科专业是为基础教育课程改革服务的新兴师范类本科专业，整合了历史学、社会学、政治学、经济学、法学、地理学、人文地理及其他人文社会学科学等多学科领域的知识，形成了核心学科，颠覆哲学文学历史艺术的综合性人文教育课程体系。"

殷企平：您说的这个关于人文教育的定义，我觉得确实是个最大的问题，正是我们今天谈话的主题，那我们就从这里开始。刚才您说的，是把人文教育定义为人文学科教育的一种理想境界，这个关键词是"理想境界"。首先，我觉得任何专业都可以是教育。我同意您的观点，即人文教育至今还是一个比较模糊的概念，各人见解不同。不过我认为，即便对于"教育"这个概念，大家也未必都了然于胸。我在几十年的教育实践中，每次开学，基本上都要问一个问题，就是学生们对于教育的理解是怎样的？什么叫作教育？英语教学是不是人文教育？在实际操作层面，我觉得我们的教学并没有真正成为"教育"，而只是培训（training），而培训跟"教育"是截然不同的概念，这一点很重要。

首先，谈一下教育。什么是教育？我觉得当一个专业训练完成之后，要后退一步，放开视野，把所学的知识放在更广阔的情境下审视。也就是说，任何学科、任何专业，都是有局限性的，任何一门专业都牵涉到对所学知识进行评价的问题，而要评价，就必须有一个标准。而标准又分成两个方面：内部标准和外部标准。如果只用内部标准来评价所学知识，那就谈不上教育，只能算作培训，这是因为只要是仅局限于学科内部进行评价，必定难以发现学科教育自身的缺陷，这恰好应了一句名言：不识庐山真面目，只缘身在此山中。

当前，在我们现有的所谓专门用途英语或大学英语教学模式里面，老师和学生在评价所学知识技能的时候，总是运用专业内、学科内的标准，而不是打开窗口，尽可能地向周边学科、专业"借光"。所谓教育，如您所说，是一个需要坚持追求的理想状态，但在操作层面，又是可以实施的。所谓实施其实就是在评价所学知识的时候，不断突破既有的疆域。比如，当我们在上文学课时，一旦就"什么是文学"提问，那就已经进入了哲学层面，涉及了本体论命题；就"我们怎么样来认识一部文学作品"提问，那就已涉及认识论命题。若问

"文学好在哪里？"这里面就有一个伦理问题。要了解狄更斯、奥斯汀的时代以及当时的社会、文化和历史背景，就需要引入历史学的概念。譬如，大家都知道狄更斯的《荒凉山庄》里蕴含法律学，你若不懂一点法律知识，就没办法对作品做出恰当的评价。这就是说，当我们打破学科间的壁垒，适当引入周边学科的原理和方法之际，就是进入教育层面之时。

另外，我想提一下纽曼（J. H. Newman）和洪堡（W. von Humboldt）的说法。纽曼通常被看作世界高等教育史上三大里程碑中的第一个代表人物，其学说的一个核心概念就是智力训练（intellectual exercise）。第二个是洪堡，他认为大学不光担负智力操练的任务，还有科研任务。大学教学除了教授现有的知识之外，还有开拓知识疆域的任务。一个好的老师，会不断地让学生知道自己在进行什么研究。你可以把课上得生动活泼，很有激情，知识的传授也很清楚，很有艺术性，但是你若不教会学生怎样拓宽学术疆界，把这个疆界往前推进一步，那就谈不上教育。就教育而言，理工科也好，医科也好，师生如果能够打开视野，把所学的专业知识放在总体知识的版图当中来审视，知道自己专业的位置，那么就已经体现教育理念了。人文教育不能是 a bit of everything，必须有主次之分。对我们英语专业的人来说，英语当然是主业，但这不可排除跟其他专业的融通性。如果有了这种融通性，我觉得至少解决了什么叫教育的问题。

现在进入一个更高的层次，或者一个更困难的领域，就是刚才您说的"人文"问题。我刚才的阐述，是把它定义在人文学科当中，但如果一定要说我们理想的人文教育要达到什么境界，那我认为可能是以"完人"为追求目标。在英国文学传统中，就长期存在着对"完人"（the Whole Man）的诉求。早在文艺复兴时期，一些人文主义者就拥有一个塑造"完人"的目标。大家耳熟能详的瑞恰慈（I. A. Richards）、燕卜荪（W. Empson）和利维斯（F. R. Leavis）等人所追求的都是博雅教育（Liberal Education），其实就是人文教育。艾略特（T. S. Eliot）也强调人文教育，强调通过教育来实现人类经验的完整性，这一思想可以追溯到阿诺德（M. Arnold）和纽曼。

阮炜：您说得太好了。我们都从事人文学或文史哲（包括语言在内）教学和研究，但人文学不等于人文教育，更不等于人文精神。若是培养"完人"，人文学科好像更占优势。若是理工科，你可能只研究一个机械臂，或某个基因，似乎很有局限性。若是人文学，古今中外的所有文科知识都得涉猎，更有人格培养，所以我们或许更接近"完人"的理想。我以为，蔡教授和其他几位同仁所理解的人文教育，大体上也是这种"完人"教育。但英文教育虽不等于人文教育，却不可以放弃对人文教育理想的追求。有大学给外语类学院取名时，不叫"外国语学院"而叫"外国语言文学学院"，简称"外文学院"，复旦大学就是如此。虽一字之差，背后的理念却大不相同。深圳大学李小均教授 2005 年在《读书》杂志上曾发表了一篇文章《从外文系到外国语学院》，讨论了我国外文教育到底应该是简单的语言训练，还是一种全面人文学素质的培育。尤其是重点大学，最好使用"英文"而非"英语"一词。英文教育或外文教育，一个"文"字，就足以表明作为管理者，甚至作为普通老师，你所坚持的理念不同，并非仅仅教授某种语言技能，而是除了语言技能外，还有该语言所承载的大量相关知识，如历史、宗教、哲学、文学、政治、社会、心理、习俗等等。

殷企平：我非常赞同。我们现在其实已经进入了另一个话题，就是怎么样才能学好语言的问题。到底是按照刚才阮老师理解的来做呢，还是按照蔡基刚教授所秉持的，我们的语言只要能服务于某种专门用途就可以了？

在我看来，如果是真正的人文学者，就不应该从英语专业分出所谓的"专门用途英语"，因为语言习得和运用势必涉及一切领域，有历史和哲思，当然还有情感，而不仅仅是知识。怎样才能学好英语？首先要有一个正确的语言观。究竟是强调碎片化的语言技能，还是强调整体、创造性的语言观？我刚才提到的利维斯，他强调语言的整体性和创造性（the collective creative achievement of language）。他所说的 collective，让人联想到 connective，又让人想到爱德华·摩根·福斯特（E. M. Forster）的名言："重要的是 connect。"在我们的学习当中也要 connect。如果一开始就把本来挺好的一个英语专业分裂了，分割成科技英语、商务英语等，学习者虽然可能上手很快，但是会缺乏后劲。举例来说，我在十九年前曾做过一个长达两年之久的调查，请浙江省所有涉外领域中一些身居要职的人物谈谈对当时刚刚变热的"实用英语"（如商务英语、经贸英语）的看法。他们都提到一个现象：那些经贸英语、商务英语的毕业生确实上手很快，可是会渐渐失去优势；一般过了两三年以后，那些走"文学道路"的毕业生却都表现出很强的后劲。因此，我想说的是，学界对"人文教育"可能有不同的理解，但至少承认它是强调人文性、思辨性的教育，这对英语语言的学习是有好处的。并且，我们强调重视人文教育的英语专业，并不排除技能。

阮炜：但根据某些同行的理解，英语只是一种技能，所以英语教育并不等于人文教育。这里有两个设定。第一，人文教育并非什么好东西。第二，英语教育就是一种语言技能的训练，不可以把它提升到一个了不起的程度；如果这么做，后果很严重，会造成巨大的教育资源浪费。我觉得这种观点不无道理，但有失偏颇。如果太强调英语教育的工具性，最后是学不好英语的。1978年以后，中国以崭新的姿态屹立于世界。这个成就是怎么取得的？共产党的领导是一个根本因素，中华文明本身的一些优秀素质也不能否认——中华民族最是世界上最勤劳的民族之一。除这些以外，通过英文和其他西方语言的深入学习，我们得以深刻理解西方这个非常不同的文明，我们不再像洋务派那样头痛医头、脚痛医脚，以为学会了造坚船利炮，就可以免遭欺负，而是通过学习西方人的思想和文学文化，真正进入他们的精神世界。要进入他们的精神世界，就得绞尽脑汁把西方语中有而汉语中没有的概念传达过来。这是一项异常艰巨的工作，得移入、创造大量新词，得赋予旧词以新义，这意味着思维方式的深刻转变。在这个过程中，我们扩大了自己的精神世界，完成了文明的转型，最终实现了文明的复兴。我以为，这是中华民族20世纪以来取得的最伟大成就之一。

殷企平：我很同意。其实您已经引出了第三个话题：我们在学习英文时，或者在从事英文教育时，是不是应该带领学生进入西方人的精神世界当中，把他们好的东西学过来？马修·阿诺德在伊顿公学所作的一次演讲中，回答了一个问题：对英国人来说，为什么还要学习外国人的语言，为什么还要学习外国文学，甚至是古老的外国文学？阿诺德的回答是：知彼才能知己。就是说，你不学习外语的话，可能对自己语言的认识也不那么透彻。因为有比较才能鉴别，至少有必要多一个比较的视角。同时，我们还要看到，在从事英语教育的时候，并不只是教会学生英语语言、文学、英国的历史和文化，同时还能够教学生提高母语和本族文化方面的很多认知。这方面的例子其实很多，我不由得又想到瑞恰慈，他对英国文学的研究，常常带有中国视角。他对孟子精神很感兴趣，曾经写过《孟子论心智》(*Mencius on the Mind*)一书。他对中国的美学思想也很感兴趣。我们在教英国文学的时候，其实离不开瑞恰慈，因为他能够自然而然地给予我们文化自信。

瑞恰慈在讨论语言的意义时，使用了三个关键词，即情感（feeling）、语气（tone）和意图（intention）。他把情感解释成"对所指的态度"（attitude towards the reference）。那种所谓的"专门用途英语"教学，很可能会忽略情感，以为在语言使用中情感是可有可无的。但专门用途专家们忘了，人们使用语言的时候，对所指的东西总带有特定的态度。例如，在从事科技的时候，对科技采取什么态度就很重要。语气也是一种态度，即"对他人的态度"（attitudes toward other people）。至于意图，则是"发声的目的"（the purpose of utterance）。目前，关于英文专业的人文教育理想，我们尚未达成共识，但是至少都认为它是一种有情感、有情怀、知识性、思辨性的英文教育。这种教育其实有一个前提，即presuppose the internalization of all language skills。也就是说，强调人文教育，绝非排除语言技能培训，而恰恰是以后者为前提的。利维斯有一本书叫作 *The Common Pursuit*《共同的追求》。所谓 common pursuit，是指 the common pursuit of true judgement，即"对任何真知灼见的共同追求"。信奉人文教育理想的英语专业并不排斥科技英语、外贸英语、商务英语等等。其实大家都有一种共同的理念，或者说有一种通约性的认知。这种通约性意味着一种应变能力，例如，眼前这把椅子，即便做得再好，如果换了环境，可能就没有用了，可是假如我们的产品不拘泥于椅子或桌子等形状，而是更注重材料本身的质地，那就会更具备应变性。当今这个变化很快的世界，恰恰更需要这种应变能力，它比某种特殊的技能更为重要。

阮炜：我认为您所谈到的那种应变能力，就是英文教育的理想状态。不管是什么用途的英语，英文本身学好了，基础打好了，都是很容易学的，或者说应变能力终究是建立在人文性英文教育的基础上的。最后还是要落实到这一点：英文不能当一个技能来学。其实，多年来大家都在讨论这个问题，甚至大体上都同意这个结论，所以并不是一个问题。但一个长期从事大学英语教育的同行看到了资源浪费的现象，提出了一些批评，引起了一些讨论，这本身不是坏事。

殷企平：接下来我们开启另外一个话题。现在很多的英语专业挂了红牌、黄牌，英语专业的毕业生已经面临就业危机，或者可以说是英语专业"生病了"。这病因到底是什么呢？人们确实看到了一些症状，但是对病因的诊断是不准的。

难道是因为我们有太多的"人文教育"吗?英语专业现在有这么大的危机,难道是因为太强调技能背后的那些东西吗?回答是否定的。

阮炜:英文教育的就业问题,不单单是英语专业学生的就业问题,其实牵涉整个社会的就业状况,非常复杂。我没做调查研究,拿不出精确的数据,但长期以来我们培养的大量毕业生,最后在工作岗位并没有使用英语,这并不等于我们的教育失败了。这种情况在全世界都是存在的,所学专业最后并没有用上。这就包含我们对大学的理解。大学并不等于你进来学了某个专业后,一辈子都要用它谋生。大学很大程度上只是一张门票,是一种淘汰或奖励机制。仅仅拿英语专业就业困难来说事,把英文教育定位成人文教育,然后加以否定,是有问题的。你并没有作一个对比,比如考虑一下其他专业就业情况如何,所有本科专业在全世界就业情况如何。2019 年暑假期间,我在波兰的一个学术会议上发言并阐明,我国的全民英文教育是世界教育史上的一个奇迹,它起到一种非凡的作用,通过英文和其他西方语言的学习,整个西方世界对我们来说变得透明了。倒过来说,西方世界看我们,未必像我们看他们那么清楚。但从长远看,我国英文专业会萎缩。甚至现在,在部分重点大学取消大学英语的必修课定位,是否应提上议事日程?也许在不久的将来,学生会有选择的权利,喜欢英文就学,不喜欢就不学。中学英文教育是强制性的,大学里仍得学英语,但读研究生还得学,读博士还得学,之后评职称,甚至评中医职称,还得学,还得考,这显然是荒谬的。

殷企平:接着您的话题谈谈我们现在有没有必要再坚持办英语专业?是不是有必要再继续坚持大学英语的教学?关于这两个问题,我的看法是这样的:首先,我同意您的意见,可能有一段时间它会缩水,即减少数量。这是自然的,因为有很多具体的、复杂的影响因素,比如跟我们的人口、国家战略需求、个人的兴趣这些都有关系。从高等教育理论来讲,高等教育有三个合力,缺一不可。一个是学科的内在逻辑,另一个是大学生的内在需求,再一个就是社会的需求。

关于另外一个问题,我同意您的观点,即人工智能崛起后会取代一部分原来英语从业者的功能。但是,我要补充的是,它虽然取代了一些功能,但是又产生了新的需求。我们前不久请了原国家外专局局长黄友义先生来做学术报告。

他是我们国家的顶尖翻译之一。他就发现,在机器翻译蓬勃发展以后,会带来新的问题,而这些新的问题恰恰需要人去解决。比如说,在一些高端的层面,包括我们现在最主要的"一带一路"倡议的翻译、"人类命运共同体"的翻译、"中国大陆"的翻译,如果翻译得不好,就会铸成大错,甚至是政治错误。当然,其中不完全是翻译问题,但如果是一个好的翻译,他应该预料到这类问题。这不由得又回到刚才的问题,就是英文专业到底有没有必要坚持人文教育?既有的事实说明,有些人文性的问题,恰恰就在英文专业中暴露出来。虽然有些问题在中国肯定暴露不出来,因为我们并无恶意,但是别人听起来会认为你有负面用意。这不仅仅是翻译的问题,而恰恰是有待于具有跨文化视野和跨学科背景的专业人士能够预先发现问题,通过黄友义先生这样的人来提醒决策部门。我认为这就是英文专业人文性的价值所在,它是不可替代的。因为我们自己的问题往往是要跨出去才能看到的。

阮炜:是的,它可以帮助我们的中文思维变得清晰起来。关于英文教育的未来,我理想中的未来状况是大学英语规模大大缩小。原因很简单,所谓特殊用途英语,机器很容易应对。数学、物理或工程学等里边的专业术语,目前翻译软件基本已能应对,不需花太多人力去修订机器译文。但文学翻译远没有这么容易。你往往拿不准,因为一个词可能有好多种用法,好多个含义。以后若少数人确实对语言有感觉,喜欢语言文学,又学得很好,就由他们来解决文学翻译的问题。最终来说,英语专业肯定不会像目前规模那么大,中国上千个 Departments of English 中或许只有一百来个可称之为"英文系"。但如果那时候仍有一些人只对英语感兴趣,非常愿意学它,甚至找不到工作也愿意学,那也得让他们学。

殷企平:如果真的把90%的英语专业办成了专门用途英语,那恐怕很快就会消亡,因为正如你所说,它们的功能马上就可以被取代了。我认为一个学生在本科阶段,其实不管学什么专业都没有决定性结果。如果这个观点成立的话,不管是学英语,还是学数学,或是学历史,都可以是 general education,我们现在把它翻译成通识教育,其实我更喜欢的说法是 liberal education(博雅教育),因为它一直可以追溯到亚里士多德,以及刚才我讲的纽曼。如果任何专业都是可以通向博雅教育的话,那么我们的英语专业多一些又何妨?正如此前谈到的,很多本科生毕业以后很可能是要换工作的，不一定就能坚守英语专业。如果他们受过良好的教育，适应能力就会很强，那么做什么都可以。所以专业并没有决定性作用，只要坚持人文教育，英语专业反而会有更强的生命力。

阮炜：从今天开始，或许我们可以把 education of English 叫作"英文教育"，把 department of English 叫作"英文系"，因为它包含人文教育的理想。从长远看，外文专业会慢慢萎缩，最终会留下一批真正对英文或其他外国语文感兴趣的人。如果我们能运用一下想象力，不难想到，最终会产生一个新职业，或可叫作翻译软件训练师。到一定时候，翻译软件需要升级了，他们就派上用场了。人类总得教会翻译软件或机器人一些最新的知识，而不是简单的几个词汇的问题。

殷企平：总之，一种狭隘的学习，或者说一种只注重技能、不具备人文性的学习，对任何一个学科来讲，都只会把自己引向绝路。今天的交流是思想的碰撞，意犹未尽。因此，如果有不同的看法是很好的，并非一定要有统一的认识不可；这本来就是一次开放式讨论。

（本文原载于《山东外语教学》2020 年第 2 期）